A MODERN RETELLING OF *LITTLE WOMEN*

Meg, Jo, Beth, and Amy

A Graphic Novel

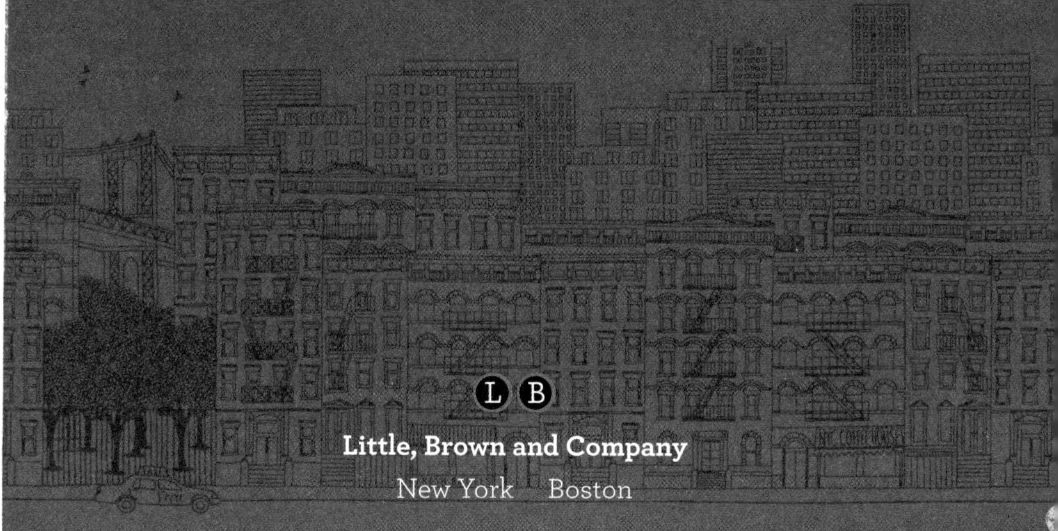

LB

Little, Brown and Company

New York Boston

The illustrations for this book were done digitally. This book was edited by Rex Ogle and designed by Christina Quintero. The production was supervised by Erika Schwartz, and the production editor was Annie McDonnell. The text was set in CCComicrazy, and the display type is Wanderlust Letters.

Little, Brown and Company
Hachette Book Group
1290 Avenue of the Americas, New York, NY 10104
Visit us at LBYR.com

First Edition: February 2019

Little, Brown and Company is a division of Hachette Book Group, Inc.
The Little, Brown name and logo are trademarks of Hachette Book Group, Inc.

The publisher is not responsible for websites (or their content) that are not owned by the publisher.

"Ooh Child," words and music by Stan Vincent. © 1970 (Re-newed) Kama Sutra Music, Inc., and Frantino Music. All rights controlled and administered by EMI Unart Catalog Inc. (publishing) and Alfred Music Publishing Co., Inc. (print). All rights reserved.

Library of Congress Control Number: 2018961610

ISBNs: 978-0-316-52286-1 (hardcover), 978-0-316-52288-5 (pbk.), 978-0-316-52359-2 (ebook), 978-0-316-52285-4 (ebook), 978-0-316-41739-6 (ebook)

Printed in the United States of America

LSC-C

Hardcover: 10 9 8 7 6 5 4 3 2 1
Paperback: 10 9 8 7 6 5 4 3 2 1

A Tapas Media, Inc Collaboration.

To Louisa May Alcott,
a writer I love.

And to my abuelita, Catalina,
who taught me what family means.

—Rey

To my brothers and sisters,
who motivate me to be the best
versions of myself. To my
parents, grandparents, and
friends' parents, who all believed
in my dream. And to my wife,
Tamiris, who has stuck with me
through thick and thin.

—Bre

FRESH BAGELS

CHAPTER 1

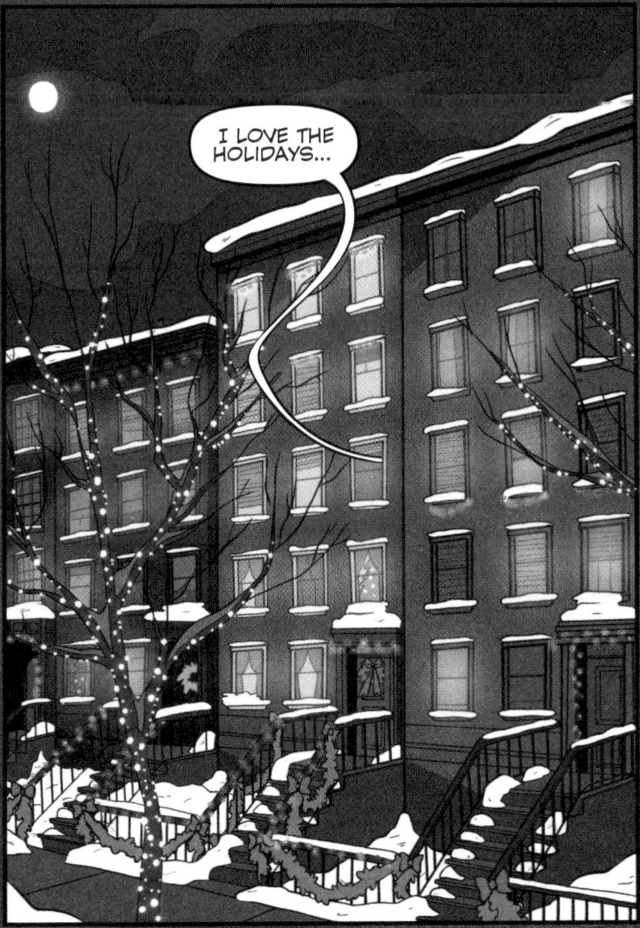
I LOVE THE HOLIDAYS...

All I Want for Christmas...

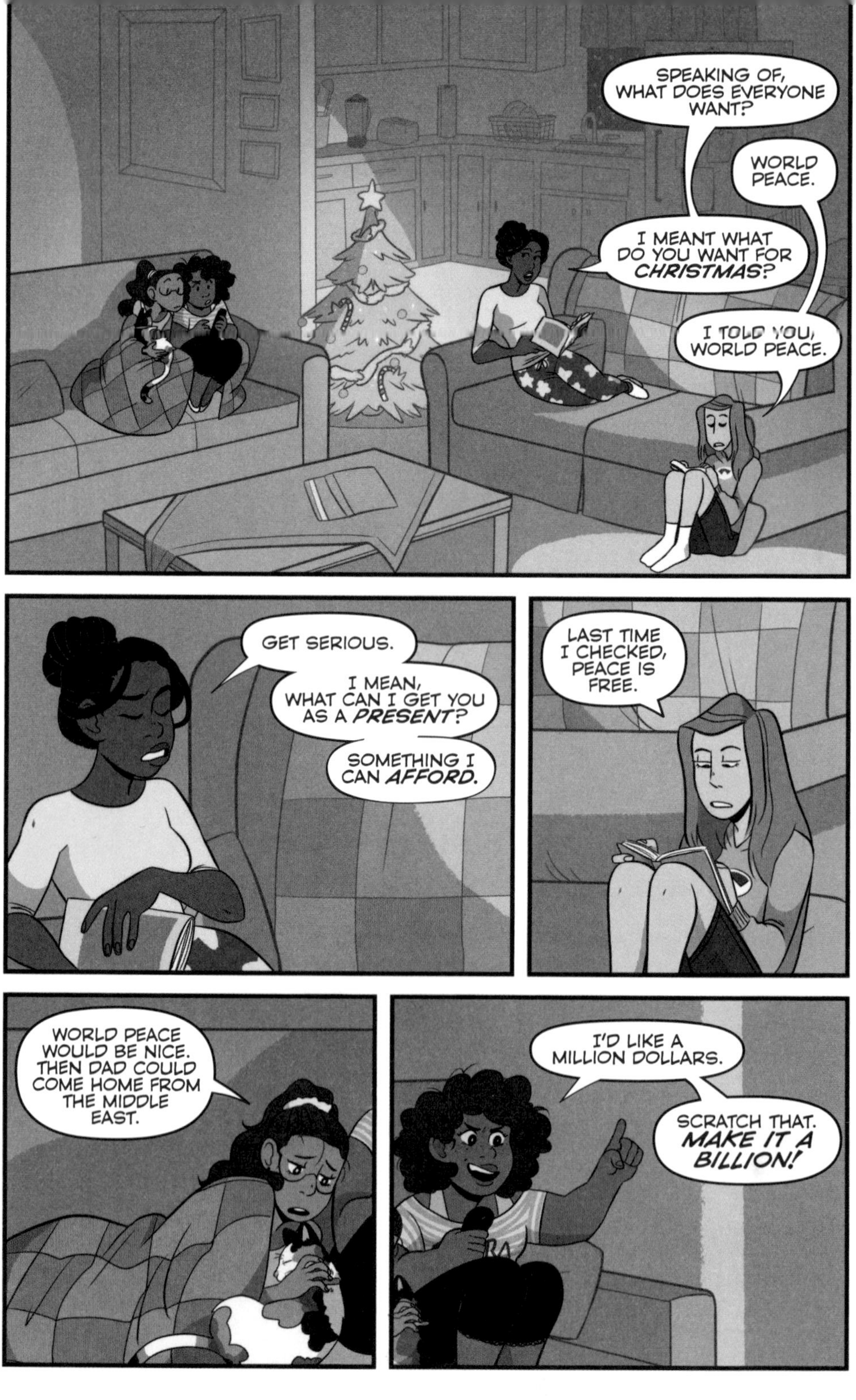
SPEAKING OF, WHAT DOES EVERYONE WANT?
WORLD PEACE.
I MEANT WHAT DO YOU WANT FOR *CHRISTMAS*?
I TOLD YOU, WORLD PEACE.
GET SERIOUS.
I MEAN, WHAT CAN I GET YOU AS A *PRESENT*?
SOMETHING I CAN *AFFORD*.
LAST TIME I CHECKED, PEACE IS FREE.
WORLD PEACE WOULD BE NICE. THEN DAD COULD COME HOME FROM THE MIDDLE EAST.
I'D LIKE A MILLION DOLLARS.
SCRATCH THAT. *MAKE IT A BILLION!*

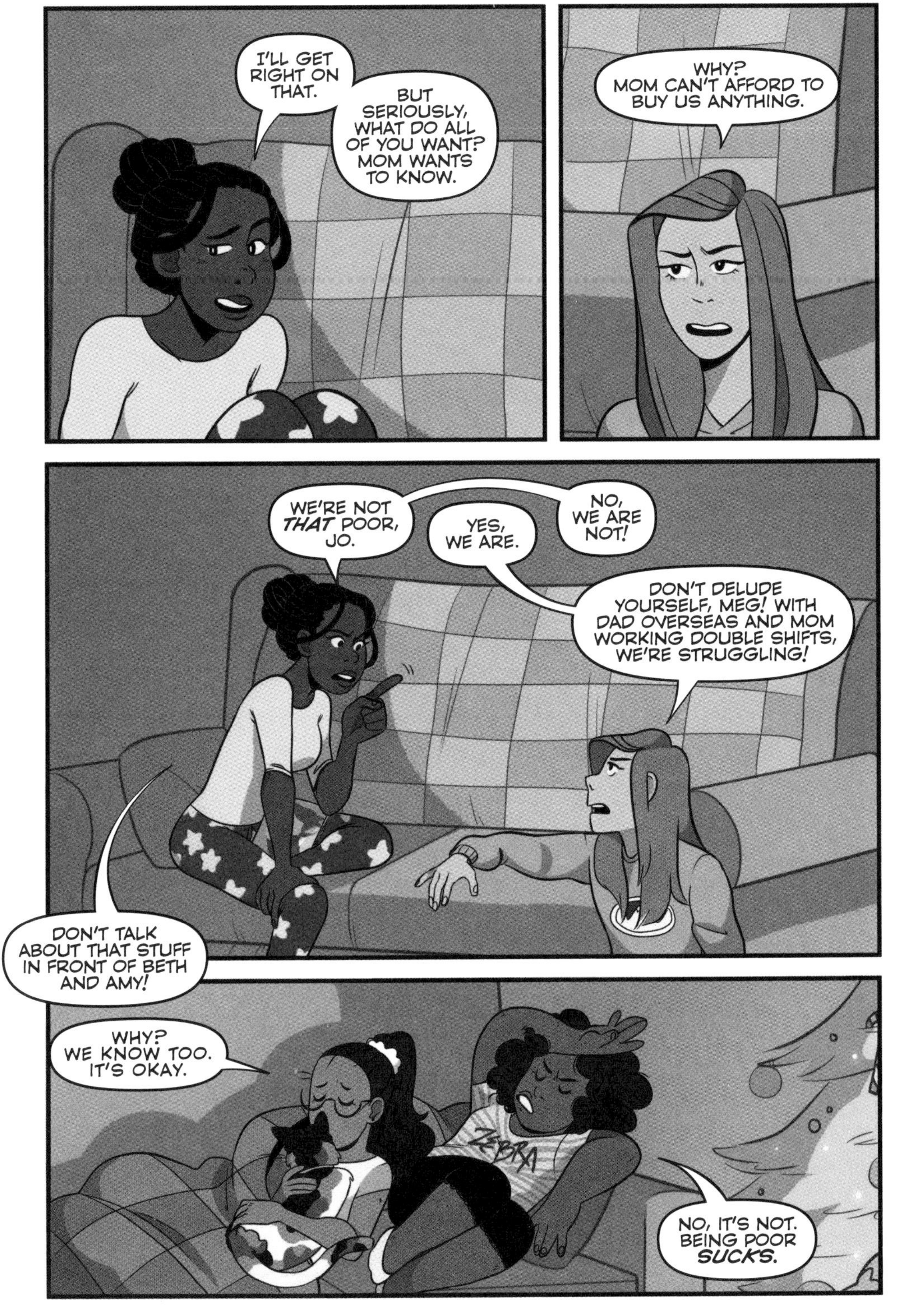
I'LL GET RIGHT ON THAT.
BUT SERIOUSLY, WHAT DO ALL OF YOU WANT? MOM WANTS TO KNOW.
WHY? MOM CAN'T AFFORD TO BUY US ANYTHING.
WE'RE NOT *THAT* POOR, JO.
YES, WE ARE.
NO, WE ARE NOT!
DON'T DELUDE YOURSELF, MEG! WITH DAD OVERSEAS AND MOM WORKING DOUBLE SHIFTS, WE'RE STRUGGLING!
DON'T TALK ABOUT THAT STUFF IN FRONT OF BETH AND AMY!
WHY? WE KNOW TOO. IT'S OKAY.
ZEBRA
NO, IT'S NOT. BEING POOR ***SUCKS***.

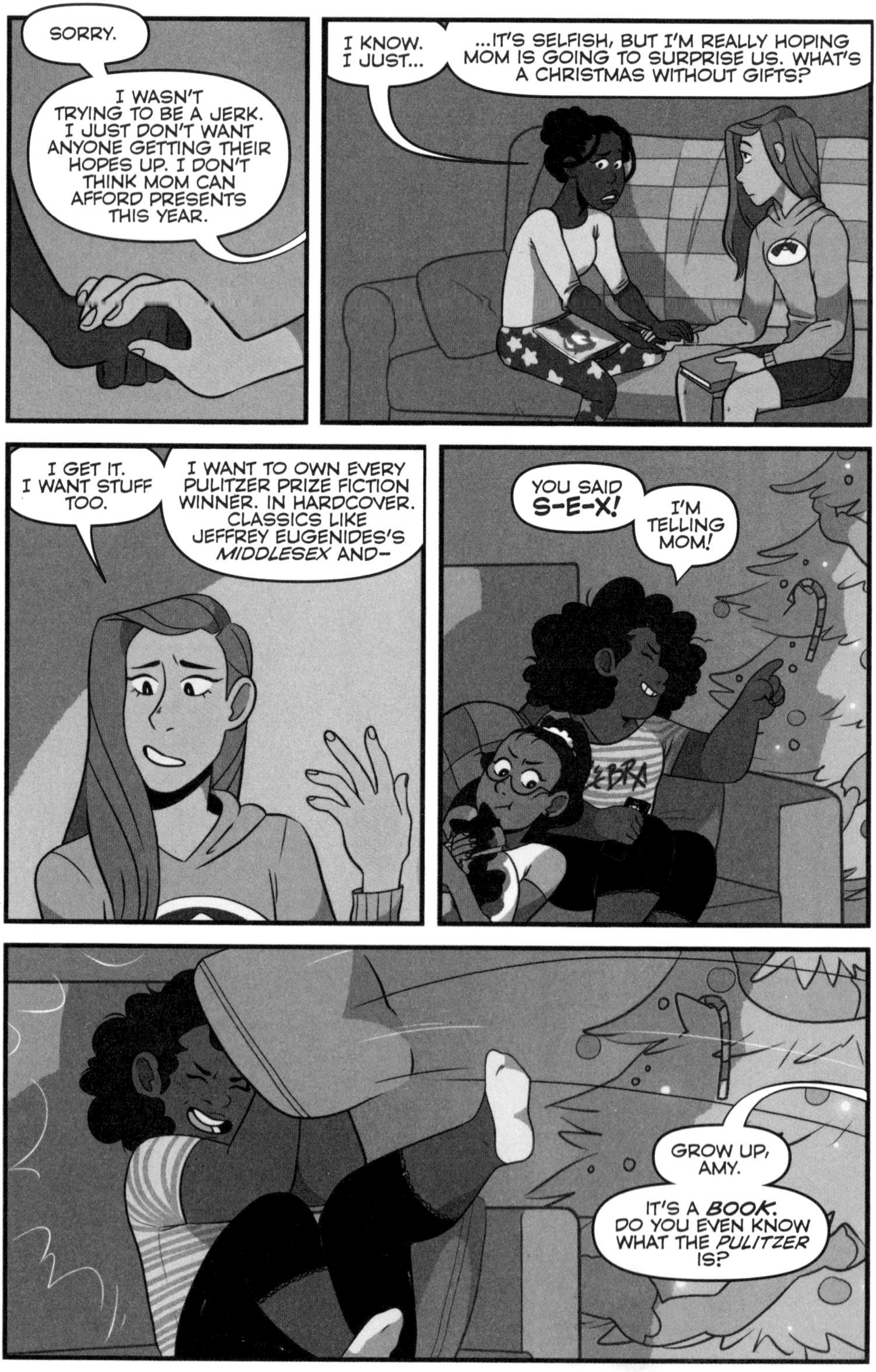
SORRY.
I WASN'T TRYING TO BE A JERK. I JUST DON'T WANT ANYONE GETTING THEIR HOPES UP. I DON'T THINK MOM CAN AFFORD PRESENTS THIS YEAR.
I KNOW. I JUST...
...IT'S SELFISH, BUT I'M REALLY HOPING MOM IS GOING TO SURPRISE US. WHAT'S A CHRISTMAS WITHOUT GIFTS?
I GET IT. I WANT STUFF TOO.
I WANT TO OWN EVERY PULITZER PRIZE FICTION WINNER. IN HARDCOVER. CLASSICS LIKE JEFFREY EUGENIDES'S *MIDDLESEX* AND–
YOU SAID **S-E-X!**
I'M TELLING MOM!
GROW UP, AMY.
IT'S A ***BOOK.*** DO YOU EVEN KNOW WHAT THE *PULITZER* IS?

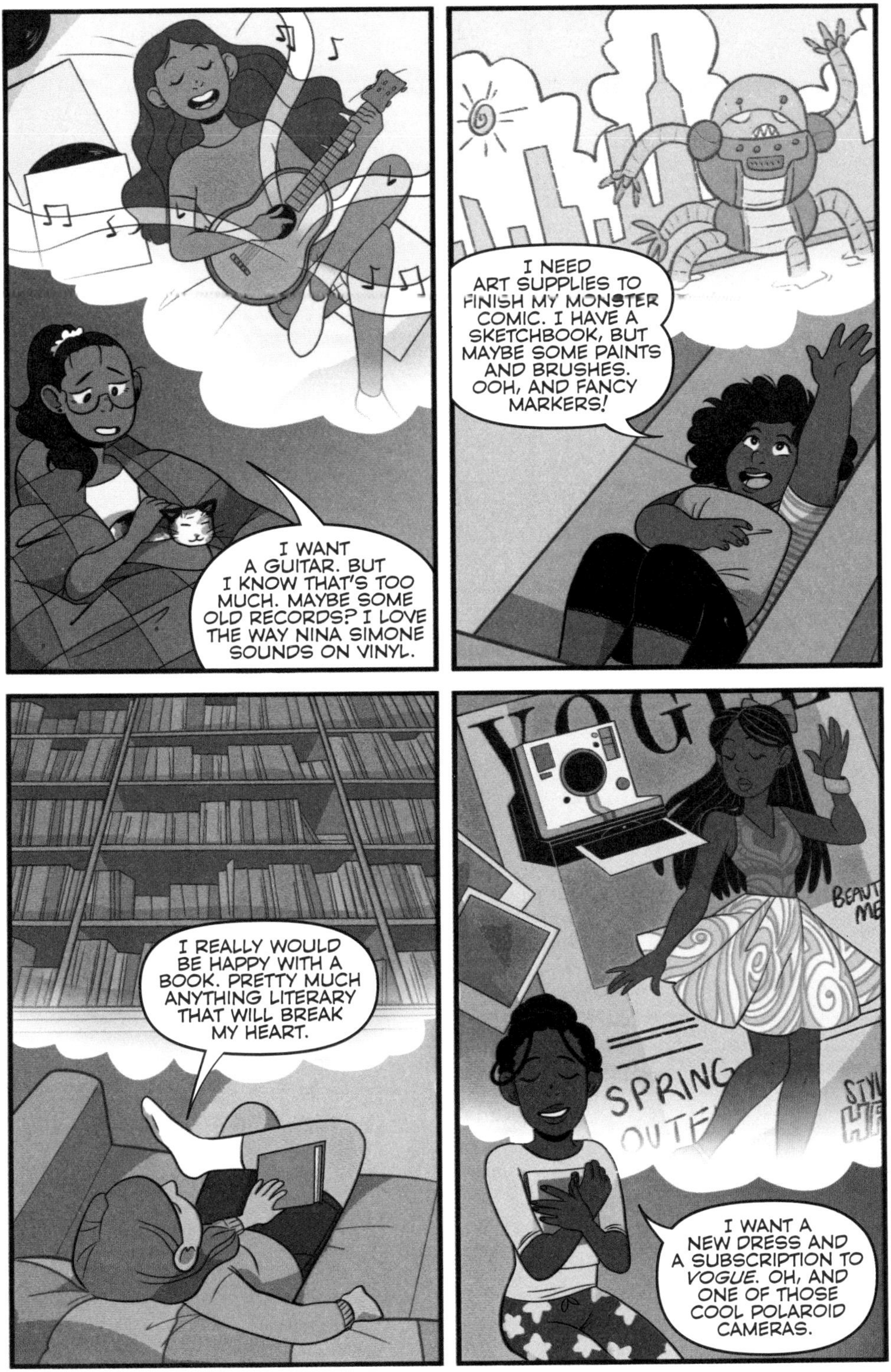
I WANT A GUITAR. BUT I KNOW THAT'S TOO MUCH. MAYBE SOME OLD RECORDS? I LOVE THE WAY NINA SIMONE SOUNDS ON VINYL.
I NEED ART SUPPLIES TO FINISH MY MONSTER COMIC. I HAVE A SKETCHBOOK, BUT MAYBE SOME PAINTS AND BRUSHES. OOH, AND FANCY MARKERS!
I REALLY WOULD BE HAPPY WITH A BOOK. PRETTY MUCH ANYTHING LITERARY THAT WILL BREAK MY HEART.
SPRING
I WANT A NEW DRESS AND A SUBSCRIPTION TO *VOGUE*. OH, AND ONE OF THOSE COOL POLAROID CAMERAS.

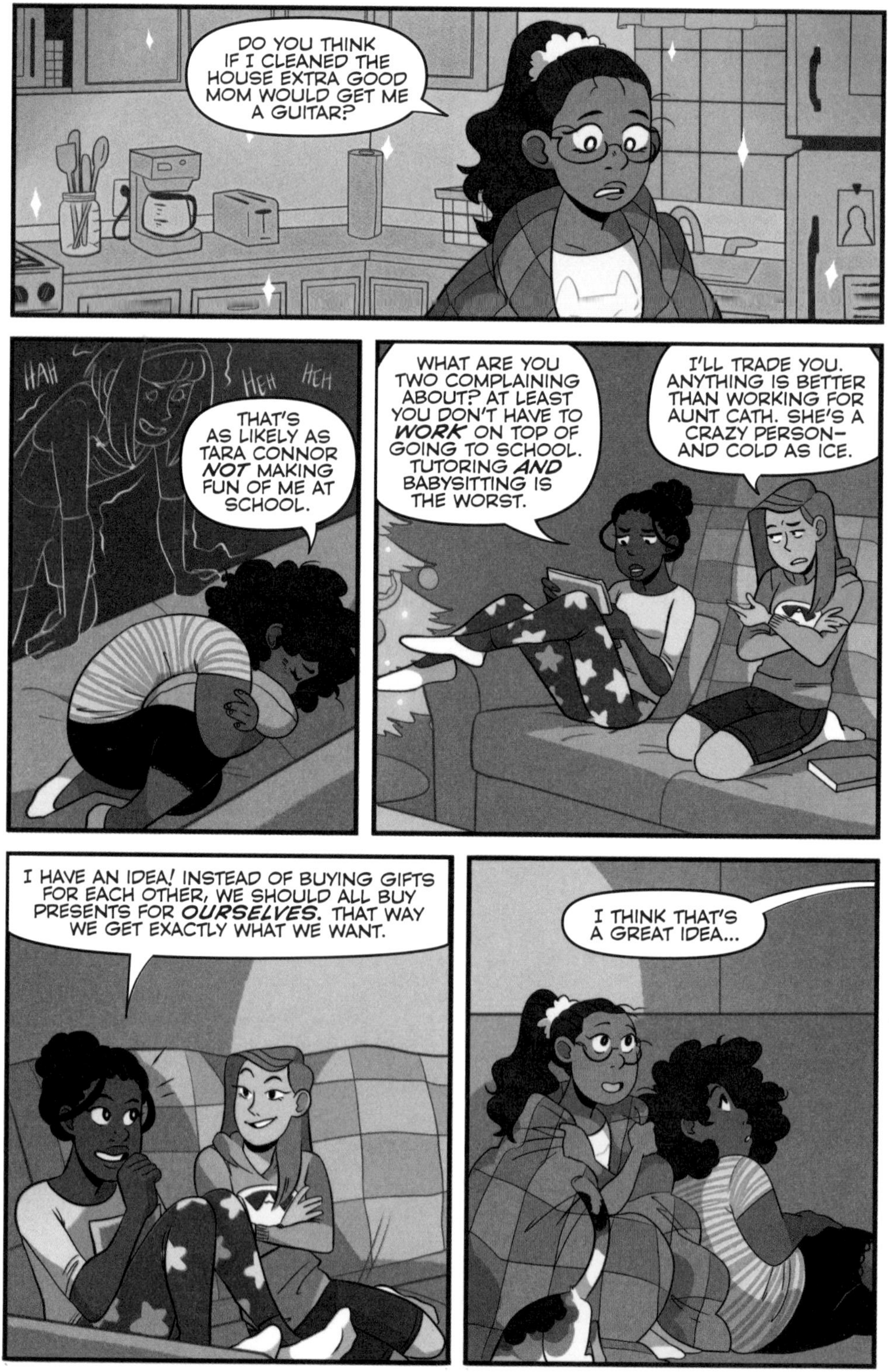
DO YOU THINK IF I CLEANED THE HOUSE EXTRA GOOD MOM WOULD GET ME A GUITAR?
HAH
HEH
HEH
THAT'S AS LIKELY AS TARA CONNOR *NOT* MAKING FUN OF ME AT SCHOOL.
WHAT ARE YOU TWO COMPLAINING ABOUT? AT LEAST YOU DON'T HAVE TO *WORK* ON TOP OF GOING TO SCHOOL. TUTORING *AND* BABYSITTING IS THE WORST.
I'LL TRADE YOU. ANYTHING IS BETTER THAN WORKING FOR AUNT CATH. SHE'S A CRAZY PERSON— AND COLD AS ICE.
I HAVE AN IDEA! INSTEAD OF BUYING GIFTS FOR EACH OTHER, WE SHOULD ALL BUY PRESENTS FOR *OURSELVES.* THAT WAY WE GET EXACTLY WHAT WE WANT.
I THINK THAT'S A GREAT IDEA...

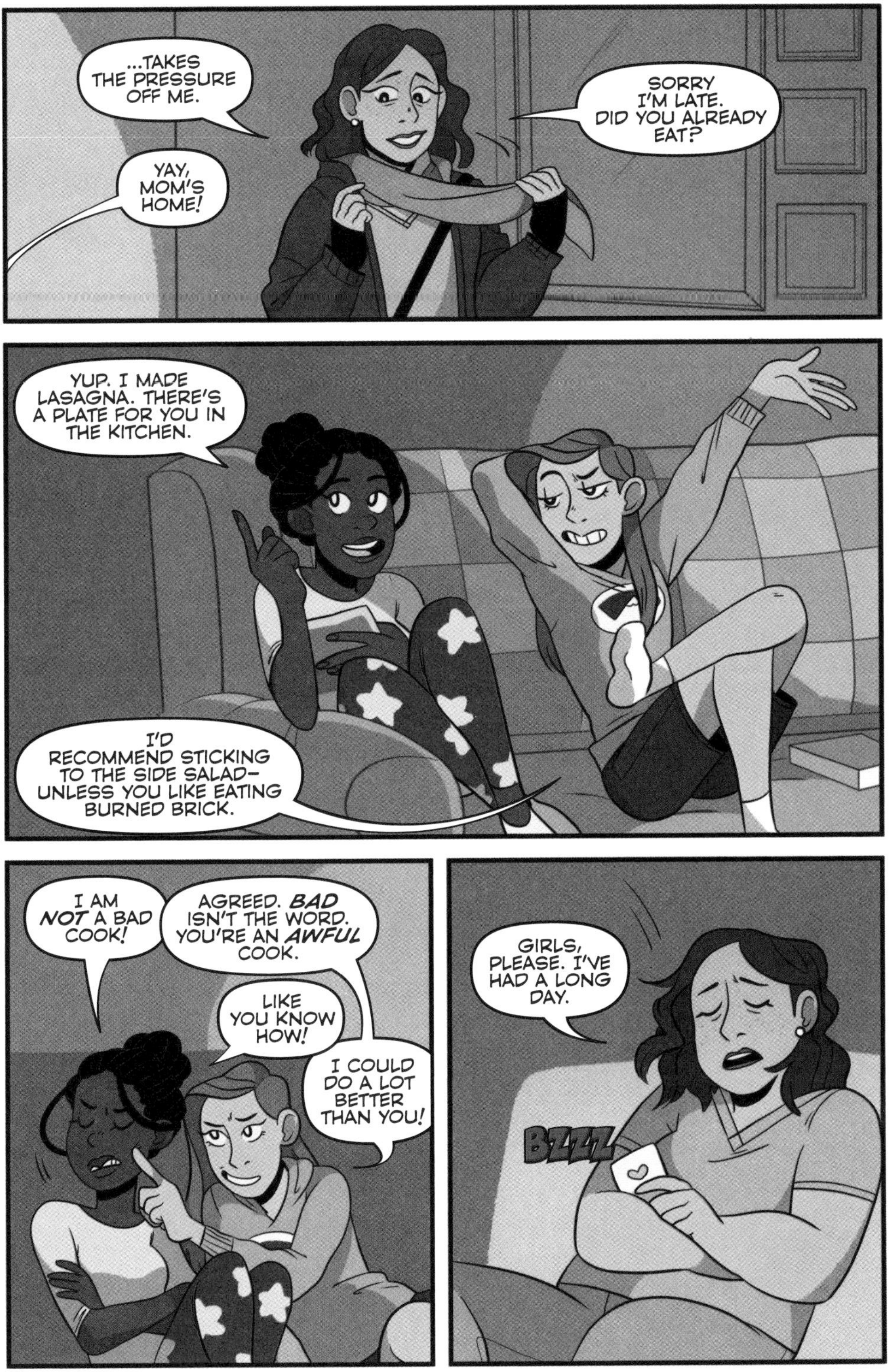
...TAKES THE PRESSURE OFF ME.
YAY, MOM'S HOME!
SORRY I'M LATE. DID YOU ALREADY EAT?
YUP. I MADE LASAGNA. THERE'S A PLATE FOR YOU IN THE KITCHEN.
I'D RECOMMEND STICKING TO THE SIDE SALAD—UNLESS YOU LIKE EATING BURNED BRICK.
I AM *NOT* A BAD COOK!
AGREED. *BAD* ISN'T THE WORD. YOU'RE AN *AWFUL* COOK.
LIKE YOU KNOW HOW!
I COULD DO A LOT BETTER THAN YOU!
GIRLS, PLEASE. I'VE HAD A LONG DAY.
BZZZ

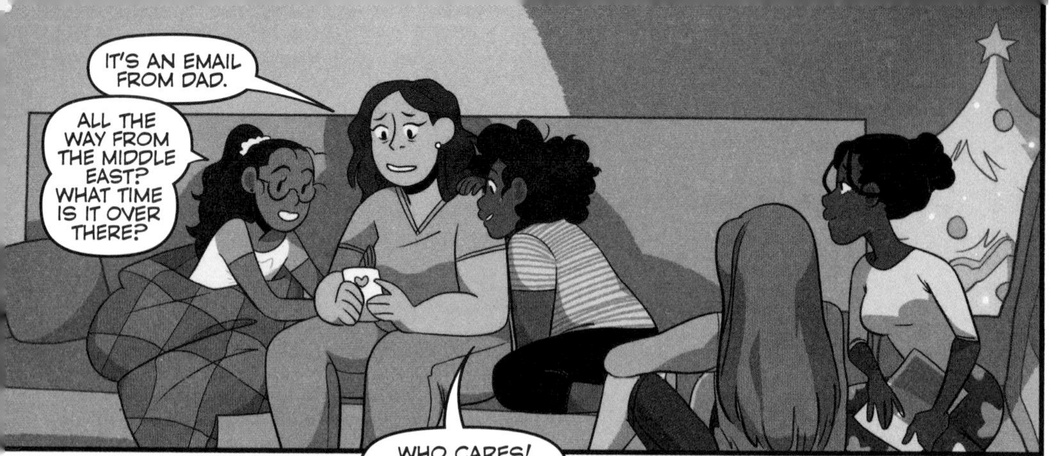
IT'S AN EMAIL FROM DAD.
ALL THE WAY FROM THE MIDDLE EAST? WHAT TIME IS IT OVER THERE?
WHO CARES! READ THE EMAIL, MOM!

New Message

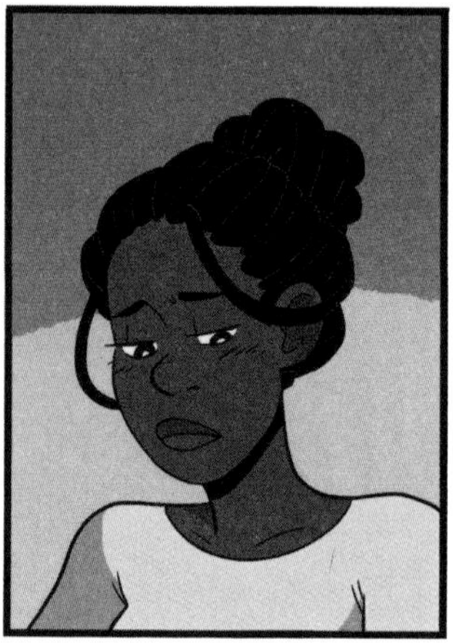

FROM: Robert March
TO: Madison March
SENT: December 19

How are all of my girls? Thanks for sending pictures of family pizza night. I can't believe how much all of you have grown in only a few months. The pics made me very happy…and very homesick. I know it's been hard, having me away, serving in the army, but it's the honorable thing to do, not just for you, but for our country.

People in America think they have it hard, but they are far better off than many. I have seen so much suffering over here. Some have lost their homes, some have lost their loved ones, and some have lost everything. War is nobody's friend. But I believe in what I'm here for: making the world a safer place for each of you.

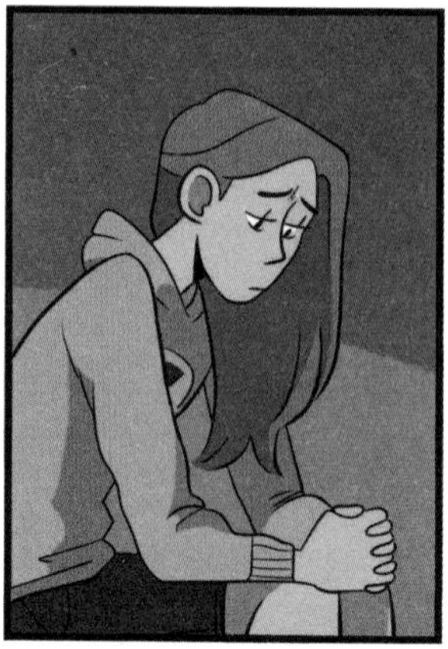

I hope all of you are behaving and taking care of each other. Make sure you take care of your mom too. Be good, my little women. I love you with all my heart.

–Dad

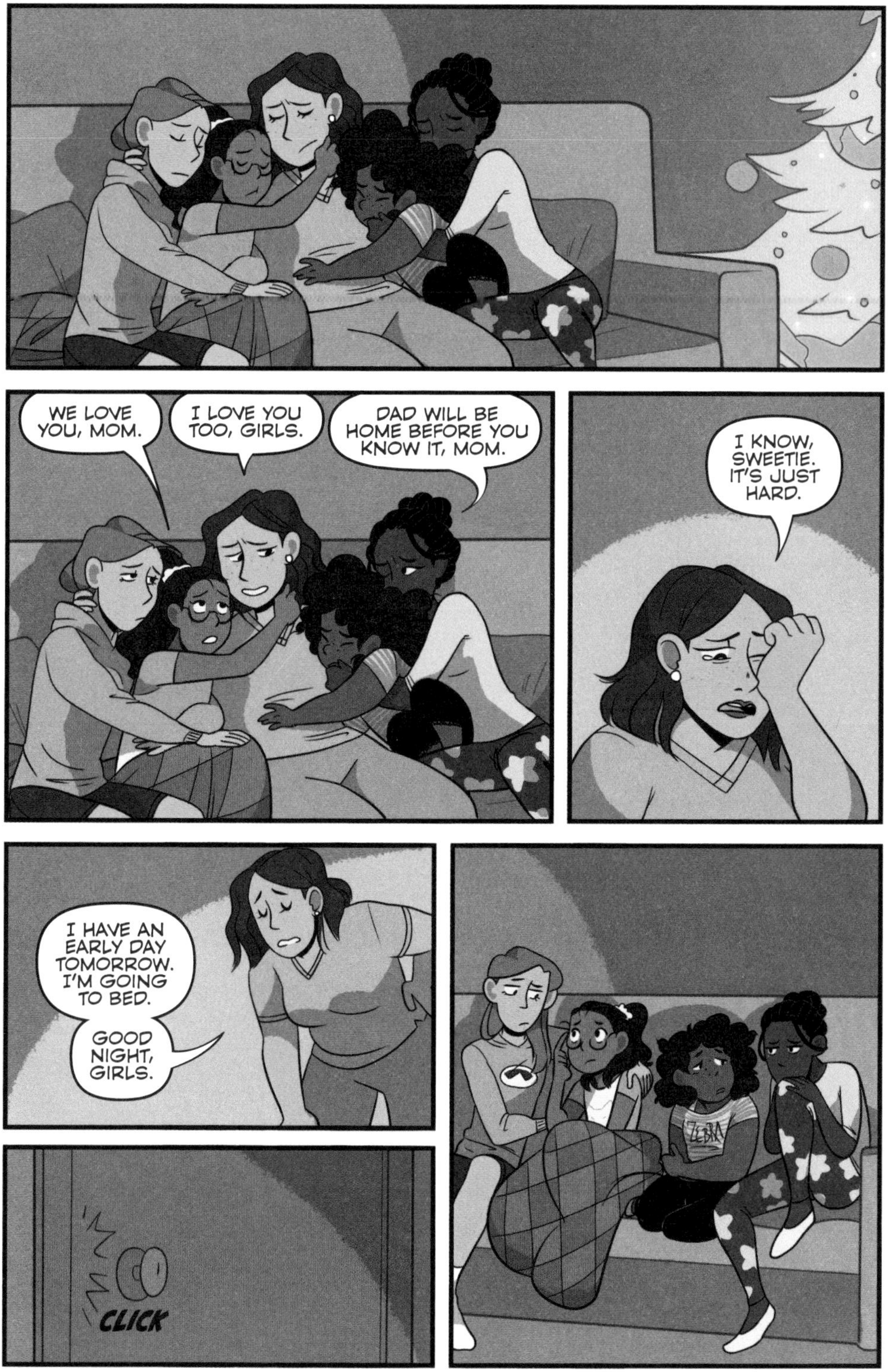
WE LOVE YOU, MOM.
I LOVE YOU TOO, GIRLS.
DAD WILL BE HOME BEFORE YOU KNOW IT, MOM.
I KNOW, SWEETIE. IT'S JUST HARD.
I HAVE AN EARLY DAY TOMORROW. I'M GOING TO BED.
GOOD NIGHT, GIRLS.
CLICK

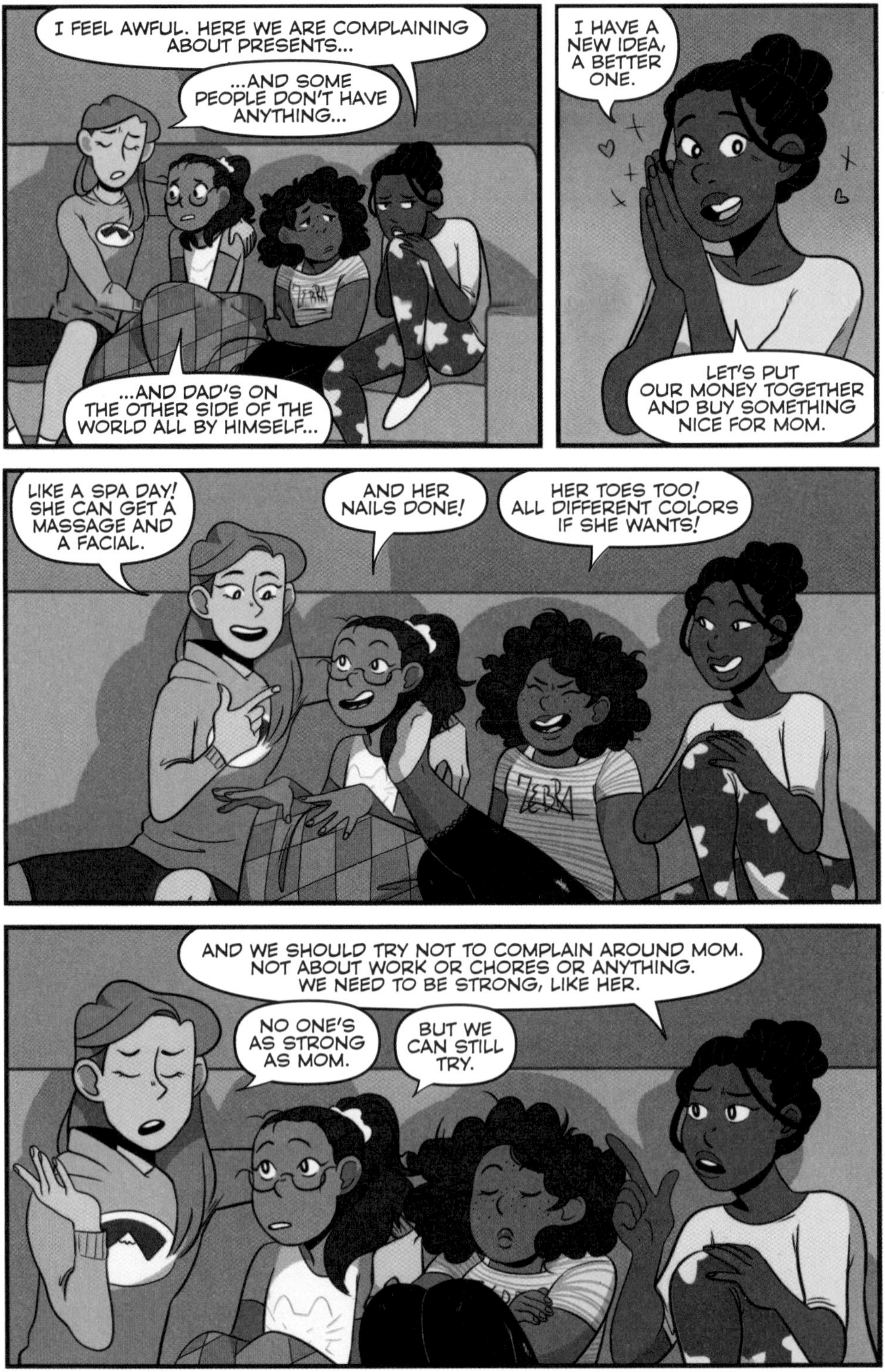
I FEEL AWFUL. HERE WE ARE COMPLAINING ABOUT PRESENTS...
...AND SOME PEOPLE DON'T HAVE ANYTHING...
...AND DAD'S ON THE OTHER SIDE OF THE WORLD ALL BY HIMSELF...
I HAVE A NEW IDEA, A BETTER ONE.
LET'S PUT OUR MONEY TOGETHER AND BUY SOMETHING NICE FOR MOM.
LIKE A SPA DAY! SHE CAN GET A MASSAGE AND A FACIAL.
AND HER NAILS DONE!
HER TOES TOO! ALL DIFFERENT COLORS IF SHE WANTS!
AND WE SHOULD TRY NOT TO COMPLAIN AROUND MOM. NOT ABOUT WORK OR CHORES OR ANYTHING. WE NEED TO BE STRONG, LIKE HER.
NO ONE'S AS STRONG AS MOM.
BUT WE CAN STILL TRY.

CHAPTER 2

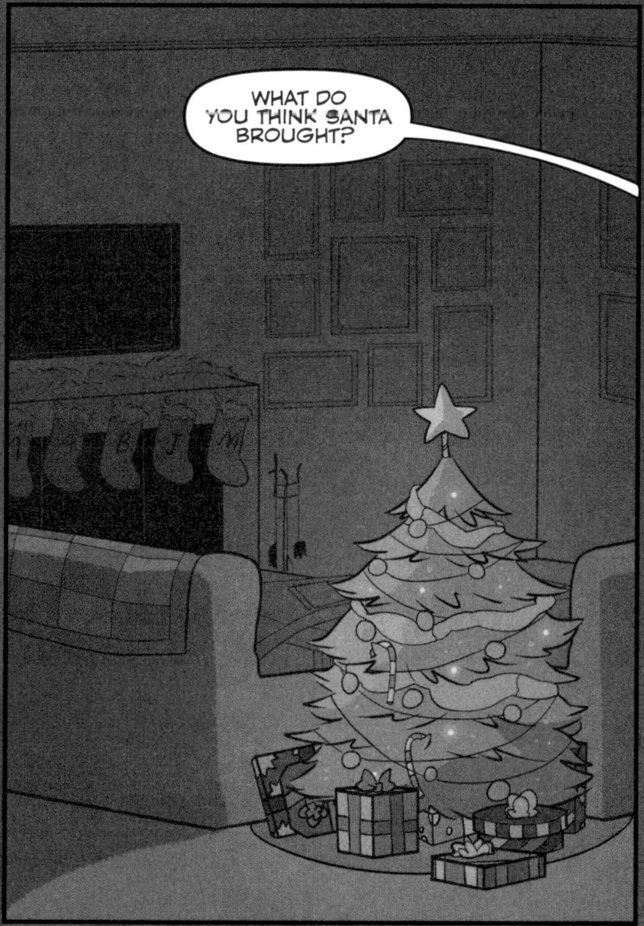
WHAT DO YOU THINK SANTA BROUGHT?

It's the Thought That Counts...

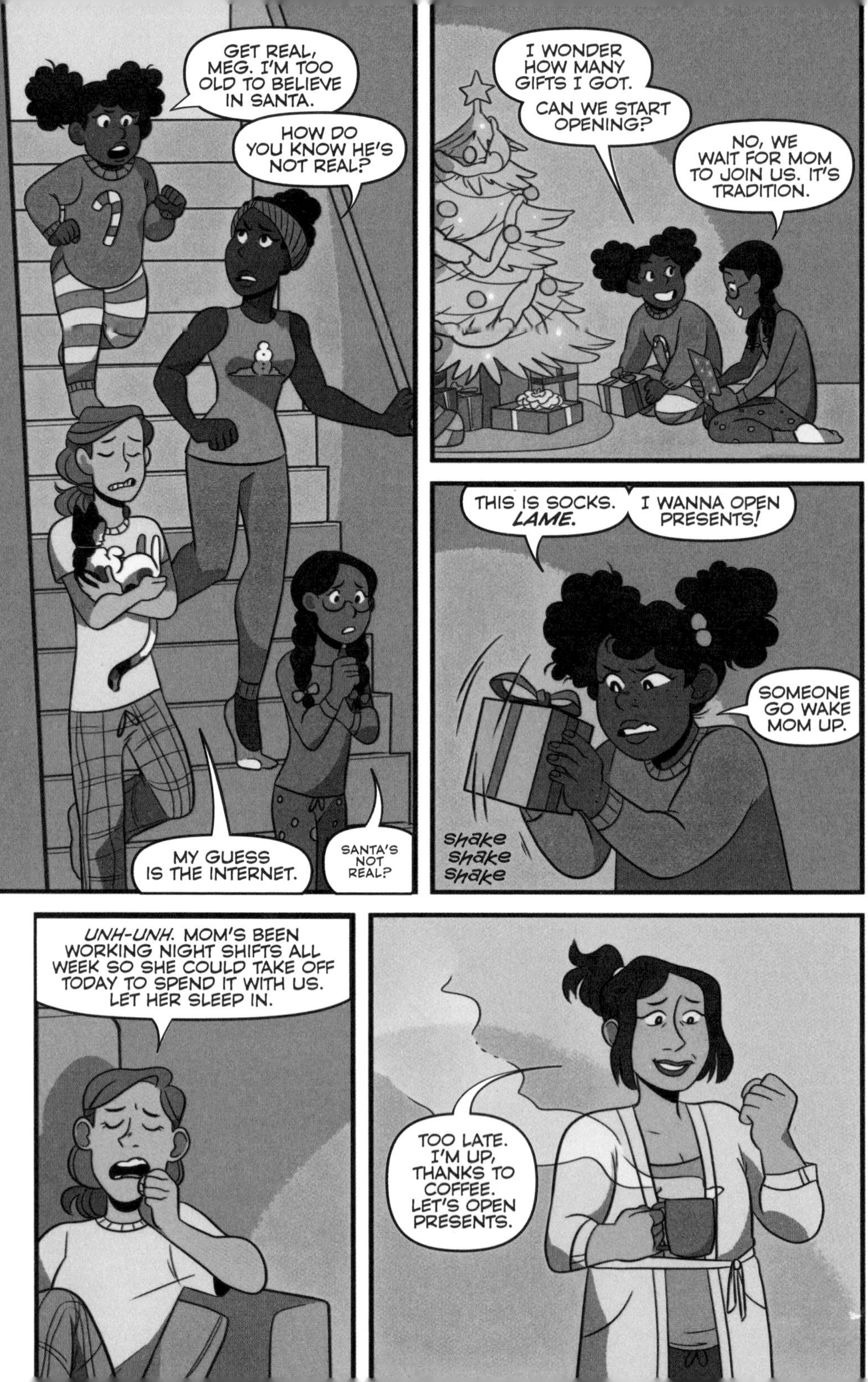
GET REAL, MEG. I'M TOO OLD TO BELIEVE IN SANTA.
HOW DO YOU KNOW HE'S NOT REAL?
MY GUESS IS THE INTERNET.
SANTA'S NOT REAL?
I WONDER HOW MANY GIFTS I GOT.
CAN WE START OPENING?
NO, WE WAIT FOR MOM TO JOIN US. IT'S TRADITION.
THIS IS SOCKS. *LAME.*
I WANNA OPEN PRESENTS!
SOMEONE GO WAKE MOM UP.
shake shake shake
UNH-UNH. MOM'S BEEN WORKING NIGHT SHIFTS ALL WEEK SO SHE COULD TAKE OFF TODAY TO SPEND IT WITH US. LET HER SLEEP IN.
TOO LATE. I'M UP, THANKS TO COFFEE. LET'S OPEN PRESENTS.

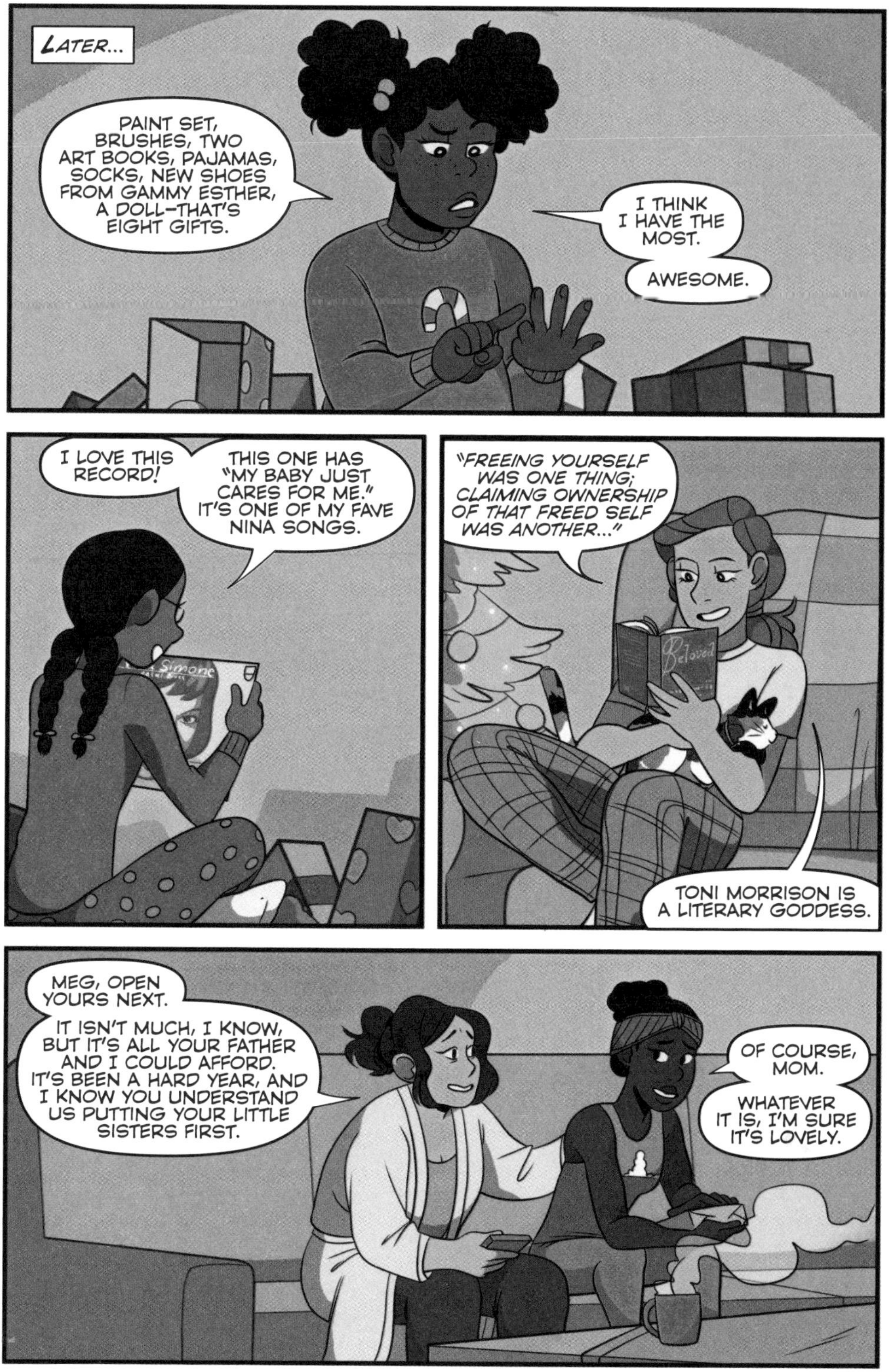
LATER...
PAINT SET, BRUSHES, TWO ART BOOKS, PAJAMAS, SOCKS, NEW SHOES FROM GAMMY ESTHER, A DOLL—THAT'S EIGHT GIFTS.
I THINK I HAVE THE MOST.
AWESOME.
I LOVE THIS RECORD!
THIS ONE HAS "MY BABY JUST CARES FOR ME." IT'S ONE OF MY FAVE NINA SONGS.
"FREEING YOURSELF WAS ONE THING; CLAIMING OWNERSHIP OF THAT FREED SELF WAS ANOTHER..."
TONI MORRISON IS A LITERARY GODDESS.
MEG, OPEN YOURS NEXT.
IT ISN'T MUCH, I KNOW, BUT IT'S ALL YOUR FATHER AND I COULD AFFORD. IT'S BEEN A HARD YEAR, AND I KNOW YOU UNDERSTAND US PUTTING YOUR LITTLE SISTERS FIRST.
OF COURSE, MOM.
WHATEVER IT IS, I'M SURE IT'S LOVELY.

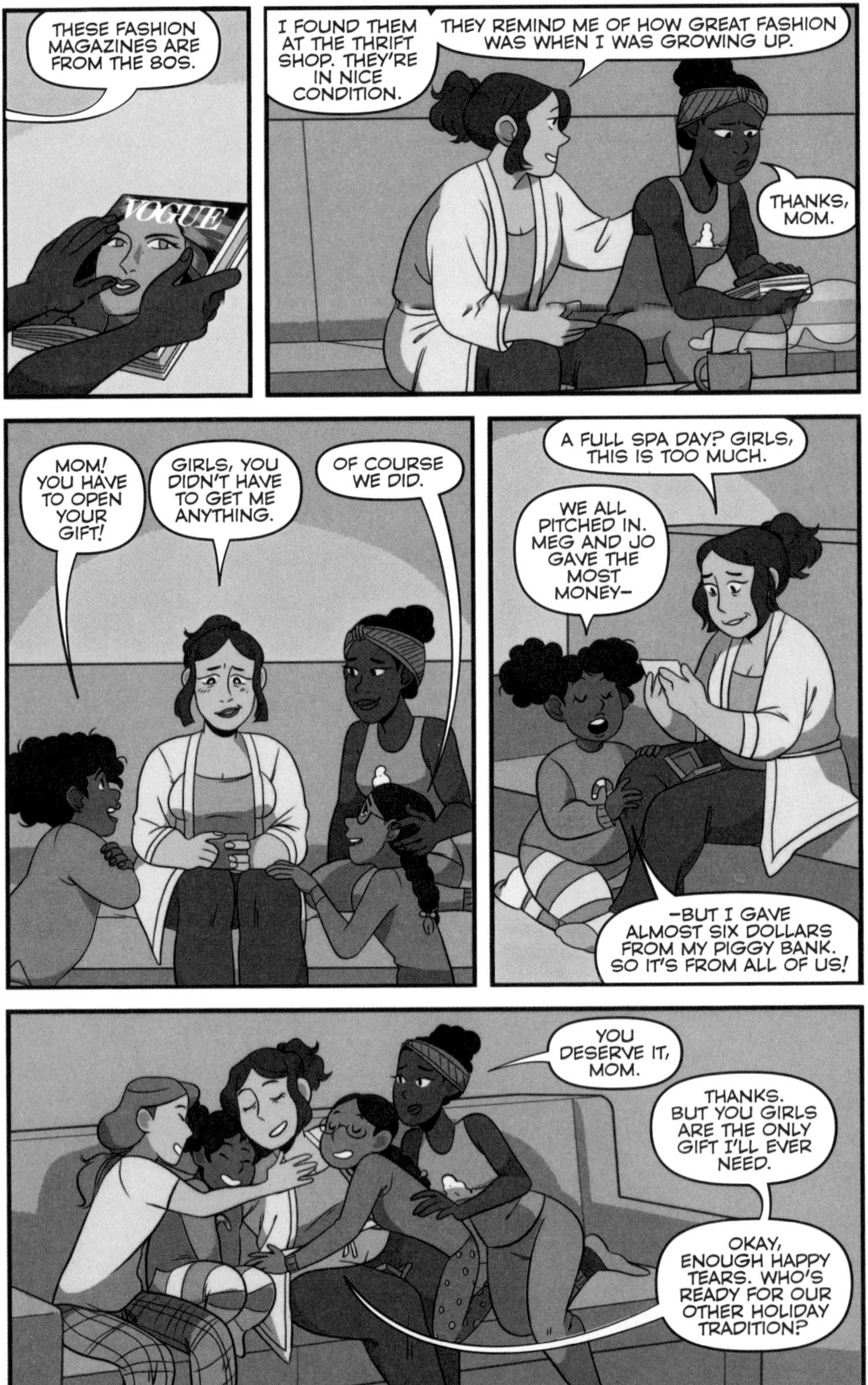
THESE FASHION MAGAZINES ARE FROM THE 80S.
VOGUE
I FOUND THEM AT THE THRIFT SHOP. THEY'RE IN NICE CONDITION.
THEY REMIND ME OF HOW GREAT FASHION WAS WHEN I WAS GROWING UP.
THANKS, MOM.
MOM! YOU HAVE TO OPEN YOUR GIFT!
GIRLS, YOU DIDN'T HAVE TO GET ME ANYTHING.
OF COURSE WE DID.
A FULL SPA DAY? GIRLS, THIS IS TOO MUCH.
WE ALL PITCHED IN. MEG AND JO GAVE THE MOST MONEY—
—BUT I GAVE ALMOST SIX DOLLARS FROM MY PIGGY BANK. SO IT'S FROM ALL OF US!
YOU DESERVE IT, MOM.
THANKS. BUT YOU GIRLS ARE THE ONLY GIFT I'LL EVER NEED.
OKAY, ENOUGH HAPPY TEARS. WHO'S READY FOR OUR OTHER HOLIDAY TRADITION?

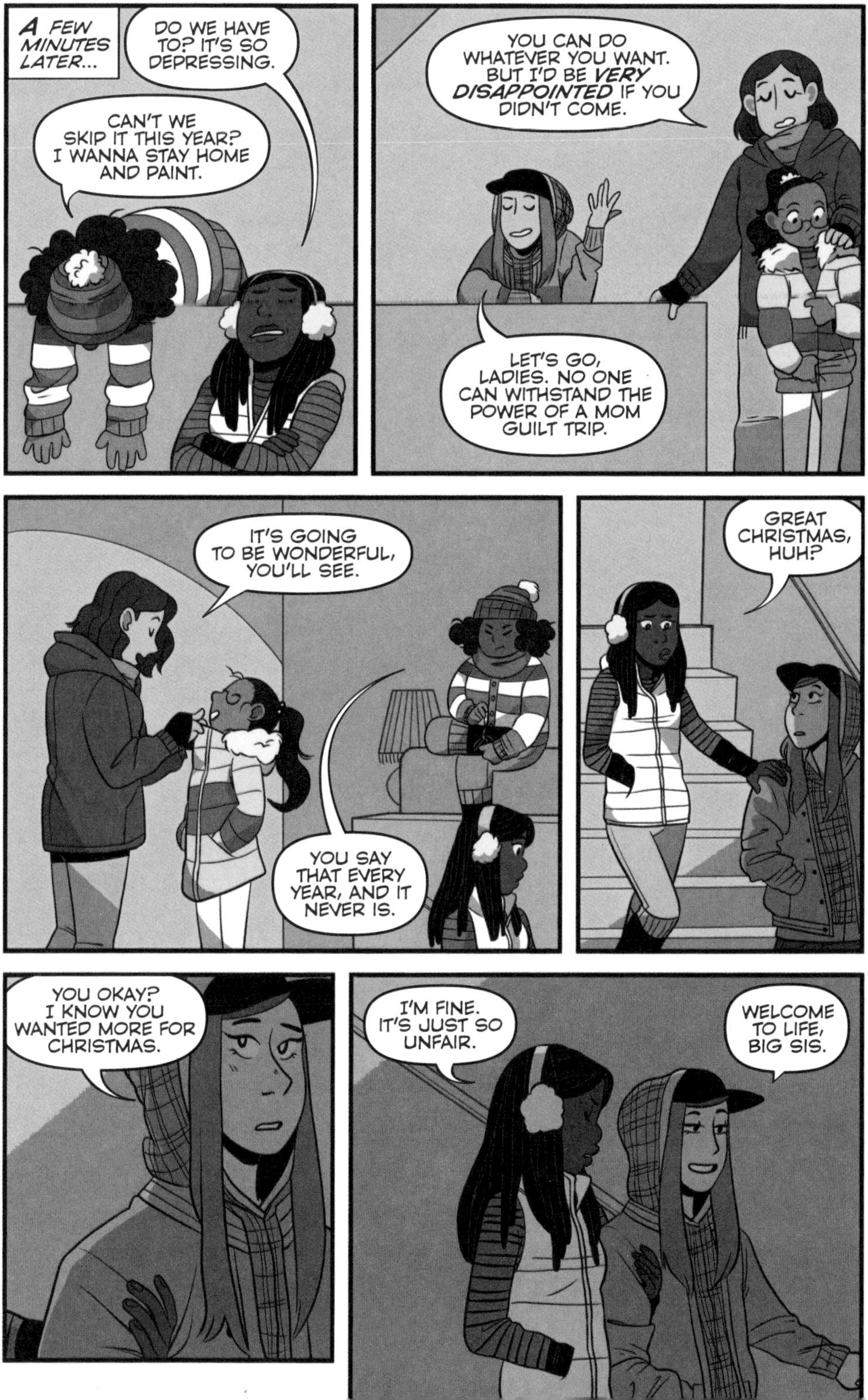
A FEW MINUTES LATER...
DO WE HAVE TO? IT'S SO DEPRESSING.
CAN'T WE SKIP IT THIS YEAR? I WANNA STAY HOME AND PAINT.
YOU CAN DO WHATEVER YOU WANT. BUT I'D BE VERY DISAPPOINTED IF YOU DIDN'T COME.
LET'S GO, LADIES. NO ONE CAN WITHSTAND THE POWER OF A MOM GUILT TRIP.
IT'S GOING TO BE WONDERFUL, YOU'LL SEE.
YOU SAY THAT EVERY YEAR, AND IT NEVER IS.
GREAT CHRISTMAS, HUH?
YOU OKAY? I KNOW YOU WANTED MORE FOR CHRISTMAS.
I'M FINE. IT'S JUST SO UNFAIR.
WELCOME TO LIFE, BIG SIS.

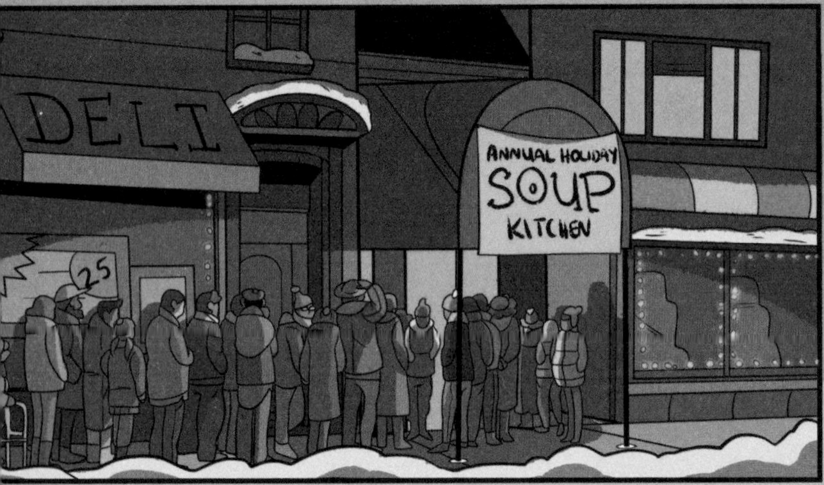
DELI
25
ANNUAL HOLIDAY
SOUP
KITCHEN

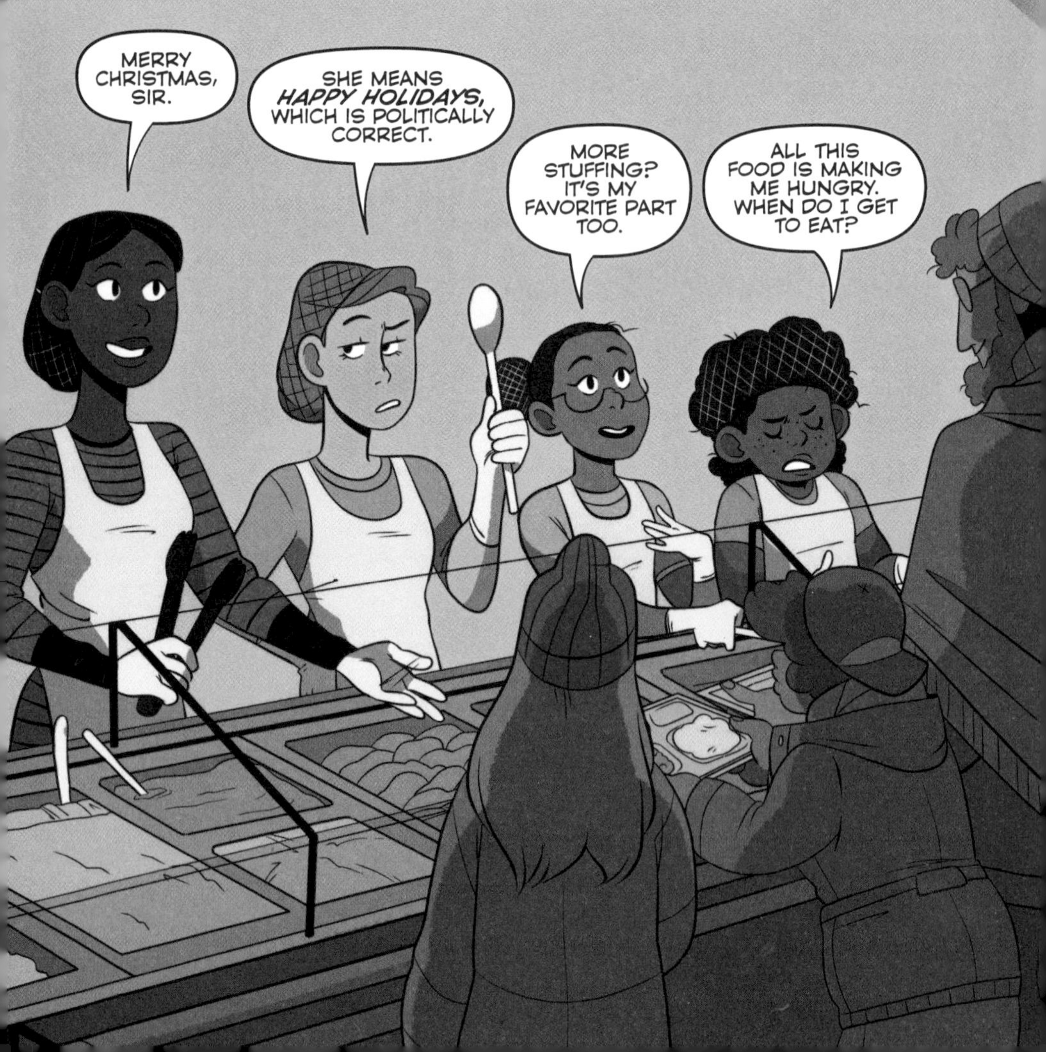
MERRY CHRISTMAS, SIR.
SHE MEANS *HAPPY HOLIDAYS,* WHICH IS POLITICALLY CORRECT.
MORE STUFFING? IT'S MY FAVORITE PART TOO.
ALL THIS FOOD IS MAKING ME HUNGRY. WHEN DO I GET TO EAT?

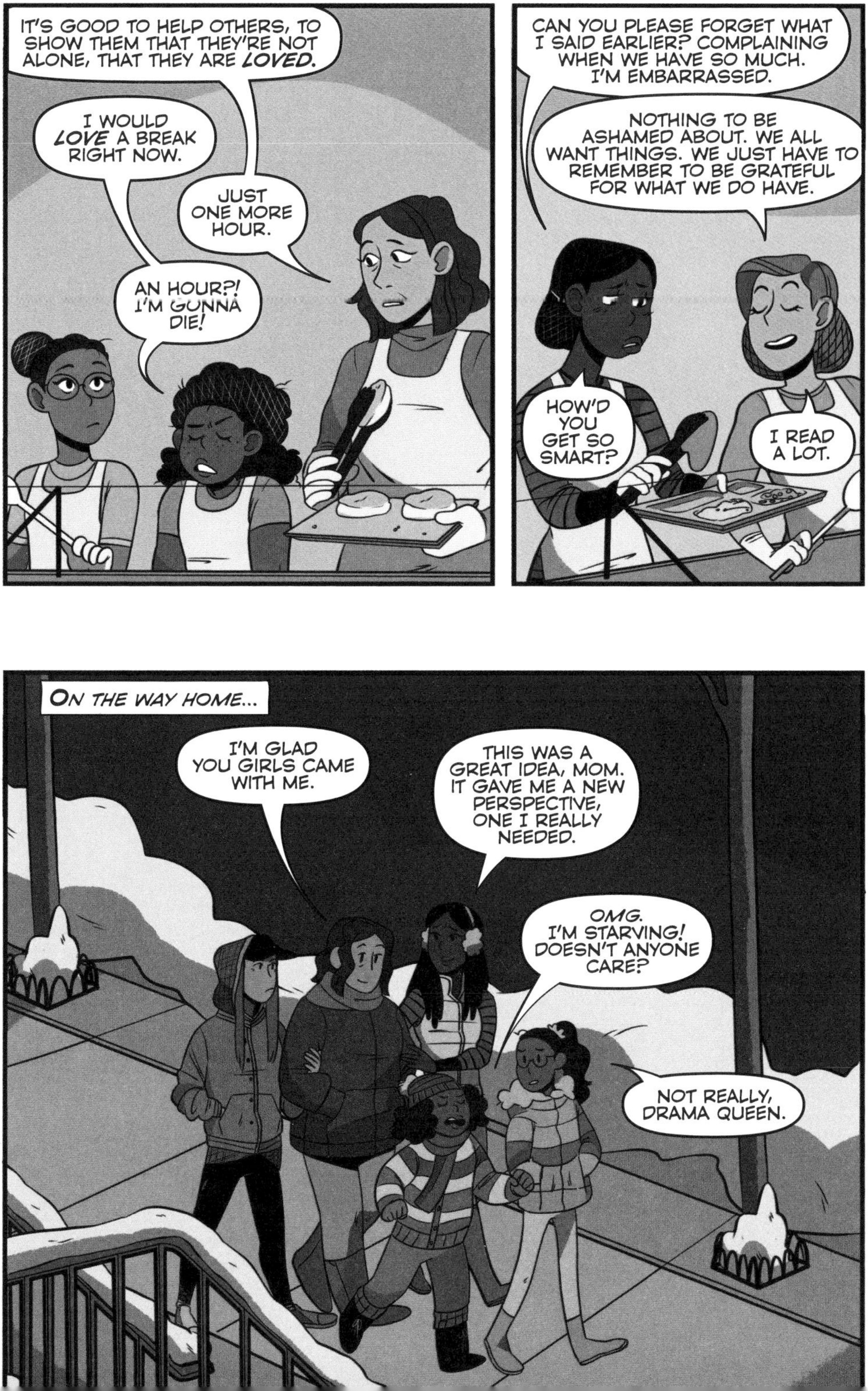
IT'S GOOD TO HELP OTHERS, TO SHOW THEM THAT THEY'RE NOT ALONE, THAT THEY ARE *LOVED.*
I WOULD *LOVE* A BREAK RIGHT NOW.
JUST ONE MORE HOUR.
AN HOUR?! I'M GONNA DIE!
CAN YOU PLEASE FORGET WHAT I SAID EARLIER? COMPLAINING WHEN WE HAVE SO MUCH. I'M EMBARRASSED.
NOTHING TO BE ASHAMED ABOUT. WE ALL WANT THINGS. WE JUST HAVE TO REMEMBER TO BE GRATEFUL FOR WHAT WE DO HAVE.
HOW'D YOU GET SO SMART?
I READ A LOT.
ON THE WAY HOME...
I'M GLAD YOU GIRLS CAME WITH ME.
THIS WAS A GREAT IDEA, MOM. IT GAVE ME A NEW PERSPECTIVE, ONE I REALLY NEEDED.
OMG. I'M STARVING! DOESN'T ANYONE CARE?
NOT REALLY, DRAMA QUEEN.

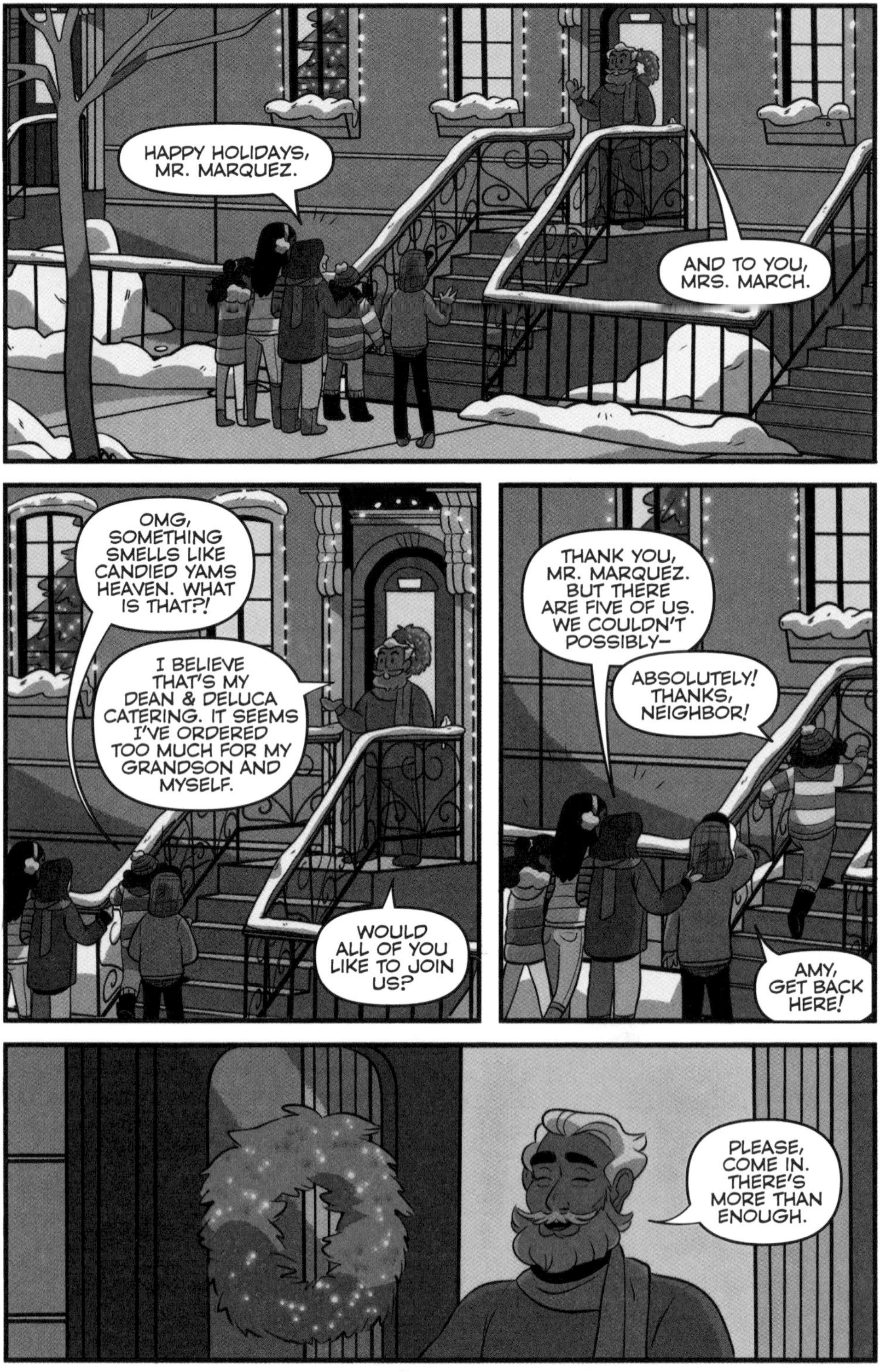
HAPPY HOLIDAYS, MR. MARQUEZ.
AND TO YOU, MRS. MARCH.
OMG, SOMETHING SMELLS LIKE CANDIED YAMS HEAVEN. WHAT IS THAT?!
I BELIEVE THAT'S MY DEAN & DELUCA CATERING. IT SEEMS I'VE ORDERED TOO MUCH FOR MY GRANDSON AND MYSELF.
WOULD ALL OF YOU LIKE TO JOIN US?
THANK YOU, MR. MARQUEZ. BUT THERE ARE FIVE OF US. WE COULDN'T POSSIBLY—
ABSOLUTELY! THANKS, NEIGHBOR!
AMY, GET BACK HERE!
PLEASE, COME IN. THERE'S MORE THAN ENOUGH.

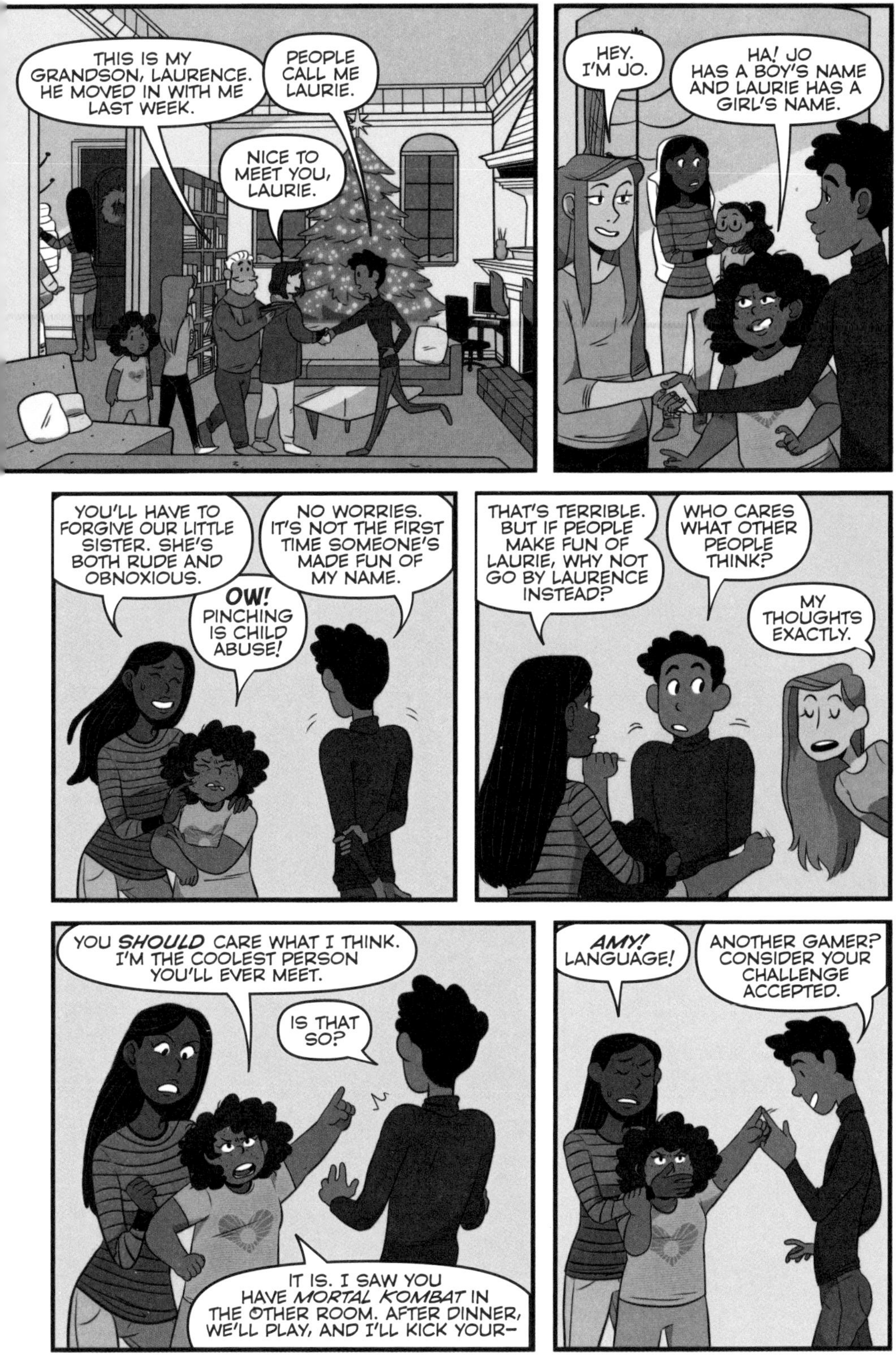
THIS IS MY GRANDSON, LAURENCE. HE MOVED IN WITH ME LAST WEEK.
PEOPLE CALL ME LAURIE.
NICE TO MEET YOU, LAURIE.
HEY. I'M JO.
HA! JO HAS A BOY'S NAME AND LAURIE HAS A GIRL'S NAME.
YOU'LL HAVE TO FORGIVE OUR LITTLE SISTER. SHE'S BOTH RUDE AND OBNOXIOUS.
NO WORRIES. IT'S NOT THE FIRST TIME SOMEONE'S MADE FUN OF MY NAME.
OW! PINCHING IS CHILD ABUSE!
THAT'S TERRIBLE. BUT IF PEOPLE MAKE FUN OF LAURIE, WHY NOT GO BY LAURENCE INSTEAD?
WHO CARES WHAT OTHER PEOPLE THINK?
MY THOUGHTS EXACTLY.
YOU SHOULD CARE WHAT I THINK. I'M THE COOLEST PERSON YOU'LL EVER MEET.
IS THAT SO?
IT IS. I SAW YOU HAVE MORTAL KOMBAT IN THE OTHER ROOM. AFTER DINNER, WE'LL PLAY, AND I'LL KICK YOUR–
AMY! LANGUAGE!
ANOTHER GAMER? CONSIDER YOUR CHALLENGE ACCEPTED.

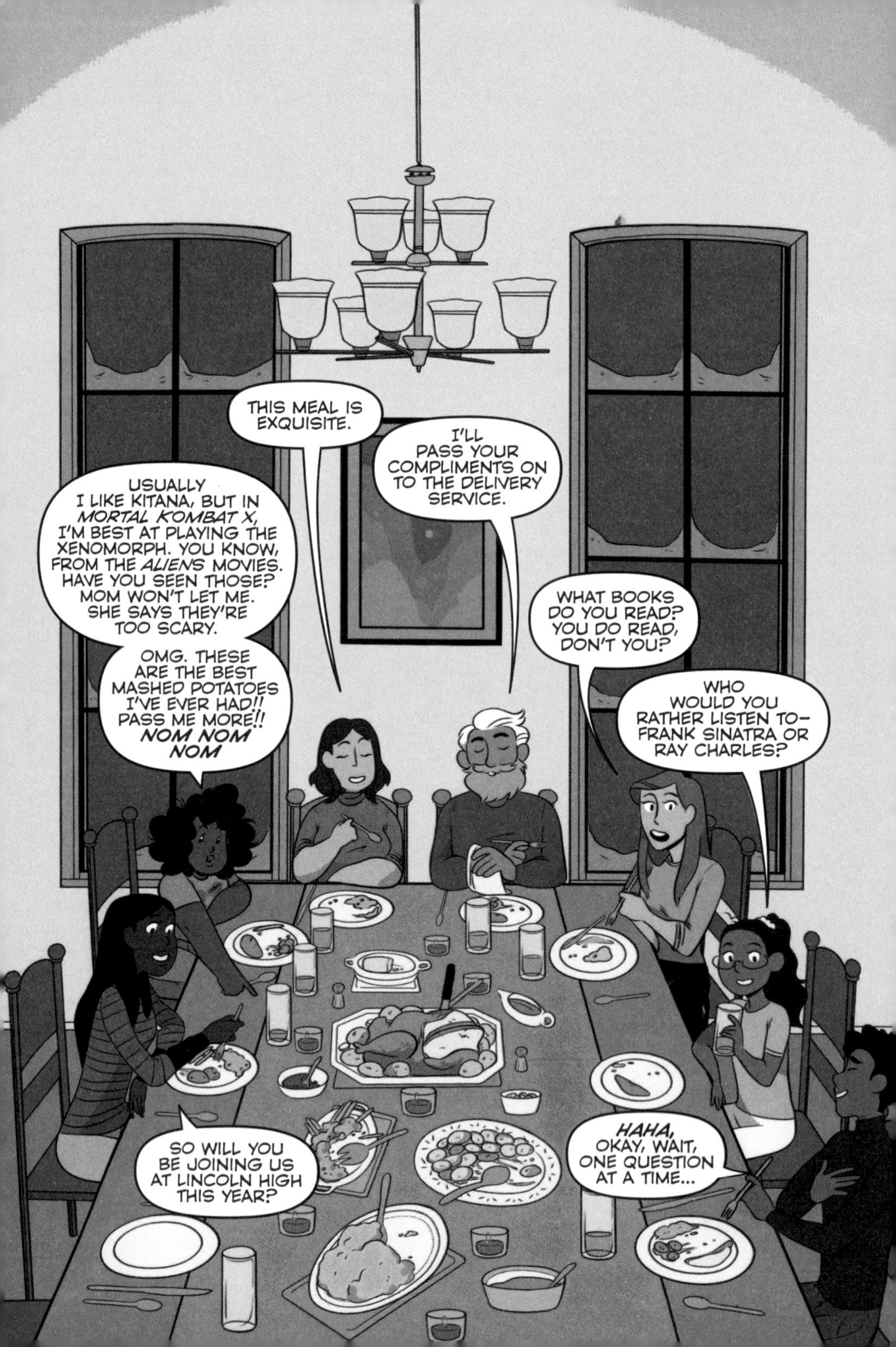
THIS MEAL IS EXQUISITE.
I'LL PASS YOUR COMPLIMENTS ON TO THE DELIVERY SERVICE.
USUALLY I LIKE KITANA, BUT IN *MORTAL KOMBAT X*, I'M BEST AT PLAYING THE XENOMORPH. YOU KNOW, FROM THE *ALIENS* MOVIES. HAVE YOU SEEN THOSE? MOM WON'T LET ME. SHE SAYS THEY'RE TOO SCARY.
OMG. THESE ARE THE BEST MASHED POTATOES I'VE EVER HAD!! PASS ME MORE!! ***NOM NOM NOM***
WHAT BOOKS DO YOU READ? YOU DO READ, DON'T YOU?
WHO WOULD YOU RATHER LISTEN TO—FRANK SINATRA OR RAY CHARLES?
SO WILL YOU BE JOINING US AT LINCOLN HIGH THIS YEAR?
HAHA, OKAY, WAIT, ONE QUESTION AT A TIME...

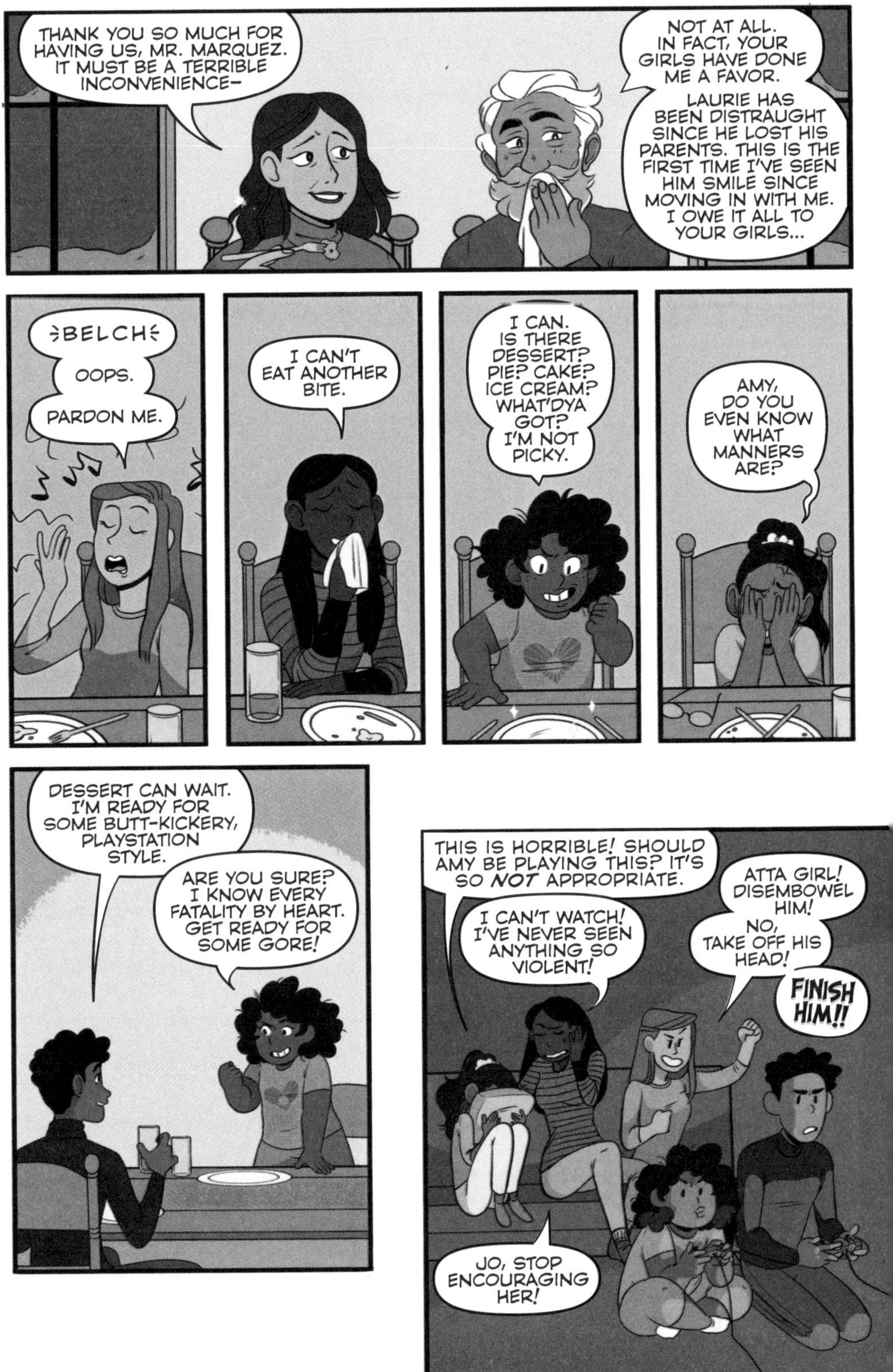
THANK YOU SO MUCH FOR HAVING US, MR. MARQUEZ. IT MUST BE A TERRIBLE INCONVENIENCE–
NOT AT ALL. IN FACT, YOUR GIRLS HAVE DONE ME A FAVOR.
LAURIE HAS BEEN DISTRAUGHT SINCE HE LOST HIS PARENTS. THIS IS THE FIRST TIME I'VE SEEN HIM SMILE SINCE MOVING IN WITH ME. I OWE IT ALL TO YOUR GIRLS...
BELCH
OOPS.
PARDON ME.
I CAN'T EAT ANOTHER BITE.
I CAN. IS THERE DESSERT? PIE? CAKE? ICE CREAM? WHAT'DYA GOT? I'M NOT PICKY.
AMY, DO YOU EVEN KNOW WHAT MANNERS ARE?
DESSERT CAN WAIT. I'M READY FOR SOME BUTT-KICKERY, PLAYSTATION STYLE.
ARE YOU SURE? I KNOW EVERY FATALITY BY HEART. GET READY FOR SOME GORE!
THIS IS HORRIBLE! SHOULD AMY BE PLAYING THIS? IT'S SO NOT APPROPRIATE.
I CAN'T WATCH! I'VE NEVER SEEN ANYTHING SO VIOLENT!
ATTA GIRL! DISEMBOWEL HIM!
NO, TAKE OFF HIS HEAD!
FINISH HIM!!
JO, STOP ENCOURAGING HER!

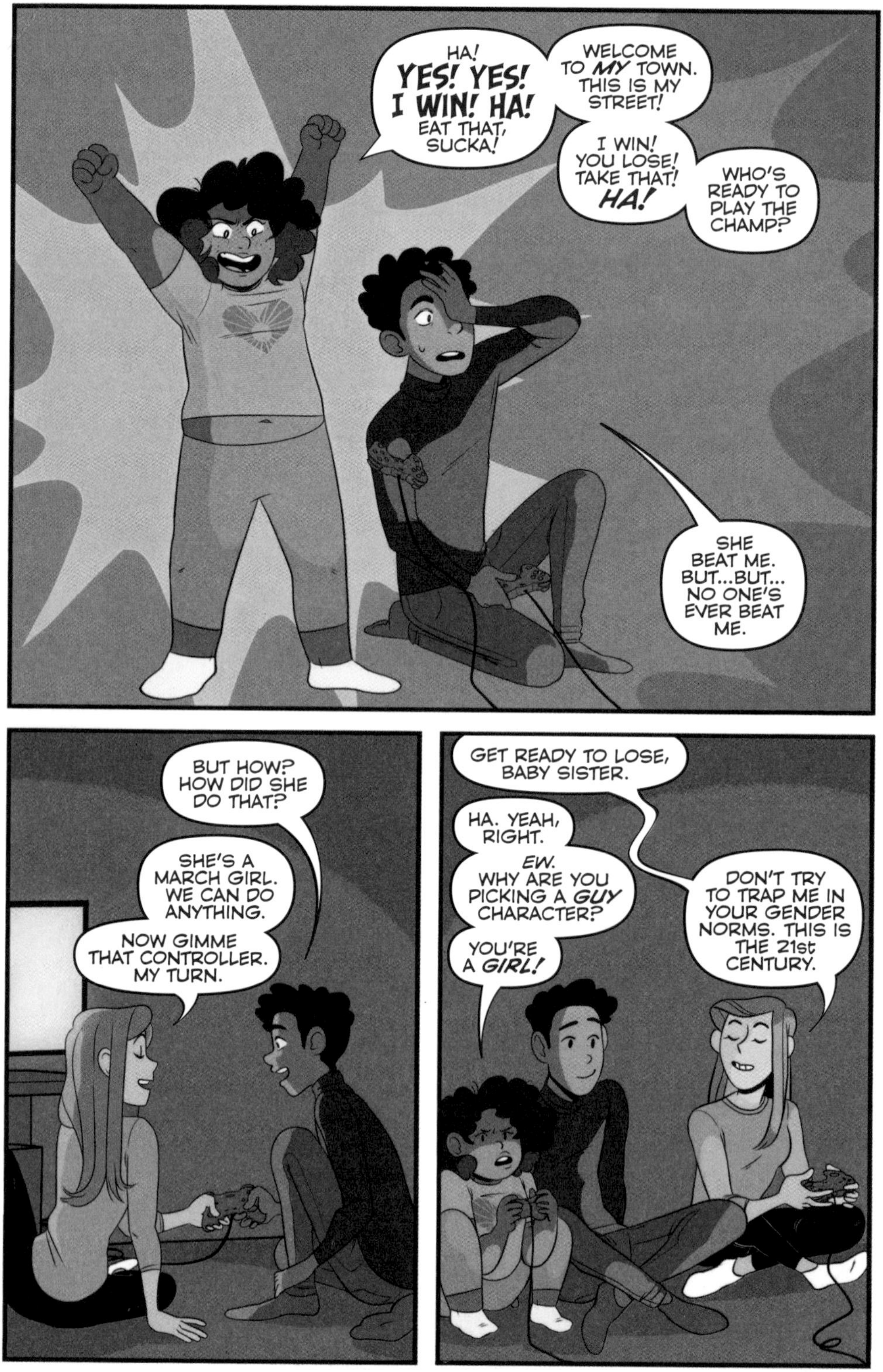
HA!
YES! YES! I WIN! HA! EAT THAT, SUCKA!
WELCOME TO *MY* TOWN. THIS IS MY STREET!
I WIN! YOU LOSE! TAKE THAT! *HA!*
WHO'S READY TO PLAY THE CHAMP?
SHE BEAT ME. BUT...BUT... NO ONE'S EVER BEAT ME.
BUT HOW? HOW DID SHE DO THAT?
SHE'S A MARCH GIRL. WE CAN DO ANYTHING.
NOW GIMME THAT CONTROLLER. MY TURN.
GET READY TO LOSE, BABY SISTER.
HA. YEAH, RIGHT.
EW. WHY ARE YOU PICKING A *GUY* CHARACTER?
YOU'RE A *GIRL!*
DON'T TRY TO TRAP ME IN YOUR GENDER NORMS. THIS IS THE 21st CENTURY.

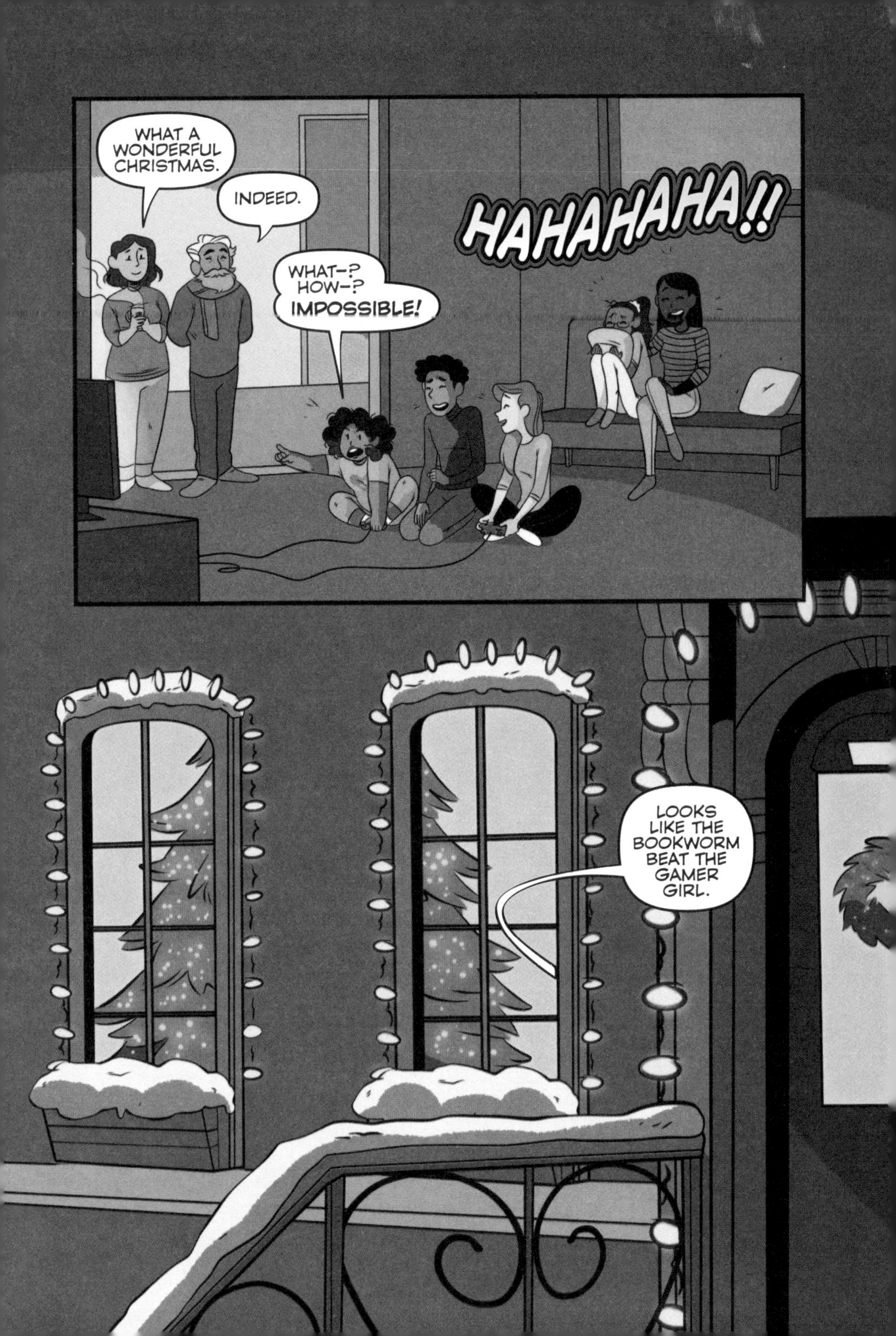
WHAT A WONDERFUL CHRISTMAS.
INDEED.
HAHAHAHAHA!!
WHAT-? HOW-? IMPOSSIBLE!
LOOKS LIKE THE BOOKWORM BEAT THE GAMER GIRL.

FROM: Megan March
TO: Robert March
SENT: December 28

Hi Dad,

Christmas wasn't the same without you. How could it be? This is the first time I've had the holidays without you.

Remember our first Christmas alone together? When it was just the two of us in that little apartment in the Village after my mom passed away? I insisted Santa wasn't real. You kept telling me he was, trying so hard to give me a good holiday. So much that you rented that ridiculous Santa outfit and that big white beard. I guess you knew me well enough to know I'd stay up late to catch a glimpse of Jolly Old Saint Nick. But your well-laid plan backfired!

You were all, "Ho ho ho, hello, little girl, I'm Santa!" I think you expected me to jump with joy. Instead, I screamed! You were shocked, but come on! I really thought you were an intruder in our apartment. I don't think you realized how terrifying it would be for me to find a stranger in our living room. I screamed so loud, I woke the neighbors and they came to make sure no one was being murdered. Ha! You must have been mortified.

I can't tell you how relieved I was when you pulled off that beard and hat. I cried until my tears turned into laughter. Then we had cookies and watched the snow fall outside. It's still one of my favorite memories. I'll cherish it forever.

I miss you so much. I know what you're doing is important, but I selfishly wish you were here with me.

At least for the holidays.

Love you, Dad.
XOXO, Meg

P.S. Attaching a picture of your "little women" in front of the Rockefeller Center Christmas tree.

CHAPTER 3

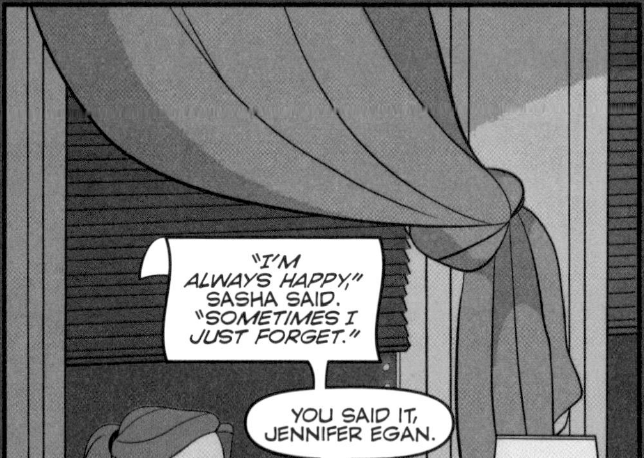
"I'M ALWAYS HAPPY," SASHA SAID. "SOMETIMES I JUST FORGET."
YOU SAID IT, JENNIFER EGAN.

How NOT to Ring in a New Year...

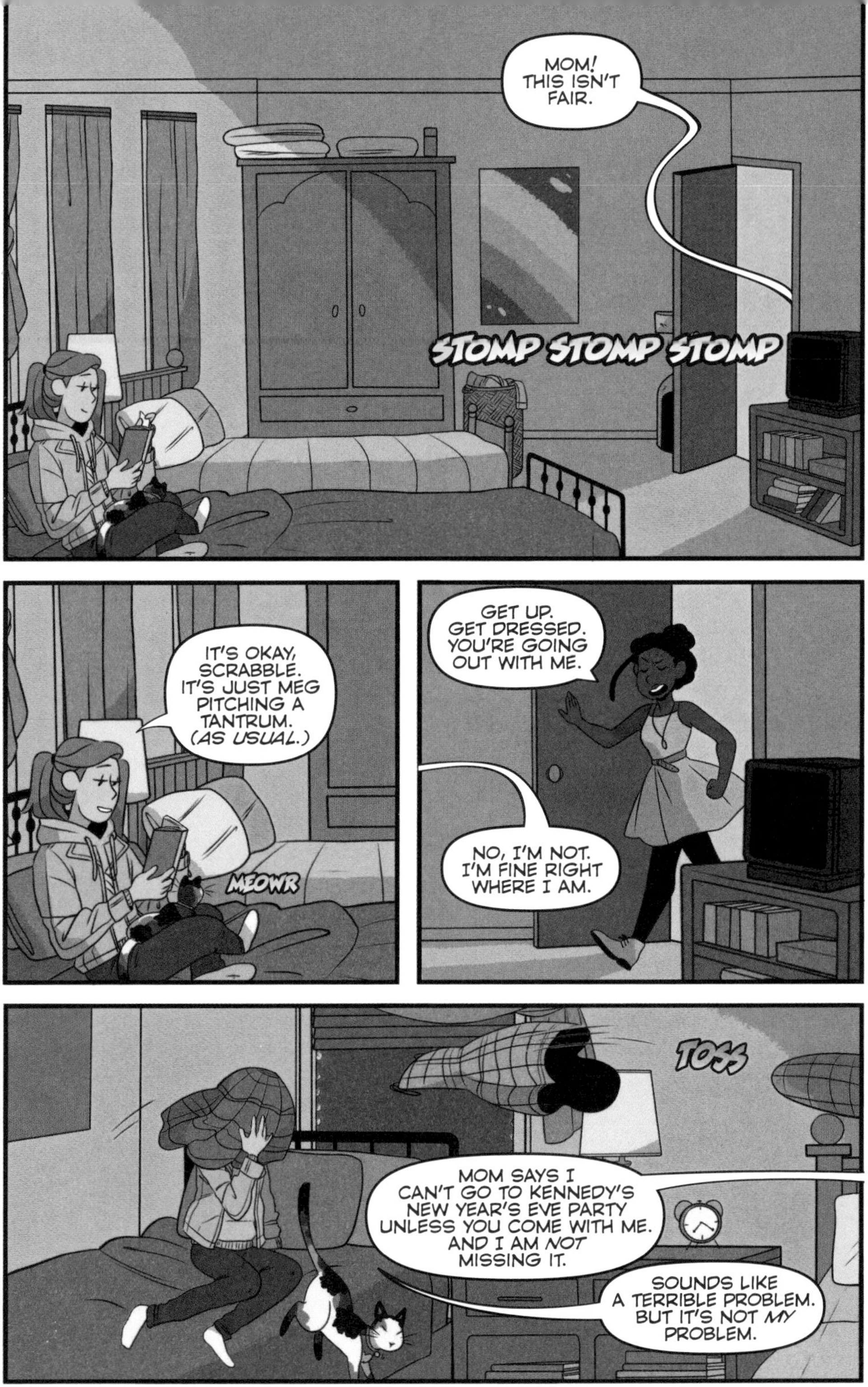
MOM! THIS ISN'T FAIR.
STOMP STOMP STOMP
IT'S OKAY, SCRABBLE. IT'S JUST MEG PITCHING A TANTRUM. (AS *USUAL*.)
MEOWR
GET UP. GET DRESSED. YOU'RE GOING OUT WITH ME.
NO, I'M NOT. I'M FINE RIGHT WHERE I AM.
TOSS
MOM SAYS I CAN'T GO TO KENNEDY'S NEW YEAR'S EVE PARTY UNLESS YOU COME WITH ME. AND I AM *NOT* MISSING IT.
SOUNDS LIKE A TERRIBLE PROBLEM. BUT IT'S NOT *MY* PROBLEM.

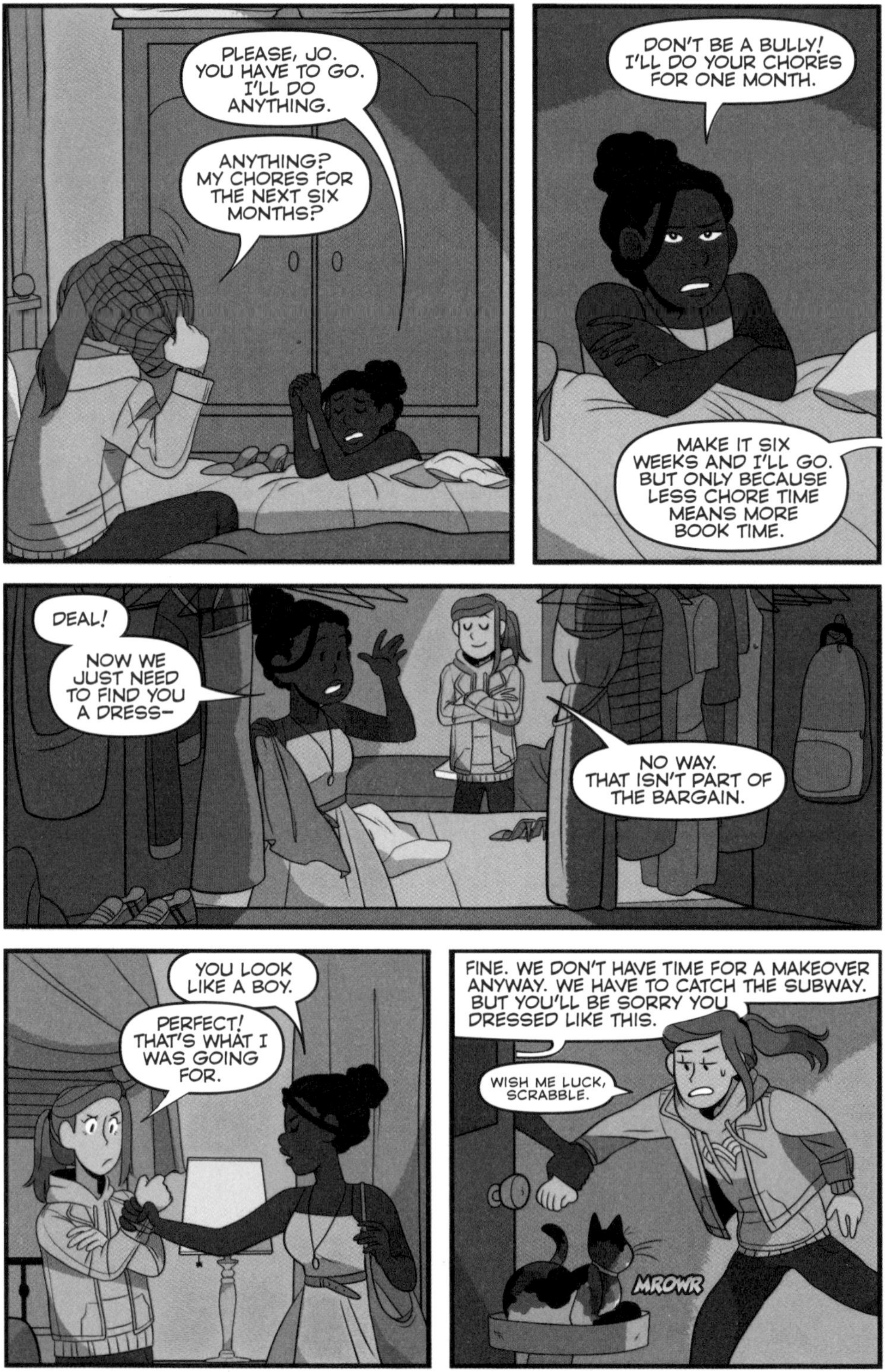
PLEASE, JO. YOU HAVE TO GO. I'LL DO ANYTHING.
ANYTHING? MY CHORES FOR THE NEXT SIX MONTHS?
DON'T BE A BULLY! I'LL DO YOUR CHORES FOR ONE MONTH.
MAKE IT SIX WEEKS AND I'LL GO. BUT ONLY BECAUSE LESS CHORE TIME MEANS MORE BOOK TIME.
DEAL!
NOW WE JUST NEED TO FIND YOU A DRESS–
NO WAY. THAT ISN'T PART OF THE BARGAIN.
YOU LOOK LIKE A BOY.
PERFECT! THAT'S WHAT I WAS GOING FOR.
FINE. WE DON'T HAVE TIME FOR A MAKEOVER ANYWAY. WE HAVE TO CATCH THE SUBWAY. BUT YOU'LL BE SORRY YOU DRESSED LIKE THIS.
WISH ME LUCK, SCRABBLE.
MROWR

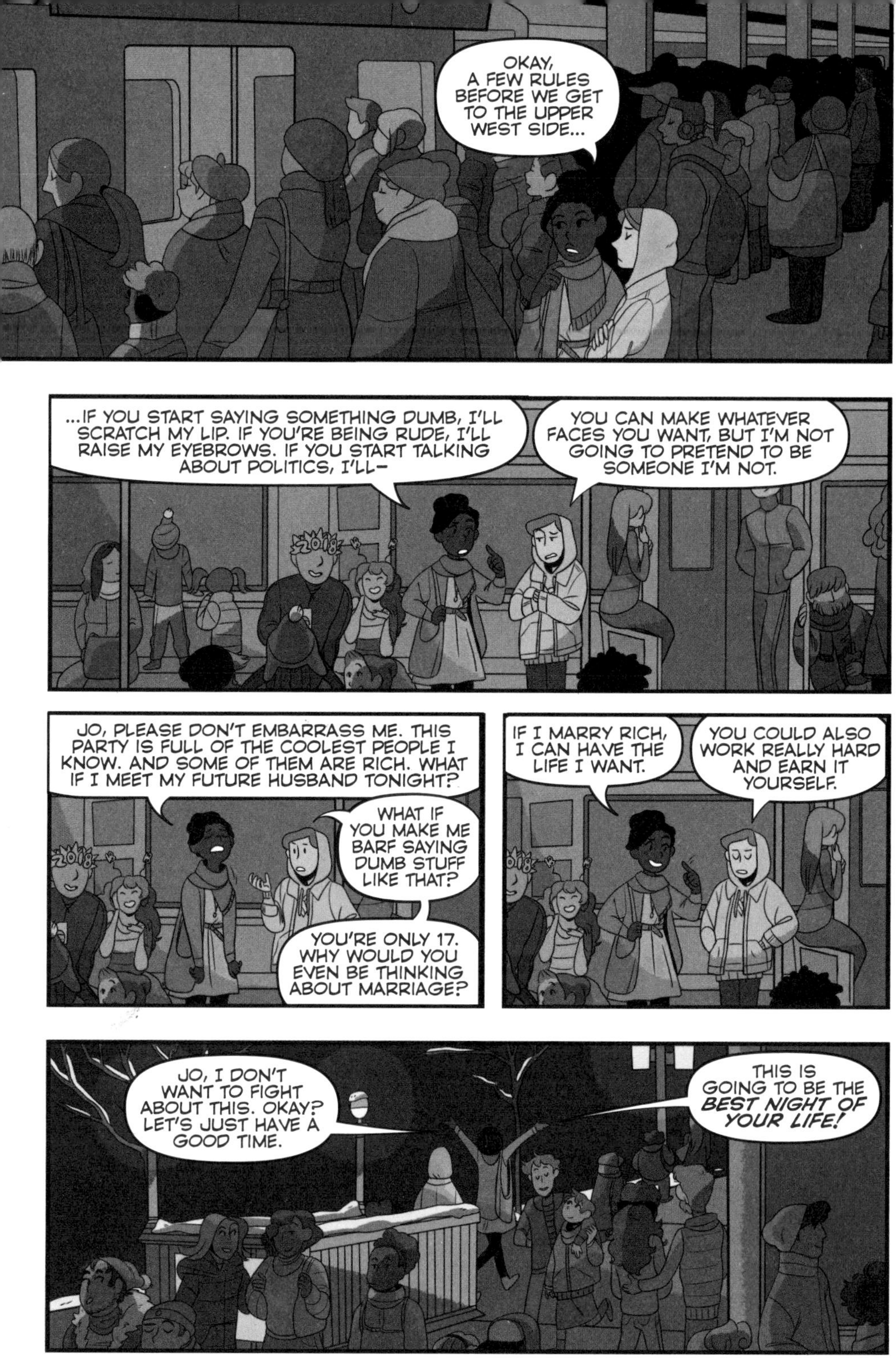
OKAY, A FEW RULES BEFORE WE GET TO THE UPPER WEST SIDE...
...IF YOU START SAYING SOMETHING DUMB, I'LL SCRATCH MY LIP. IF YOU'RE BEING RUDE, I'LL RAISE MY EYEBROWS. IF YOU START TALKING ABOUT POLITICS, I'LL—
YOU CAN MAKE WHATEVER FACES YOU WANT, BUT I'M NOT GOING TO PRETEND TO BE SOMEONE I'M NOT.
2018
JO, PLEASE DON'T EMBARRASS ME. THIS PARTY IS FULL OF THE COOLEST PEOPLE I KNOW. AND SOME OF THEM ARE RICH. WHAT IF I MEET MY FUTURE HUSBAND TONIGHT?
WHAT IF YOU MAKE ME BARF SAYING DUMB STUFF LIKE THAT?
YOU'RE ONLY 17. WHY WOULD YOU EVEN BE THINKING ABOUT MARRIAGE?
IF I MARRY RICH, I CAN HAVE THE LIFE I WANT.
YOU COULD ALSO WORK REALLY HARD AND EARN IT YOURSELF.
JO, I DON'T WANT TO FIGHT ABOUT THIS. OKAY? LET'S JUST HAVE A GOOD TIME.
THIS IS GOING TO BE THE *BEST NIGHT OF YOUR LIFE!*

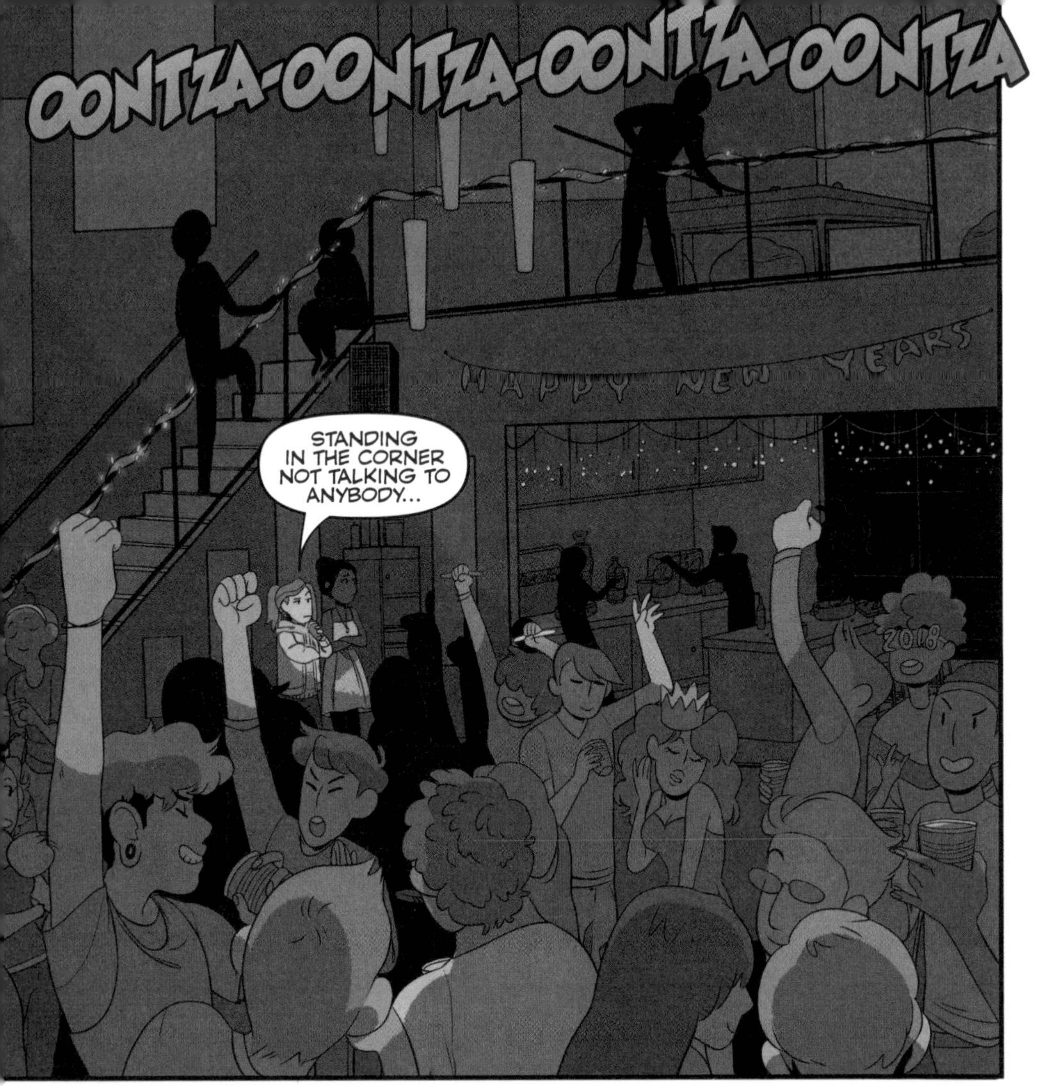
OONTZA-OONTZA-OONTZA-OONTZA
HAPPY NEW YEARS
STANDING IN THE CORNER NOT TALKING TO ANYBODY...
2018

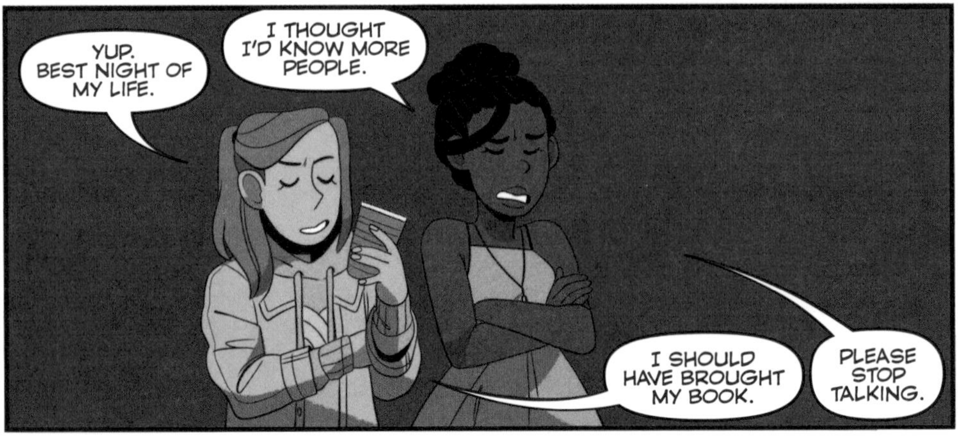
YUP. BEST NIGHT OF MY LIFE.
I THOUGHT I'D KNOW MORE PEOPLE.
I SHOULD HAVE BROUGHT MY BOOK.
PLEASE STOP TALKING.

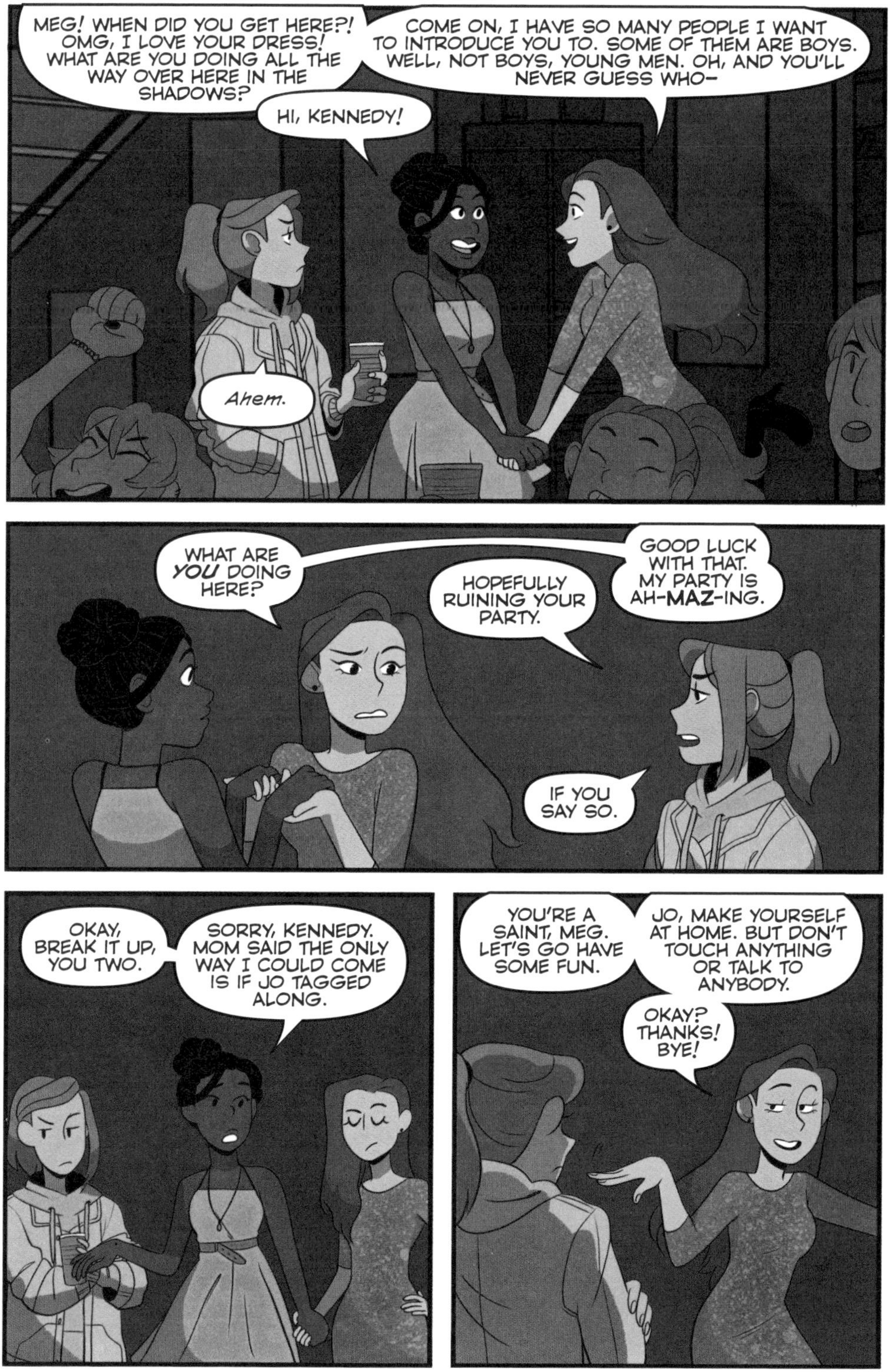

MEG! WHEN DID YOU GET HERE?! OMG, I LOVE YOUR DRESS! WHAT ARE YOU DOING ALL THE WAY OVER HERE IN THE SHADOWS?
HI, KENNEDY!
COME ON, I HAVE SO MANY PEOPLE I WANT TO INTRODUCE YOU TO. SOME OF THEM ARE BOYS. WELL, NOT BOYS, YOUNG MEN. OH, AND YOU'LL NEVER GUESS WHO–
Ahem.
WHAT ARE *YOU* DOING HERE?
HOPEFULLY RUINING YOUR PARTY.
GOOD LUCK WITH THAT. MY PARTY IS AH-MAZ-ING.
IF YOU SAY SO.
OKAY, BREAK IT UP, YOU TWO.
SORRY, KENNEDY. MOM SAID THE ONLY WAY I COULD COME IS IF JO TAGGED ALONG.
YOU'RE A SAINT, MEG. LET'S GO HAVE SOME FUN.
JO, MAKE YOURSELF AT HOME. BUT DON'T TOUCH ANYTHING OR TALK TO ANYBODY.
OKAY? THANKS! BYE!

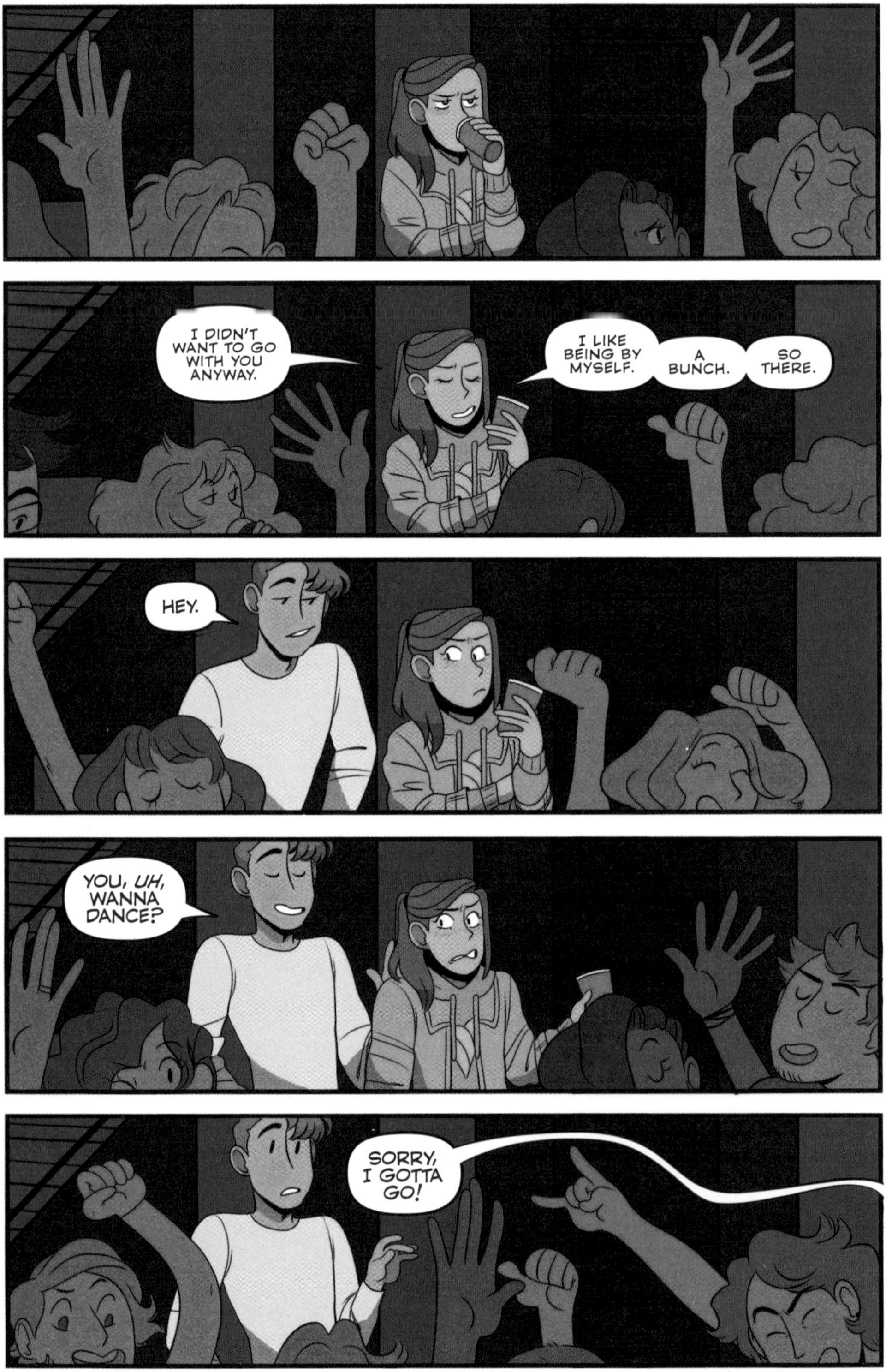
I DIDN'T WANT TO GO WITH YOU ANYWAY.
I LIKE BEING BY MYSELF.
A BUNCH.
SO THERE.
HEY.
YOU, *UH,* WANNA DANCE?
SORRY, I GOTTA GO!

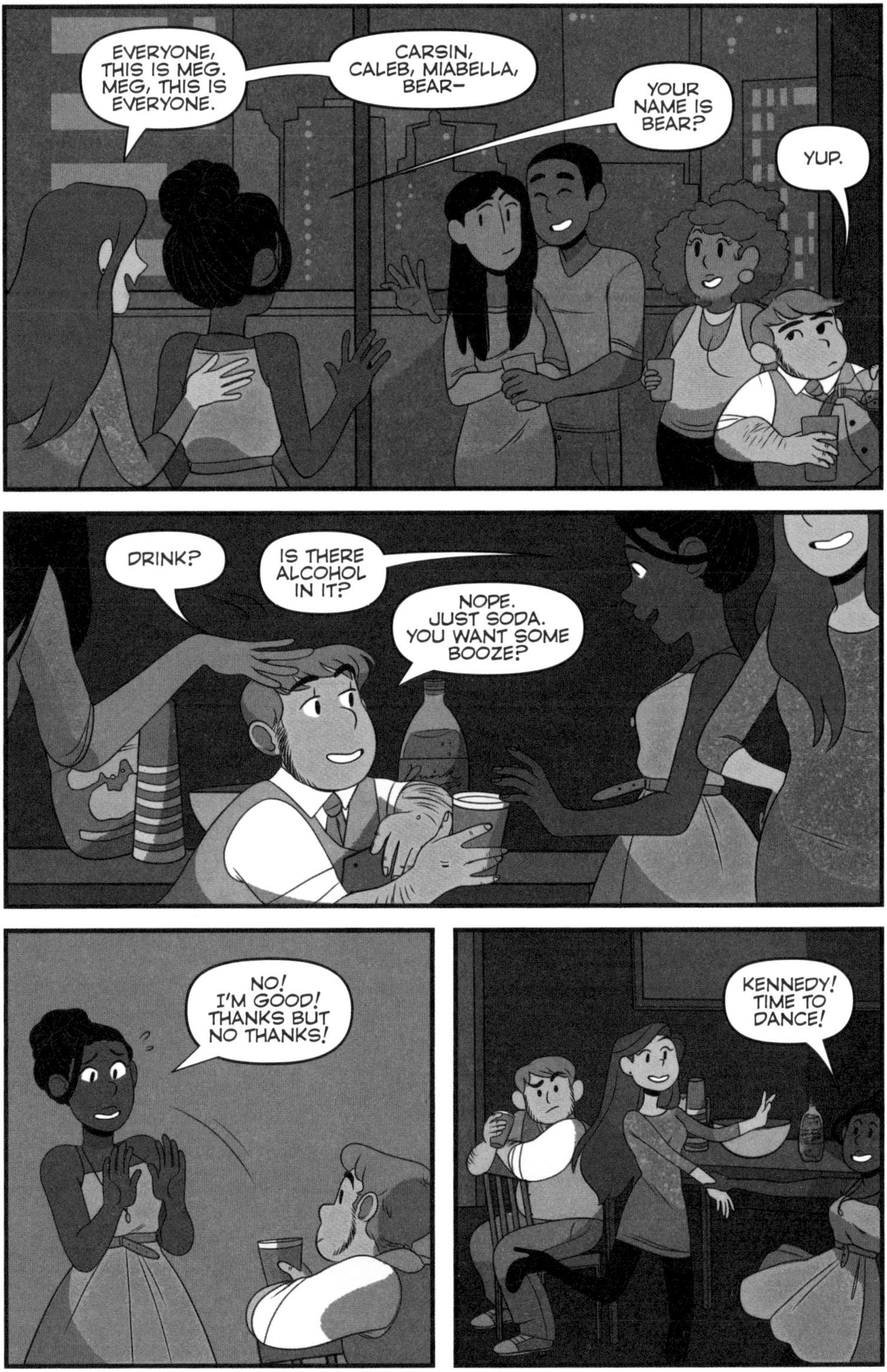
EVERYONE, THIS IS MEG. MEG, THIS IS EVERYONE.
CARSIN, CALEB, MIABELLA, BEAR–
YOUR NAME IS BEAR?
YUP.
DRINK?
IS THERE ALCOHOL IN IT?
NOPE. JUST SODA. YOU WANT SOME BOOZE?
NO! I'M GOOD! THANKS BUT NO THANKS!
KENNEDY! TIME TO DANCE!

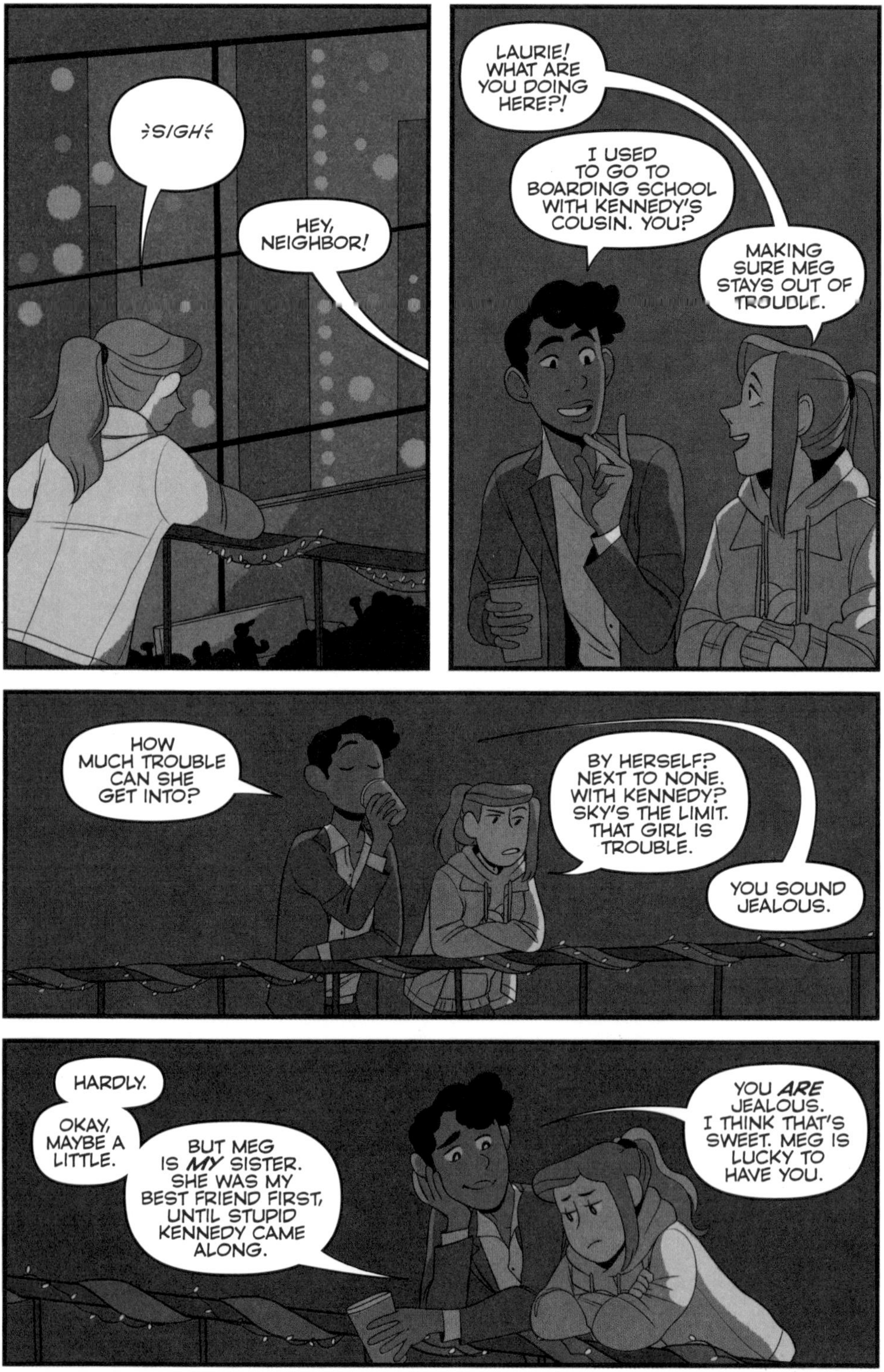

⁃SIGH⁃
HEY, NEIGHBOR!
LAURIE! WHAT ARE YOU DOING HERE?!
I USED TO GO TO BOARDING SCHOOL WITH KENNEDY'S COUSIN. YOU?
MAKING SURE MEG STAYS OUT OF TROUBLE.
HOW MUCH TROUBLE CAN SHE GET INTO?
BY HERSELF? NEXT TO NONE. WITH KENNEDY? SKY'S THE LIMIT. THAT GIRL IS TROUBLE.
YOU SOUND JEALOUS.
HARDLY.
OKAY, MAYBE A LITTLE.
BUT MEG IS *MY* SISTER. SHE WAS MY BEST FRIEND FIRST, UNTIL STUPID KENNEDY CAME ALONG.
YOU *ARE* JEALOUS. I THINK THAT'S SWEET. MEG IS LUCKY TO HAVE YOU.

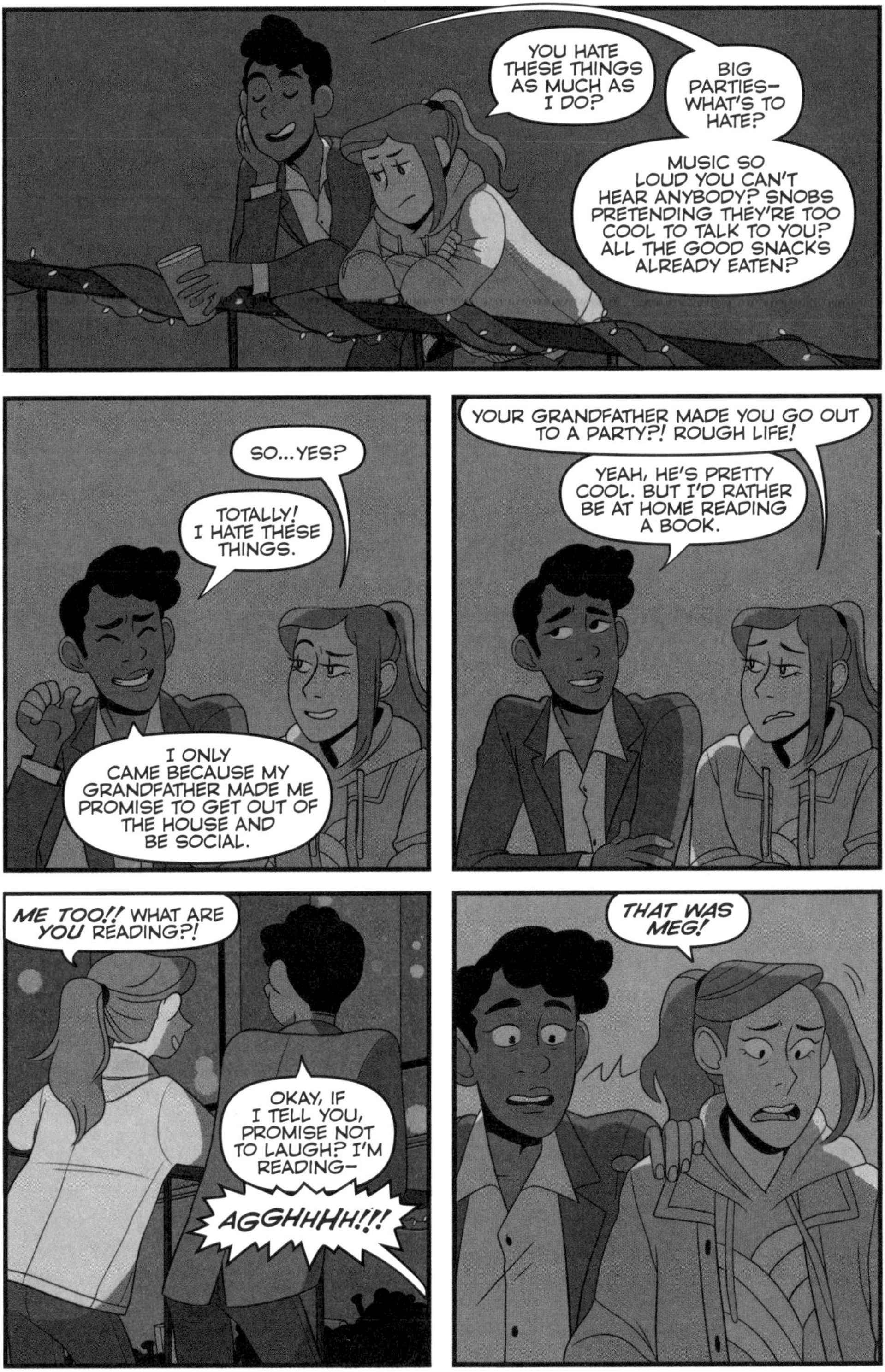
YOU HATE THESE THINGS AS MUCH AS I DO?
BIG PARTIES– WHAT'S TO HATE?
MUSIC SO LOUD YOU CAN'T HEAR ANYBODY? SNOBS PRETENDING THEY'RE TOO COOL TO TALK TO YOU? ALL THE GOOD SNACKS ALREADY EATEN?
SO...YES?
TOTALLY! I HATE THESE THINGS.
I ONLY CAME BECAUSE MY GRANDFATHER MADE ME PROMISE TO GET OUT OF THE HOUSE AND BE SOCIAL.
YOUR GRANDFATHER MADE YOU GO OUT TO A PARTY?! ROUGH LIFE!
YEAH, HE'S PRETTY COOL. BUT I'D RATHER BE AT HOME READING A BOOK.
ME TOO!! WHAT ARE *YOU* READING?!
OKAY, IF I TELL YOU, PROMISE NOT TO LAUGH? I'M READING–
AGGHHHH!!!
THAT WAS MEG!

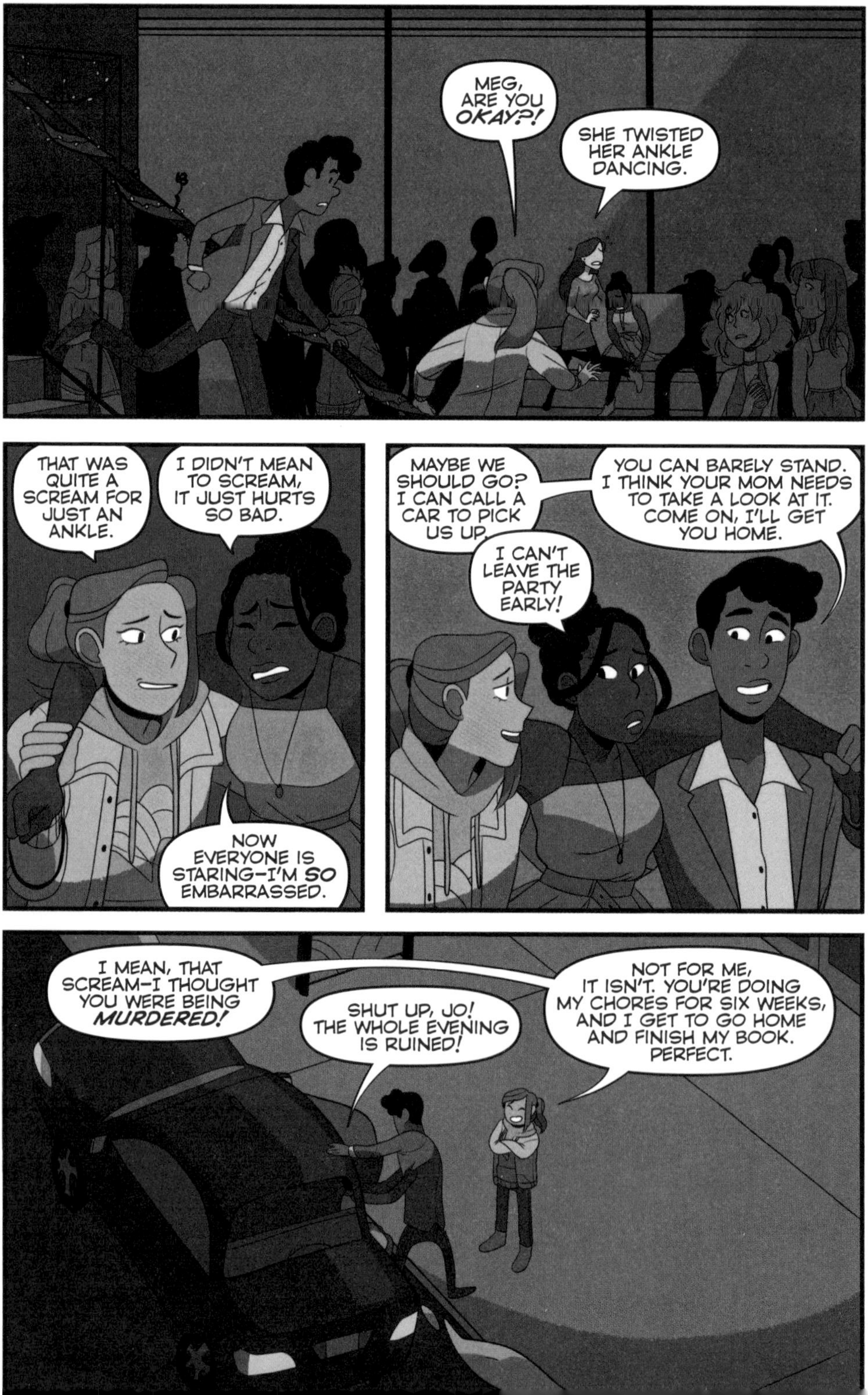
MEG, ARE YOU OKAY?!
SHE TWISTED HER ANKLE DANCING.
THAT WAS QUITE A SCREAM FOR JUST AN ANKLE.
I DIDN'T MEAN TO SCREAM, IT JUST HURTS SO BAD.
NOW EVERYONE IS STARING—I'M SO EMBARRASSED.
MAYBE WE SHOULD GO? I CAN CALL A CAR TO PICK US UP.
I CAN'T LEAVE THE PARTY EARLY!
YOU CAN BARELY STAND. I THINK YOUR MOM NEEDS TO TAKE A LOOK AT IT. COME ON, I'LL GET YOU HOME.
I MEAN, THAT SCREAM—I THOUGHT YOU WERE BEING MURDERED!
SHUT UP, JO! THE WHOLE EVENING IS RUINED!
NOT FOR ME, IT ISN'T. YOU'RE DOING MY CHORES FOR SIX WEEKS, AND I GET TO GO HOME AND FINISH MY BOOK. PERFECT.

FROM: Josephine March
TO: Robert March
SENT: January 3

Hey-hey Dad!

It's a new year now, and everything feels different and yet somehow the same. Amy is still the family baby and the life of the party. Beth is still quiet and shy, and a true connoisseur of fine music. Meg is still obsessed with fashion and marrying rich. (Don't tell her I said that.) And Mom still works too hard and misses you every day. Same as the rest of us.

While I don't agree with war, I understand your desire to protect your family and country. But I wish you could just come home already. Of course, if I were making wishes, I would wish for a utopia where the world is at peace. Then we could all create art and live in harmony and all people would be free to be themselves. That must sound naive. But since I'm only sixteen, I am granting myself a few more years of remaining blissfully optimistic.

After all, I've lived something of a charmed life. My biological father left Mom and me before I turned two. And when I was four, Mom met you. I remember the first time I met you and Meg. As we walked up to that diner, Mom's hands were so sweaty. She said to me, "Please, please behave. I really like Robert." When we got to the diner, I didn't know what to expect. Mom had already told me you were black, which was funny to me, because I didn't see how that mattered.

When you saw Mom, your face lit up. I could tell you liked Mom as much as she liked you. Then you turned to me. You bent down on your knee, looked me in the eye, and shook my hand. "I heard you like books," you said. Then you handed me *Alice in Wonderland*. (The original one with the Sir John Tenniel illustrations, which is the best one, of course.) And you added, "I hope we can be friends."

And somehow—perhaps a child's intuition—I knew. You weren't like my birth father, who left. You were a good man. So I wrapped my arms around your neck and said, "Silly bear, we already are friends."

The day would have been perfect if it had ended there. Instead, Meg pulled my hair, and I started crying. Ha! Mom looked like she was going to have a heart attack. You just smiled that warm smile of yours and said, "They're already acting like sisters." And we were. And we still are. Except it's not acting. We still fight, but I love Meg. I am the luckiest girl on the planet to have the family that I do. I know that. Well, most of the time anyways. But on days when I want to scream or throw things, I take a deep breath and remember one of my happiest memories....

After the wedding, with Mom still in her dress and you in your tux, you bent your knee and said: "My last name is March. That means I'm a March. So is Meg, and so is your mom too now. How would you feel if I adopted you, so you could have my last name too? How would you feel about being my daughter?"

No one had ever given me a choice like that. I mean, my own father wanted nothing to do with me. He left me and Mom without a second thought. But you? You could have ignored me, or treated me like a fairy-tale stepchild, or just let things stay as they were. But you were different. You wanted me to feel loved. You wanted me to feel like I belonged. I will always remember the day, how proud I was when we went to the courthouse, and how I got to tell the judge I wanted to change my last name because I was a March.

I love you, Dad.

P.S. I love this photo of us...

P.P.S. A quote I found just for you...

"I believe that what we become depends on what our fathers teach us at odd moments, when they aren't trying to teach us. We are formed by little scraps of wisdom."

—Umberto Eco,
Foucault's Pendulum

CHAPTER 4

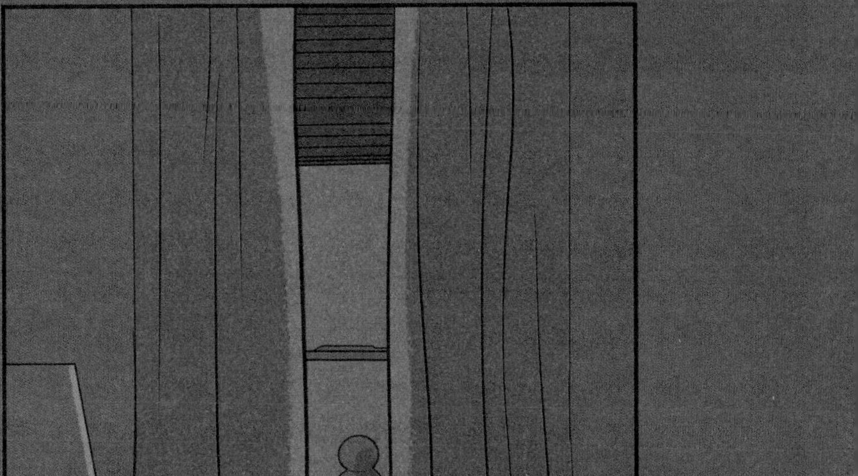
NNN NNN NNN NN
NOOO...
...I DON'T WANT TO GO BACK TO SCHOOL...
...OR TUTORING RICH KIDS...
...OR BEING AWAKE.

Back to the Grind...

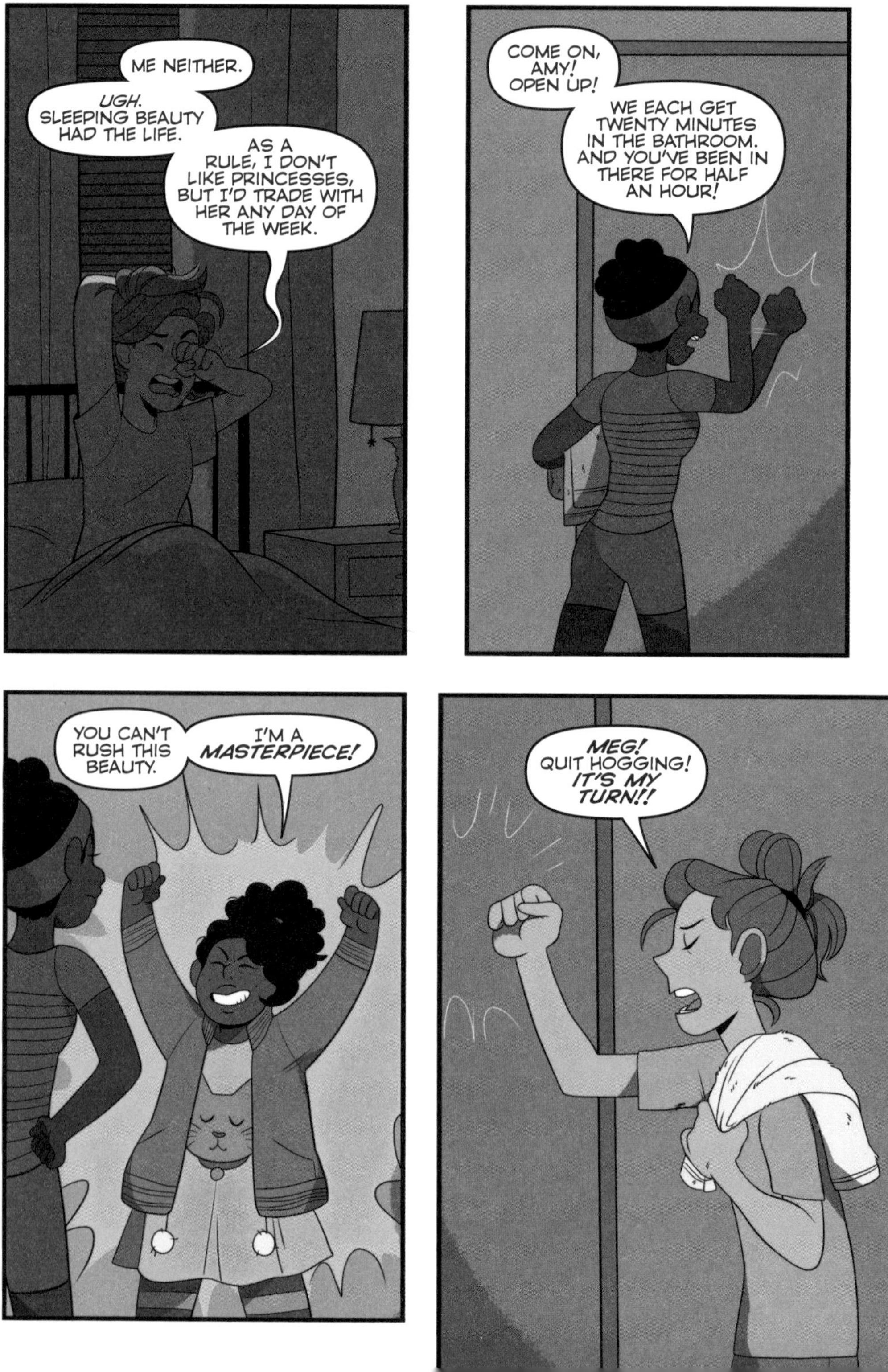
ME NEITHER.
UGH. SLEEPING BEAUTY HAD THE LIFE.
AS A RULE, I DON'T LIKE PRINCESSES, BUT I'D TRADE WITH HER ANY DAY OF THE WEEK.
COME ON, AMY! OPEN UP!
WE EACH GET TWENTY MINUTES IN THE BATHROOM. AND YOU'VE BEEN IN THERE FOR HALF AN HOUR!
YOU CAN'T RUSH THIS BEAUTY.
I'M A MASTERPIECE!
MEG! QUIT HOGGING! IT'S MY TURN!!

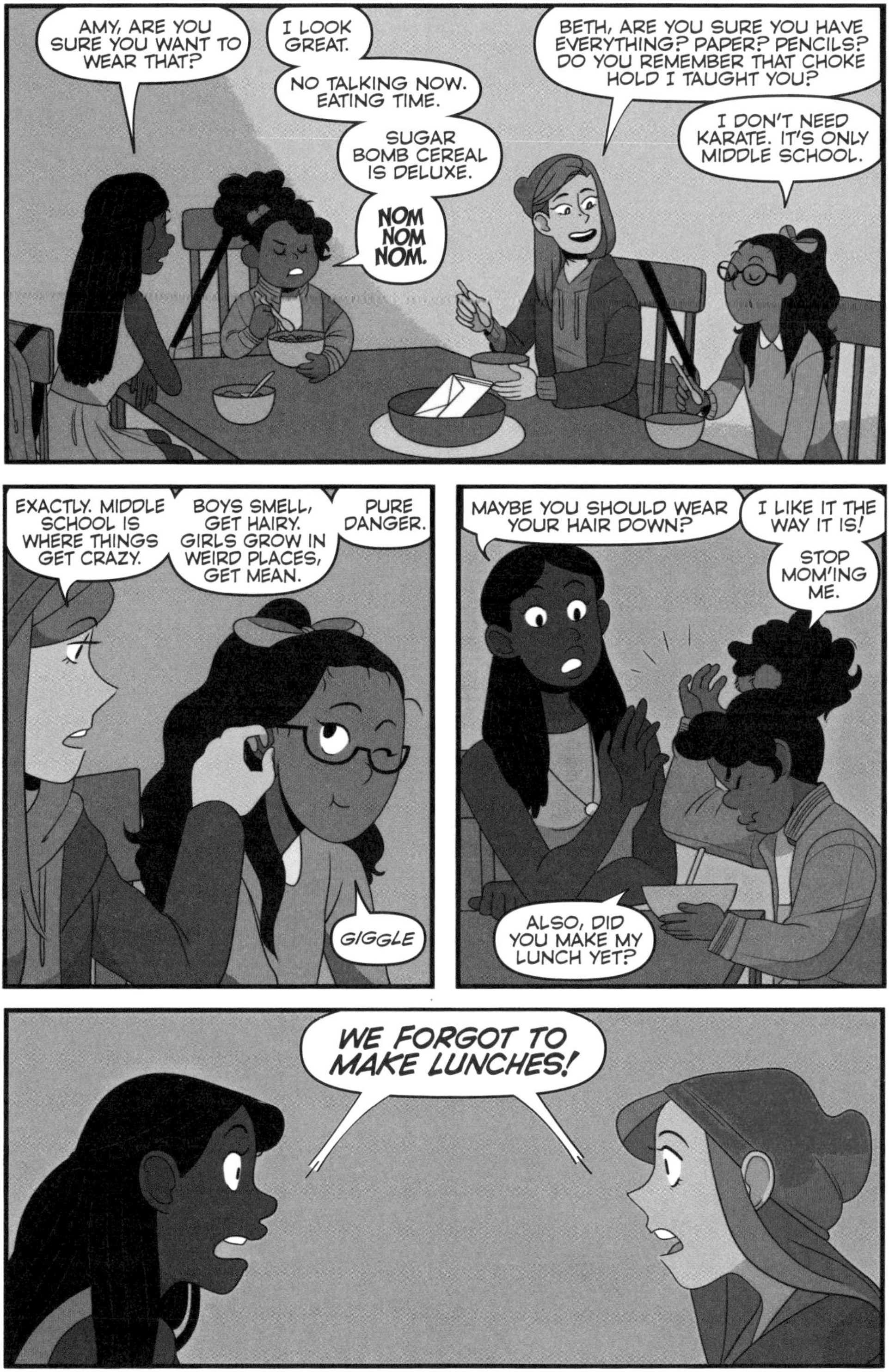
AMY, ARE YOU SURE YOU WANT TO WEAR THAT?
I LOOK GREAT.
NO TALKING NOW. EATING TIME.
SUGAR BOMB CEREAL IS DELUXE.
NOM NOM NOM.
BETH, ARE YOU SURE YOU HAVE EVERYTHING? PAPER? PENCILS? DO YOU REMEMBER THAT CHOKE HOLD I TAUGHT YOU?
I DON'T NEED KARATE. IT'S ONLY MIDDLE SCHOOL.
EXACTLY. MIDDLE SCHOOL IS WHERE THINGS GET CRAZY.
BOYS SMELL, GET HAIRY. GIRLS GROW IN WEIRD PLACES, GET MEAN.
PURE DANGER.
GIGGLE
MAYBE YOU SHOULD WEAR YOUR HAIR DOWN?
I LIKE IT THE WAY IT IS!
STOP MOM'ING ME.
ALSO, DID YOU MAKE MY LUNCH YET?
WE FORGOT TO MAKE LUNCHES!

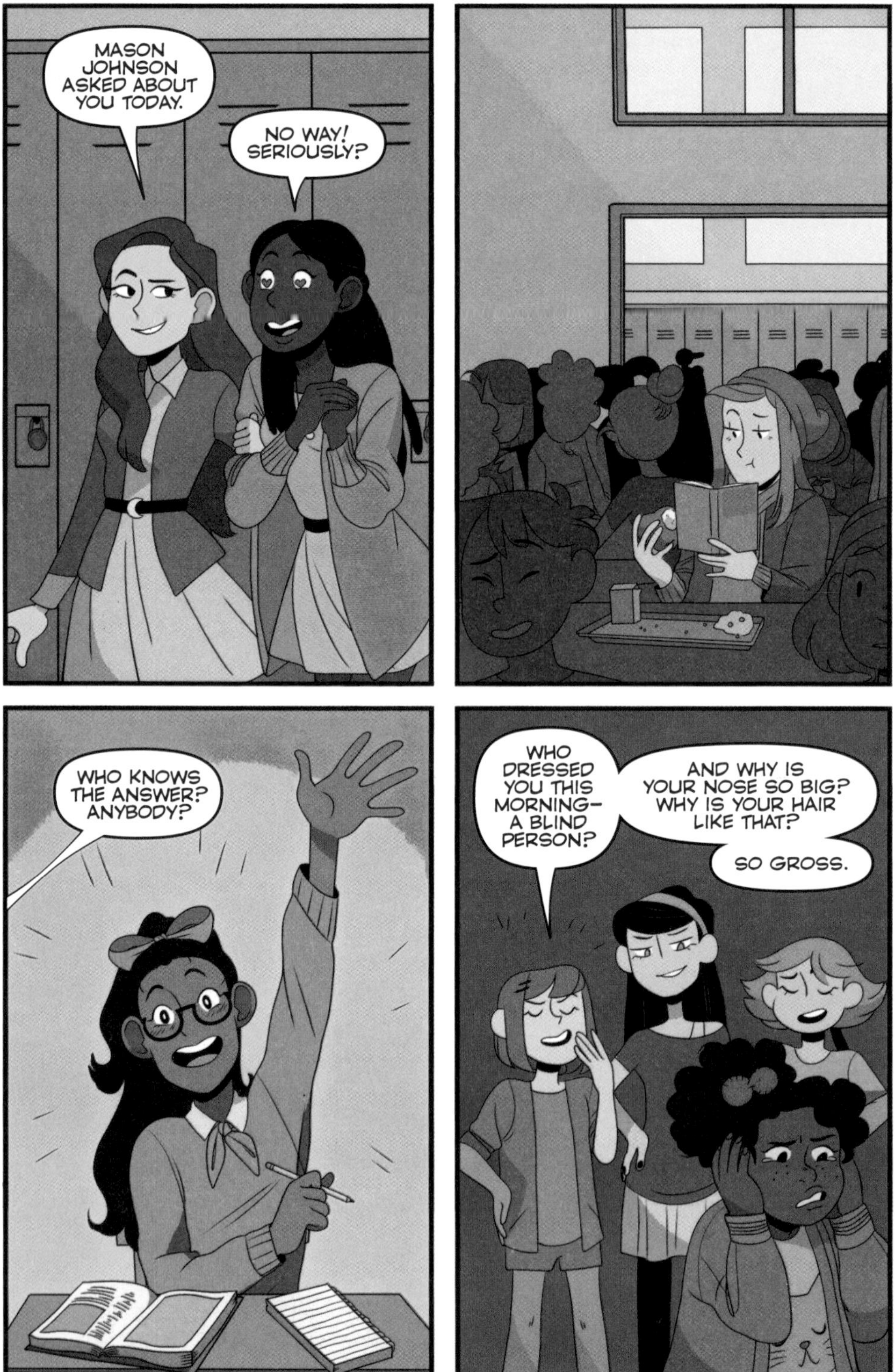
MASON JOHNSON ASKED ABOUT YOU TODAY.
NO WAY! SERIOUSLY?
WHO KNOWS THE ANSWER? ANYBODY?
WHO DRESSED YOU THIS MORNING— A BLIND PERSON?
AND WHY IS YOUR NOSE SO BIG? WHY IS YOUR HAIR LIKE THAT?
SO GROSS.

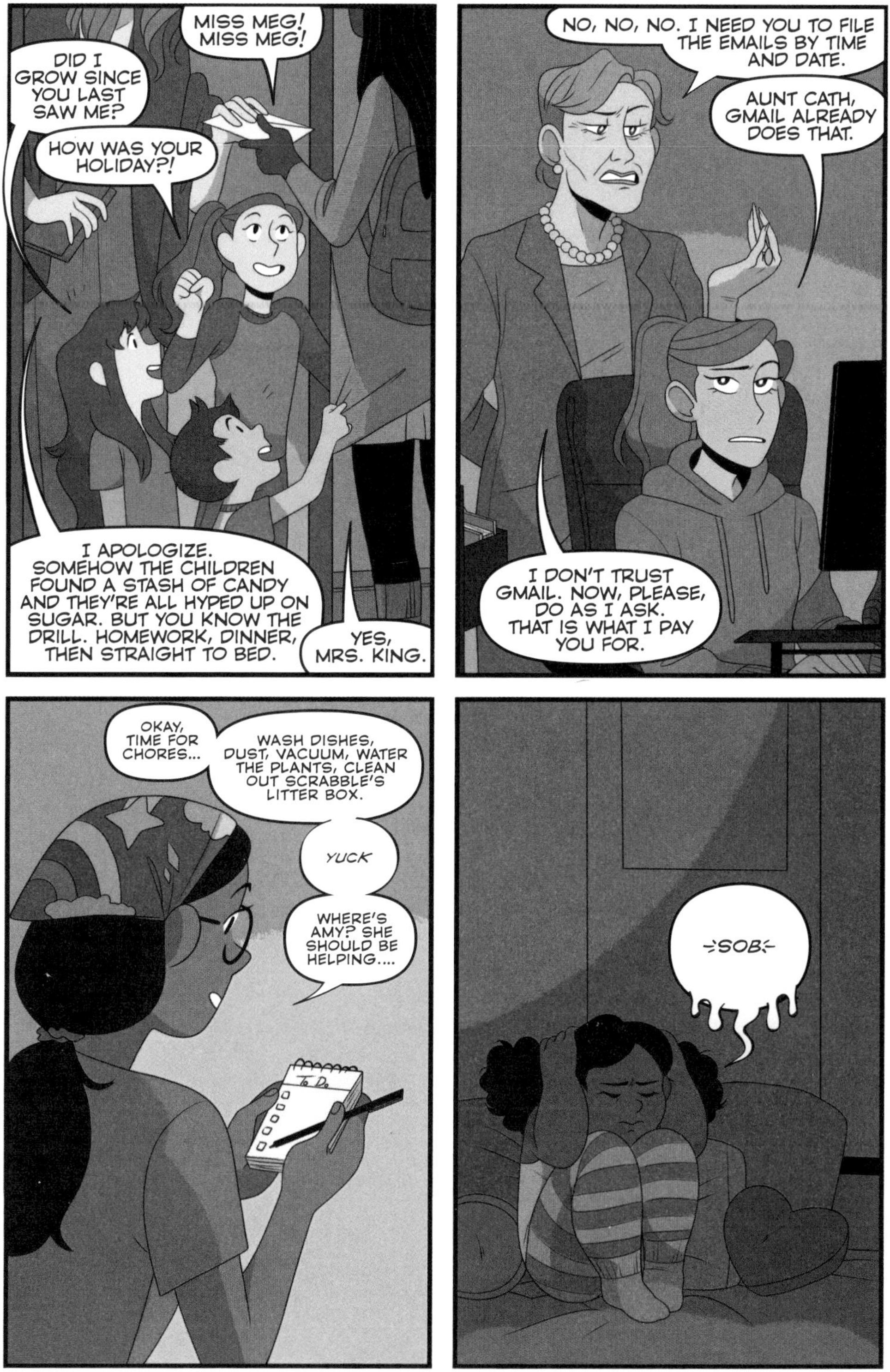
MISS MEG! MISS MEG!
DID I GROW SINCE YOU LAST SAW ME?
HOW WAS YOUR HOLIDAY?!
I APOLOGIZE. SOMEHOW THE CHILDREN FOUND A STASH OF CANDY AND THEY'RE ALL HYPED UP ON SUGAR. BUT YOU KNOW THE DRILL. HOMEWORK, DINNER, THEN STRAIGHT TO BED.
YES, MRS. KING.
NO, NO, NO. I NEED YOU TO FILE THE EMAILS BY TIME AND DATE.
AUNT CATH, GMAIL ALREADY DOES THAT.
I DON'T TRUST GMAIL. NOW, PLEASE, DO AS I ASK. THAT IS WHAT I PAY YOU FOR.
OKAY, TIME FOR CHORES...
WASH DISHES, DUST, VACUUM, WATER THE PLANTS, CLEAN OUT SCRABBLE'S LITTER BOX.
YUCK
WHERE'S AMY? SHE SHOULD BE HELPING....
To Do
SOB

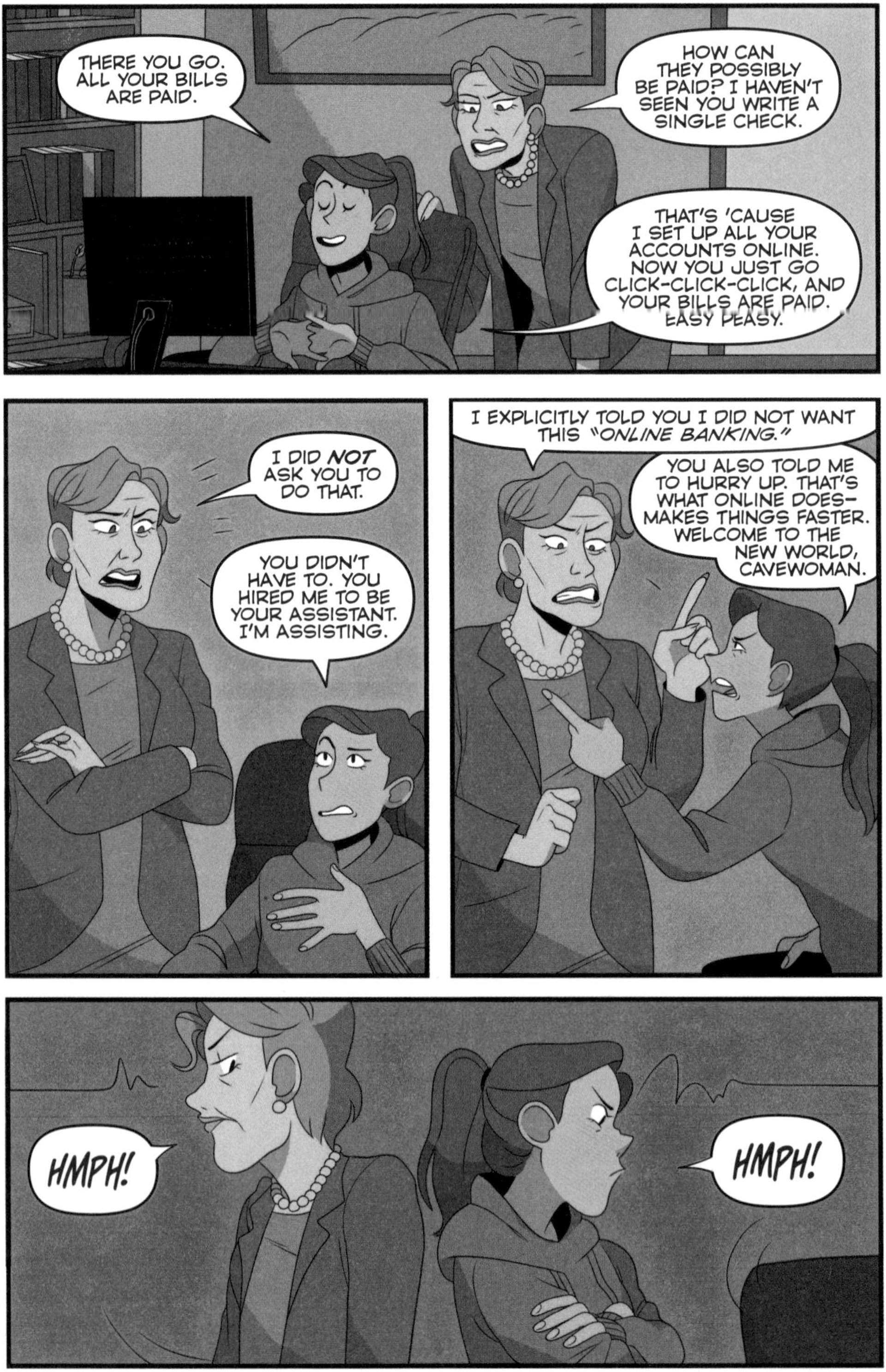
THERE YOU GO. ALL YOUR BILLS ARE PAID.
HOW CAN THEY POSSIBLY BE PAID? I HAVEN'T SEEN YOU WRITE A SINGLE CHECK.
THAT'S 'CAUSE I SET UP ALL YOUR ACCOUNTS ONLINE. NOW YOU JUST GO CLICK-CLICK-CLICK, AND YOUR BILLS ARE PAID. EASY PEASY.
I DID ***NOT*** ASK YOU TO DO THAT.
YOU DIDN'T HAVE TO. YOU HIRED ME TO BE YOUR ASSISTANT. I'M ASSISTING.
I EXPLICITLY TOLD YOU I DID NOT WANT THIS *"ONLINE BANKING."*
YOU ALSO TOLD ME TO HURRY UP. THAT'S WHAT ONLINE DOES—MAKES THINGS FASTER. WELCOME TO THE NEW WORLD, CAVEWOMAN.
HMPH!
HMPH!

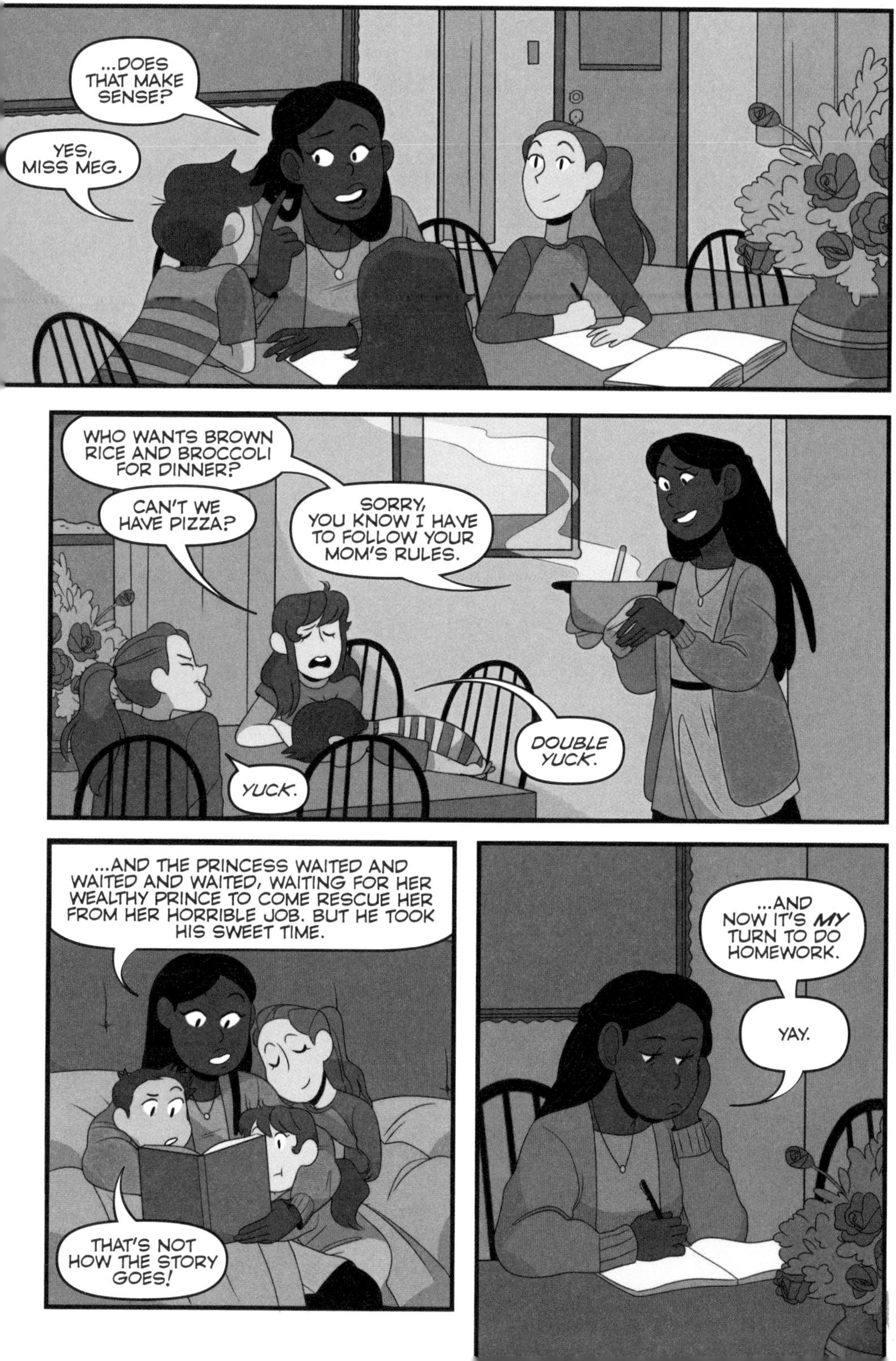
...DOES THAT MAKE SENSE?
YES, MISS MEG.
WHO WANTS BROWN RICE AND BROCCOLI FOR DINNER?
CAN'T WE HAVE PIZZA?
SORRY, YOU KNOW I HAVE TO FOLLOW YOUR MOM'S RULES.
YUCK.
DOUBLE YUCK.
...AND THE PRINCESS WAITED AND WAITED AND WAITED, WAITING FOR HER WEALTHY PRINCE TO COME RESCUE HER FROM HER HORRIBLE JOB. BUT HE TOOK HIS SWEET TIME.
THAT'S NOT HOW THE STORY GOES!
...AND NOW IT'S *MY* TURN TO DO HOMEWORK.
YAY.

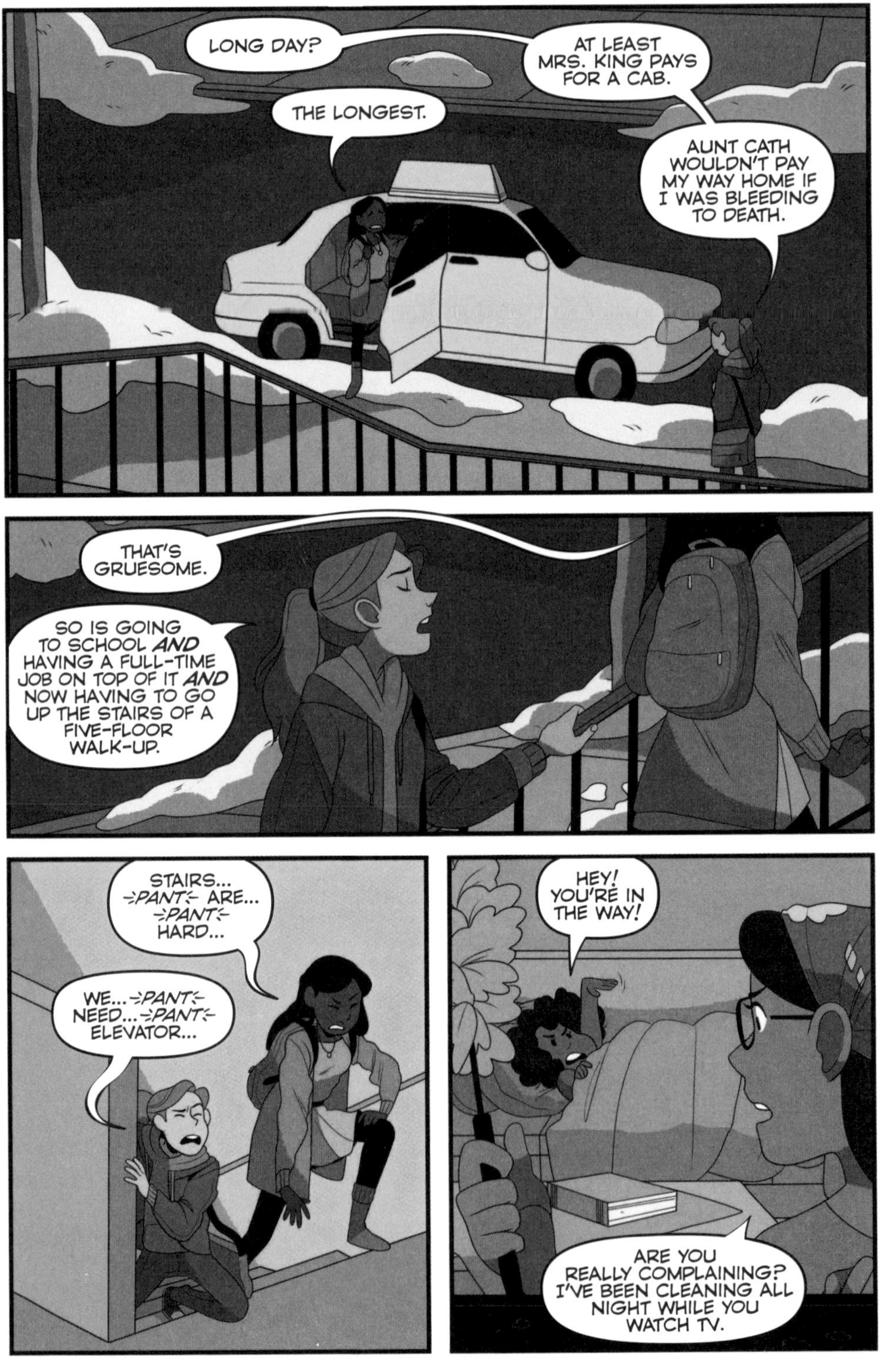
LONG DAY?
THE LONGEST.
AT LEAST MRS. KING PAYS FOR A CAB.
AUNT CATH WOULDN'T PAY MY WAY HOME IF I WAS BLEEDING TO DEATH.
THAT'S GRUESOME.
SO IS GOING TO SCHOOL *AND* HAVING A FULL-TIME JOB ON TOP OF IT *AND* NOW HAVING TO GO UP THE STAIRS OF A FIVE-FLOOR WALK-UP.
STAIRS... *PANT* ARE... *PANT* HARD...
WE... *PANT* NEED... *PANT* ELEVATOR...
HEY! YOU'RE IN THE WAY!
ARE YOU REALLY COMPLAINING? I'VE BEEN CLEANING ALL NIGHT WHILE YOU WATCH TV.

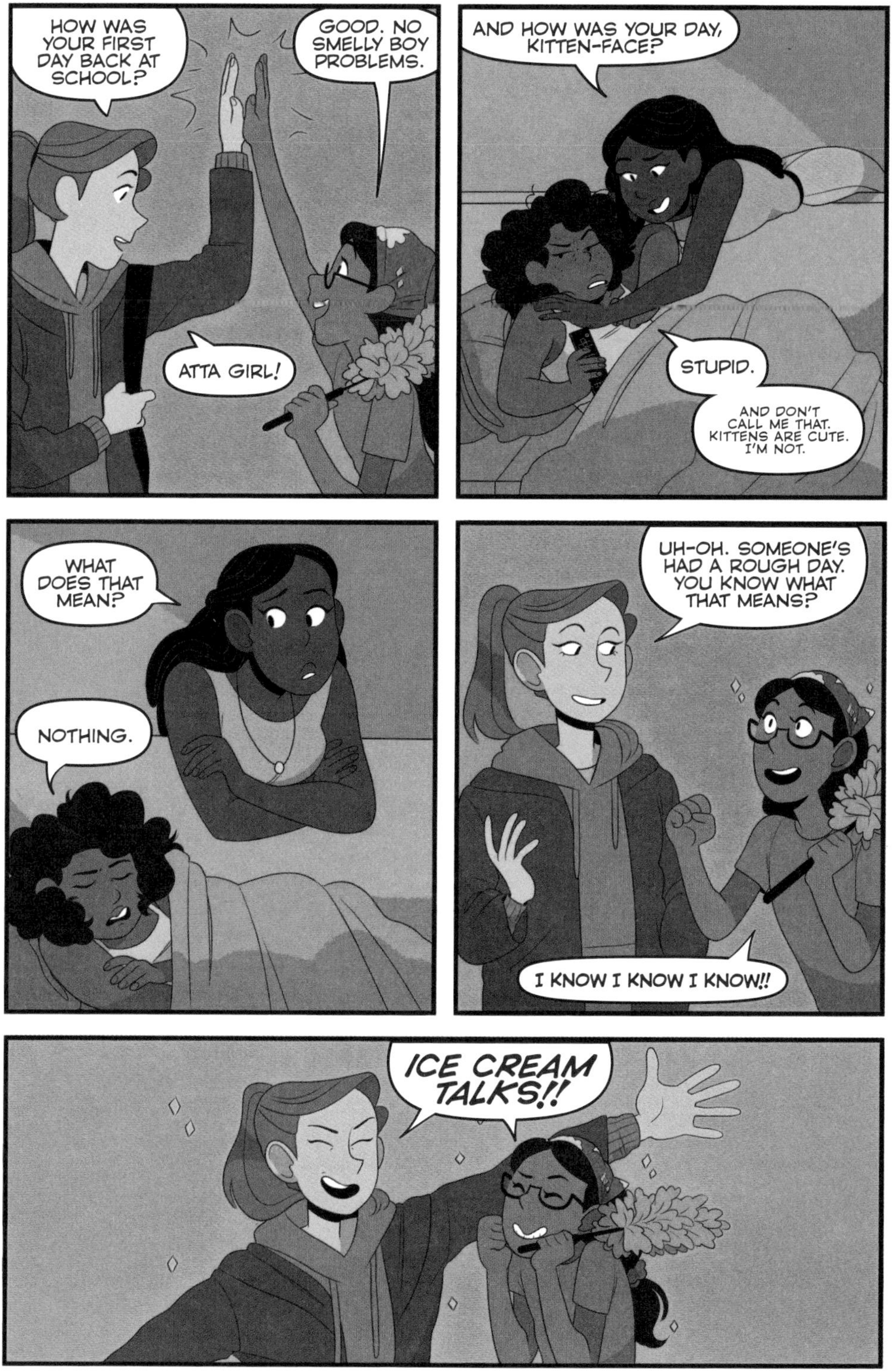
HOW WAS YOUR FIRST DAY BACK AT SCHOOL?
GOOD. NO SMELLY BOY PROBLEMS.
ATTA GIRL!
AND HOW WAS YOUR DAY, KITTEN-FACE?
STUPID.
AND DON'T CALL ME THAT. KITTENS ARE CUTE. I'M NOT.
WHAT DOES THAT MEAN?
NOTHING.
UH-OH. SOMEONE'S HAD A ROUGH DAY. YOU KNOW WHAT THAT MEANS?
I KNOW I KNOW I KNOW!!
ICE CREAM TALKS!!

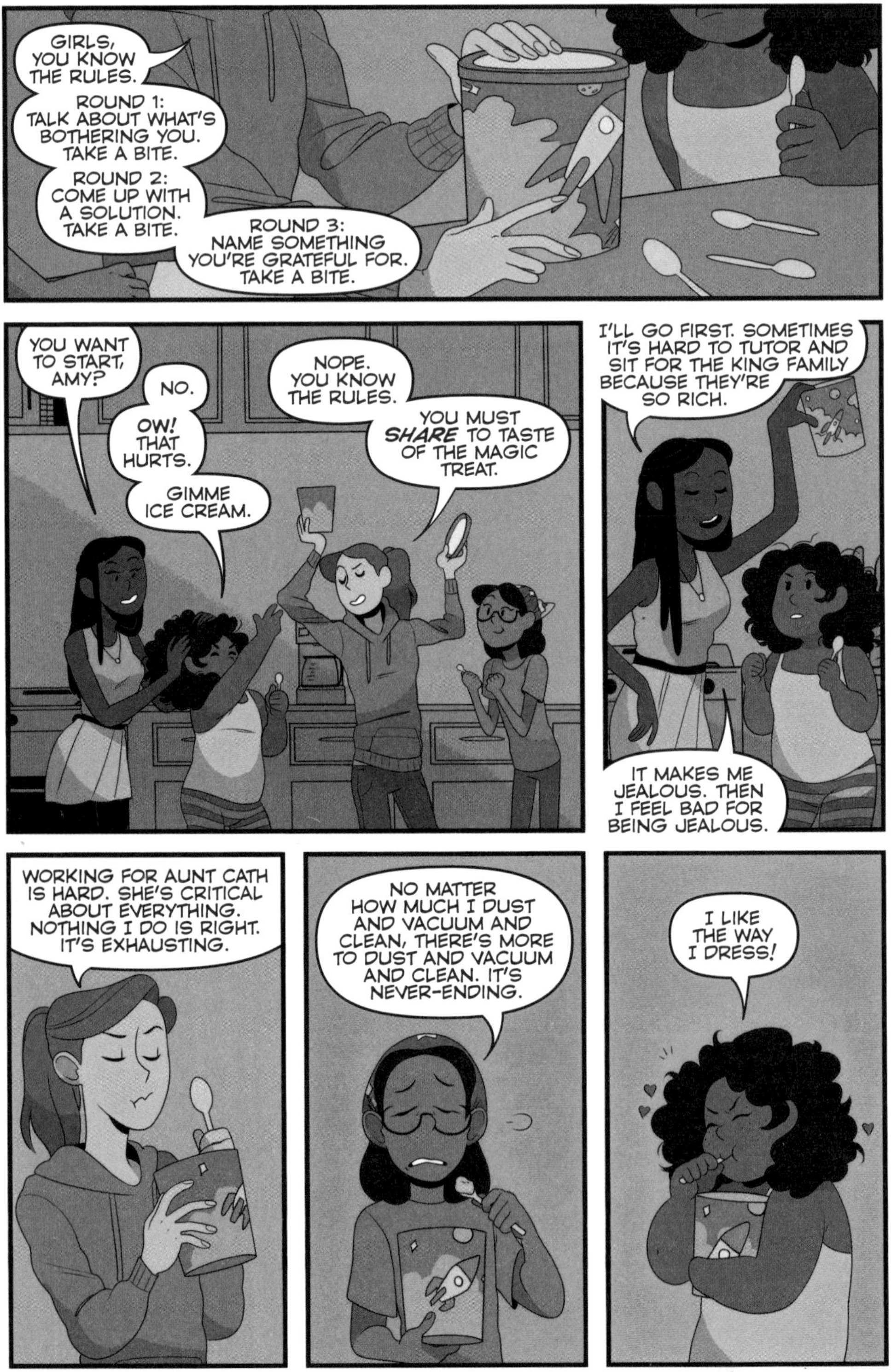
GIRLS, YOU KNOW THE RULES.
ROUND 1: TALK ABOUT WHAT'S BOTHERING YOU. TAKE A BITE.
ROUND 2: COME UP WITH A SOLUTION. TAKE A BITE.
ROUND 3: NAME SOMETHING YOU'RE GRATEFUL FOR. TAKE A BITE.
YOU WANT TO START, AMY?
NO.
OW! THAT HURTS.
GIMME ICE CREAM.
NOPE. YOU KNOW THE RULES.
YOU MUST *SHARE* TO TASTE OF THE MAGIC TREAT.
I'LL GO FIRST. SOMETIMES IT'S HARD TO TUTOR AND SIT FOR THE KING FAMILY BECAUSE THEY'RE SO RICH.
IT MAKES ME JEALOUS. THEN I FEEL BAD FOR BEING JEALOUS.
WORKING FOR AUNT CATH IS HARD. SHE'S CRITICAL ABOUT EVERYTHING. NOTHING I DO IS RIGHT. IT'S EXHAUSTING.
NO MATTER HOW MUCH I DUST AND VACUUM AND CLEAN, THERE'S MORE TO DUST AND VACUUM AND CLEAN. IT'S NEVER-ENDING.
I LIKE THE WAY I DRESS!

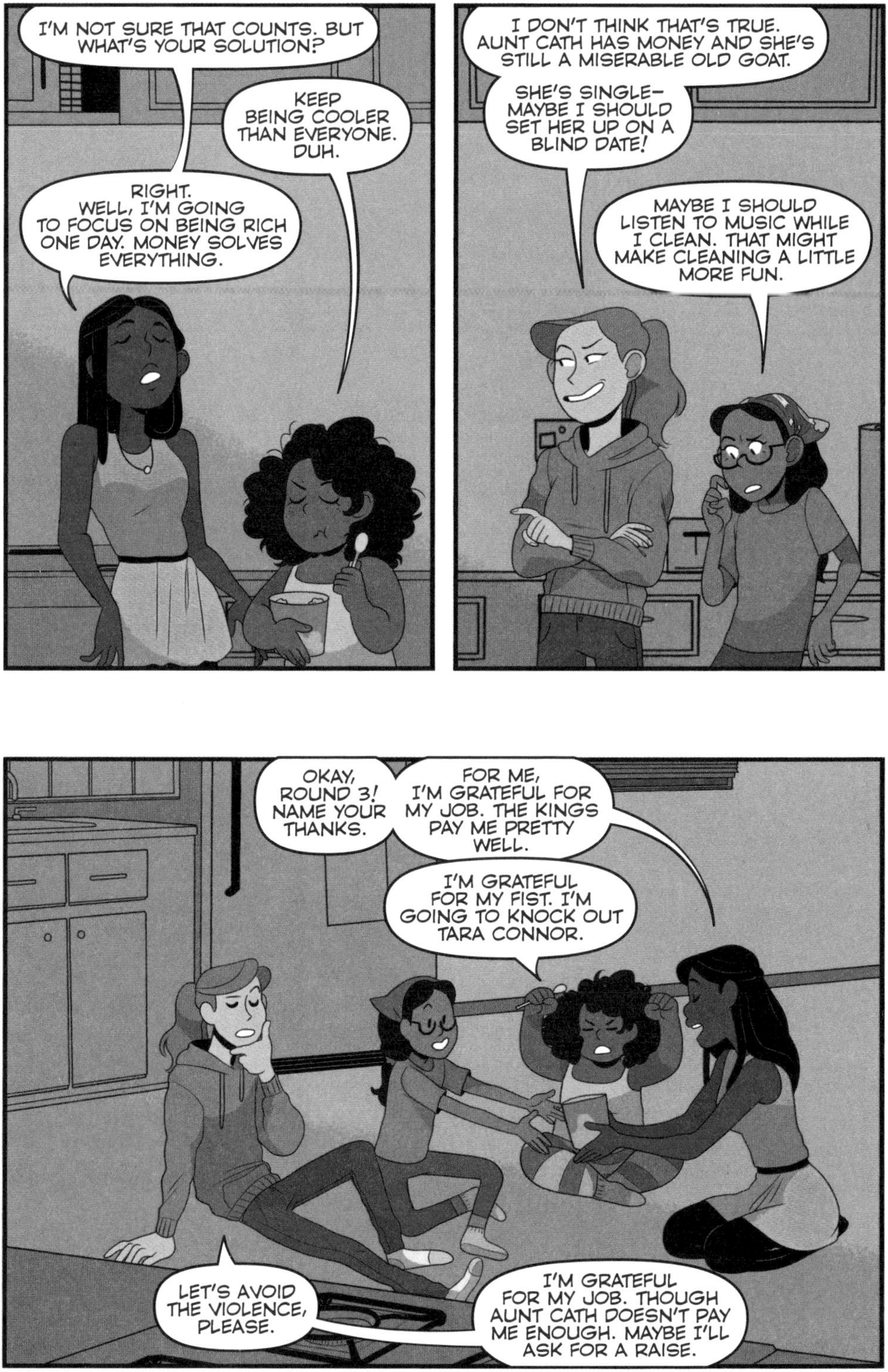
I'M NOT SURE THAT COUNTS. BUT WHAT'S YOUR SOLUTION?
KEEP BEING COOLER THAN EVERYONE. DUH.
RIGHT. WELL, I'M GOING TO FOCUS ON BEING RICH ONE DAY. MONEY SOLVES EVERYTHING.
I DON'T THINK THAT'S TRUE. AUNT CATH HAS MONEY AND SHE'S STILL A MISERABLE OLD GOAT.
SHE'S SINGLE– MAYBE I SHOULD SET HER UP ON A BLIND DATE!
MAYBE I SHOULD LISTEN TO MUSIC WHILE I CLEAN. THAT MIGHT MAKE CLEANING A LITTLE MORE FUN.
OKAY, ROUND 3! NAME YOUR THANKS.
FOR ME, I'M GRATEFUL FOR MY JOB. THE KINGS PAY ME PRETTY WELL.
I'M GRATEFUL FOR MY FIST. I'M GOING TO KNOCK OUT TARA CONNOR.
LET'S AVOID THE VIOLENCE, PLEASE.
I'M GRATEFUL FOR MY JOB. THOUGH AUNT CATH DOESN'T PAY ME ENOUGH. MAYBE I'LL ASK FOR A RAISE.

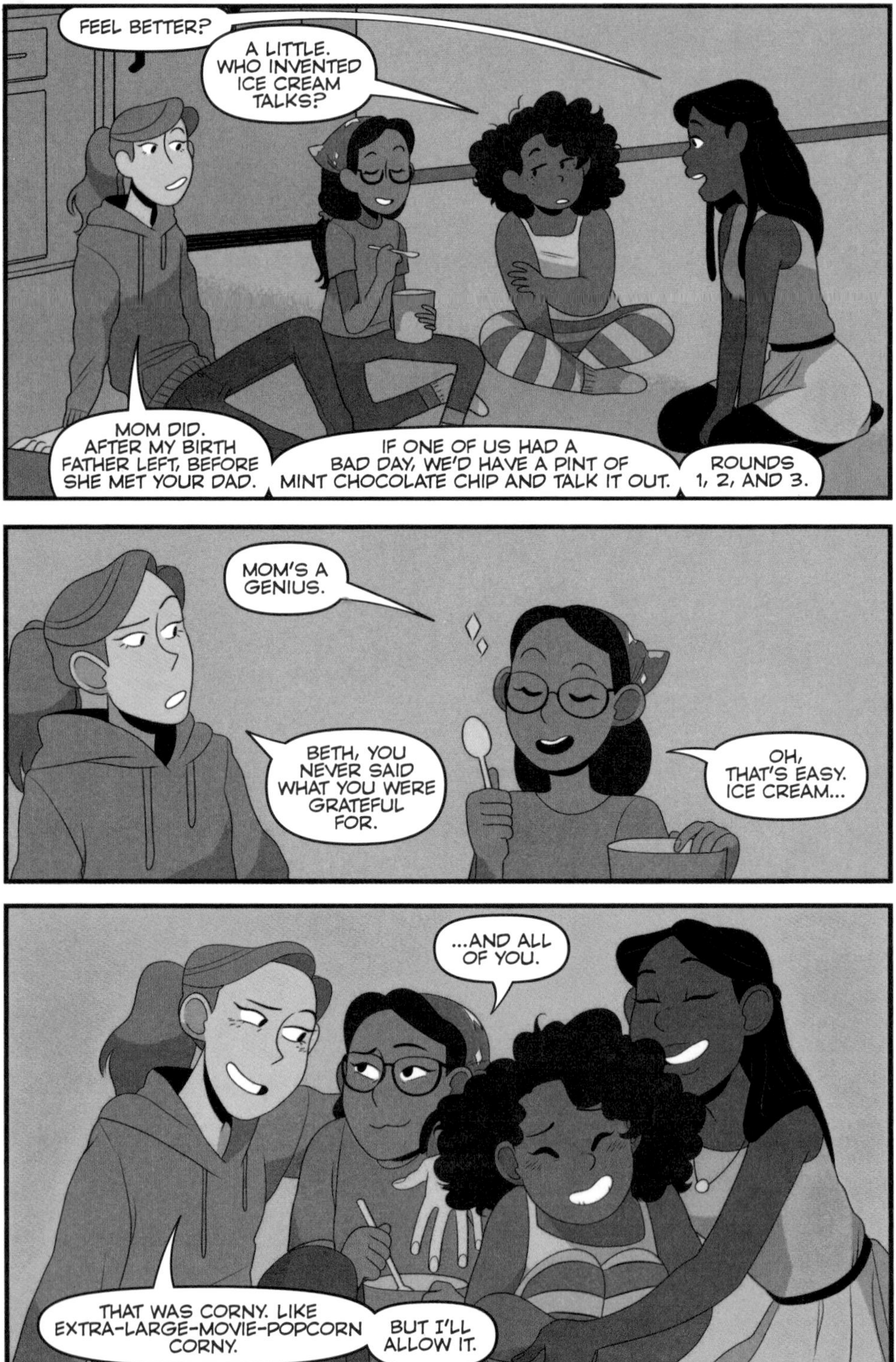
FEEL BETTER?
A LITTLE. WHO INVENTED ICE CREAM TALKS?
MOM DID. AFTER MY BIRTH FATHER LEFT, BEFORE SHE MET YOUR DAD.
IF ONE OF US HAD A BAD DAY, WE'D HAVE A PINT OF MINT CHOCOLATE CHIP AND TALK IT OUT.
ROUNDS 1, 2, AND 3.
MOM'S A GENIUS.
BETH, YOU NEVER SAID WHAT YOU WERE GRATEFUL FOR.
OH, THAT'S EASY. ICE CREAM...
...AND ALL OF YOU.
THAT WAS CORNY. LIKE EXTRA-LARGE-MOVIE-POPCORN CORNY.
BUT I'LL ALLOW IT.

New Message

FROM: Beth March
TO: Robert March
SENT: January 28

Hi Daddy!

How are you? I am fine. Middle school is fun. The kids are okay, but the classes are real fun. Did I tell you we have something called electives—that means classes we get to choose. And I chose music! We get to play different instruments. I thought I would like the piano or maybe the flute more, but it turns out I really like playing guitar.

Oh, and Jo found this old vintage record store in Bushwick. She took me there and bought me two records. I chose The Ronettes and Ella Fitzgerald. I love old music! When you're back, can I play them for you? I bet you and Mom would like to dance to them.

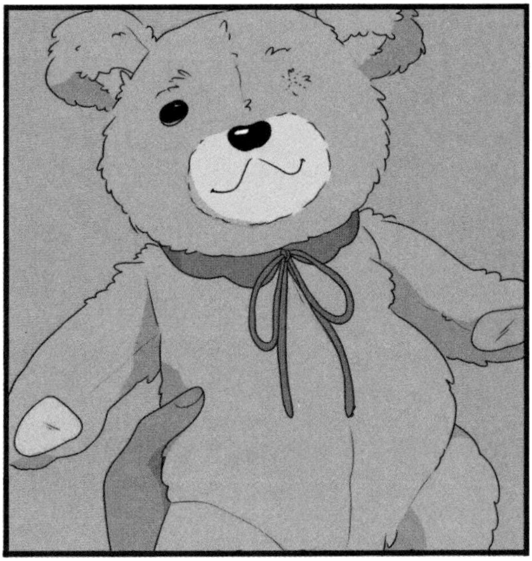

I miss you a whole whole bunch. Don't tell my sisters, but I still sleep with Mr. Furry Burry, the bear you brought me back from Kabul when I was little. He kinda smells and he's missing an eye, but he reminds me of you. (I included a pic for you!)

Come home soon—and safe!
Love you forever, Beth!

Send

CHAPTER 5

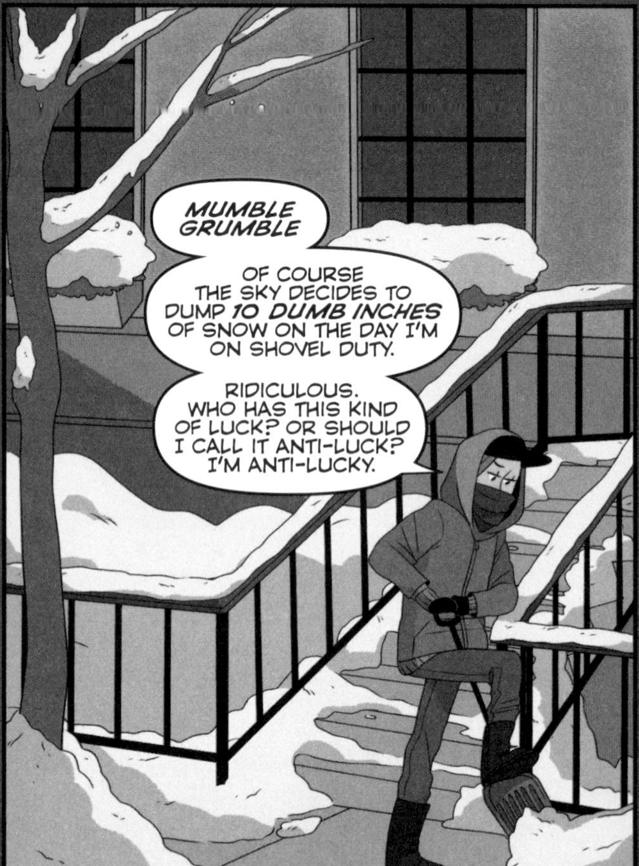
MUMBLE GRUMBLE
OF COURSE THE SKY DECIDES TO DUMP 10 DUMB INCHES OF SNOW ON THE DAY I'M ON SHOVEL DUTY.
RIDICULOUS. WHO HAS THIS KIND OF LUCK? OR SHOULD I CALL IT ANTI-LUCK? I'M ANTI-LUCKY.

Neighbors

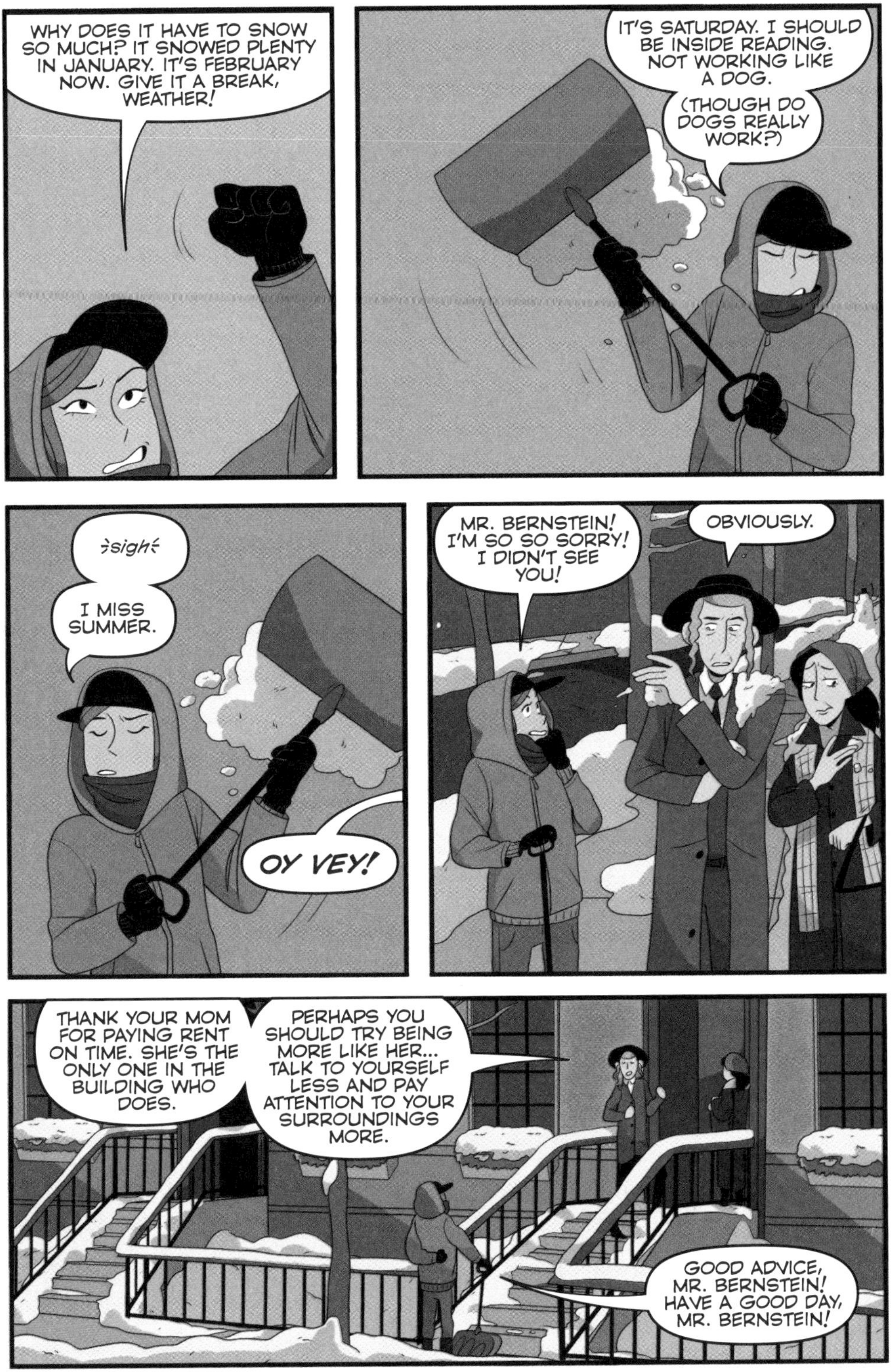
WHY DOES IT HAVE TO SNOW SO MUCH? IT SNOWED PLENTY IN JANUARY. IT'S FEBRUARY NOW. GIVE IT A BREAK, WEATHER!
IT'S SATURDAY. I SHOULD BE INSIDE READING. NOT WORKING LIKE A DOG.
(THOUGH DO DOGS REALLY WORK?)
sigh
I MISS SUMMER.
OY VEY!
MR. BERNSTEIN! I'M SO SO SORRY! I DIDN'T SEE YOU!
OBVIOUSLY.
THANK YOUR MOM FOR PAYING RENT ON TIME. SHE'S THE ONLY ONE IN THE BUILDING WHO DOES.
PERHAPS YOU SHOULD TRY BEING MORE LIKE HER... TALK TO YOURSELF LESS AND PAY ATTENTION TO YOUR SURROUNDINGS MORE.
GOOD ADVICE, MR. BERNSTEIN! HAVE A GOOD DAY, MR. BERNSTEIN!

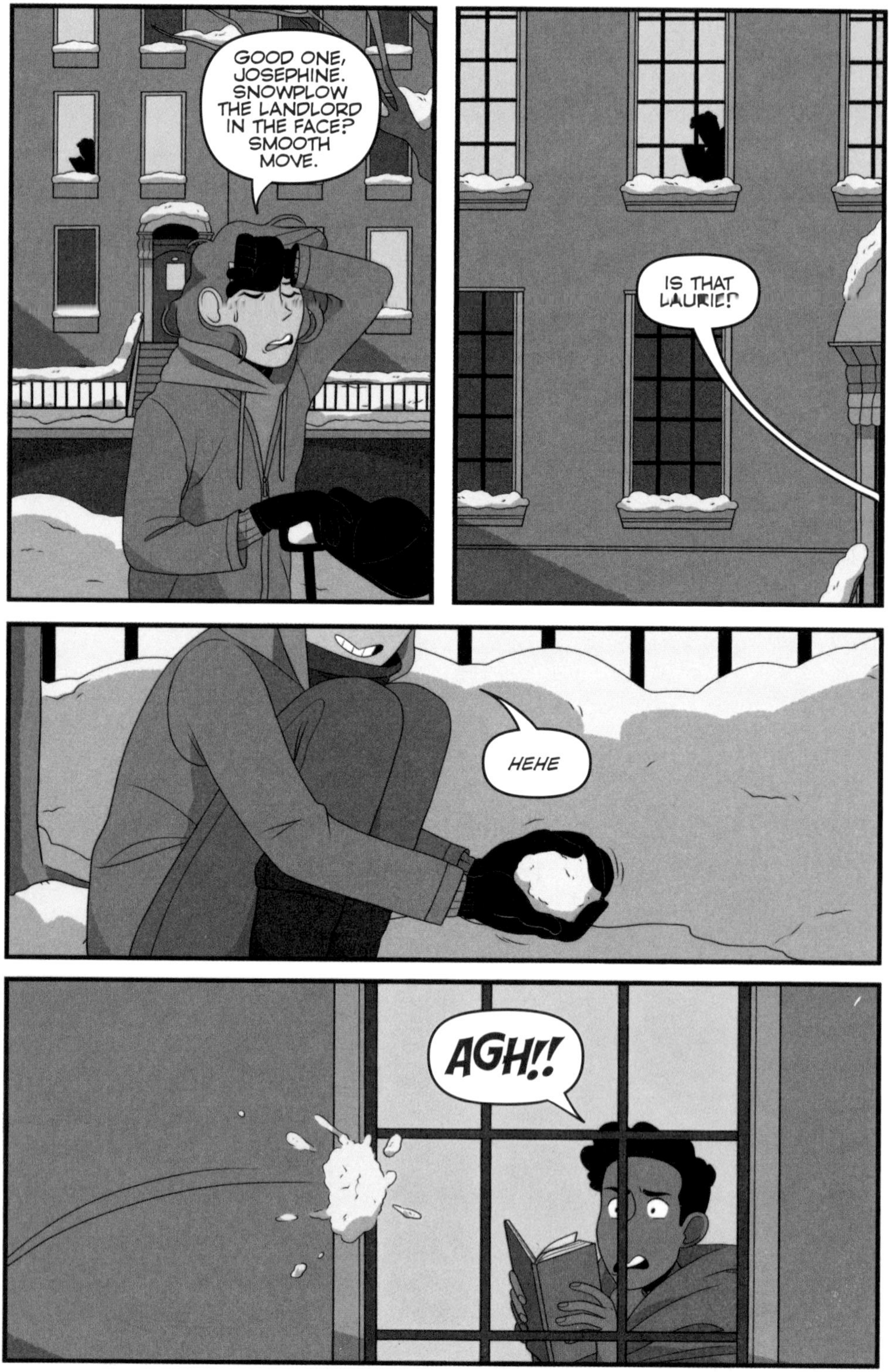
GOOD ONE, JOSEPHINE. SNOWPLOW THE LANDLORD IN THE FACE? SMOOTH MOVE.
IS THAT LAURIE?
HEHE
AGH!!

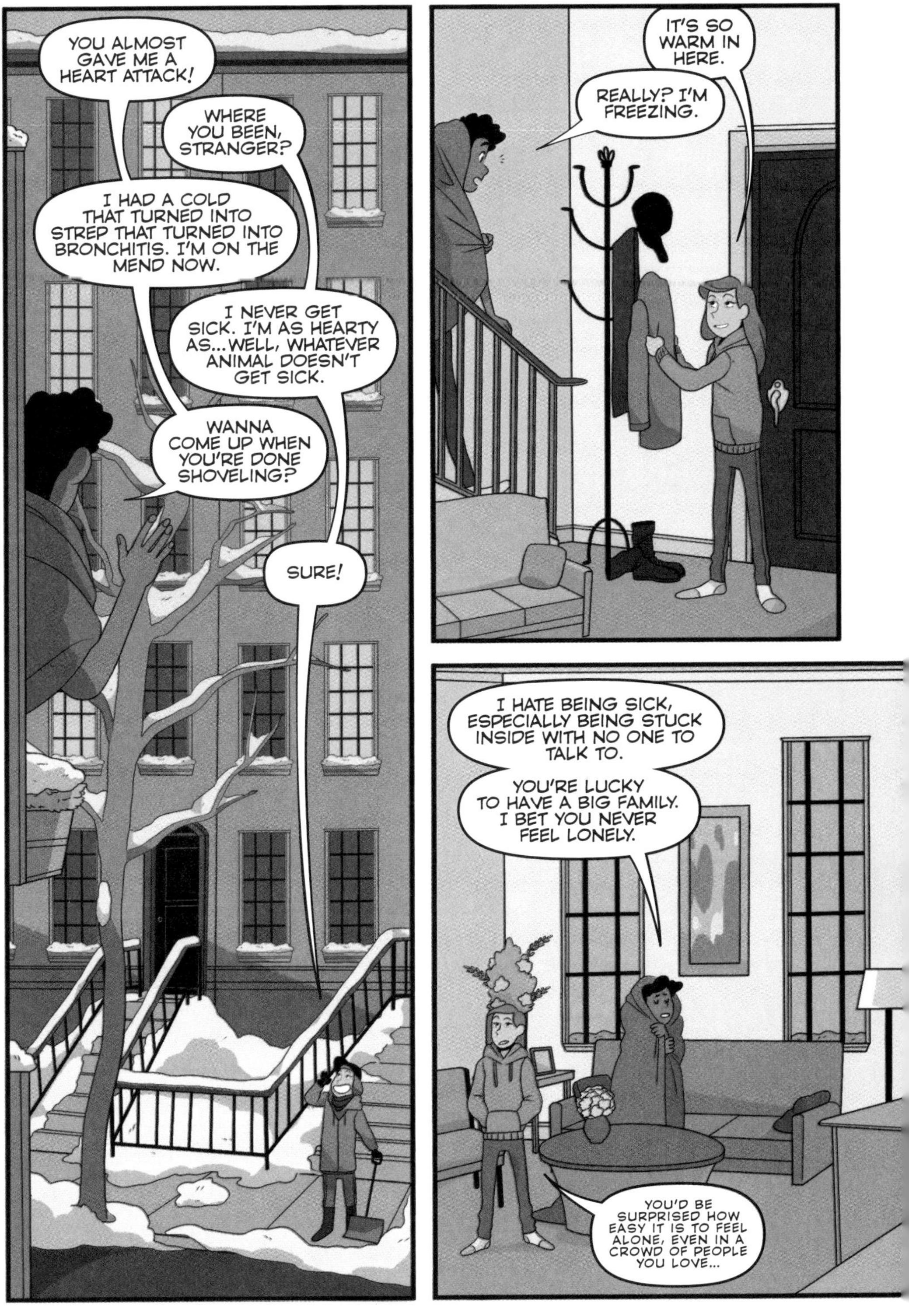
YOU ALMOST GAVE ME A HEART ATTACK!
WHERE YOU BEEN, STRANGER?
I HAD A COLD THAT TURNED INTO STREP THAT TURNED INTO BRONCHITIS. I'M ON THE MEND NOW.
I NEVER GET SICK. I'M AS HEARTY AS...WELL, WHATEVER ANIMAL DOESN'T GET SICK.
WANNA COME UP WHEN YOU'RE DONE SHOVELING?
SURE!
IT'S SO WARM IN HERE.
REALLY? I'M FREEZING.
I HATE BEING SICK, ESPECIALLY BEING STUCK INSIDE WITH NO ONE TO TALK TO.
YOU'RE LUCKY TO HAVE A BIG FAMILY. I BET YOU NEVER FEEL LONELY.
YOU'D BE SURPRISED HOW EASY IT IS TO FEEL ALONE, EVEN IN A CROWD OF PEOPLE YOU LOVE...

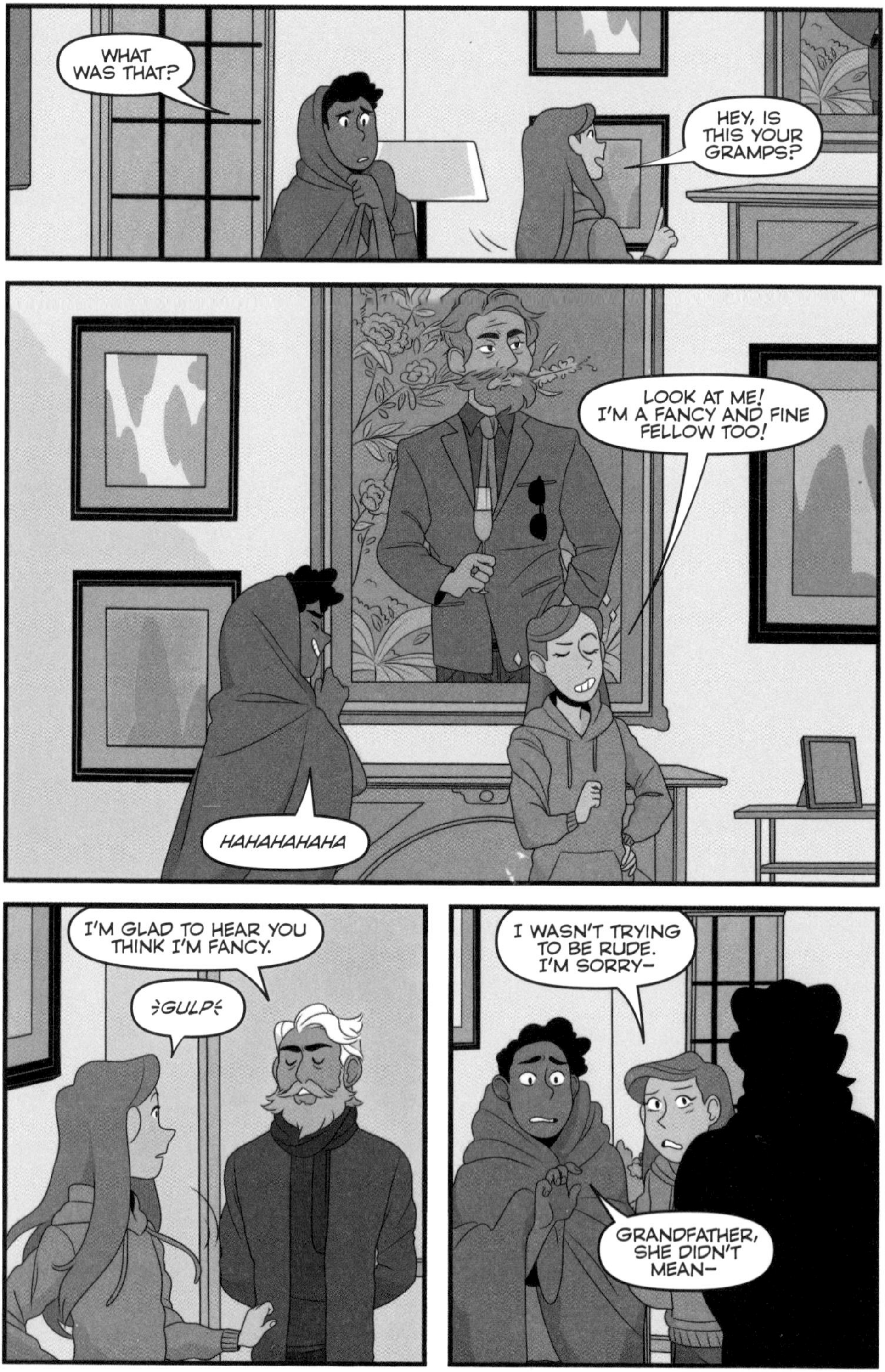
WHAT WAS THAT?
HEY, IS THIS YOUR GRAMPS?
LOOK AT ME! I'M A FANCY AND FINE FELLOW TOO!
HAHAHAHAHA
I'M GLAD TO HEAR YOU THINK I'M FANCY.
GULP
I WASN'T TRYING TO BE RUDE. I'M SORRY–
GRANDFATHER, SHE DIDN'T MEAN–

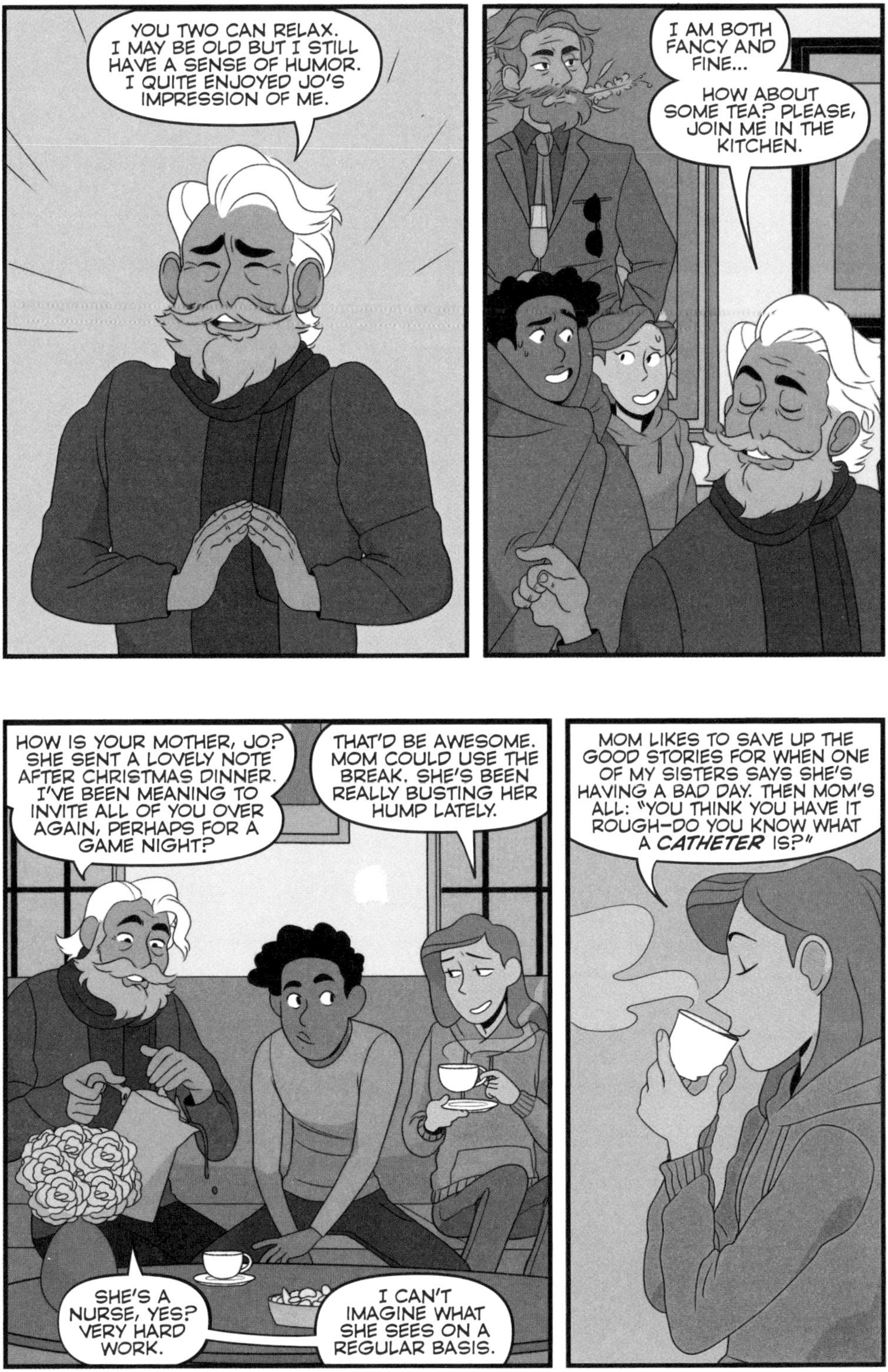

YOU TWO CAN RELAX. I MAY BE OLD BUT I STILL HAVE A SENSE OF HUMOR. I QUITE ENJOYED JO'S IMPRESSION OF ME.
I AM BOTH FANCY AND FINE...
HOW ABOUT SOME TEA? PLEASE, JOIN ME IN THE KITCHEN.
HOW IS YOUR MOTHER, JO? SHE SENT A LOVELY NOTE AFTER CHRISTMAS DINNER. I'VE BEEN MEANING TO INVITE ALL OF YOU OVER AGAIN, PERHAPS FOR A GAME NIGHT?
THAT'D BE AWESOME. MOM COULD USE THE BREAK. SHE'S BEEN REALLY BUSTING HER HUMP LATELY.
SHE'S A NURSE, YES? VERY HARD WORK.
I CAN'T IMAGINE WHAT SHE SEES ON A REGULAR BASIS.
MOM LIKES TO SAVE UP THE GOOD STORIES FOR WHEN ONE OF MY SISTERS SAYS SHE'S HAVING A BAD DAY. THEN MOM'S ALL: "YOU THINK YOU HAVE IT ROUGH–DO YOU KNOW WHAT A *CATHETER* IS?"

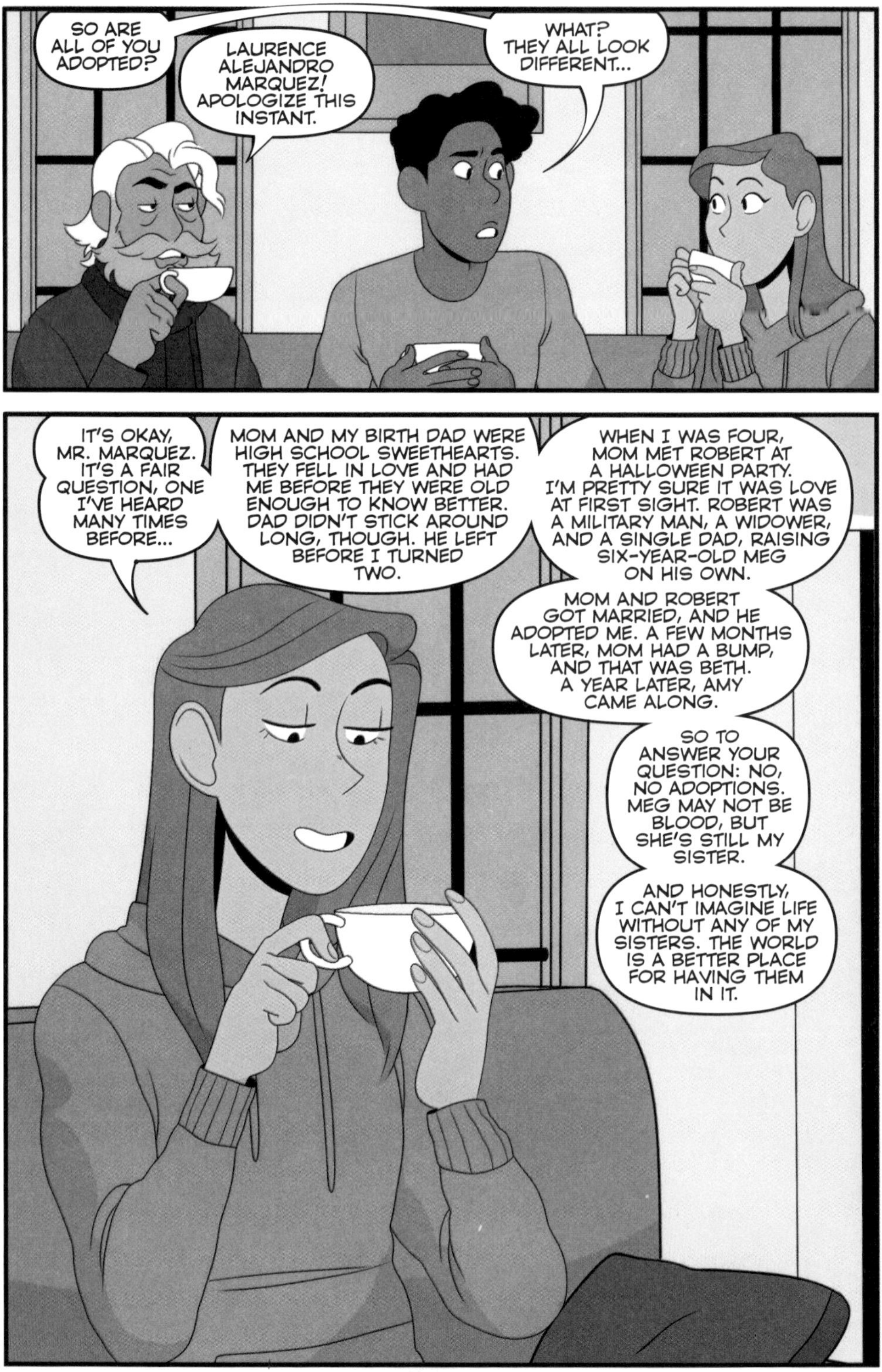
SO ARE ALL OF YOU ADOPTED?
LAURENCE ALEJANDRO MARQUEZ! APOLOGIZE THIS INSTANT.
WHAT? THEY ALL LOOK DIFFERENT...
IT'S OKAY, MR. MARQUEZ. IT'S A FAIR QUESTION, ONE I'VE HEARD MANY TIMES BEFORE...
MOM AND MY BIRTH DAD WERE HIGH SCHOOL SWEETHEARTS. THEY FELL IN LOVE AND HAD ME BEFORE THEY WERE OLD ENOUGH TO KNOW BETTER. DAD DIDN'T STICK AROUND LONG, THOUGH. HE LEFT BEFORE I TURNED TWO.
WHEN I WAS FOUR, MOM MET ROBERT AT A HALLOWEEN PARTY. I'M PRETTY SURE IT WAS LOVE AT FIRST SIGHT. ROBERT WAS A MILITARY MAN, A WIDOWER, AND A SINGLE DAD, RAISING SIX-YEAR-OLD MEG ON HIS OWN.
MOM AND ROBERT GOT MARRIED, AND HE ADOPTED ME. A FEW MONTHS LATER, MOM HAD A BUMP, AND THAT WAS BETH. A YEAR LATER, AMY CAME ALONG.
SO TO ANSWER YOUR QUESTION: NO, NO ADOPTIONS. MEG MAY NOT BE BLOOD, BUT SHE'S STILL MY SISTER.
AND HONESTLY, I CAN'T IMAGINE LIFE WITHOUT ANY OF MY SISTERS. THE WORLD IS A BETTER PLACE FOR HAVING THEM IN IT.

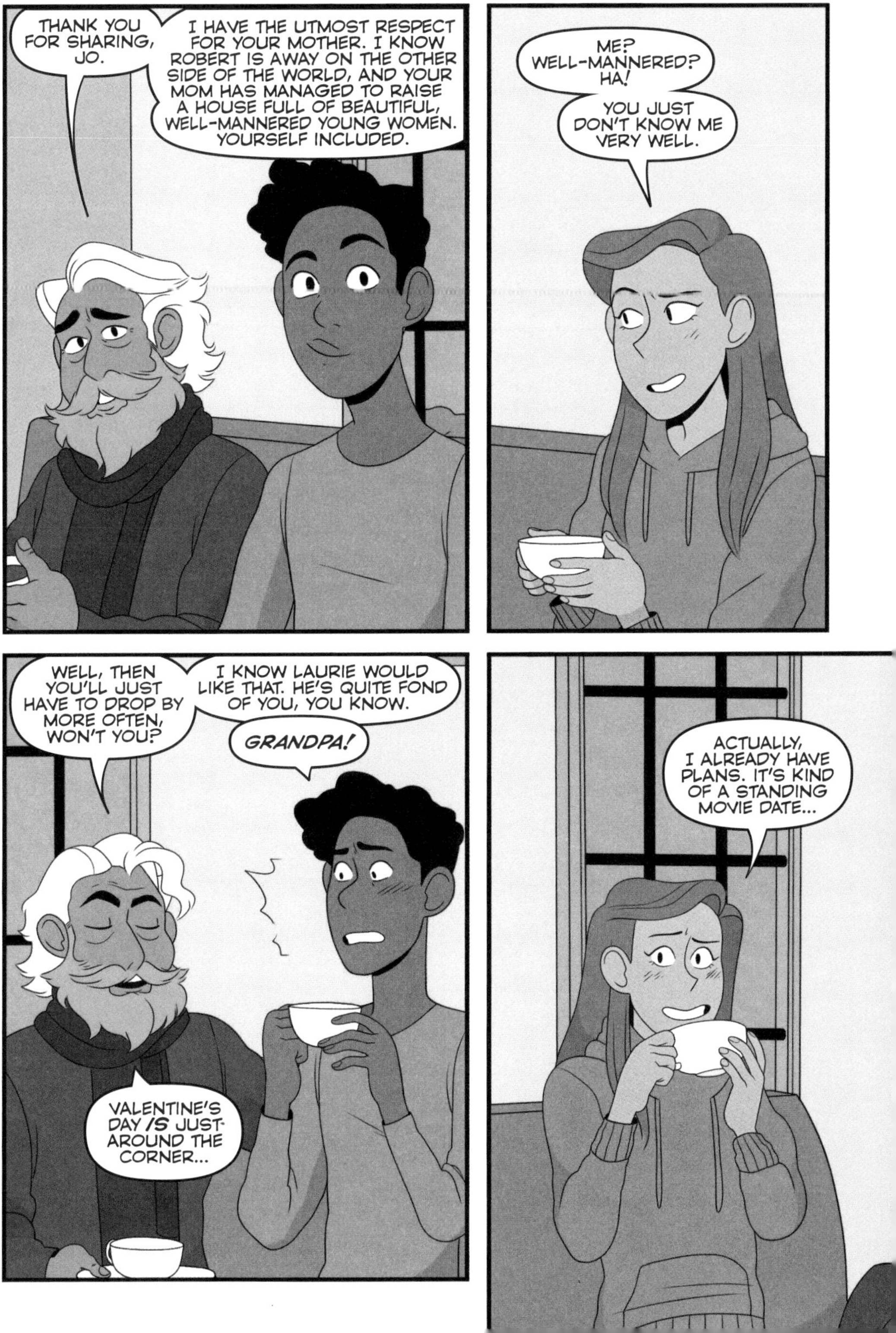

THANK YOU FOR SHARING, JO.
I HAVE THE UTMOST RESPECT FOR YOUR MOTHER. I KNOW ROBERT IS AWAY ON THE OTHER SIDE OF THE WORLD, AND YOUR MOM HAS MANAGED TO RAISE A HOUSE FULL OF BEAUTIFUL, WELL-MANNERED YOUNG WOMEN. YOURSELF INCLUDED.
ME? WELL-MANNERED? HA!
YOU JUST DON'T KNOW ME VERY WELL.
WELL, THEN YOU'LL JUST HAVE TO DROP BY MORE OFTEN, WON'T YOU?
I KNOW LAURIE WOULD LIKE THAT. HE'S QUITE FOND OF YOU, YOU KNOW.
GRANDPA!
VALENTINE'S DAY *IS* JUST-AROUND THE CORNER...
ACTUALLY, I ALREADY HAVE PLANS. IT'S KIND OF A STANDING MOVIE DATE...

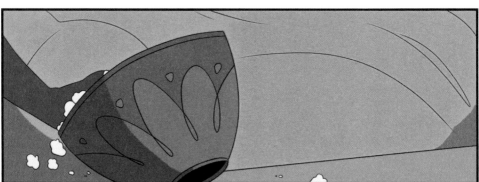

I LOVE ROMANCE MOVIES.

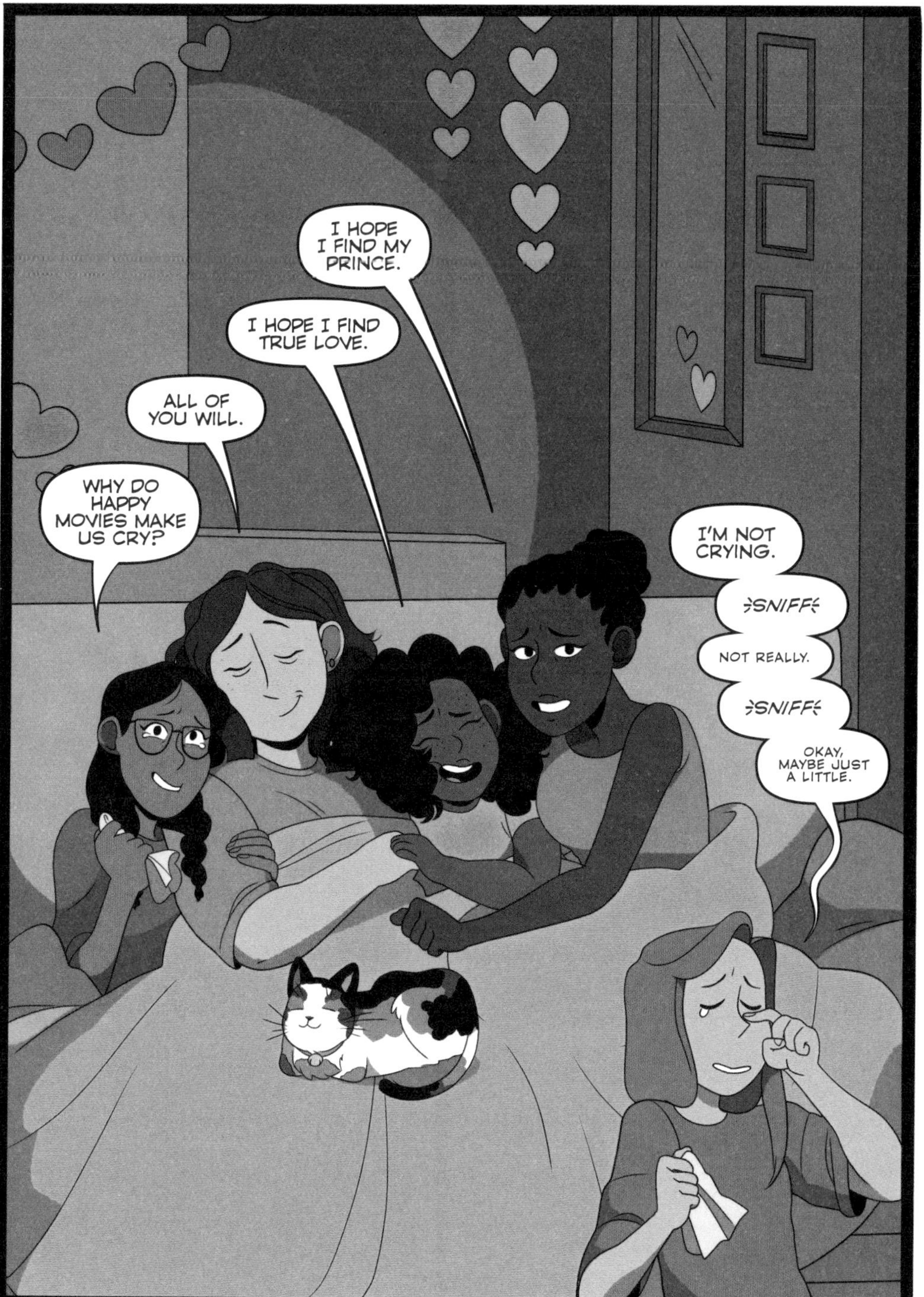
WHY DO HAPPY MOVIES MAKE US CRY?
ALL OF YOU WILL.
I HOPE I FIND TRUE LOVE.
I HOPE I FIND MY PRINCE.
I'M NOT CRYING.
SNIFF
NOT REALLY.
SNIFF
OKAY, MAYBE JUST A LITTLE.

New Message

FROM: Amy March
TO: Robert March
SENT: Feb 21

daddy!

meg & jo & beth said i should email u, so i am. i would write u more, but i hate writing cause it feels like HOMEWOKR. yuck! i rather talk to u on the phone. or skype!

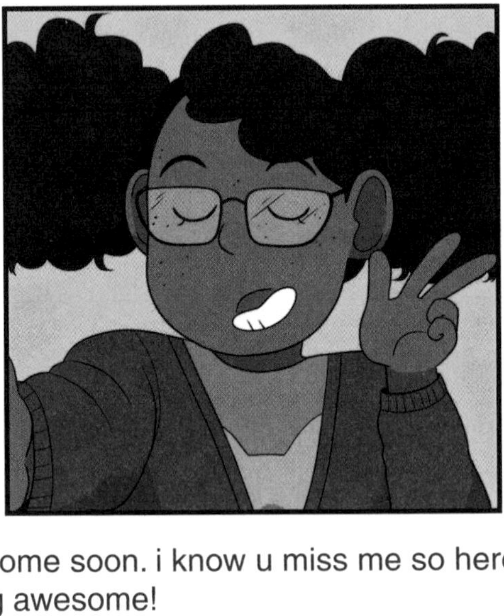

i hope u come home soon. i know u miss me so here are pics of me ebing awesome!

Send

XOXOXOXOXOX
OXOXOXOXOXO
XOXOXOXOXOX
OXOXOXOXOXO
XOXOXOXOXOX
OXOXOXOXOXO,
your FAVE
daughter, AMY!

CHAPTER 6

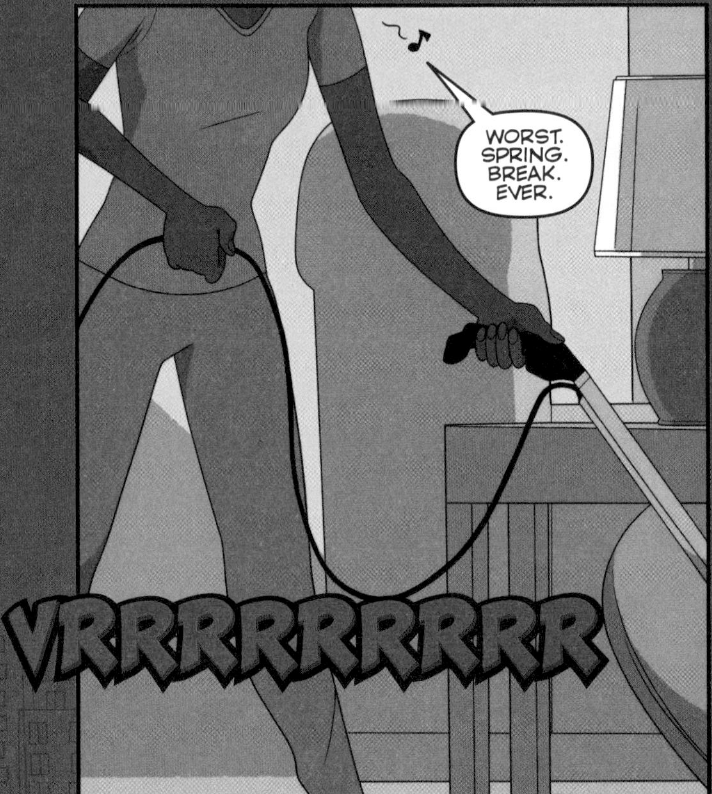
WORST. SPRING. BREAK. EVER.
VRRRRRRRRRR

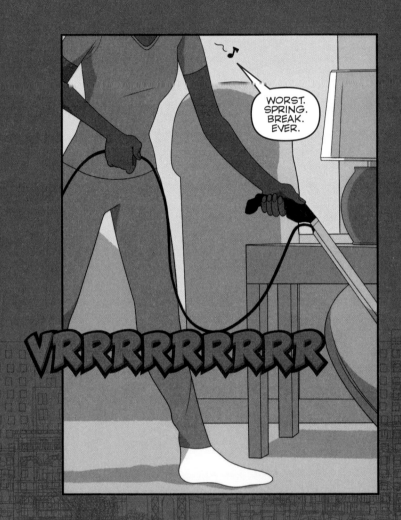

The Gift of Music

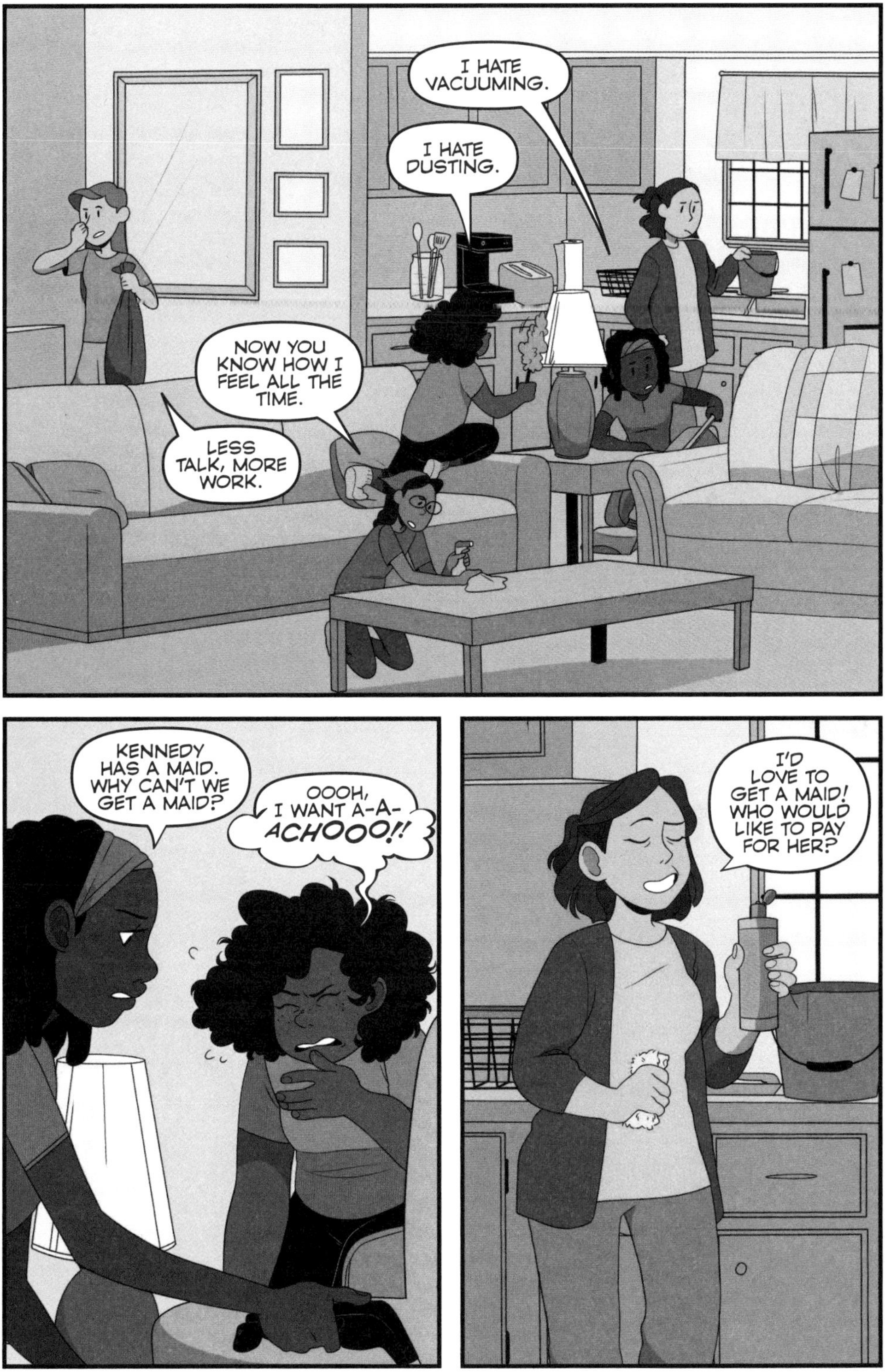
I HATE VACUUMING.
I HATE DUSTING.
NOW YOU KNOW HOW I FEEL ALL THE TIME.
LESS TALK, MORE WORK.
KENNEDY HAS A MAID. WHY CAN'T WE GET A MAID?
OOOH, I WANT A-A-ACHOOO!!
I'D LOVE TO GET A MAID! WHO WOULD LIKE TO PAY FOR HER?

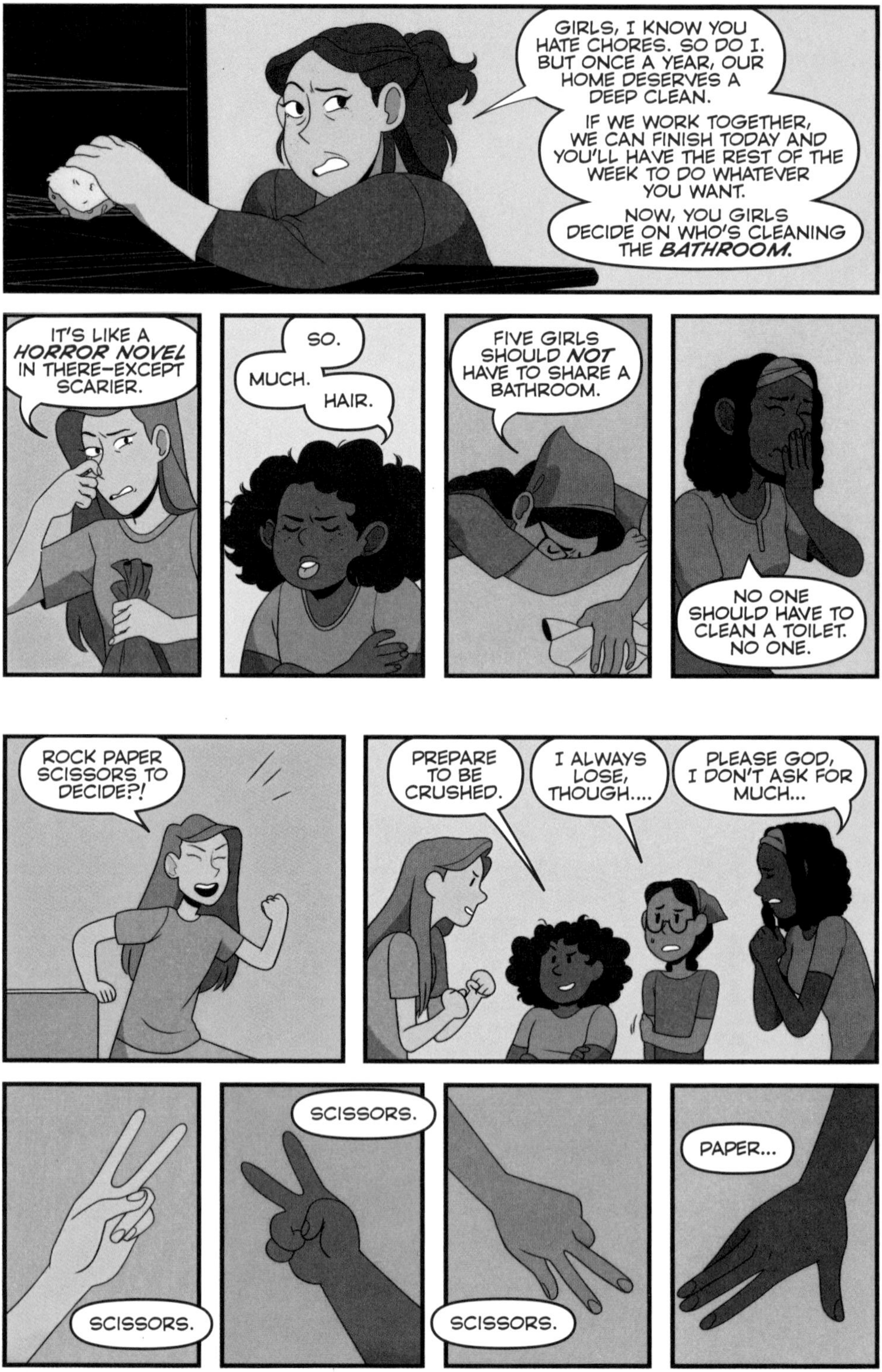
GIRLS, I KNOW YOU HATE CHORES. SO DO I. BUT ONCE A YEAR, OUR HOME DESERVES A DEEP CLEAN.
IF WE WORK TOGETHER, WE CAN FINISH TODAY AND YOU'LL HAVE THE REST OF THE WEEK TO DO WHATEVER YOU WANT.
NOW, YOU GIRLS DECIDE ON WHO'S CLEANING THE *BATHROOM.*
IT'S LIKE A *HORROR NOVEL* IN THERE—EXCEPT SCARIER.
SO.
MUCH.
HAIR.
FIVE GIRLS SHOULD *NOT* HAVE TO SHARE A BATHROOM.
NO ONE SHOULD HAVE TO CLEAN A TOILET. NO ONE.
ROCK PAPER SCISSORS TO DECIDE?!
PREPARE TO BE CRUSHED.
I ALWAYS LOSE, THOUGH....
PLEASE GOD, I DON'T ASK FOR MUCH...
SCISSORS.
SCISSORS.
SCISSORS.
PAPER...

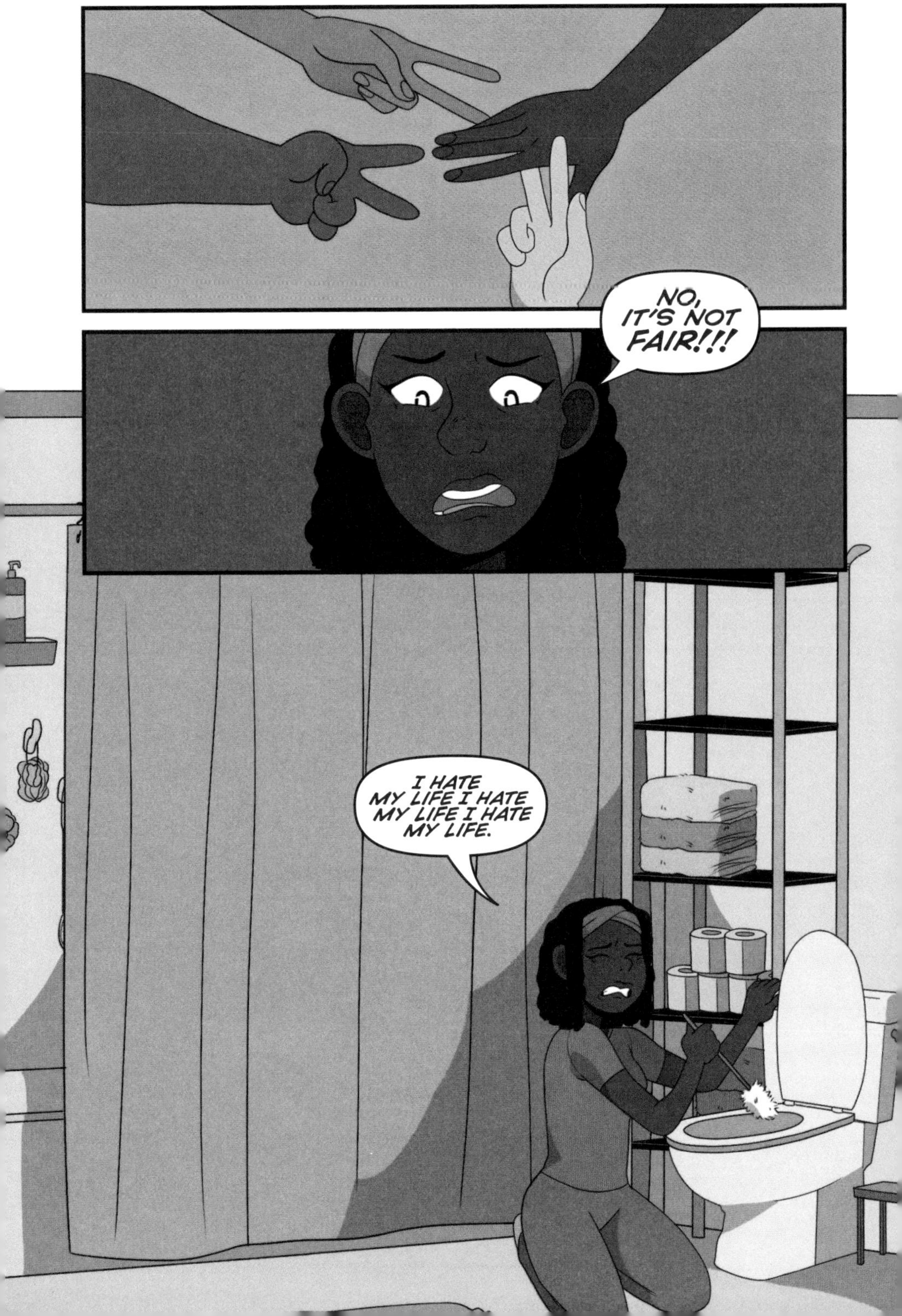
NO, IT'S NOT FAIR!!!
I HATE MY LIFE I HATE MY LIFE I HATE MY LIFE.

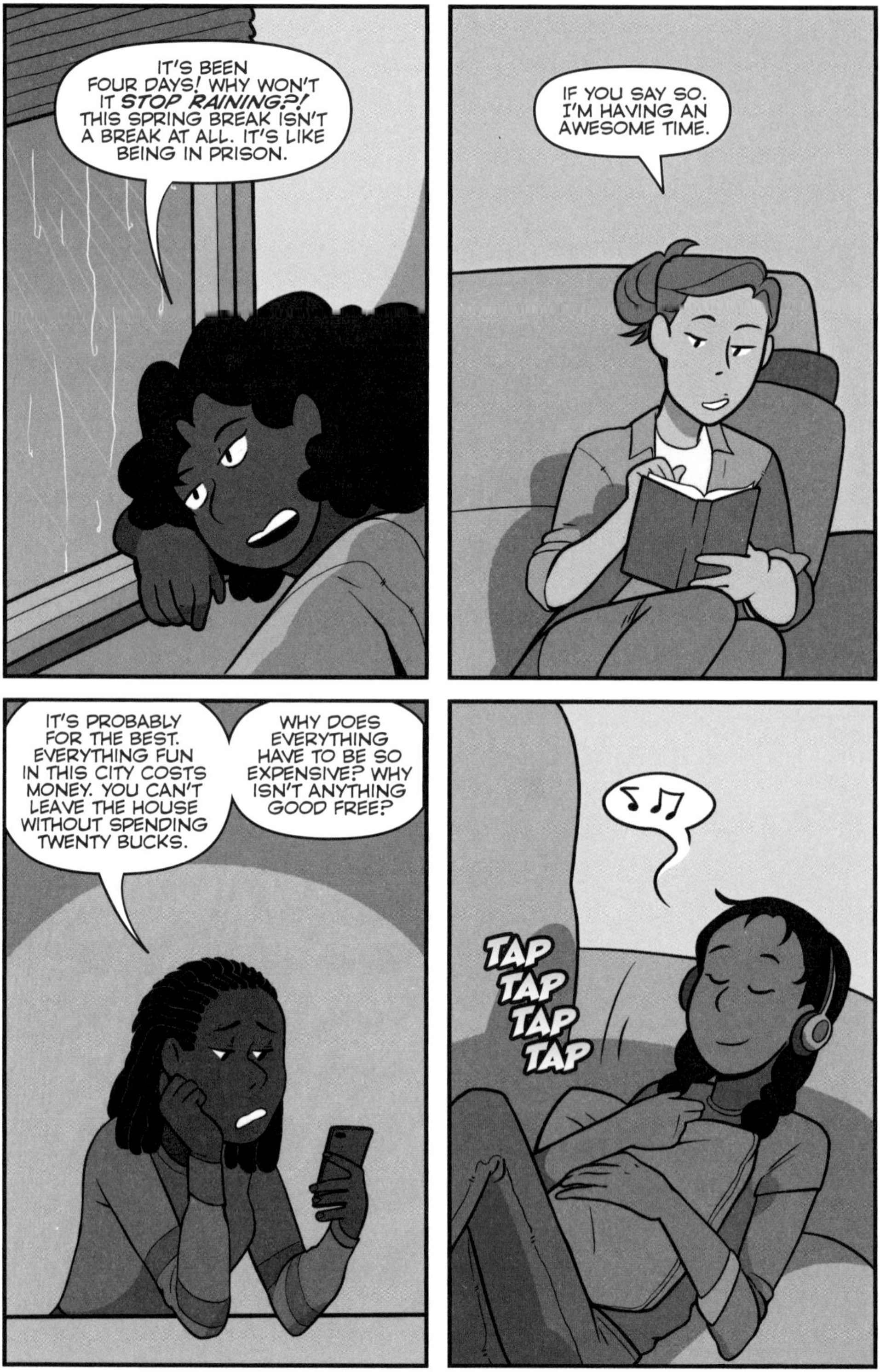
IT'S BEEN FOUR DAYS! WHY WON'T IT STOP RAINING?! THIS SPRING BREAK ISN'T A BREAK AT ALL. IT'S LIKE BEING IN PRISON.
IF YOU SAY SO. I'M HAVING AN AWESOME TIME.
IT'S PROBABLY FOR THE BEST. EVERYTHING FUN IN THIS CITY COSTS MONEY. YOU CAN'T LEAVE THE HOUSE WITHOUT SPENDING TWENTY BUCKS.
WHY DOES EVERYTHING HAVE TO BE SO EXPENSIVE? WHY ISN'T ANYTHING GOOD FREE?
TAP TAP TAP TAP

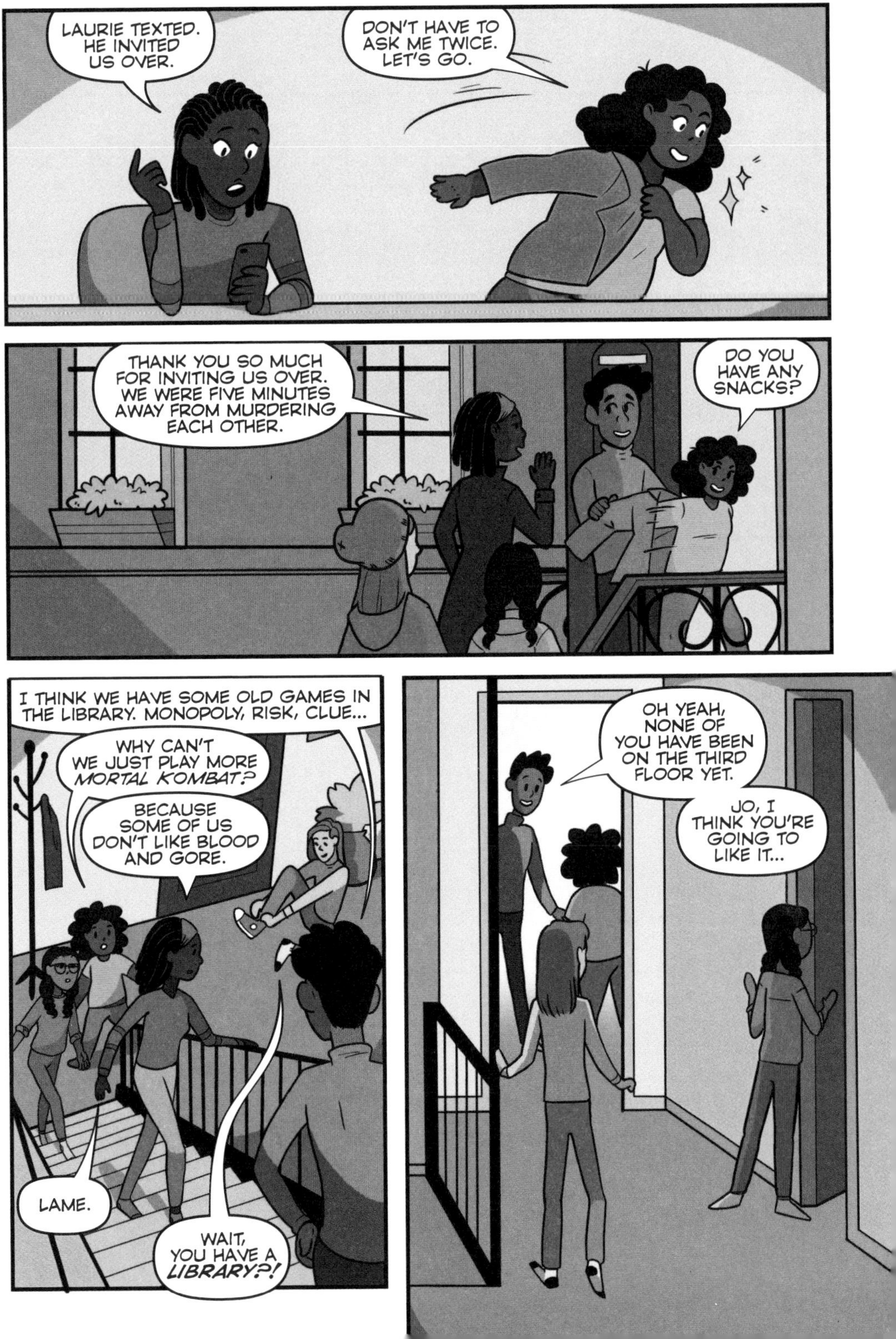
LAURIE TEXTED. HE INVITED US OVER.
DON'T HAVE TO ASK ME TWICE. LET'S GO.
THANK YOU SO MUCH FOR INVITING US OVER. WE WERE FIVE MINUTES AWAY FROM MURDERING EACH OTHER.
DO YOU HAVE ANY SNACKS?
I THINK WE HAVE SOME OLD GAMES IN THE LIBRARY. MONOPOLY, RISK, CLUE...
WHY CAN'T WE JUST PLAY MORE *MORTAL KOMBAT?*
BECAUSE SOME OF US DON'T LIKE BLOOD AND GORE.
LAME.
WAIT, YOU HAVE A ***LIBRARY?!***
OH YEAH, NONE OF YOU HAVE BEEN ON THE THIRD FLOOR YET.
JO, I THINK YOU'RE GOING TO LIKE IT...

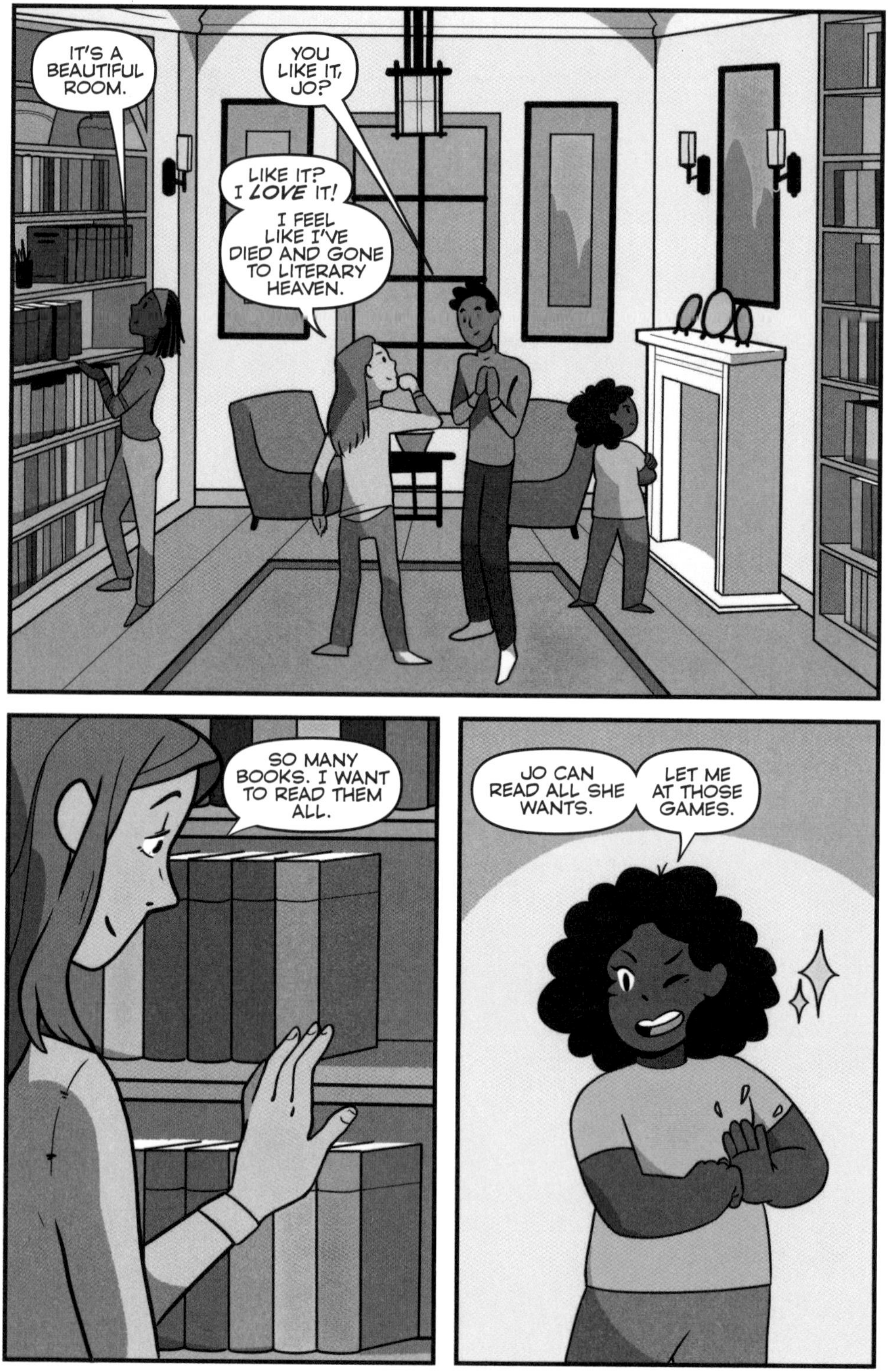
IT'S A BEAUTIFUL ROOM.
YOU LIKE IT, JO?
LIKE IT? I *LOVE* IT!
I FEEL LIKE I'VE DIED AND GONE TO LITERARY HEAVEN.
SO MANY BOOKS. I WANT TO READ THEM ALL.
JO CAN READ ALL SHE WANTS.
LET ME AT THOSE GAMES.

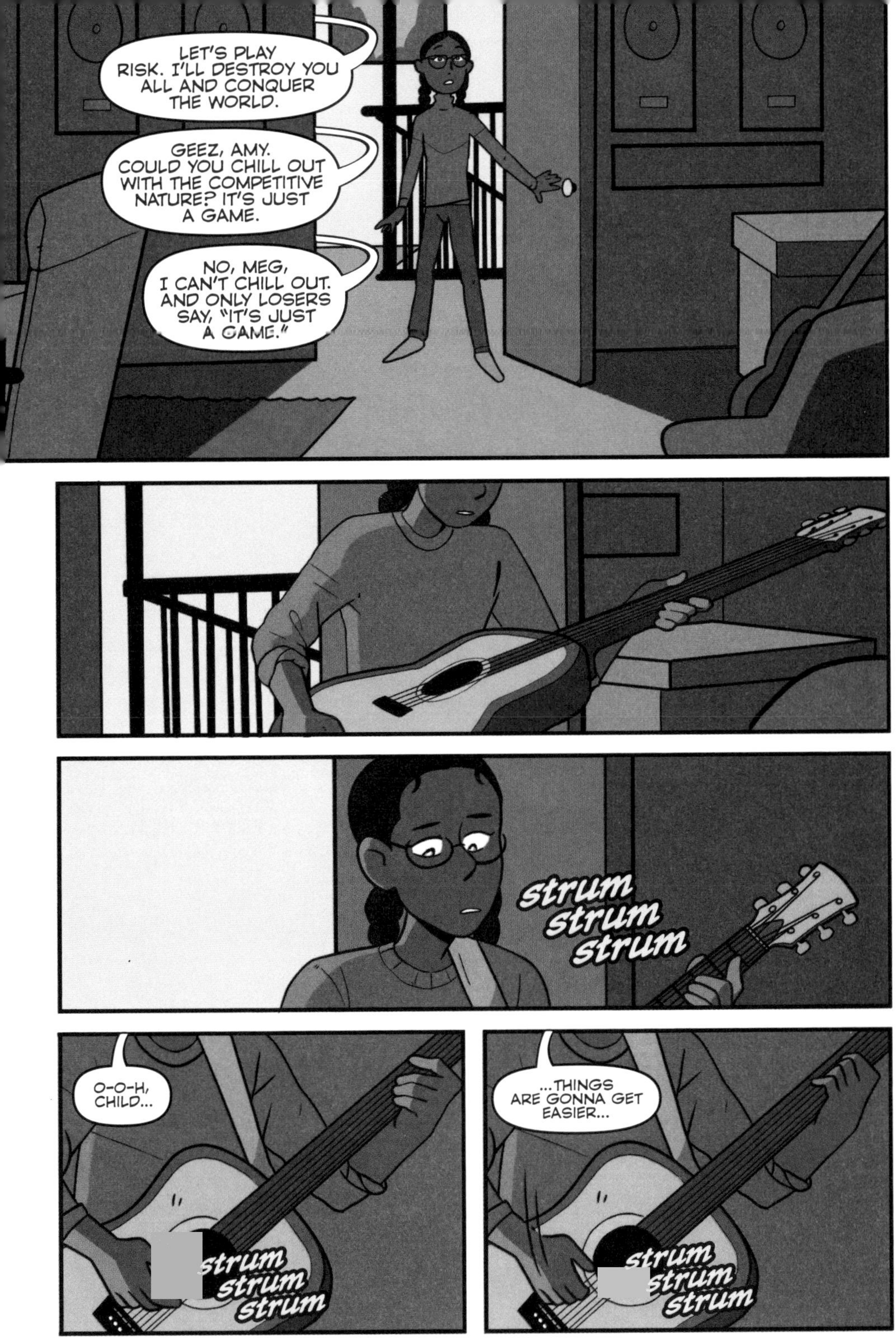
LET'S PLAY RISK. I'LL DESTROY YOU ALL AND CONQUER THE WORLD.
GEEZ, AMY. COULD YOU CHILL OUT WITH THE COMPETITIVE NATURE? IT'S JUST A GAME.
NO, MEG, I CAN'T CHILL OUT. AND ONLY LOSERS SAY, "IT'S JUST A GAME."
strum strum strum
O-O-H, CHILD...
strum strum strum
...THINGS ARE GONNA GET EASIER...
strum strum strum

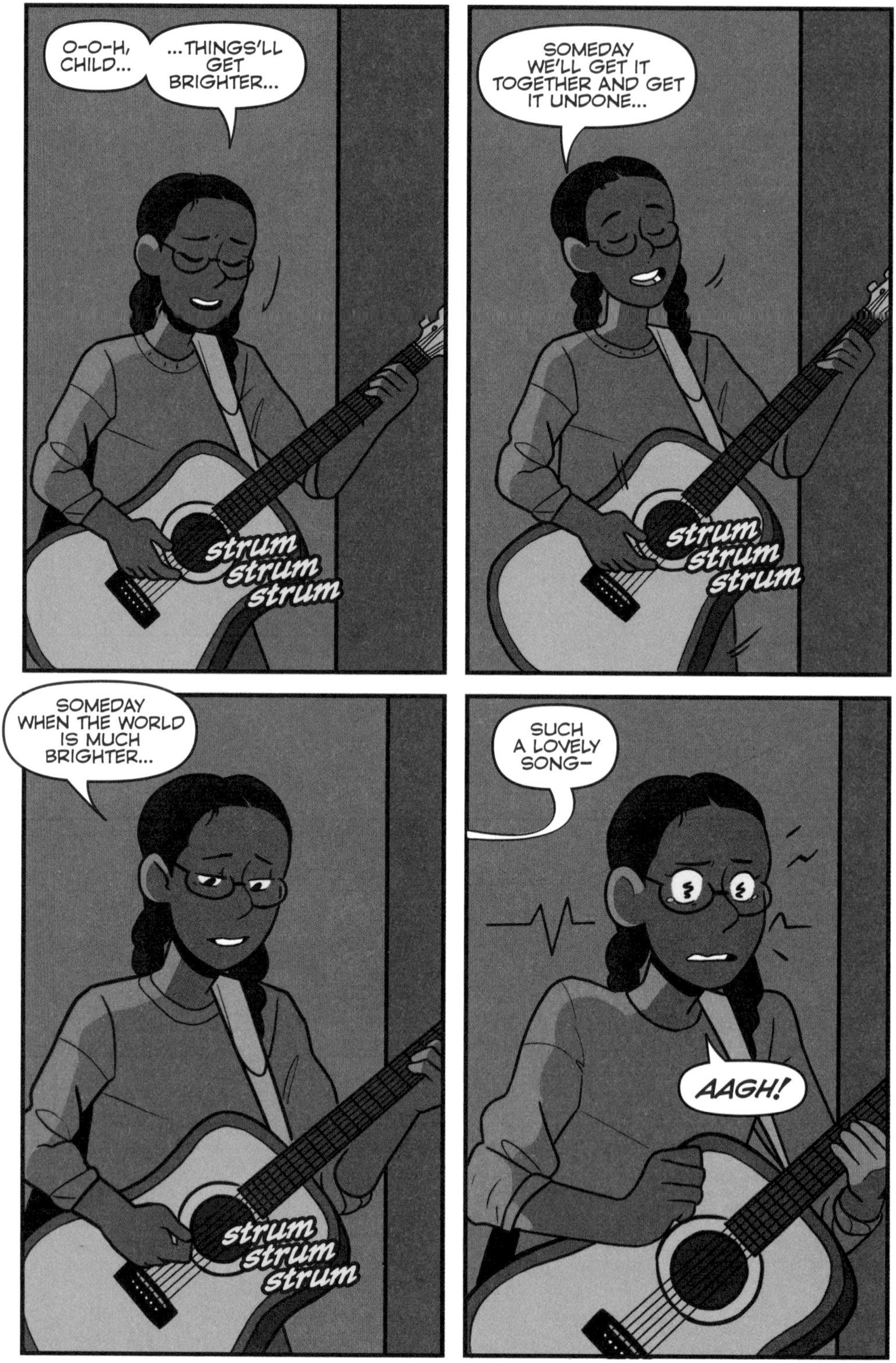
O-O-H, CHILD...
...THINGS'LL GET BRIGHTER...
strum strum strum
SOMEDAY WE'LL GET IT TOGETHER AND GET IT UNDONE...
strum strum strum
SOMEDAY WHEN THE WORLD IS MUCH BRIGHTER...
strum strum strum
SUCH A LOVELY SONG-
AAGH!

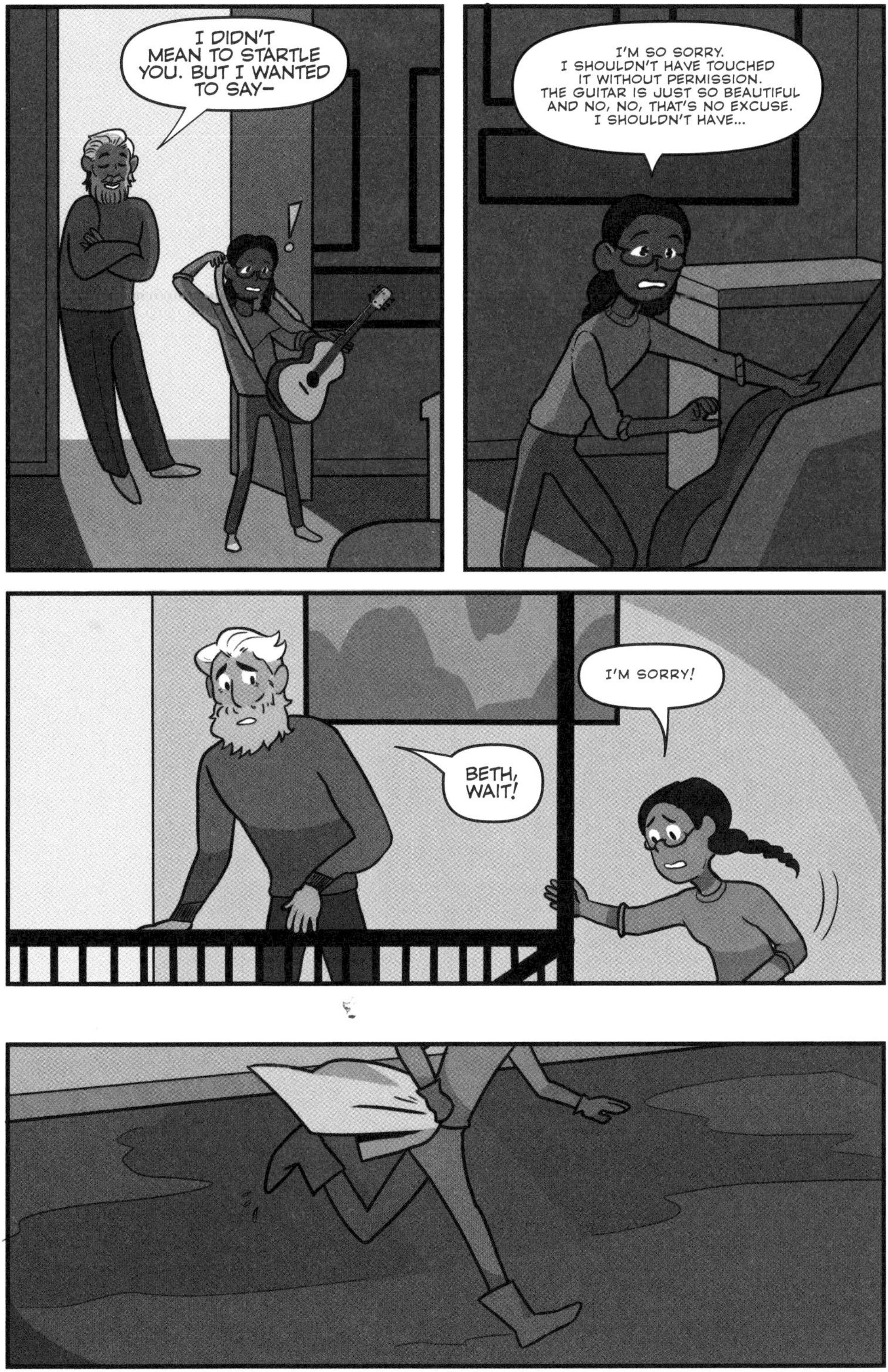

I DIDN'T MEAN TO STARTLE YOU. BUT I WANTED TO SAY–
!
I'M SO SORRY. I SHOULDN'T HAVE TOUCHED IT WITHOUT PERMISSION. THE GUITAR IS JUST SO BEAUTIFUL AND NO, NO, THAT'S NO EXCUSE. I SHOULDN'T HAVE...
I'M SORRY!
BETH, WAIT!

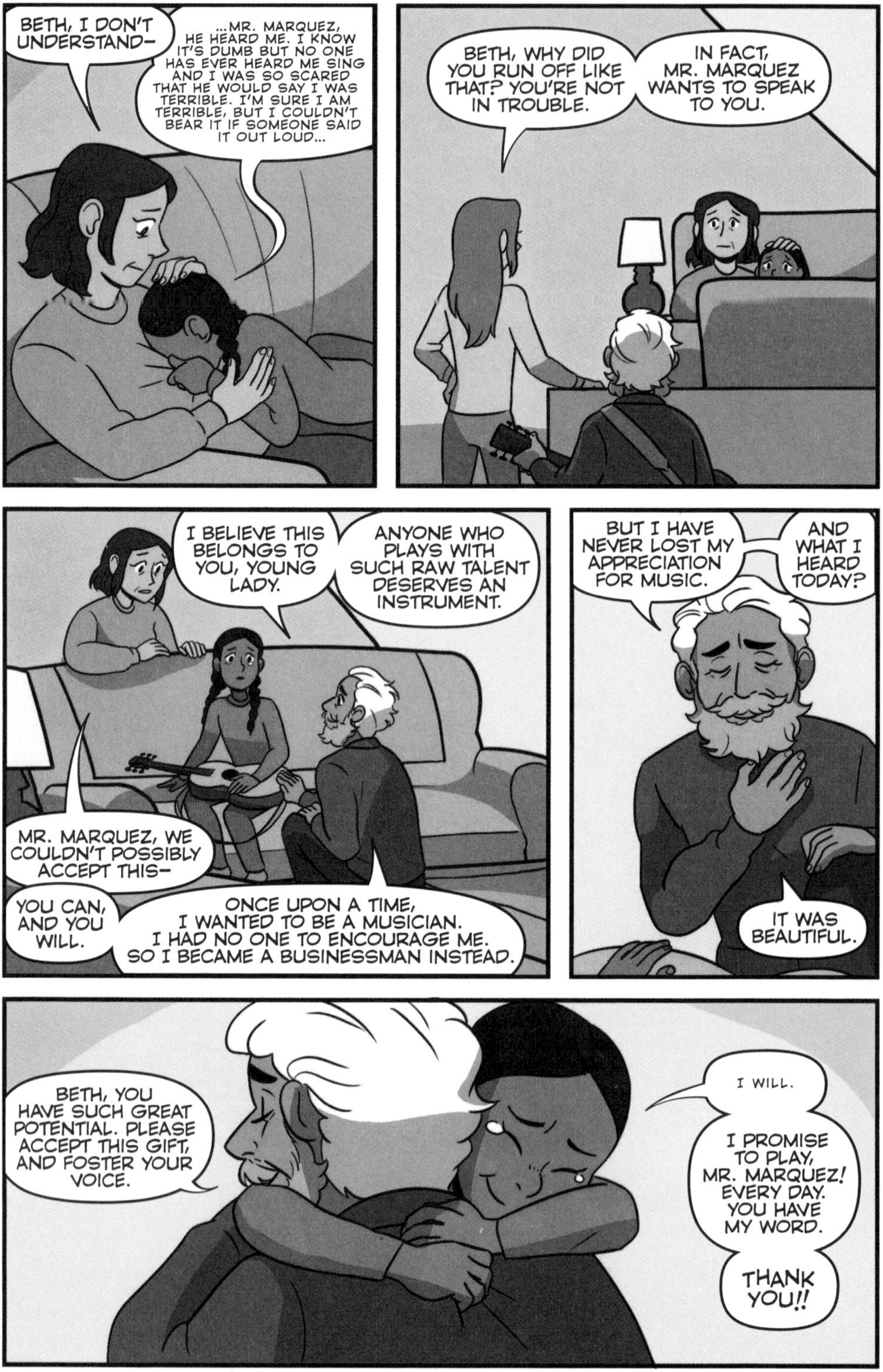
BETH, I DON'T UNDERSTAND–
...MR. MARQUEZ, HE HEARD ME. I KNOW IT'S DUMB BUT NO ONE HAS EVER HEARD ME SING AND I WAS SO SCARED THAT HE WOULD SAY I WAS TERRIBLE. I'M SURE I AM TERRIBLE, BUT I COULDN'T BEAR IT IF SOMEONE SAID IT OUT LOUD...
BETH, WHY DID YOU RUN OFF LIKE THAT? YOU'RE NOT IN TROUBLE.
IN FACT, MR. MARQUEZ WANTS TO SPEAK TO YOU.
I BELIEVE THIS BELONGS TO YOU, YOUNG LADY.
ANYONE WHO PLAYS WITH SUCH RAW TALENT DESERVES AN INSTRUMENT.
MR. MARQUEZ, WE COULDN'T POSSIBLY ACCEPT THIS–
YOU CAN, AND YOU WILL.
ONCE UPON A TIME, I WANTED TO BE A MUSICIAN. I HAD NO ONE TO ENCOURAGE ME. SO I BECAME A BUSINESSMAN INSTEAD.
BUT I HAVE NEVER LOST MY APPRECIATION FOR MUSIC.
AND WHAT I HEARD TODAY?
IT WAS BEAUTIFUL.
BETH, YOU HAVE SUCH GREAT POTENTIAL. PLEASE ACCEPT THIS GIFT, AND FOSTER YOUR VOICE.
I WILL.
I PROMISE TO PLAY, MR. MARQUEZ! EVERY DAY. YOU HAVE MY WORD.
THANK YOU!!

FROM: Beth March
TO: Robert March
SENT: March 22

Oh Dad! The most wonderful thing happened—I got a guitar! Mr. Marquez from across the street gave it to me. Mom tried to talk him out of it, but he insisted. He heard me playing and says I have real talent. Do you think it's possible? Meg loves clothes and Jo loves books and Amy loves art (and video games). And I love music so much, but it scares me to death to play in front of others. Jo said that shouldn't stop me. She told me that some of the best musicians just write the songs. They don't have to get up on stage and play in front of anybody. They just get to make music and sell it to other people. I think that's what I want to be when I grow up—a songwriter.

There's just something about music. It comes from deep inside, from that special place in a soul that connects with everyone else. Some songs make me want to dance or cry or laugh or hug Mom. It's amazing how a few words and an instrument can do that. Every song, no matter what it is, makes everyone feel something. People either love it or hate it. (I mean I guess some people might just like it, but even liking something is a feeling.) And I want to make that kind of music.

Now I just have to decide what kind of music I like most. Pop? (Maybe.) Country? (I don't know if I'd be good at that.) Rap? (Definitely not!) Haha. I asked Meg what she thought, and she said I should make the kind of music I want to hear. But I like so much! I like Beyoncé and Stevie Wonder and Stevie Nicks and Dolly Parton and Nina Simone and Prince and Tina Turner and Joni Mitchell and Alicia Keys and The Temptations and Norah Jones and those are just my favorites!

I don't know where to begin....Actually, this email just gave me an idea. I think I'll write a song about YOU. I miss you Daddy.

Love you love you love you.
Yours, Beth

CHAPTER 7

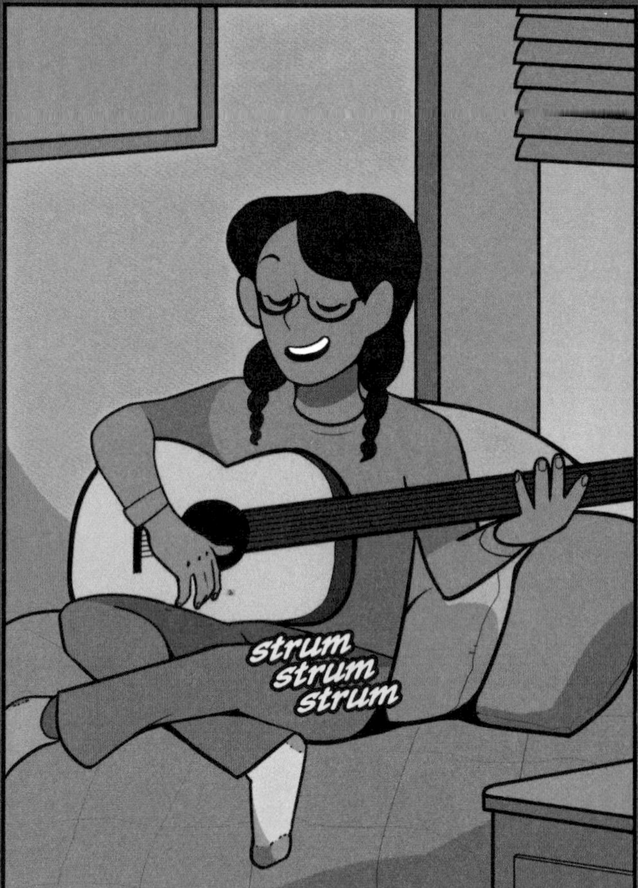
strum
strum
strum

Hell Hath No Fury Like a Sister Scorned...

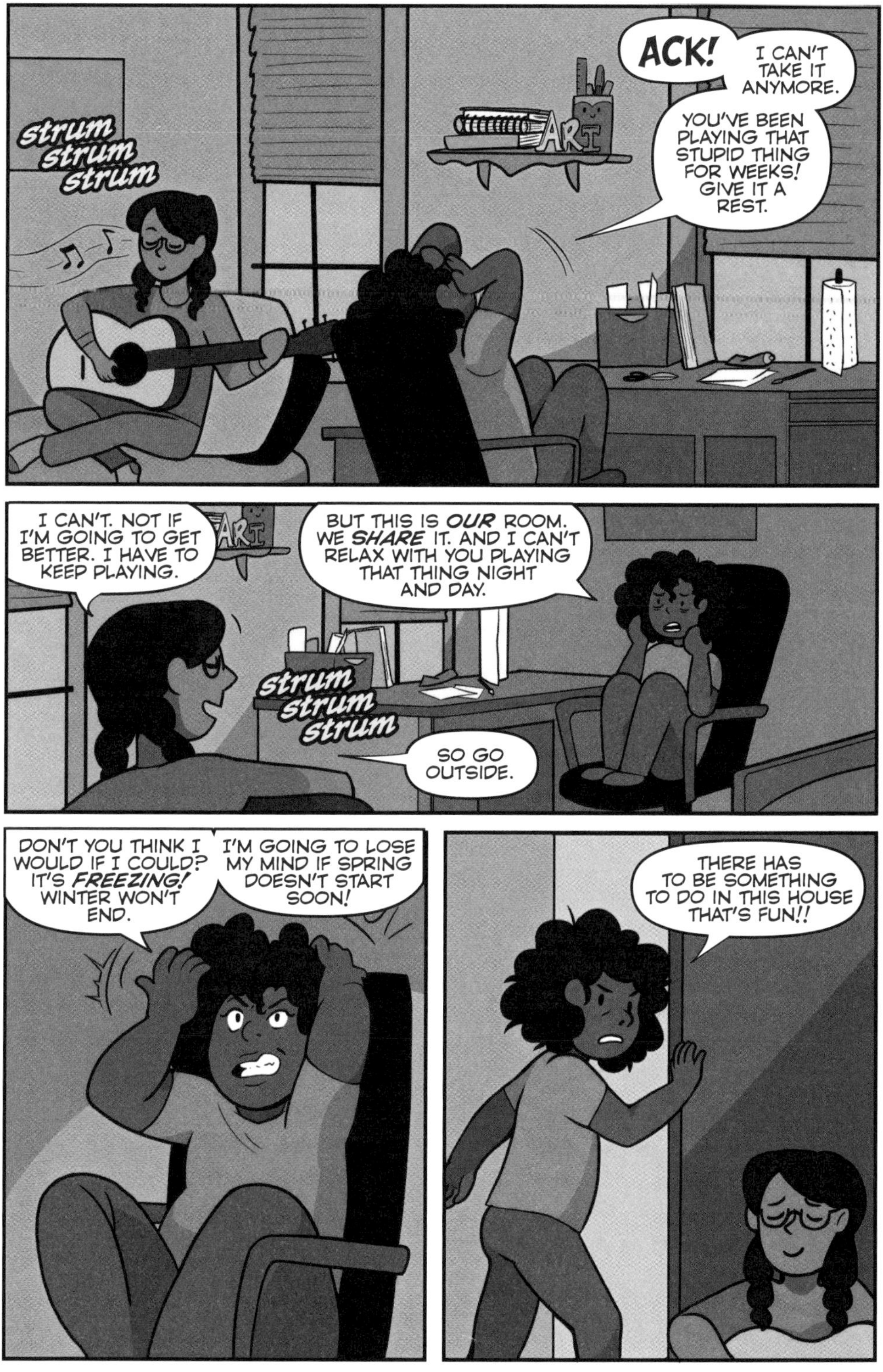

strum strum strum
ACK!
I CAN'T TAKE IT ANYMORE.
YOU'VE BEEN PLAYING THAT STUPID THING FOR WEEKS! GIVE IT A REST.
I CAN'T. NOT IF I'M GOING TO GET BETTER. I HAVE TO KEEP PLAYING.
BUT THIS IS *OUR* ROOM. WE *SHARE* IT. AND I CAN'T RELAX WITH YOU PLAYING THAT THING NIGHT AND DAY.
strum strum strum
SO GO OUTSIDE.
DON'T YOU THINK I WOULD IF I COULD? IT'S *FREEZING!* WINTER WON'T END.
I'M GOING TO LOSE MY MIND IF SPRING DOESN'T START SOON!
THERE HAS TO BE SOMETHING TO DO IN THIS HOUSE THAT'S FUN!!

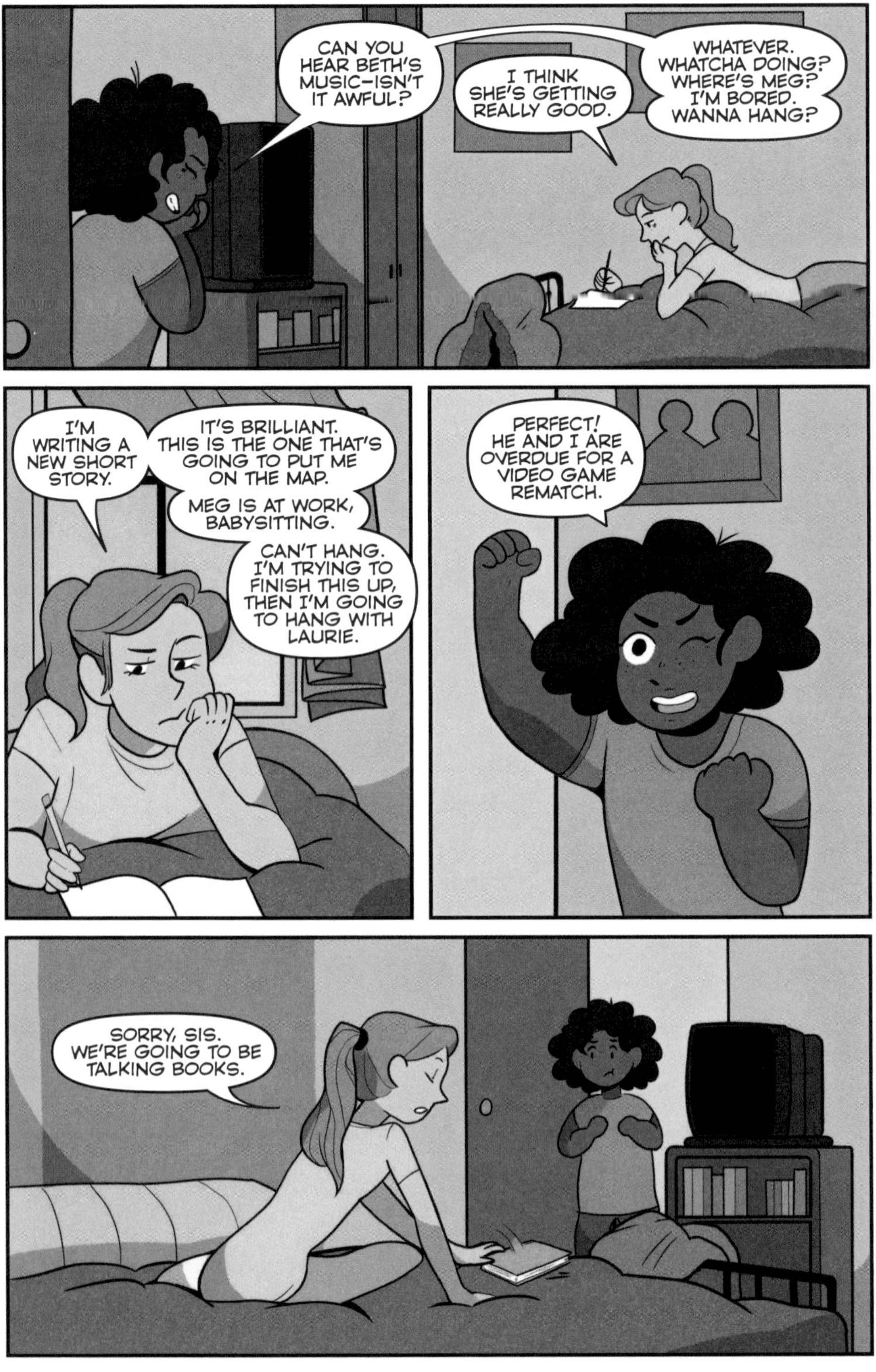
CAN YOU HEAR BETH'S MUSIC–ISN'T IT AWFUL?
I THINK SHE'S GETTING REALLY GOOD.
WHATEVER. WHATCHA DOING? WHERE'S MEG? I'M BORED. WANNA HANG?
I'M WRITING A NEW SHORT STORY.
IT'S BRILLIANT. THIS IS THE ONE THAT'S GOING TO PUT ME ON THE MAP.
MEG IS AT WORK, BABYSITTING.
CAN'T HANG. I'M TRYING TO FINISH THIS UP, THEN I'M GOING TO HANG WITH LAURIE.
PERFECT! HE AND I ARE OVERDUE FOR A VIDEO GAME REMATCH.
SORRY, SIS. WE'RE GOING TO BE TALKING BOOKS.

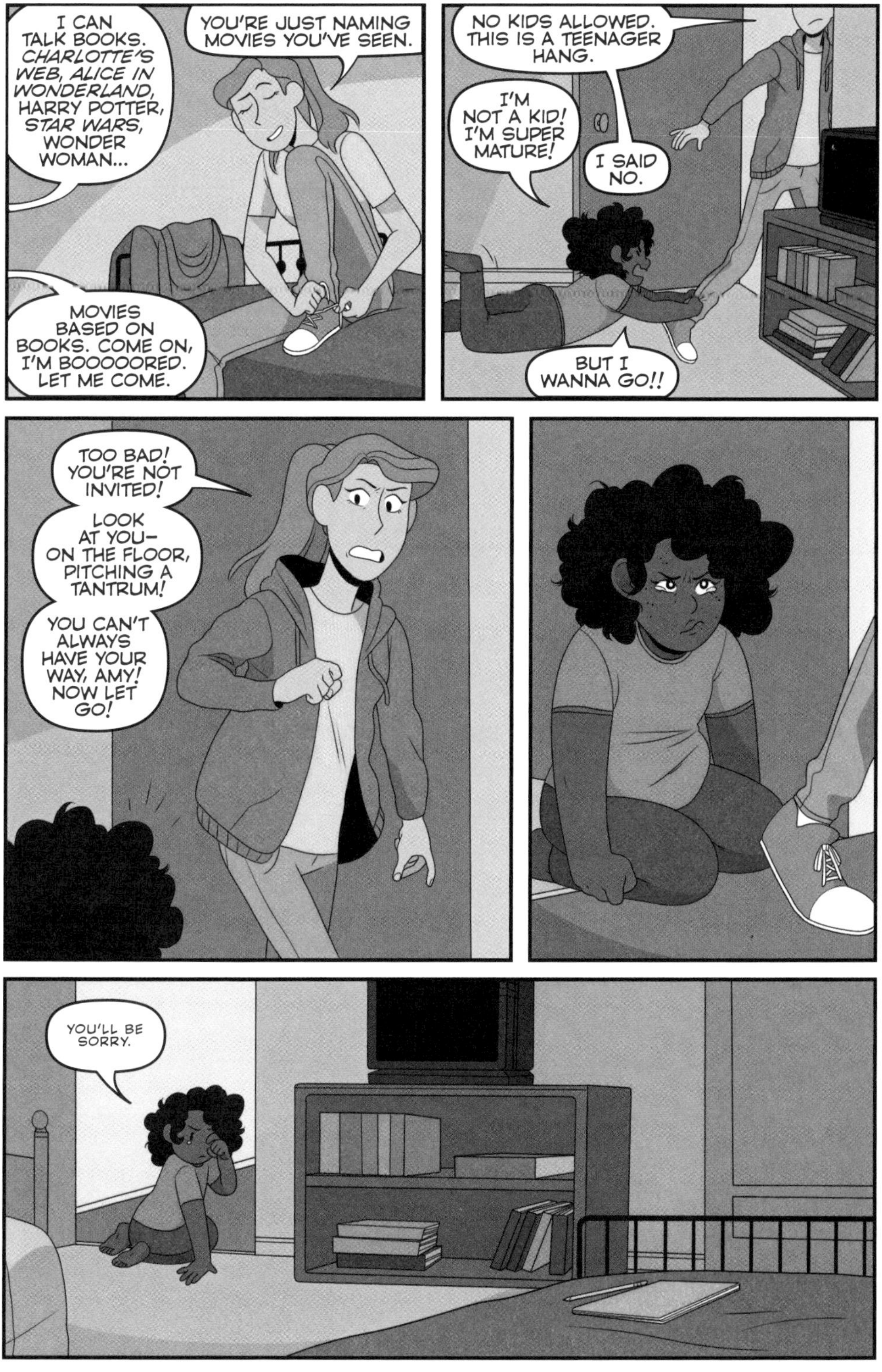
I CAN TALK BOOKS. *CHARLOTTE'S WEB, ALICE IN WONDERLAND,* HARRY POTTER, *STAR WARS,* WONDER WOMAN...
YOU'RE JUST NAMING MOVIES YOU'VE SEEN.
MOVIES BASED ON BOOKS. COME ON, I'M BOOOOORED. LET ME COME.
NO KIDS ALLOWED. THIS IS A TEENAGER HANG.
I'M NOT A KID! I'M SUPER MATURE!
I SAID NO.
BUT I WANNA GO!!
TOO BAD! YOU'RE NOT INVITED!
LOOK AT YOU— ON THE FLOOR, PITCHING A TANTRUM!
YOU CAN'T ALWAYS HAVE YOUR WAY, AMY! NOW LET GO!
YOU'LL BE SORRY.

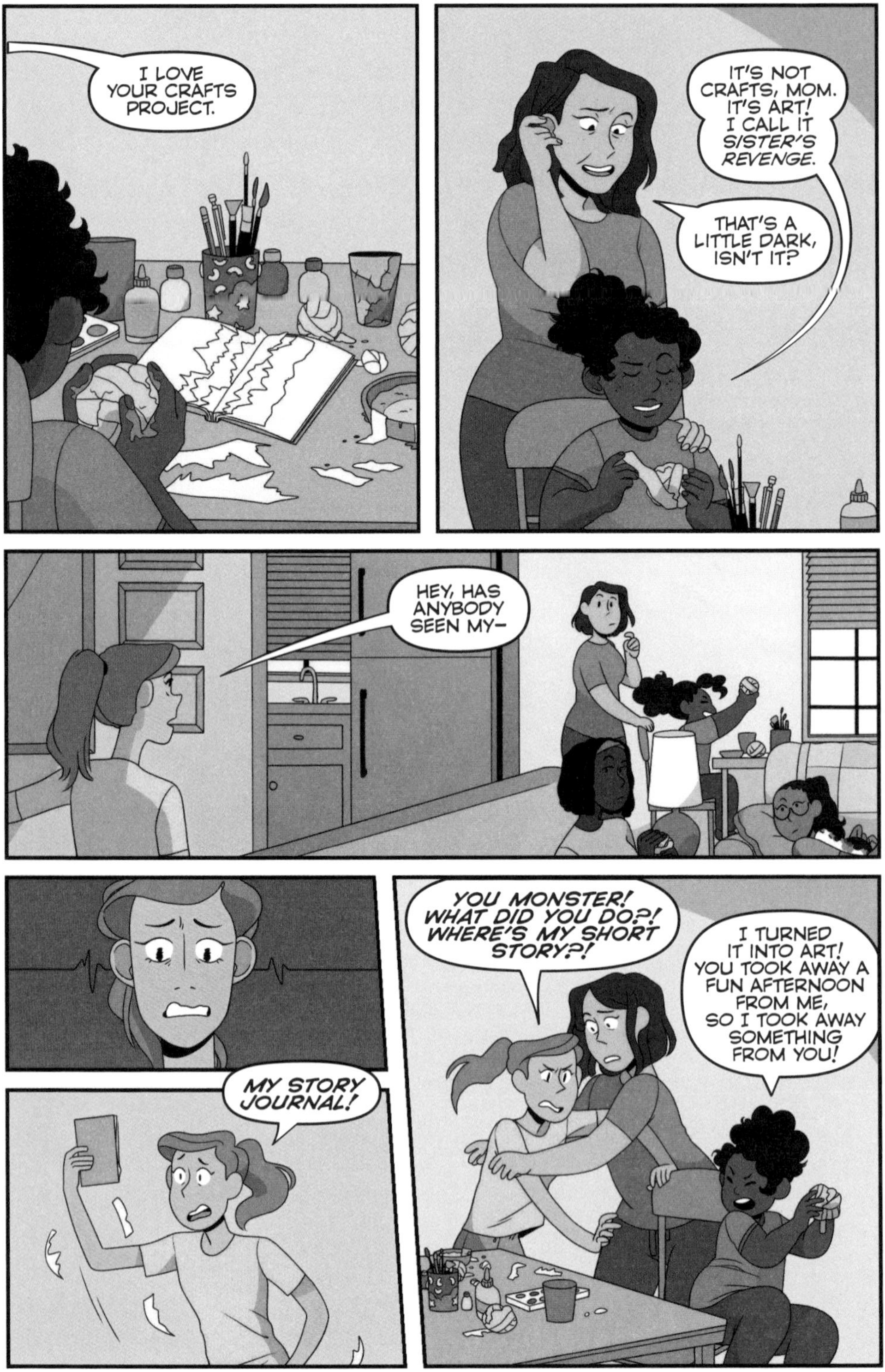
I LOVE YOUR CRAFTS PROJECT.
IT'S NOT CRAFTS, MOM. IT'S ART! I CALL IT *SISTER'S REVENGE*.
THAT'S A LITTLE DARK, ISN'T IT?
HEY, HAS ANYBODY SEEN MY—
MY STORY JOURNAL!
YOU MONSTER! WHAT DID YOU DO?! WHERE'S MY SHORT STORY?!
I TURNED IT INTO ART! YOU TOOK AWAY A FUN AFTERNOON FROM ME, SO I TOOK AWAY SOMETHING FROM YOU!

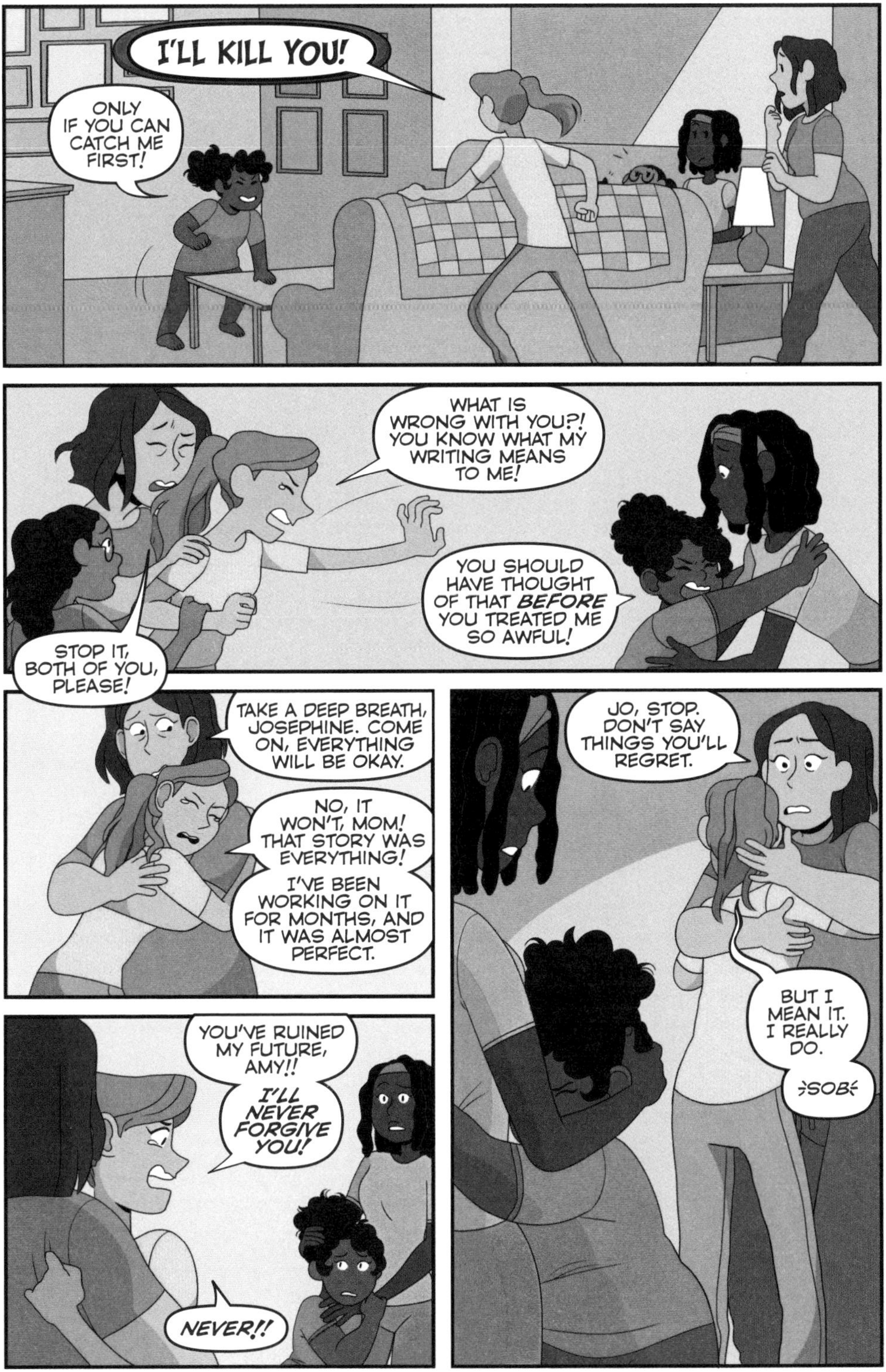
I'LL KILL YOU!
ONLY IF YOU CAN CATCH ME FIRST!
WHAT IS WRONG WITH YOU?! YOU KNOW WHAT MY WRITING MEANS TO ME!
YOU SHOULD HAVE THOUGHT OF THAT BEFORE YOU TREATED ME SO AWFUL!
STOP IT, BOTH OF YOU, PLEASE!
TAKE A DEEP BREATH, JOSEPHINE. COME ON, EVERYTHING WILL BE OKAY.
NO, IT WON'T, MOM! THAT STORY WAS EVERYTHING!
I'VE BEEN WORKING ON IT FOR MONTHS, AND IT WAS ALMOST PERFECT.
YOU'VE RUINED MY FUTURE, AMY!!
I'LL NEVER FORGIVE YOU!
NEVER!!
JO, STOP. DON'T SAY THINGS YOU'LL REGRET.
BUT I MEAN IT. I REALLY DO.
SOB

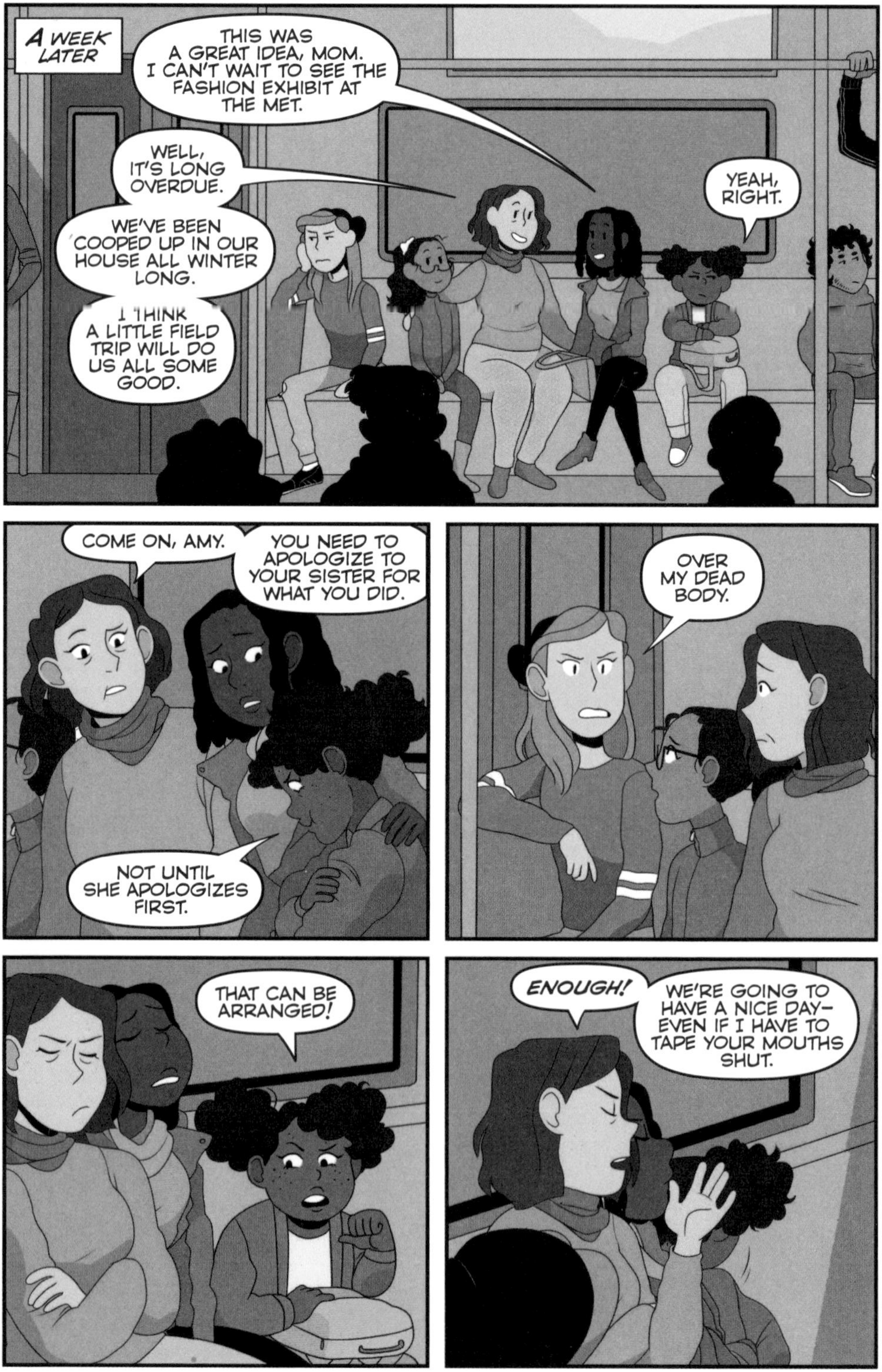
A WEEK LATER
THIS WAS A GREAT IDEA, MOM. I CAN'T WAIT TO SEE THE FASHION EXHIBIT AT THE MET.
WELL, IT'S LONG OVERDUE.
WE'VE BEEN COOPED UP IN OUR HOUSE ALL WINTER LONG.
I THINK A LITTLE FIELD TRIP WILL DO US ALL SOME GOOD.
YEAH, RIGHT.
COME ON, AMY.
YOU NEED TO APOLOGIZE TO YOUR SISTER FOR WHAT YOU DID.
NOT UNTIL SHE APOLOGIZES FIRST.
OVER MY DEAD BODY.
THAT CAN BE ARRANGED!
ENOUGH!
WE'RE GOING TO HAVE A NICE DAY— EVEN IF I HAVE TO TAPE YOUR MOUTHS SHUT.

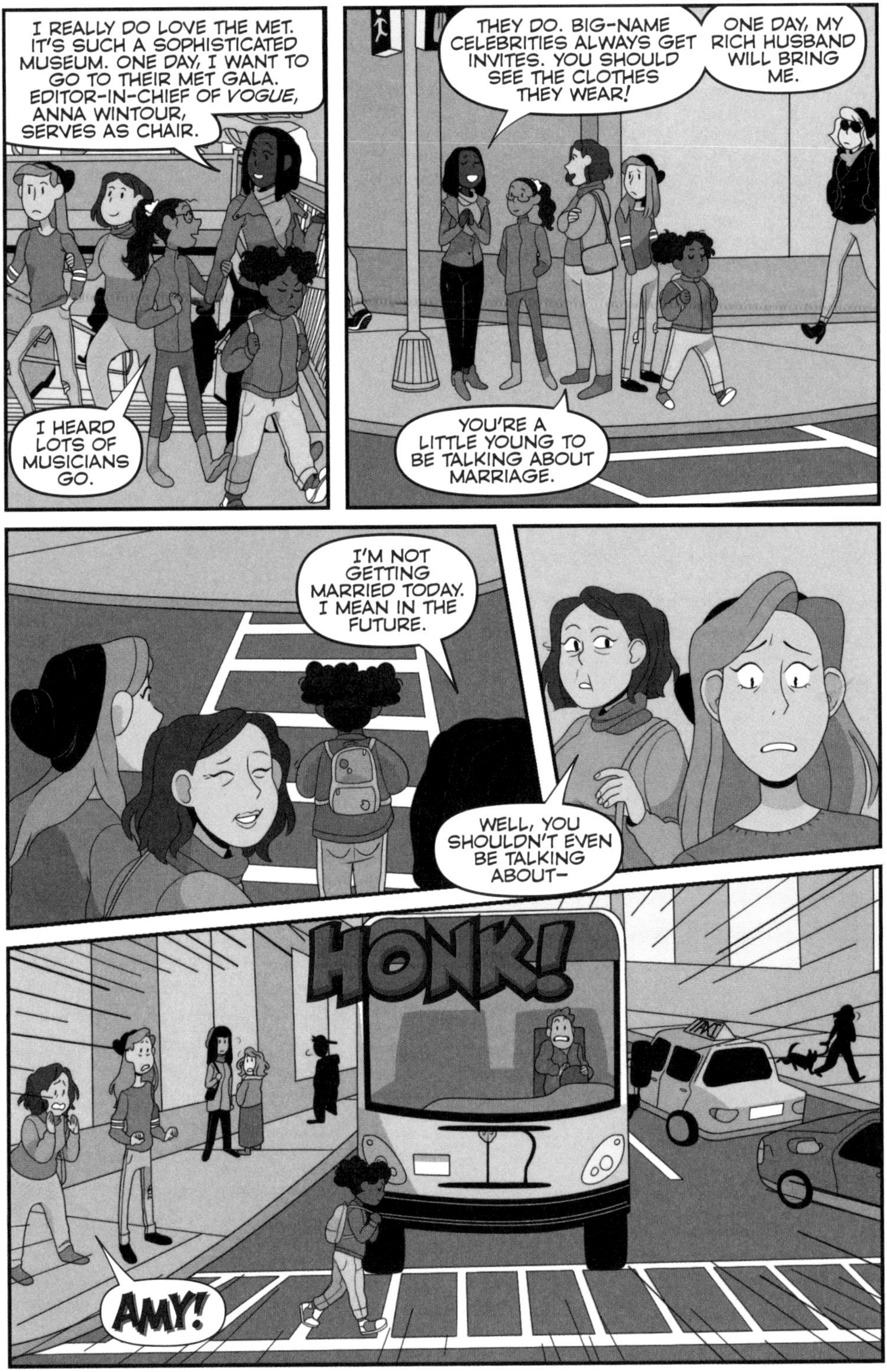
I REALLY DO LOVE THE MET. IT'S SUCH A SOPHISTICATED MUSEUM. ONE DAY, I WANT TO GO TO THEIR MET GALA. EDITOR-IN-CHIEF OF *VOGUE*, ANNA WINTOUR, SERVES AS CHAIR.
I HEARD LOTS OF MUSICIANS GO.
THEY DO. BIG-NAME CELEBRITIES ALWAYS GET INVITES. YOU SHOULD SEE THE CLOTHES THEY WEAR!
ONE DAY, MY RICH HUSBAND WILL BRING ME.
YOU'RE A LITTLE YOUNG TO BE TALKING ABOUT MARRIAGE.
I'M NOT GETTING MARRIED TODAY. I MEAN IN THE FUTURE.
WELL, YOU SHOULDN'T EVEN BE TALKING ABOUT—
HONK!
TAXI
AMY!

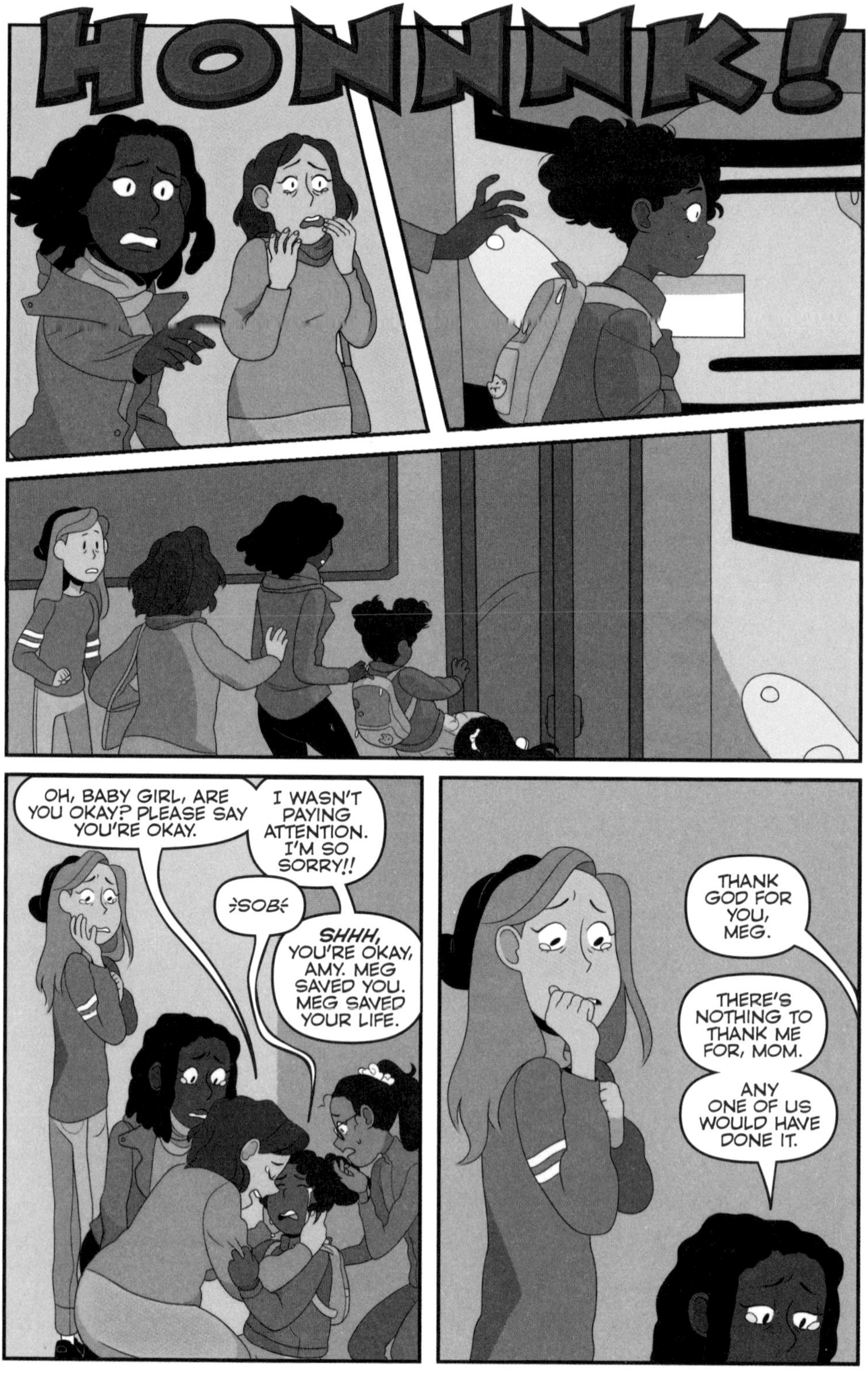

HONNNK!
OH, BABY GIRL, ARE YOU OKAY? PLEASE SAY YOU'RE OKAY.
I WASN'T PAYING ATTENTION. I'M SO SORRY!!
SOB
SHHH, YOU'RE OKAY, AMY. MEG SAVED YOU. MEG SAVED YOUR LIFE.
THANK GOD FOR YOU, MEG.
THERE'S NOTHING TO THANK ME FOR, MOM.
ANY ONE OF US WOULD HAVE DONE IT.

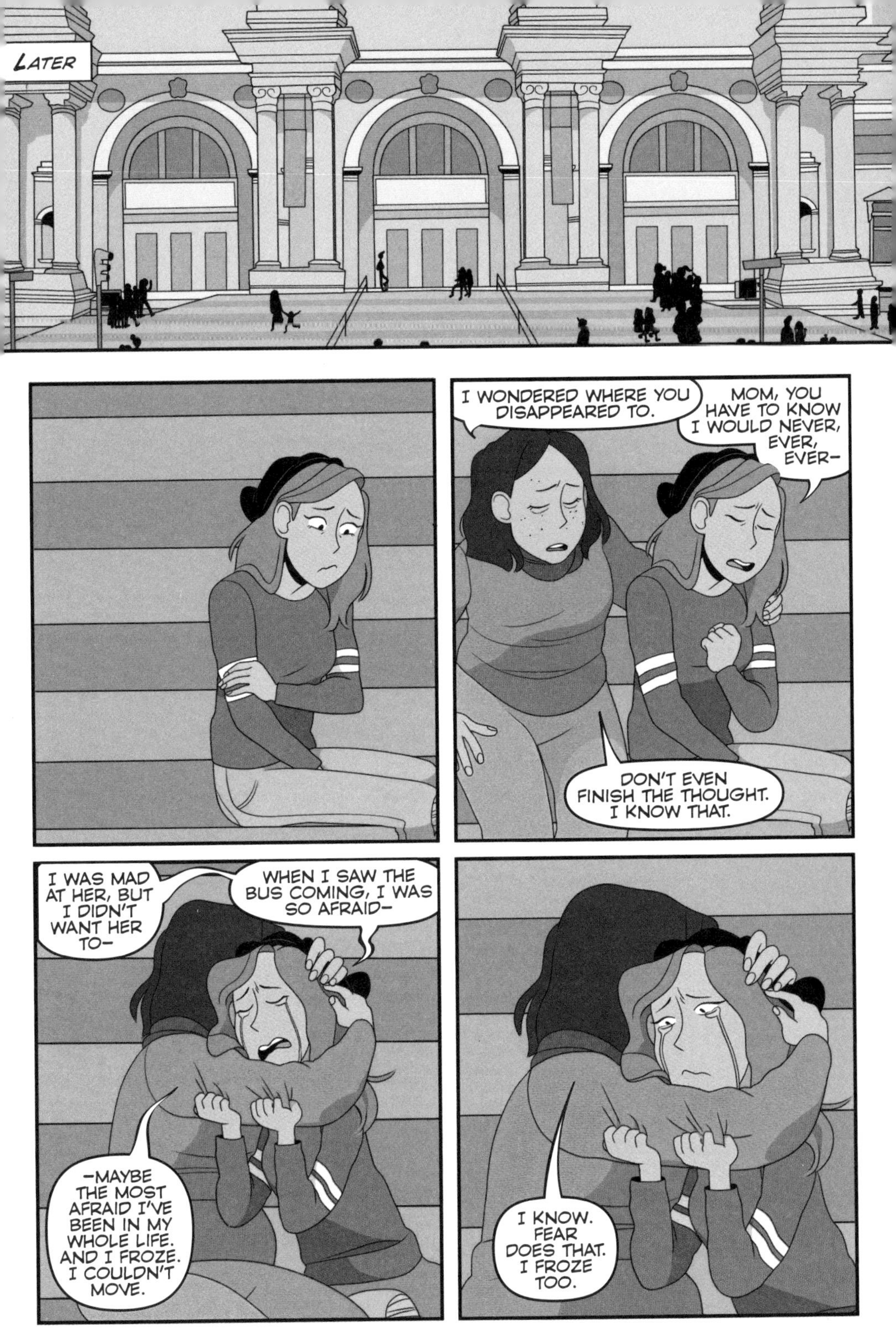
LATER
I WONDERED WHERE YOU DISAPPEARED TO.
MOM, YOU HAVE TO KNOW I WOULD NEVER, EVER, EVER–
DON'T EVEN FINISH THE THOUGHT. I KNOW THAT.
I WAS MAD AT HER, BUT I DIDN'T WANT HER TO–
WHEN I SAW THE BUS COMING, I WAS SO AFRAID–
–MAYBE THE MOST AFRAID I'VE BEEN IN MY WHOLE LIFE. AND I FROZE. I COULDN'T MOVE.
I KNOW. FEAR DOES THAT. I FROZE TOO.

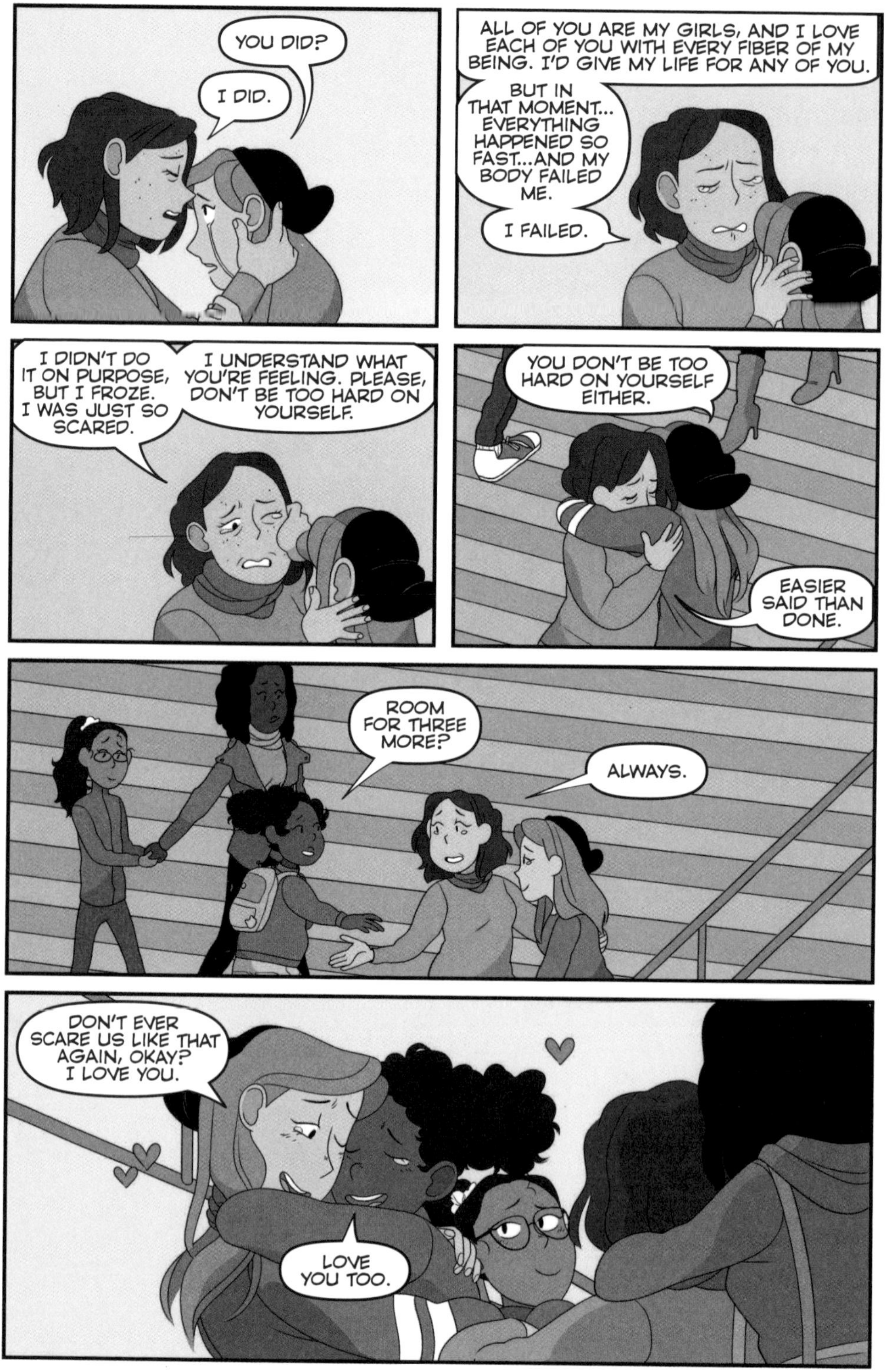
YOU DID?
I DID.
ALL OF YOU ARE MY GIRLS, AND I LOVE EACH OF YOU WITH EVERY FIBER OF MY BEING. I'D GIVE MY LIFE FOR ANY OF YOU.
BUT IN THAT MOMENT... EVERYTHING HAPPENED SO FAST...AND MY BODY FAILED ME.
I FAILED.
I DIDN'T DO IT ON PURPOSE, BUT I FROZE. I WAS JUST SO SCARED.
I UNDERSTAND WHAT YOU'RE FEELING. PLEASE, DON'T BE TOO HARD ON YOURSELF.
YOU DON'T BE TOO HARD ON YOURSELF EITHER.
EASIER SAID THAN DONE.
ROOM FOR THREE MORE?
ALWAYS.
DON'T EVER SCARE US LIKE THAT AGAIN, OKAY? I LOVE YOU.
LOVE YOU TOO.

April 4

I'm a horrible person. A monster.

No, I mean it. I've been so mad at Amy, and
today—today she almost died. We had gone to
the museum and she stepped in front of a bus.
I was so scared. It's like her whole life flashed
before my eyes. I know it sounds like a cliché,
but that's what happened. I remembered
when she was a bump in Mom's tummy. I
remembered when she was born, and how tiny
her fingers were, and when they squeezed mine.
I remembered changing her dirty diapers. I
remembered the first time she had a bad dream
and crawled into bed with me because Meg was
at Kennedy's. I remembered everything. And I
froze.

The bus would have hit her. It would have—I
can't even write it. But Meg saved her. Like some
kind of superhero, Meg moved faster than I
could have imagined and she pulled Amy back.
Two feet. Twenty-four inches. That's all that
stood between Amy and

Sorry. I had to stop writing for a minute. I can't stop crying. Mom told me not to be hard on myself, but I should have been the one to save her. I was closest. Yet fear got the better of me. I pray there's never a next time. But if there is, I'll move. Mind over matter, I'll force my body to act, to be a hero.

It was such a powerful moment. One I don't think I'll ever forget. When it was over, I sat on the steps of the museum thinking about the whole of life, and how it can all just be taken away in a split second. Who knows how much time any of us has on this big silly planet, but I plan to take full advantage. If I could just get over my fears of what everyone will think if they knew the real me...if they knew my secret...

CHAPTER 8

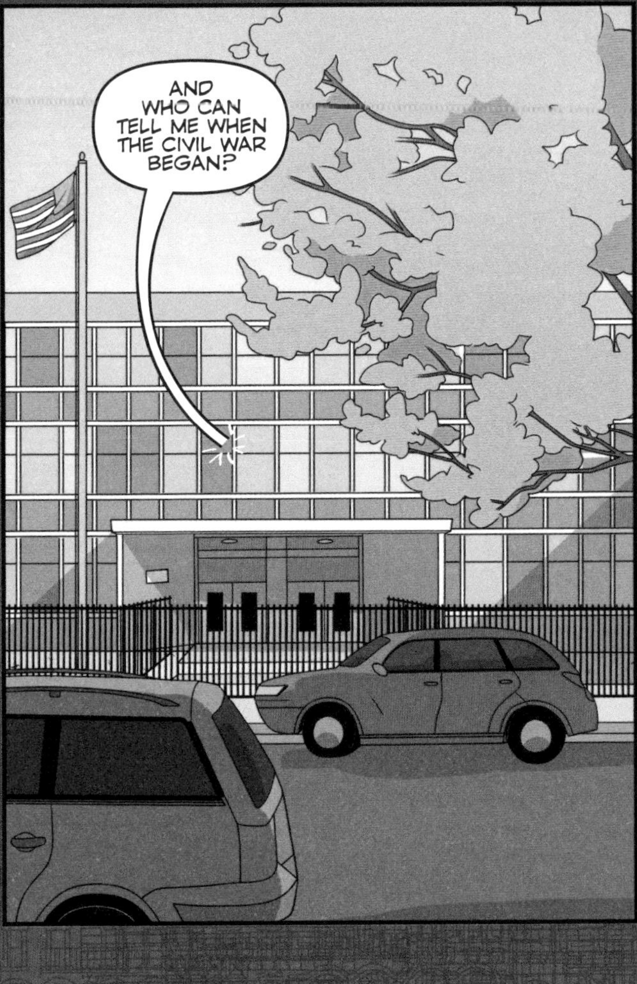
AND WHO CAN TELL ME WHEN THE CIVIL WAR BEGAN?

School Drama...

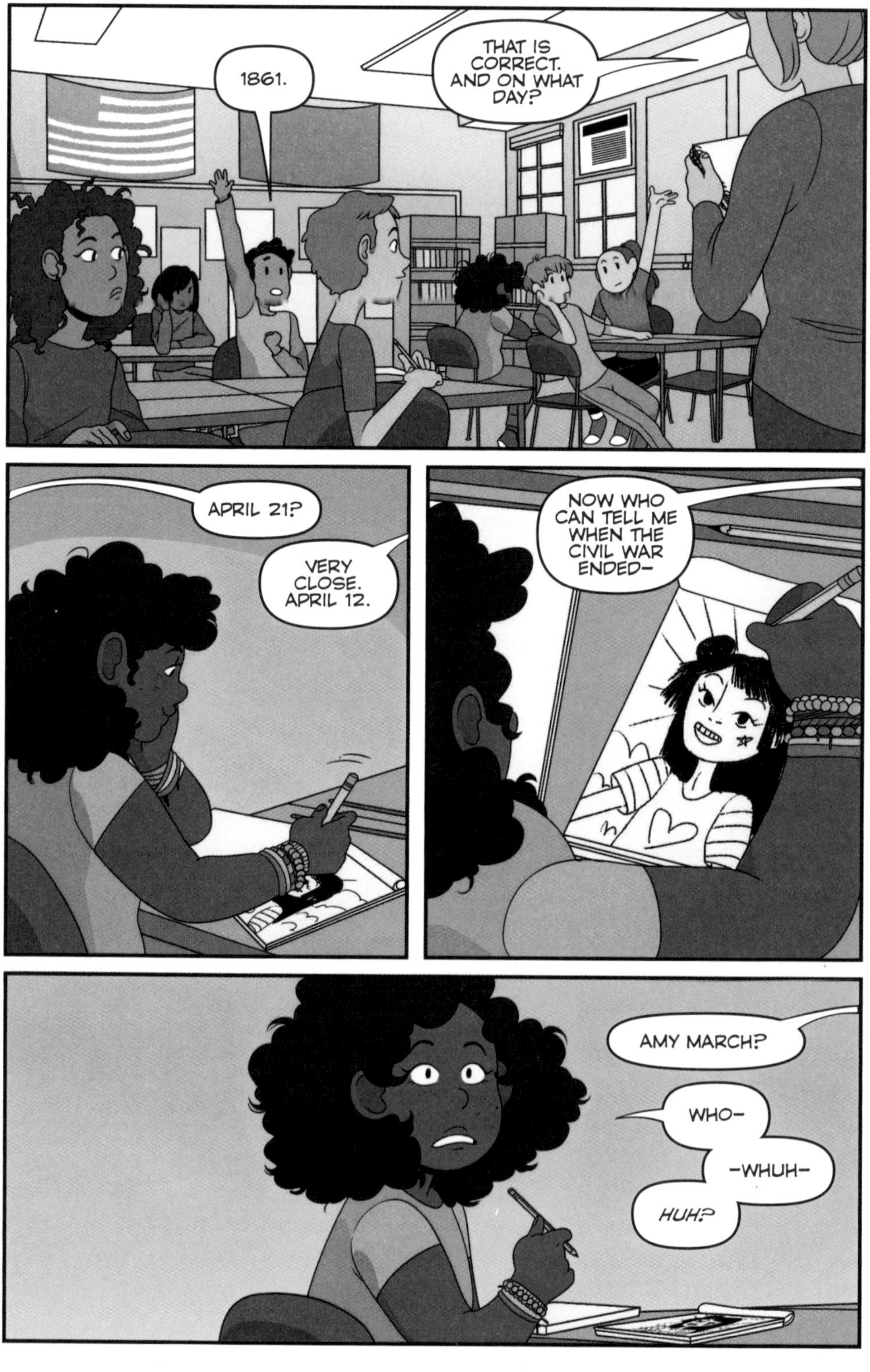
1861.
THAT IS CORRECT. AND ON WHAT DAY?
APRIL 21?
VERY CLOSE. APRIL 12.
NOW WHO CAN TELL ME WHEN THE CIVIL WAR ENDED–
AMY MARCH?
WHO–
–WHUH–
HUH?

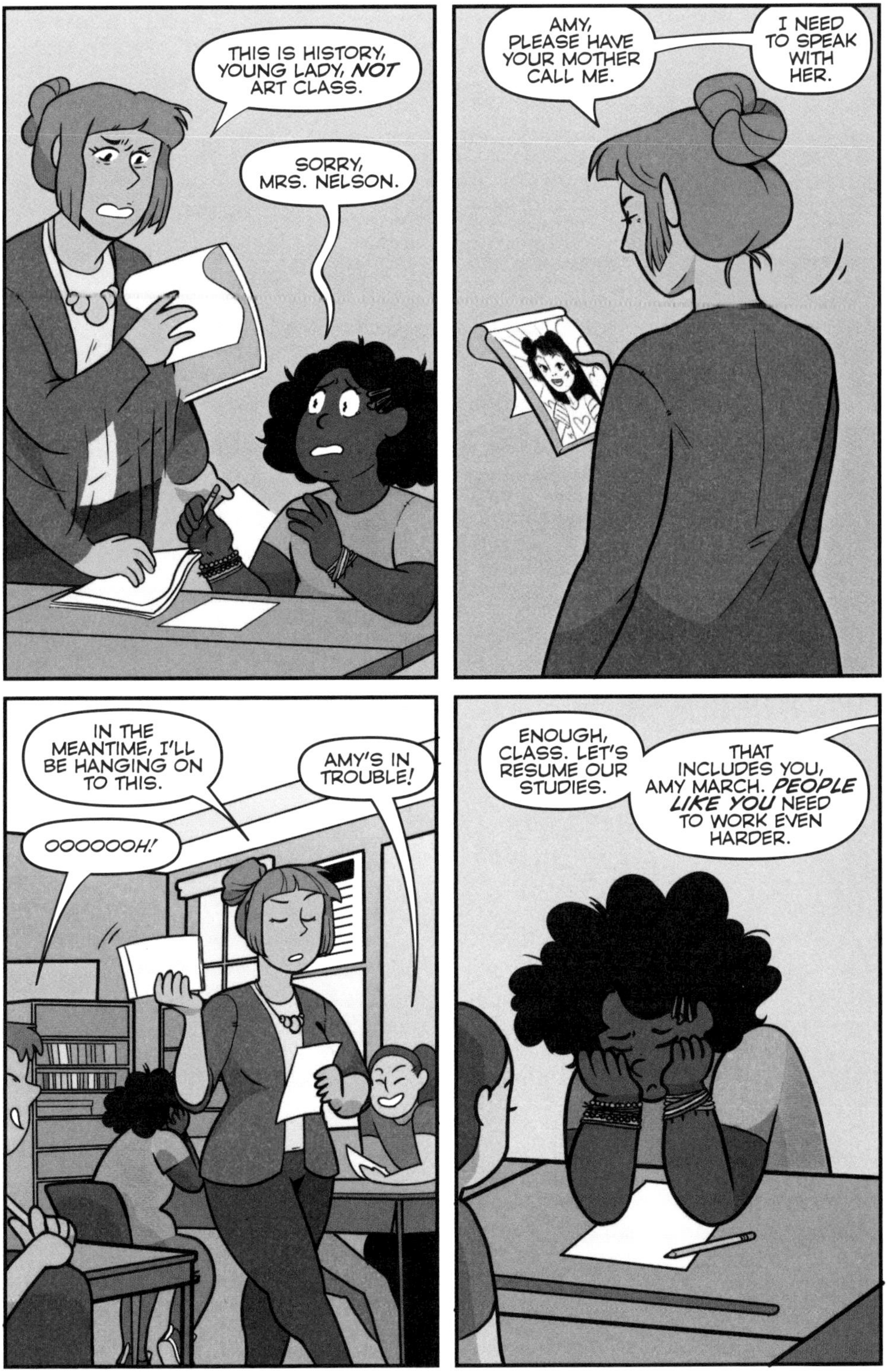
THIS IS HISTORY, YOUNG LADY, *NOT* ART CLASS.
SORRY, MRS. NELSON.
AMY, PLEASE HAVE YOUR MOTHER CALL ME.
I NEED TO SPEAK WITH HER.
IN THE MEANTIME, I'LL BE HANGING ON TO THIS.
AMY'S IN TROUBLE!
OOOOOOH!
ENOUGH, CLASS. LET'S RESUME OUR STUDIES.
THAT INCLUDES YOU, AMY MARCH. ***PEOPLE LIKE YOU*** NEED TO WORK EVEN HARDER.

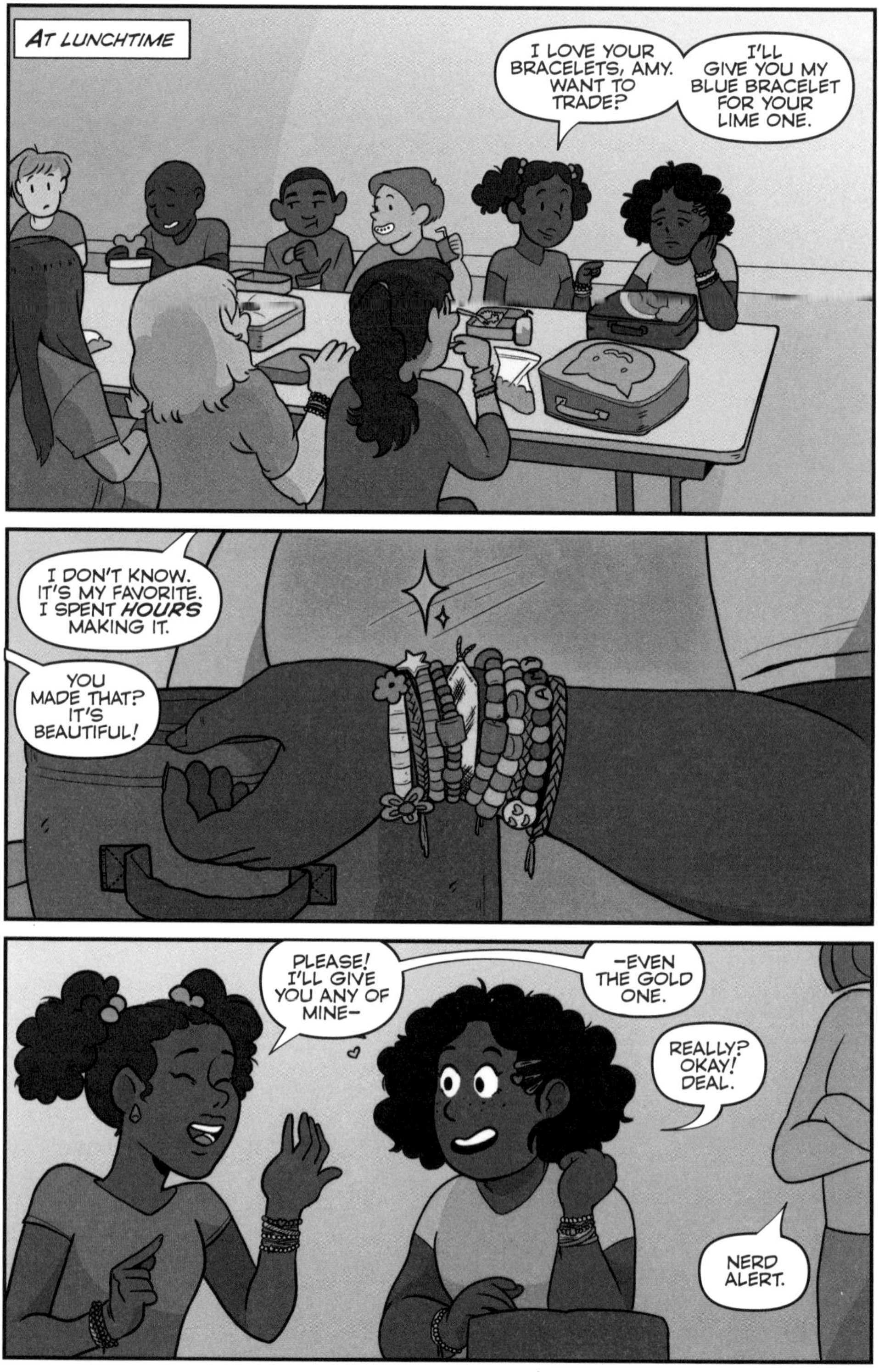
AT LUNCHTIME
I LOVE YOUR BRACELETS, AMY. WANT TO TRADE?
I'LL GIVE YOU MY BLUE BRACELET FOR YOUR LIME ONE.
I DON'T KNOW. IT'S MY FAVORITE. I SPENT **HOURS** MAKING IT.
YOU MADE THAT? IT'S BEAUTIFUL!
PLEASE! I'LL GIVE YOU ANY OF MINE–
–EVEN THE GOLD ONE.
REALLY? OKAY! DEAL.
NERD ALERT.

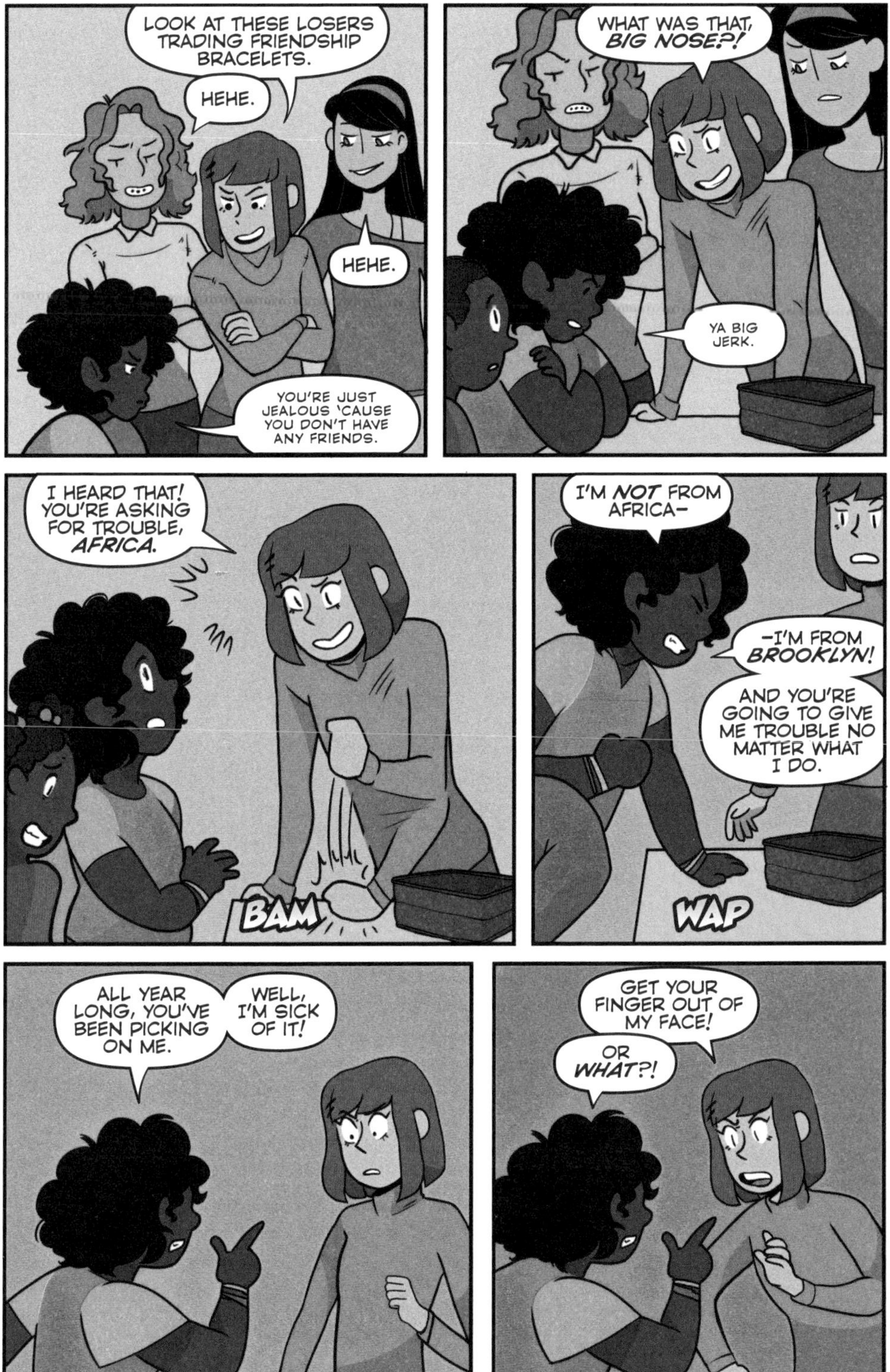
LOOK AT THESE LOSERS TRADING FRIENDSHIP BRACELETS.
HEHE.
HEHE.
YOU'RE JUST JEALOUS 'CAUSE YOU DON'T HAVE ANY FRIENDS.
WHAT WAS THAT, *BIG NOSE?!*
YA BIG JERK.
I HEARD THAT! YOU'RE ASKING FOR TROUBLE, *AFRICA.*
BAM
I'M *NOT* FROM AFRICA—
—I'M FROM *BROOKLYN!*
AND YOU'RE GOING TO GIVE ME TROUBLE NO MATTER WHAT I DO.
WAP
ALL YEAR LONG, YOU'VE BEEN PICKING ON ME.
WELL, I'M SICK OF IT!
GET YOUR FINGER OUT OF MY FACE!
OR *WHAT?!*

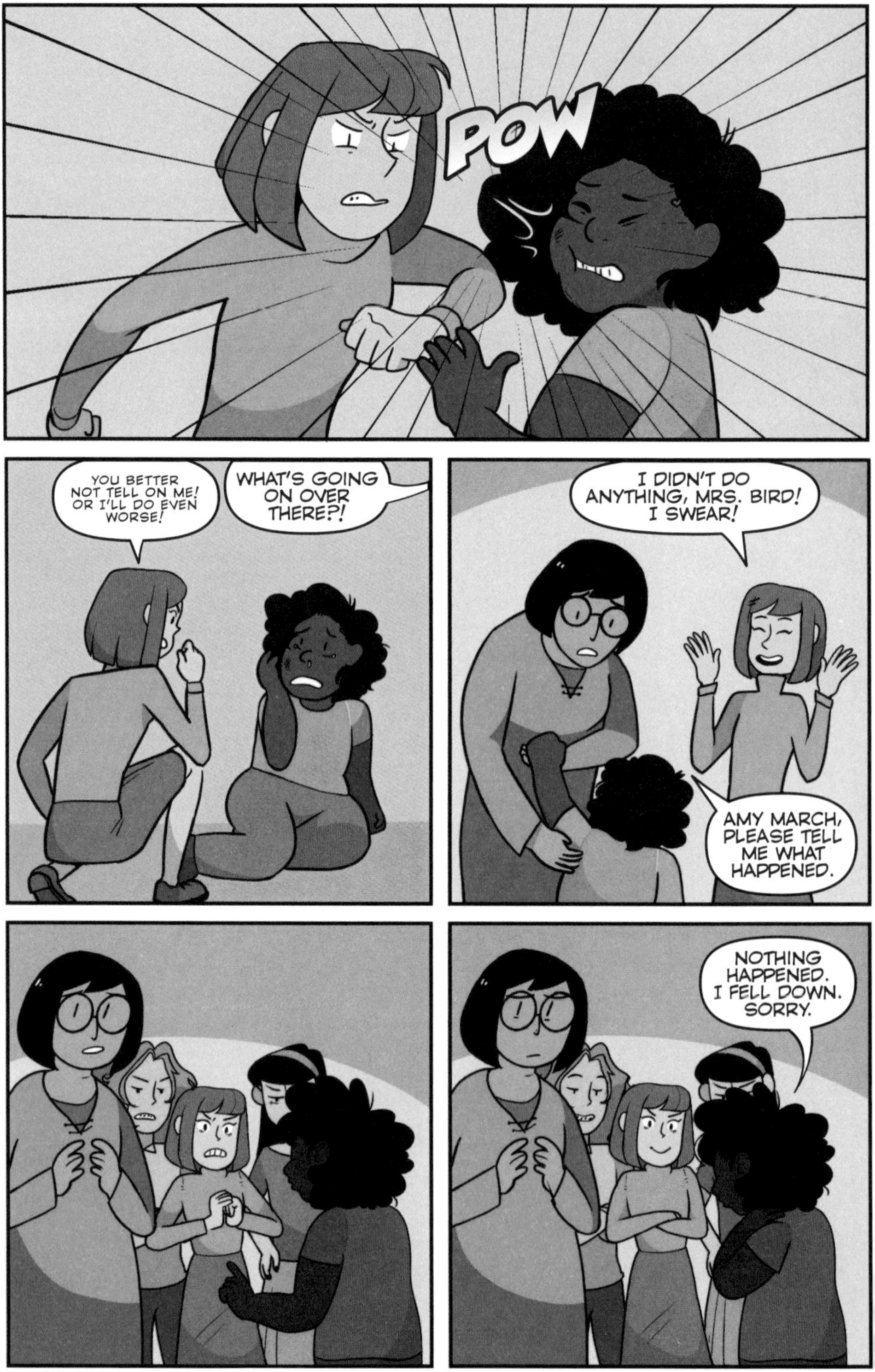
POW
YOU BETTER NOT TELL ON ME! OR I'LL DO EVEN WORSE!
WHAT'S GOING ON OVER THERE?!
I DIDN'T DO ANYTHING, MRS. BIRD! I SWEAR!
AMY MARCH, PLEASE TELL ME WHAT HAPPENED.
NOTHING HAPPENED. I FELL DOWN. SORRY.

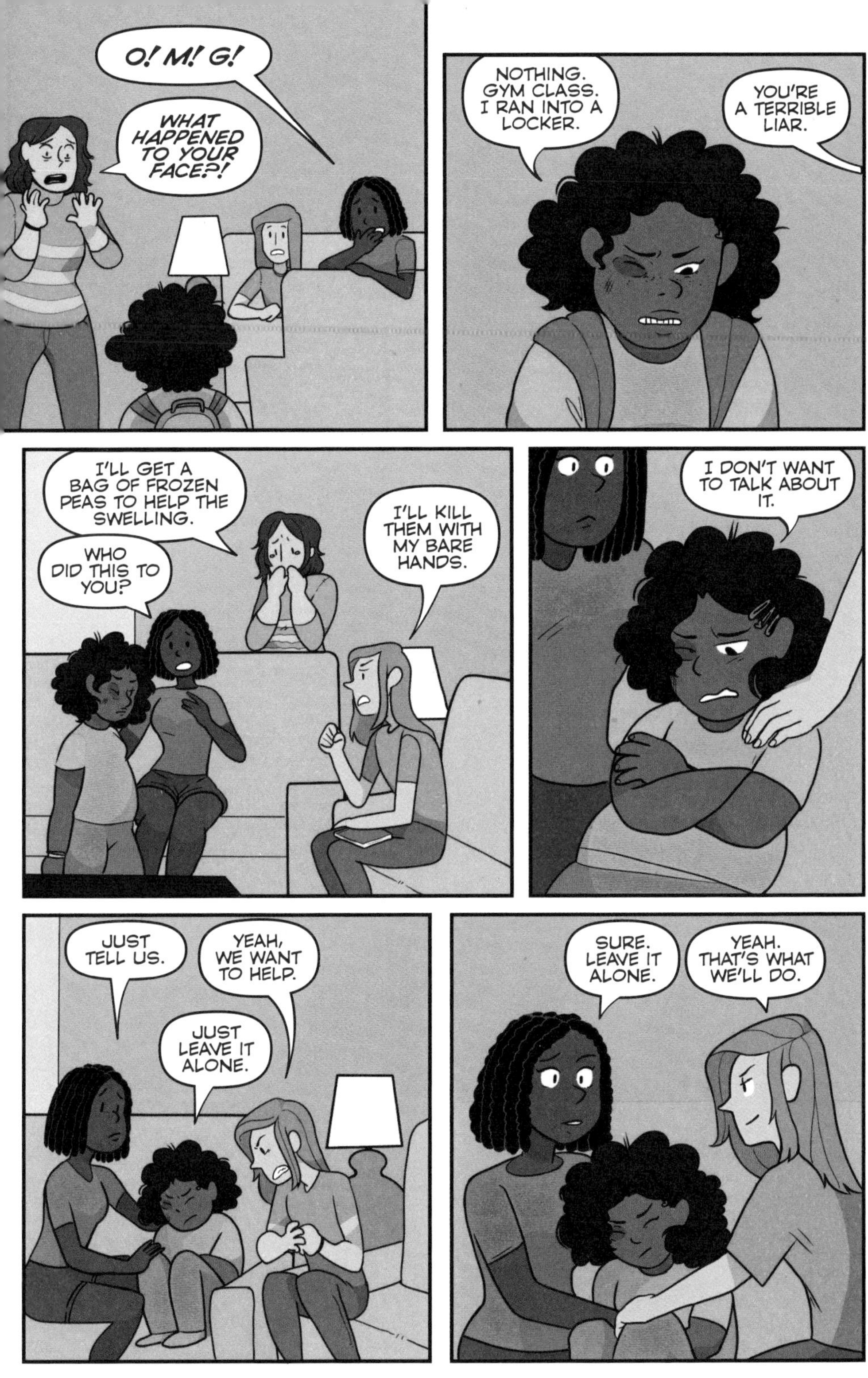
O! M! G!
WHAT HAPPENED TO YOUR FACE?!
NOTHING. GYM CLASS. I RAN INTO A LOCKER.
YOU'RE A TERRIBLE LIAR.
I'LL GET A BAG OF FROZEN PEAS TO HELP THE SWELLING.
WHO DID THIS TO YOU?
I'LL KILL THEM WITH MY BARE HANDS.
I DON'T WANT TO TALK ABOUT IT.
JUST TELL US.
YEAH, WE WANT TO HELP.
JUST LEAVE IT ALONE.
SURE. LEAVE IT ALONE.
YEAH. THAT'S WHAT WE'LL DO.

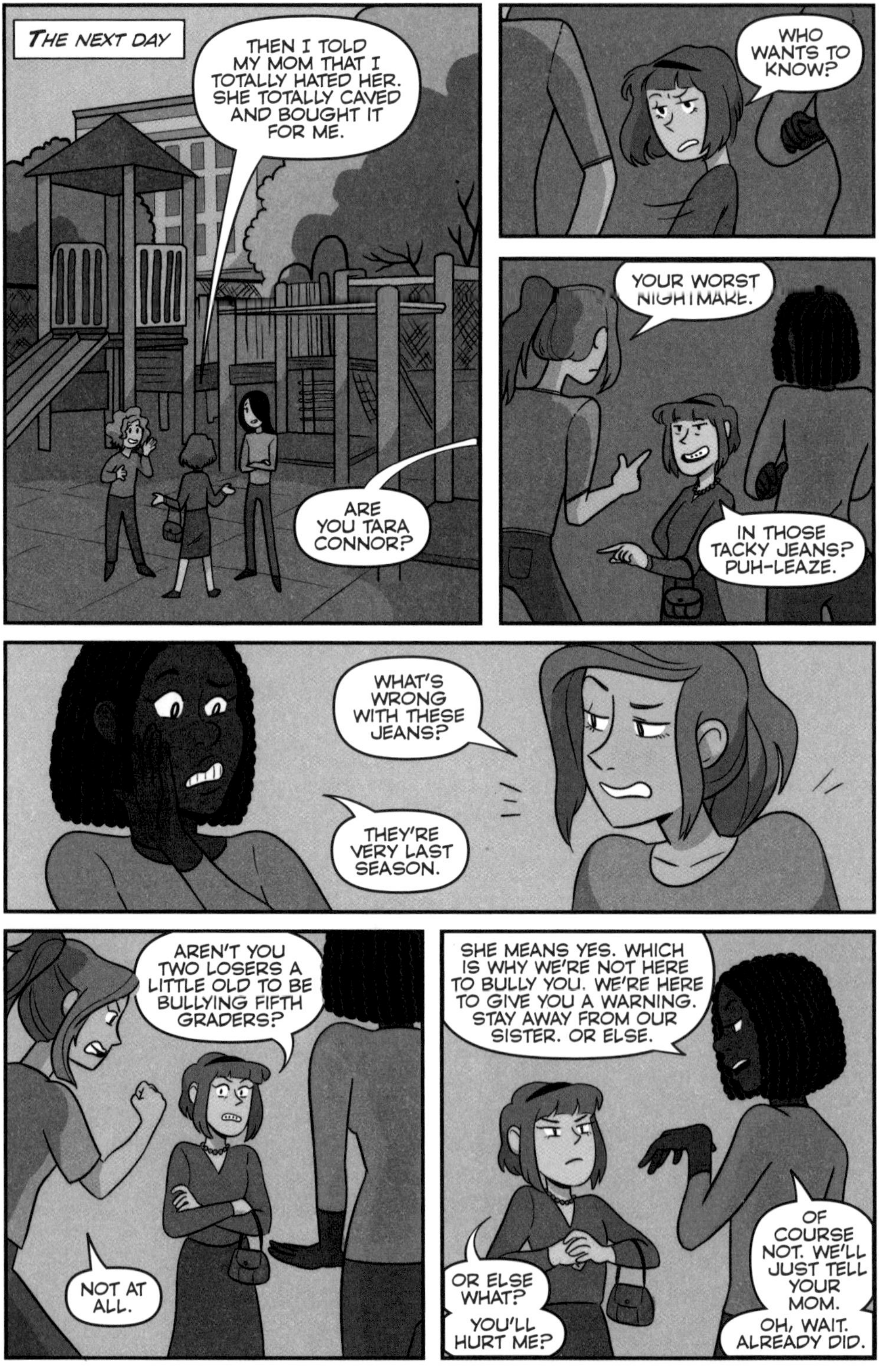
THE NEXT DAY
THEN I TOLD MY MOM THAT I TOTALLY HATED HER. SHE TOTALLY CAVED AND BOUGHT IT FOR ME.
ARE YOU TARA CONNOR?
WHO WANTS TO KNOW?
YOUR WORST NIGHTMARE.
IN THOSE TACKY JEANS? PUH-LEAZE.
WHAT'S WRONG WITH THESE JEANS?
THEY'RE VERY LAST SEASON.
AREN'T YOU TWO LOSERS A LITTLE OLD TO BE BULLYING FIFTH GRADERS?
NOT AT ALL.
SHE MEANS YES. WHICH IS WHY WE'RE NOT HERE TO BULLY YOU. WE'RE HERE TO GIVE YOU A WARNING. STAY AWAY FROM OUR SISTER. OR ELSE.
OR ELSE WHAT?
YOU'LL HURT ME?
OF COURSE NOT. WE'LL JUST TELL YOUR MOM.
OH, WAIT. ALREADY DID.

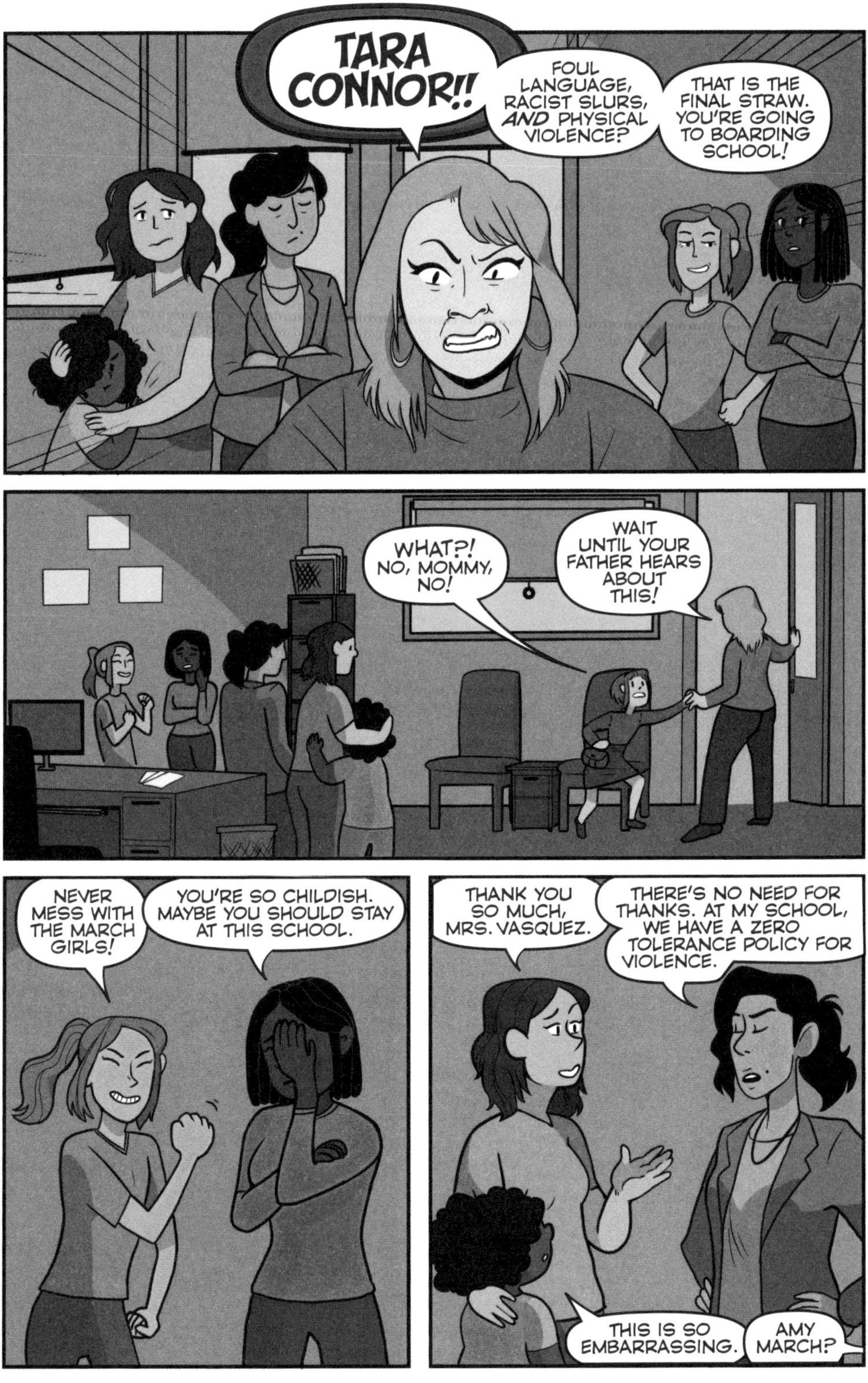
TARA CONNOR!!
FOUL LANGUAGE, RACIST SLURS, AND PHYSICAL VIOLENCE?
THAT IS THE FINAL STRAW. YOU'RE GOING TO BOARDING SCHOOL!
WHAT?! NO, MOMMY, NO!
WAIT UNTIL YOUR FATHER HEARS ABOUT THIS!
NEVER MESS WITH THE MARCH GIRLS!
YOU'RE SO CHILDISH. MAYBE YOU SHOULD STAY AT THIS SCHOOL.
THANK YOU SO MUCH, MRS. VASQUEZ.
THERE'S NO NEED FOR THANKS. AT MY SCHOOL, WE HAVE A ZERO TOLERANCE POLICY FOR VIOLENCE.
THIS IS SO EMBARRASSING.
AMY MARCH?

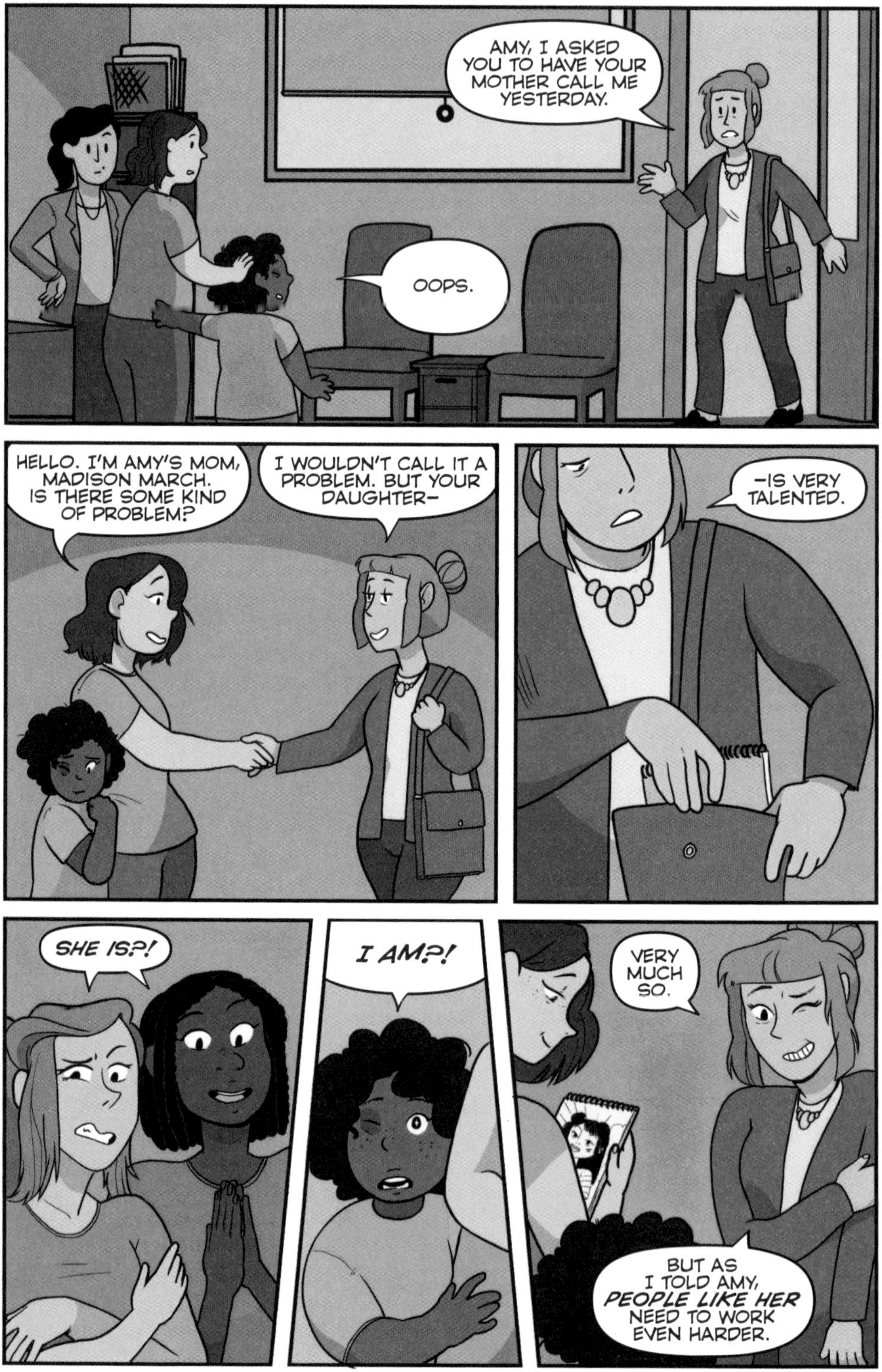
AMY, I ASKED YOU TO HAVE YOUR MOTHER CALL ME YESTERDAY.
OOPS.
HELLO. I'M AMY'S MOM, MADISON MARCH. IS THERE SOME KIND OF PROBLEM?
I WOULDN'T CALL IT A PROBLEM. BUT YOUR DAUGHTER—
—IS VERY TALENTED.
SHE IS?!
I AM?!
VERY MUCH SO.
BUT AS I TOLD AMY, *PEOPLE LIKE HER* NEED TO WORK EVEN HARDER.

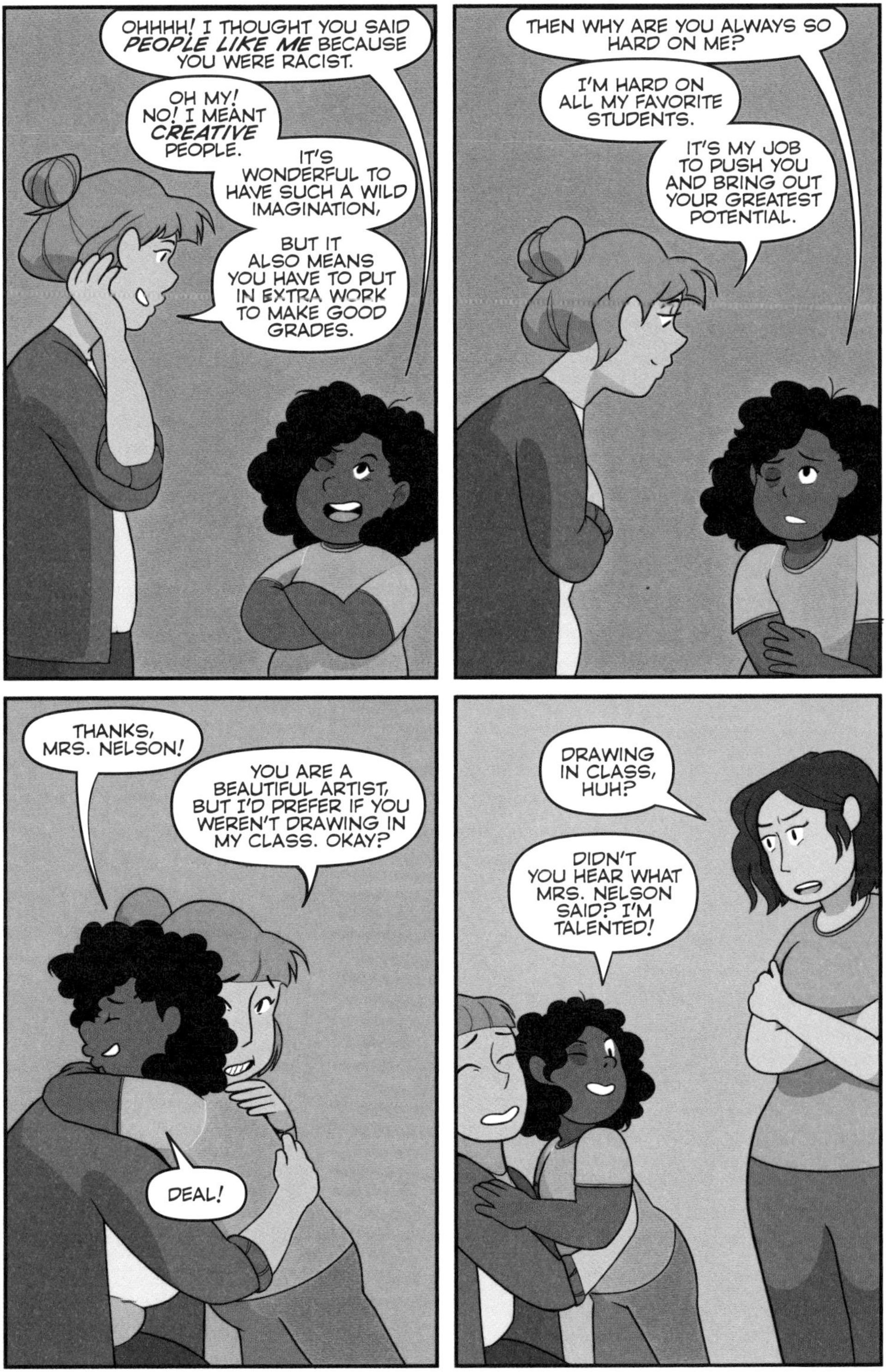
OHHHH! I THOUGHT YOU SAID *PEOPLE LIKE ME* BECAUSE YOU WERE RACIST.
OH MY! NO! I MEANT *CREATIVE* PEOPLE.
IT'S WONDERFUL TO HAVE SUCH A WILD IMAGINATION,
BUT IT ALSO MEANS YOU HAVE TO PUT IN EXTRA WORK TO MAKE GOOD GRADES.
THEN WHY ARE YOU ALWAYS SO HARD ON ME?
I'M HARD ON ALL MY FAVORITE STUDENTS.
IT'S MY JOB TO PUSH YOU AND BRING OUT YOUR GREATEST POTENTIAL.
THANKS, MRS. NELSON!
YOU ARE A BEAUTIFUL ARTIST, BUT I'D PREFER IF YOU WEREN'T DRAWING IN MY CLASS. OKAY?
DEAL!
DRAWING IN CLASS, HUH?
DIDN'T YOU HEAR WHAT MRS. NELSON SAID? I'M TALENTED!

FROM: Amy March
TO: Robert March
SENT: April 18

hi Daddy!

meg and jo say i should write u more, so that's what i'm doing. i dont know what to rite about so i guess i will tell you about my week, which was kinda crazy. this girl tara connor is awful to me all the time, makes fun of my hair and my skin and especially my nose, which is pretty dumb because i like my nose. i mean i guess sometimes i dont but that's because tara made fun of it so much, it made me so mad, but i didnt want to fight her or anything because i thought i'd probably get in more trouble than her, cuz she's white and i'm black, and thats what happens. my teacher mrs nelson makes us read news articles cuz she says its important to know whats happening in the world and its always in the news that black people are getting hurt or worse by people in our country, like cops and other people too. it makes me really sad. but mrs nelson says the world is getting better, too slowly she says, but i think slow is better than not moving forward at all, right? mrs nelson is teaching about the civil war which is really intresting cuz it ended the confedrcy (the south), and abolished slavery and freed 4 million slaves.

its weird to think we might have been related to slaves, and we probably were because we are from here and not from africa, which is one of the mean names tara always called me. but mom says i shouldnt be insulted cuz Africa is a beautiful place and all people are beautiful no matter

Send

where they from. anyways, she punched me, not mom, tara did, tara punched me right in the face and the only reason I didn't hit her back was because she is white, and I got really scared that if i hit her i would go to jail. but then meg and jo and mom figured out what happened and told the prinipcal, mrs vasquez who i've never met but turns out is really nice, and she called tara's mom, and boy did her head hit the roof! tara's mom was so mad! she dragged tara out of school in front of everyone and tara was crying cuz her mom is sending her to boarding school cuz she's so horrible. i would feel bad, but i dont. tara was mean to a lot of people not just me. anyway, it turns out mrs nelson who i thought was racist isn't racist at all. she says i'm one of her favorite students, and i'm glad cuz i think she's really nice! and she likes my art! she even told mom i should take art for my elective in middle school. of course mom got mad cuz i was drawing in history and told me i need to pay better attention. now that i like mrs. nelson i'll definitly try harder. probably not with science lessons tho. i hate science

wow! i wrote a lot, didn't i? coolio. i'm gonna go doodle and draw some before bed. love you daddy. come home already!
your FAVORITe daughter, AMY!

CHAPTER 9

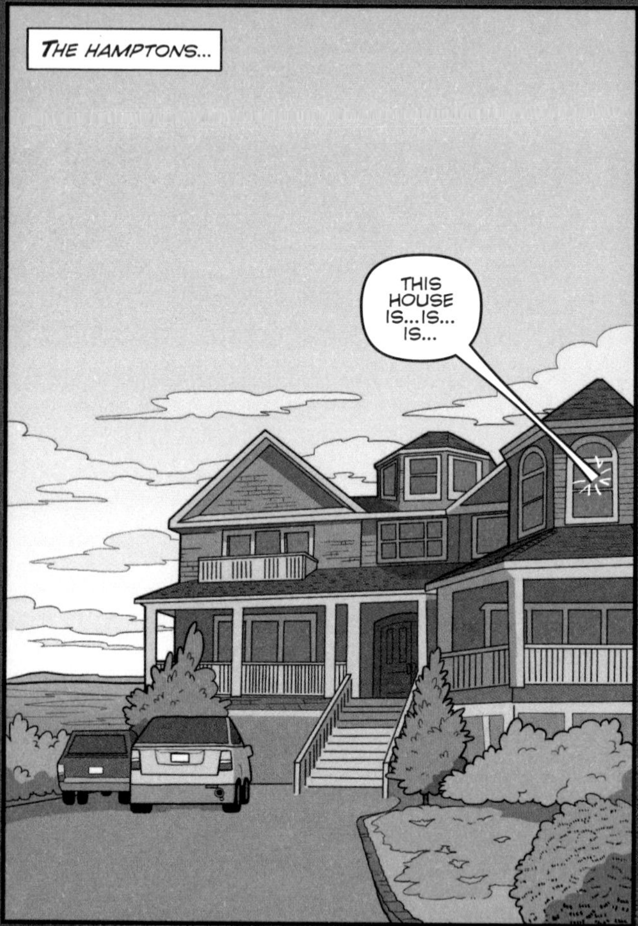

THE HAMPTONS...
THIS HOUSE IS...IS... IS...

Money and Freedom...

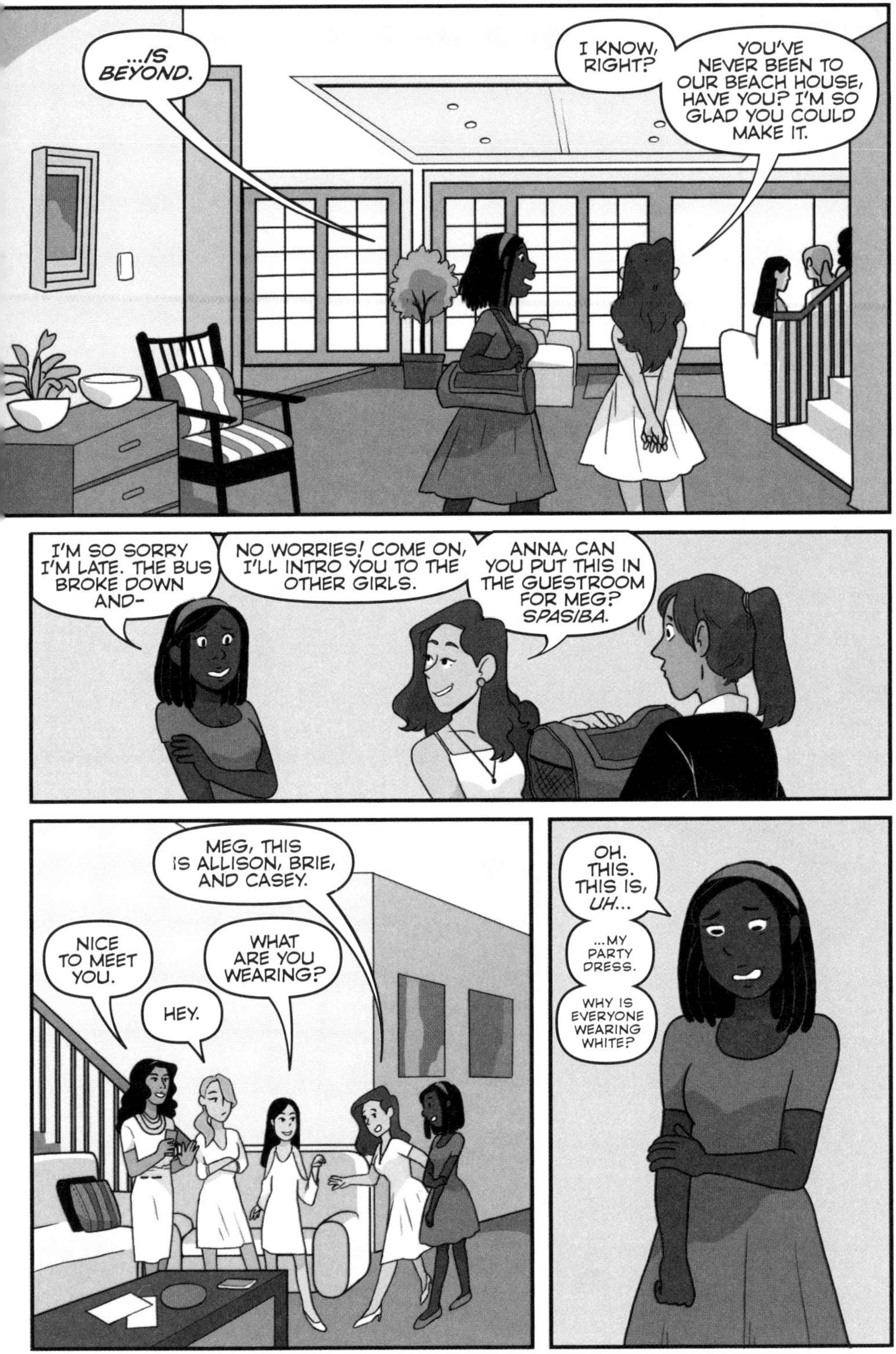
...IS BEYOND.
I KNOW, RIGHT?
YOU'VE NEVER BEEN TO OUR BEACH HOUSE, HAVE YOU? I'M SO GLAD YOU COULD MAKE IT.
I'M SO SORRY I'M LATE. THE BUS BROKE DOWN AND-
NO WORRIES! COME ON, I'LL INTRO YOU TO THE OTHER GIRLS.
ANNA, CAN YOU PUT THIS IN THE GUESTROOM FOR MEG? SPASIBA.
MEG, THIS IS ALLISON, BRIE, AND CASEY.
NICE TO MEET YOU.
HEY.
WHAT ARE YOU WEARING?
OH. THIS. THIS IS, UH...
...MY PARTY DRESS.
WHY IS EVERYONE WEARING WHITE?

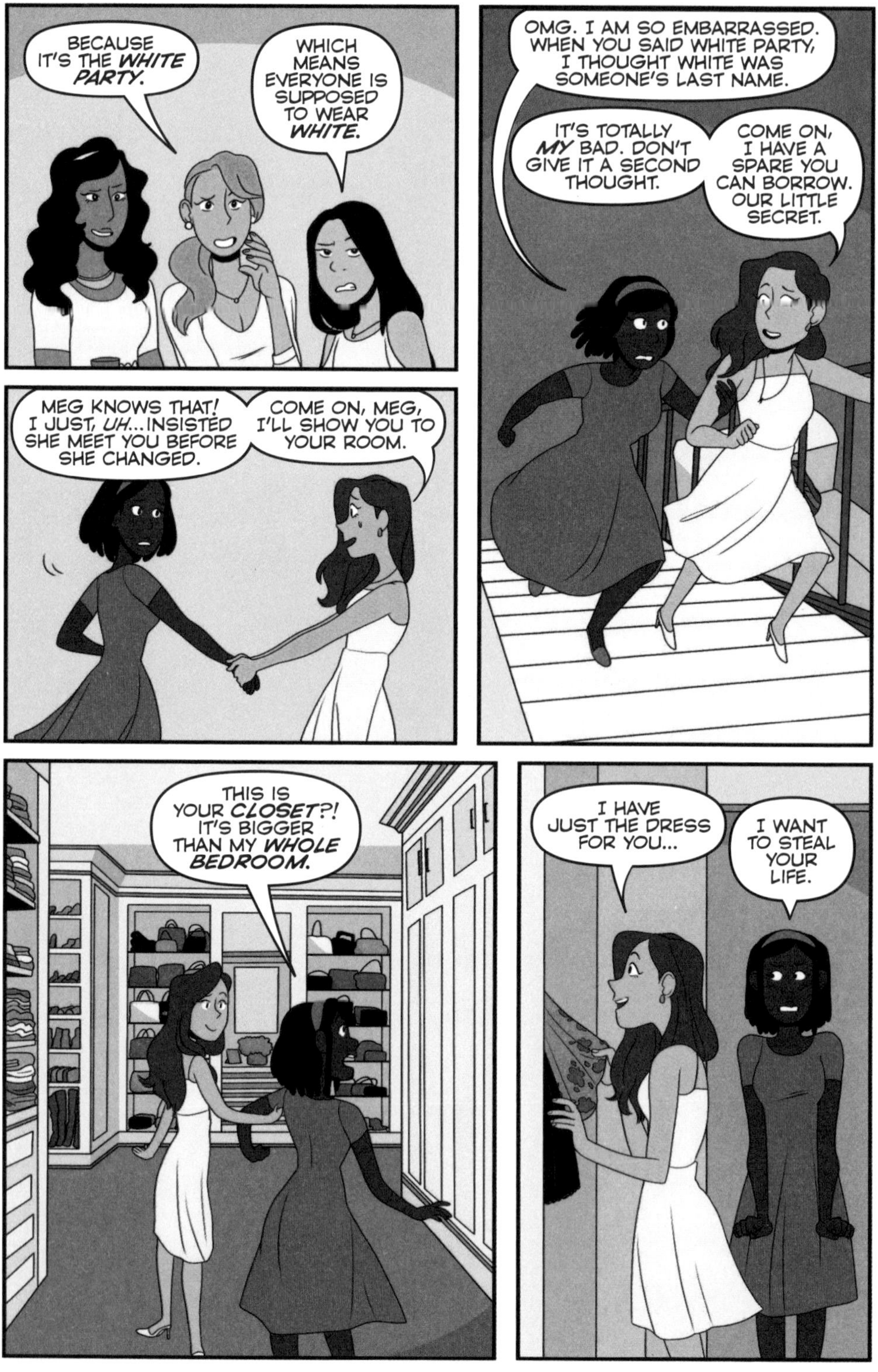
BECAUSE IT'S THE *WHITE PARTY.*
WHICH MEANS EVERYONE IS SUPPOSED TO WEAR *WHITE.*
OMG. I AM SO EMBARRASSED. WHEN YOU SAID WHITE PARTY, I THOUGHT WHITE WAS SOMEONE'S LAST NAME.
IT'S TOTALLY *MY* BAD. DON'T GIVE IT A SECOND THOUGHT.
COME ON, I HAVE A SPARE YOU CAN BORROW. OUR LITTLE SECRET.
MEG KNOWS THAT! I JUST, *UH*...INSISTED SHE MEET YOU BEFORE SHE CHANGED.
COME ON, MEG, I'LL SHOW YOU TO YOUR ROOM.
THIS IS YOUR *CLOSET?!* IT'S BIGGER THAN MY *WHOLE BEDROOM.*
I HAVE JUST THE DRESS FOR YOU...
I WANT TO STEAL YOUR LIFE.

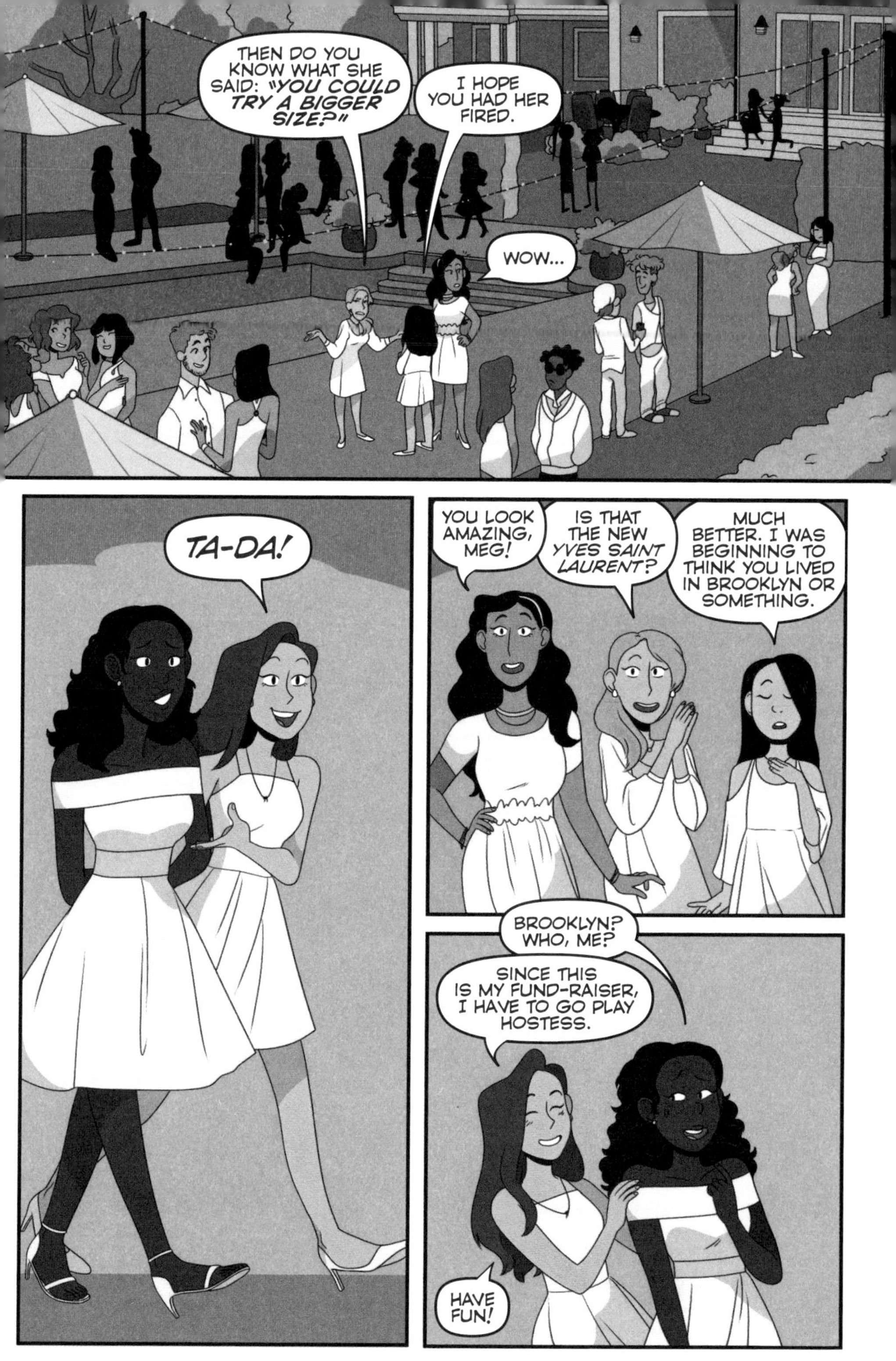
THEN DO YOU KNOW WHAT SHE SAID: "YOU COULD TRY A BIGGER SIZE?"
I HOPE YOU HAD HER FIRED.
WOW...
TA-DA!
YOU LOOK AMAZING, MEG!
IS THAT THE NEW YVES SAINT LAURENT?
MUCH BETTER. I WAS BEGINNING TO THINK YOU LIVED IN BROOKLYN OR SOMETHING.
BROOKLYN? WHO, ME?
SINCE THIS IS MY FUND-RAISER, I HAVE TO GO PLAY HOSTESS.
HAVE FUN!

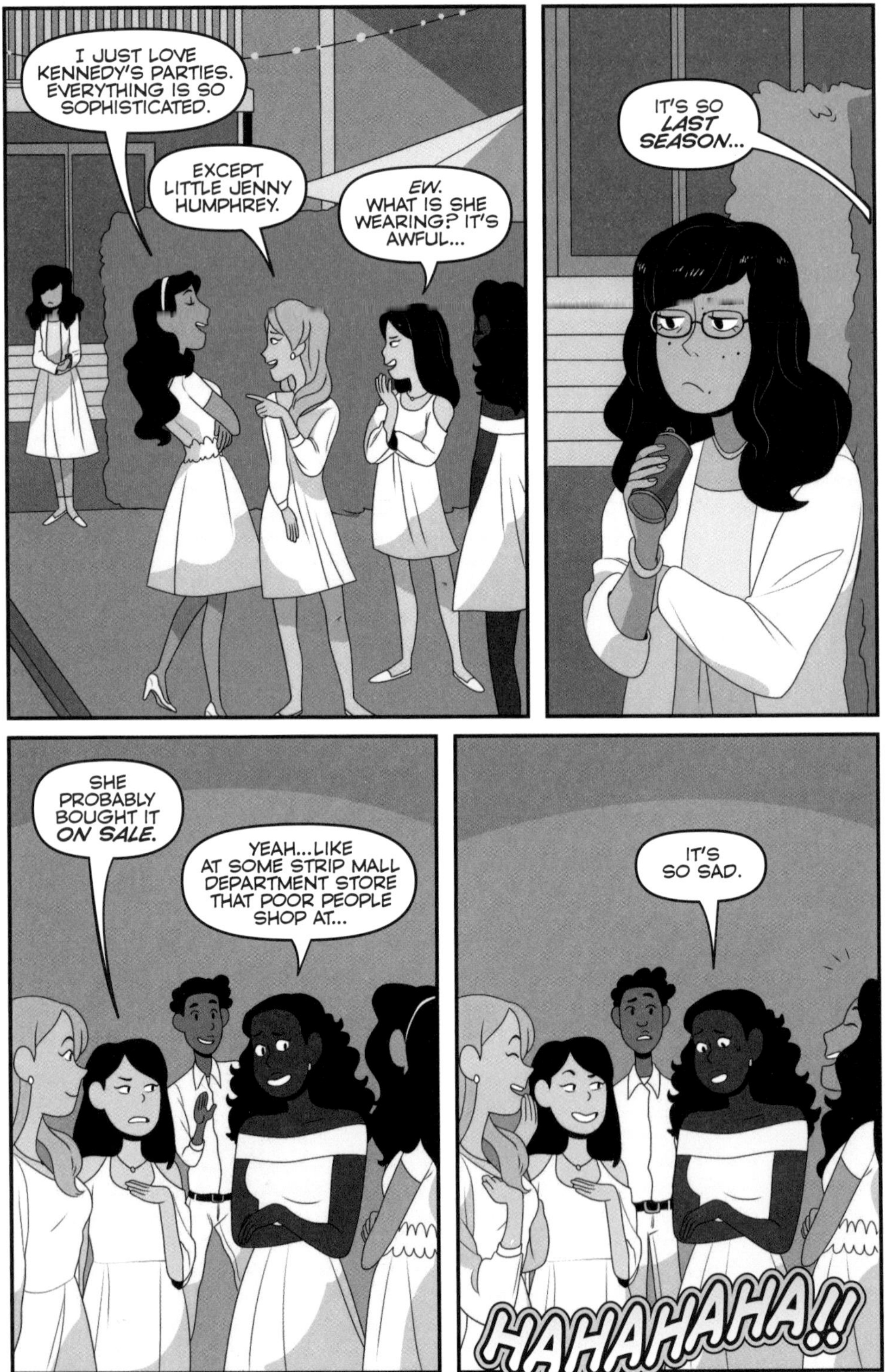
I JUST LOVE KENNEDY'S PARTIES. EVERYTHING IS SO SOPHISTICATED.
EXCEPT LITTLE JENNY HUMPHREY.
EW. WHAT IS SHE WEARING? IT'S AWFUL...
IT'S SO LAST SEASON...
SHE PROBABLY BOUGHT IT ON SALE.
YEAH...LIKE AT SOME STRIP MALL DEPARTMENT STORE THAT POOR PEOPLE SHOP AT...
IT'S SO SAD.
HAHAHAHAHA!!

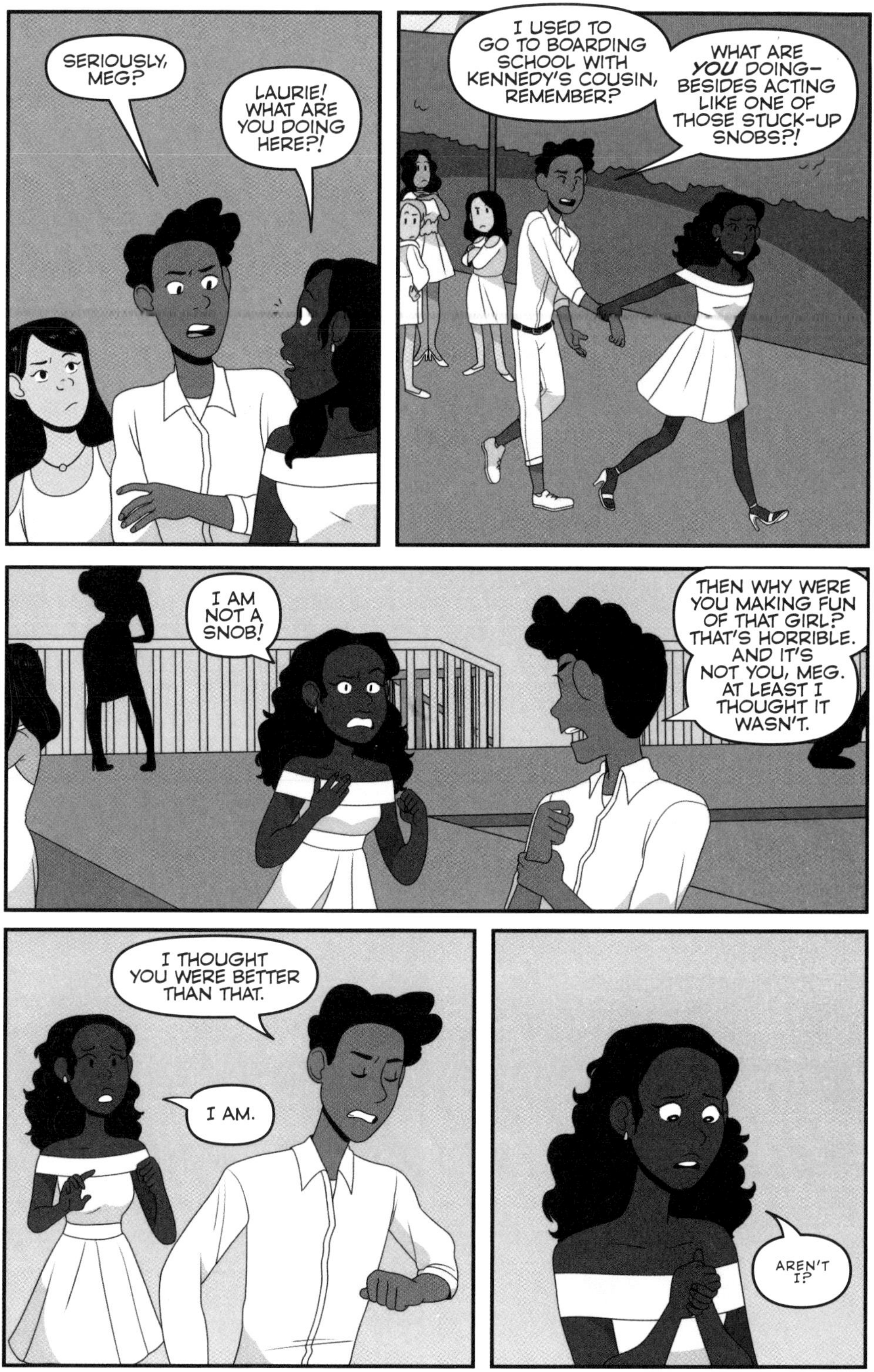
SERIOUSLY, MEG?
LAURIE! WHAT ARE YOU DOING HERE?!
I USED TO GO TO BOARDING SCHOOL WITH KENNEDY'S COUSIN, REMEMBER?
WHAT ARE *YOU* DOING–BESIDES ACTING LIKE ONE OF THOSE STUCK-UP SNOBS?!
I AM NOT A SNOB!
THEN WHY WERE YOU MAKING FUN OF THAT GIRL? THAT'S HORRIBLE. AND IT'S NOT YOU, MEG. AT LEAST I THOUGHT IT WASN'T.
I THOUGHT YOU WERE BETTER THAN THAT.
I AM.
AREN'T I?

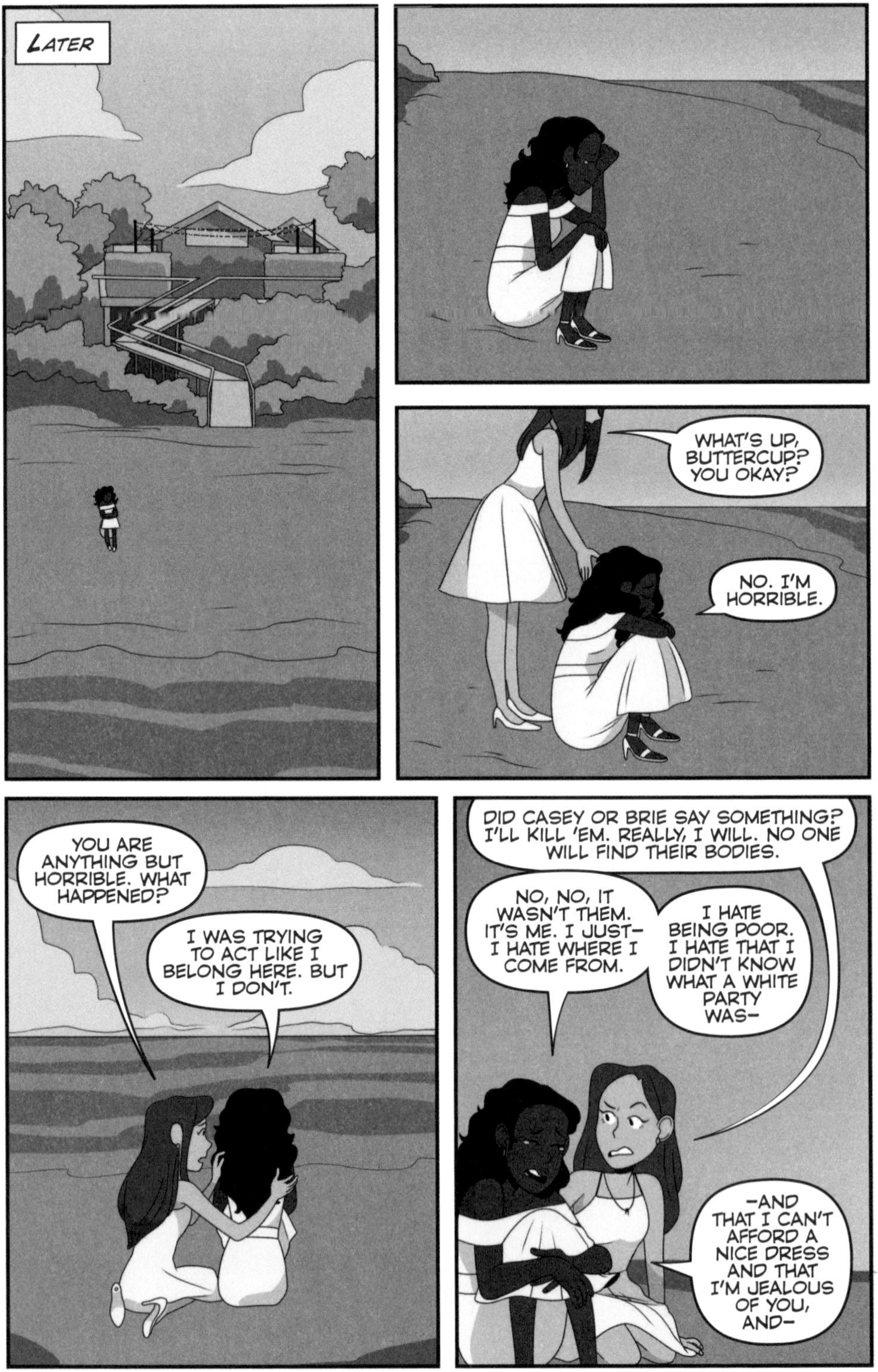
LATER
WHAT'S UP, BUTTERCUP? YOU OKAY?
NO. I'M HORRIBLE.
YOU ARE ANYTHING BUT HORRIBLE. WHAT HAPPENED?
I WAS TRYING TO ACT LIKE I BELONG HERE. BUT I DON'T.
DID CASEY OR BRIE SAY SOMETHING? I'LL KILL 'EM. REALLY, I WILL. NO ONE WILL FIND THEIR BODIES.
NO, NO, IT WASN'T THEM. IT'S ME. I JUST— I HATE WHERE I COME FROM.
I HATE BEING POOR. I HATE THAT I DIDN'T KNOW WHAT A WHITE PARTY WAS—
—AND THAT I CAN'T AFFORD A NICE DRESS AND THAT I'M JEALOUS OF YOU, AND—

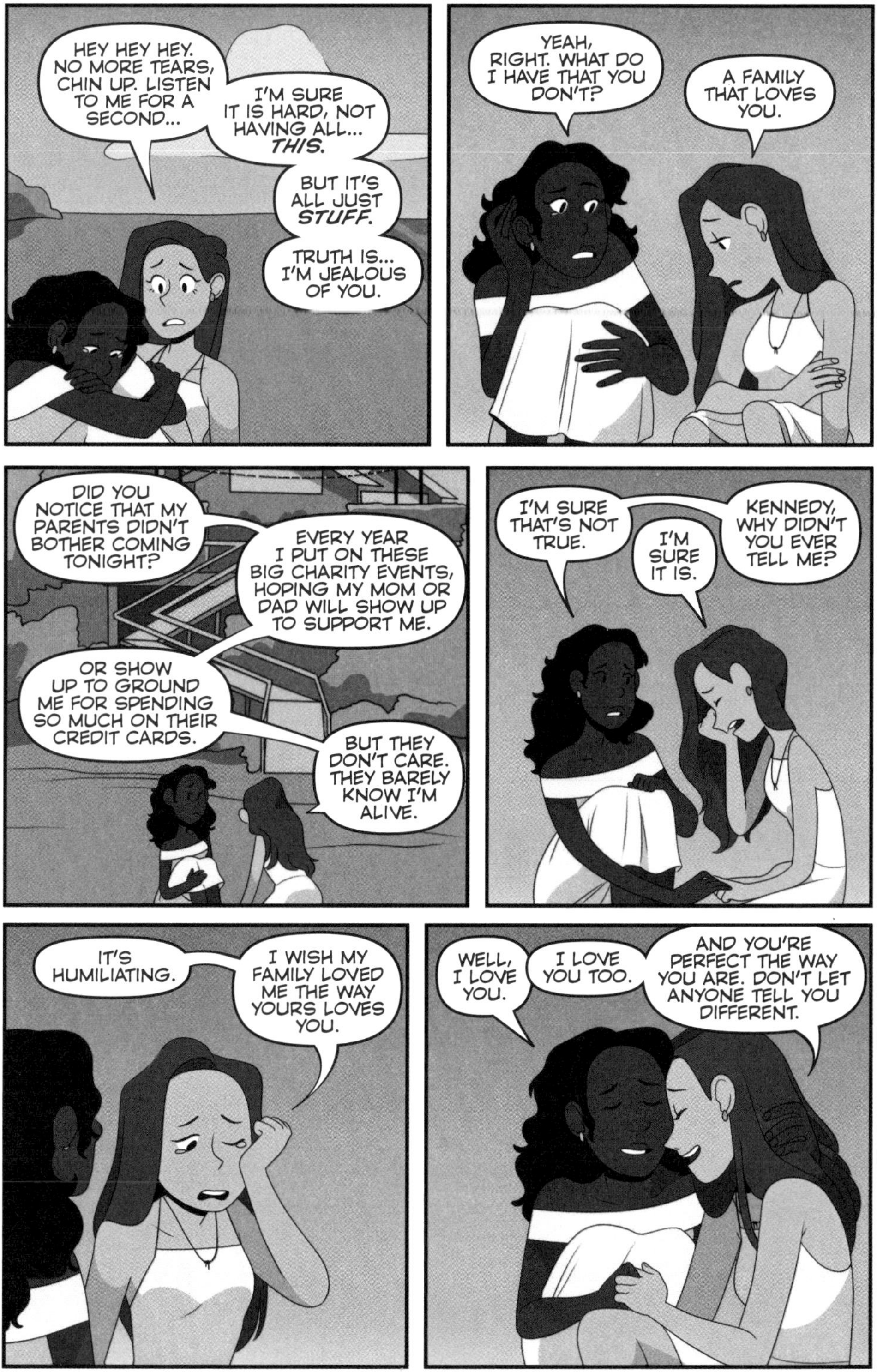
HEY HEY HEY. NO MORE TEARS, CHIN UP. LISTEN TO ME FOR A SECOND...
I'M SURE IT IS HARD, NOT HAVING ALL... *THIS*.
BUT IT'S ALL JUST *STUFF*.
TRUTH IS... I'M JEALOUS OF YOU.
YEAH, RIGHT. WHAT DO I HAVE THAT YOU DON'T?
A FAMILY THAT LOVES YOU.
DID YOU NOTICE THAT MY PARENTS DIDN'T BOTHER COMING TONIGHT?
EVERY YEAR I PUT ON THESE BIG CHARITY EVENTS, HOPING MY MOM OR DAD WILL SHOW UP TO SUPPORT ME.
OR SHOW UP TO GROUND ME FOR SPENDING SO MUCH ON THEIR CREDIT CARDS.
BUT THEY DON'T CARE. THEY BARELY KNOW I'M ALIVE.
I'M SURE THAT'S NOT TRUE.
I'M SURE IT IS.
KENNEDY, WHY DIDN'T YOU EVER TELL ME?
IT'S HUMILIATING.
I WISH MY FAMILY LOVED ME THE WAY YOURS LOVES YOU.
WELL, I LOVE YOU.
I LOVE YOU TOO.
AND YOU'RE PERFECT THE WAY YOU ARE. DON'T LET ANYONE TELL YOU DIFFERENT.

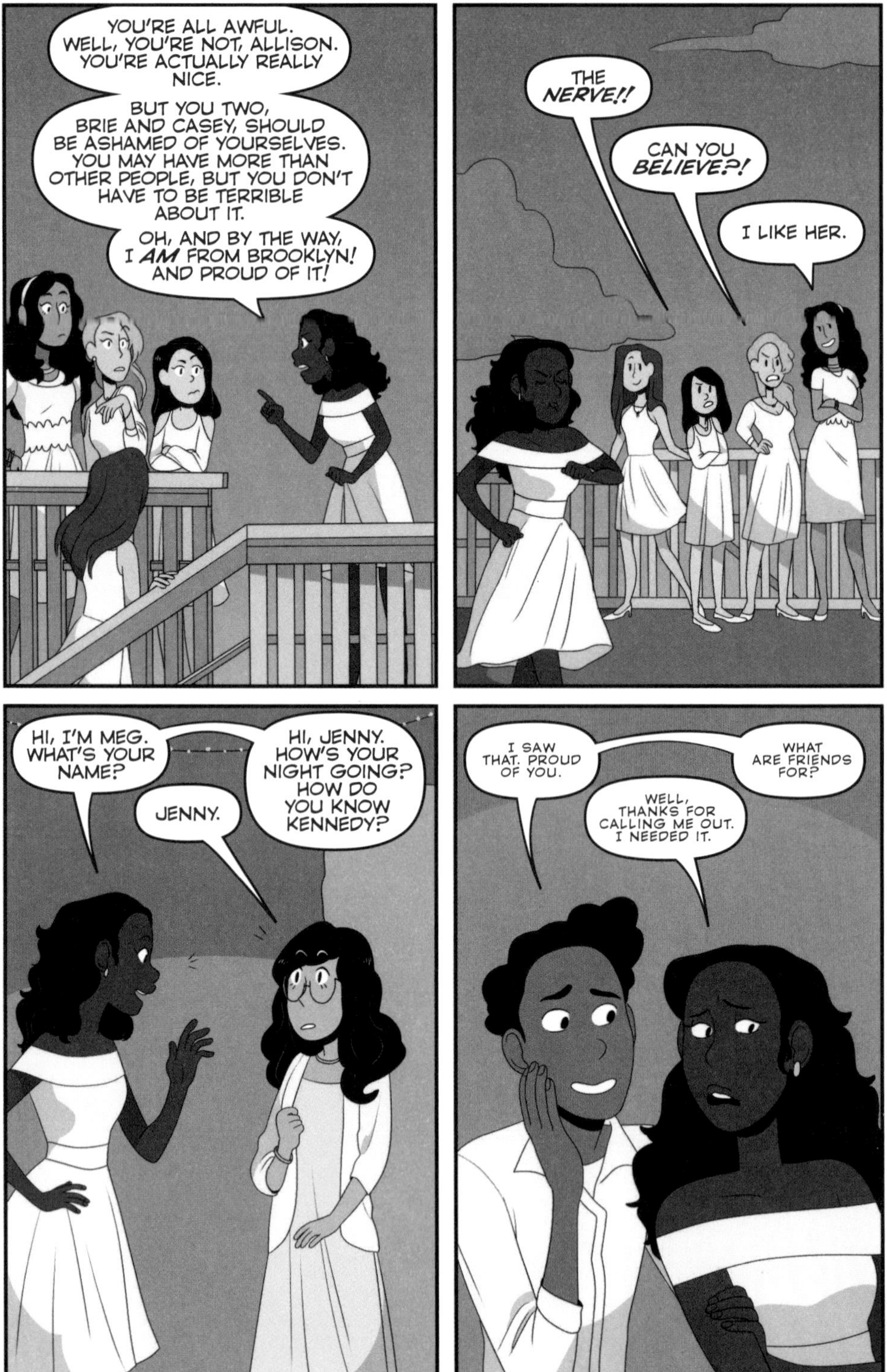
YOU'RE ALL AWFUL. WELL, YOU'RE NOT, ALLISON. YOU'RE ACTUALLY REALLY NICE.
BUT YOU TWO, BRIE AND CASEY, SHOULD BE ASHAMED OF YOURSELVES. YOU MAY HAVE MORE THAN OTHER PEOPLE, BUT YOU DON'T HAVE TO BE TERRIBLE ABOUT IT.
OH, AND BY THE WAY, I *AM* FROM BROOKLYN! AND PROUD OF IT!
THE *NERVE!!*
CAN YOU *BELIEVE?!*
I LIKE HER.
HI, I'M MEG. WHAT'S YOUR NAME?
JENNY.
HI, JENNY. HOW'S YOUR NIGHT GOING? HOW DO YOU KNOW KENNEDY?
I SAW THAT. PROUD OF YOU.
WHAT ARE FRIENDS FOR?
WELL, THANKS FOR CALLING ME OUT. I NEEDED IT.

FROM: Megan March
TO: Robert March
SENT: May 18

Hi Dad,

I just wanted to tell you how proud I am of you and the sacrifices you're making for us. You never lose patience, never doubt, never complain, yet always manage to hope. You work hard, and you wait so cheerfully that I'm ashamed to admit that I have done otherwise. But I'm turning over a new leaf.

Starting today, I want to be more like you. I want to be stronger, kinder, and more patient. Not just with my sisters but with everyone. For some time now, I've been ashamed of being poor. But this weekend (in the Hamptons of all places!), I realized that I'm not. I'm rich in the only way that counts: I have a family that values and loves me.

I am the luckiest girl in the world. And I am proud to be your daughter.

I love you, always and forever,
Meg

Send

CHAPTER 10

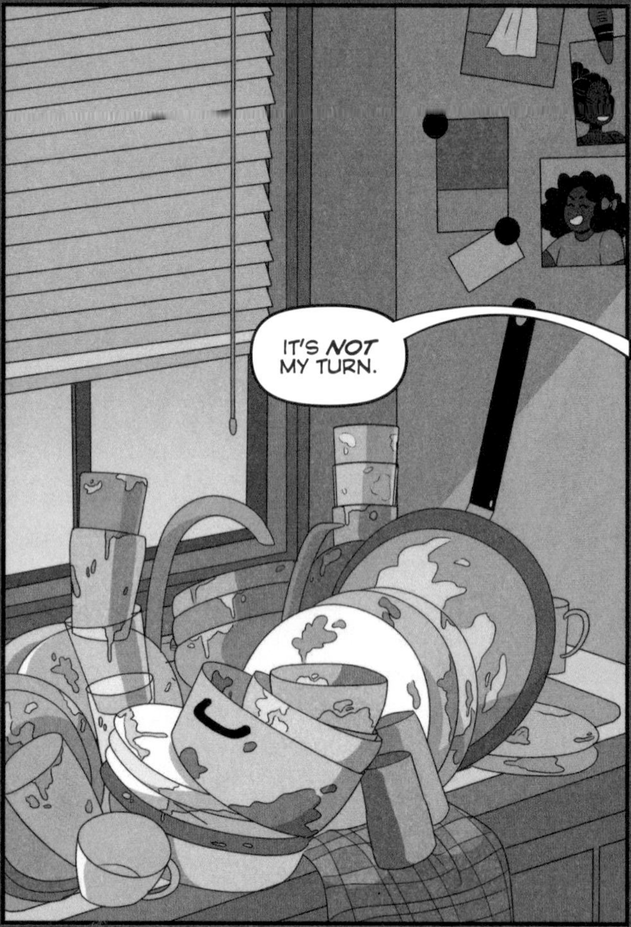
IT'S *NOT* MY TURN.

Dirty Dishes

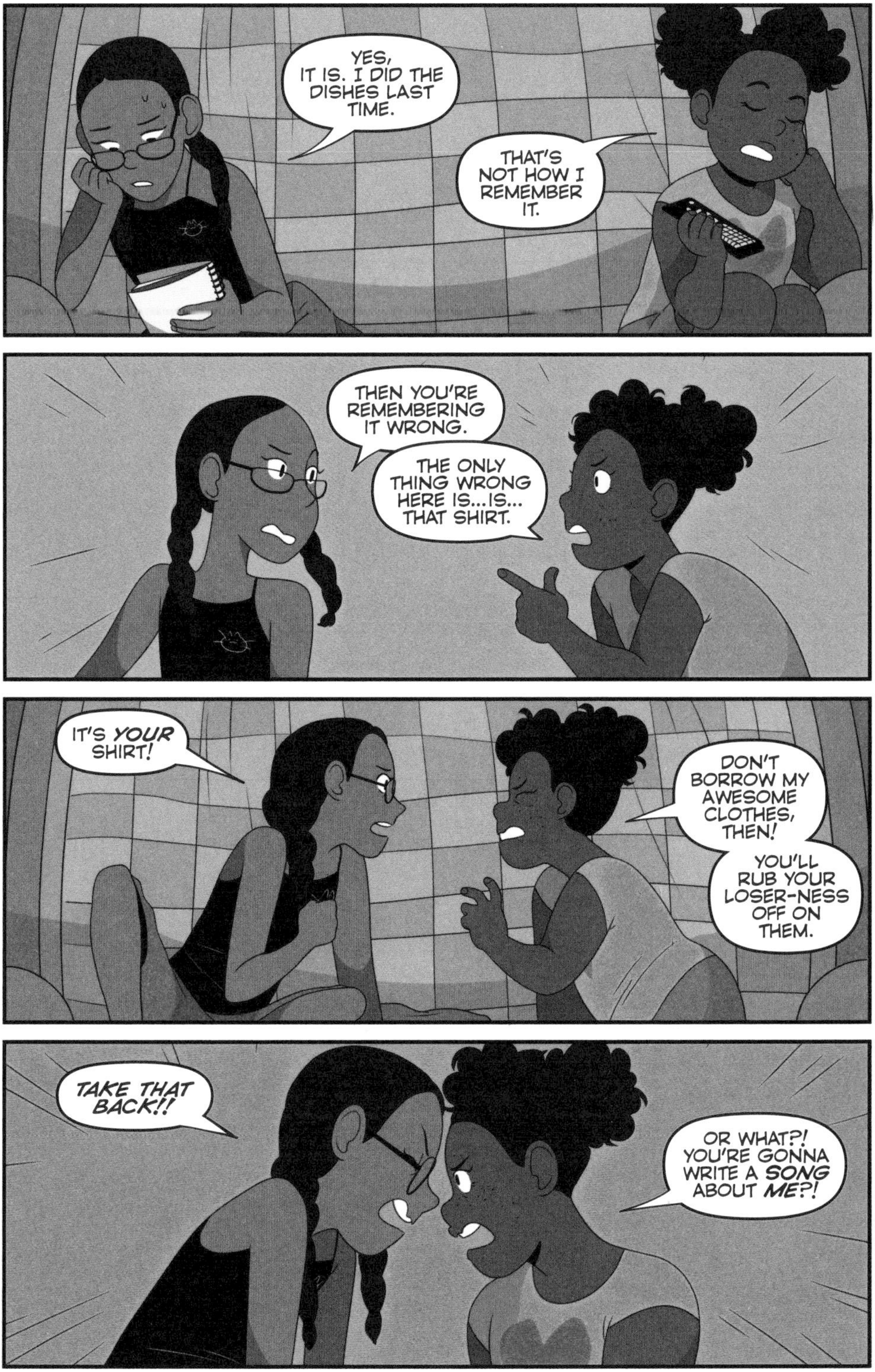
YES, IT IS. I DID THE DISHES LAST TIME.
THAT'S NOT HOW I REMEMBER IT.
THEN YOU'RE REMEMBERING IT WRONG.
THE ONLY THING WRONG HERE IS...IS... THAT SHIRT.
IT'S *YOUR* SHIRT!
DON'T BORROW MY AWESOME CLOTHES, THEN!
YOU'LL RUB YOUR LOSER-NESS OFF ON THEM.
TAKE THAT BACK!!
OR WHAT?! YOU'RE GONNA WRITE A *SONG* ABOUT *ME*?!

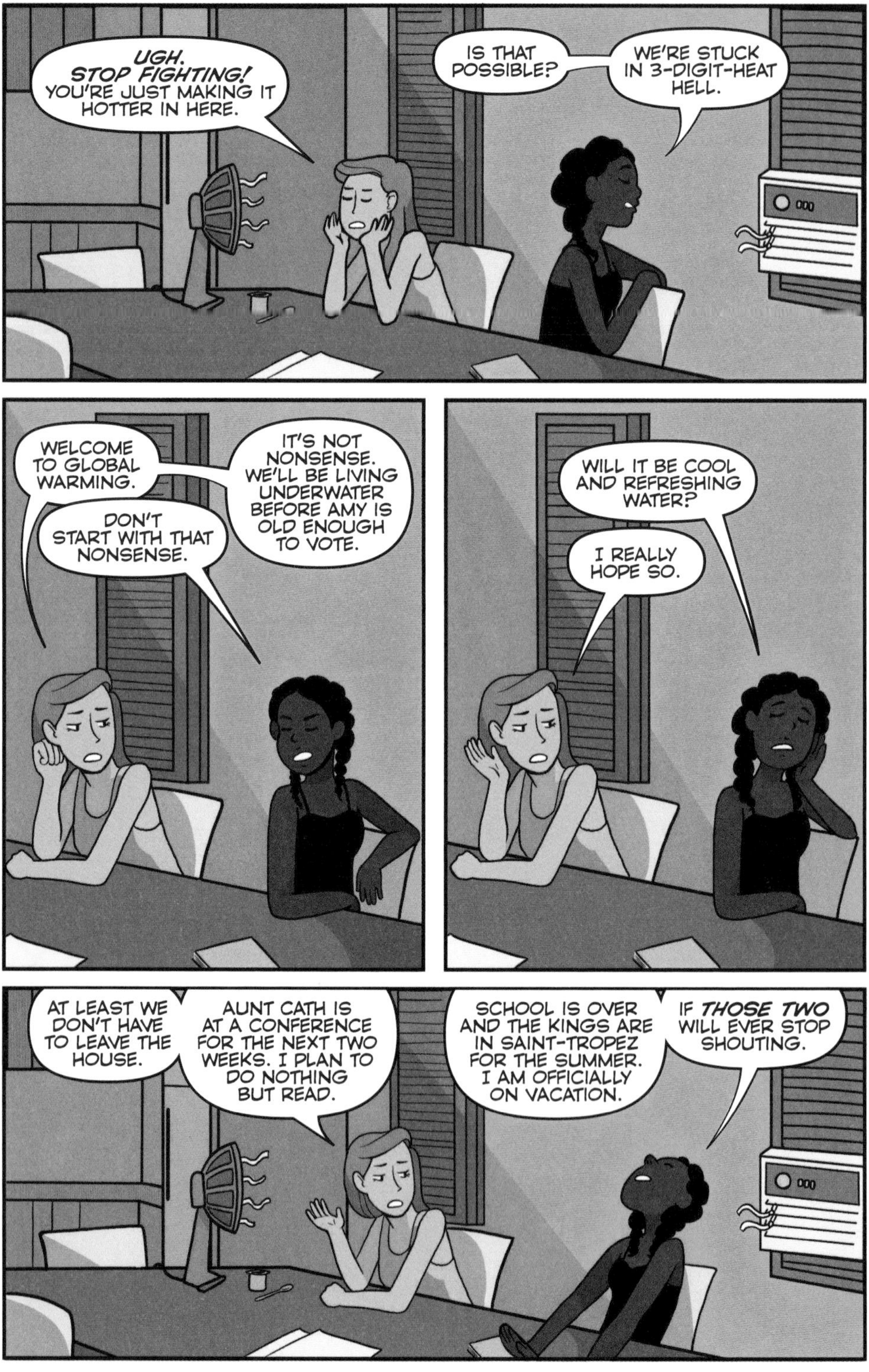
UGH. *STOP FIGHTING!* YOU'RE JUST MAKING IT HOTTER IN HERE.
WE'RE STUCK IN 3-DIGIT-HEAT HELL.
IS THAT POSSIBLE?
WELCOME TO GLOBAL WARMING.
DON'T START WITH THAT NONSENSE.
IT'S NOT NONSENSE. WE'LL BE LIVING UNDERWATER BEFORE AMY IS OLD ENOUGH TO VOTE.
WILL IT BE COOL AND REFRESHING WATER?
I REALLY HOPE SO.
AT LEAST WE DON'T HAVE TO LEAVE THE HOUSE.
AUNT CATH IS AT A CONFERENCE FOR THE NEXT TWO WEEKS. I PLAN TO DO NOTHING BUT READ.
SCHOOL IS OVER AND THE KINGS ARE IN SAINT-TROPEZ FOR THE SUMMER. I AM OFFICIALLY ON VACATION.
IF *THOSE TWO* WILL EVER STOP SHOUTING.

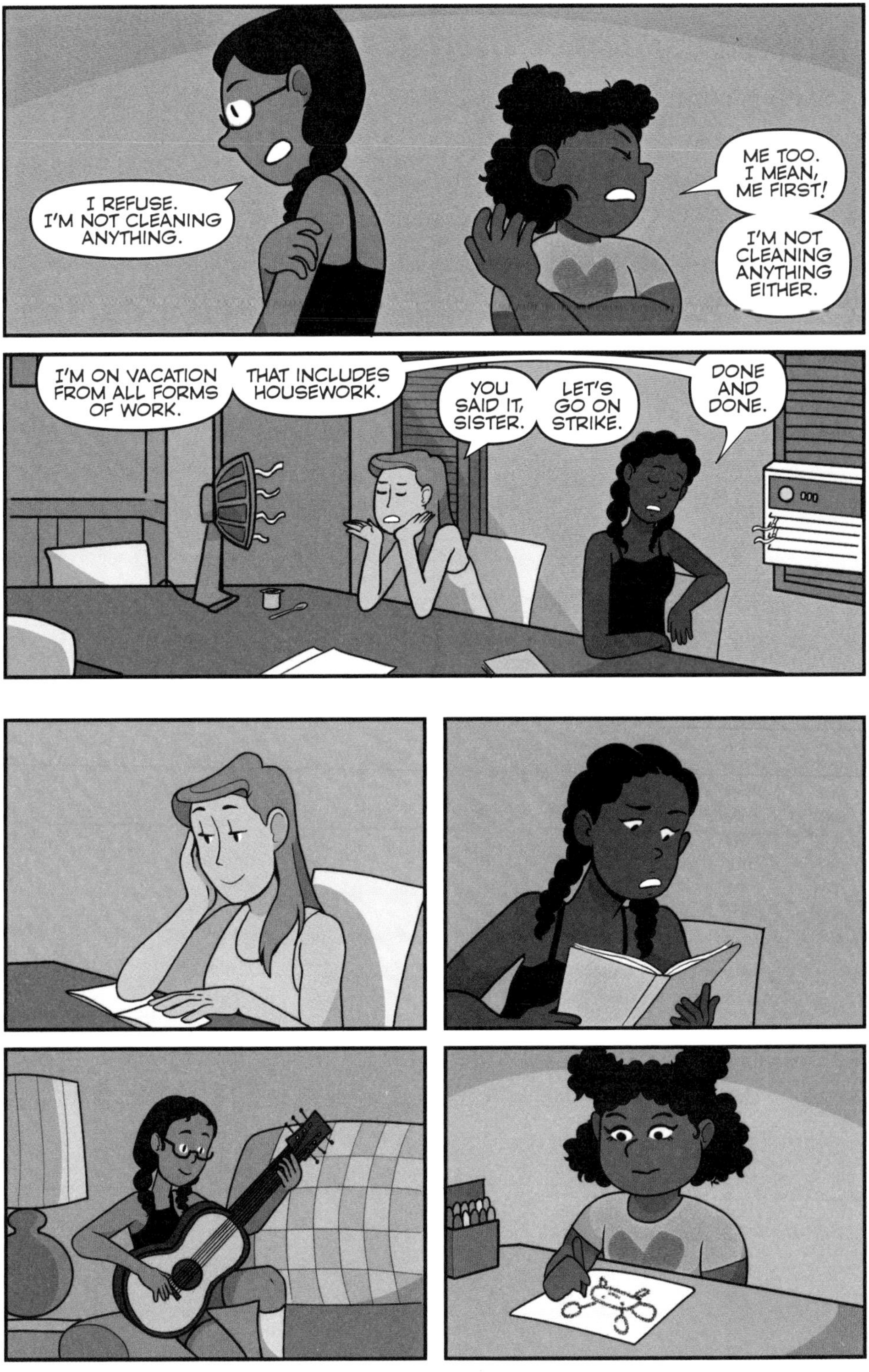
I REFUSE. I'M NOT CLEANING ANYTHING.
ME TOO. I MEAN, ME FIRST!
I'M NOT CLEANING ANYTHING EITHER.
I'M ON VACATION FROM ALL FORMS OF WORK.
THAT INCLUDES HOUSEWORK.
YOU SAID IT, SISTER.
LET'S GO ON STRIKE.
DONE AND DONE.

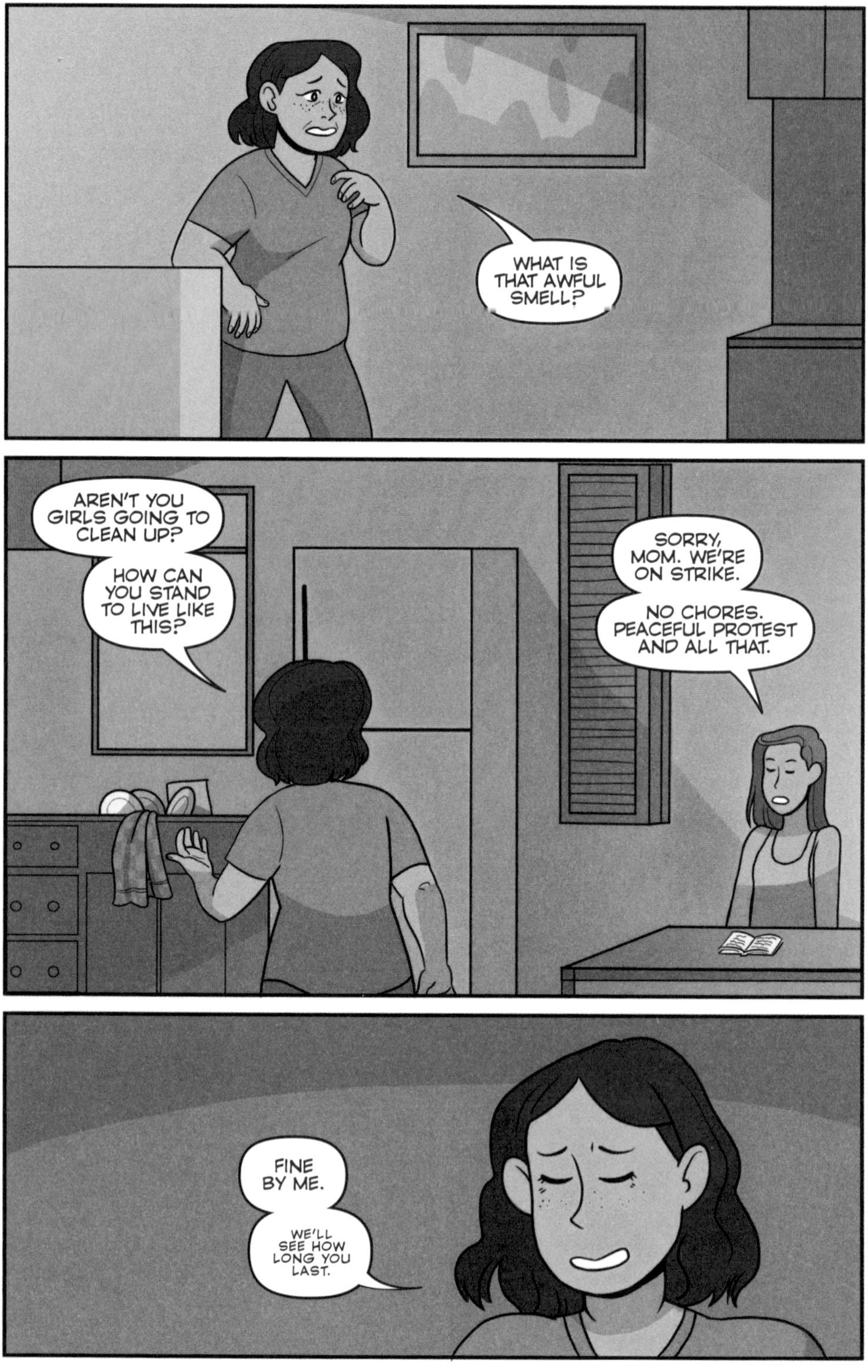
WHAT IS THAT AWFUL SMELL?
AREN'T YOU GIRLS GOING TO CLEAN UP?
HOW CAN YOU STAND TO LIVE LIKE THIS?
SORRY, MOM. WE'RE ON STRIKE.
NO CHORES. PEACEFUL PROTEST AND ALL THAT.
FINE BY ME.
WE'LL SEE HOW LONG YOU LAST.

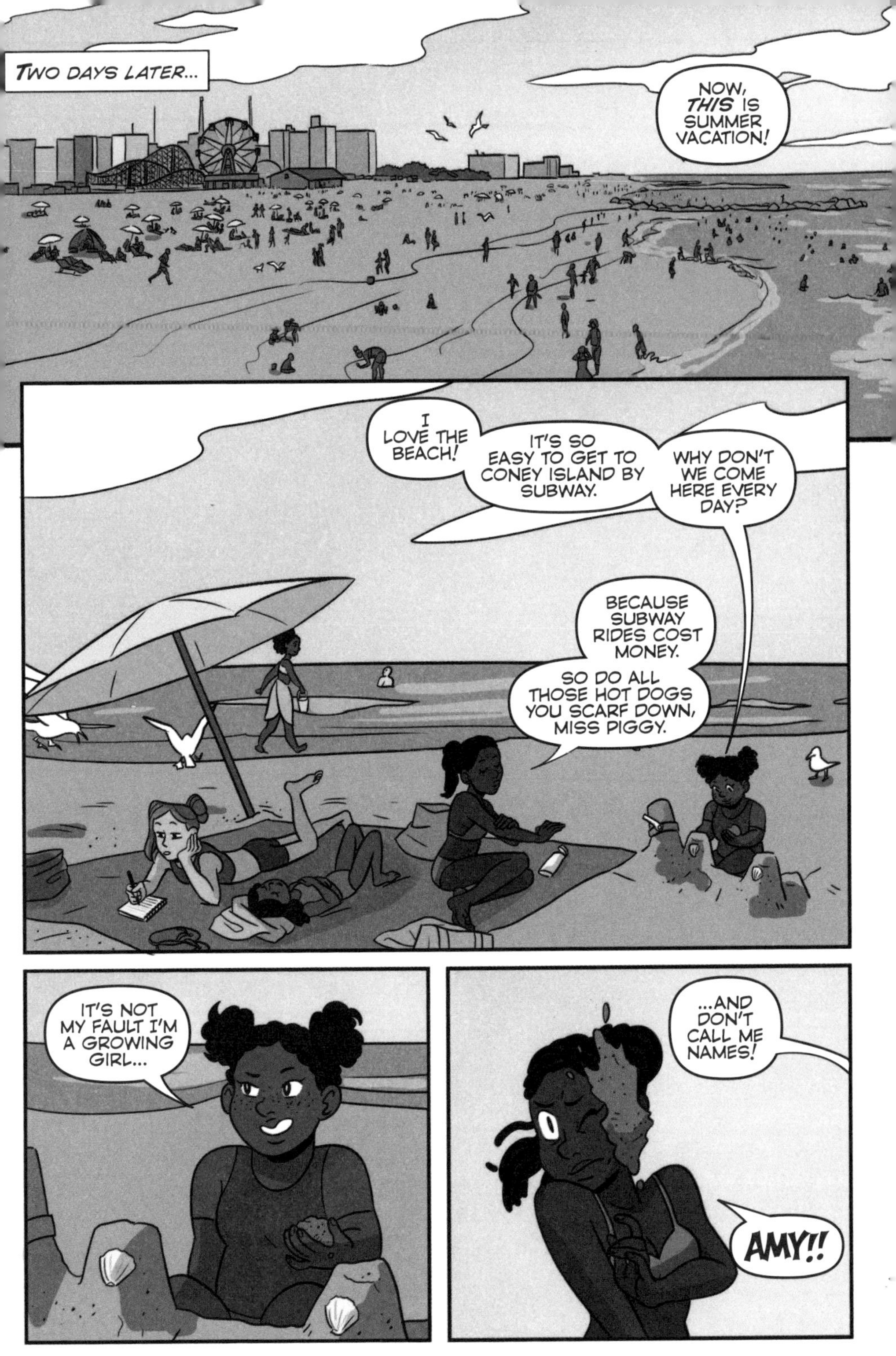
TWO DAYS LATER...
NOW, THIS IS SUMMER VACATION!
I LOVE THE BEACH!
IT'S SO EASY TO GET TO CONEY ISLAND BY SUBWAY.
WHY DON'T WE COME HERE EVERY DAY?
BECAUSE SUBWAY RIDES COST MONEY.
SO DO ALL THOSE HOT DOGS YOU SCARF DOWN, MISS PIGGY.
IT'S NOT MY FAULT I'M A GROWING GIRL...
...AND DON'T CALL ME NAMES!
AMY!!

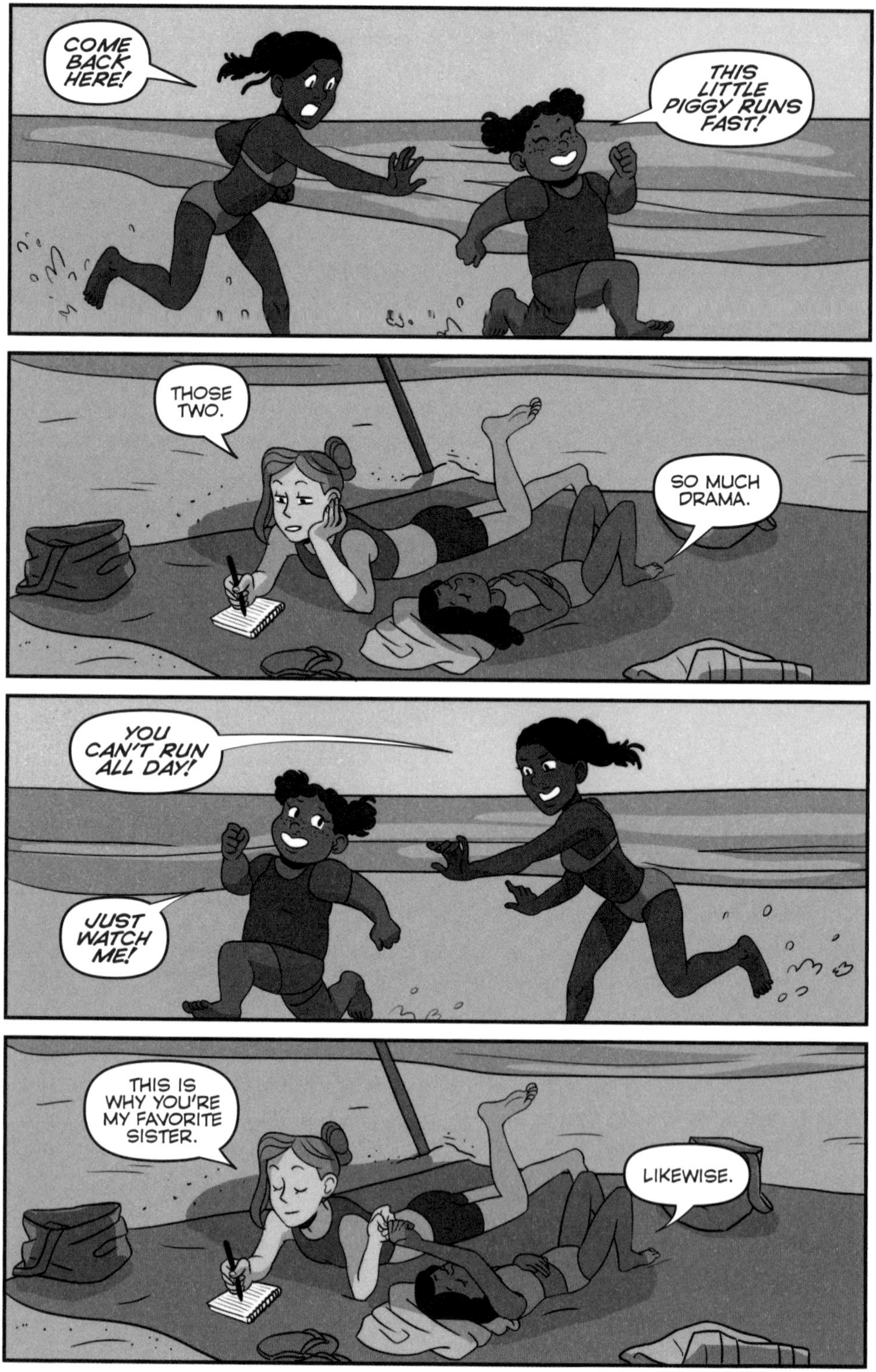
COME BACK HERE!
THIS LITTLE PIGGY RUNS FAST!
THOSE TWO.
SO MUCH DRAMA.
YOU CAN'T RUN ALL DAY!
JUST WATCH ME!
THIS IS WHY YOU'RE MY FAVORITE SISTER.
LIKEWISE.

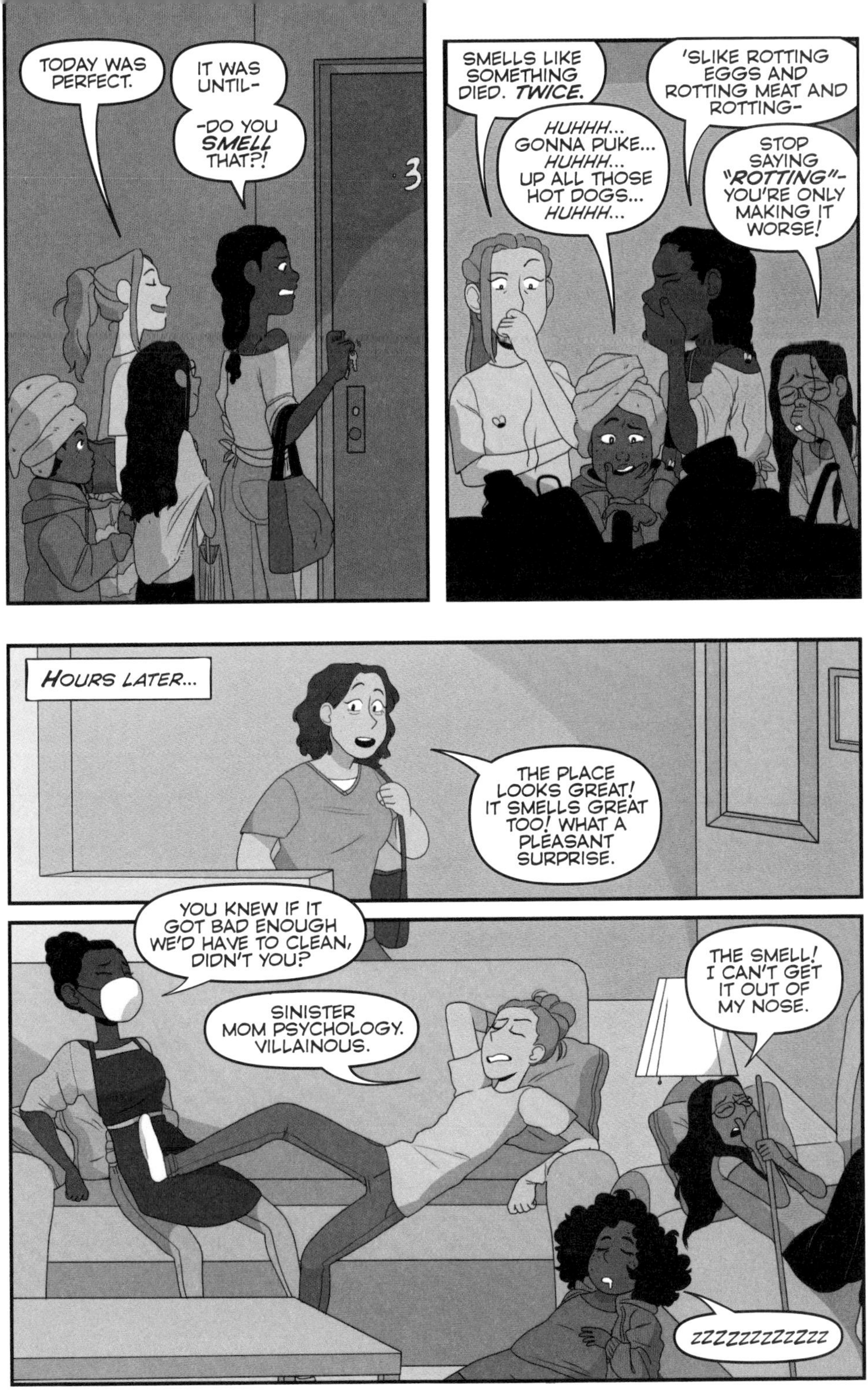
TODAY WAS PERFECT.
IT WAS UNTIL-
-DO YOU *SMELL* THAT?!
3
SMELLS LIKE SOMETHING DIED. *TWICE.*
HUHHH... GONNA PUKE... *HUHHH*... UP ALL THOSE HOT DOGS... *HUHHH*...
'SLIKE ROTTING EGGS AND ROTTING MEAT AND ROTTING-
STOP SAYING *"ROTTING"*- YOU'RE ONLY MAKING IT WORSE!
HOURS LATER...
THE PLACE LOOKS GREAT! IT SMELLS GREAT TOO! WHAT A PLEASANT SURPRISE.
YOU KNEW IF IT GOT BAD ENOUGH WE'D HAVE TO CLEAN, DIDN'T YOU?
SINISTER MOM PSYCHOLOGY. VILLAINOUS.
THE SMELL! I CAN'T GET IT OUT OF MY NOSE.
ZZZZZZZZZZZZ

FROM: Beth March
TO: Robert March
SENT: June 19

Hey Dad,

How are you? I am fine. School just ended and all of us sisters are going to enjoy our summer break. Though it would be better if you were here too. I'd love to go to the beach, just the two of us. I know that's selfish, but I want to play you a song on my guitar that I've been working on. I'm too embarrassed to play it for anyone else. But I would play it for you.

What else? Um, I don't know. I just woke up and it's almost noon. Please don't think I'm lazy, I'm really not! Lately, I've been getting bad headaches, and I'm really tired all the time. Jo says it's the heat from global warming. It is really hot here. Is it hot where you are?

Anyways, it's nice being out of school. I've been staying up late watching movies. Not bad ones! Just Disney princess ones. I know I'm too old for them, but I still like them. (Though I wish they had more black princesses.)

Okay, I'm going to go take a nap. Just kidding! (Or maybe I'm not.)

I miss you. Please come home soon.
Love you forever,
Beth

Jo's Journal: KEEP OUT

"Carpe diem. Seize the day, boys. Make your lives extraordinary."

I wish I had written that. But I can't take credit. Robin Williams said it in that movie <u>Dead Poets Society</u>. I admit that I've watched it FOUR times this summer, but I can't help it. It hits me on so many levels. And it's so true. Seize the day! Because who knows, it could be your last. (Yeesh. Morbid much?)

I don't mean to be, but it's true. Life flies by. Take this summer, for instance. It's already the end of June. Summer only just began, and the first month is almost done and gone. The last two weeks have flown by as if nothing more than an orange leaf on an autumn wind, a fall that is just around the corner.

That's why I'm trying to read one book a week this summer. So far I've read <u>The Color Purple</u> by Alice Walker (and cried through most of it) and <u>The Hours</u> by Michael Cunningham. Both are heartbreaking and beautiful and so wonderful, and I only hope that one day I can write so exquisitely. But there is this thing that worries me...

After I read a great book, I am left wanting more. It takes every effort not to turn the last page and start again on the first. (I mean, if I read every book I loved over and over, I'd never get to the next.) So instead, I go online and look up what I can about the author. I want to know what inspired them, what moved them to craft such wonderful words and perfect vernacular. And do you know what I've found? They've all endured some horrible, tragic circumstance that forever changed them. And it terrifies me.

Why? Because on one hand, I want to write beautifully, but I don't want to suffer to do it. On the other hand, it makes me feel as though I am overdue for some terrible event.

Yikes. I just got goose pimples all over my body. I am thoroughly freaking myself out. I do want to write, and I want to write well, and I want to win the Pulitzer for fiction one day, which is kind of ridiculous because there are so many amazing writers out there and who am I? I mean, I don't want to be famous, and I don't want to be rich (though I wouldn't complain about that), but ultimately, I just want to be recognized as worthy....

That's it, isn't it? I want to be worthy. Because right now, with my... secret... I don't feel worthy. I feel dishonest. I feel like a liar, a charlatan, a con artist. I suppose, in my own way, I am suffering. But it's not as though I can't breathe each day. Our world has changed. People—society—they're more tolerant than ever. Heck, just a few decades ago, Mom and Dad wouldn't have been able to get married. Now, they're celebrated. And I want to be celebrated too. But I don't have the courage to say the words. I don't know what I'm scared of... that Mom and Dad won't love me anymore. That Meg and Beth and Amy will look at me different. I don't think they would, but what if? What if it bothers them? What if they hate me? I can't bear the thought of that. So I don't say anything.

So I guess my point is, if I can't be me, if I can't be celebrated... then maybe (at the very least) my writing can.

I shouldn't feel sorry for myself. I have a good life. I have two parents who love me, three sisters who have my back, friends who I can tell anything to.... Well, almost anything. See? I am happy. And what does a happy person have to write about? Nothing!

Ugh. There goes that feeling again! That sense that something terrible is coming, something that will test me, some awful personal tragedy. I don't know what it is, and that terrifies me. I like my life as it is. I don't want it to change. But change is constant. And I guess all of us have to face something sooner or later. So carpe diem!

In that vein, I'll end this entry with my second favorite quote from <u>Dead Poet's Society</u>...

KEATING: "Seize the day. Gather ye rosebuds while ye may." Why does the writer use these lines?

CHARLIE: Because he's in a hurry.

KEATING: No. Ding! Thank you for playing anyway. Because we are food for worms, lads. Because, believe it or not, each and every one of us in this room is one day going to stop breathing, turn cold and die.

Me? Josephine March? I'm not ready to die. Not even close. No worm food for me, not yet! I have more to write. So much more...

CHAPTER 11

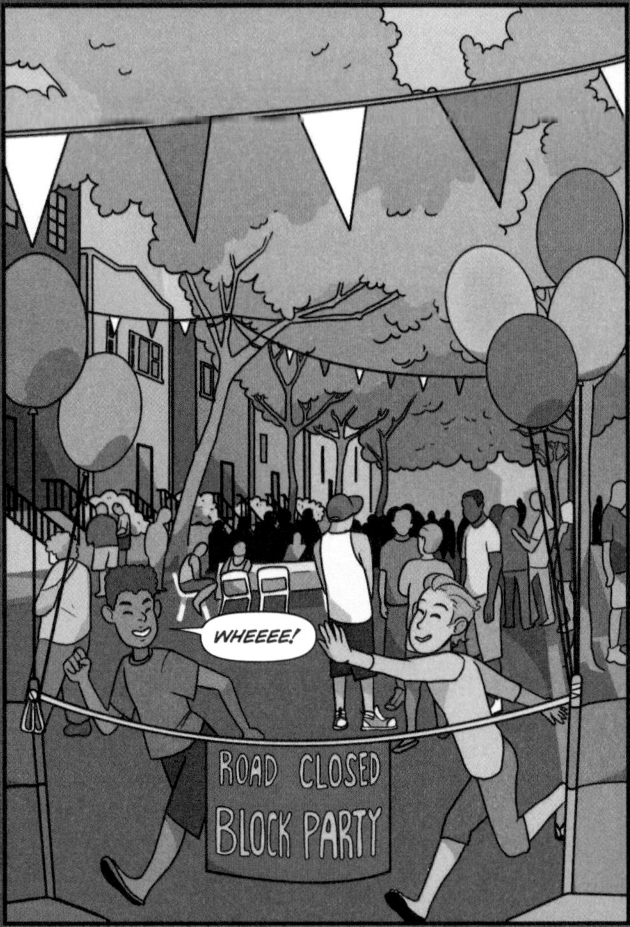
WHEEEE!
ROAD CLOSED
BLOCK PARTY

Fireworks

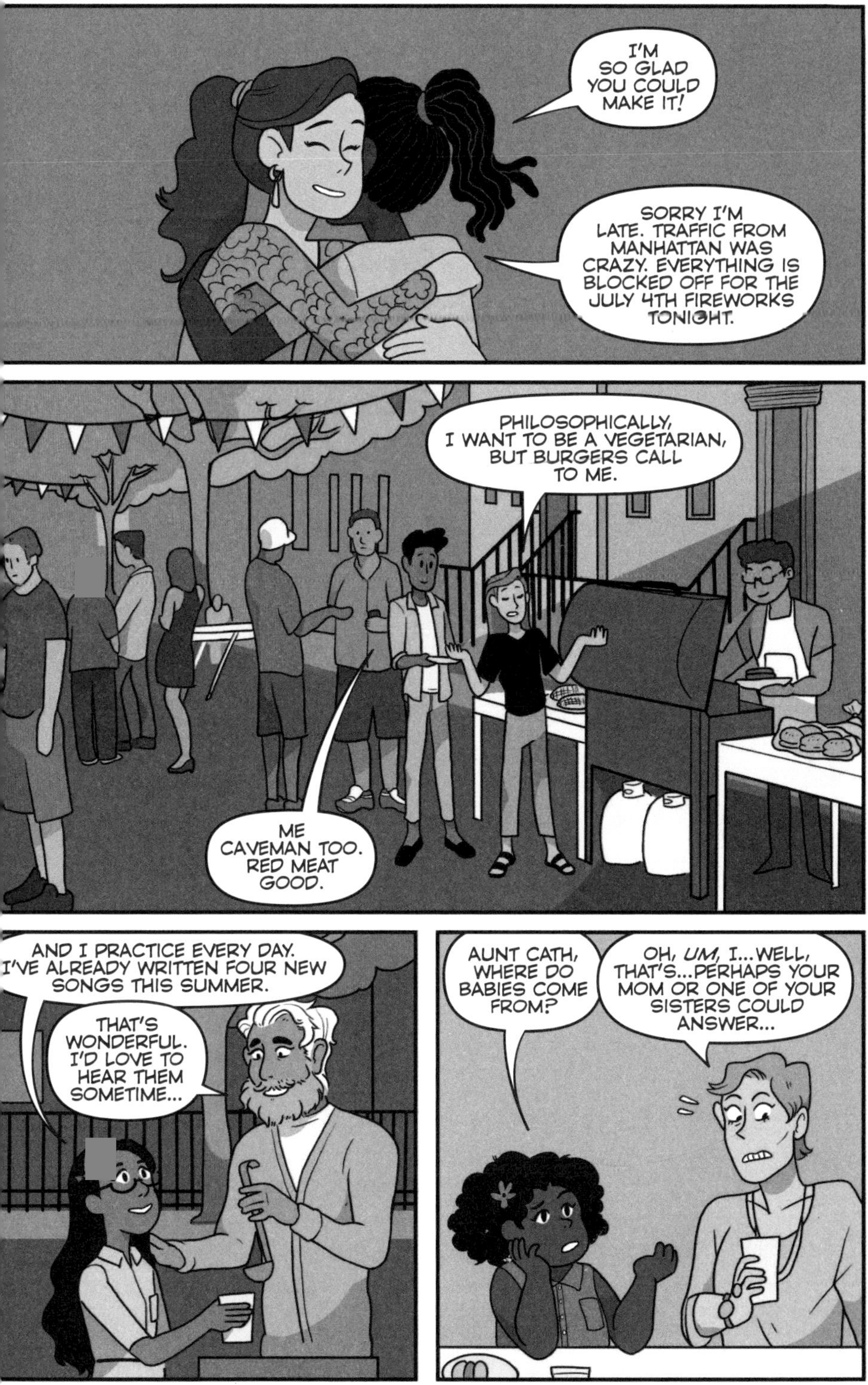
I'M SO GLAD YOU COULD MAKE IT!
SORRY I'M LATE. TRAFFIC FROM MANHATTAN WAS CRAZY. EVERYTHING IS BLOCKED OFF FOR THE JULY 4TH FIREWORKS TONIGHT.
PHILOSOPHICALLY, I WANT TO BE A VEGETARIAN, BUT BURGERS CALL TO ME.
ME CAVEMAN TOO. RED MEAT GOOD.
AND I PRACTICE EVERY DAY. I'VE ALREADY WRITTEN FOUR NEW SONGS THIS SUMMER.
THAT'S WONDERFUL. I'D LOVE TO HEAR THEM SOMETIME...
AUNT CATH, WHERE DO BABIES COME FROM?
OH, *UM,* I...WELL, THAT'S...PERHAPS YOUR MOM OR ONE OF YOUR SISTERS COULD ANSWER...

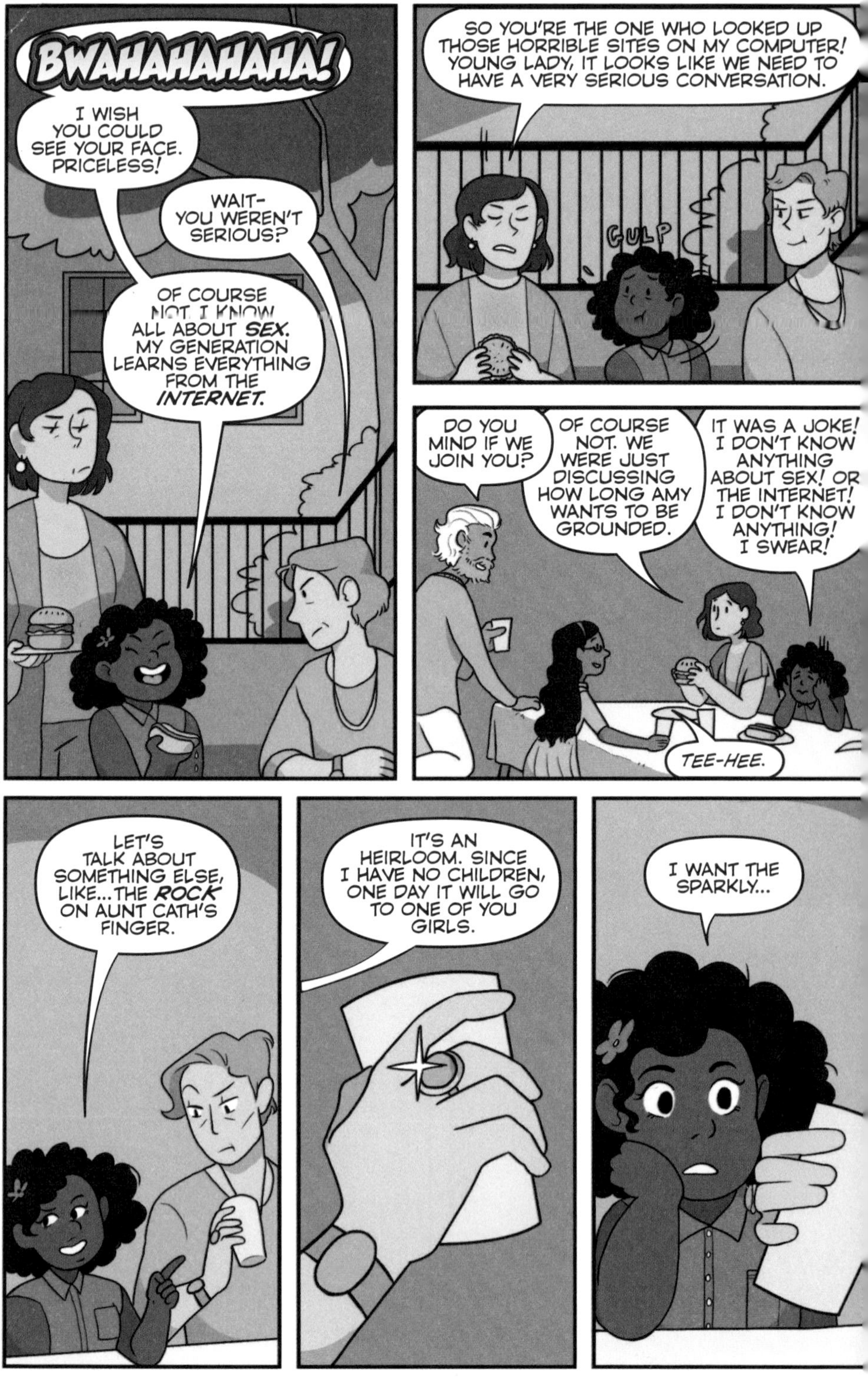
BWAHAHAHAHA!
I WISH YOU COULD SEE YOUR FACE. PRICELESS!
WAIT- YOU WEREN'T SERIOUS?
OF COURSE NOT. I KNOW ALL ABOUT SEX. MY GENERATION LEARNS EVERYTHING FROM THE INTERNET.
SO YOU'RE THE ONE WHO LOOKED UP THOSE HORRIBLE SITES ON MY COMPUTER! YOUNG LADY, IT LOOKS LIKE WE NEED TO HAVE A VERY SERIOUS CONVERSATION.
GULP
DO YOU MIND IF WE JOIN YOU?
OF COURSE NOT. WE WERE JUST DISCUSSING HOW LONG AMY WANTS TO BE GROUNDED.
IT WAS A JOKE! I DON'T KNOW ANYTHING ABOUT SEX! OR THE INTERNET! I DON'T KNOW ANYTHING! I SWEAR!
TEE-HEE.
LET'S TALK ABOUT SOMETHING ELSE, LIKE...THE ROCK ON AUNT CATH'S FINGER.
IT'S AN HEIRLOOM. SINCE I HAVE NO CHILDREN, ONE DAY IT WILL GO TO ONE OF YOU GIRLS.
I WANT THE SPARKLY...

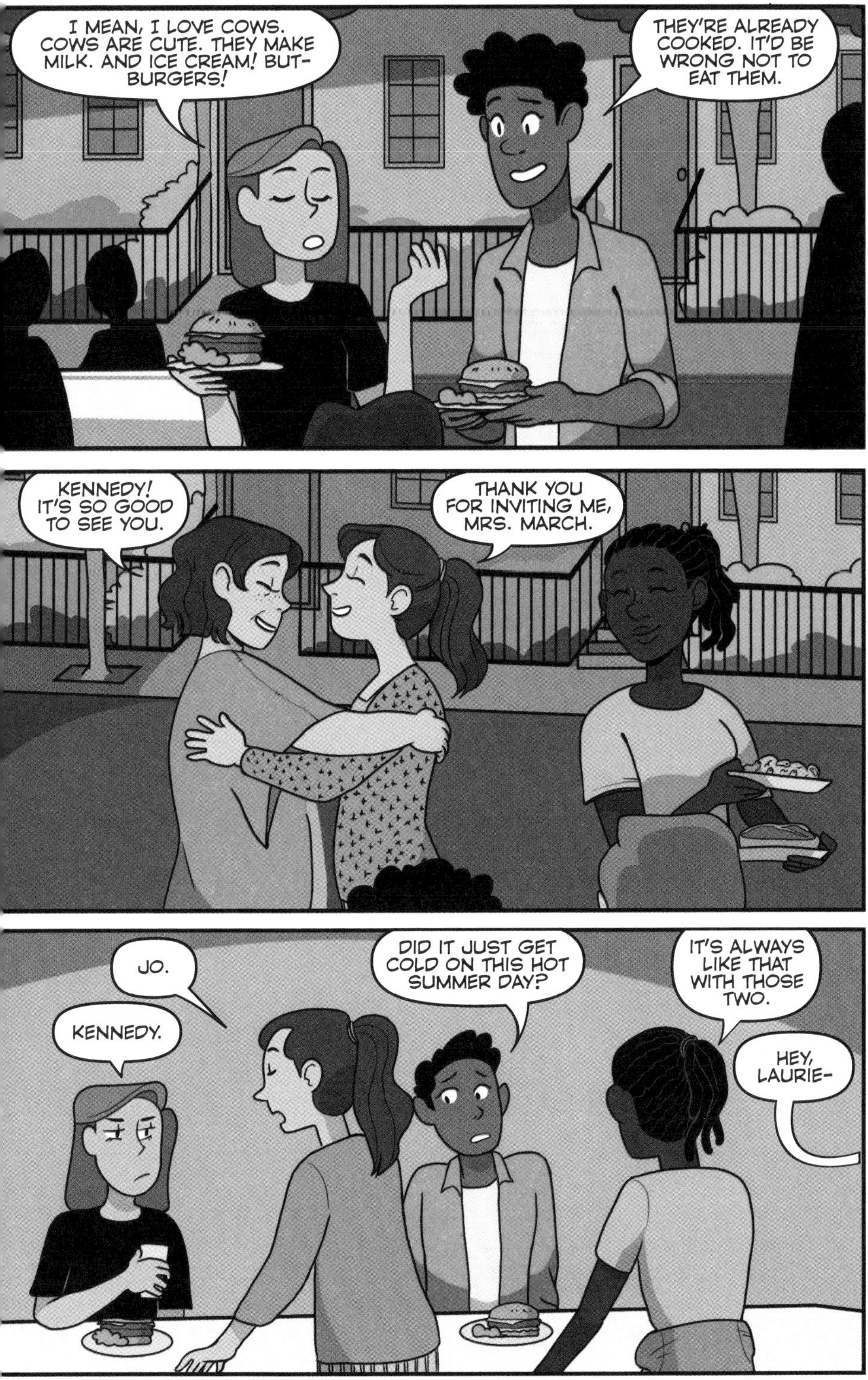
I MEAN, I LOVE COWS. COWS ARE CUTE. THEY MAKE MILK. AND ICE CREAM! BUT- BURGERS!
THEY'RE ALREADY COOKED. IT'D BE WRONG NOT TO EAT THEM.
KENNEDY! IT'S SO GOOD TO SEE YOU.
THANK YOU FOR INVITING ME, MRS. MARCH.
JO.
KENNEDY.
DID IT JUST GET COLD ON THIS HOT SUMMER DAY?
IT'S ALWAYS LIKE THAT WITH THOSE TWO.
HEY, LAURIE-

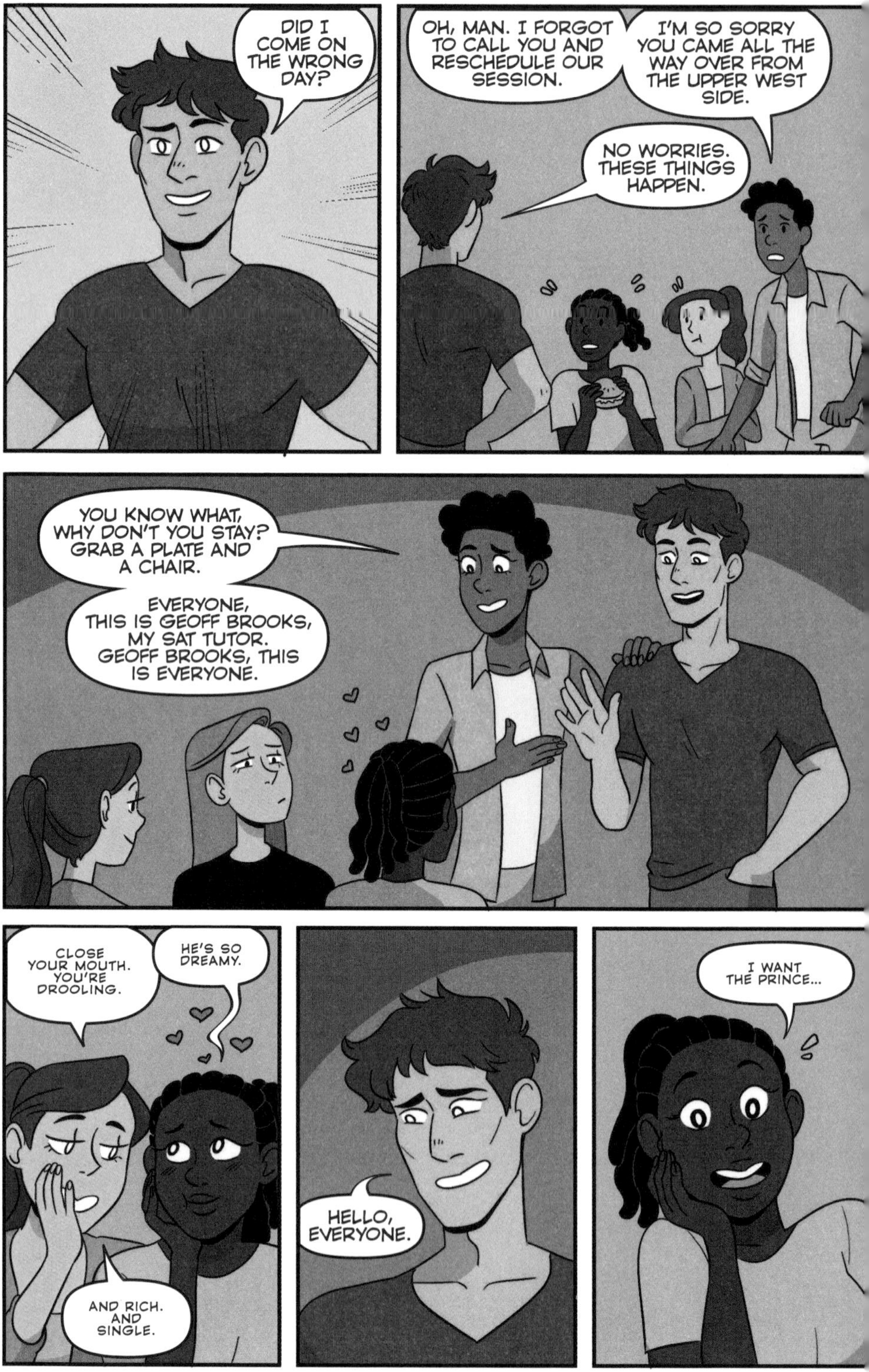
DID I COME ON THE WRONG DAY?
OH, MAN. I FORGOT TO CALL YOU AND RESCHEDULE OUR SESSION.
I'M SO SORRY YOU CAME ALL THE WAY OVER FROM THE UPPER WEST SIDE.
NO WORRIES. THESE THINGS HAPPEN.
YOU KNOW WHAT, WHY DON'T YOU STAY? GRAB A PLATE AND A CHAIR.
EVERYONE, THIS IS GEOFF BROOKS, MY SAT TUTOR. GEOFF BROOKS, THIS IS EVERYONE.
CLOSE YOUR MOUTH. YOU'RE DROOLING.
HE'S SO DREAMY.
AND RICH. AND SINGLE.
HELLO, EVERYONE.
I WANT THE PRINCE...

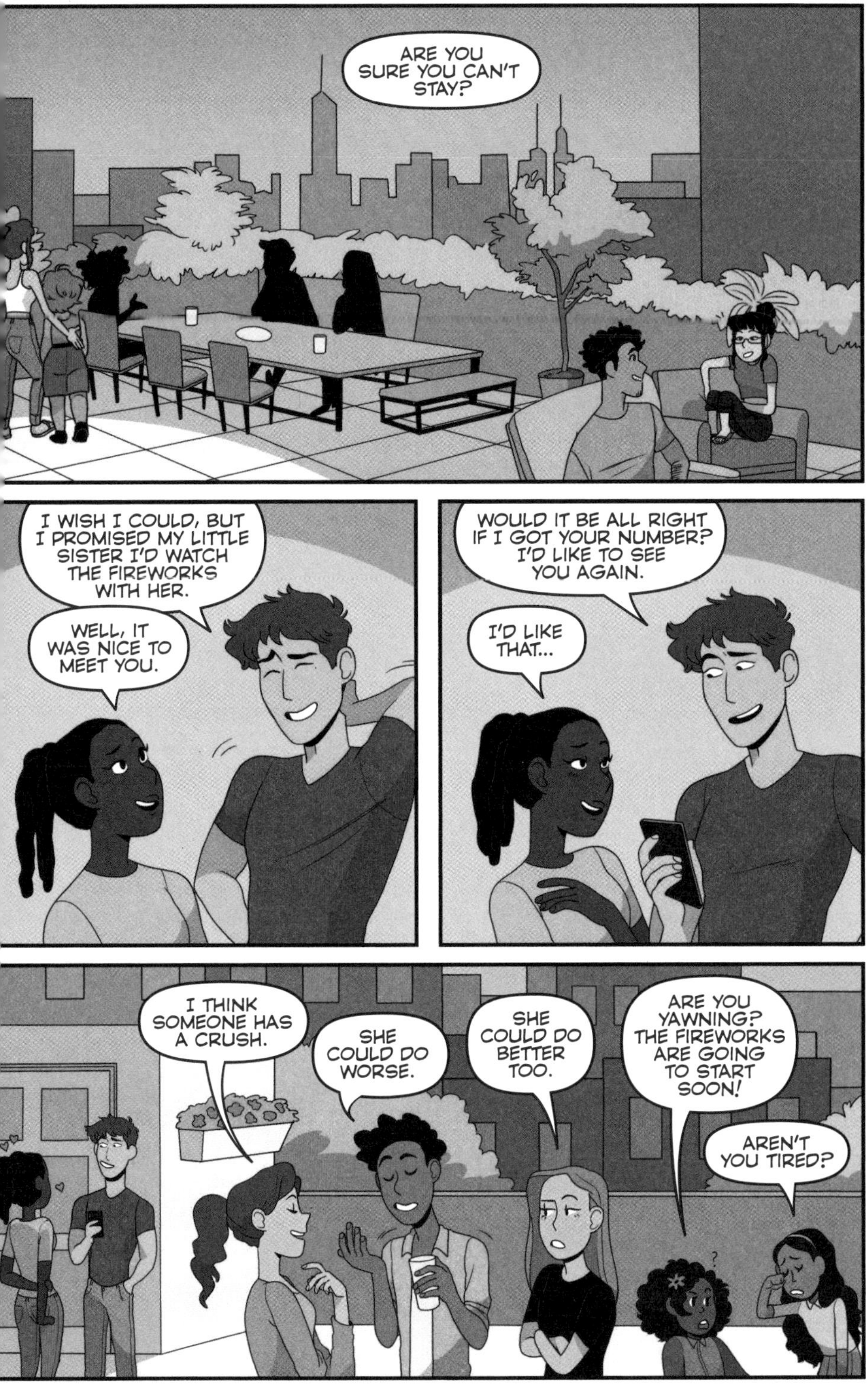
ARE YOU SURE YOU CAN'T STAY?
I WISH I COULD, BUT I PROMISED MY LITTLE SISTER I'D WATCH THE FIREWORKS WITH HER.
WELL, IT WAS NICE TO MEET YOU.
WOULD IT BE ALL RIGHT IF I GOT YOUR NUMBER? I'D LIKE TO SEE YOU AGAIN.
I'D LIKE THAT...
I THINK SOMEONE HAS A CRUSH.
SHE COULD DO WORSE.
SHE COULD DO BETTER TOO.
ARE YOU YAWNING? THE FIREWORKS ARE GOING TO START SOON!
AREN'T YOU TIRED?

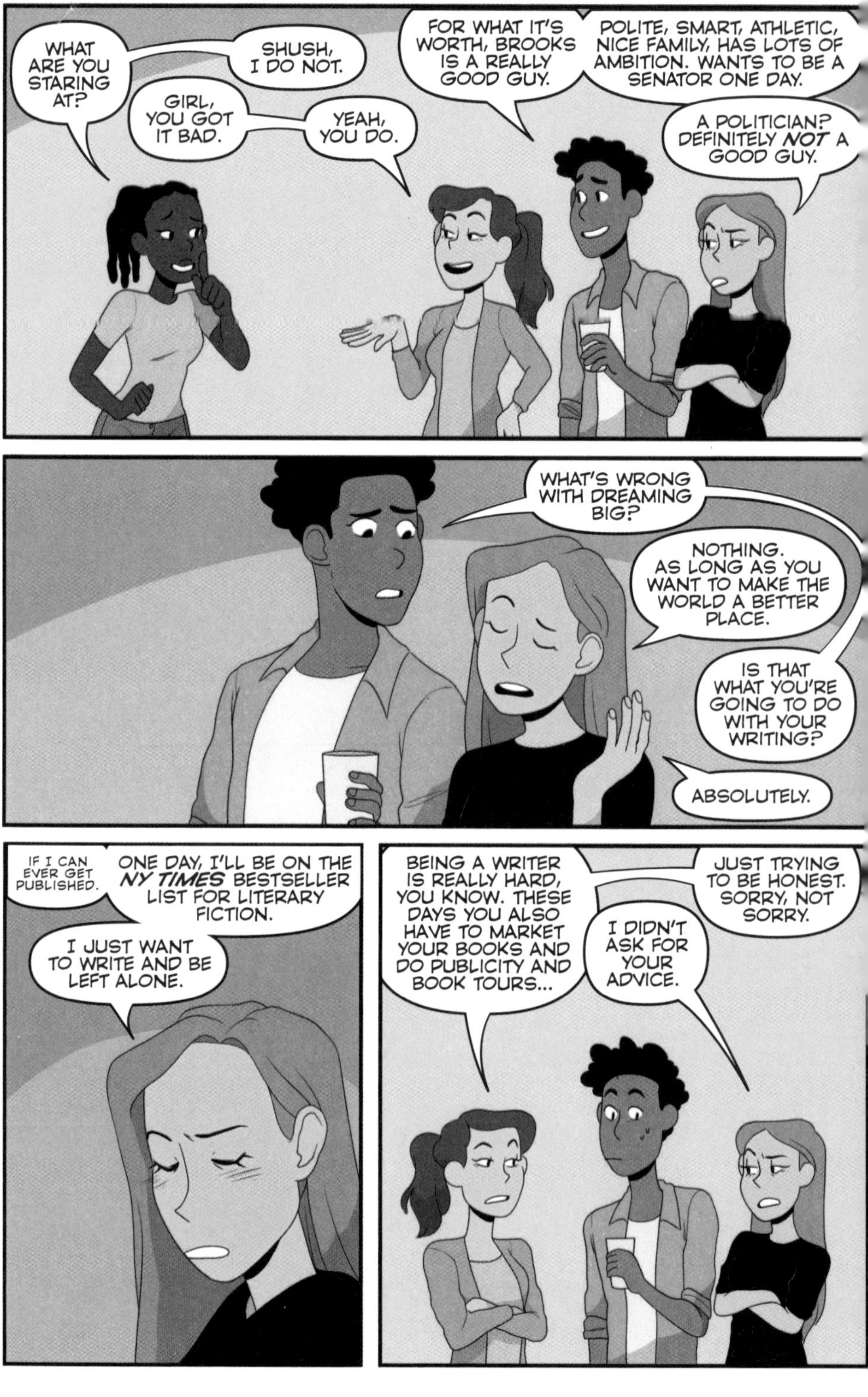
WHAT ARE YOU STARING AT?
SHUSH, I DO NOT.
GIRL, YOU GOT IT BAD.
YEAH, YOU DO.
FOR WHAT IT'S WORTH, BROOKS IS A REALLY GOOD GUY.
POLITE, SMART, ATHLETIC, NICE FAMILY, HAS LOTS OF AMBITION. WANTS TO BE A SENATOR ONE DAY.
A POLITICIAN? DEFINITELY NOT A GOOD GUY.
WHAT'S WRONG WITH DREAMING BIG?
NOTHING. AS LONG AS YOU WANT TO MAKE THE WORLD A BETTER PLACE.
IS THAT WHAT YOU'RE GOING TO DO WITH YOUR WRITING?
ABSOLUTELY.
ONE DAY, I'LL BE ON THE NY TIMES BESTSELLER LIST FOR LITERARY FICTION.
IF I CAN EVER GET PUBLISHED.
I JUST WANT TO WRITE AND BE LEFT ALONE.
BEING A WRITER IS REALLY HARD, YOU KNOW. THESE DAYS YOU ALSO HAVE TO MARKET YOUR BOOKS AND DO PUBLICITY AND BOOK TOURS...
I DIDN'T ASK FOR YOUR ADVICE.
JUST TRYING TO BE HONEST. SORRY, NOT SORRY.

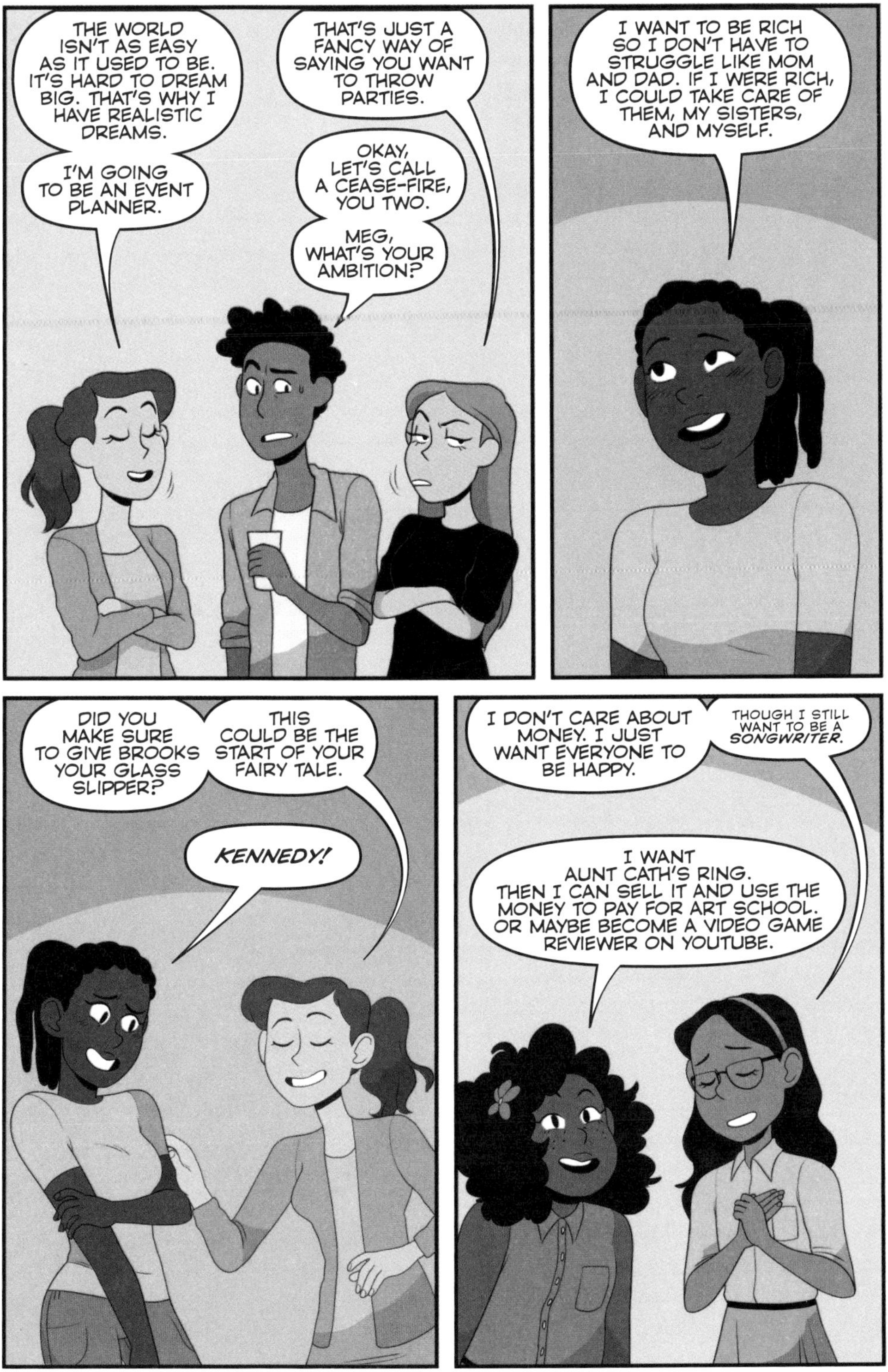
THE WORLD ISN'T AS EASY AS IT USED TO BE. IT'S HARD TO DREAM BIG. THAT'S WHY I HAVE REALISTIC DREAMS.
I'M GOING TO BE AN EVENT PLANNER.
THAT'S JUST A FANCY WAY OF SAYING YOU WANT TO THROW PARTIES.
OKAY, LET'S CALL A CEASE-FIRE, YOU TWO.
MEG, WHAT'S YOUR AMBITION?
I WANT TO BE RICH SO I DON'T HAVE TO STRUGGLE LIKE MOM AND DAD. IF I WERE RICH, I COULD TAKE CARE OF THEM, MY SISTERS, AND MYSELF.
DID YOU MAKE SURE TO GIVE BROOKS YOUR GLASS SLIPPER?
THIS COULD BE THE START OF YOUR FAIRY TALE.
KENNEDY!
I DON'T CARE ABOUT MONEY. I JUST WANT EVERYONE TO BE HAPPY.
THOUGH I STILL WANT TO BE A SONGWRITER.
I WANT AUNT CATH'S RING. THEN I CAN SELL IT AND USE THE MONEY TO PAY FOR ART SCHOOL. OR MAYBE BECOME A VIDEO GAME REVIEWER ON YOUTUBE.

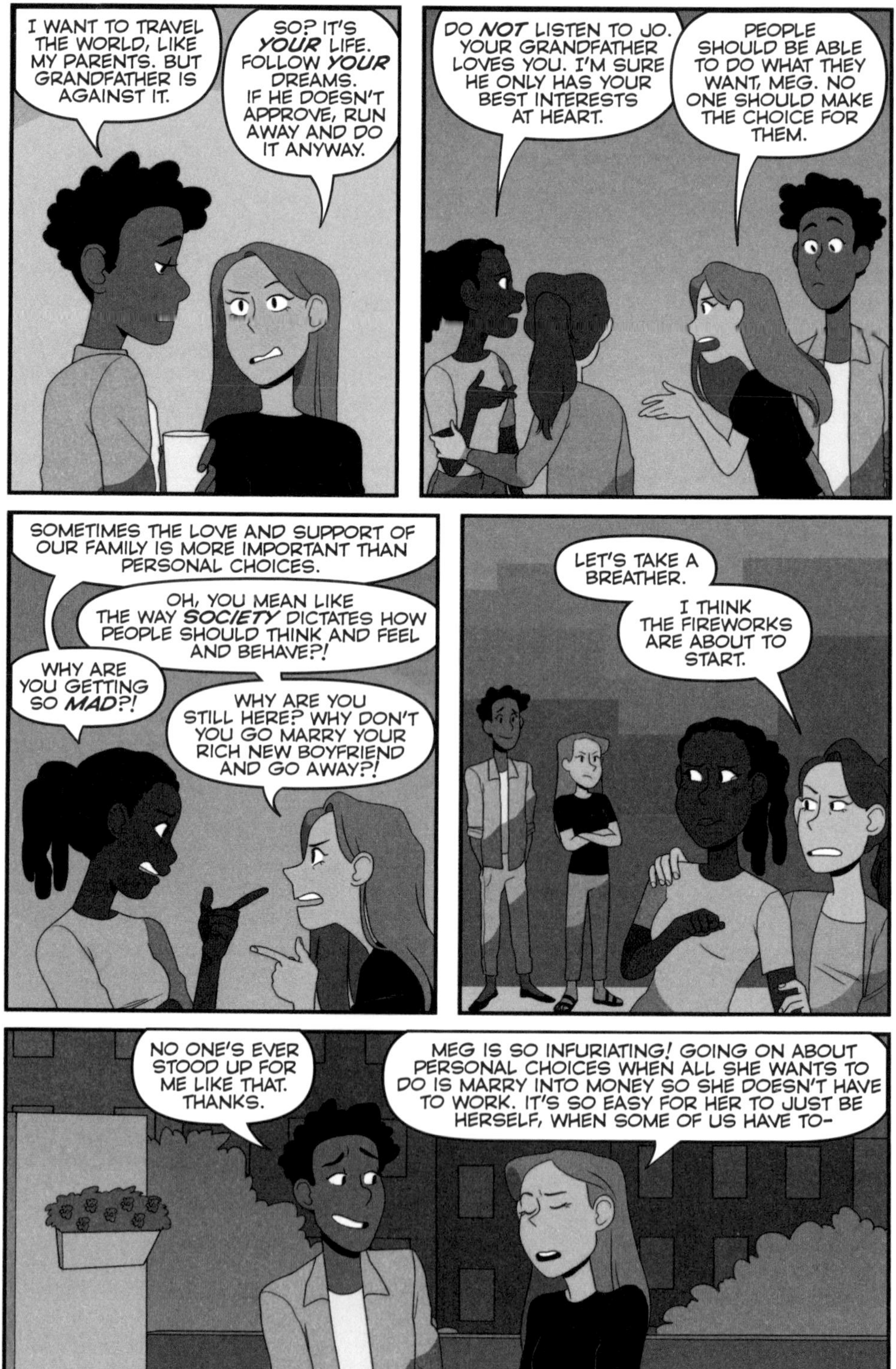
I WANT TO TRAVEL THE WORLD, LIKE MY PARENTS. BUT GRANDFATHER IS AGAINST IT.
SO? IT'S *YOUR* LIFE. FOLLOW *YOUR* DREAMS. IF HE DOESN'T APPROVE, RUN AWAY AND DO IT ANYWAY.
DO *NOT* LISTEN TO JO. YOUR GRANDFATHER LOVES YOU. I'M SURE HE ONLY HAS YOUR BEST INTERESTS AT HEART.
PEOPLE SHOULD BE ABLE TO DO WHAT THEY WANT, MEG. NO ONE SHOULD MAKE THE CHOICE FOR THEM.
SOMETIMES THE LOVE AND SUPPORT OF OUR FAMILY IS MORE IMPORTANT THAN PERSONAL CHOICES.
OH, YOU MEAN LIKE THE WAY *SOCIETY* DICTATES HOW PEOPLE SHOULD THINK AND FEEL AND BEHAVE?!
WHY ARE YOU GETTING SO *MAD*?!
WHY ARE YOU STILL HERE? WHY DON'T YOU GO MARRY YOUR RICH NEW BOYFRIEND AND GO AWAY?!
LET'S TAKE A BREATHER.
I THINK THE FIREWORKS ARE ABOUT TO START.
NO ONE'S EVER STOOD UP FOR ME LIKE THAT. THANKS.
MEG IS SO INFURIATING! GOING ON ABOUT PERSONAL CHOICES WHEN ALL SHE WANTS TO DO IS MARRY INTO MONEY SO SHE DOESN'T HAVE TO WORK. IT'S SO EASY FOR HER TO JUST BE HERSELF, WHEN SOME OF US HAVE TO-

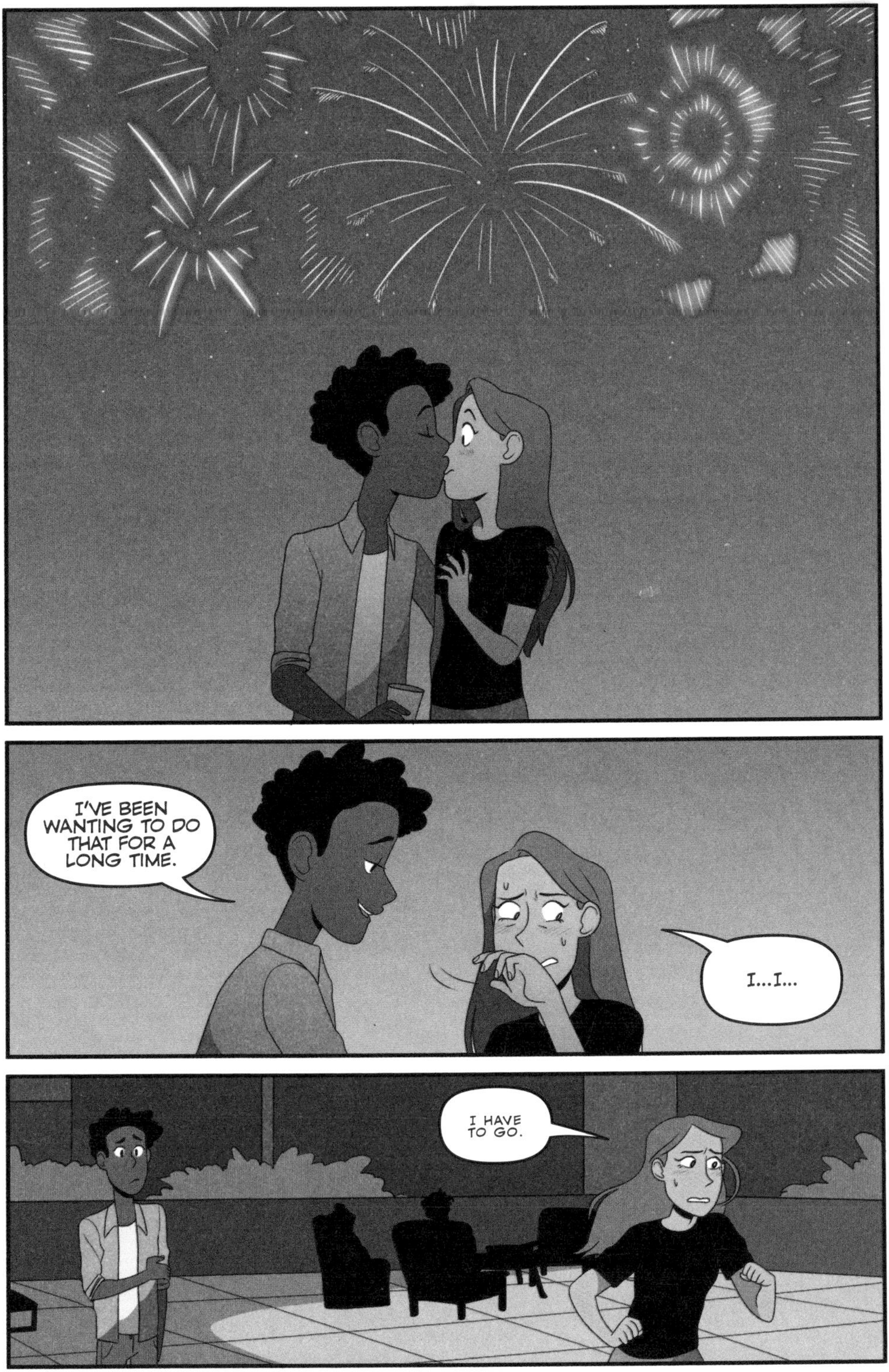
I'VE BEEN WANTING TO DO THAT FOR A LONG TIME.
I...I...
I HAVE TO GO.

July 4

Laurie has ruined everything! I'm so upset, and I don't know what to do. I think I've just lost my best friend. Okay, deep breaths, like Mom says. Writing will calm me down. Let me start at the beginning...

Today began so perfectly. We Skyped with Dad, and each of us got to speak with him for as long as we wanted. Then Mom and Mr. Marquez and our neighbors had a block party to celebrate the 4th of July. Mr. Chang cooked all day at the grill so people could have as many burgers and hot dogs as they wanted. The Rodriguez family made homemade tamales and seven-layer bean dip. And Mr. Bernstein even brought out a karaoke machine. We ate and we sang and we laughed and we danced, and everything was just so perfect...

Then we all went to the roof to watch the fireworks. We were having a great time until we started talking about our futures. Meg got all preachy and started talking about family and doing what they want us to. Okay, so that's not exactly what she said, but that's what I heard, because...well, you know. Of course, rather than deal with my own stuff, I started screaming at Meg. I just got so mad, because I can't be me...the real me. I know... real mature, right?

Meanwhile, Laurie thought I was sticking up for him. Telling him he should live his own life and not care what his family thinks. Me and my stupid mouth...I wish I could take my own advice. I'm such a hypocrite. So yeah, that's when Laurie had to go and kiss me!

That kiss could destroy our friendship. What was he thinking?!
Why did he have to kiss me? Why couldn't he have kissed Meg?
Or someone who wanted it? Instead, he had to go and kiss me.
And what did I do? I ran away! Of course I ran away. He's one
of my closest friends—my best friend (if I don't count Meg).
I don't want to lose that. And now how am I supposed to face
him?!

I just don't know why he would do that. I certainly didn't lead him
to the conclusion that that's what I wanted. I don't flirt. I don't
dress like a girl. I don't even let him open doors for me. Maybe it's
true what they say: Guys only want what they can't have.

Ugh. Maybe I am to blame. After all, I'm the one keeping
secrets. Not just from my family and friends, but from myself.
I know who and what I really am, but I'm not ready to face it.
So what I viewed as a friendship, maybe Laurie assumed was
something more. I wish I could go along with it. After all, Laurie
would be a wonderful partner. He's lovely and funny and smart
and we both like to read. But for me, the magic spark just isn't
there, not like the chemistry I feel when...

God. I am such a coward. I can't even write it. It's like being
afraid of my own shadow. But this is the world we live in, one in
which not all men and women are created equal. People are still
prejudiced against others, whether for the color of their skin,
the shape of their bodies, the beliefs in their gods, or the love in
their hearts. Why can't everyone just accept everyone for who
they are?

I want to tell Laurie the truth, but I'm scared to, just like I'm
scared to tell my family. Maybe one day...but not today.

CHAPTER 12

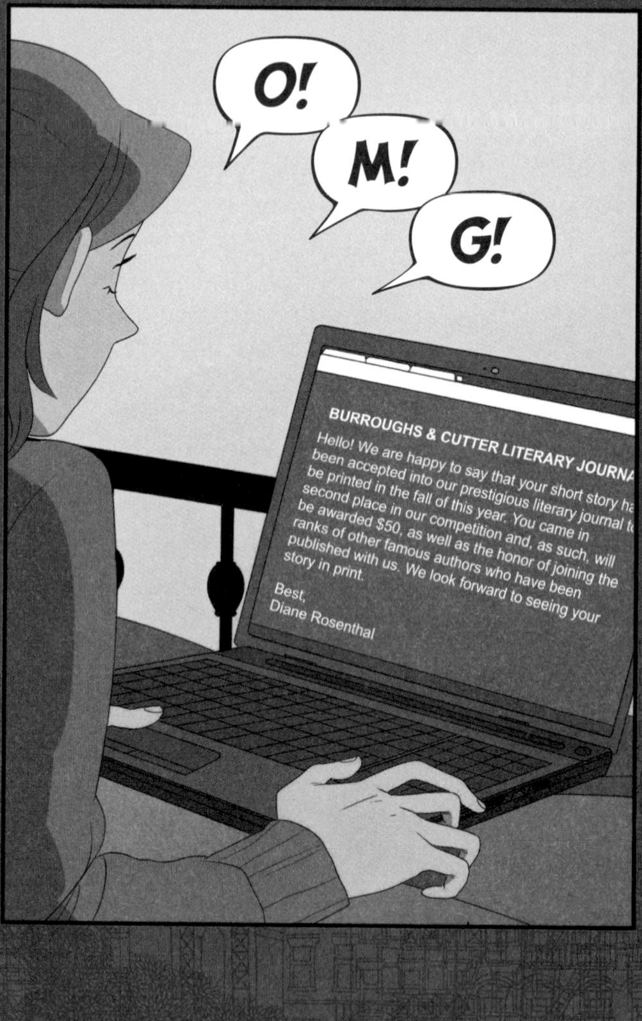
O!
M!
G!
BURROUGHS & CUTTER LITERARY JOURNA
Hello! We are happy to say that your short story ha
been accepted into our prestigious literary journal t
be printed in the fall of this year. You came in
second place in our competition and, as such, will
be awarded $50, as well as the honor of joining the
ranks of other famous authors who have been
published with us. We look forward to seeing your
story in print.
Best,
Diane Rosenthal

Good News, Bad News...

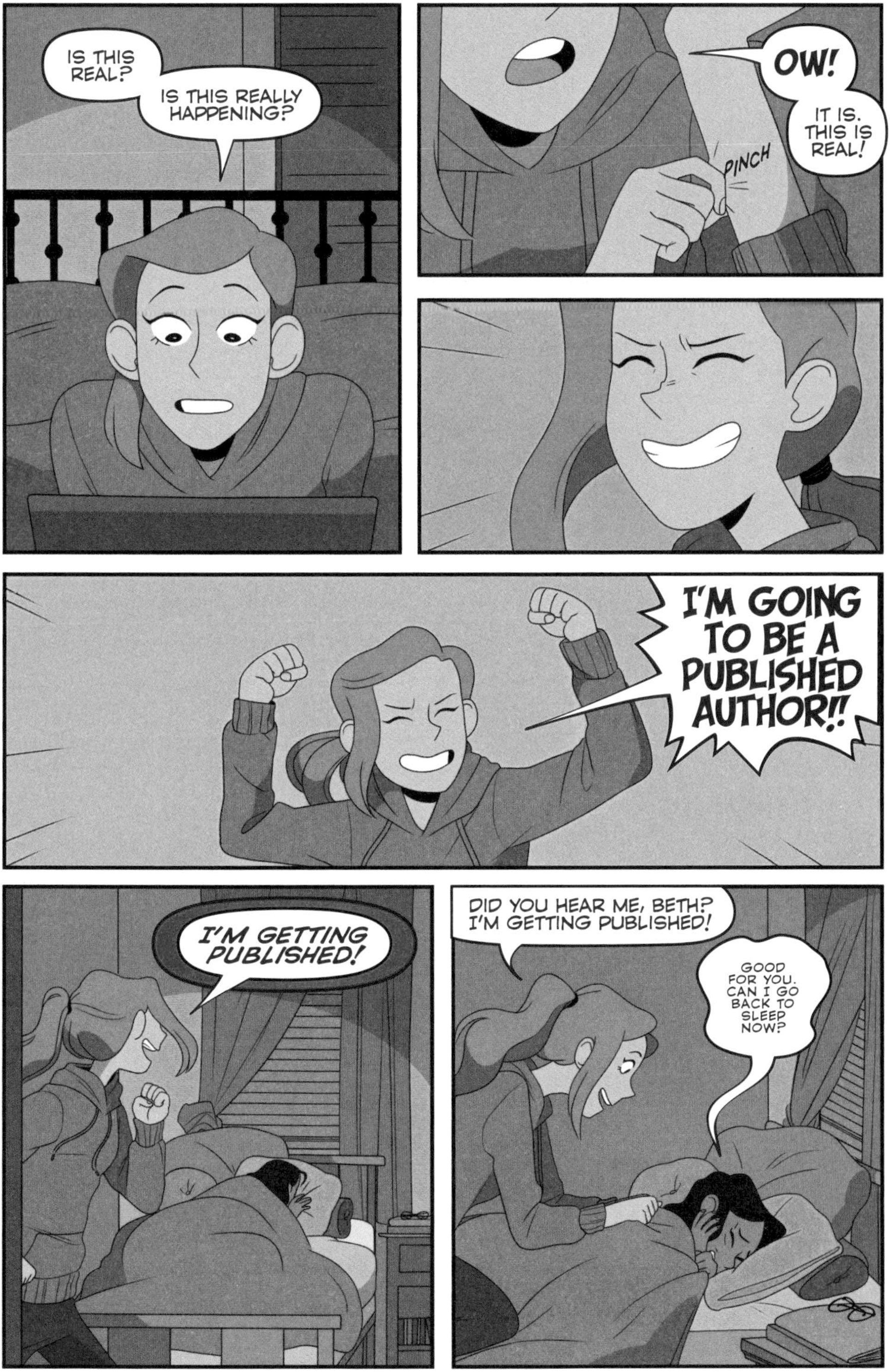
IS THIS REAL?
IS THIS REALLY HAPPENING?
OW!
IT IS. THIS IS REAL!
PINCH
I'M GOING TO BE A PUBLISHED AUTHOR!!
I'M GETTING PUBLISHED!
DID YOU HEAR ME, BETH? I'M GETTING PUBLISHED!
GOOD FOR YOU. CAN I GO BACK TO SLEEP NOW?

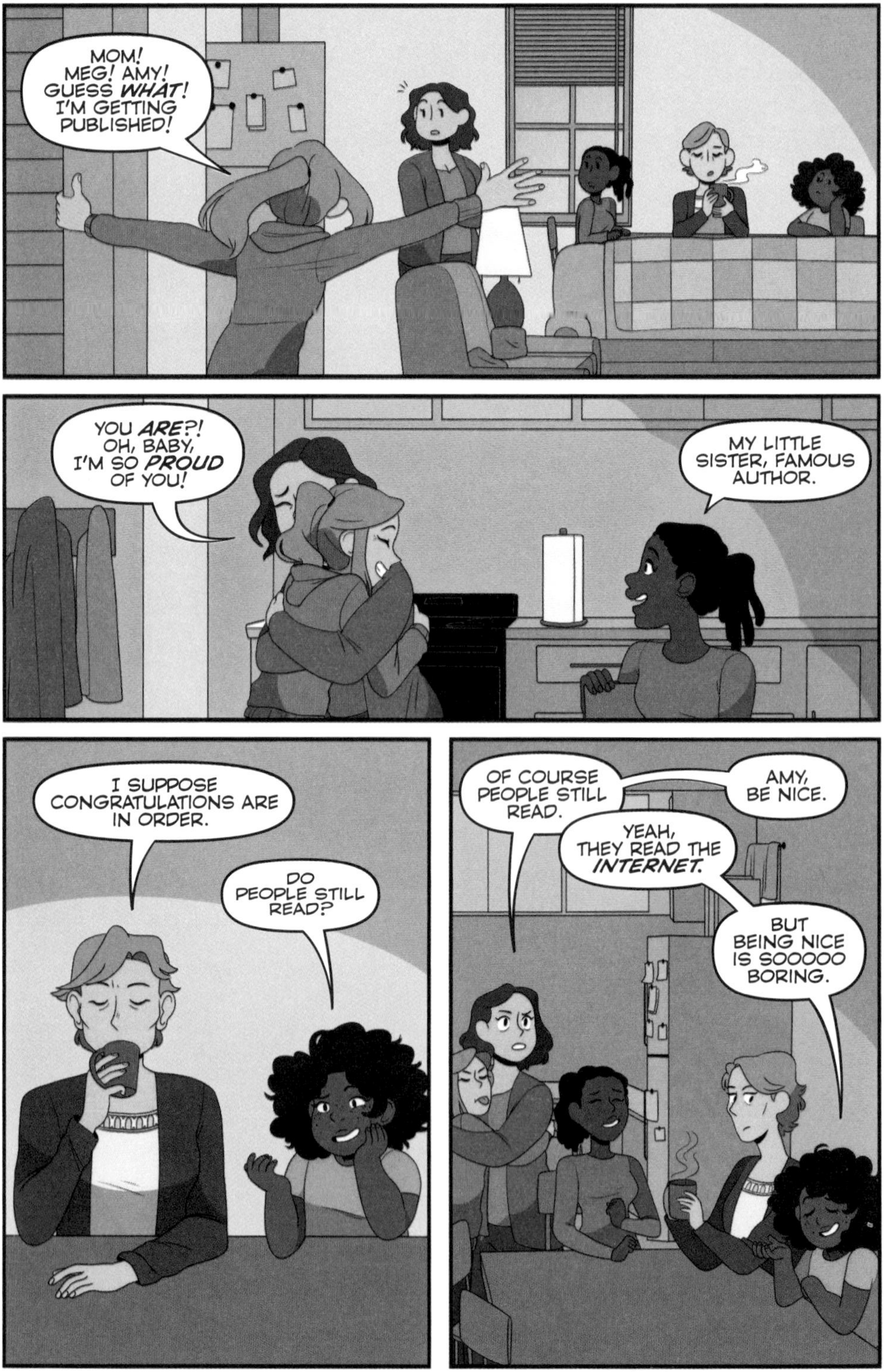
MOM! MEG! AMY! GUESS *WHAT*! I'M GETTING PUBLISHED!
YOU *ARE*?! OH, BABY, I'M SO *PROUD* OF YOU!
MY LITTLE SISTER, FAMOUS AUTHOR.
I SUPPOSE CONGRATULATIONS ARE IN ORDER.
DO PEOPLE STILL READ?
OF COURSE PEOPLE STILL READ.
AMY, BE NICE.
YEAH, THEY READ THE *INTERNET.*
BUT BEING NICE IS SOOOOO BORING.

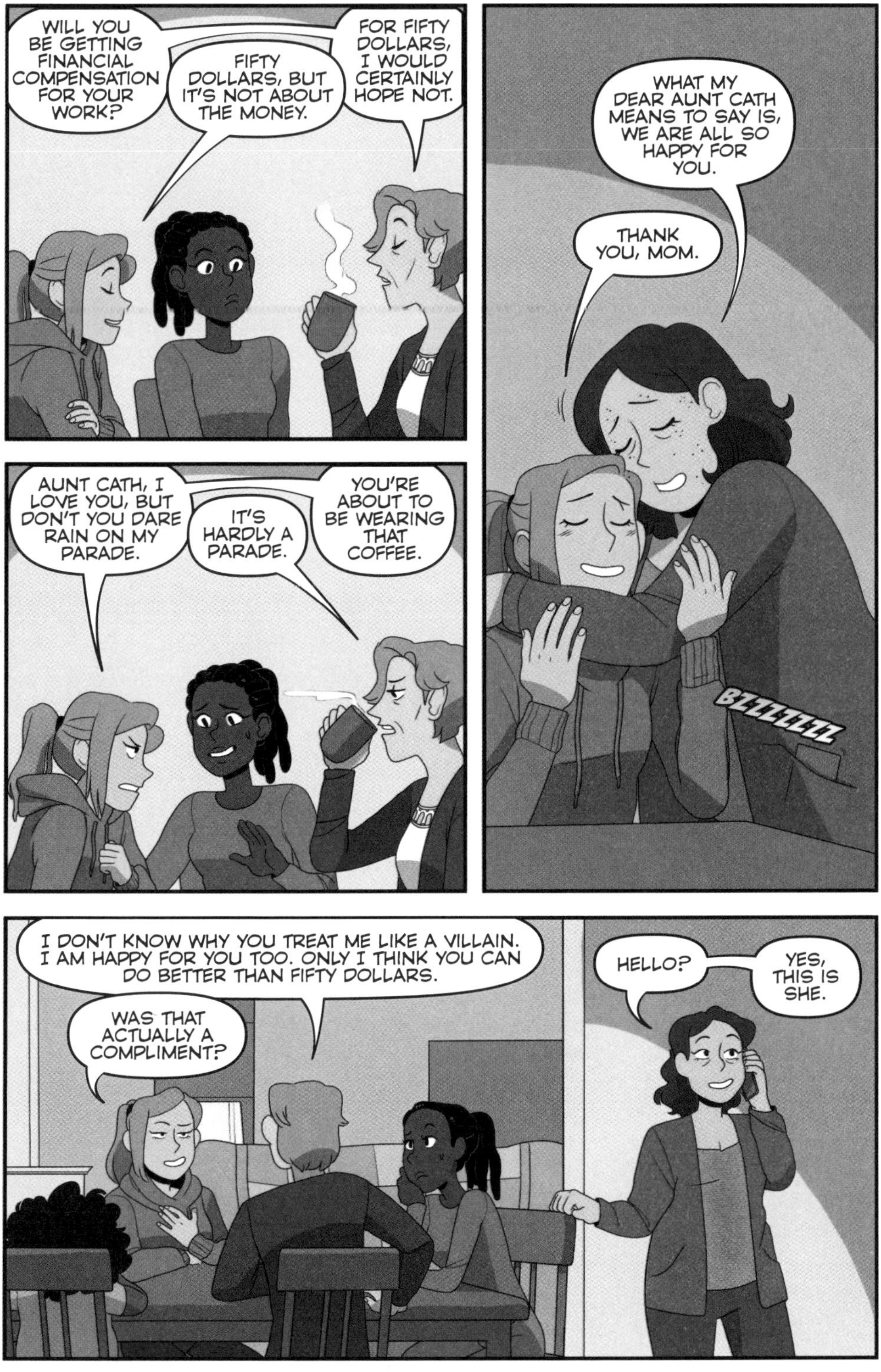
WILL YOU BE GETTING FINANCIAL COMPENSATION FOR YOUR WORK?
FIFTY DOLLARS, BUT IT'S NOT ABOUT THE MONEY.
FOR FIFTY DOLLARS, I WOULD CERTAINLY HOPE NOT.
AUNT CATH, I LOVE YOU, BUT DON'T YOU DARE RAIN ON MY PARADE.
IT'S HARDLY A PARADE.
YOU'RE ABOUT TO BE WEARING THAT COFFEE.
WHAT MY DEAR AUNT CATH MEANS TO SAY IS, WE ARE ALL SO HAPPY FOR YOU.
THANK YOU, MOM.
BZZZZZZZ
I DON'T KNOW WHY YOU TREAT ME LIKE A VILLAIN. I AM HAPPY FOR YOU TOO. ONLY I THINK YOU CAN DO BETTER THAN FIFTY DOLLARS.
WAS THAT ACTUALLY A COMPLIMENT?
HELLO?
YES, THIS IS SHE.

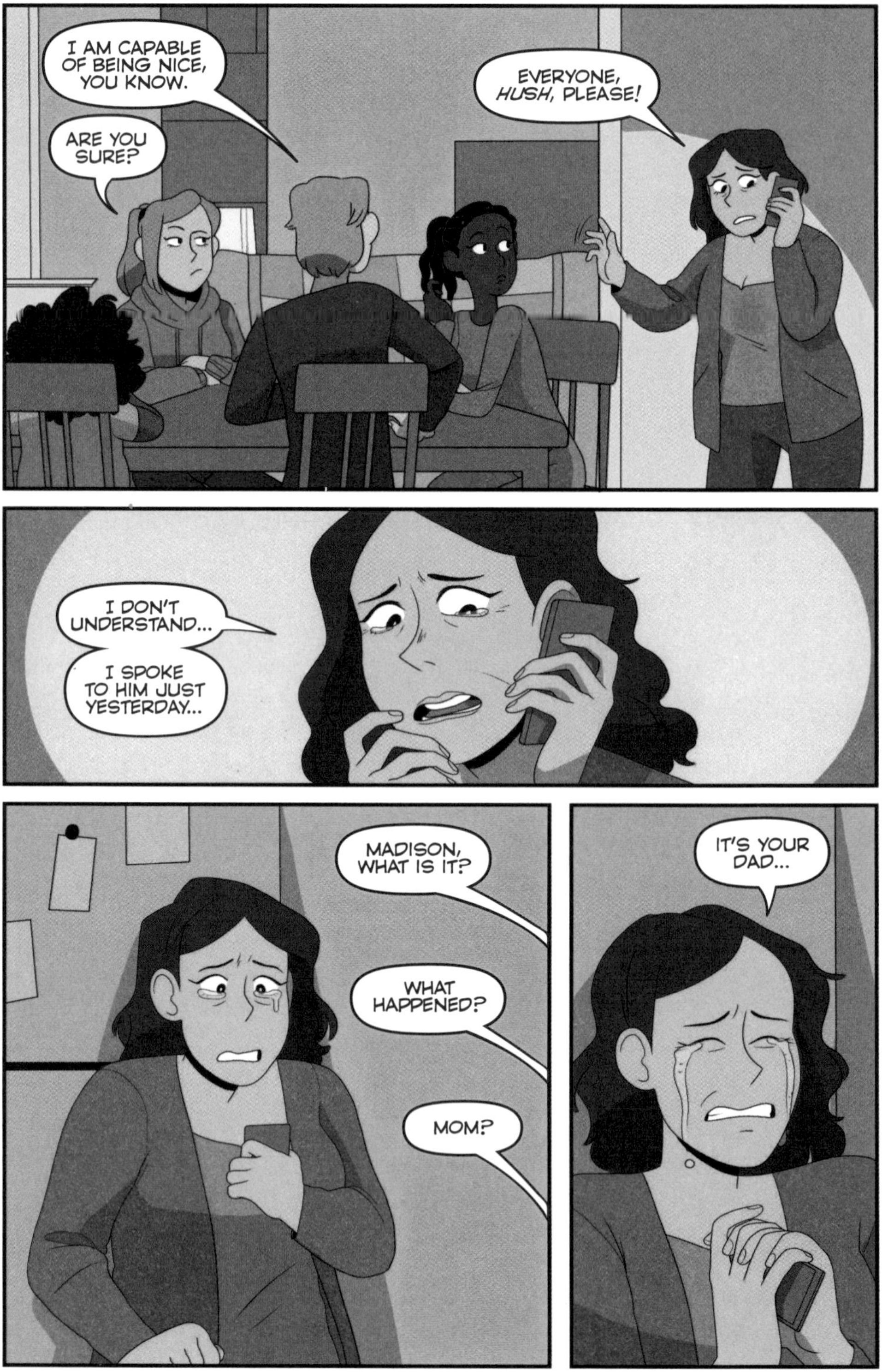
I AM CAPABLE OF BEING NICE, YOU KNOW.
ARE YOU SURE?
EVERYONE, *HUSH*, PLEASE!
I DON'T UNDERSTAND...
I SPOKE TO HIM JUST YESTERDAY...
MADISON, WHAT IS IT?
WHAT HAPPENED?
MOM?
IT'S YOUR DAD...

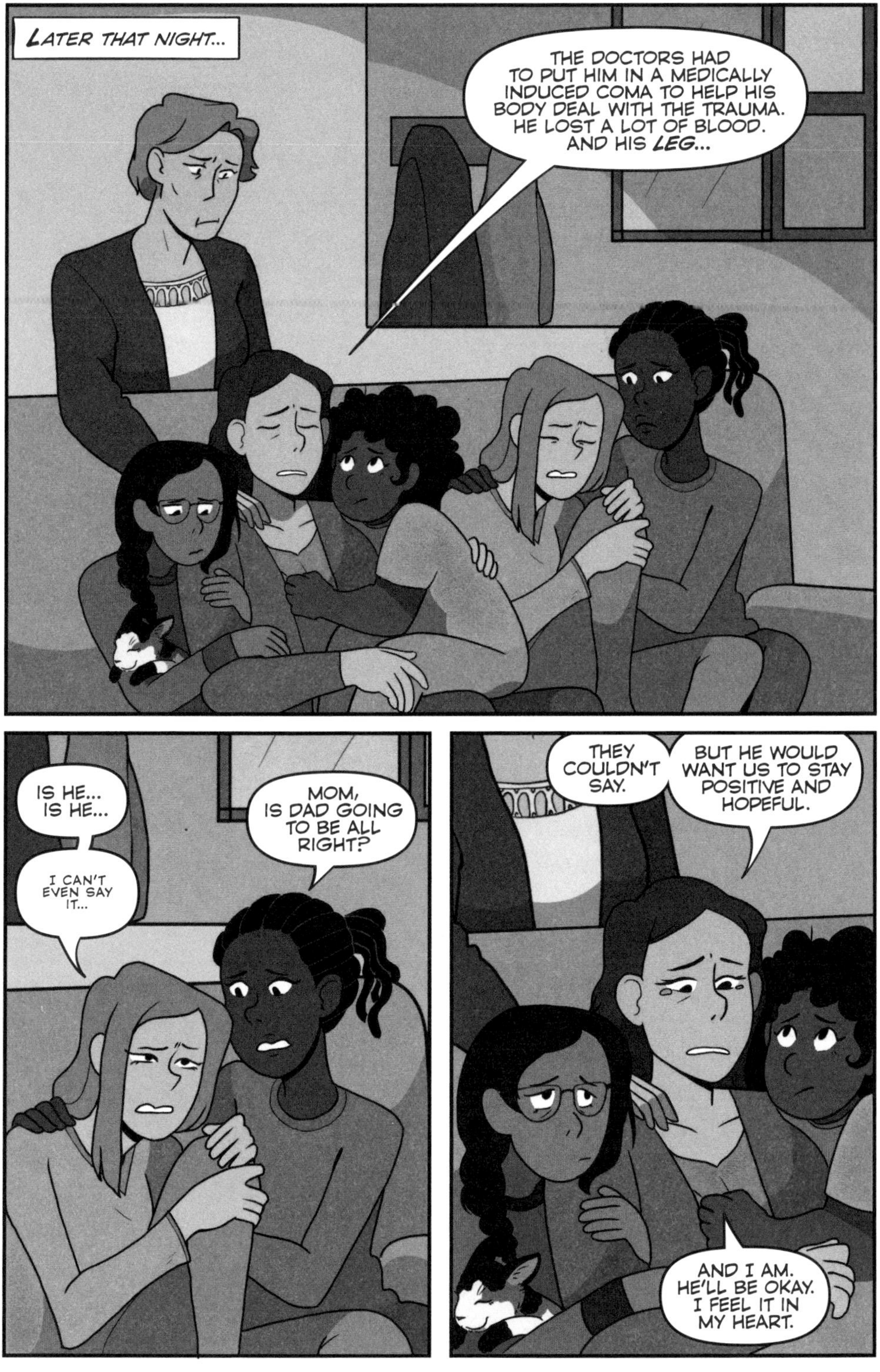
LATER THAT NIGHT...
THE DOCTORS HAD TO PUT HIM IN A MEDICALLY INDUCED COMA TO HELP HIS BODY DEAL WITH THE TRAUMA. HE LOST A LOT OF BLOOD. AND HIS LEG...
IS HE... IS HE...
I CAN'T EVEN SAY IT...
MOM, IS DAD GOING TO BE ALL RIGHT?
THEY COULDN'T SAY.
BUT HE WOULD WANT US TO STAY POSITIVE AND HOPEFUL.
AND I AM. HE'LL BE OKAY. I FEEL IT IN MY HEART.

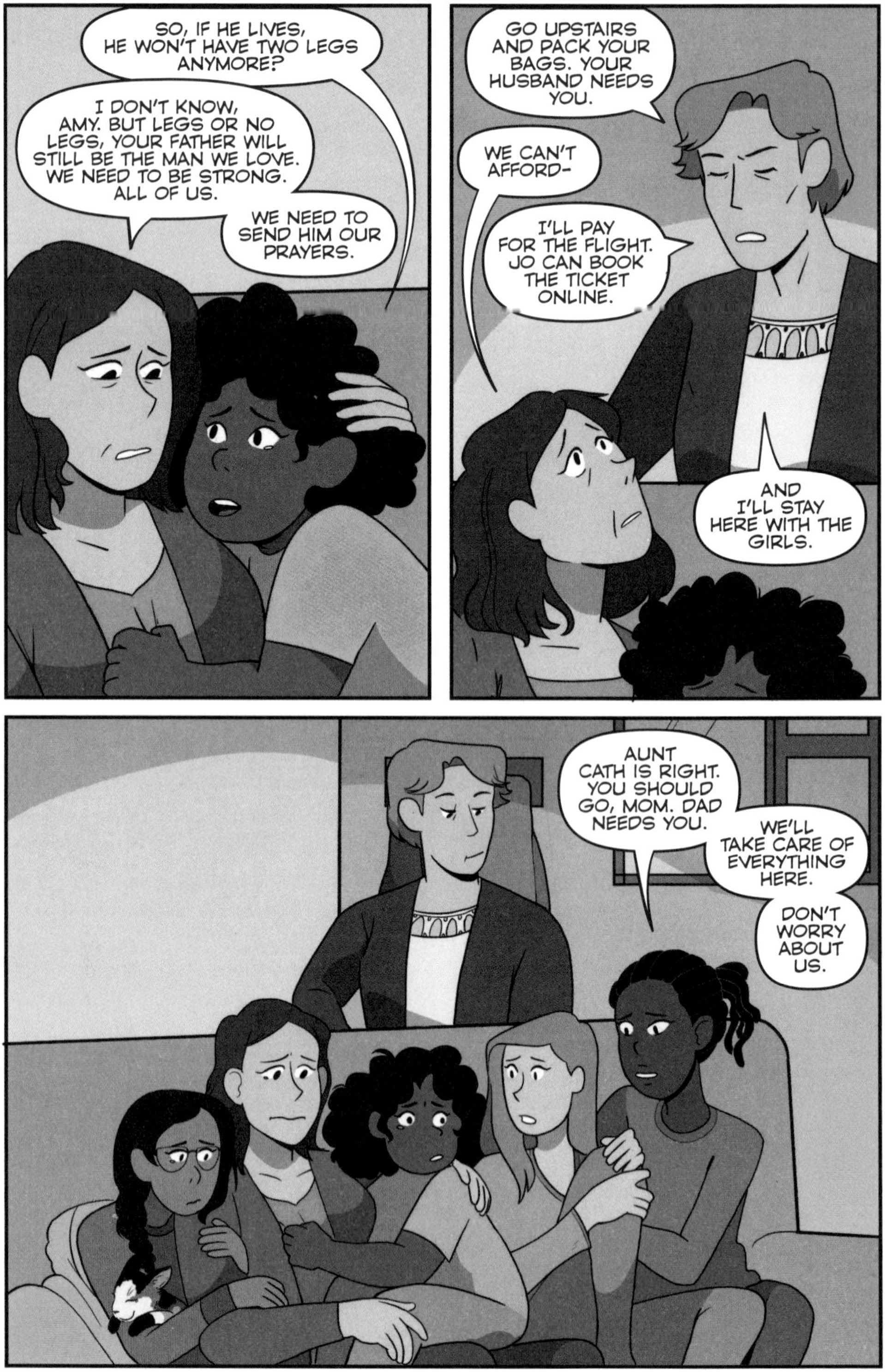
SO, IF HE LIVES, HE WON'T HAVE TWO LEGS ANYMORE?
I DON'T KNOW, AMY. BUT LEGS OR NO LEGS, YOUR FATHER WILL STILL BE THE MAN WE LOVE. WE NEED TO BE STRONG. ALL OF US.
WE NEED TO SEND HIM OUR PRAYERS.
GO UPSTAIRS AND PACK YOUR BAGS. YOUR HUSBAND NEEDS YOU.
WE CAN'T AFFORD-
I'LL PAY FOR THE FLIGHT. JO CAN BOOK THE TICKET ONLINE.
AND I'LL STAY HERE WITH THE GIRLS.
AUNT CATH IS RIGHT. YOU SHOULD GO, MOM. DAD NEEDS YOU.
WE'LL TAKE CARE OF EVERYTHING HERE.
DON'T WORRY ABOUT US.

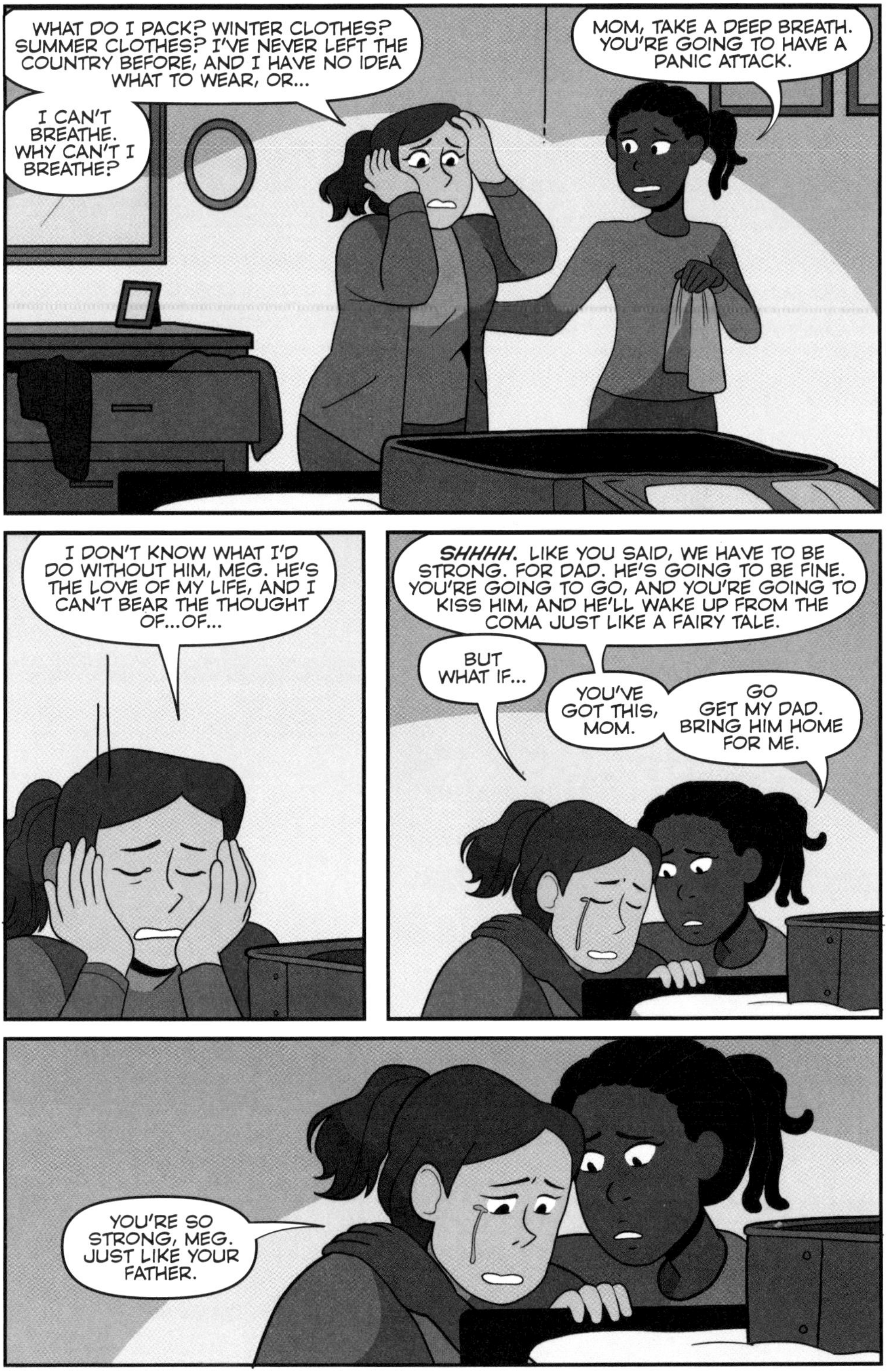
WHAT DO I PACK? WINTER CLOTHES? SUMMER CLOTHES? I'VE NEVER LEFT THE COUNTRY BEFORE, AND I HAVE NO IDEA WHAT TO WEAR, OR...
I CAN'T BREATHE. WHY CAN'T I BREATHE?
MOM, TAKE A DEEP BREATH. YOU'RE GOING TO HAVE A PANIC ATTACK.
I DON'T KNOW WHAT I'D DO WITHOUT HIM, MEG. HE'S THE LOVE OF MY LIFE, AND I CAN'T BEAR THE THOUGHT OF...OF...
SHHHH. LIKE YOU SAID, WE HAVE TO BE STRONG. FOR DAD. HE'S GOING TO BE FINE. YOU'RE GOING TO GO, AND YOU'RE GOING TO KISS HIM, AND HE'LL WAKE UP FROM THE COMA JUST LIKE A FAIRY TALE.
BUT WHAT IF...
YOU'VE GOT THIS, MOM.
GO GET MY DAD. BRING HIM HOME FOR ME.
YOU'RE SO STRONG, MEG. JUST LIKE YOUR FATHER.

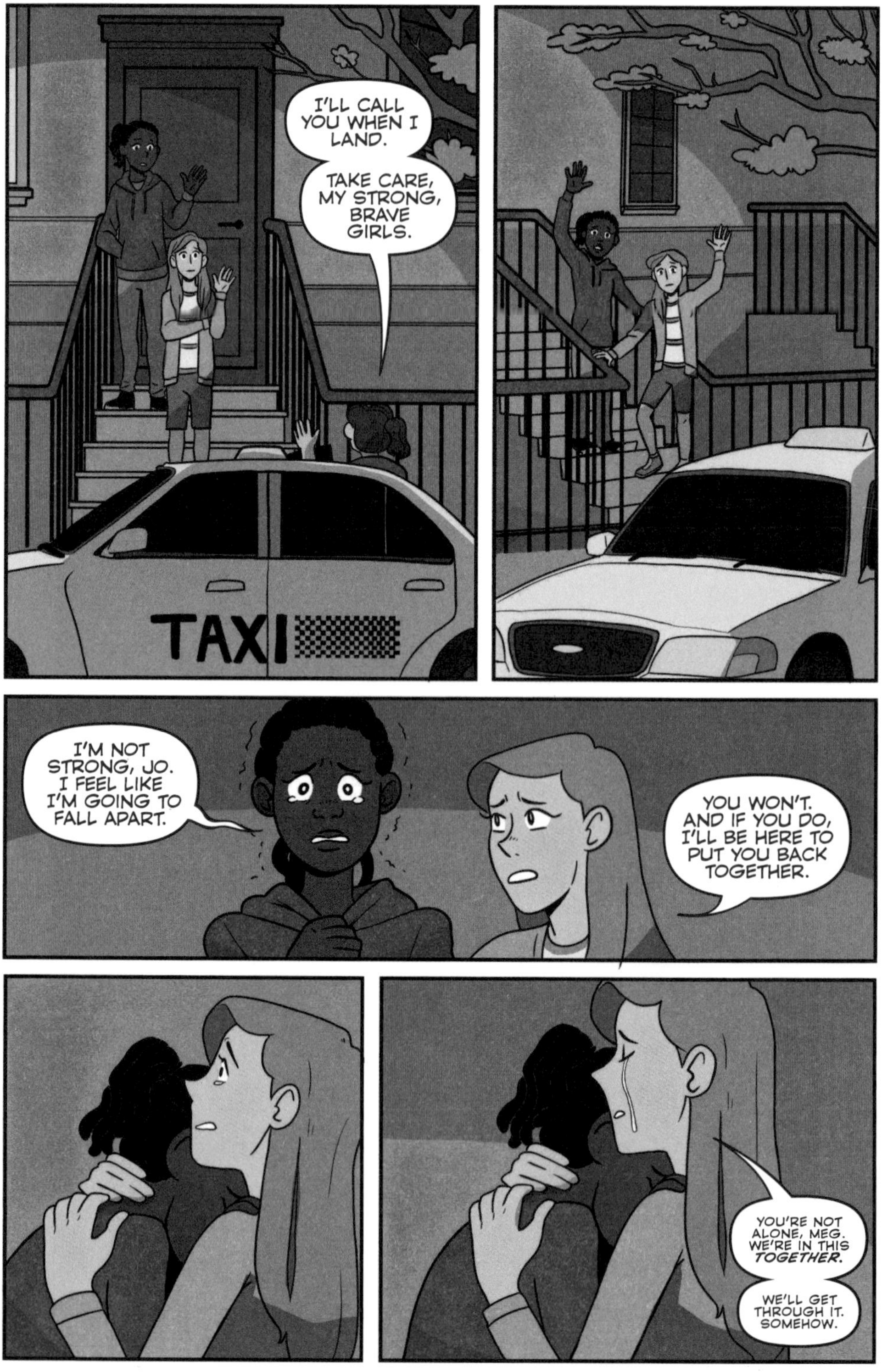
I'LL CALL YOU WHEN I LAND.
TAKE CARE, MY STRONG, BRAVE GIRLS.
TAXI
I'M NOT STRONG, JO. I FEEL LIKE I'M GOING TO FALL APART.
YOU WON'T. AND IF YOU DO, I'LL BE HERE TO PUT YOU BACK TOGETHER.
YOU'RE NOT ALONE, MEG. WE'RE IN THIS *TOGETHER*.
WE'LL GET THROUGH IT. SOMEHOW.

July 27

I feel so helpless. Jo said I should channel my
feelings. She suggested a punching bag or running,
but I hate exercise. So I thought I'd do what she does,
and write down what I'm feeling. Maybe it'll help.
It certainly couldn't make me feel worse. I've never felt
so horrible in my whole life.

Dad is hurt and on the other side of the world. Mom
says there was a stray blast, and he got caught in
it. The doctors wouldn't tell her how bad it was on
the phone, only that he lost one of his legs, and that
they're doing everything they can. They are moving
him from the Middle East to a hospital in Germany.
That's where Mom is heading right now.

I can't imagine what Dad must be going through. I'm
almost grateful he's in a coma. But does he feel pain?
Is he dreaming? Is he thinking of his family? Is he
going to be okay? I wish I could go be with him too.
All I want is to hold his hand and let him know
he'll get better. But will he?

I feel so lost. Like the whole world took a wrong turn. How could this happen to my dad? We all know military service is dangerous, but it didn't seem real until the phone rang and Mom collapsed. Then suddenly it was all too real. And there's nothing I can do. Why isn't there anything I can do?!

Maybe...maybe...I should ask myself, what would Dad do? What would he want me to do? That's easy. He'd want me to stay strong and take care of my sisters. So that's what I'll do. That's all I can do...

I love you, Daddy. Please come home.

Meg

CHAPTER 13

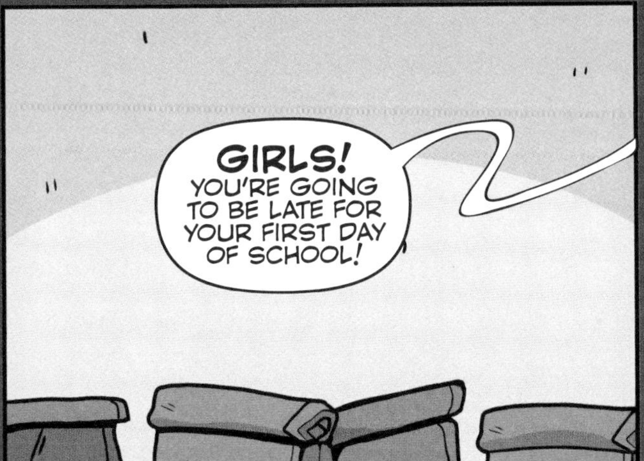
GIRLS! YOU'RE GOING TO BE LATE FOR YOUR FIRST DAY OF SCHOOL!
MEG
JO
BETH
AMY

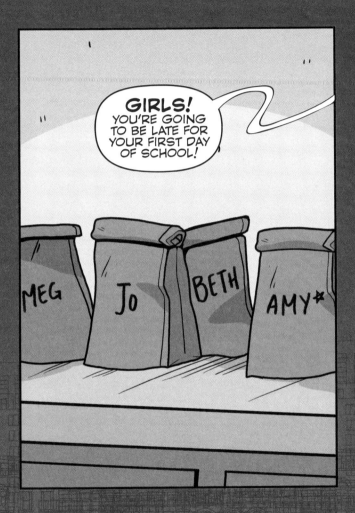

Words Across the World...

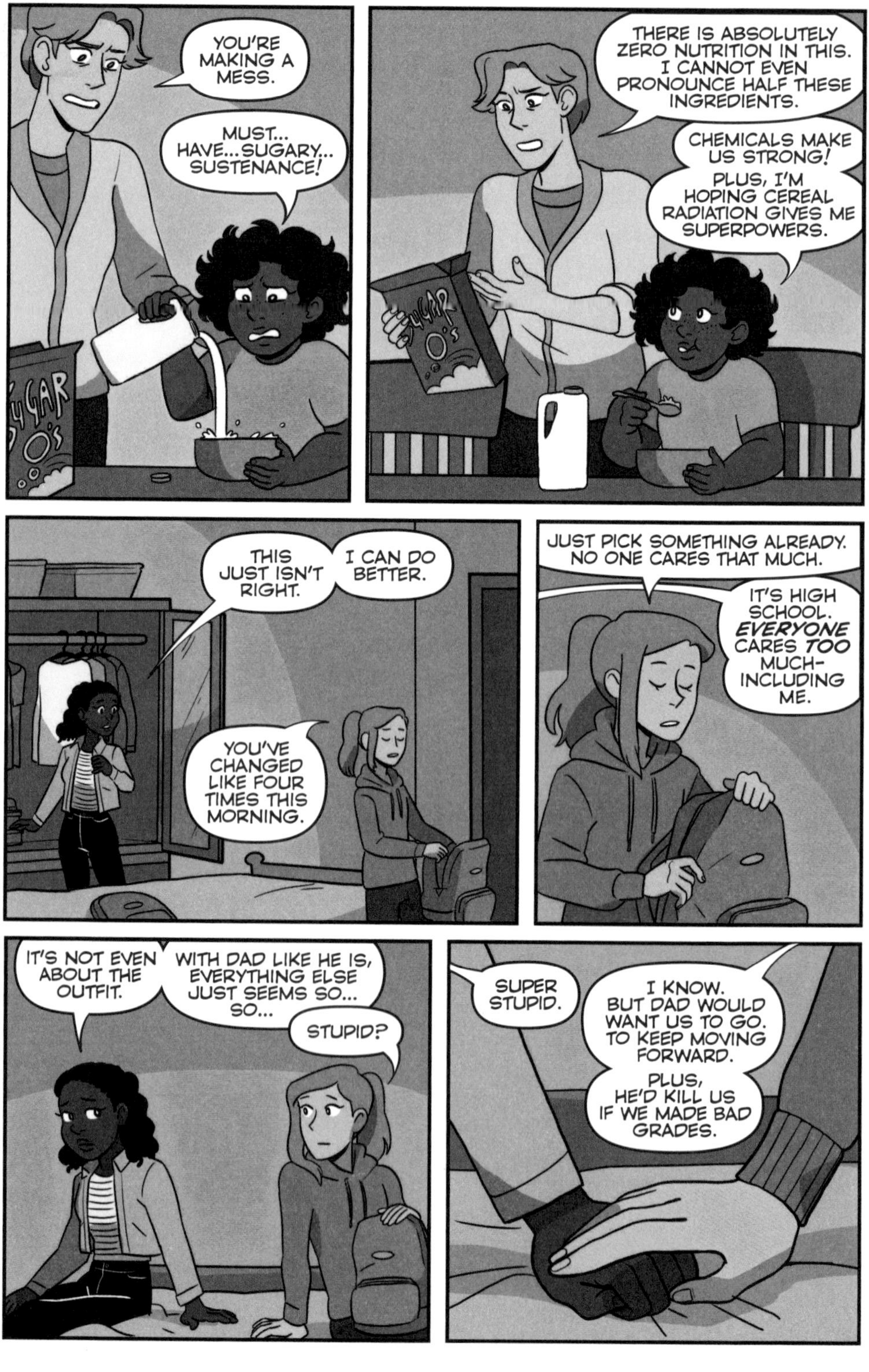
YOU'RE MAKING A MESS.
MUST... HAVE...SUGARY... SUSTENANCE!
SUGAR O's
THERE IS ABSOLUTELY ZERO NUTRITION IN THIS. I CANNOT EVEN PRONOUNCE HALF THESE INGREDIENTS.
CHEMICALS MAKE US STRONG!
PLUS, I'M HOPING CEREAL RADIATION GIVES ME SUPERPOWERS.
SUGAR O's
THIS JUST ISN'T RIGHT.
I CAN DO BETTER.
YOU'VE CHANGED LIKE FOUR TIMES THIS MORNING.
JUST PICK SOMETHING ALREADY. NO ONE CARES THAT MUCH.
IT'S HIGH SCHOOL. ***EVERYONE*** CARES ***TOO*** MUCH-INCLUDING ME.
IT'S NOT EVEN ABOUT THE OUTFIT.
WITH DAD LIKE HE IS, EVERYTHING ELSE JUST SEEMS SO... SO...
STUPID?
SUPER STUPID.
I KNOW. BUT DAD WOULD WANT US TO GO. TO KEEP MOVING FORWARD.
PLUS, HE'D KILL US IF WE MADE BAD GRADES.

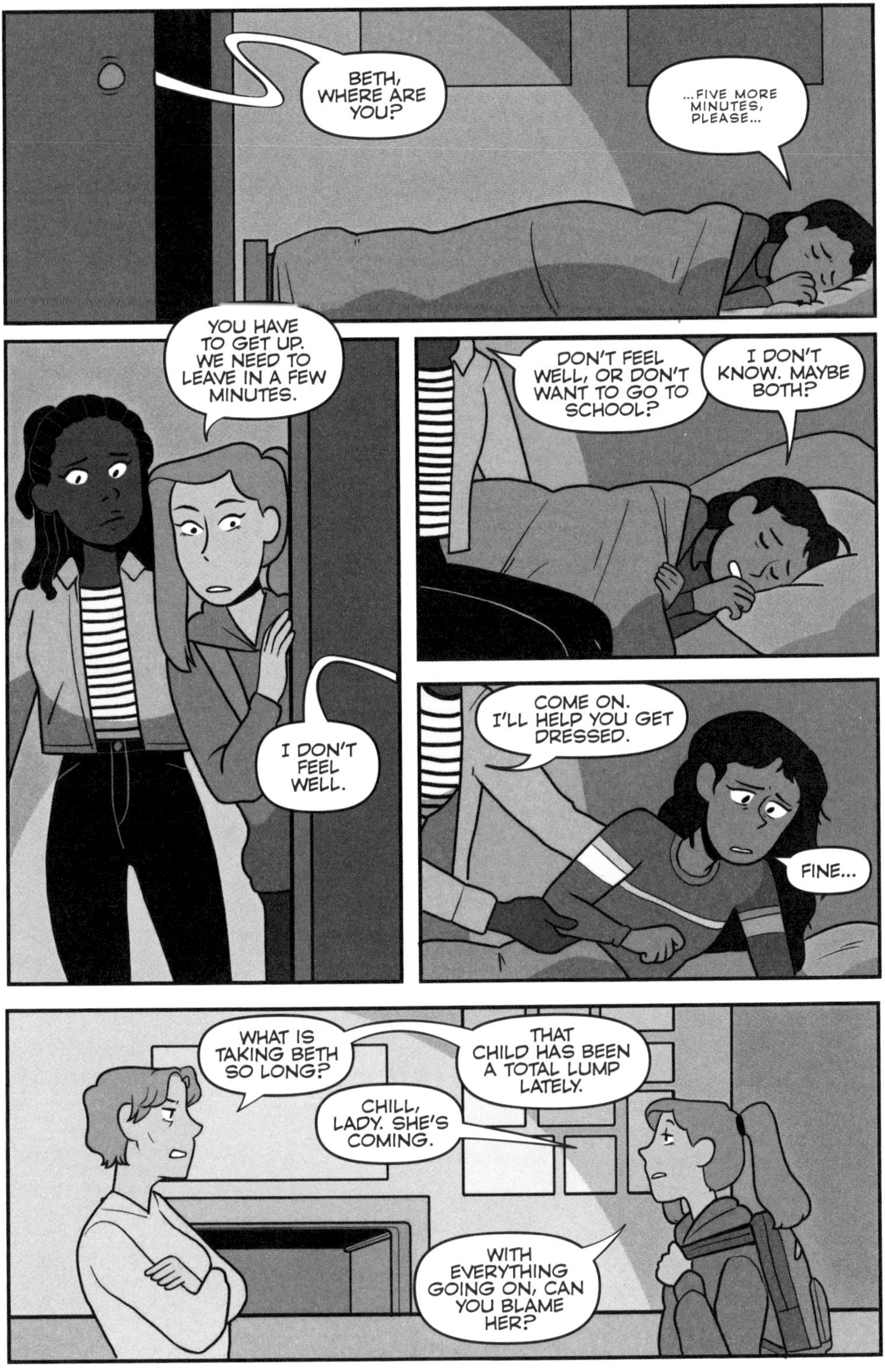
BETH, WHERE ARE YOU?
...FIVE MORE MINUTES, PLEASE...
YOU HAVE TO GET UP. WE NEED TO LEAVE IN A FEW MINUTES.
I DON'T FEEL WELL.
DON'T FEEL WELL, OR DON'T WANT TO GO TO SCHOOL?
I DON'T KNOW. MAYBE BOTH?
COME ON. I'LL HELP YOU GET DRESSED.
FINE...
WHAT IS TAKING BETH SO LONG?
THAT CHILD HAS BEEN A TOTAL LUMP LATELY.
CHILL, LADY. SHE'S COMING.
WITH EVERYTHING GOING ON, CAN YOU BLAME HER?

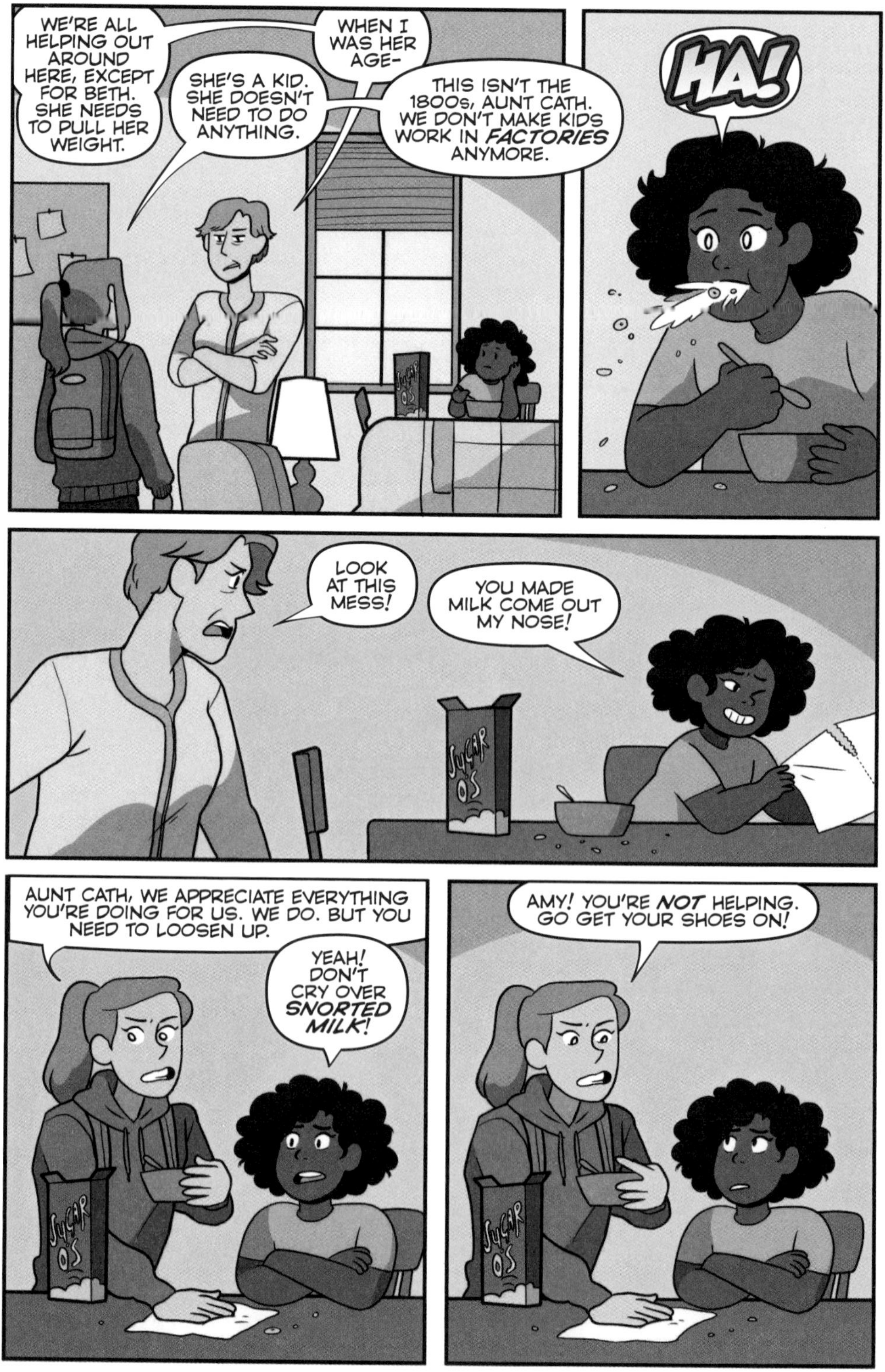
WE'RE ALL HELPING OUT AROUND HERE, EXCEPT FOR BETH. SHE NEEDS TO PULL HER WEIGHT.
WHEN I WAS HER AGE-
SHE'S A KID. SHE DOESN'T NEED TO DO ANYTHING.
THIS ISN'T THE 1800s, AUNT CATH. WE DON'T MAKE KIDS WORK IN ***FACTORIES*** ANYMORE.
SUGAR O'S
HA!
LOOK AT THIS MESS!
YOU MADE MILK COME OUT MY NOSE!
SUGAR O'S
AUNT CATH, WE APPRECIATE EVERYTHING YOU'RE DOING FOR US. WE DO. BUT YOU NEED TO LOOSEN UP.
YEAH! DON'T CRY OVER ***SNORTED MILK!***
SUGAR O'S
AMY! YOU'RE ***NOT*** HELPING. GO GET YOUR SHOES ON!
SUGAR O'S

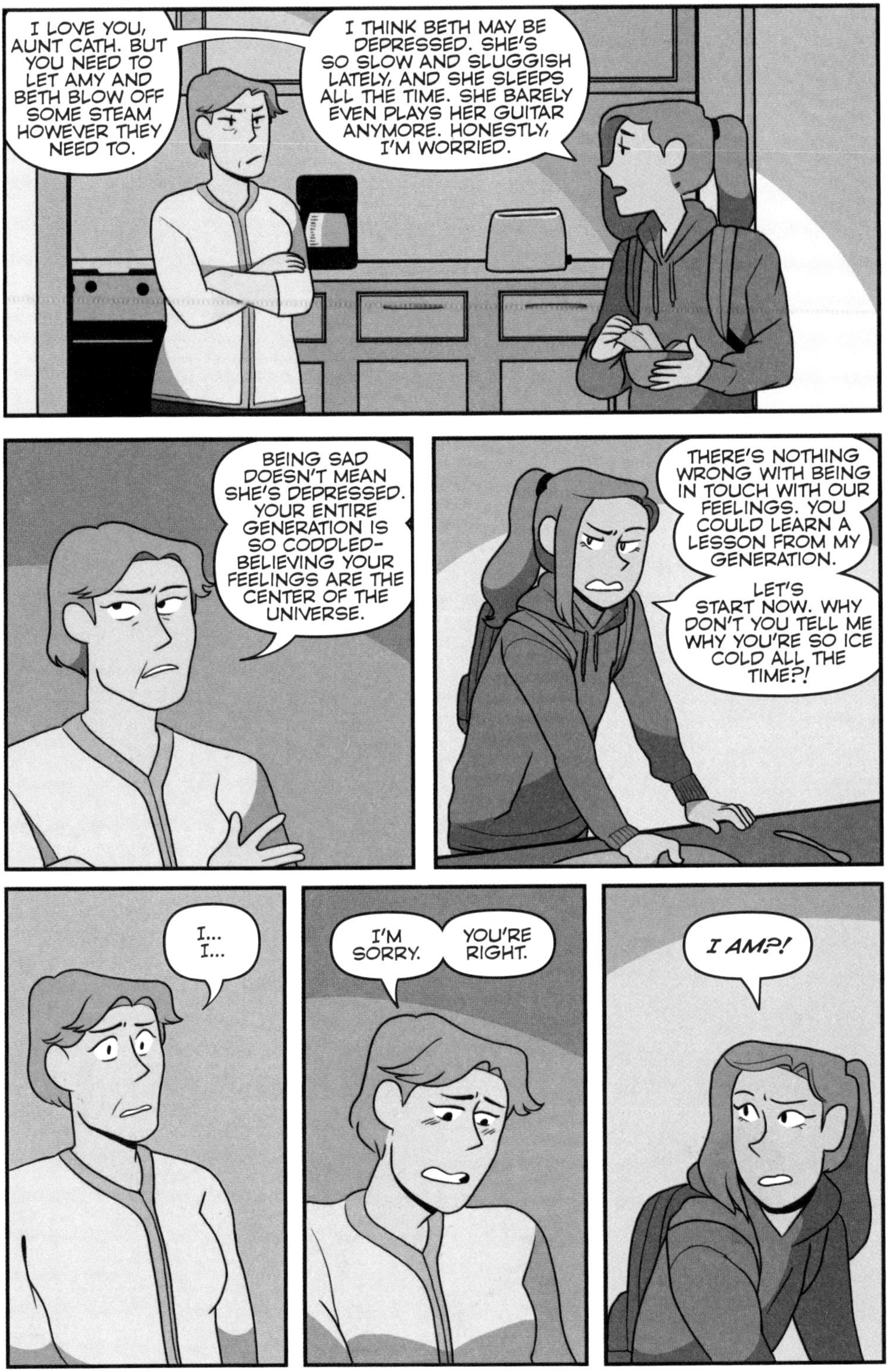
I LOVE YOU, AUNT CATH. BUT YOU NEED TO LET AMY AND BETH BLOW OFF SOME STEAM HOWEVER THEY NEED TO.
I THINK BETH MAY BE DEPRESSED. SHE'S SO SLOW AND SLUGGISH LATELY, AND SHE SLEEPS ALL THE TIME. SHE BARELY EVEN PLAYS HER GUITAR ANYMORE. HONESTLY, I'M WORRIED.
BEING SAD DOESN'T MEAN SHE'S DEPRESSED. YOUR ENTIRE GENERATION IS SO CODDLED-BELIEVING YOUR FEELINGS ARE THE CENTER OF THE UNIVERSE.
THERE'S NOTHING WRONG WITH BEING IN TOUCH WITH OUR FEELINGS. YOU COULD LEARN A LESSON FROM MY GENERATION.
LET'S START NOW. WHY DON'T YOU TELL ME WHY YOU'RE SO ICE COLD ALL THE TIME?!
I... I...
I'M SORRY.
YOU'RE RIGHT.
I AM?!

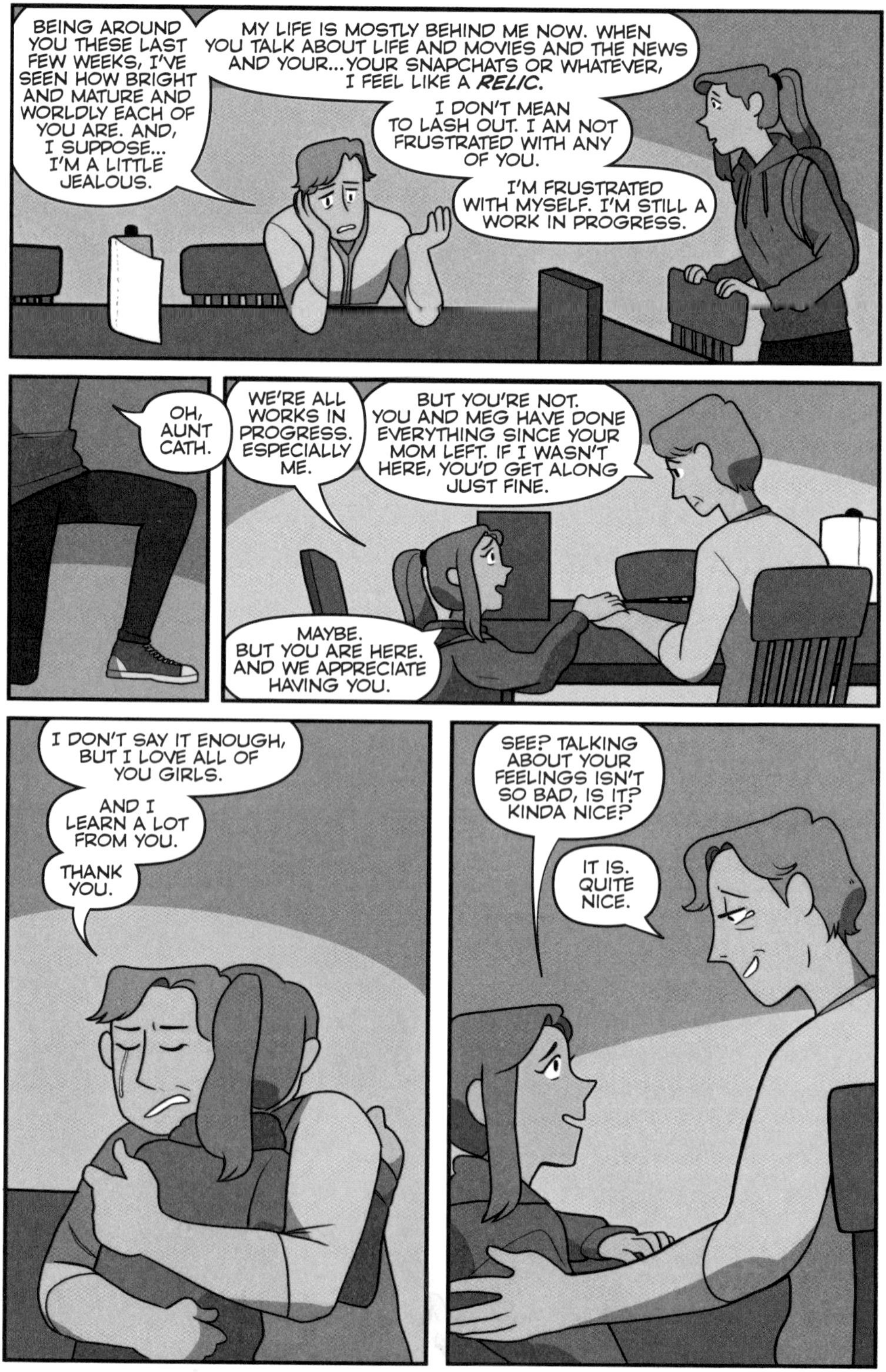
BEING AROUND YOU THESE LAST FEW WEEKS, I'VE SEEN HOW BRIGHT AND MATURE AND WORLDLY EACH OF YOU ARE. AND, I SUPPOSE... I'M A LITTLE JEALOUS.
MY LIFE IS MOSTLY BEHIND ME NOW. WHEN YOU TALK ABOUT LIFE AND MOVIES AND THE NEWS AND YOUR...YOUR SNAPCHATS OR WHATEVER, I FEEL LIKE A *RELIC*.
I DON'T MEAN TO LASH OUT. I AM NOT FRUSTRATED WITH ANY OF YOU.
I'M FRUSTRATED WITH MYSELF. I'M STILL A WORK IN PROGRESS.
OH, AUNT CATH.
WE'RE ALL WORKS IN PROGRESS. ESPECIALLY ME.
BUT YOU'RE NOT. YOU AND MEG HAVE DONE EVERYTHING SINCE YOUR MOM LEFT. IF I WASN'T HERE, YOU'D GET ALONG JUST FINE.
MAYBE. BUT YOU ARE HERE. AND WE APPRECIATE HAVING YOU.
I DON'T SAY IT ENOUGH, BUT I LOVE ALL OF YOU GIRLS.
AND I LEARN A LOT FROM YOU.
THANK YOU.
SEE? TALKING ABOUT YOUR FEELINGS ISN'T SO BAD, IS IT? KINDA NICE?
IT IS. QUITE NICE.

FROM: Josephine March
TO: Madison March
SENT: August 26

Hey Mom,

I tried Skyping you but forgot about the time difference over there. You probably fell asleep in Dad's room again. No worries. But call when you can. I know hearing your voice would help everyone over here. We're staying strong, like you asked, but we miss you both every day.

Everything is good on this end. School started this week, and I like my teachers. Well, except Mr. Tucker. He's my chemistry teacher and I don't understand half the words coming out of his mouth. But my English teacher, Mrs. Humphrey, might be the best teacher I've ever had. She also teaches an elective class called Literature and World Culture. It sounds like a college course, right? I can't wait to take it next semester.

As for everyone else, we're all okay. Meg has been a total boss. She's practically taken your place, making sure everyone gets fed and brushes their teeth before bed. She won't even let me watch TV after ten! But she's been so good about juggling her own job and taking care of our family.

Amy is…well, Amy. Like they said in the 1920s, she's full of "piss and vinegar." That one is so full of life, she's like a juggernaut of energy. But if nothing else, she keeps all of us laughing.

I am a little worried about Beth. Her appetite isn't what it used to be, and she wants to sleep all the time. I think she's taking the news about Dad's leg the hardest. She did pick up her guitar tonight and start playing, but she chose such a melancholy song and went to bed after. Meg and I will make sure to give her extra attention this weekend and see if we can snap her out of it.

We love you so very very very much. My fingers are crossed you can both come home soon.
Love, Jo

FROM: Megan March
TO: Robert March
SENT: August 30

Dad!

You're awake! I'm so happy and grateful and just over-the-moon happy to know you're on the mend. When we Skype Mom, we always hope for good news. But tonight, when she said, "There's someone who wants to speak to you," my heart swelled so big I thought it would burst. Seeing your smile again made everything right in the world.

I know we only just finished speaking, but Amy was hogging the whole conversation. So I thought I'd write to say how relieved I am that you're awake. I can't imagine what you've been through. Or what you are about to go through. But Mom says she is friends with everyone in the physical therapy department at the hospital and you'll be in good hands when you get home. The next few months are going to be hard, but you have Mom with you now, and all of us at home, praying for your quick recovery. Come home soon.

We love you so very much. Can't wait to see you. —Meg

New Message

FROM: Amy March
TO: Robert March
SENT: August 31

Daddy!

Meg said I could only get on the computer if I emailed you, which is what I was going to do anyways. She thinks I only get on here to look at Youtube clips, which is maybe usually kinda true, but not today, cuz I made you some pictures. I'm really talented, I know. I was going to mail them to you, but Jo said they'll take forever in snail mail, and you'll probably be home before then, right?

How are u? I miss you! What's new? Besides your leg? Beth seems freaked out about your leg, but I'm not. I think it's cool. You should get a robot leg, like Cyborg from Justice League. Or maybe an animal leg. If I could have any animal leg, I'd probably get a cheetah, cuz its fast. I love u a whole bunch but I'm tired of writing now so I'm going to do more art and watch TV. Come home fast!

Love u 4-ever. Ur fave girl, Amy

ROBOT D4D!
BAM
POW!

Send

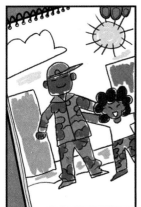

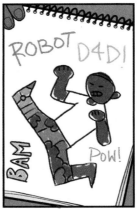

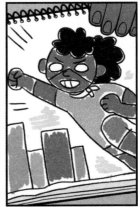

CHAPTER 14

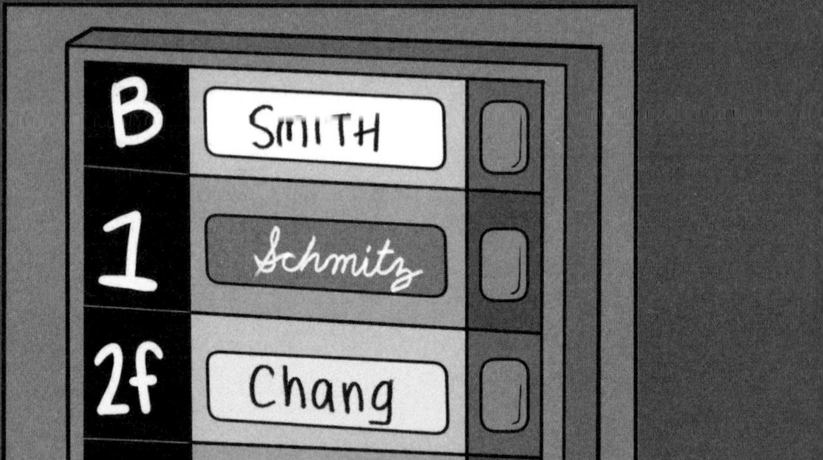
B
SMITH
1
Schmitz
2f
Chang
2R
Reyes-Green
3
MARCH
BZZZZZ

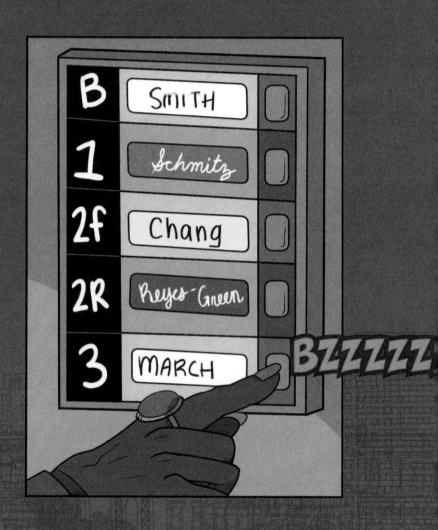

The Doctor Is In...

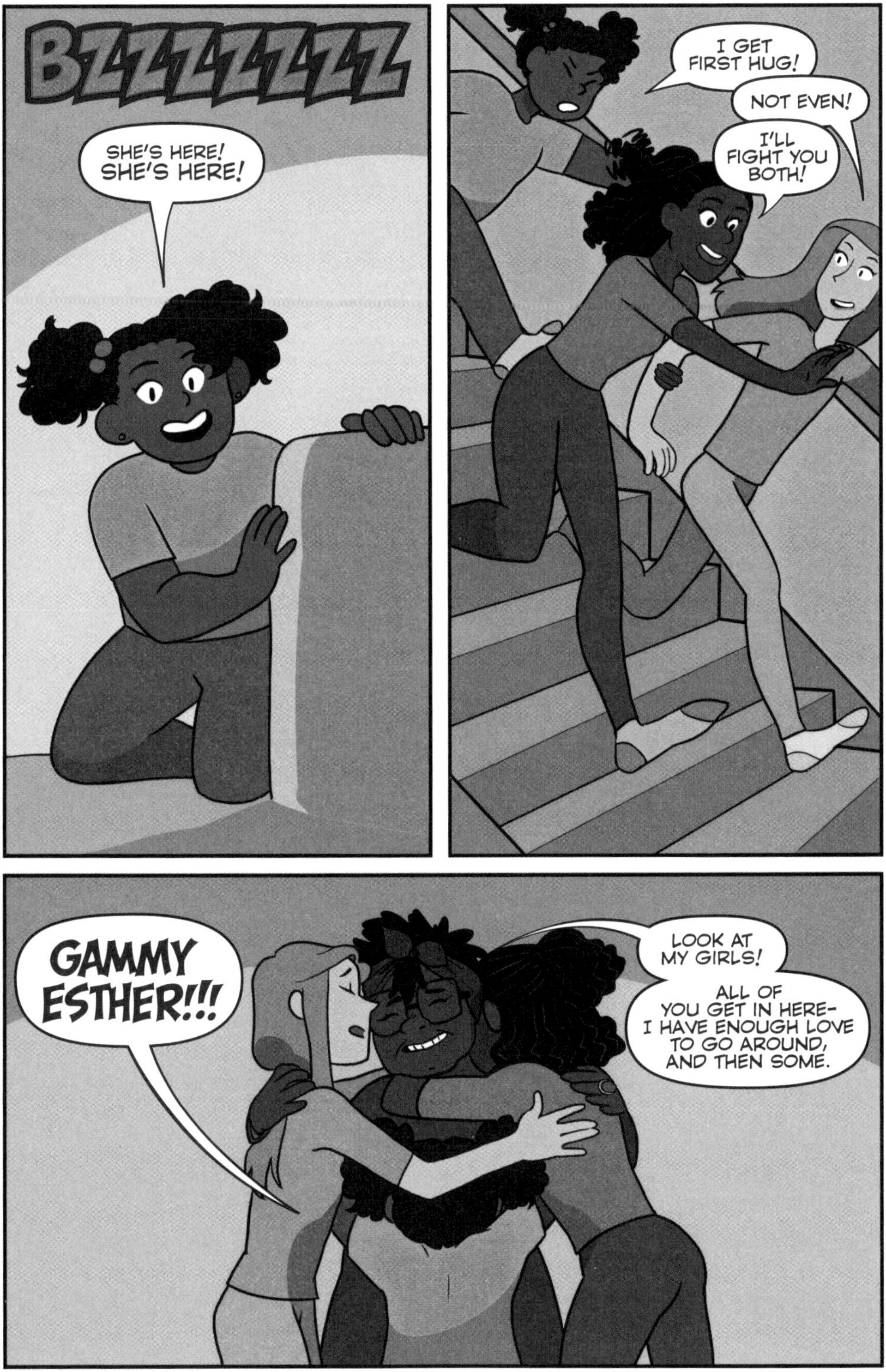
BZZZZZZZ
SHE'S HERE! SHE'S HERE!
I GET FIRST HUG!
NOT EVEN!
I'LL FIGHT YOU BOTH!
GAMMY ESTHER!!!
LOOK AT MY GIRLS!
ALL OF YOU GET IN HERE- I HAVE ENOUGH LOVE TO GO AROUND, AND THEN SOME.

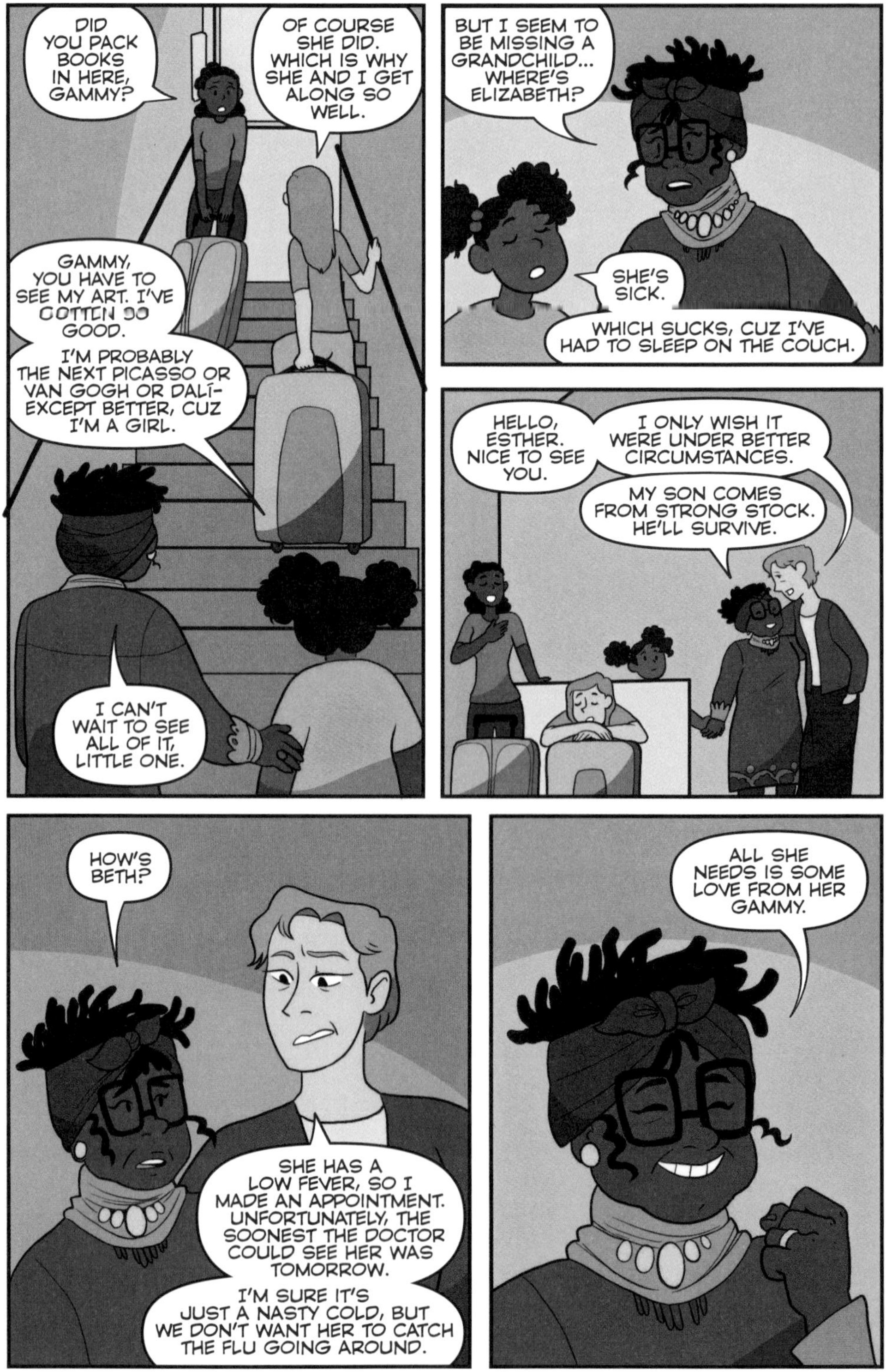

DID YOU PACK BOOKS IN HERE, GAMMY?
OF COURSE SHE DID. WHICH IS WHY SHE AND I GET ALONG SO WELL.
GAMMY, YOU HAVE TO SEE MY ART. I'VE GOTTEN SO GOOD.
I'M PROBABLY THE NEXT PICASSO OR VAN GOGH OR DALÍ—EXCEPT BETTER, CUZ I'M A GIRL.
I CAN'T WAIT TO SEE ALL OF IT, LITTLE ONE.
BUT I SEEM TO BE MISSING A GRANDCHILD... WHERE'S ELIZABETH?
SHE'S SICK.
WHICH SUCKS, CUZ I'VE HAD TO SLEEP ON THE COUCH.
HELLO, ESTHER. NICE TO SEE YOU.
I ONLY WISH IT WERE UNDER BETTER CIRCUMSTANCES.
MY SON COMES FROM STRONG STOCK. HE'LL SURVIVE.
HOW'S BETH?
SHE HAS A LOW FEVER, SO I MADE AN APPOINTMENT. UNFORTUNATELY, THE SOONEST THE DOCTOR COULD SEE HER WAS TOMORROW.
I'M SURE IT'S JUST A NASTY COLD, BUT WE DON'T WANT HER TO CATCH THE FLU GOING AROUND.
ALL SHE NEEDS IS SOME LOVE FROM HER GAMMY.

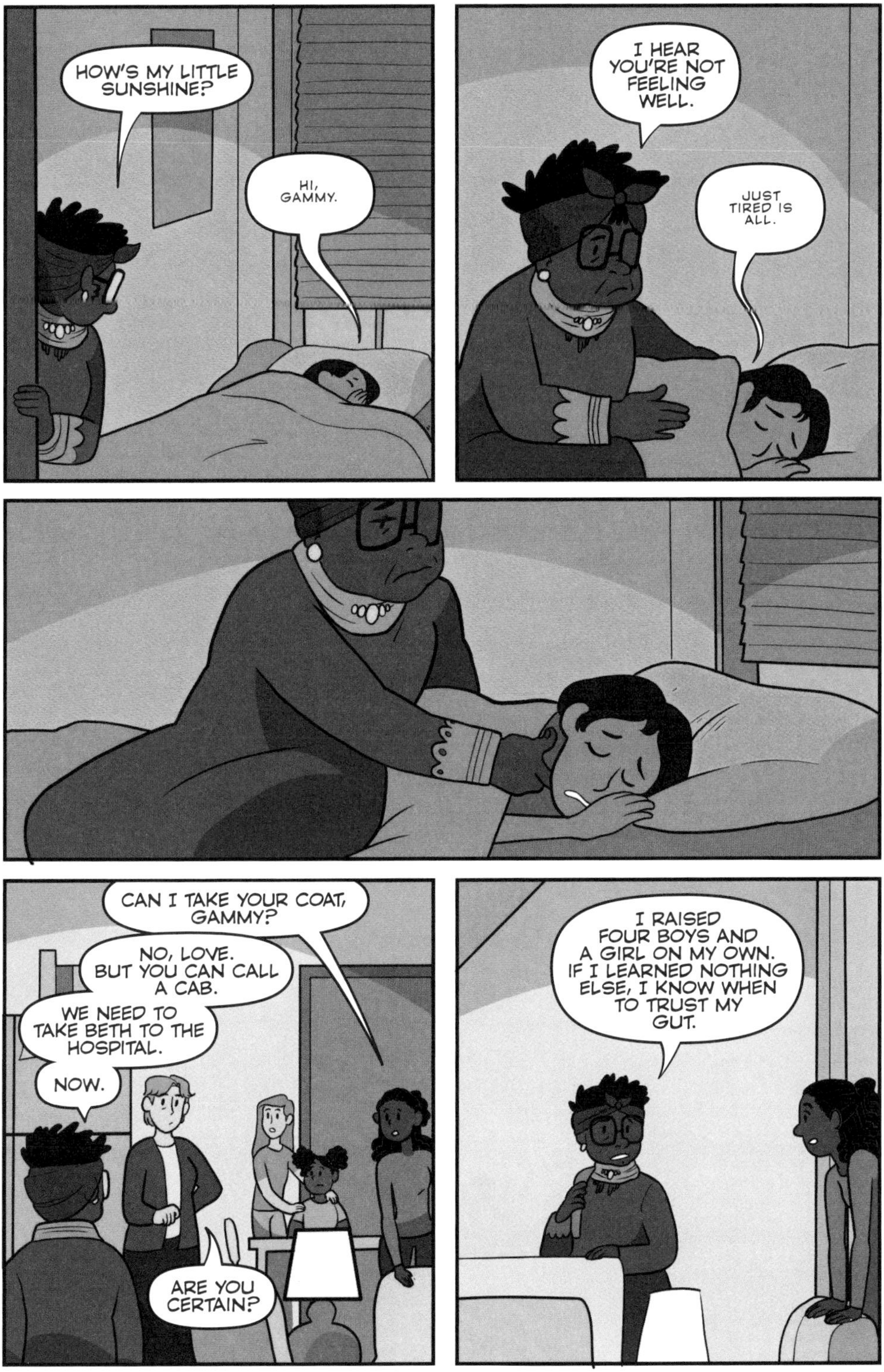
HOW'S MY LITTLE SUNSHINE?
HI, GAMMY.
I HEAR YOU'RE NOT FEELING WELL.
JUST TIRED IS ALL.
CAN I TAKE YOUR COAT, GAMMY?
NO, LOVE. BUT YOU CAN CALL A CAB.
WE NEED TO TAKE BETH TO THE HOSPITAL.
NOW.
ARE YOU CERTAIN?
I RAISED FOUR BOYS AND A GIRL ON MY OWN. IF I LEARNED NOTHING ELSE, I KNOW WHEN TO TRUST MY GUT.

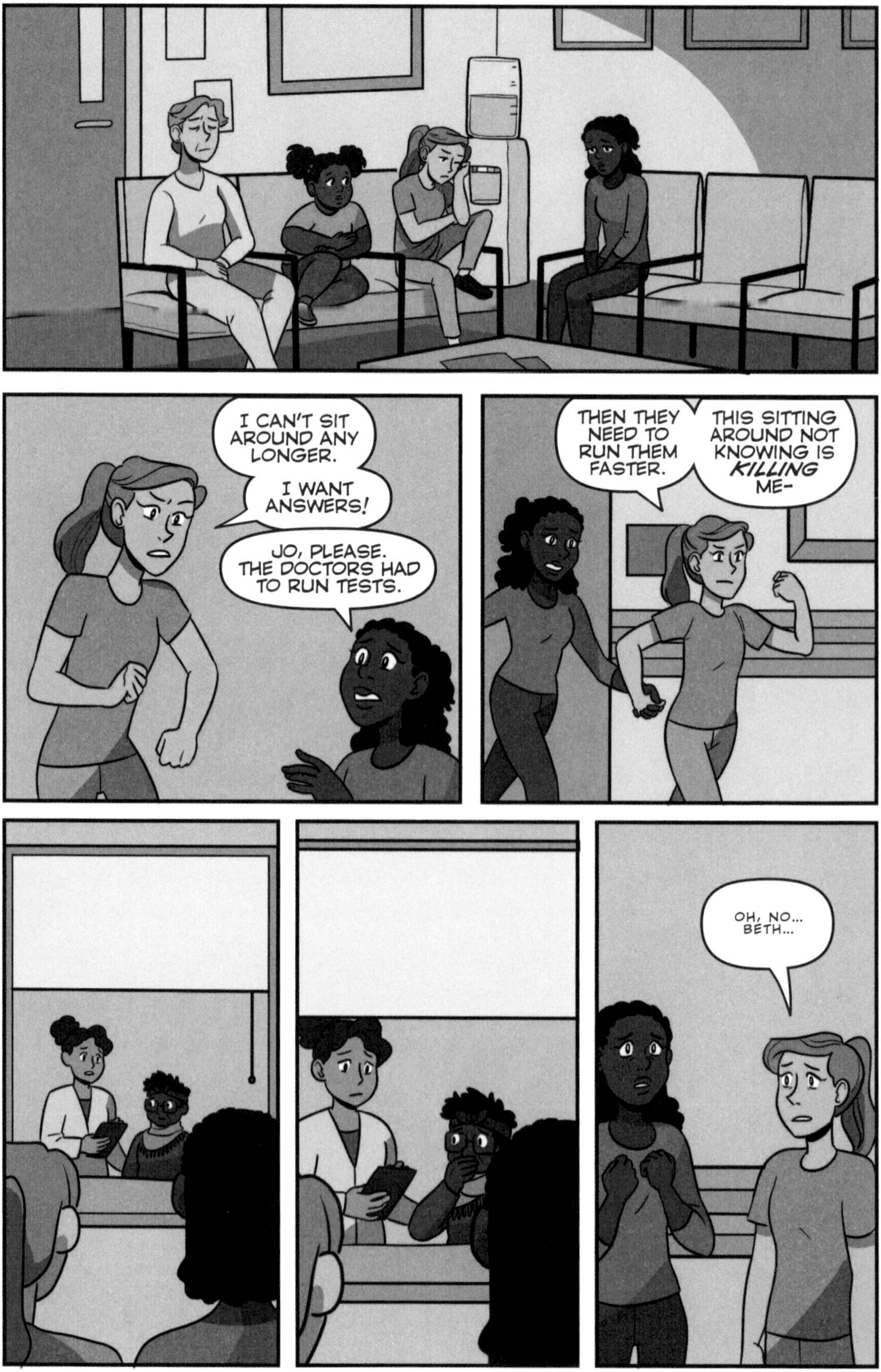
I CAN'T SIT AROUND ANY LONGER.
I WANT ANSWERS!
JO, PLEASE. THE DOCTORS HAD TO RUN TESTS.
THEN THEY NEED TO RUN THEM FASTER.
THIS SITTING AROUND NOT KNOWING IS *KILLING* ME-
OH, NO... BETH...

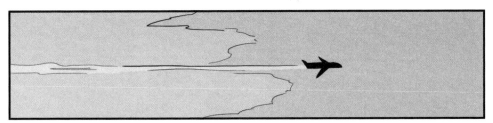

MRS. MARCH. MAY I SPEAK WITH YOU?

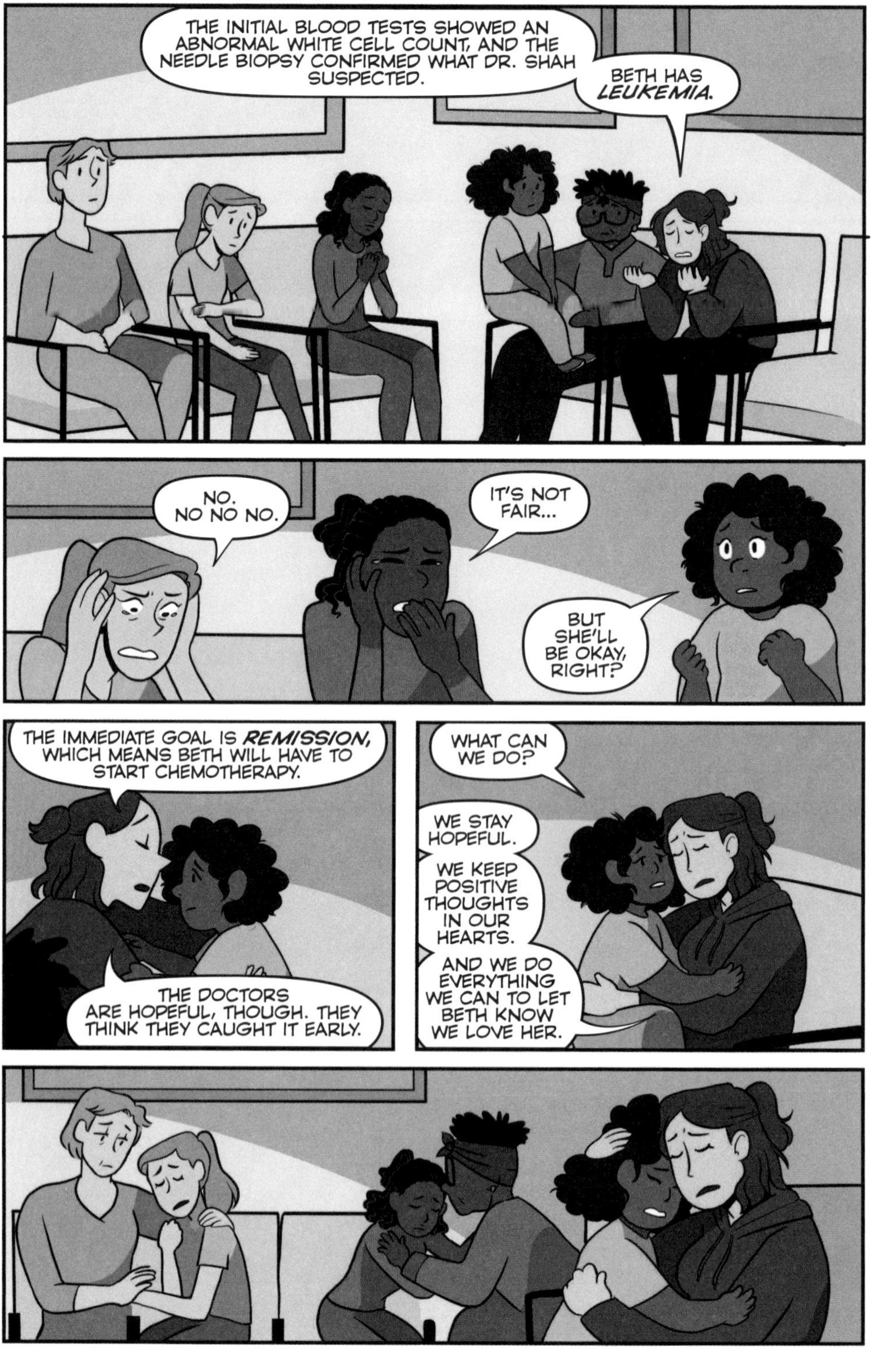
THE INITIAL BLOOD TESTS SHOWED AN ABNORMAL WHITE CELL COUNT, AND THE NEEDLE BIOPSY CONFIRMED WHAT DR. SHAH SUSPECTED.
BETH HAS *LEUKEMIA.*
NO. NO NO NO.
IT'S NOT FAIR...
BUT SHE'LL BE OKAY, RIGHT?
THE IMMEDIATE GOAL IS *REMISSION,* WHICH MEANS BETH WILL HAVE TO START CHEMOTHERAPY.
THE DOCTORS ARE HOPEFUL, THOUGH. THEY THINK THEY CAUGHT IT EARLY.
WHAT CAN WE DO?
WE STAY HOPEFUL.
WE KEEP POSITIVE THOUGHTS IN OUR HEARTS.
AND WE DO EVERYTHING WE CAN TO LET BETH KNOW WE LOVE HER.

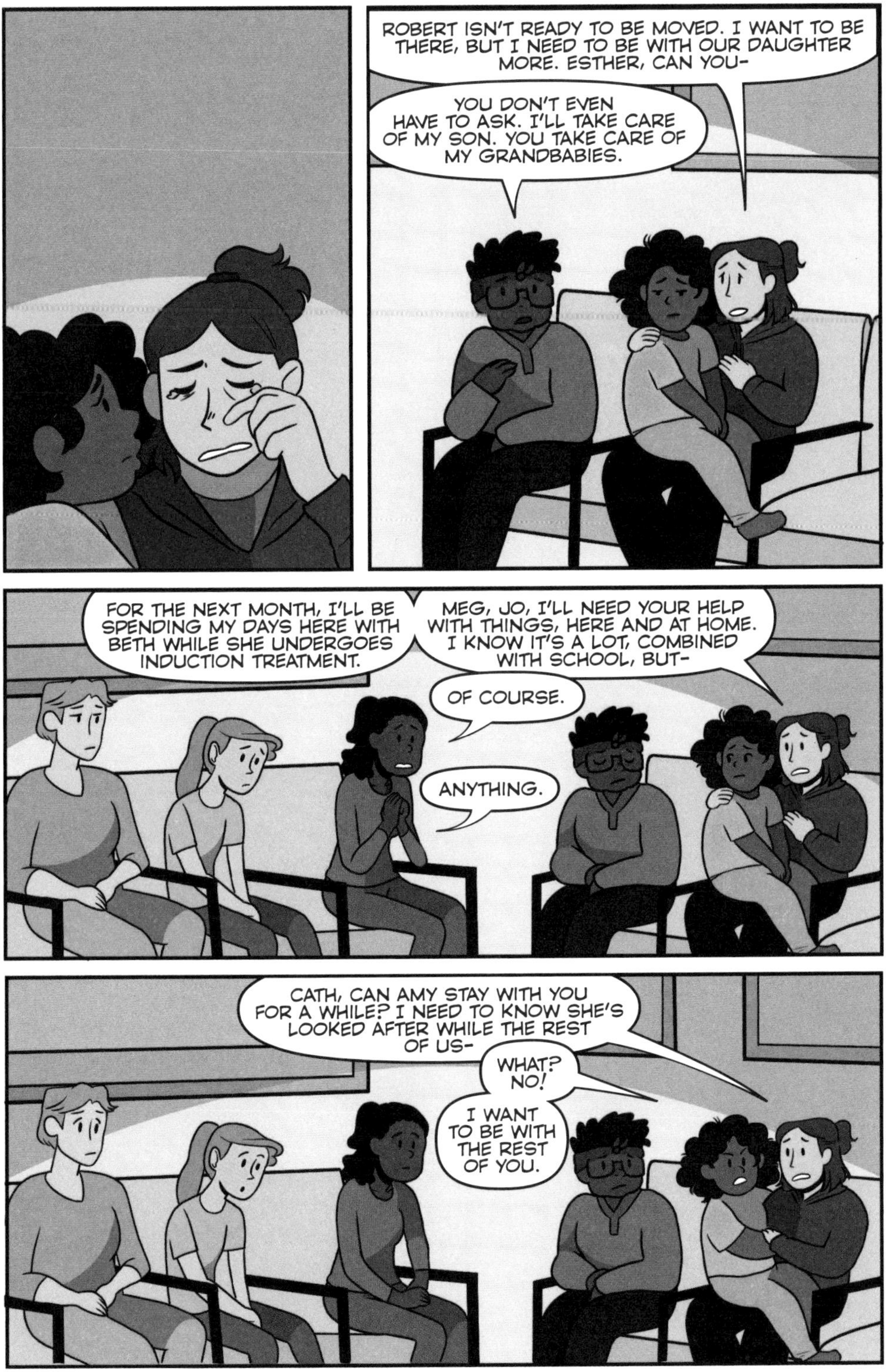
ROBERT ISN'T READY TO BE MOVED. I WANT TO BE THERE, BUT I NEED TO BE WITH OUR DAUGHTER MORE. ESTHER, CAN YOU-
YOU DON'T EVEN HAVE TO ASK. I'LL TAKE CARE OF MY SON. YOU TAKE CARE OF MY GRANDBABIES.
FOR THE NEXT MONTH, I'LL BE SPENDING MY DAYS HERE WITH BETH WHILE SHE UNDERGOES INDUCTION TREATMENT.
MEG, JO, I'LL NEED YOUR HELP WITH THINGS, HERE AND AT HOME. I KNOW IT'S A LOT, COMBINED WITH SCHOOL, BUT-
OF COURSE.
ANYTHING.
CATH, CAN AMY STAY WITH YOU FOR A WHILE? I NEED TO KNOW SHE'S LOOKED AFTER WHILE THE REST OF US-
WHAT? NO!
I WANT TO BE WITH THE REST OF YOU.

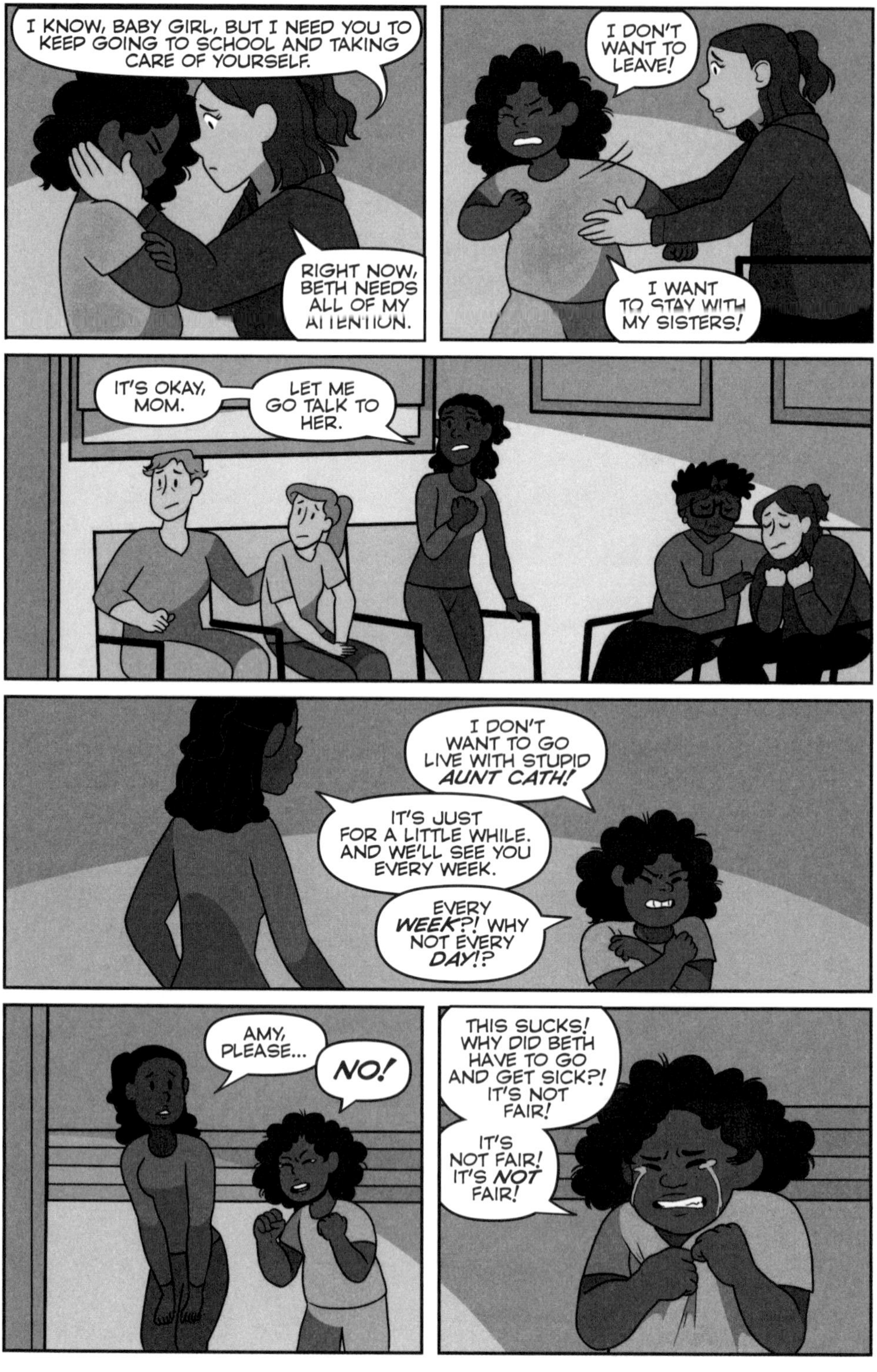
I KNOW, BABY GIRL, BUT I NEED YOU TO KEEP GOING TO SCHOOL AND TAKING CARE OF YOURSELF.
RIGHT NOW, BETH NEEDS ALL OF MY ATTENTION.
I DON'T WANT TO LEAVE!
I WANT TO STAY WITH MY SISTERS!
IT'S OKAY, MOM.
LET ME GO TALK TO HER.
I DON'T WANT TO GO LIVE WITH STUPID *AUNT CATH!*
IT'S JUST FOR A LITTLE WHILE. AND WE'LL SEE YOU EVERY WEEK.
EVERY *WEEK*?! WHY NOT EVERY *DAY*!?
AMY, PLEASE...
NO!
THIS SUCKS! WHY DID BETH HAVE TO GO AND GET SICK?! IT'S NOT FAIR!
IT'S NOT FAIR! IT'S *NOT* FAIR!

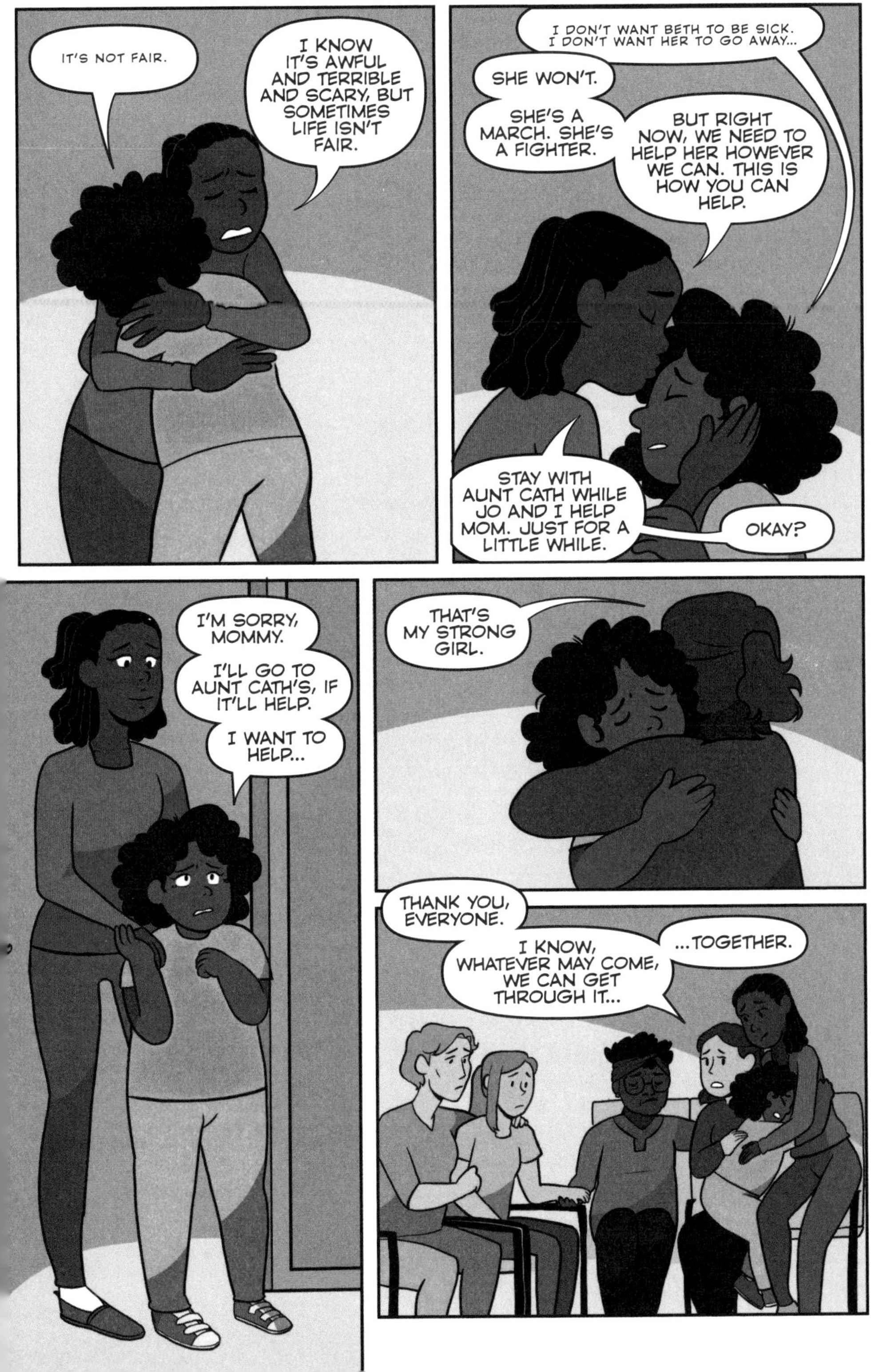

IT'S NOT FAIR.
I KNOW IT'S AWFUL AND TERRIBLE AND SCARY, BUT SOMETIMES LIFE ISN'T FAIR.
I DON'T WANT BETH TO BE SICK. I DON'T WANT HER TO GO AWAY...
SHE WON'T.
SHE'S A MARCH. SHE'S A FIGHTER.
BUT RIGHT NOW, WE NEED TO HELP HER HOWEVER WE CAN. THIS IS HOW YOU CAN HELP.
STAY WITH AUNT CATH WHILE JO AND I HELP MOM. JUST FOR A LITTLE WHILE.
OKAY?
I'M SORRY, MOMMY.
I'LL GO TO AUNT CATH'S, IF IT'LL HELP.
I WANT TO HELP...
THAT'S MY STRONG GIRL.
THANK YOU, EVERYONE.
I KNOW, WHATEVER MAY COME, WE CAN GET THROUGH IT...
...TOGETHER.

FROM: Megan March
TO: Esther March
SENT: September 10

Hi Gammy,

Thanks for calling me last night. I'm sorry I cried the whole time. I just couldn't keep it in. It's like, most of the time, I can hold it together, and be strong—for Beth, for Dad, for Mom—but when I heard your voice, the floodgates opened. I know you say I can always be myself with you, and I guess that *was* me being myself. I really needed that cry.

I've been trying to be so strong for everyone, and I think I have been. But all of it is wearing me down. I'm tired and exhausted and there's still so much to do. I wake up and pick up the house. Then, I go to school and try to concentrate, which is practically impossible. Then, I go to the hospital, so Mom can go home and take a shower, or I bring her clothes and food. And some nights, I still have to go to the Kings' to watch their kids when all I want to be doing is staying at Beth's side. And after all that, there's still homework left to do. The worst part is— nothing seems as important right now as spending time with Beth or with Dad. And he's on the other side of the planet.

But I'm glad you're there with him now. It was good to talk to him tonight too. But I can't cry with him the way I do with you. I'm his firstborn, and I don't want him to think I'm weak. I feel like I'm letting everyone down, even though you keep saying I'm not.

Send

That thing you said on the phone, about staying in the present moment, it struck a chord with me. And that quote: "This too shall pass." It helps remembering that. Every time I feel a wave of stress coming at me, I say it, and take a deep breath. It seems to be helping. Somehow, you always know the right thing to say. Thank you for being there, Gammy. I don't know what we'd do without you.

Give my love to Dad. And I'll give your love to Beth. —Meg

P.S. Thank you for keeping my secret about my boyfriend. I don't think my sisters could understand me dating someone right now, but Brooks is the only thing that helps me forget the pain. He's handsome and charming, and he's been so wonderfully supportive through the last few months. I can't wait for you to meet him when everything gets better…

Sept 16

Jo's Journal: KEEP OUT

Everything is falling apart. And it's not fair. How much is one family supposed to bear? How much more can we take? My father is hurt and unable to come home. My little sister has cancer and the chemo seems to take more and more away from her with each treatment. And at the end of every long day, I lie down to go to sleep, and I can't. I lie there, wide awake, wondering if I'll see Beth tomorrow.

I know it's morbid and horrible, but I can't control my thoughts. I want her to get better, for everything to go back to the way it was before the whole world crashed down around our ears. But there's nothing I can do. I can't control this. I can't fix it. I can't punch or scream at cancer. It makes the mightiest of men into mice. I am trying to trust in modern medicine and the doctors and the hospital staff, but every time I go there, I want to know why people aren't doing more. We live in the 21st century—how can we not have a cure for cancer yet? We can talk instantaneously to people on the other side of the globe and we can fly to the moon and send satellites to the far reaches of space—so why don't we have a cure for disease?

Why does life have to be this hard? At least for kids. Beth is an innocent. She shouldn't have to suffer this. If I could, I would take her pain. I would. But I can't. All I can do is write, letting my words be a prayer, a plea to God or Jesus or Allah or Buddha or whoever is up there, hoping that my words sway their hearts and let me keep my sister—even if for just another day...

CHAPTER 15

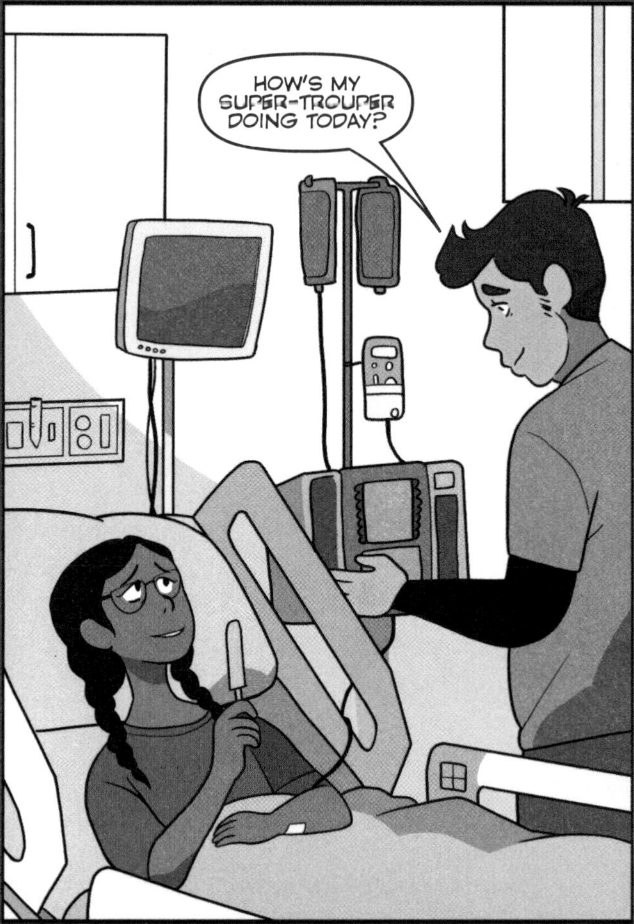
HOW'S MY SUPER-TROUPER DOING TODAY?

The Falling of Leaves...

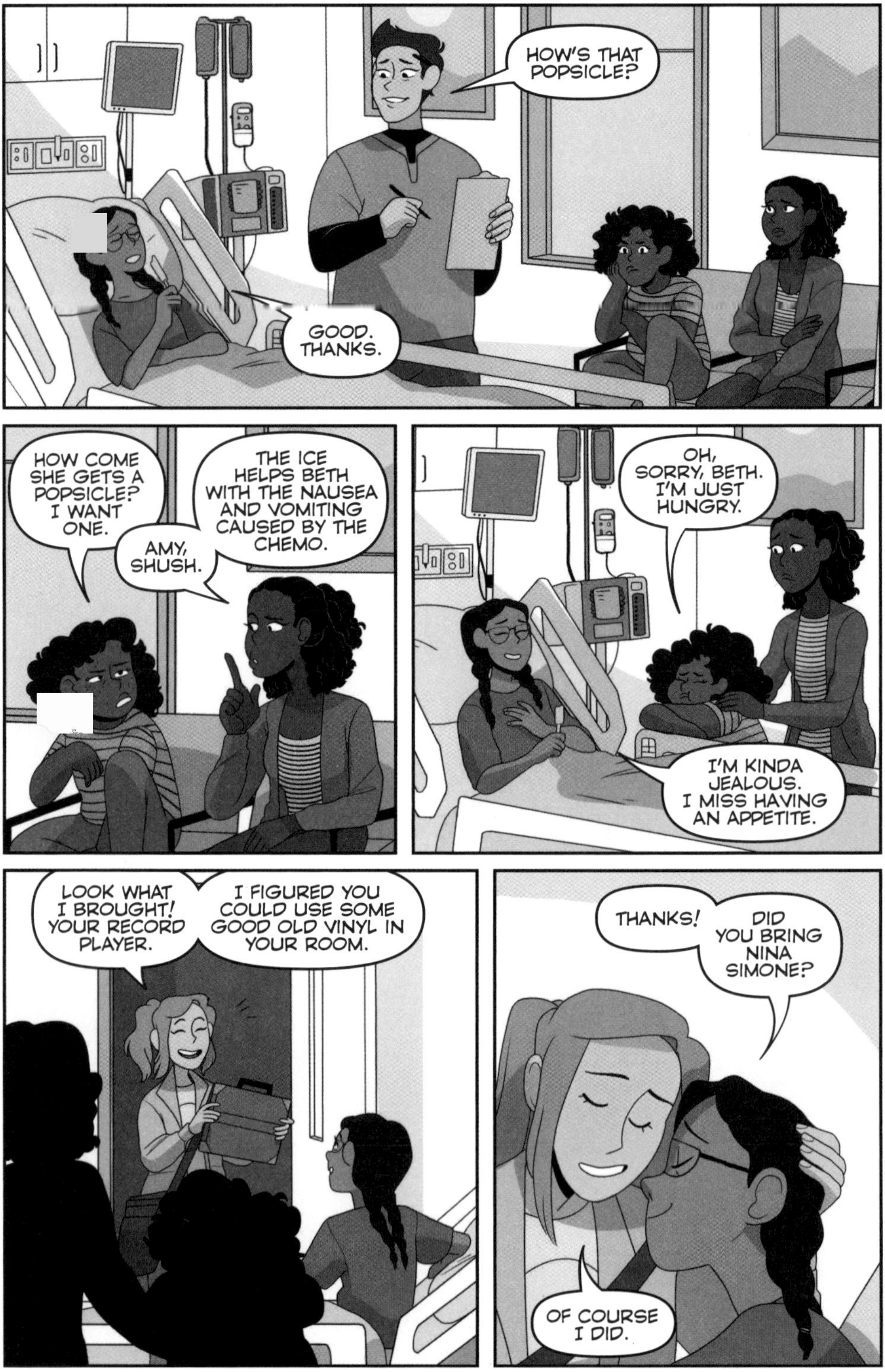
HOW'S THAT POPSICLE?
GOOD. THANKS.
HOW COME SHE GETS A POPSICLE? I WANT ONE.
AMY, SHUSH.
THE ICE HELPS BETH WITH THE NAUSEA AND VOMITING CAUSED BY THE CHEMO.
OH, SORRY, BETH. I'M JUST HUNGRY.
I'M KINDA JEALOUS. I MISS HAVING AN APPETITE.
LOOK WHAT I BROUGHT! YOUR RECORD PLAYER.
I FIGURED YOU COULD USE SOME GOOD OLD VINYL IN YOUR ROOM.
THANKS!
DID YOU BRING NINA SIMONE?
OF COURSE I DID.

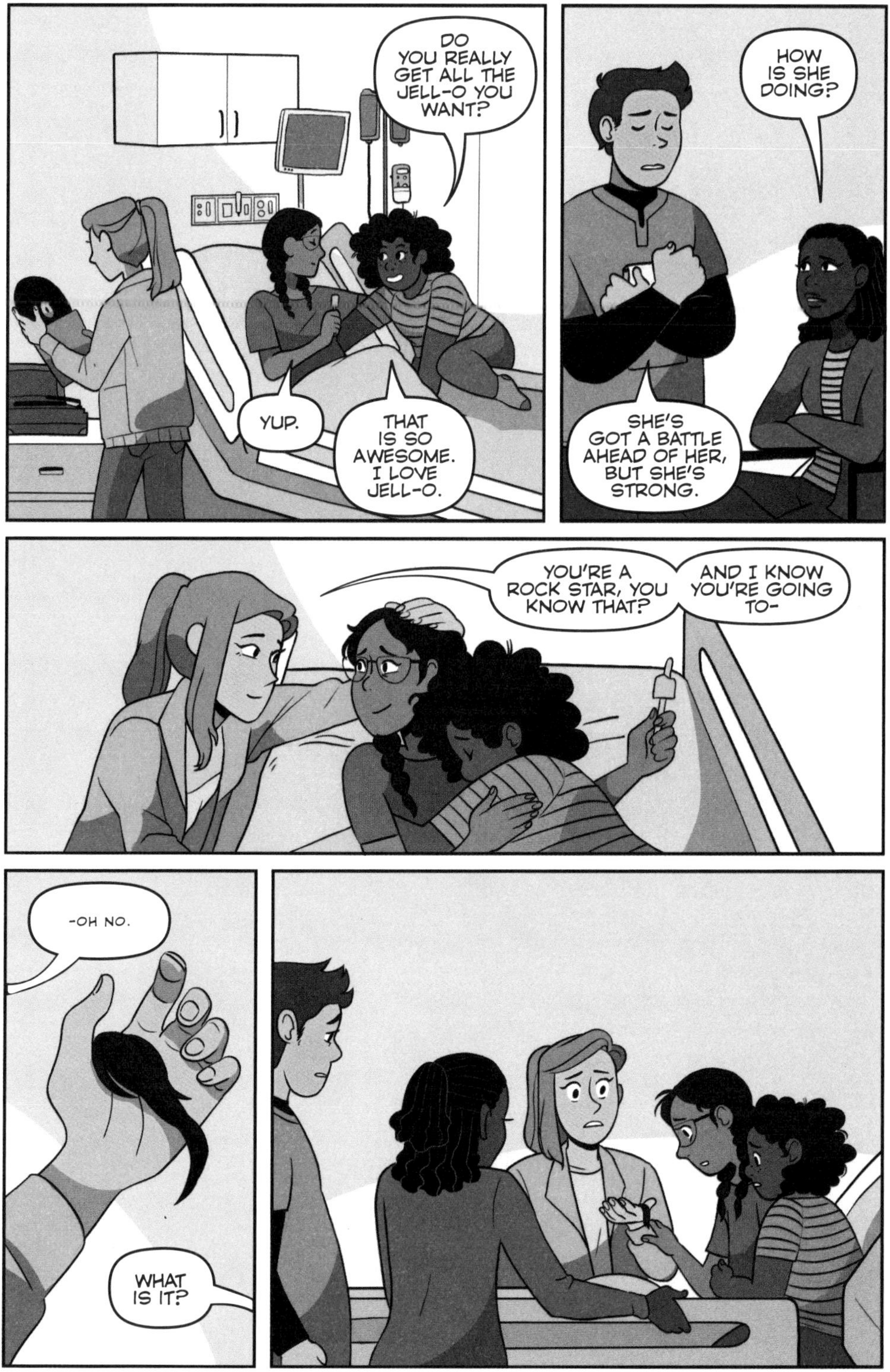
DO YOU REALLY GET ALL THE JELL-O YOU WANT?
YUP.
THAT IS SO AWESOME. I LOVE JELL-O.
HOW IS SHE DOING?
SHE'S GOT A BATTLE AHEAD OF HER, BUT SHE'S STRONG.
YOU'RE A ROCK STAR, YOU KNOW THAT?
AND I KNOW YOU'RE GOING TO-
-OH NO.
WHAT IS IT?

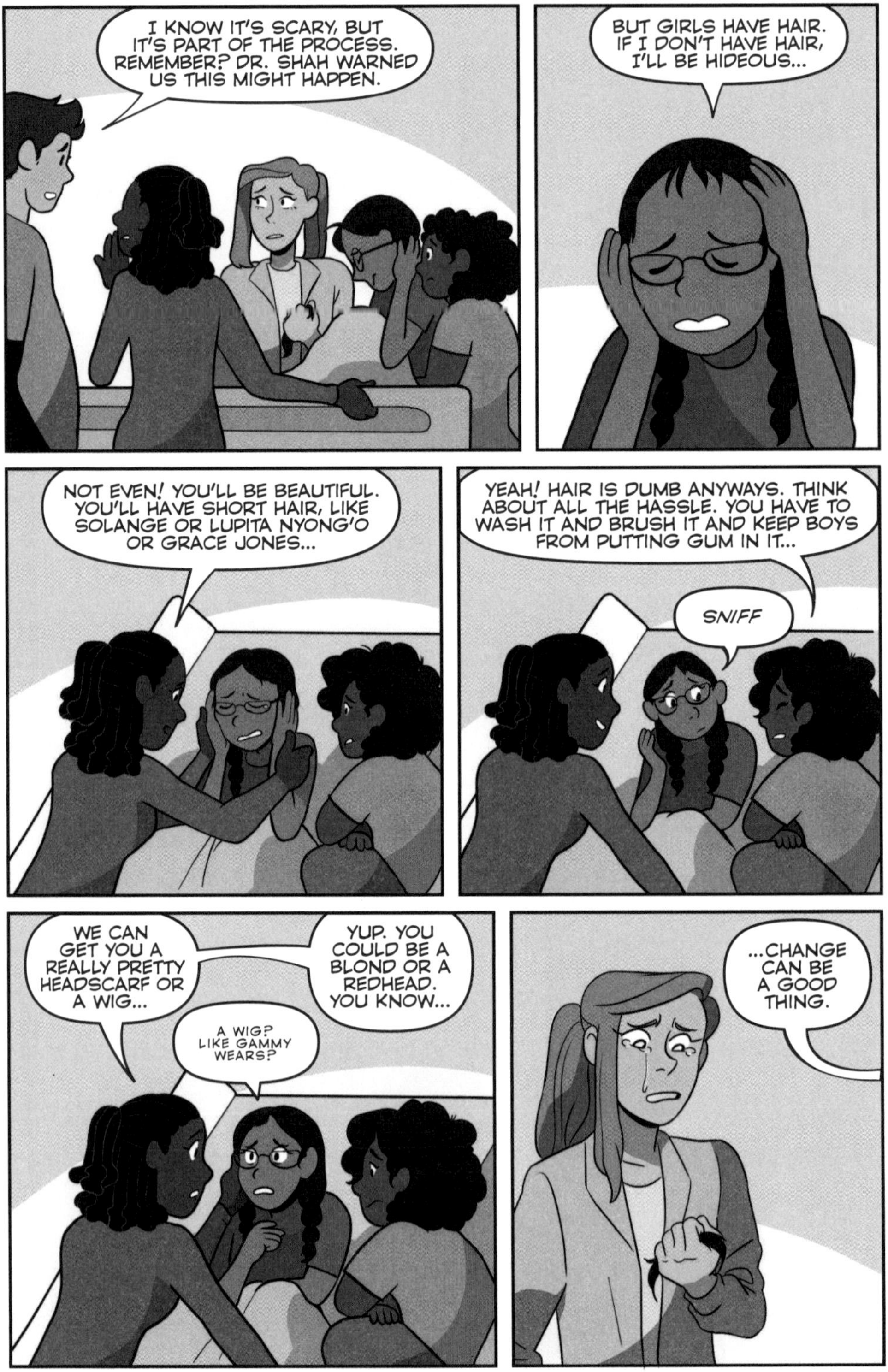
I KNOW IT'S SCARY, BUT IT'S PART OF THE PROCESS. REMEMBER? DR. SHAH WARNED US THIS MIGHT HAPPEN.
BUT GIRLS HAVE HAIR. IF I DON'T HAVE HAIR, I'LL BE HIDEOUS...
NOT EVEN! YOU'LL BE BEAUTIFUL. YOU'LL HAVE SHORT HAIR, LIKE SOLANGE OR LUPITA NYONG'O OR GRACE JONES...
YEAH! HAIR IS DUMB ANYWAYS. THINK ABOUT ALL THE HASSLE. YOU HAVE TO WASH IT AND BRUSH IT AND KEEP BOYS FROM PUTTING GUM IN IT...
SNIFF
WE CAN GET YOU A REALLY PRETTY HEADSCARF OR A WIG...
YUP. YOU COULD BE A BLOND OR A REDHEAD. YOU KNOW...
A WIG? LIKE GAMMY WEARS?
...CHANGE CAN BE A GOOD THING.

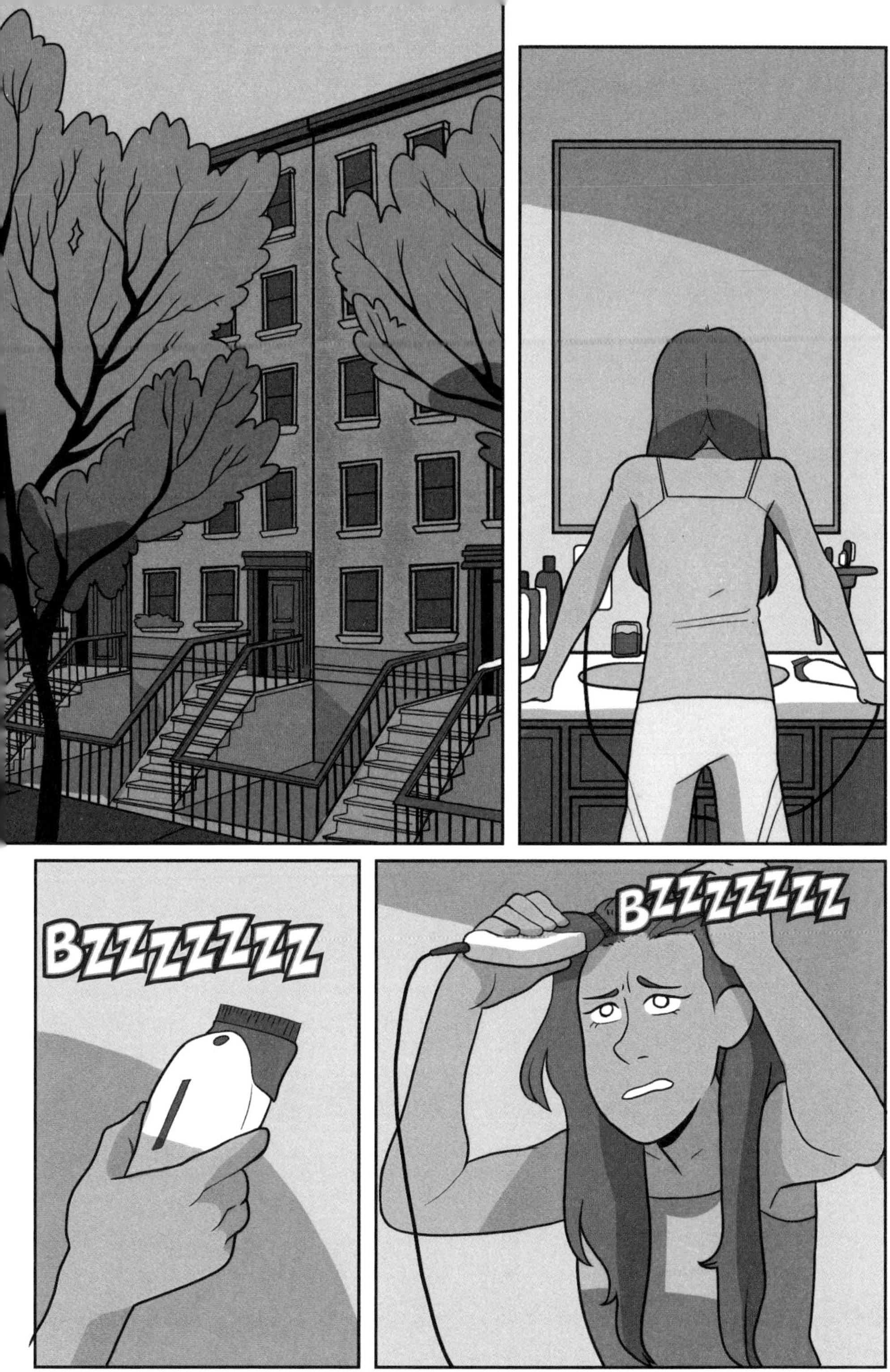
BZZZZZZZZ
BZZZZZZZZ

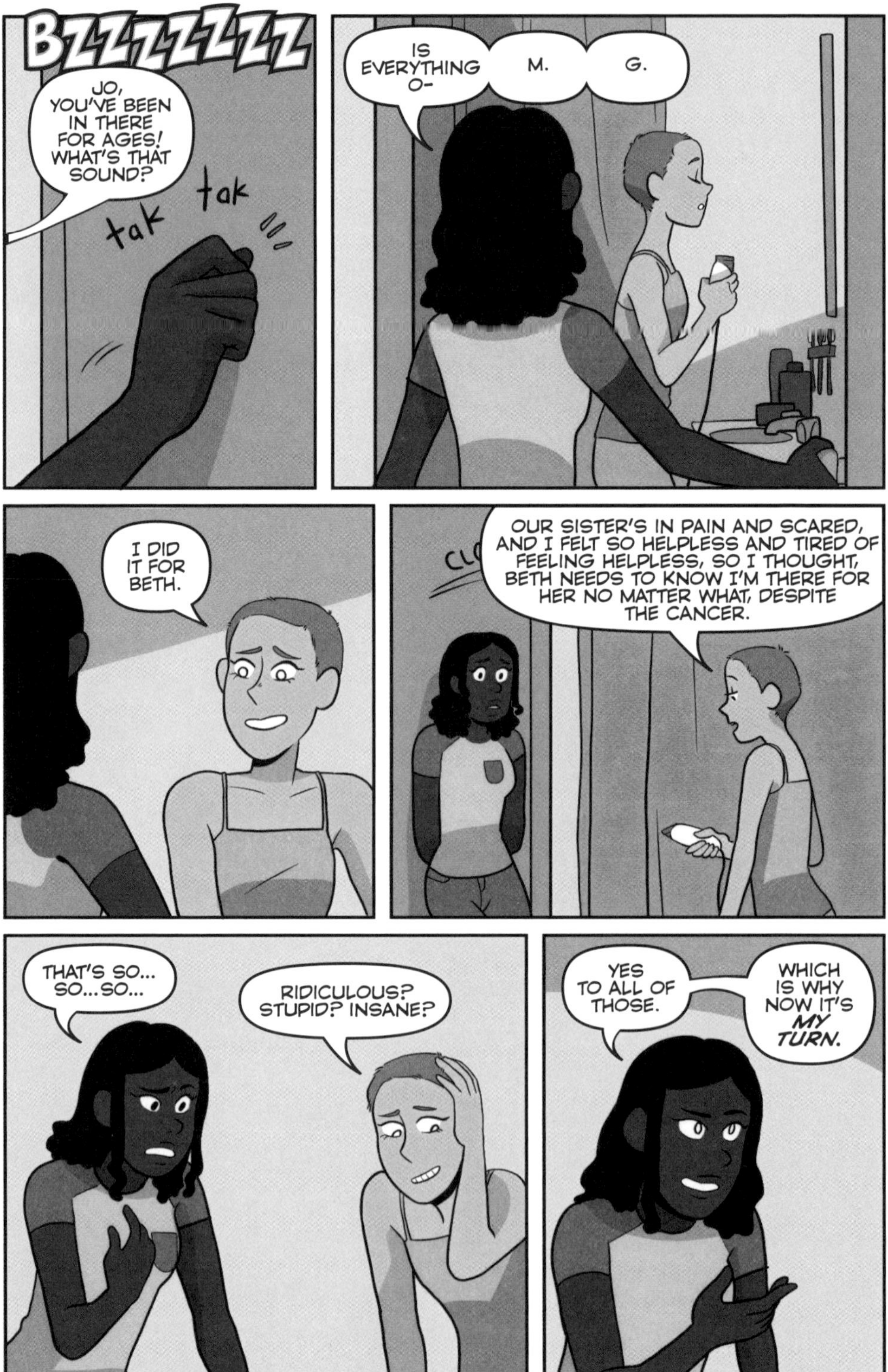
BZZZZZZZZ
JO, YOU'VE BEEN IN THERE FOR AGES! WHAT'S THAT SOUND?
tak tak
IS EVERYTHING O-
M.
G.
I DID IT FOR BETH.
CL
OUR SISTER'S IN PAIN AND SCARED, AND I FELT SO HELPLESS AND TIRED OF FEELING HELPLESS, SO I THOUGHT, BETH NEEDS TO KNOW I'M THERE FOR HER NO MATTER WHAT, DESPITE THE CANCER.
THAT'S SO... SO...SO...
RIDICULOUS? STUPID? INSANE?
YES TO ALL OF THOSE.
WHICH IS WHY NOW IT'S *MY TURN*.

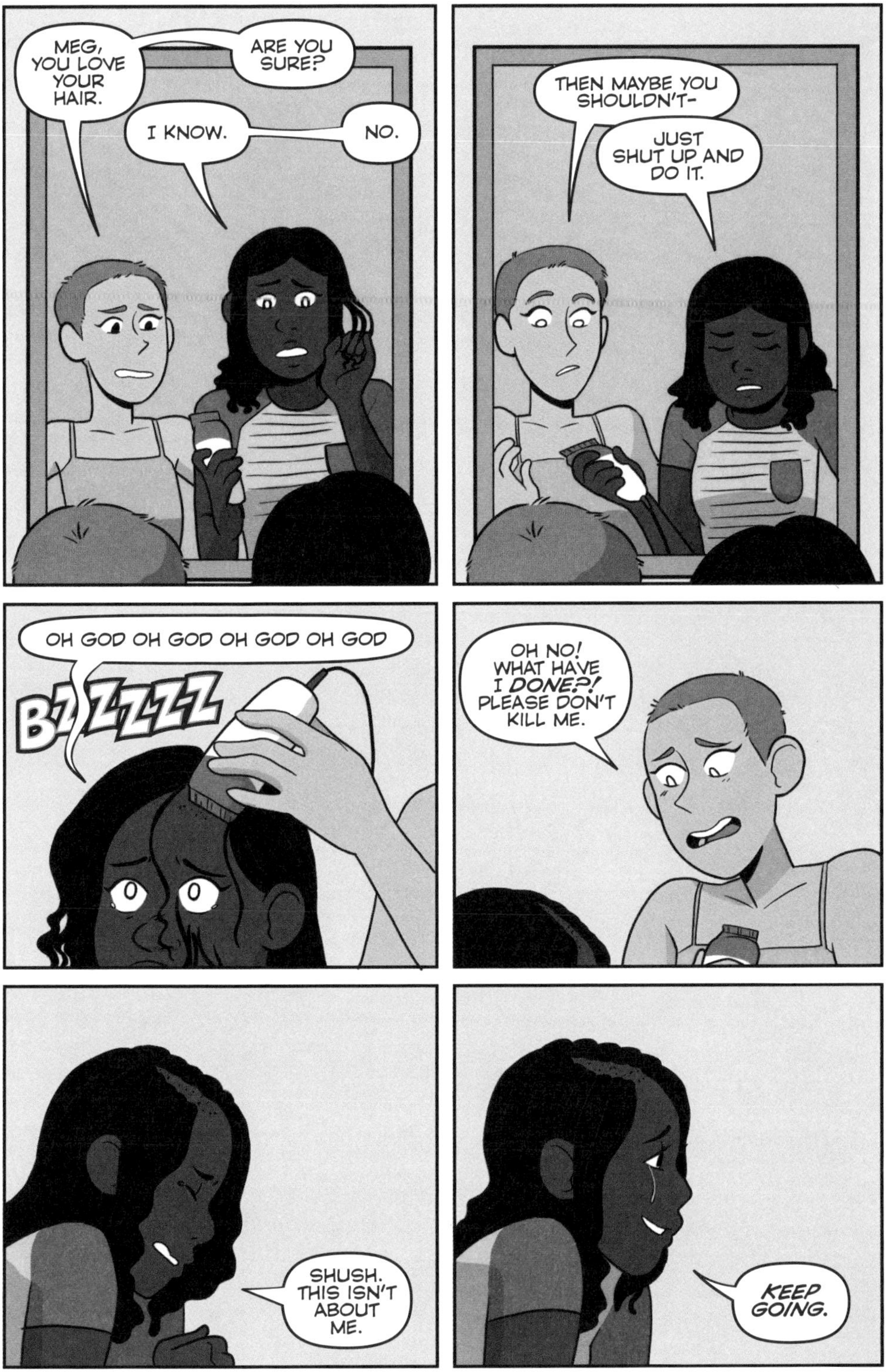
MEG, YOU LOVE YOUR HAIR.
ARE YOU SURE?
I KNOW.
NO.
THEN MAYBE YOU SHOULDN'T-
JUST SHUT UP AND DO IT.
OH GOD OH GOD OH GOD OH GOD
BZZZZZ
OH NO! WHAT HAVE I *DONE?!* PLEASE DON'T KILL ME.
SHUSH. THIS ISN'T ABOUT ME.
KEEP GOING.

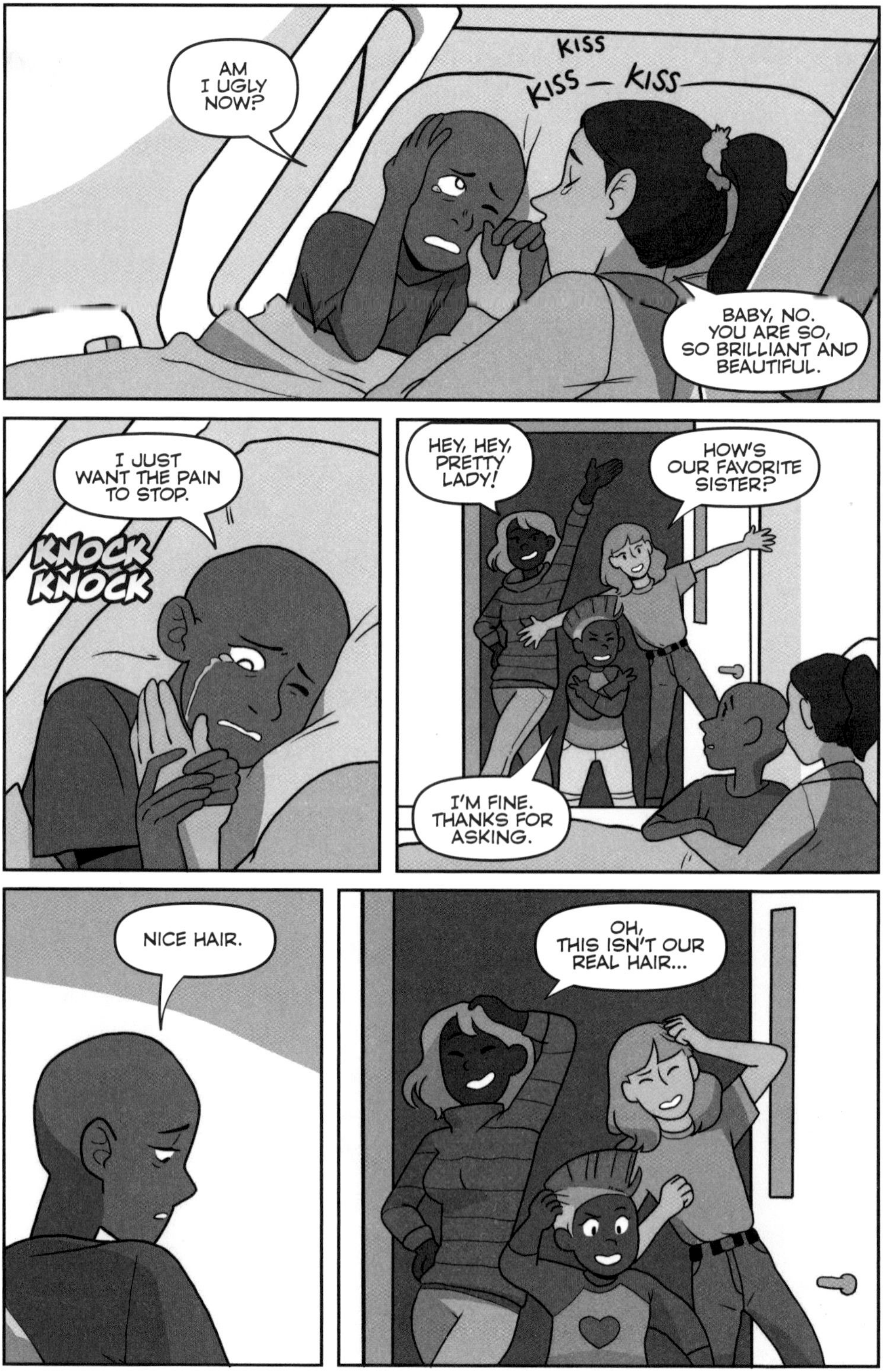
AM I UGLY NOW?
KISS
KISS — KISS
BABY, NO. YOU ARE SO, SO BRILLIANT AND BEAUTIFUL.
I JUST WANT THE PAIN TO STOP.
KNOCK KNOCK
HEY, HEY, PRETTY LADY!
HOW'S OUR FAVORITE SISTER?
I'M FINE. THANKS FOR ASKING.
NICE HAIR.
OH, THIS ISN'T OUR REAL HAIR...

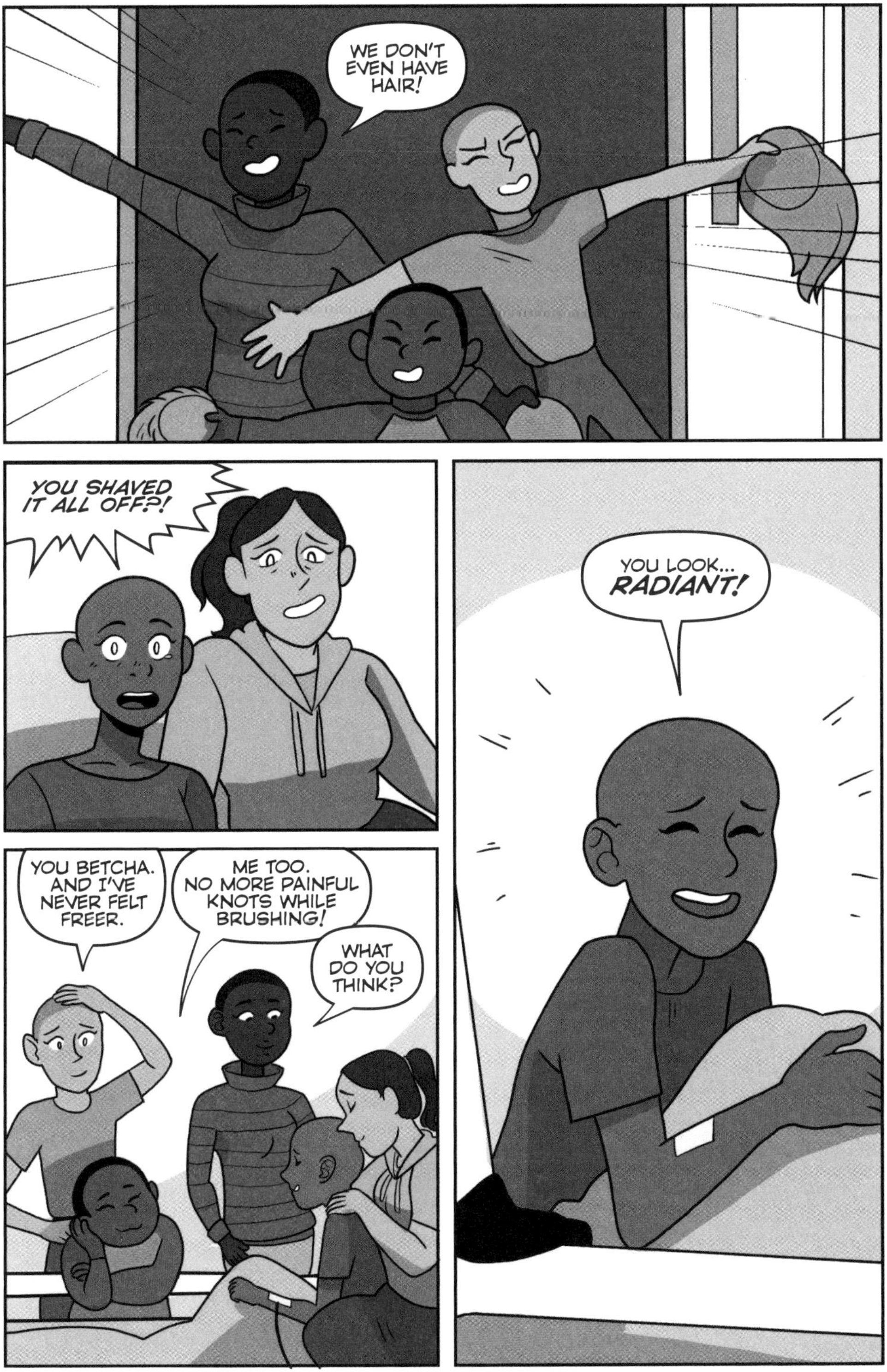
WE DON'T EVEN HAVE HAIR!
YOU SHAVED IT ALL OFF?!
YOU BETCHA. AND I'VE NEVER FELT FREER.
ME TOO. NO MORE PAINFUL KNOTS WHILE BRUSHING!
WHAT DO YOU THINK?
YOU LOOK... RADIANT!

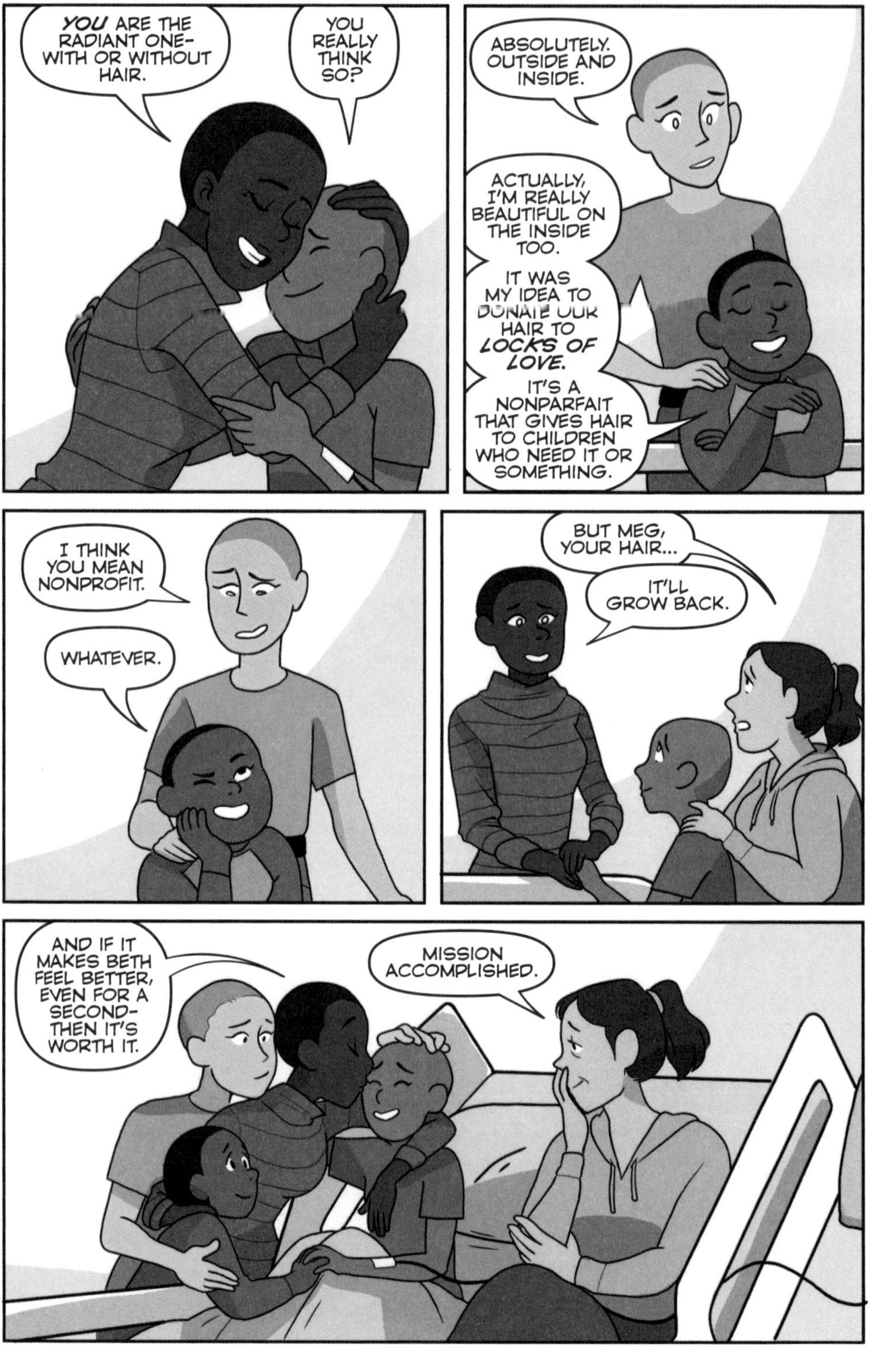
YOU ARE THE RADIANT ONE- WITH OR WITHOUT HAIR.
YOU REALLY THINK SO?
ABSOLUTELY. OUTSIDE AND INSIDE.
ACTUALLY, I'M REALLY BEAUTIFUL ON THE INSIDE TOO.
IT WAS MY IDEA TO DONATE OUR HAIR TO ***LOCKS OF LOVE.***
IT'S A NONPARFAIT THAT GIVES HAIR TO CHILDREN WHO NEED IT OR SOMETHING.
I THINK YOU MEAN NONPROFIT.
WHATEVER.
BUT MEG, YOUR HAIR...
IT'LL GROW BACK.
AND IF IT MAKES BETH FEEL BETTER, EVEN FOR A SECOND- THEN IT'S WORTH IT.
MISSION ACCOMPLISHED.

Jo's Journal: KEEP OUT

Change is good. It's necessary. Sometimes I forget that and try to cling to how things are. But then autumn comes and the leaves fall off the trees, and everywhere I go, I see green has turned to orange and brown, and fallen away to reveal something beneath....It doesn't mean things are ending, just changing.

Tonight, as I was getting ready for bed, I found myself staring into the mirror, not recognizing myself—but in the best possible way.

I don't have any hair anymore. A few days ago, I shaved my head. For Beth. The chemo is making her hair fall out, and I can tell it's upsetting her. Right now, she needs to have a positive outlook on life. But how can she do that when the chemo that's killing the cancer is making her sick? I felt so powerless, and I wanted to help, but I didn't know how. Then it just occurred to me:

Like the leaves falling outside, what if I cut my hair? Maybe if I shaved my head, Beth wouldn't feel so alone. Then Meg did it too. So did Amy. And when Beth saw—it's like the fear drained away from her eyes. The four of us are sisters. We always have been, and we always will be. I think the cancer made Beth feel like she was different. But now that we all have the same haircut? That worry is gone. I only pray it helps her recovery.

So yeah. Josephine March is bald. I know guys shave their heads all the time, but for a girl it's different. After I did it, for a minute I was like, in total shock. But almost instantly, I was okay. I kinda love it. I'm excited to see what I look like with a crew cut. Or maybe a pixie cut. Either way, I don't want to grow it out long again. This feels right. I feel more like... me. Like I'm closer to the real version of myself.

Me aside, I'm really proud of Meg. I wanted to ask her, but I never thought she would even consider it—not in a million years! Meg loves fashion and beauty and worries what others think about her. Cutting her hair meant sacrificing something that she considered beautiful and feminine and important to her appearance. By shaving it off, I think she learned that she doesn't have to rely on other's perceptions of herself to feel validated. In a way, I think what she did makes her even braver than me. Not to mention that it is so hard and takes so long for a woman to grow her hair out long and healthy. Good for Meg.

And she's not the only one. Amy is learning to be more self-aware, maybe even modest. I think that it shows she's becoming more empathetic—not that she wasn't already. Of course, every day, she calls us from Aunt Cath's when she's getting ready and says, "Where will I put my barrettes? Should I glue them to the side of my head?" Hahaha. That girl is crazy. But I love her. I love all my sisters.

Yes, it's autumn now, and the leaves will fall, and winter will come, and things will change. But I know we'll come out the other side of this stronger.

CHAPTER 16

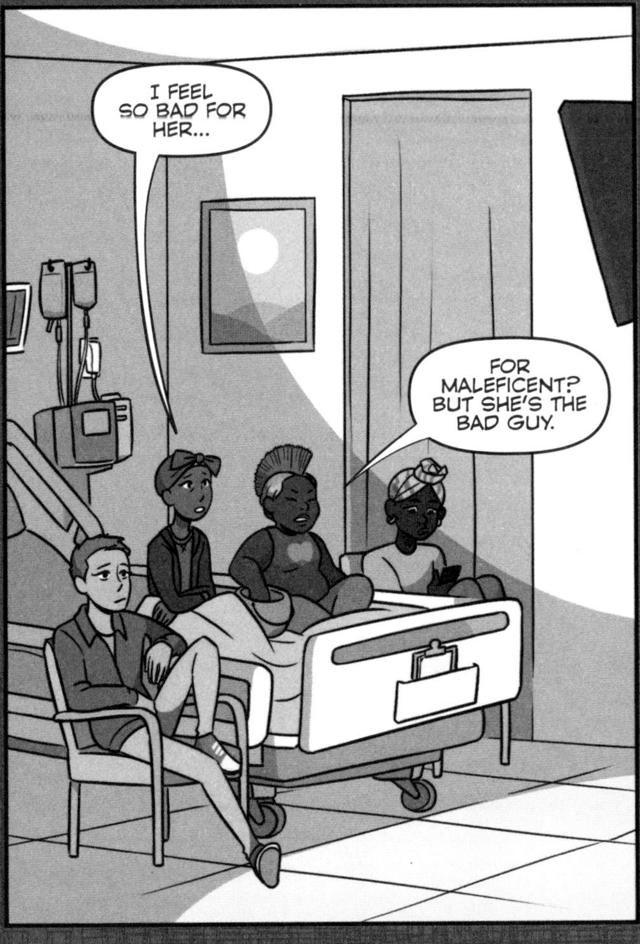
I FEEL SO BAD FOR HER...
FOR MALEFICENT? BUT SHE'S THE BAD GUY.

Dark Days and Darker Nights...

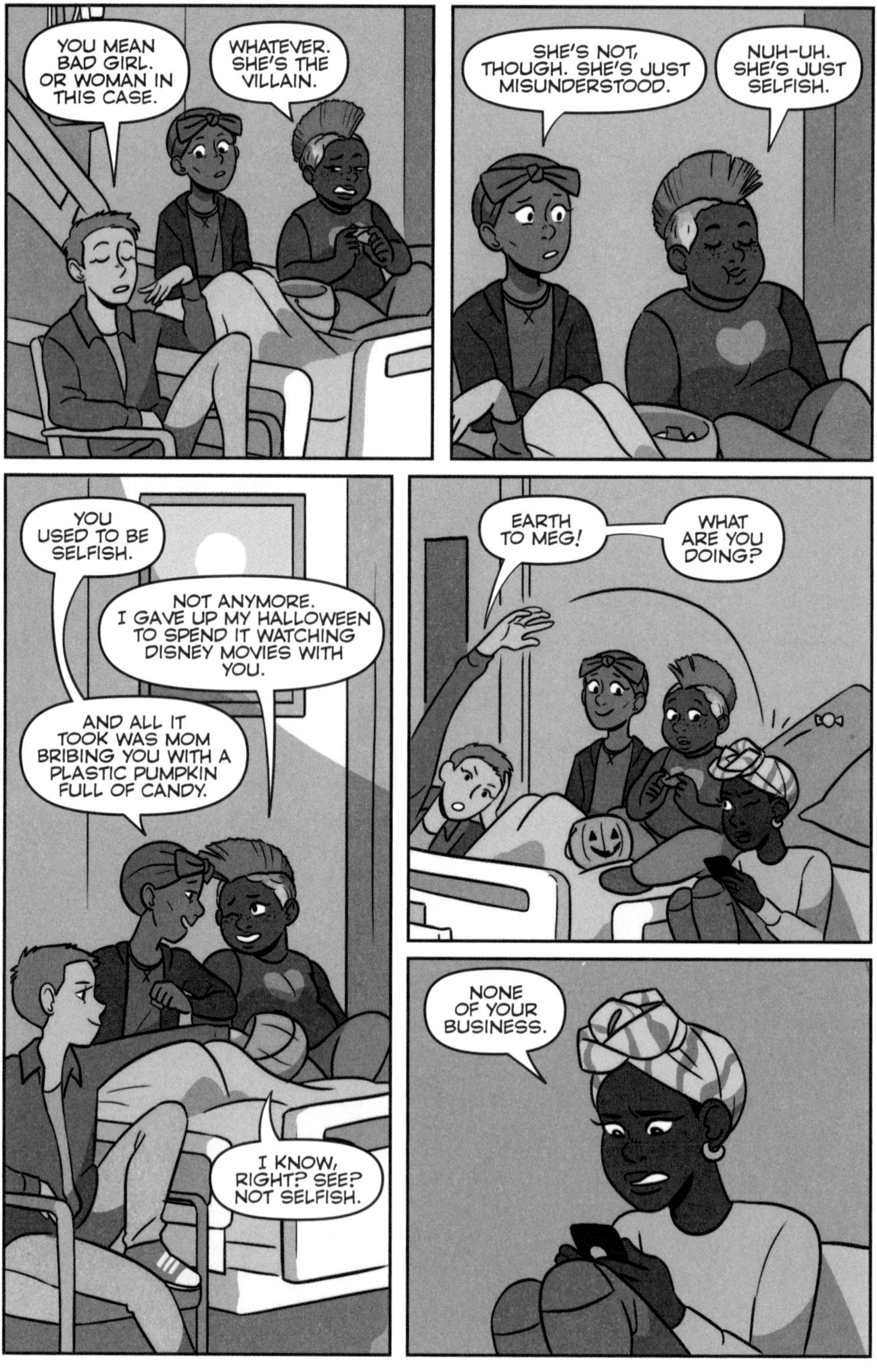
YOU MEAN BAD GIRL. OR WOMAN IN THIS CASE.
WHATEVER. SHE'S THE VILLAIN.
SHE'S NOT, THOUGH. SHE'S JUST MISUNDERSTOOD.
NUH-UH. SHE'S JUST SELFISH.
YOU USED TO BE SELFISH.
NOT ANYMORE. I GAVE UP MY HALLOWEEN TO SPEND IT WATCHING DISNEY MOVIES WITH YOU.
AND ALL IT TOOK WAS MOM BRIBING YOU WITH A PLASTIC PUMPKIN FULL OF CANDY.
I KNOW, RIGHT? SEE? NOT SELFISH.
EARTH TO MEG!
WHAT ARE YOU DOING?
NONE OF YOUR BUSINESS.

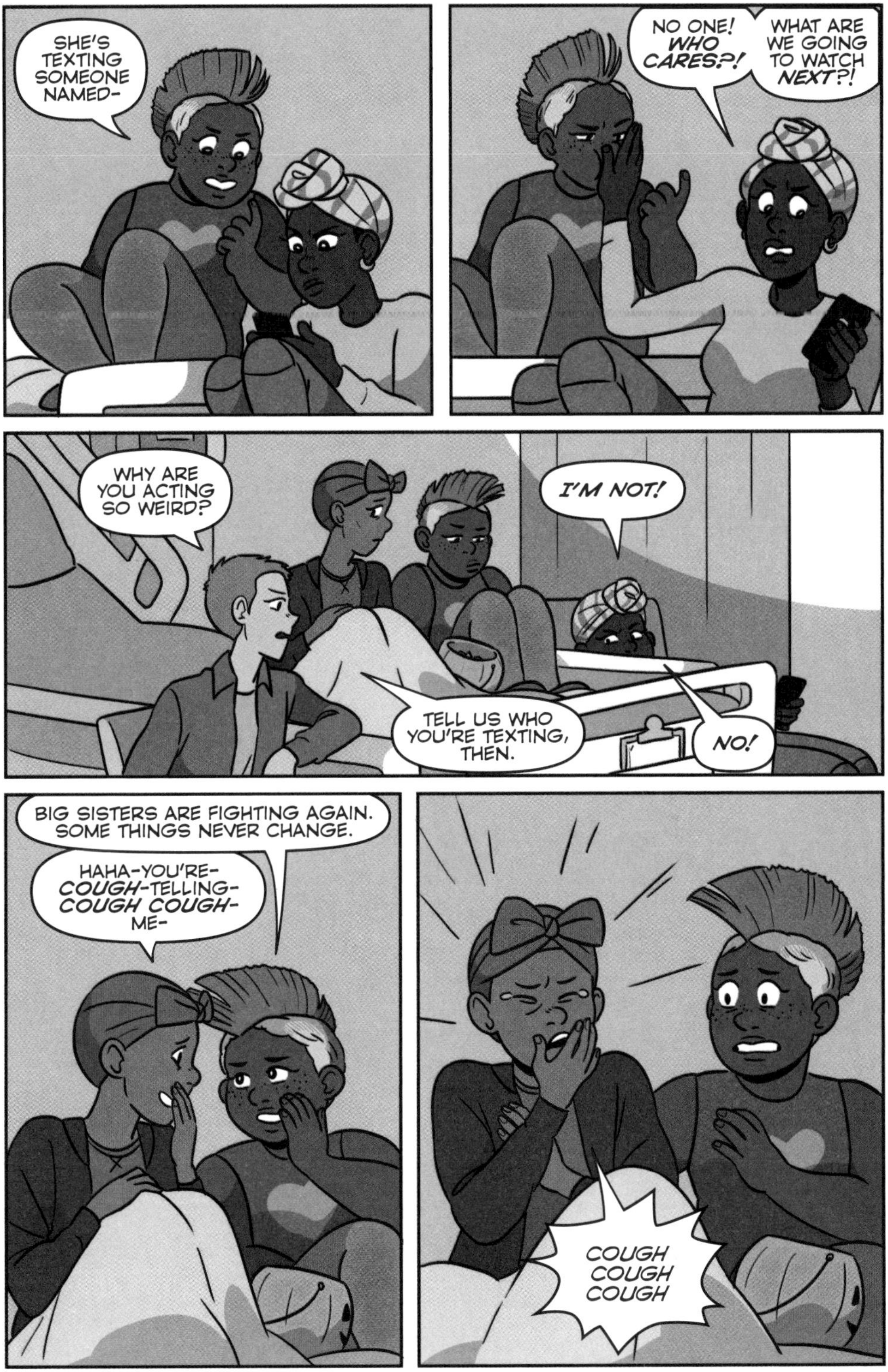
SHE'S TEXTING SOMEONE NAMED-
NO ONE! WHO CARES?!
WHAT ARE WE GOING TO WATCH NEXT?!
WHY ARE YOU ACTING SO WEIRD?
I'M NOT!
TELL US WHO YOU'RE TEXTING, THEN.
NO!
BIG SISTERS ARE FIGHTING AGAIN. SOME THINGS NEVER CHANGE.
HAHA-YOU'RE-COUGH-TELLING-COUGH COUGH-ME-
COUGH COUGH COUGH

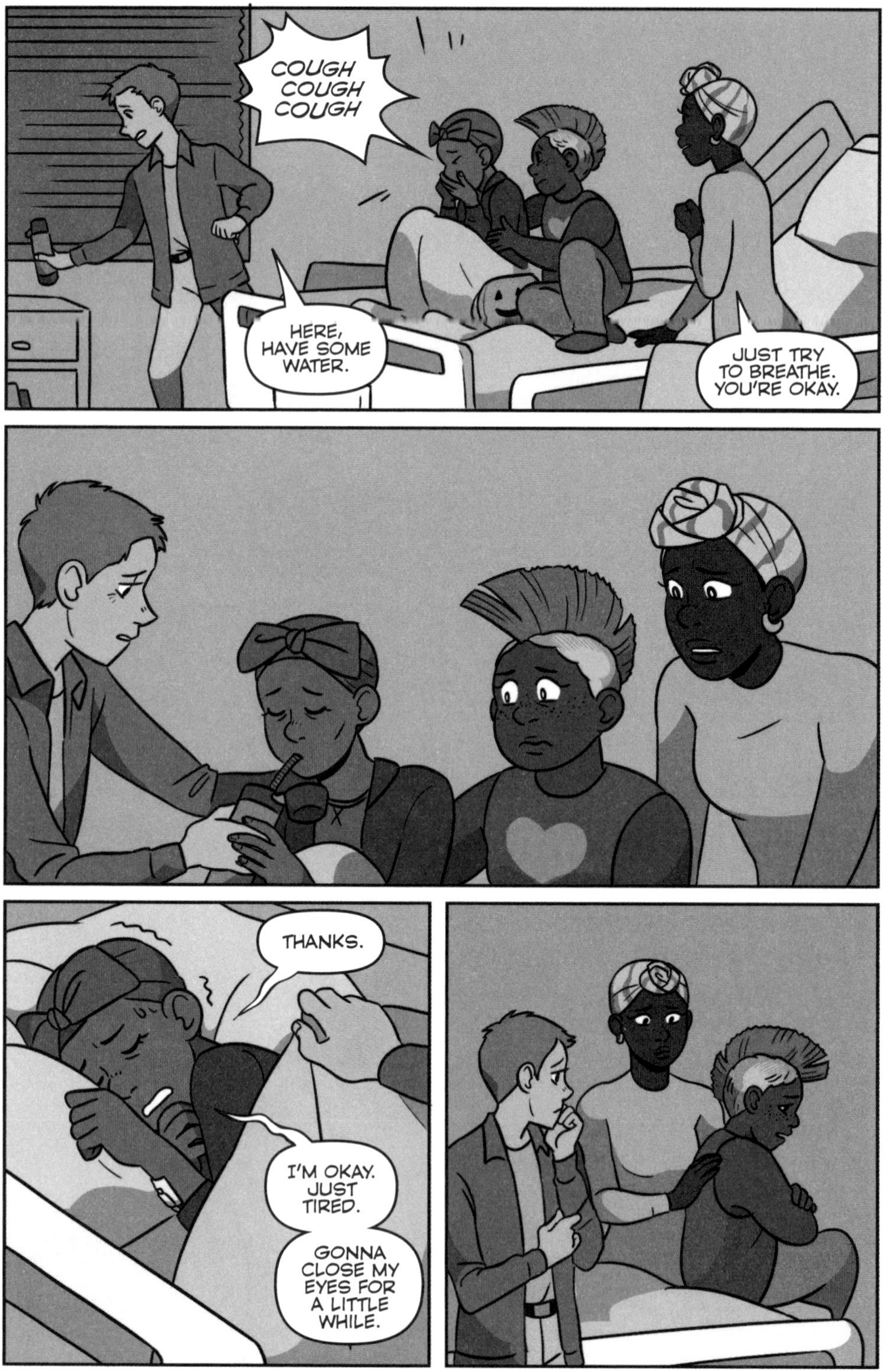
COUGH COUGH COUGH
HERE, HAVE SOME WATER.
JUST TRY TO BREATHE. YOU'RE OKAY.
THANKS.
I'M OKAY. JUST TIRED.
GONNA CLOSE MY EYES FOR A LITTLE WHILE.

FROM: Megan March
TO: Robert March
SENT: November 1

Hi Dad,

I'm sorry I didn't get a chance to call last night. We were staying with Beth at the hospital for Halloween and it got too late. I didn't want to wake you. But I promise I'll call today when I get home from school.

This autumn feels so strange. Usually I don't even notice the changing of the leaves or the shortening of the days. But this year, everything feels so sad. You know it's tradition for us to go trick or treating and then watch a scary movie. But this year Beth asked if we could do Disney movies instead. I don't mind, but it just felt so odd, us trying to watch movies while Beth battles cancer and you recover from your injuries.

When are you coming home? We really miss you.
I really miss you.

Your daughter, forever and always, Meg

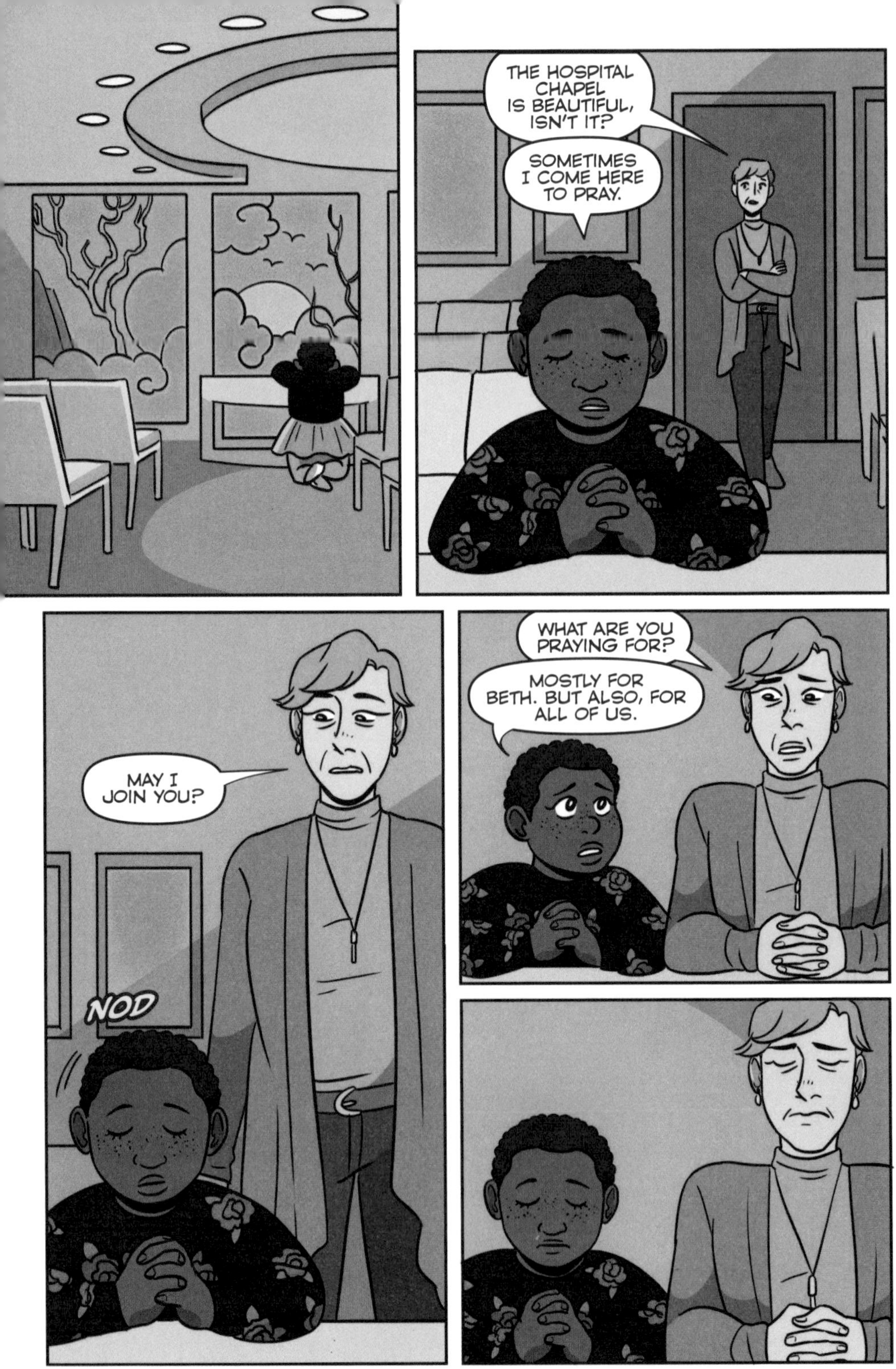
THE HOSPITAL CHAPEL IS BEAUTIFUL, ISN'T IT?
SOMETIMES I COME HERE TO PRAY.
MAY I JOIN YOU?
NOD
WHAT ARE YOU PRAYING FOR?
MOSTLY FOR BETH. BUT ALSO, FOR ALL OF US.

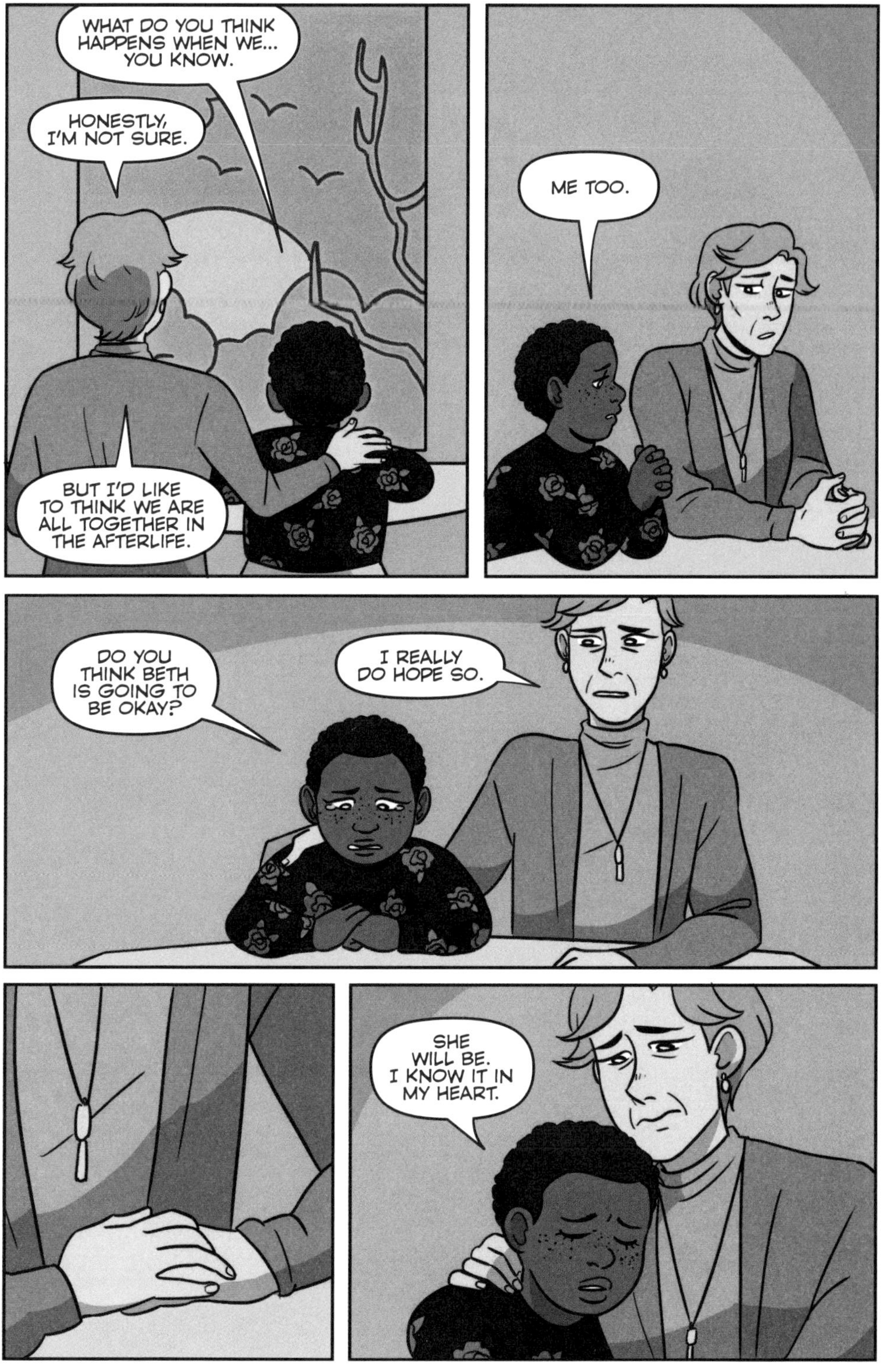
WHAT DO YOU THINK HAPPENS WHEN WE... YOU KNOW.
HONESTLY, I'M NOT SURE.
BUT I'D LIKE TO THINK WE ARE ALL TOGETHER IN THE AFTERLIFE.
ME TOO.
DO YOU THINK BETH IS GOING TO BE OKAY?
I REALLY DO HOPE SO.
SHE WILL BE. I KNOW IT IN MY HEART.

FROM: Amy March
TO: Robert March
SENT: November 1

Heya Daddy,

Beth is still sick. And everyone is sad. And we miss you.
I know your legs won't be the same, but I don't care.
Please come home soon. Please?

—Amy

Send

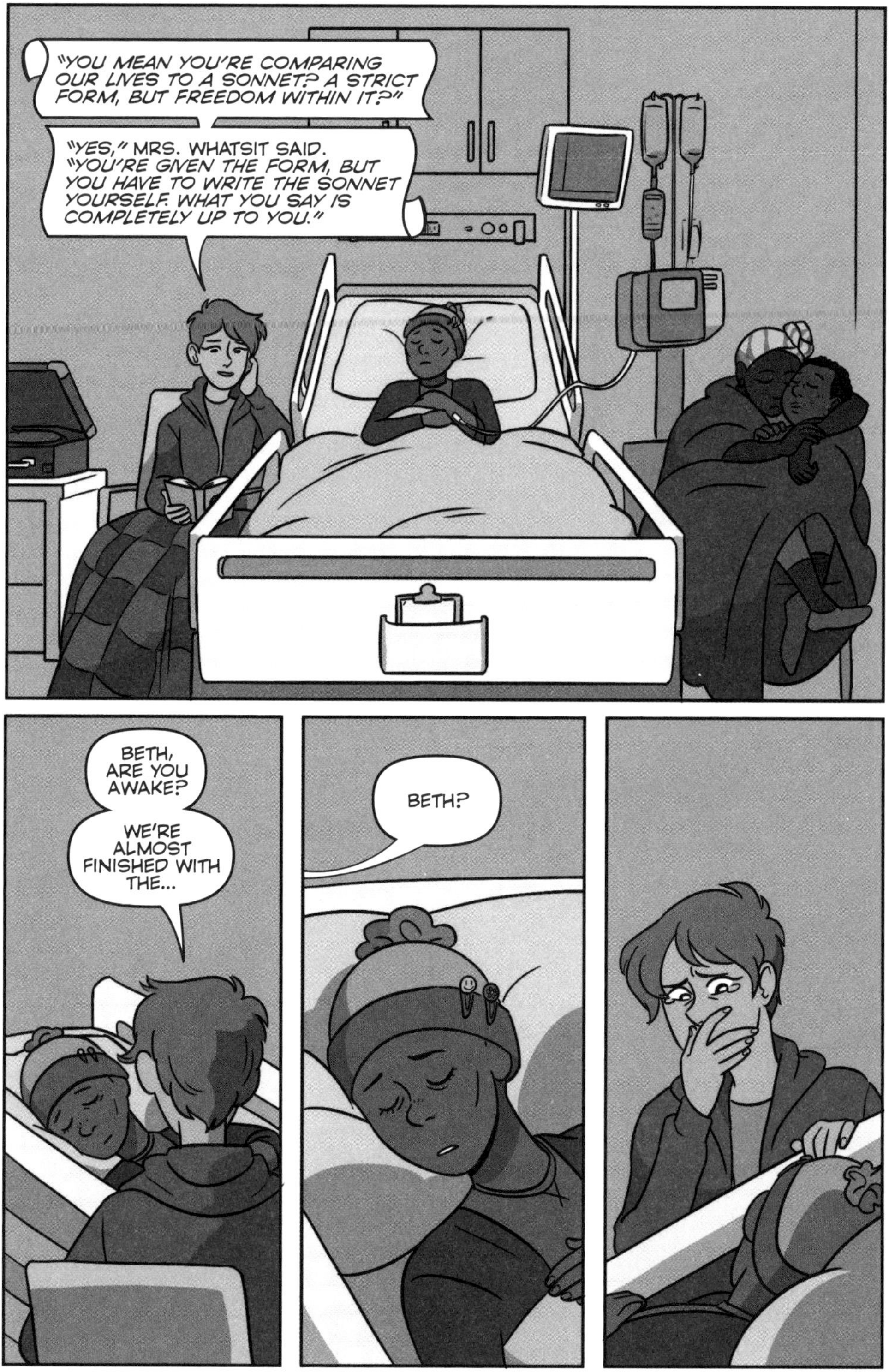
"YOU MEAN YOU'RE COMPARING OUR LIVES TO A SONNET? A STRICT FORM, BUT FREEDOM WITHIN IT?"
"YES," MRS. WHATSIT SAID. "YOU'RE GIVEN THE FORM, BUT YOU HAVE TO WRITE THE SONNET YOURSELF. WHAT YOU SAY IS COMPLETELY UP TO YOU."
BETH, ARE YOU AWAKE?
WE'RE ALMOST FINISHED WITH THE...
BETH?

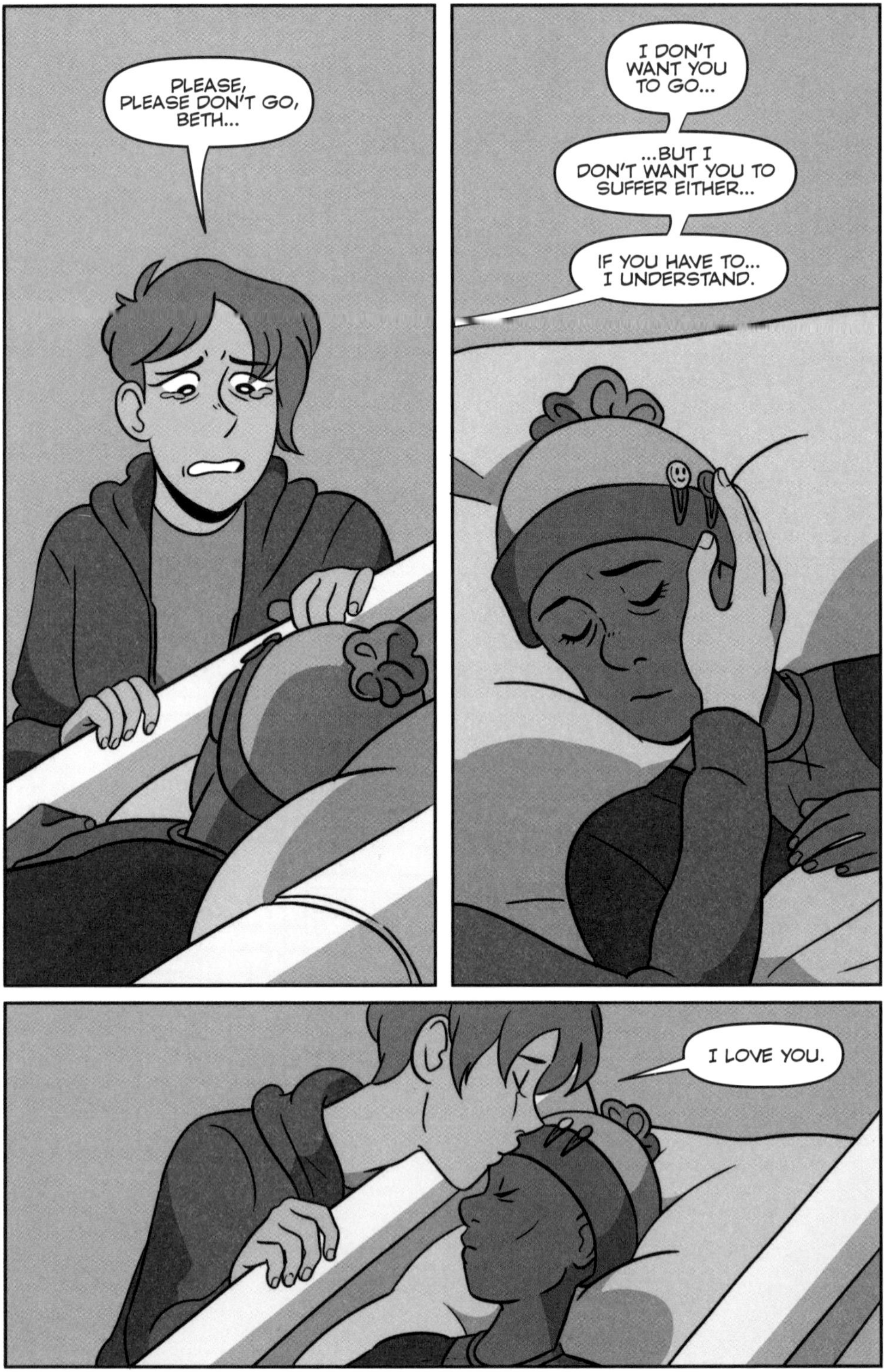
PLEASE, PLEASE DON'T GO, BETH...
I DON'T WANT YOU TO GO...
...BUT I DON'T WANT YOU TO SUFFER EITHER...
IF YOU HAVE TO... I UNDERSTAND.
I LOVE YOU.

November 7

I've never been so afraid.

I think Beth is dying.

I don't know how long I have left with her, so I refuse to leave her side. Mom and Meg tried to get me to go home, but I refused. I know they understand. We're all going through this together, but it's Beth. My Beth. She is more than my sister. She's my best friend, my kindred spirit. She's my favorite. I know we're not supposed to have favorite sisters, but I do. Beth is like me. She is a creator, of words, and music, and...

I'm afraid that her song is over.

Tonight I looked at her, lying there, pale and gaunt, like a ghost of her former self. And I thought, this is it. I kissed her and I said my goodbyes.

Please don't let this be it.

I want to be hopeful, like the others, but I can't. The rest of my family has faith, but if I'm being honest...I don't think I do. Our world is a terrible and dark place. If it weren't, then how do you explain innocent children getting sick?

It's not fair. It's not!

This life feels unbearable right now. Like I can't breathe. I wish I could change places with Beth. I would in an instant. My life for hers. If only it were that simple.

I love you, Beth.

I love you so much.

And if this is our last night together....I only hope that I will see you again. Perhaps on the other side...

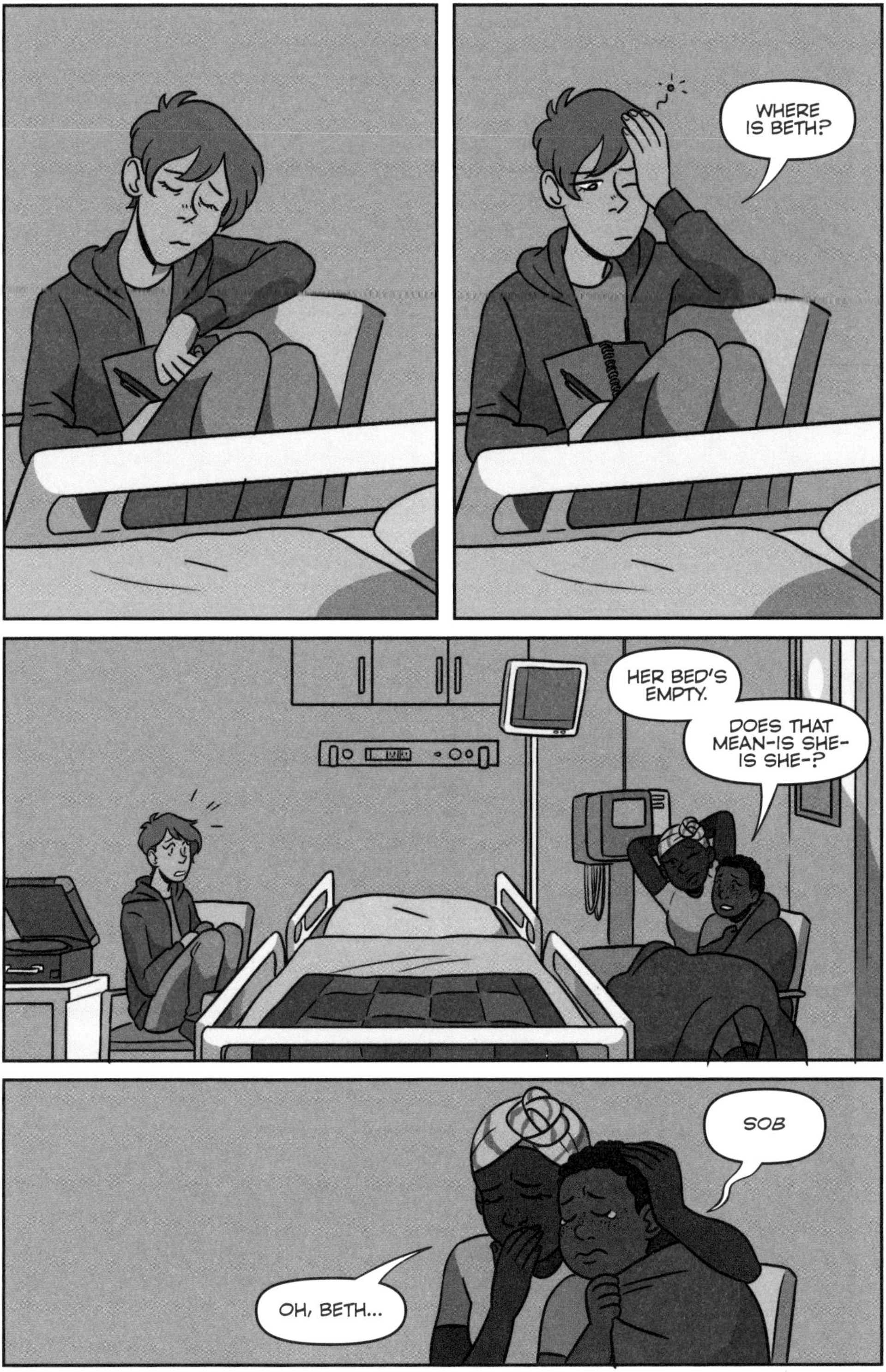
WHERE IS BETH?
HER BED'S EMPTY.
DOES THAT MEAN-IS SHE- IS SHE-?
SOB
OH, BETH...

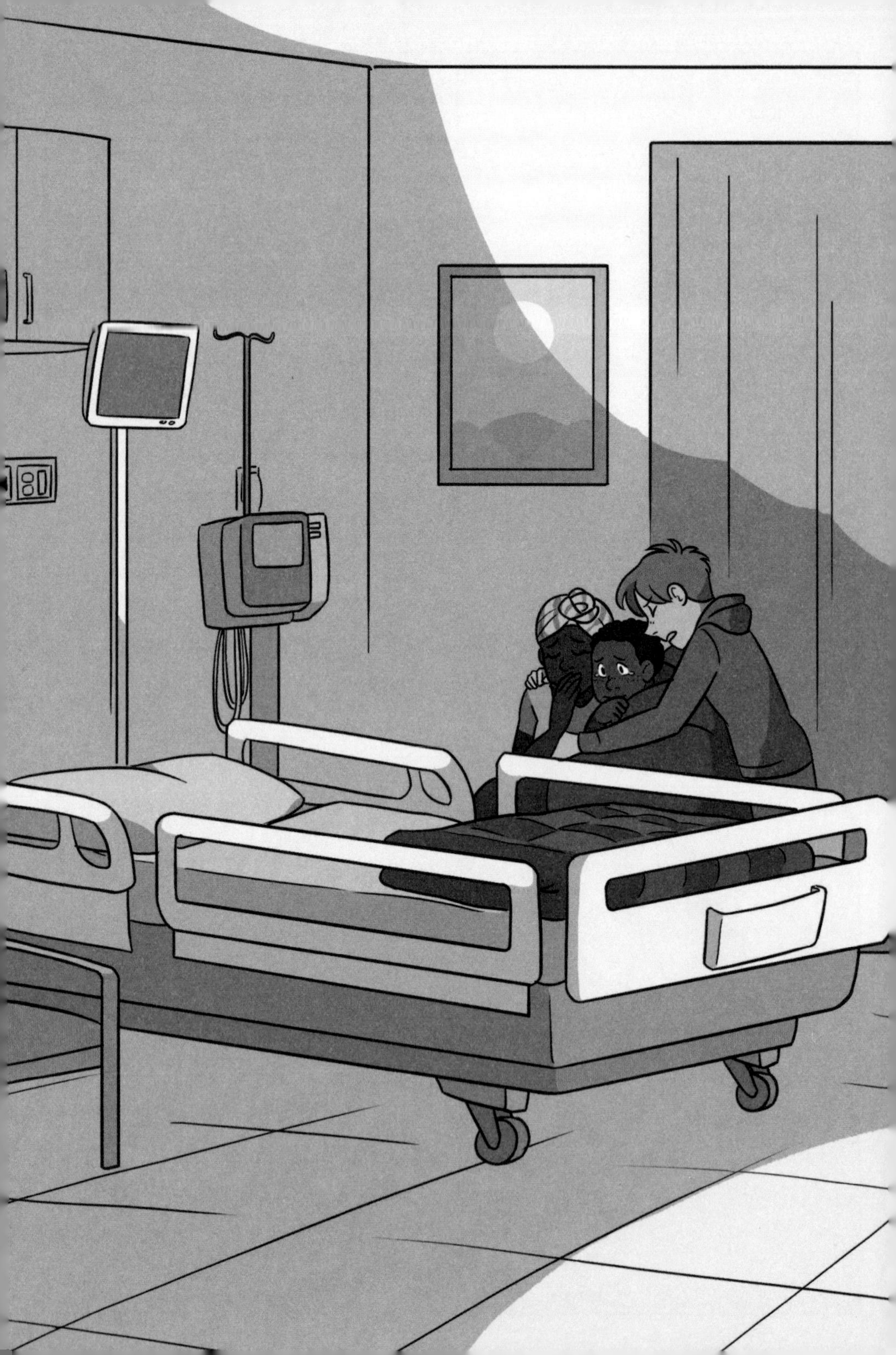

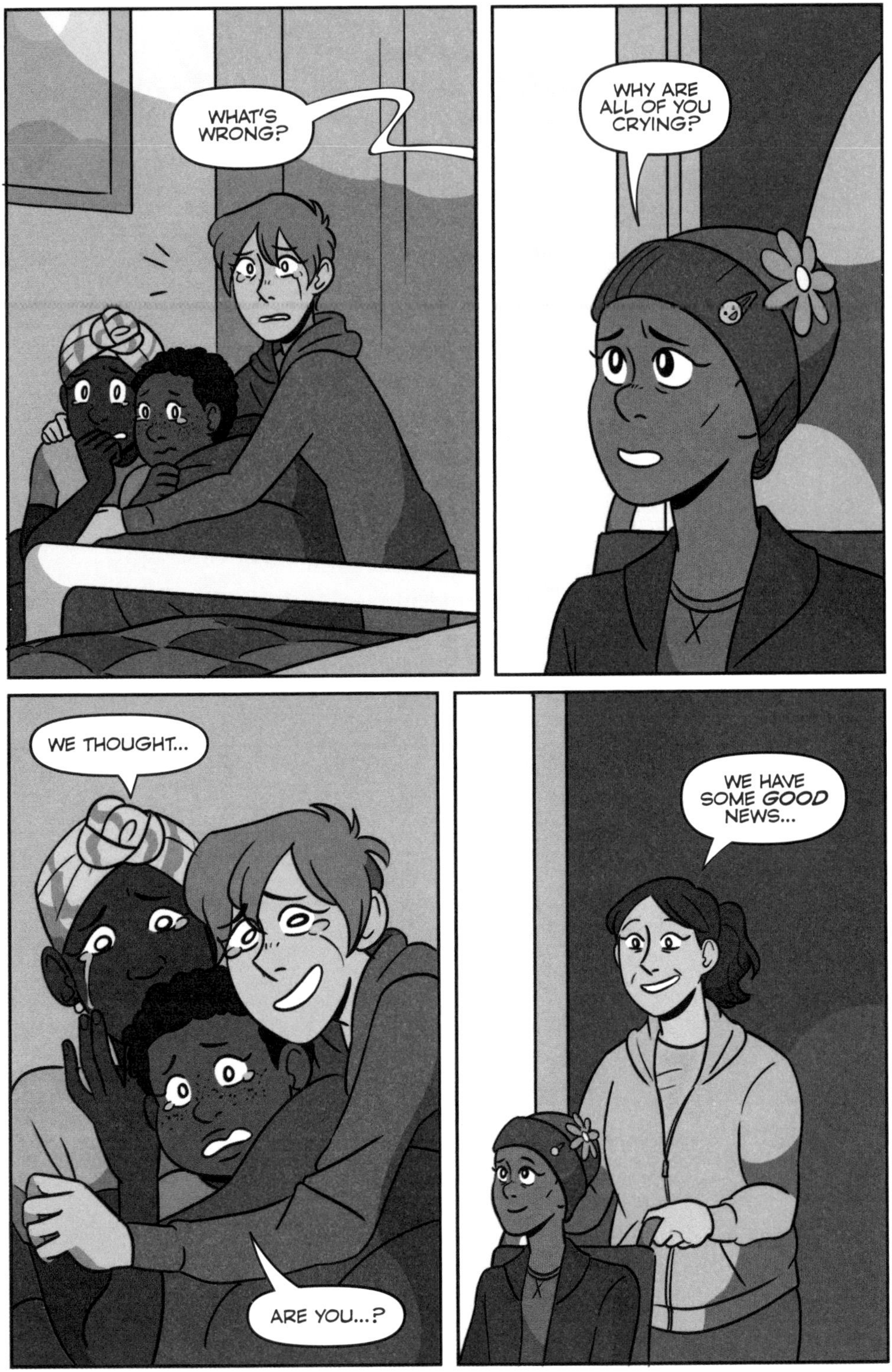
WHAT'S WRONG?
WHY ARE ALL OF YOU CRYING?
WE THOUGHT...
ARE YOU...?
WE HAVE SOME *GOOD* NEWS...

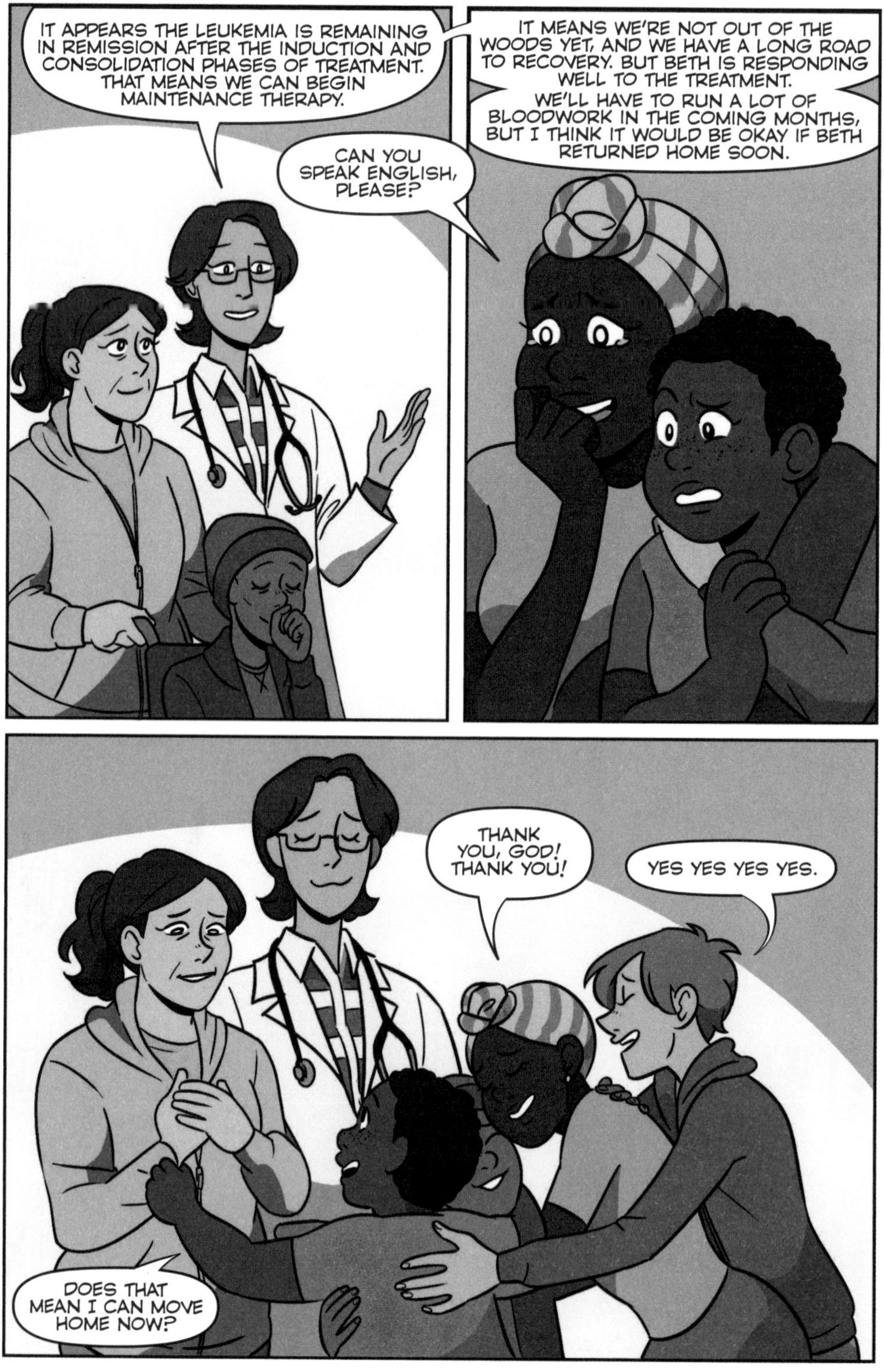
IT APPEARS THE LEUKEMIA IS REMAINING IN REMISSION AFTER THE INDUCTION AND CONSOLIDATION PHASES OF TREATMENT. THAT MEANS WE CAN BEGIN MAINTENANCE THERAPY.
CAN YOU SPEAK ENGLISH, PLEASE?
IT MEANS WE'RE NOT OUT OF THE WOODS YET, AND WE HAVE A LONG ROAD TO RECOVERY. BUT BETH IS RESPONDING WELL TO THE TREATMENT.
WE'LL HAVE TO RUN A LOT OF BLOODWORK IN THE COMING MONTHS, BUT I THINK IT WOULD BE OKAY IF BETH RETURNED HOME SOON.
THANK YOU, GOD! THANK YOU!
YES YES YES YES.
DOES THAT MEAN I CAN MOVE HOME NOW?

November 14

Jo's Journal: KEEP OUT

Beth is going to be okay. At least I think she is. I was never that good at science. But I think I understand some of this stuff now.

When leukemia gets diagnosed, there are about 100 billion cancer cells in the body. (Can you even imagine?). During the first part of treatment (called Induction), they try to kill 99.9% of the leukemia cells. That's enough to achieve "Remission." But that still leaves about 100 million cancer cells in the body. These also have to be destroyed. So the next phase is called Consolidation. That lasts about one to two months. And it's really really intense. That's why Beth had to stay at the hospital, so she didn't get a serious infection or in case of complications. But she came through. Like a total champ!

The last couple of months have been exhausting for everyone, but Dr. Shah says now is where the real work begins. We have about two years of maintenance chemotherapy ahead of us. The goal is to destroy the remaining cancer cells. Two years seems like a lifetime, but if it'll help Beth, then I'll do it. We all will.

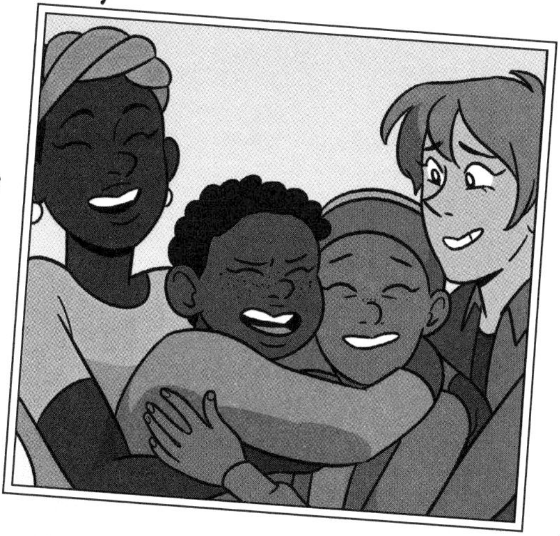

Bring it on, life. March girls can take anything you throw at us.

CHAPTER 17

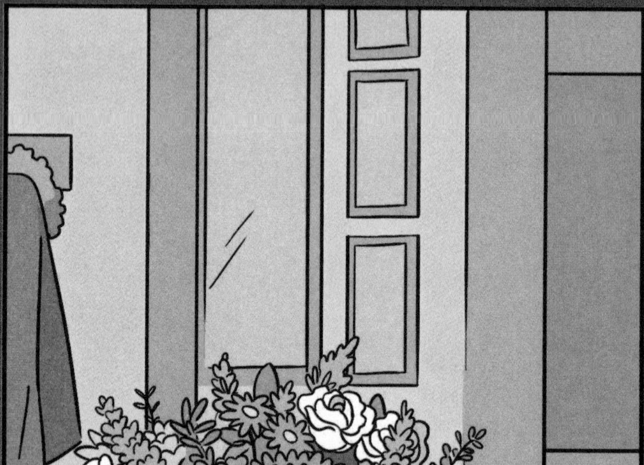
Sorry you feel like

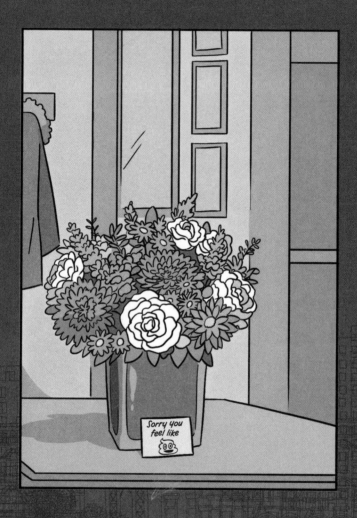

Colder and Warmer...

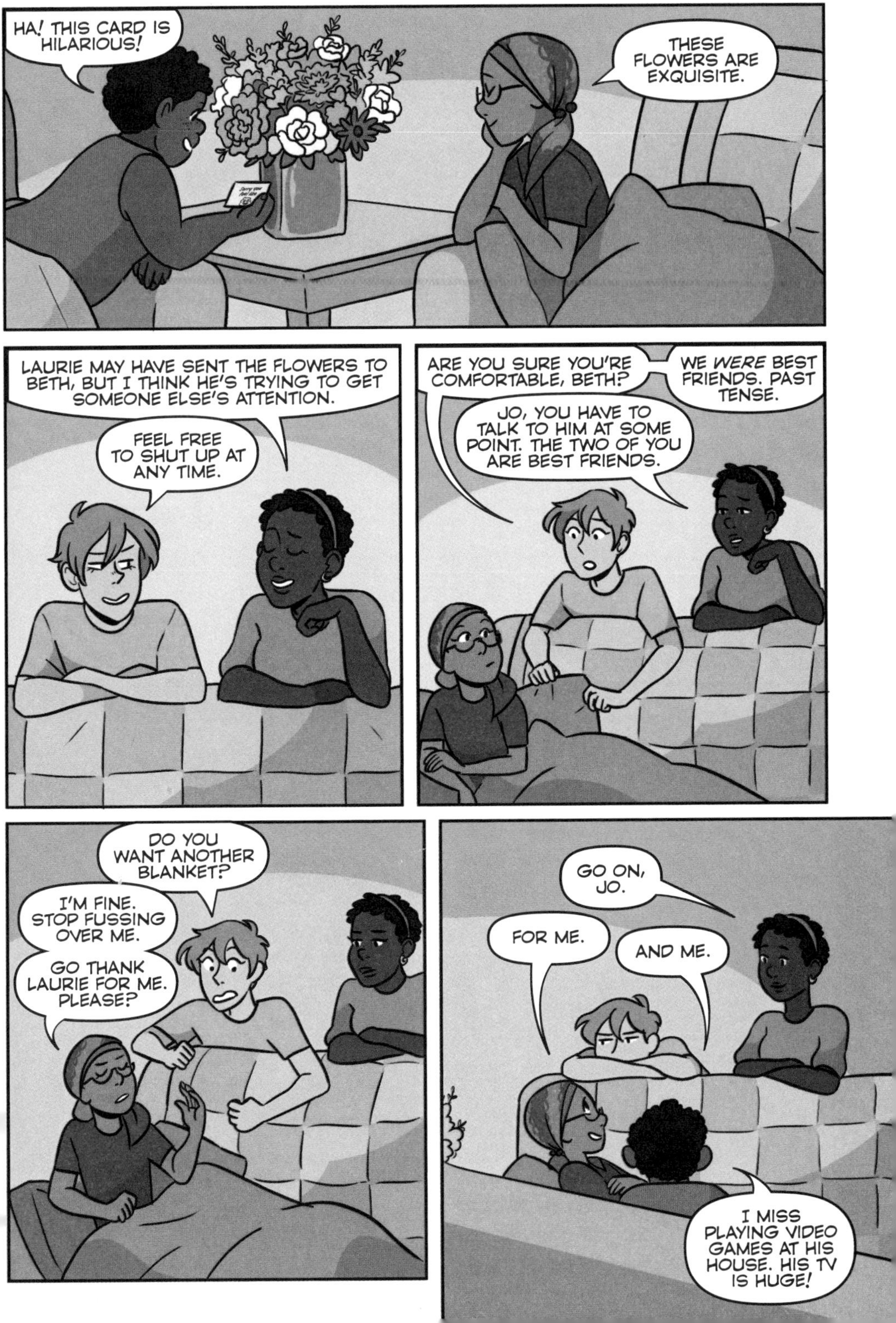
HA! THIS CARD IS HILARIOUS!
THESE FLOWERS ARE EXQUISITE.
LAURIE MAY HAVE SENT THE FLOWERS TO BETH, BUT I THINK HE'S TRYING TO GET SOMEONE ELSE'S ATTENTION.
FEEL FREE TO SHUT UP AT ANY TIME.
ARE YOU SURE YOU'RE COMFORTABLE, BETH?
WE *WERE* BEST FRIENDS. PAST TENSE.
JO, YOU HAVE TO TALK TO HIM AT SOME POINT. THE TWO OF YOU ARE BEST FRIENDS.
DO YOU WANT ANOTHER BLANKET?
I'M FINE. STOP FUSSING OVER ME.
GO THANK LAURIE FOR ME. PLEASE?
GO ON, JO.
FOR ME.
AND ME.
I MISS PLAYING VIDEO GAMES AT HIS HOUSE. HIS TV IS HUGE!

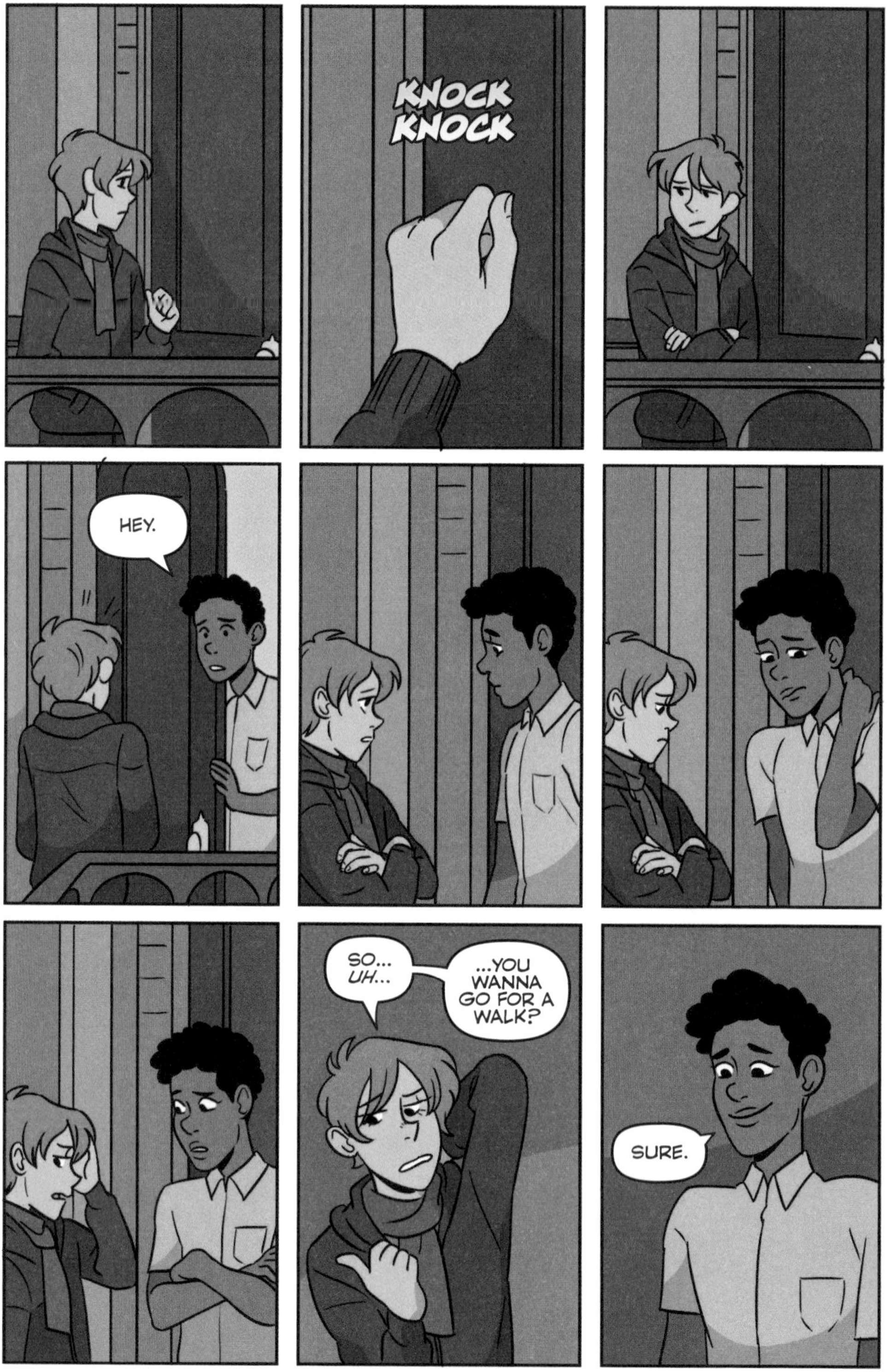
KNOCK
KNOCK
HEY.
SO... UH...
...YOU WANNA GO FOR A WALK?
SURE.

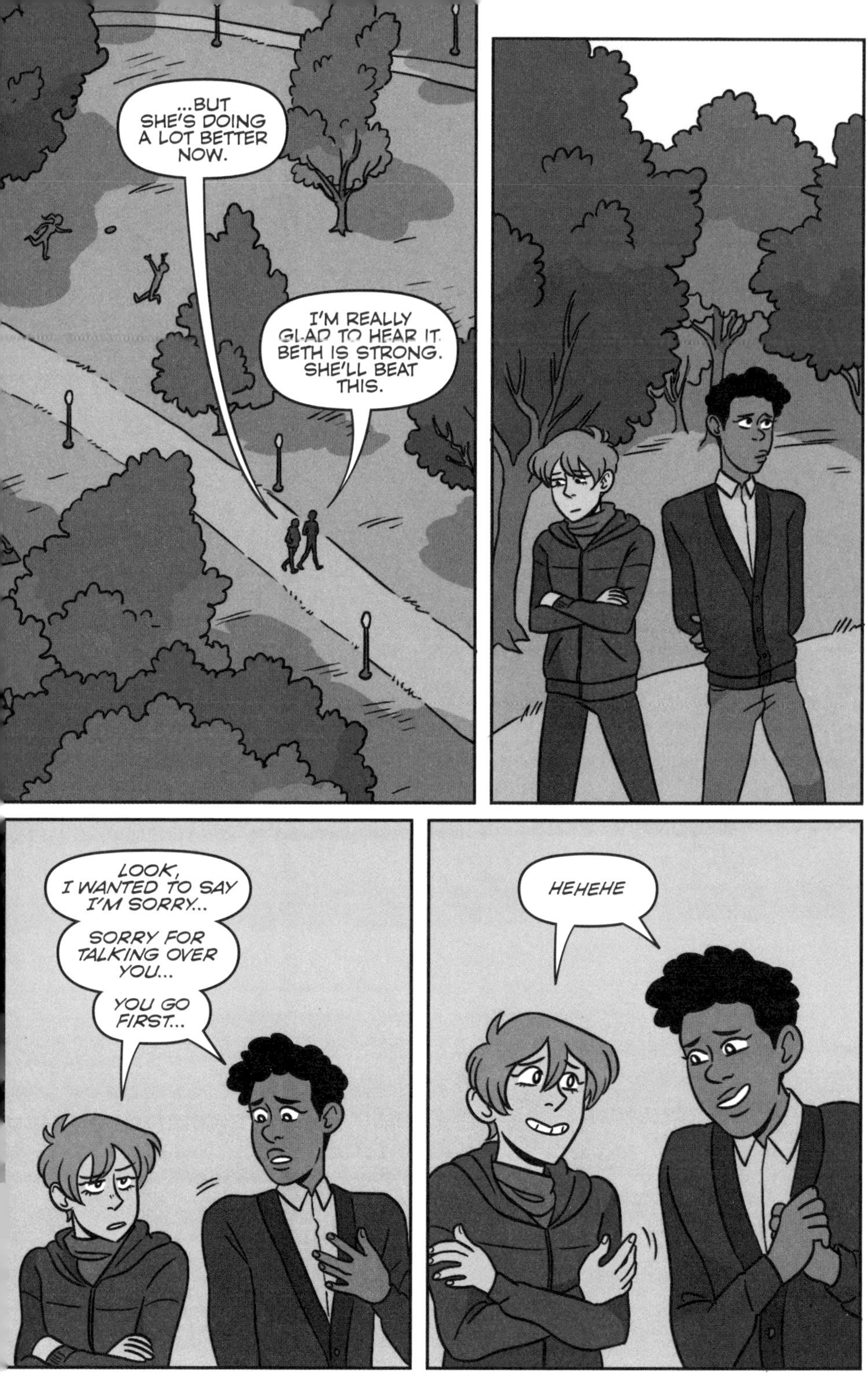
...BUT SHE'S DOING A LOT BETTER NOW.
I'M REALLY GLAD TO HEAR IT. BETH IS STRONG. SHE'LL BEAT THIS.
LOOK, I WANTED TO SAY I'M SORRY...
SORRY FOR TALKING OVER YOU...
YOU GO FIRST...
HEHEHE

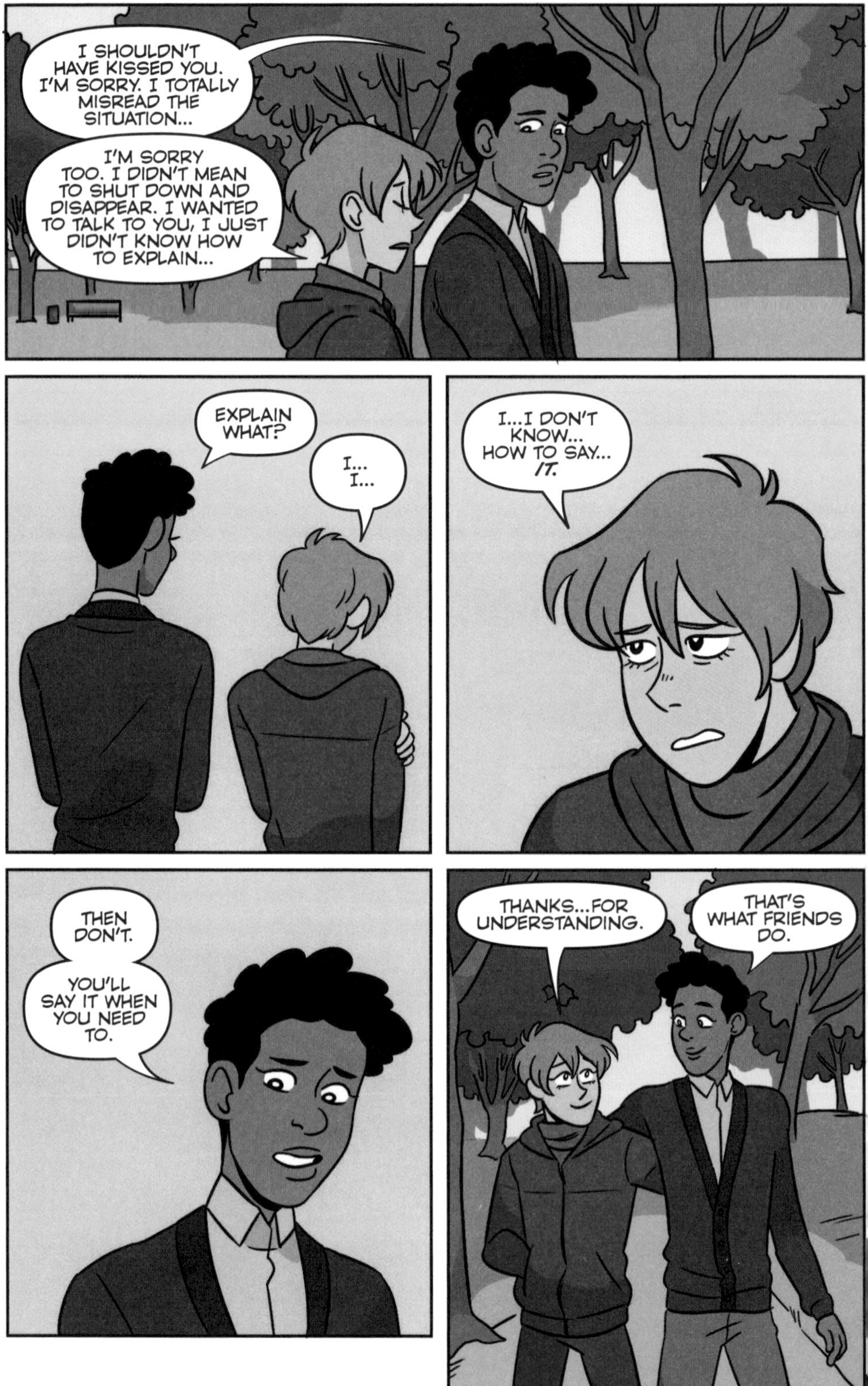
I SHOULDN'T HAVE KISSED YOU. I'M SORRY. I TOTALLY MISREAD THE SITUATION...
I'M SORRY TOO. I DIDN'T MEAN TO SHUT DOWN AND DISAPPEAR. I WANTED TO TALK TO YOU, I JUST DIDN'T KNOW HOW TO EXPLAIN...
EXPLAIN WHAT?
I... I...
I...I DON'T KNOW... HOW TO SAY... *IT.*
THEN DON'T.
YOU'LL SAY IT WHEN YOU NEED TO.
THANKS...FOR UNDERSTANDING.
THAT'S WHAT FRIENDS DO.

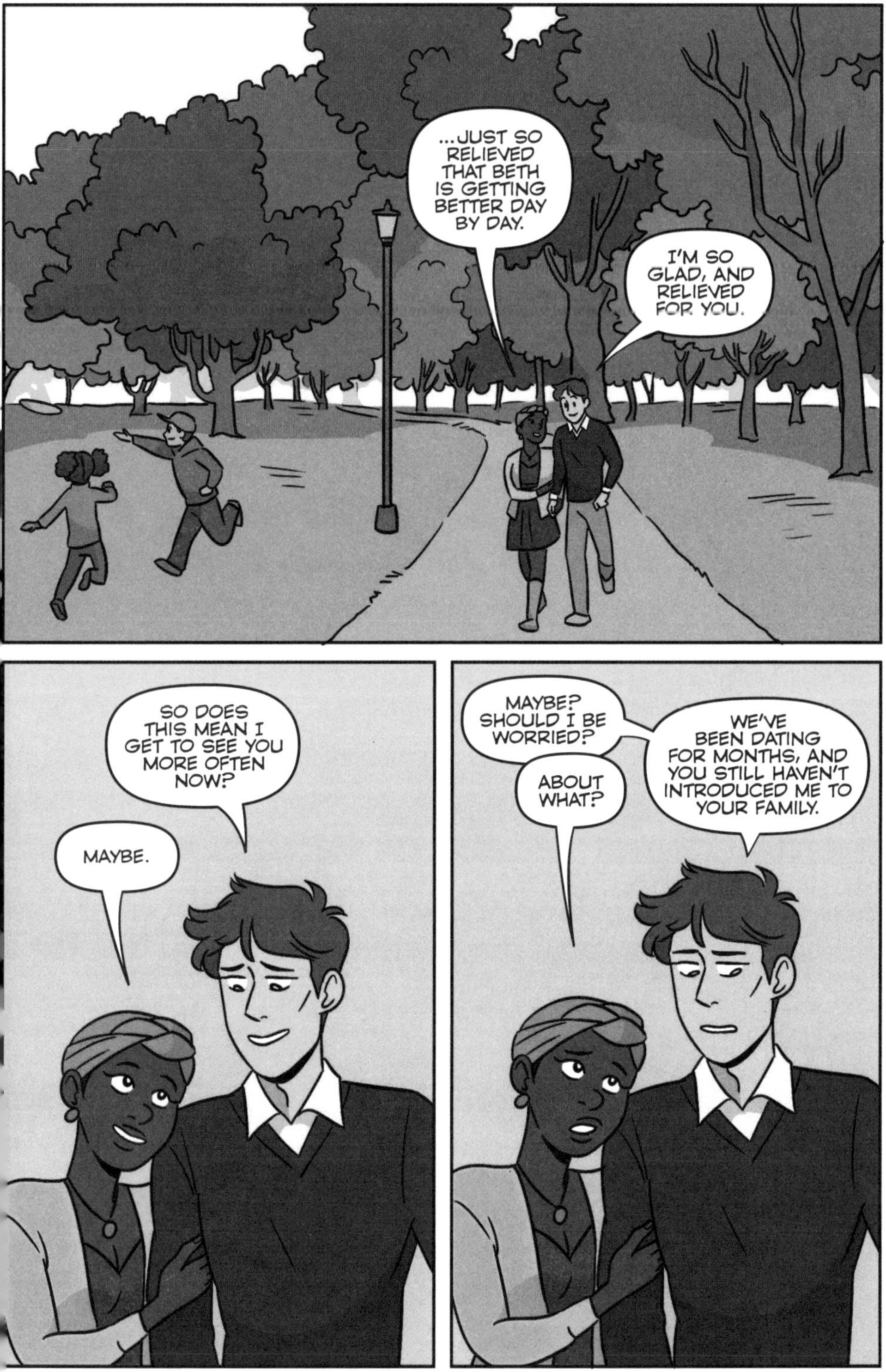
...JUST SO RELIEVED THAT BETH IS GETTING BETTER DAY BY DAY.
I'M SO GLAD, AND RELIEVED FOR YOU.
SO DOES THIS MEAN I GET TO SEE YOU MORE OFTEN NOW?
MAYBE.
MAYBE? SHOULD I BE WORRIED?
ABOUT WHAT?
WE'VE BEEN DATING FOR MONTHS, AND YOU STILL HAVEN'T INTRODUCED ME TO YOUR FAMILY.

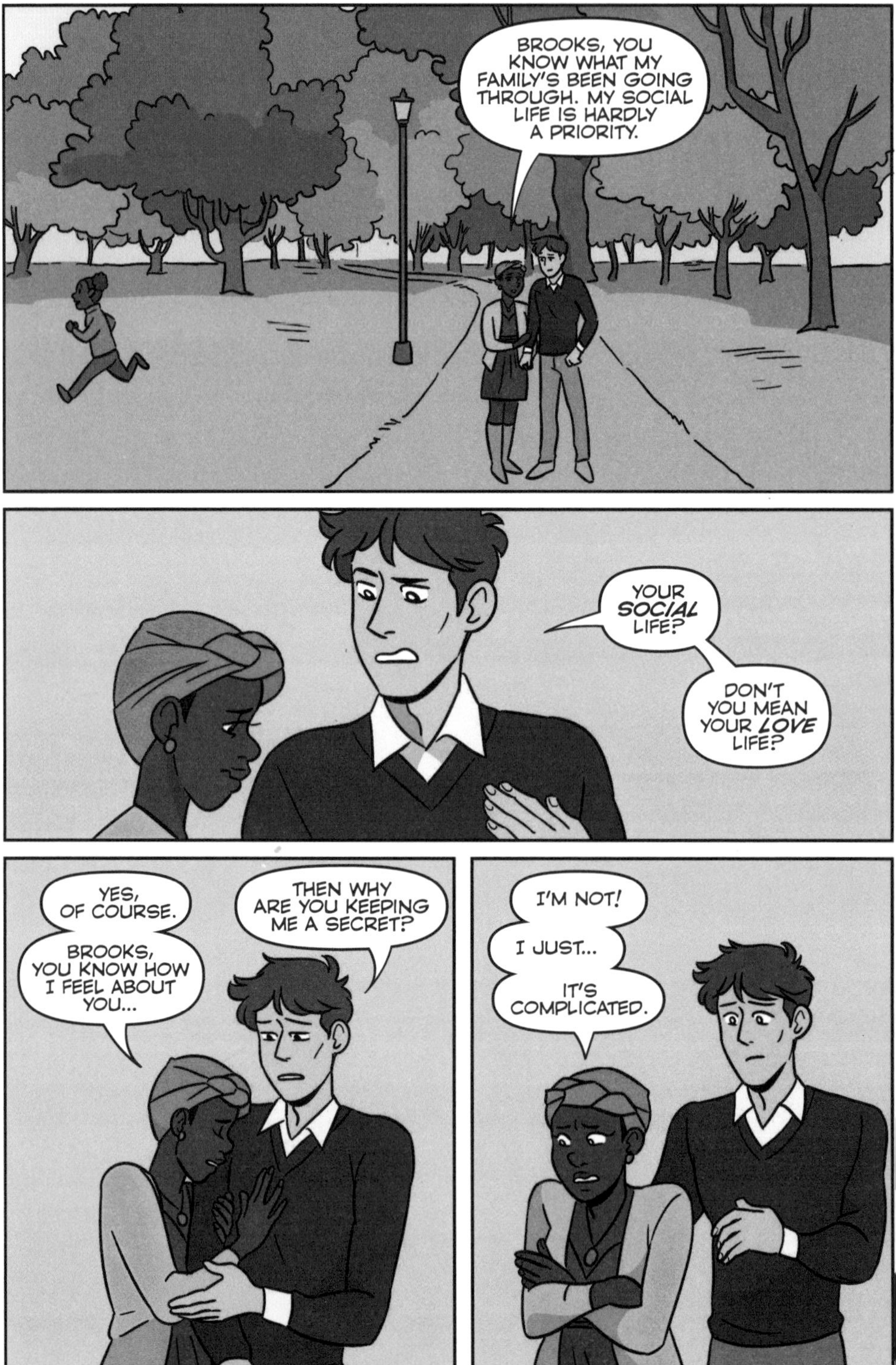
BROOKS, YOU KNOW WHAT MY FAMILY'S BEEN GOING THROUGH. MY SOCIAL LIFE IS HARDLY A PRIORITY.
YOUR *SOCIAL* LIFE?
DON'T YOU MEAN YOUR *LOVE* LIFE?
YES, OF COURSE.
BROOKS, YOU KNOW HOW I FEEL ABOUT YOU...
THEN WHY ARE YOU KEEPING ME A SECRET?
I'M NOT!
I JUST...
IT'S COMPLICATED.

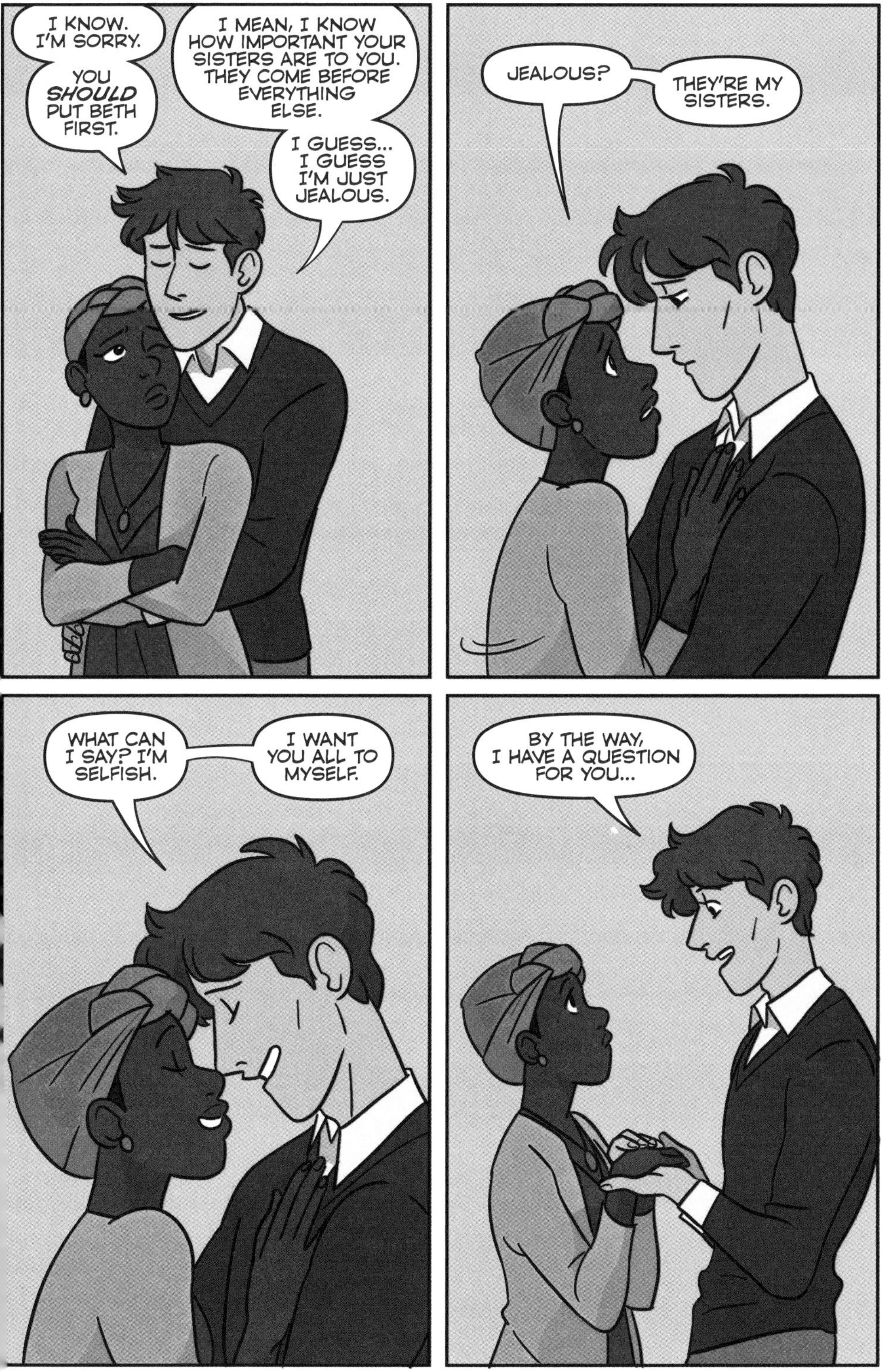
I KNOW. I'M SORRY.
YOU *SHOULD* PUT BETH FIRST.
I MEAN, I KNOW HOW IMPORTANT YOUR SISTERS ARE TO YOU. THEY COME BEFORE EVERYTHING ELSE.
I GUESS... I GUESS I'M JUST JEALOUS.
JEALOUS?
THEY'RE MY SISTERS.
WHAT CAN I SAY? I'M SELFISH.
I WANT YOU ALL TO MYSELF.
BY THE WAY, I HAVE A QUESTION FOR YOU...

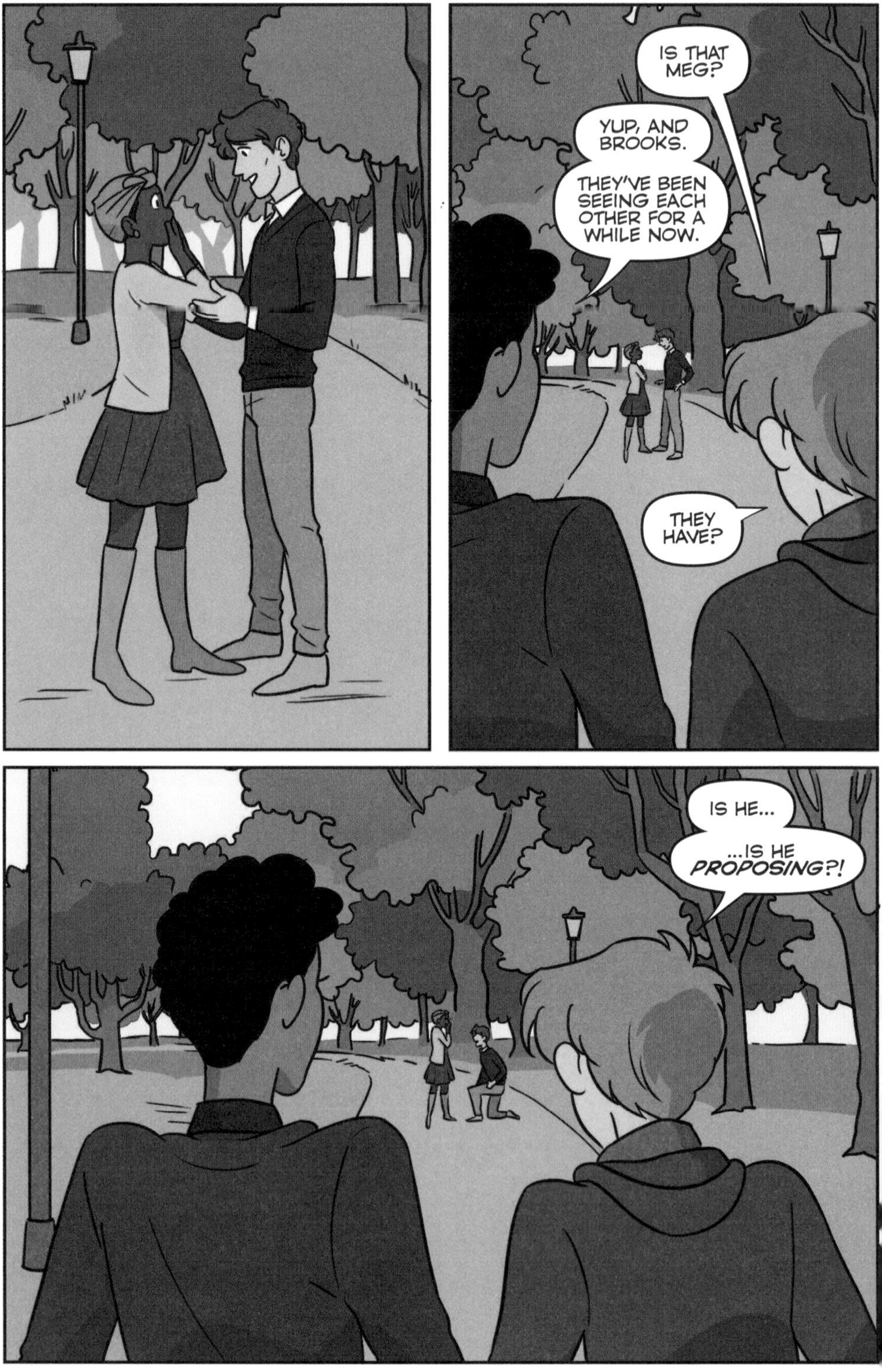
IS THAT MEG?
YUP, AND BROOKS.
THEY'VE BEEN SEEING EACH OTHER FOR A WHILE NOW.
THEY HAVE?
IS HE...
...IS HE *PROPOSING*?!

November 20

Meg is a liar!

Laurie and I were in the park, and I saw her...with Brooks. Laurie told me they've been dating for months. MONTHS! I guess it started just after they met at the 4th of July party we had. Meg's been so secretive and annoying with her texts and calls, and I was certain it was just Kennedy, but now I know the truth. I can't believe Meg would lie to me. I mean, no, I guess she didn't LIE-lie, but she withheld the truth, which is practically the same thing. If I was dating someone, I would tell her. But here she is, keeping a secret—a huge secret.

I should confront Meg, but I want to give her the chance to tell me. Though it's already been two days since I saw her in the park, and not a word! Brooks was on his knee, her hand in his. I think we all know what that means, what he asked her. They're engaged! Meg is going to be married! It's ridiculous. This isn't 1868. She hasn't even finished high school! Mom and Dad are going to FLIP OUT when they find out.

I am furious. Meg isn't just my sister, she's my best friend. Why wouldn't she tell me that she and Brooks were seeing each other? I mean, if she loves him, why be ashamed of it? He's exactly what she always wanted: handsome, educated, RICH. According to Laurie, he's a trust fund kid with a work ethic. That's a modern-day Prince Charming if I've ever heard of one. Of course, Meg would say yes. I can't believe she's getting married! She's going to skip college to be some stupid bride and probably have kids and...OMG. I'm going to be an aunt before I finish high school.

Meg is making a huge mistake. She has her whole life ahead of her, and she has so much potential that she'll waste if she gets married before she finds out who she really is....I don't know what to do. Should I tell Mom? Should I keep quiet? UGH. I hate secrets!!! And yes, I understand the complete and total irony of ME, of all people, loathing secrets. I may be a hypocrite, but at least I'm not some child bride like Meg!

CHAPTER 18

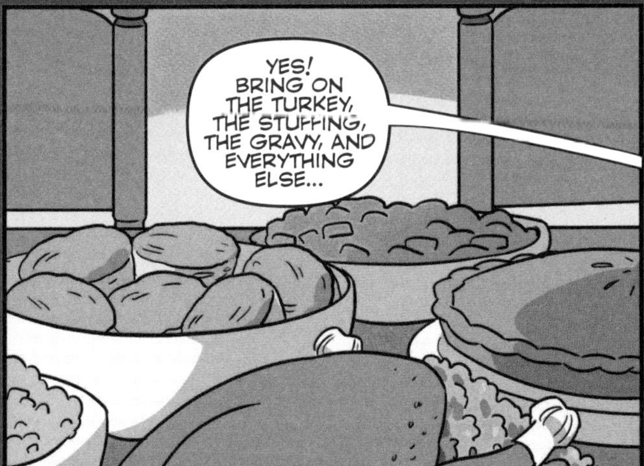
YES! BRING ON THE TURKEY, THE STUFFING, THE GRAVY, AND EVERYTHING ELSE...

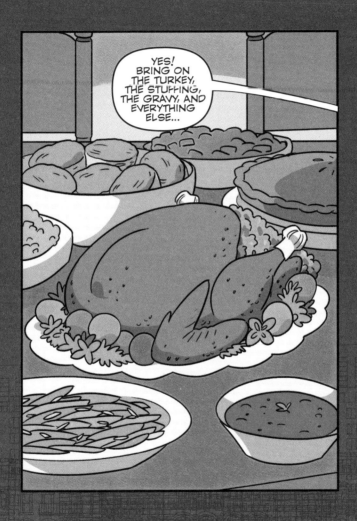

Giving Thanks...

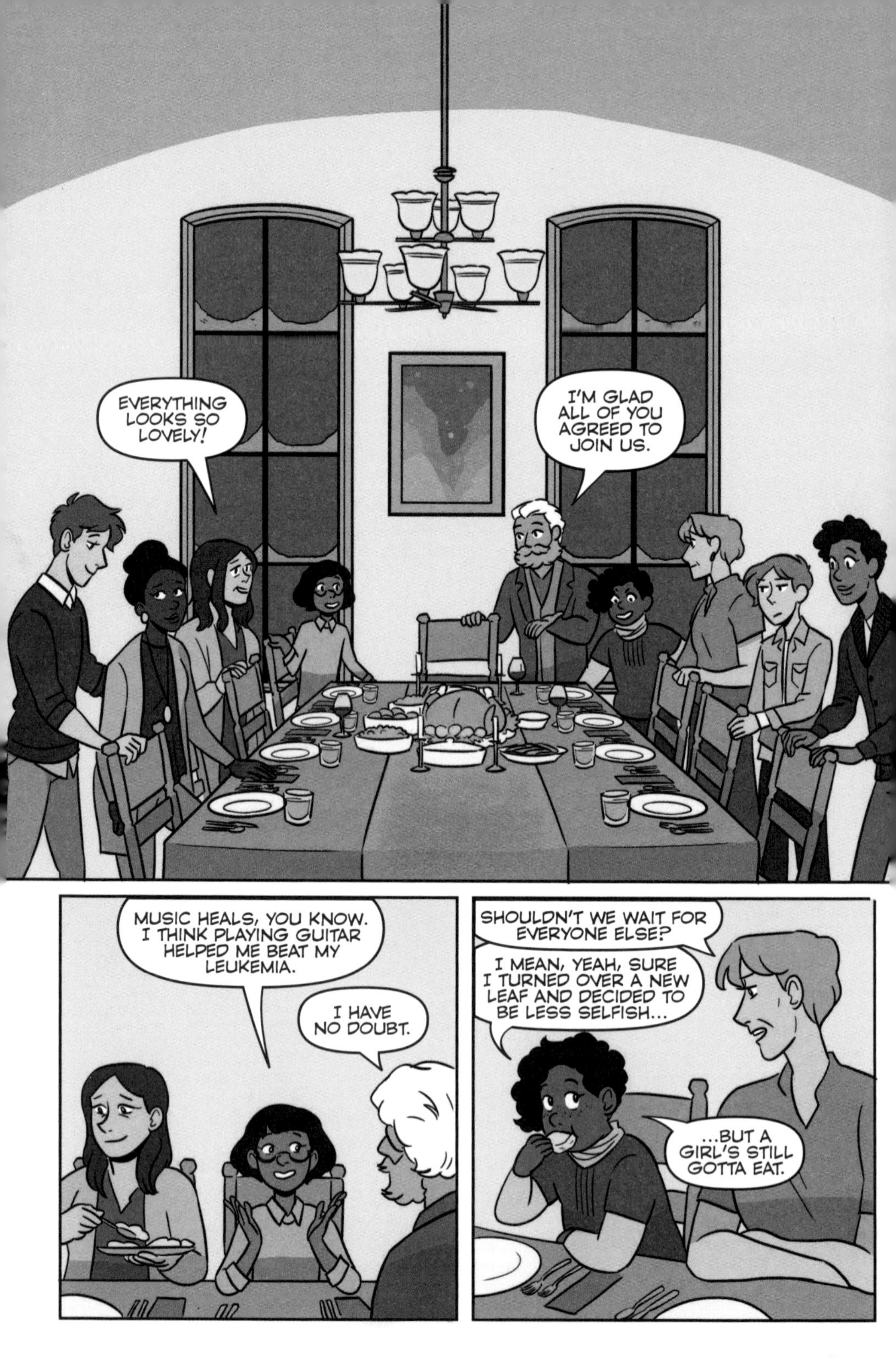

EVERYTHING LOOKS SO LOVELY!
I'M GLAD ALL OF YOU AGREED TO JOIN US.
MUSIC HEALS, YOU KNOW. I THINK PLAYING GUITAR HELPED ME BEAT MY LEUKEMIA.
I HAVE NO DOUBT.
SHOULDN'T WE WAIT FOR EVERYONE ELSE?
I MEAN, YEAH, SURE I TURNED OVER A NEW LEAF AND DECIDED TO BE LESS SELFISH...
...BUT A GIRL'S STILL GOTTA EAT.

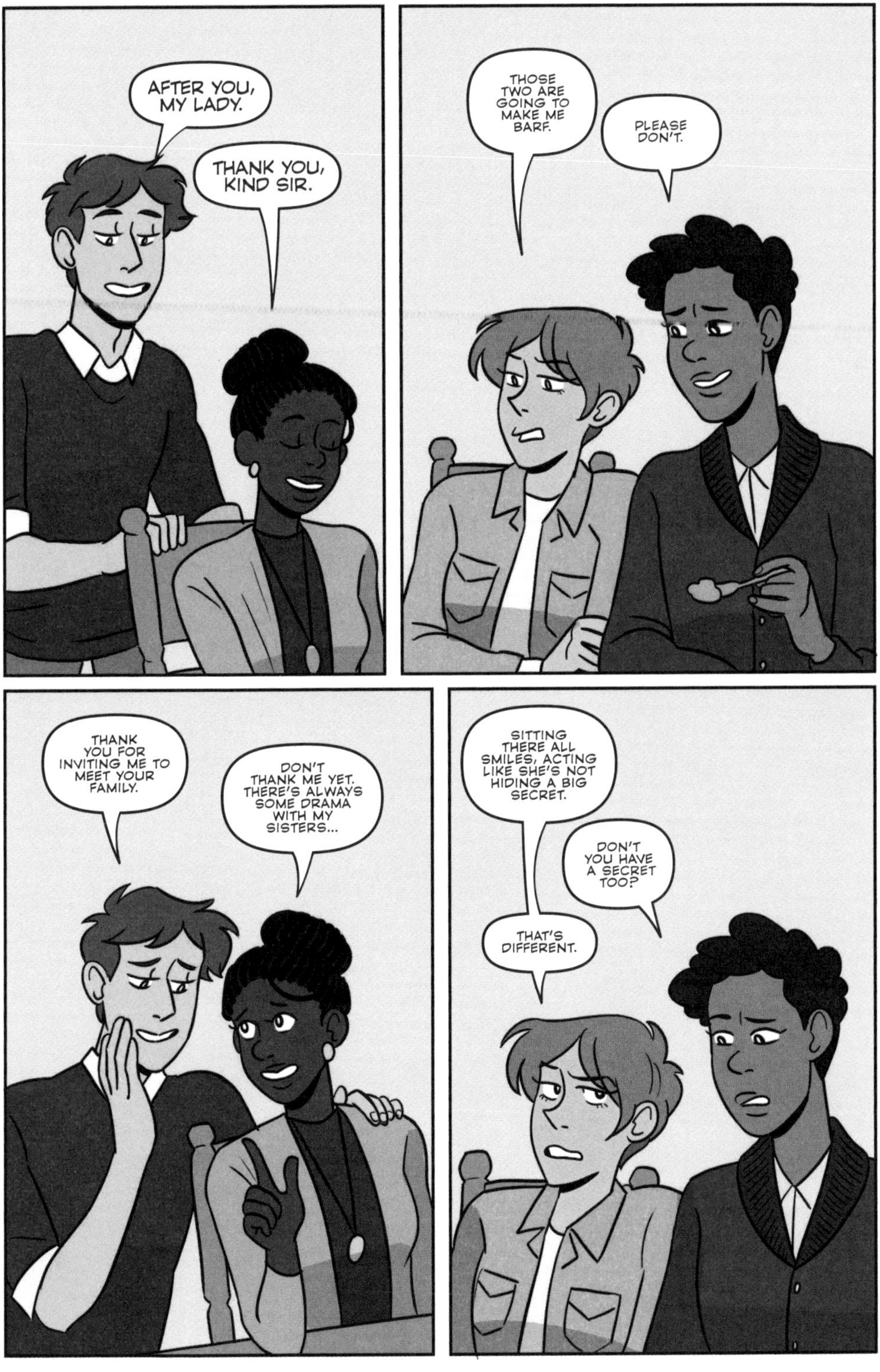
AFTER YOU, MY LADY.
THANK YOU, KIND SIR.
THOSE TWO ARE GOING TO MAKE ME BARF.
PLEASE DON'T.
THANK YOU FOR INVITING ME TO MEET YOUR FAMILY.
DON'T THANK ME YET. THERE'S ALWAYS SOME DRAMA WITH MY SISTERS...
SITTING THERE ALL SMILES, ACTING LIKE SHE'S NOT HIDING A BIG SECRET.
DON'T YOU HAVE A SECRET TOO?
THAT'S DIFFERENT.

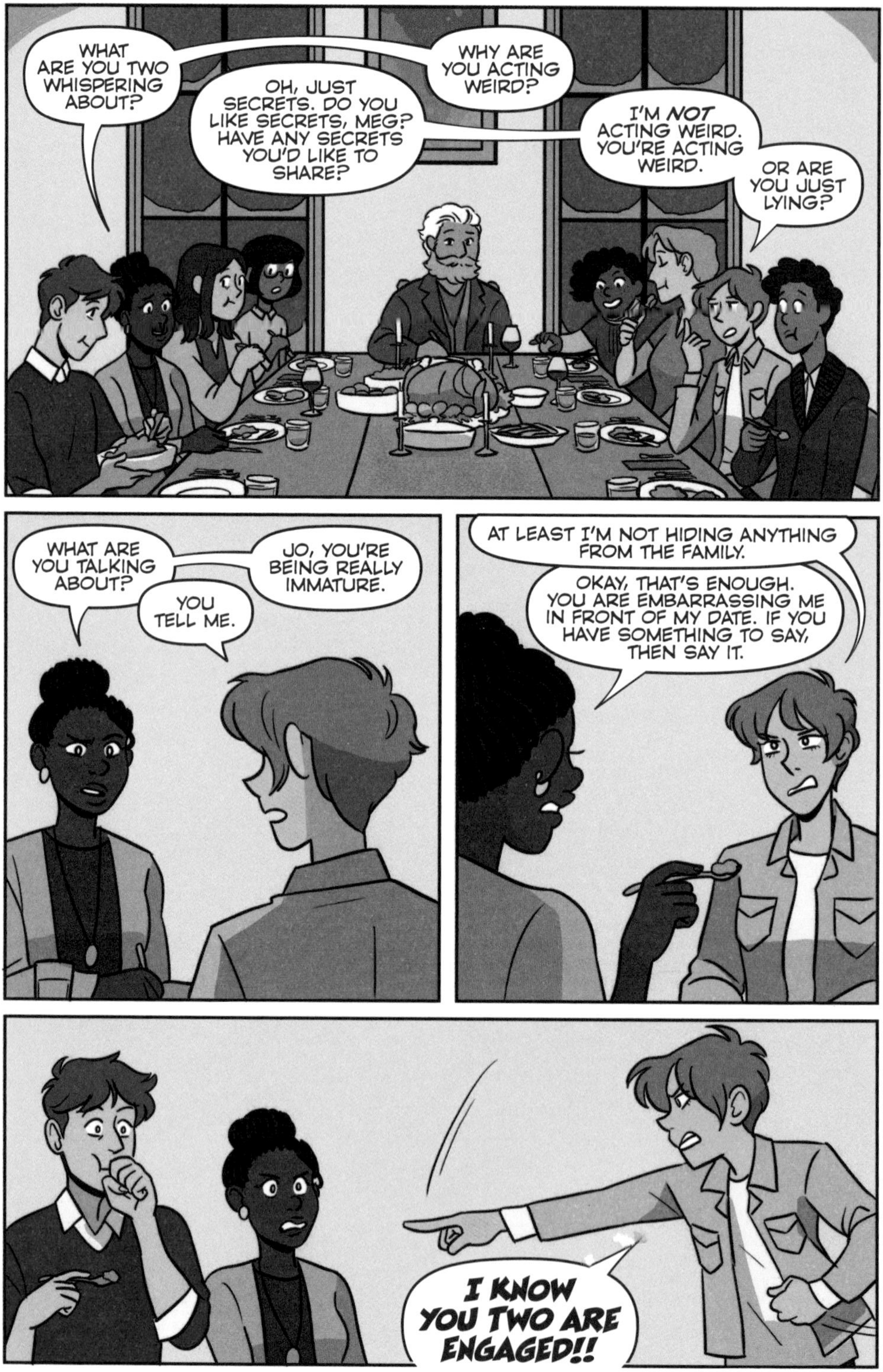
WHAT ARE YOU TWO WHISPERING ABOUT?
OH, JUST SECRETS. DO YOU LIKE SECRETS, MEG? HAVE ANY SECRETS YOU'D LIKE TO SHARE?
WHY ARE YOU ACTING WEIRD?
I'M *NOT* ACTING WEIRD. YOU'RE ACTING WEIRD.
OR ARE YOU JUST LYING?
WHAT ARE YOU TALKING ABOUT?
YOU TELL ME.
JO, YOU'RE BEING REALLY IMMATURE.
AT LEAST I'M NOT HIDING ANYTHING FROM THE FAMILY.
OKAY, THAT'S ENOUGH. YOU ARE EMBARRASSING ME IN FRONT OF MY DATE. IF YOU HAVE SOMETHING TO SAY, THEN SAY IT.
I KNOW YOU TWO ARE ENGAGED!!

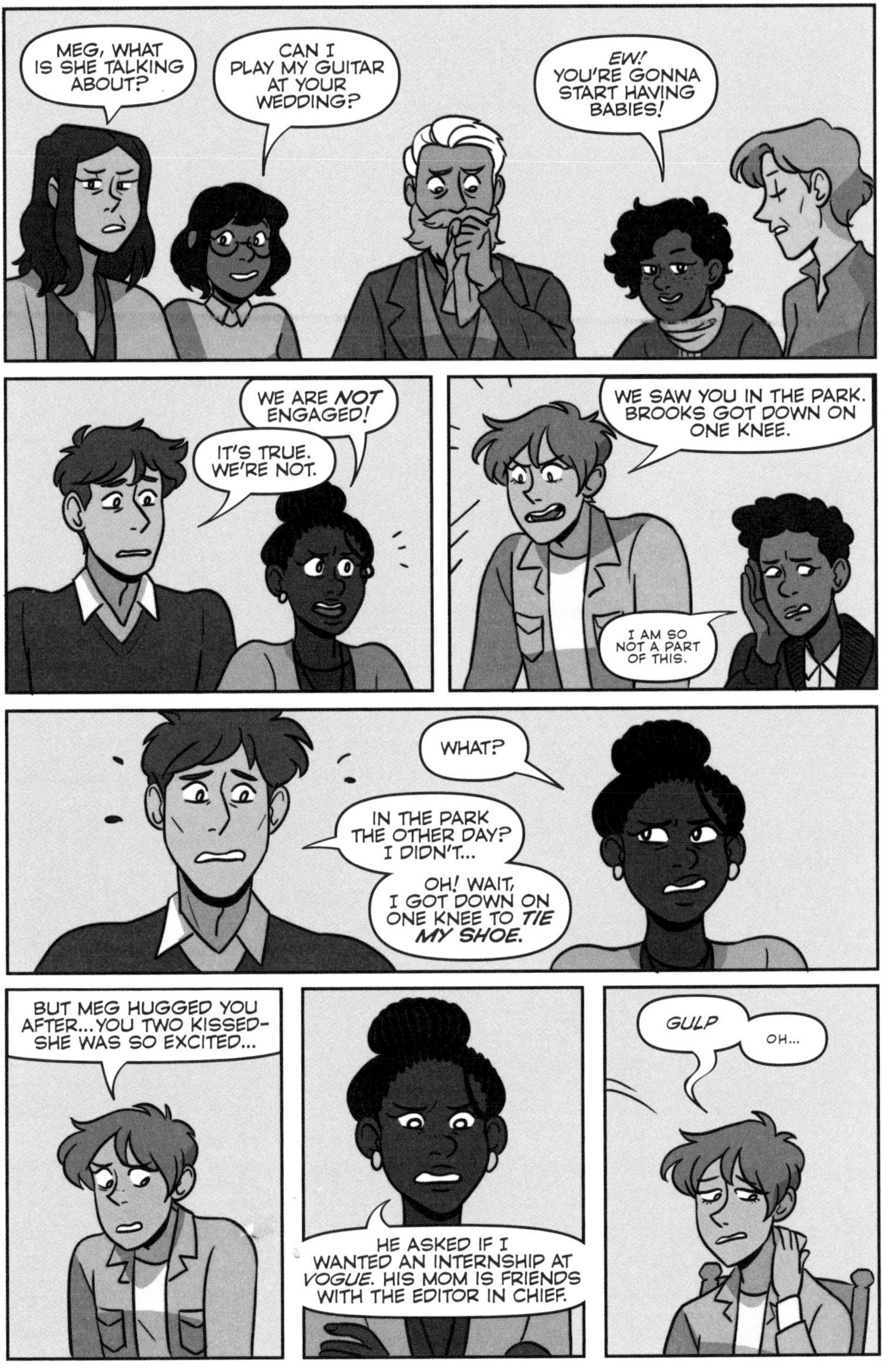
MEG, WHAT IS SHE TALKING ABOUT?
CAN I PLAY MY GUITAR AT YOUR WEDDING?
EW! YOU'RE GONNA START HAVING BABIES!
WE ARE NOT ENGAGED!
IT'S TRUE. WE'RE NOT.
WE SAW YOU IN THE PARK. BROOKS GOT DOWN ON ONE KNEE.
I AM SO NOT A PART OF THIS.
WHAT?
IN THE PARK THE OTHER DAY? I DIDN'T...
OH! WAIT, I GOT DOWN ON ONE KNEE TO TIE MY SHOE.
BUT MEG HUGGED YOU AFTER...YOU TWO KISSED-SHE WAS SO EXCITED...
HE ASKED IF I WANTED AN INTERNSHIP AT VOGUE. HIS MOM IS FRIENDS WITH THE EDITOR IN CHIEF.
GULP
OH...

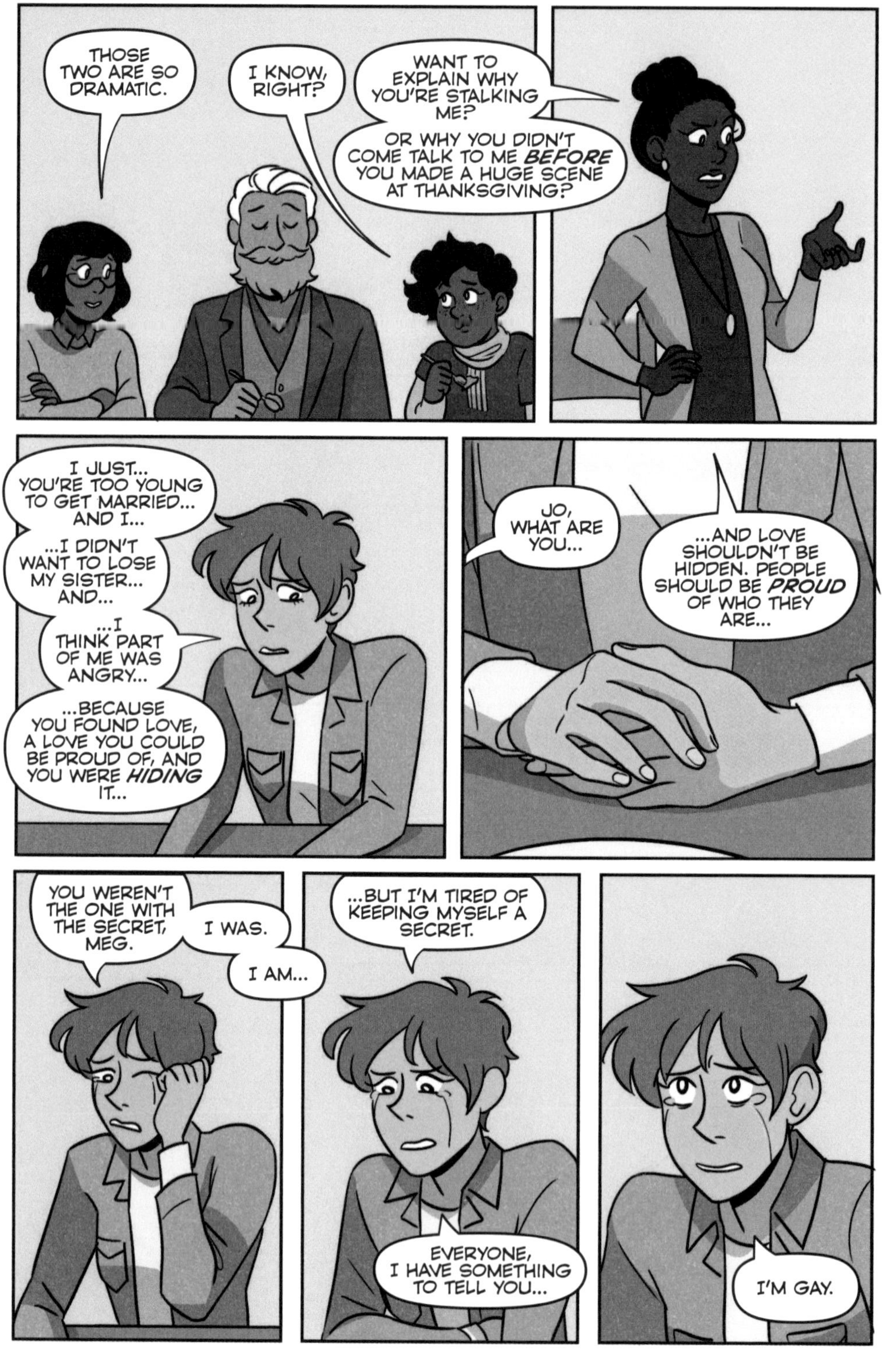
THOSE TWO ARE SO DRAMATIC.
I KNOW, RIGHT?
WANT TO EXPLAIN WHY YOU'RE STALKING ME?
OR WHY YOU DIDN'T COME TALK TO ME *BEFORE* YOU MADE A HUGE SCENE AT THANKSGIVING?
I JUST... YOU'RE TOO YOUNG TO GET MARRIED... AND I...
...I DIDN'T WANT TO LOSE MY SISTER... AND...
...I THINK PART OF ME WAS ANGRY...
...BECAUSE YOU FOUND LOVE, A LOVE YOU COULD BE PROUD OF, AND YOU WERE *HIDING* IT...
JO, WHAT ARE YOU...
...AND LOVE SHOULDN'T BE HIDDEN. PEOPLE SHOULD BE *PROUD* OF WHO THEY ARE...
YOU WEREN'T THE ONE WITH THE SECRET, MEG.
I WAS.
I AM...
...BUT I'M TIRED OF KEEPING MYSELF A SECRET.
EVERYONE, I HAVE SOMETHING TO TELL YOU...
I'M GAY.

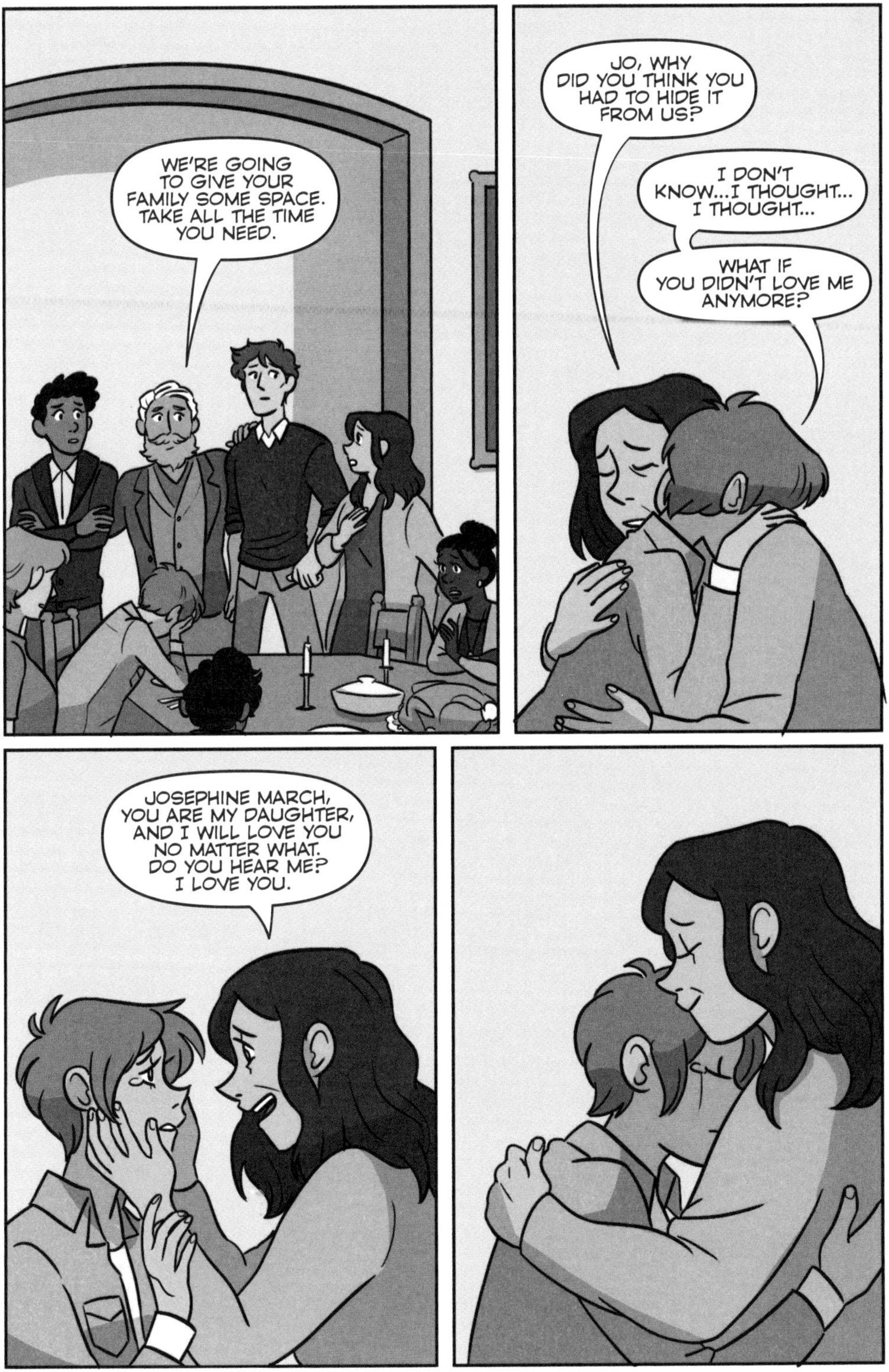
WE'RE GOING TO GIVE YOUR FAMILY SOME SPACE. TAKE ALL THE TIME YOU NEED.
JO, WHY DID YOU THINK YOU HAD TO HIDE IT FROM US?
I DON'T KNOW...I THOUGHT... I THOUGHT...
WHAT IF YOU DIDN'T LOVE ME ANYMORE?
JOSEPHINE MARCH, YOU ARE MY DAUGHTER, AND I WILL LOVE YOU NO MATTER WHAT. DO YOU HEAR ME? I LOVE YOU.

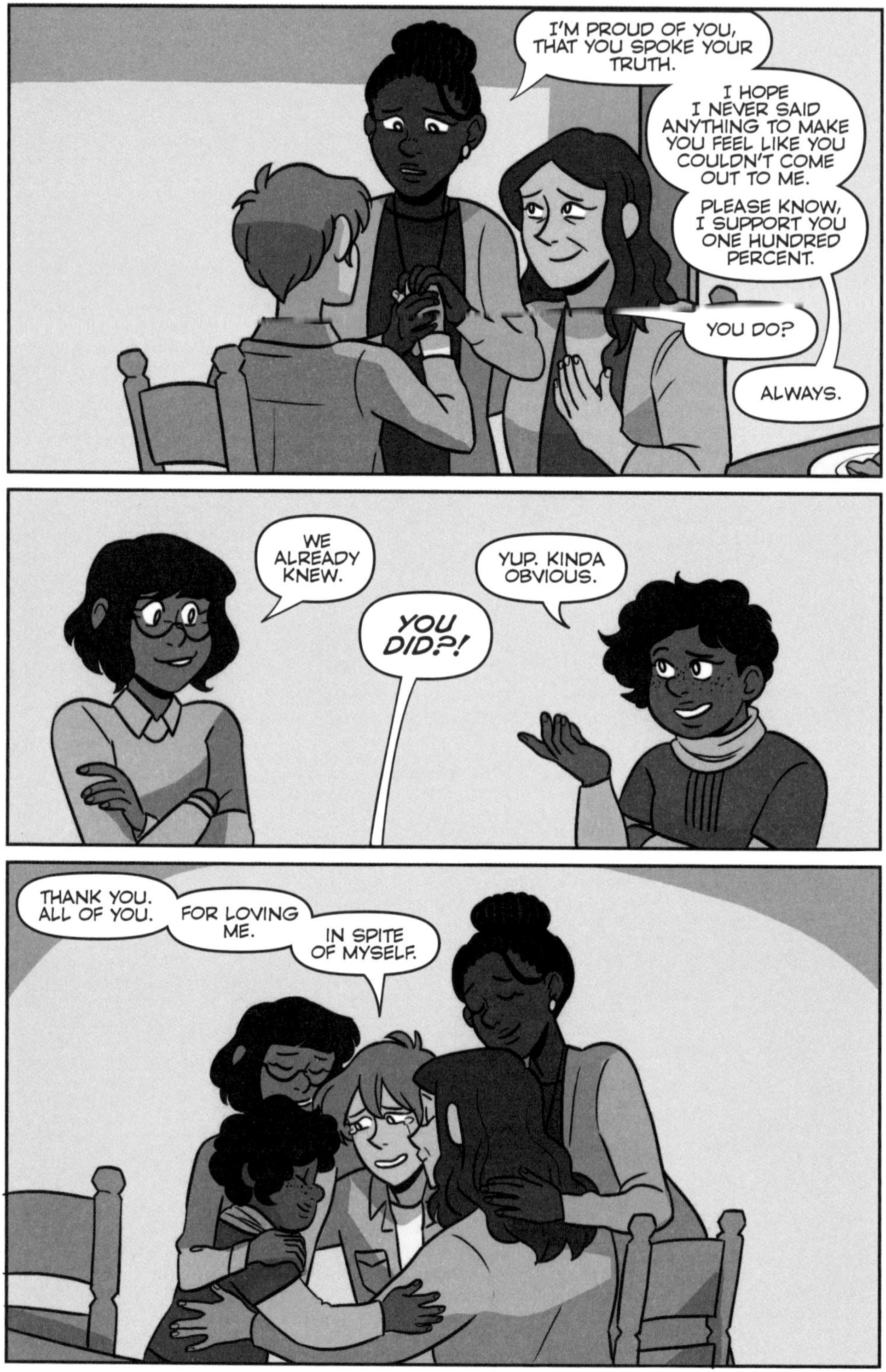
I'M PROUD OF YOU, THAT YOU SPOKE YOUR TRUTH.
I HOPE I NEVER SAID ANYTHING TO MAKE YOU FEEL LIKE YOU COULDN'T COME OUT TO ME.
PLEASE KNOW, I SUPPORT YOU ONE HUNDRED PERCENT.
YOU DO?
ALWAYS.
WE ALREADY KNEW.
YOU DID?!
YUP. KINDA OBVIOUS.
THANK YOU. ALL OF YOU.
FOR LOVING ME.
IN SPITE OF MYSELF.

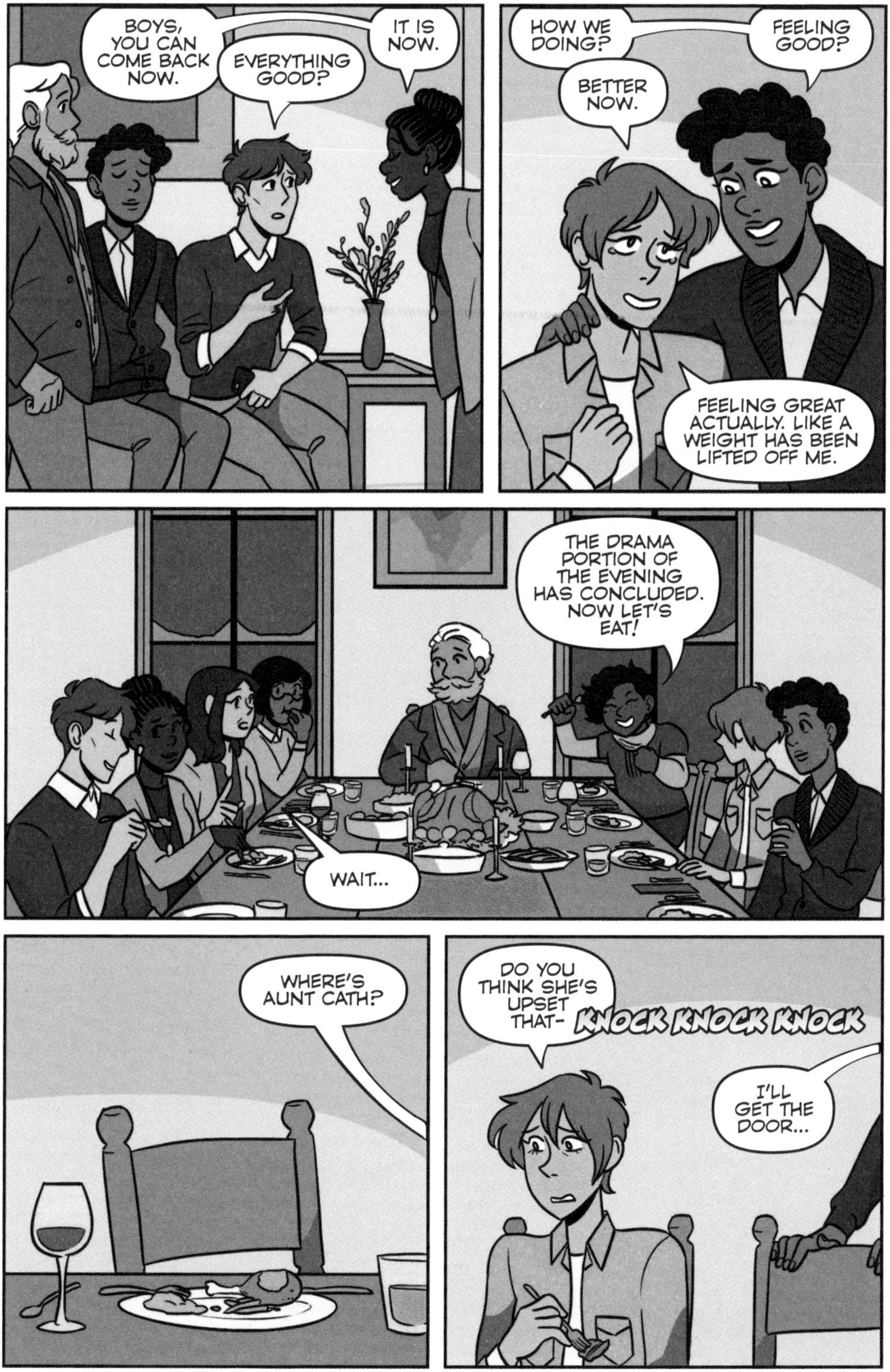
BOYS, YOU CAN COME BACK NOW.
EVERYTHING GOOD?
IT IS NOW.
HOW WE DOING?
FEELING GOOD?
BETTER NOW.
FEELING GREAT ACTUALLY. LIKE A WEIGHT HAS BEEN LIFTED OFF ME.
THE DRAMA PORTION OF THE EVENING HAS CONCLUDED. NOW LET'S EAT!
WAIT...
WHERE'S AUNT CATH?
DO YOU THINK SHE'S UPSET THAT-
KNOCK KNOCK KNOCK
I'LL GET THE DOOR...

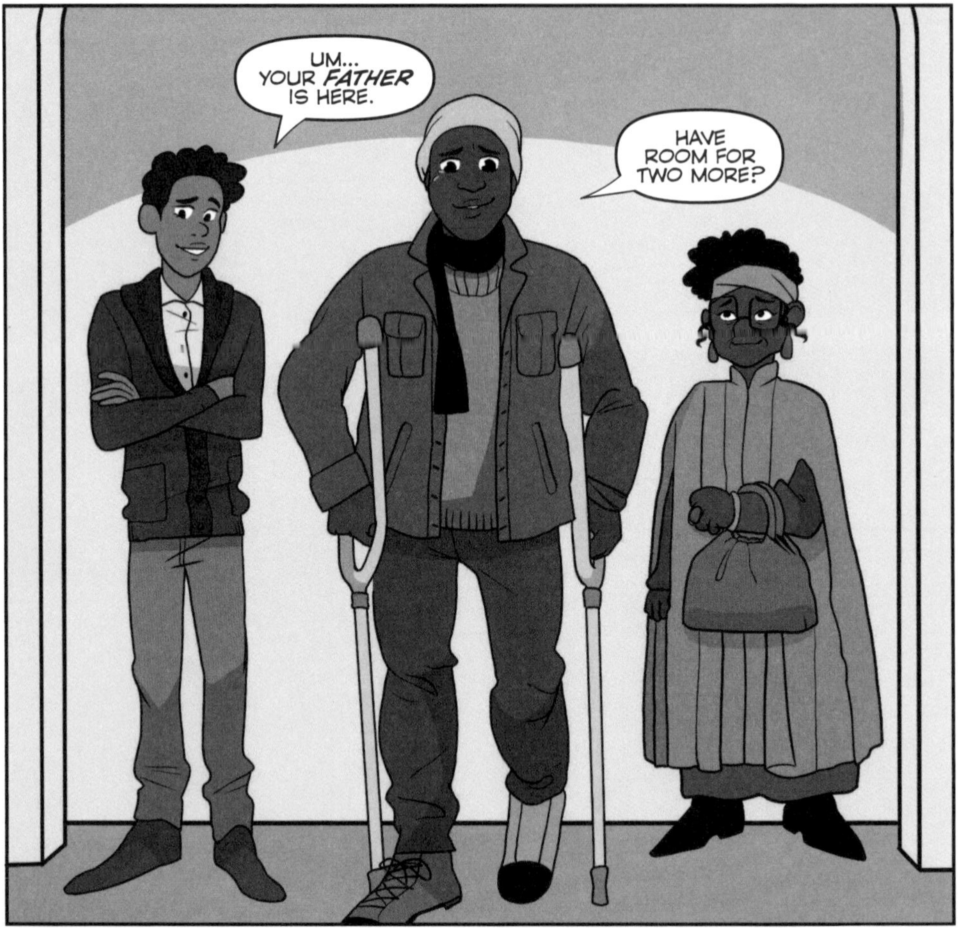
UM...
YOUR FATHER
IS HERE.
HAVE
ROOM FOR
TWO MORE?

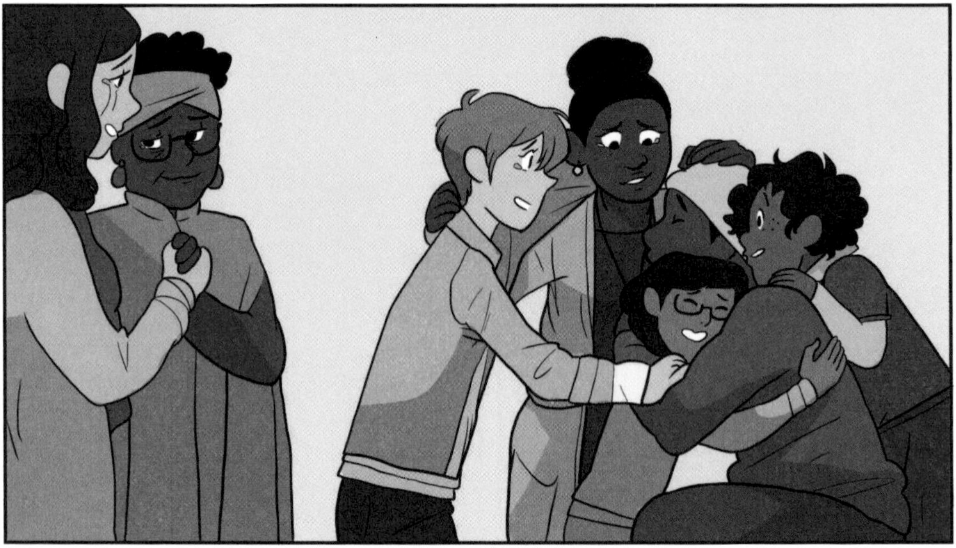

Jo's Journal: KEEP OUT

December 1

My name is Jo March, and I am gay.

I can't believe I just wrote that. I've thought it a million times, but I've never put it down on paper. I was too scared to. But then at Thanksgiving, there was all this drama (my fault), and it just came out. The words, I mean. But then so did I. I came out to my sisters and Mom. And they were fine with it. They didn't even care. Later, Mom admitted that she suspected, but she never wanted to press it. She wanted me to figure it out for myself. Beth and Amy said they knew. Really, only Meg was surprised. But she pointed out that my lack of fashion sense should have been an indicator—which I quickly busted her for being a stereotype! Silly Meg. She apologized like a hundred times for saying it.

Of course, no sooner had I come out than Dad came home. It turns out Mr. Marquez paid for him (and Gammy!) to fly home first-class. He said a family should be together for the holidays. It was so sweet of him. Though if you ask me, he did it because he has a crush on Gammy Esther. They spent the rest of the evening sipping wine in the corner while the rest of us caught up.

The day after Thanksgiving, I pulled Dad aside so I could tell him my own news. At first, he was really quiet. I've heard so many horrible coming-out stories that I started to grow anxious he was going to disown me. Instead, he kissed my forehead and said, "At some point, you're going to encounter intolerance. When that happens, I want you to hold your head high and be proud of who you are. The world's gotten a lot better, but it still has a ways to go. Until then, know that you are never alone. You have me, and you have your family to back you up."

We hugged for a long time. Then he told me how the Black Panther Party were allies with the LGBTQ community in the 1970s. Both groups struggled to be recognized as equal to the rest of the populace. Jean Genet, a famous French gay writer and activist, became friends with David Hilliard, Black Panther chief of staff. They toured the U.S., traveling state to state, speaking to promote tolerance. I had no idea.

Looks like Dad still has some things to teach me. ☺

There's only one person I need to reach: Aunt Cath. She disappeared after I came out. I called and left messages but she hasn't returned them. She only sent me a text saying to take the month of December off to reconnect with my dad. I asked Mom if Aunt Cath was maybe homophobic, and Mom didn't say anything except that she loved me and so did Aunt Cath. I don't know why, but it really bothers me that Aunt Cath would react like this. I thought we were closer than that...But I won't stop trying. She'll come around. Won't she?

But Dad is home! I can hardly believe it. It makes home feel like...well, home again. With Beth getting better day by day, and Dad in physical therapy for his leg, it's like everything is on the mend. We're all healing, physically, mentally, and spiritually. And now that we're all together, I am certain we will heal a lot faster.

New Message

FROM: Beth March
TO: Alejandro Marquez
SENT: December 4

Dear Mr. Marquez,

I wanted to thank you again for everything you've done for me this year. All the flowers you sent while I was in the hospital were nice. And Gammy Esther told me you paid for her and Dad to come home in time for Thanksgiving. And of course, you gave me my guitar. (I named him Mr. Strings.)

Now that I'm feeling better, I've been playing Mr. Strings every day. I've written two new songs. And I am playing in my school's holiday talent show. Six months ago, I would have never played in front of anybody. But after fighting cancer, things don't seem quite as scary.

Anyways, that is the reason I am writing. I would like you to see me play. Would you like to come to the holiday talent show?

The information is below.

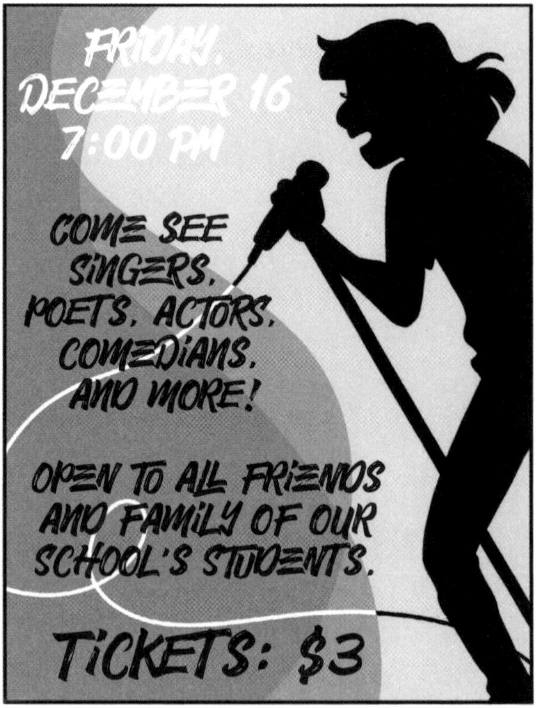
FRIDAY, DECEMBER 16
7:00 PM
COME SEE SINGERS, POETS, ACTORS, COMEDIANS, AND MORE!
OPEN TO ALL FRIENDS AND FAMILY OF OUR SCHOOL'S STUDENTS.
TICKETS: $3

Sincerely,
Beth

Send

December 6

Dear Diary, it's me, Meg. Duh.

Life has been so crazy lately and I feel I have to write it down before I burst into tears.

First, Dad is home—which is wonderful. I couldn't be happier. Second, Beth is getting stronger every day. Again, more good news. Third, Jo is gay. Ever since she came out, she seems lighter, able to breathe and smile more easily. I'm pleased for her...and also a little jealous.

I didn't go to war, or have cancer, or feel like I had to hide a secret from the world. So why am I so confused?

Today, I had an interview at Vogue. I mean, that's a dream job for any girl who has ever liked fashion. A year ago, I would have killed for this meeting. Then last week, Brooks's mom made a call and got it for me, just like that. But when I was there, all

I thought about was Dad and about Beth...about the doctors who saved their lives. And I thought, fashion is wonderful, and it's art, and I love it, but I want to use my life to make a bigger difference. I think I want to be a lawyer.

Crazy, right? I'd never thought about it until I was sitting there in that interview. Maybe I've never admitted it to myself because of my obsession with being rich or taken care of. Or maybe because I didn't believe in myself enough to think I could do it. But after this last year? I feel like I'm stronger than I realized. And I don't want a job because my boyfriend's mom made a call. I want to earn it myself. But I guess that brings me to the next thing...

Brooks is wonderful. He's everything I've ever dreamed of in a man. He is handsome and charming and dresses well. He has ambition and wants to do good in the world. And yes, he comes from money, which doesn't hurt. He's perfect! In my head, he is the perfect catch. But in my heart...I'm not sure how I feel about him. I really really really like Brooks. But I'm not sure I love him.

A hundred years ago, a girl didn't have a lot of choices. She could either get married or be a spinster. She'd probably only know one or two eligible bachelors, and would have to just settle and make it work with whichever man chose her. Options were limited. But now? Now a woman can do anything. She can become an explorer, or a doctor, or a politician. She can be an editor or a model or a designer. She can fly to the moon, or become a teacher, or be a stay-at-home mom. There's no limit to what we can do.

After everything that's happened this year—with Dad, with Beth, with life—I'm just not sure I'm ready to settle...for either a job or a partner. I think I need to take some time to figure things out—to sort out what is best for me. And I think I know where to start...

Dear Santa,

Amy March here. U probly know this, but last year I stopped believing in you. Well, this year I changed my mind. Lots of good stuff happened, so I decided miracles are reel. And what's more miracle-u-lus (I don't know how to spell good) than a fat guy who flys all over the world and gives free presentz?

Anywaze, I wanted to tell you what I want for X-mas:

* Make ~~Physikal~~ Physical Therapy easier for Dad. He says its no fun.

* Help Beth to get totally better. No cancer! Also, get her some guitar picks—the kind with glitter in them.

* Get Meg some new lipstick and make-up. (She doesn't know I used hers to finish an art project.)

* Jo likes books so get her those.

* Mom needs a vacation! Maybe help her win a contest to a tropical island for her and Dad.

* Aunt Cath needs a vacation too.

* Get Gammy Esther a new house, one close to us. I think she would like to live nearby.

* Oh, and make sure every kid gets a present. I know some kid's families are poor and can't afford stuff. So make sure you take care of those ones first.

That's it! If you're wondering bout me, I don't need anything. I have ~~everyting~~ everything I need.

Thx, dude! —Amy

CHAPTER 19

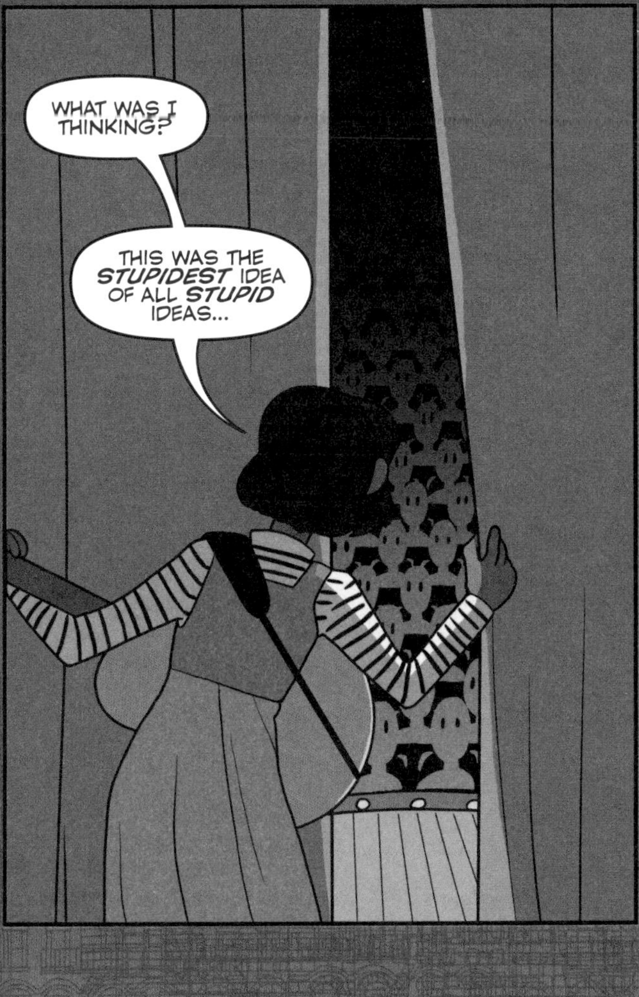
WHAT WAS I THINKING?
THIS WAS THE STUPIDEST IDEA OF ALL STUPID IDEAS...

Songs and Secrets...

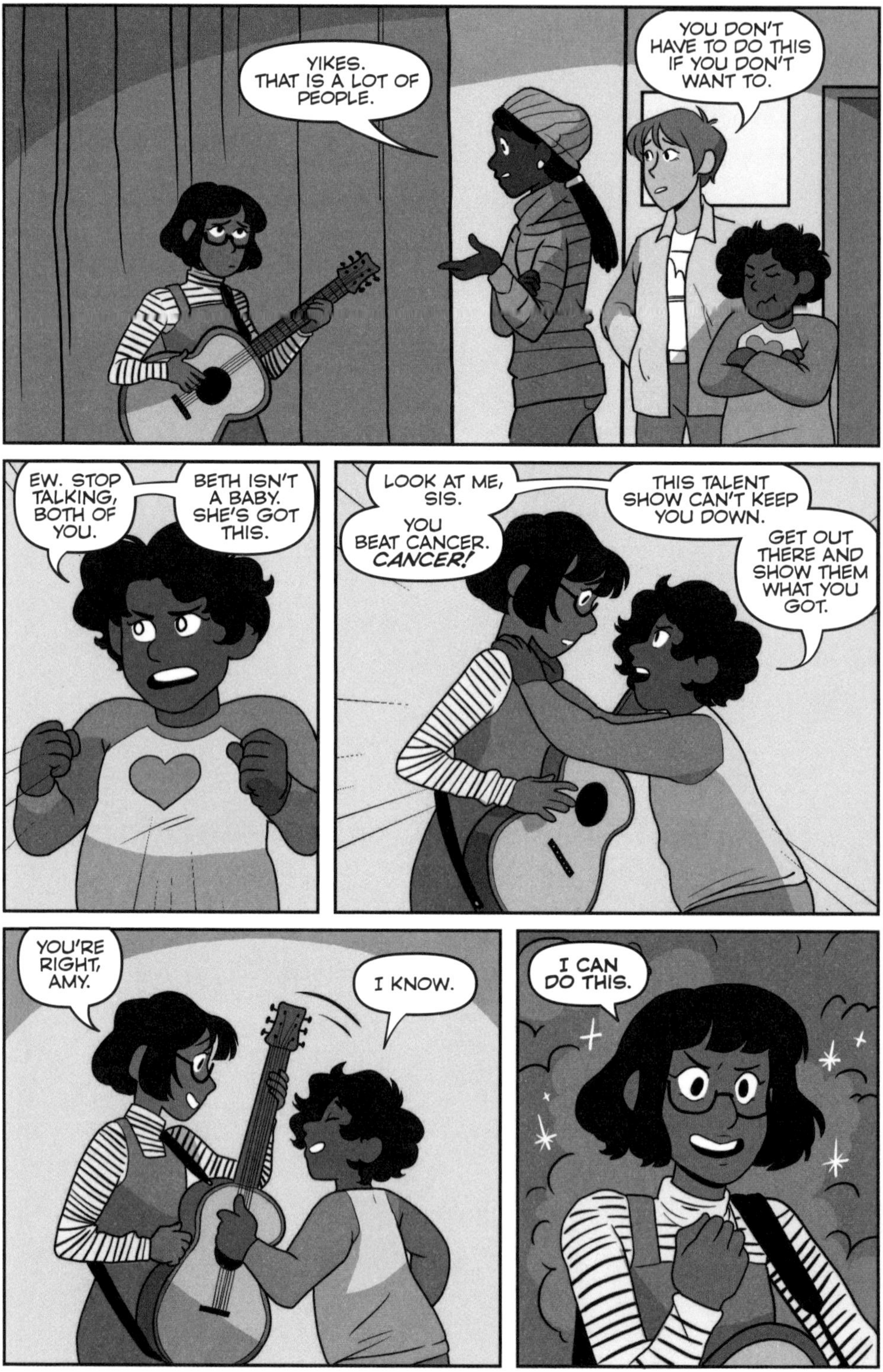
YIKES. THAT IS A LOT OF PEOPLE.
YOU DON'T HAVE TO DO THIS IF YOU DON'T WANT TO.
EW. STOP TALKING, BOTH OF YOU.
BETH ISN'T A BABY. SHE'S GOT THIS.
LOOK AT ME, SIS.
YOU BEAT CANCER. *CANCER!*
THIS TALENT SHOW CAN'T KEEP YOU DOWN.
GET OUT THERE AND SHOW THEM WHAT YOU GOT.
YOU'RE RIGHT, AMY.
I KNOW.
I CAN DO THIS.

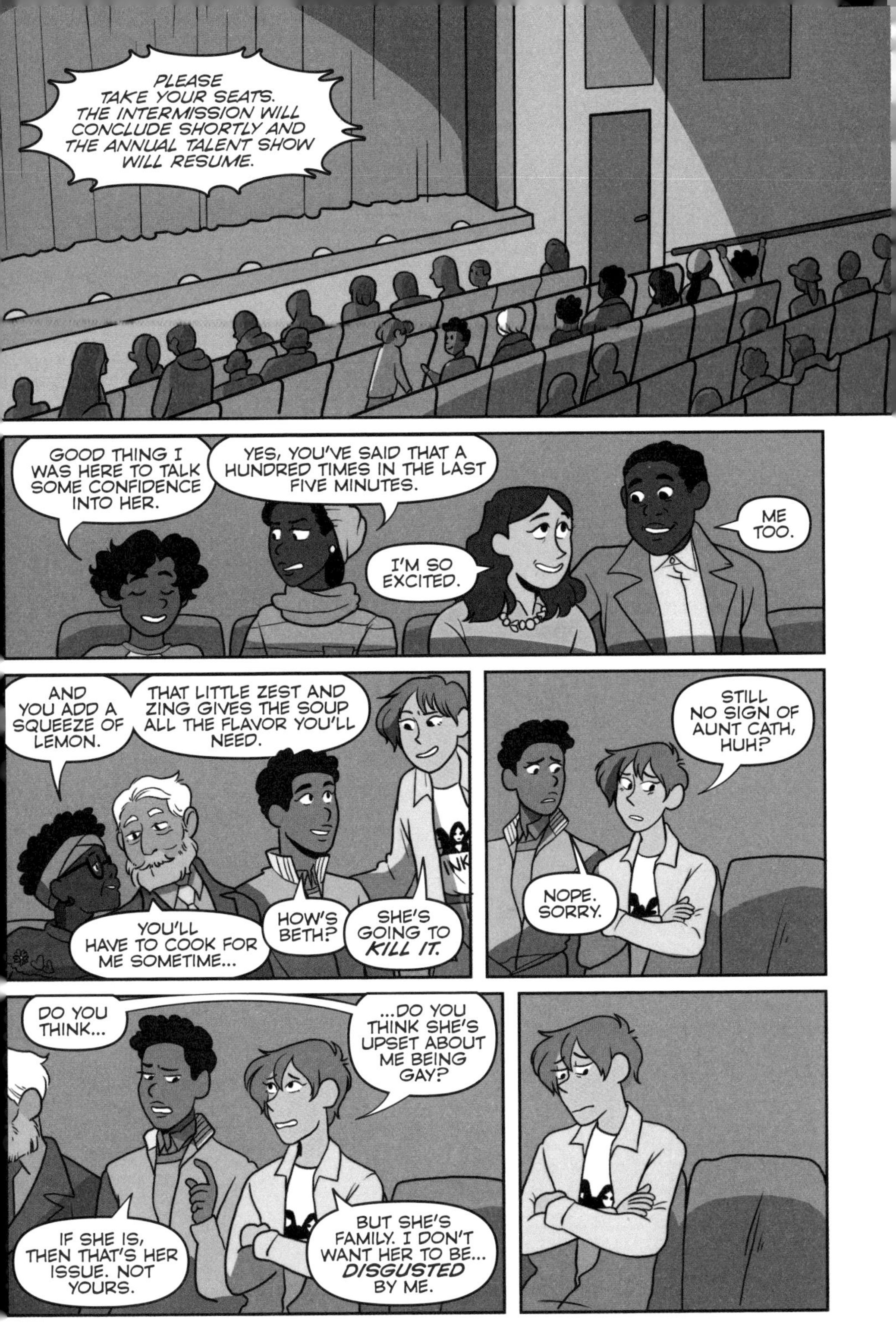
PLEASE TAKE YOUR SEATS. THE INTERMISSION WILL CONCLUDE SHORTLY AND THE ANNUAL TALENT SHOW WILL RESUME.
GOOD THING I WAS HERE TO TALK SOME CONFIDENCE INTO HER.
YES, YOU'VE SAID THAT A HUNDRED TIMES IN THE LAST FIVE MINUTES.
I'M SO EXCITED.
ME TOO.
AND YOU ADD A SQUEEZE OF LEMON.
THAT LITTLE ZEST AND ZING GIVES THE SOUP ALL THE FLAVOR YOU'LL NEED.
YOU'LL HAVE TO COOK FOR ME SOMETIME...
HOW'S BETH?
SHE'S GOING TO *KILL IT.*
STILL NO SIGN OF AUNT CATH, HUH?
NOPE. SORRY.
DO YOU THINK...
...DO YOU THINK SHE'S UPSET ABOUT ME BEING GAY?
IF SHE IS, THEN THAT'S HER ISSUE. NOT YOURS.
BUT SHE'S FAMILY. I DON'T WANT HER TO BE... *DISGUSTED* BY ME.

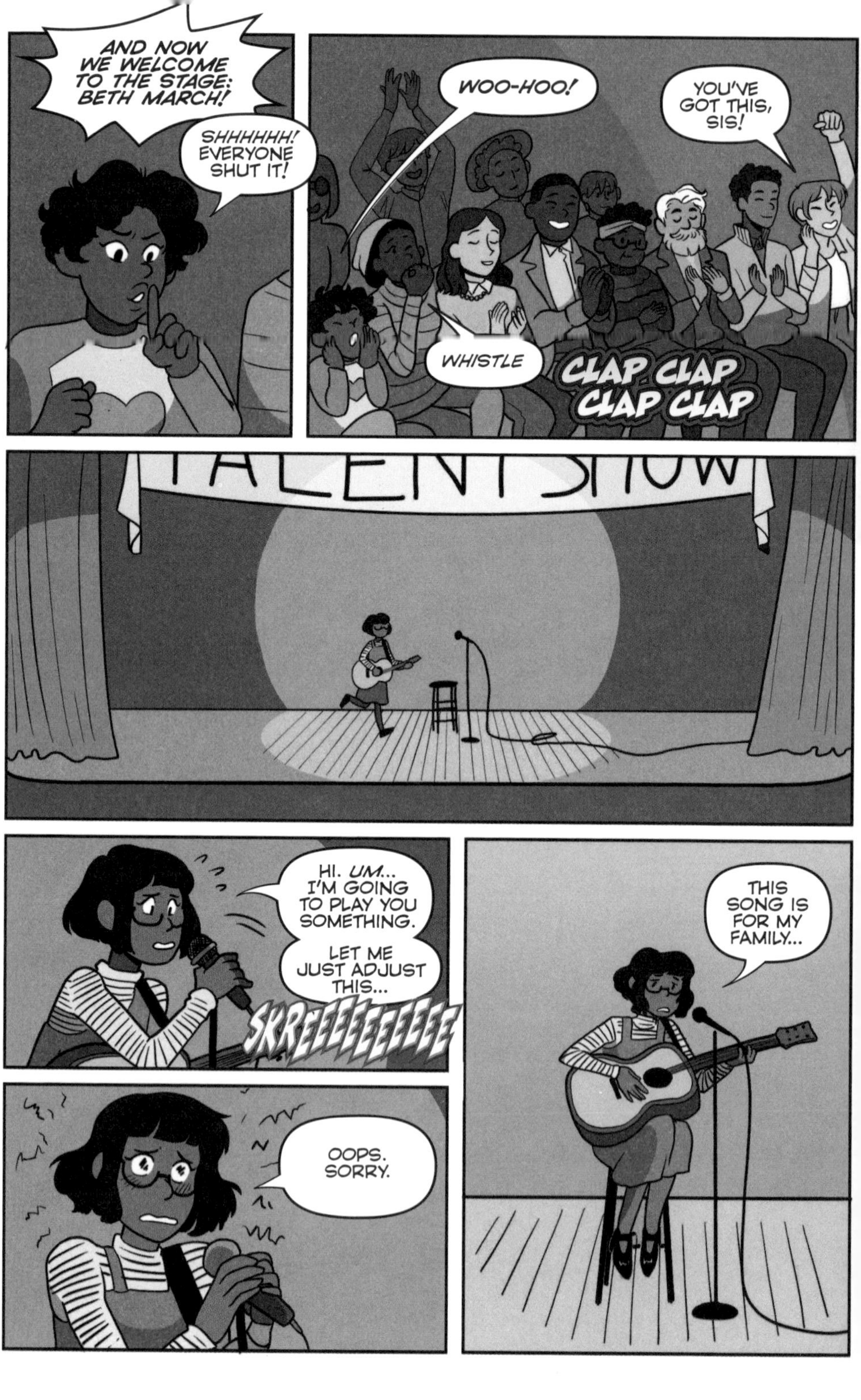
AND NOW WE WELCOME TO THE STAGE: BETH MARCH!
SHHHHHH! EVERYONE SHUT IT!
WOO-HOO!
YOU'VE GOT THIS, SIS!
WHISTLE
CLAP CLAP CLAP CLAP
TALENT SHOW
HI. UM... I'M GOING TO PLAY YOU SOMETHING.
LET ME JUST ADJUST THIS...
SKREEEEEEEEEE
THIS SONG IS FOR MY FAMILY...
OOPS. SORRY.

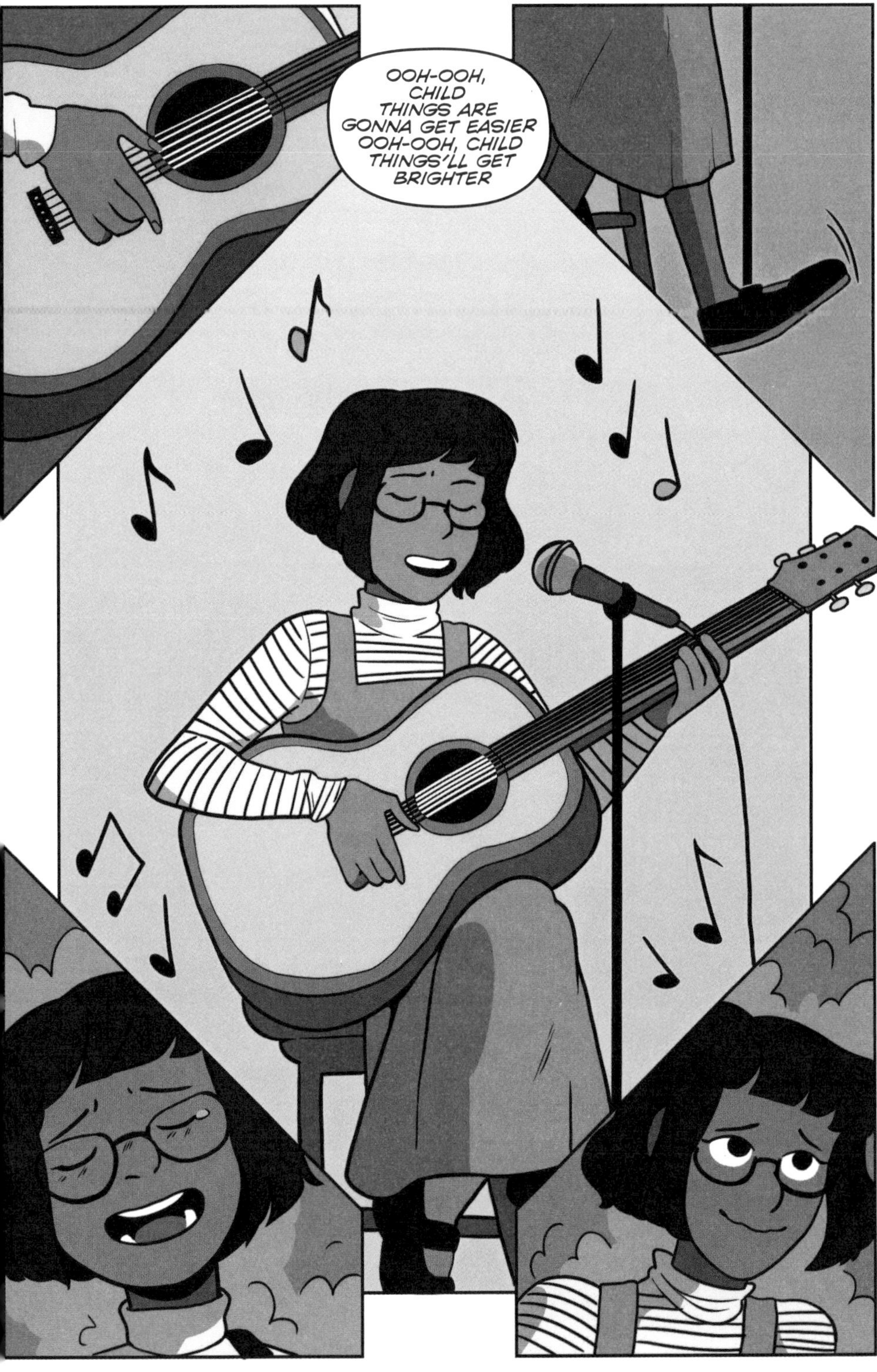
OOH-OOH, CHILD THINGS ARE GONNA GET EASIER OOH-OOH, CHILD THINGS'LL GET BRIGHTER

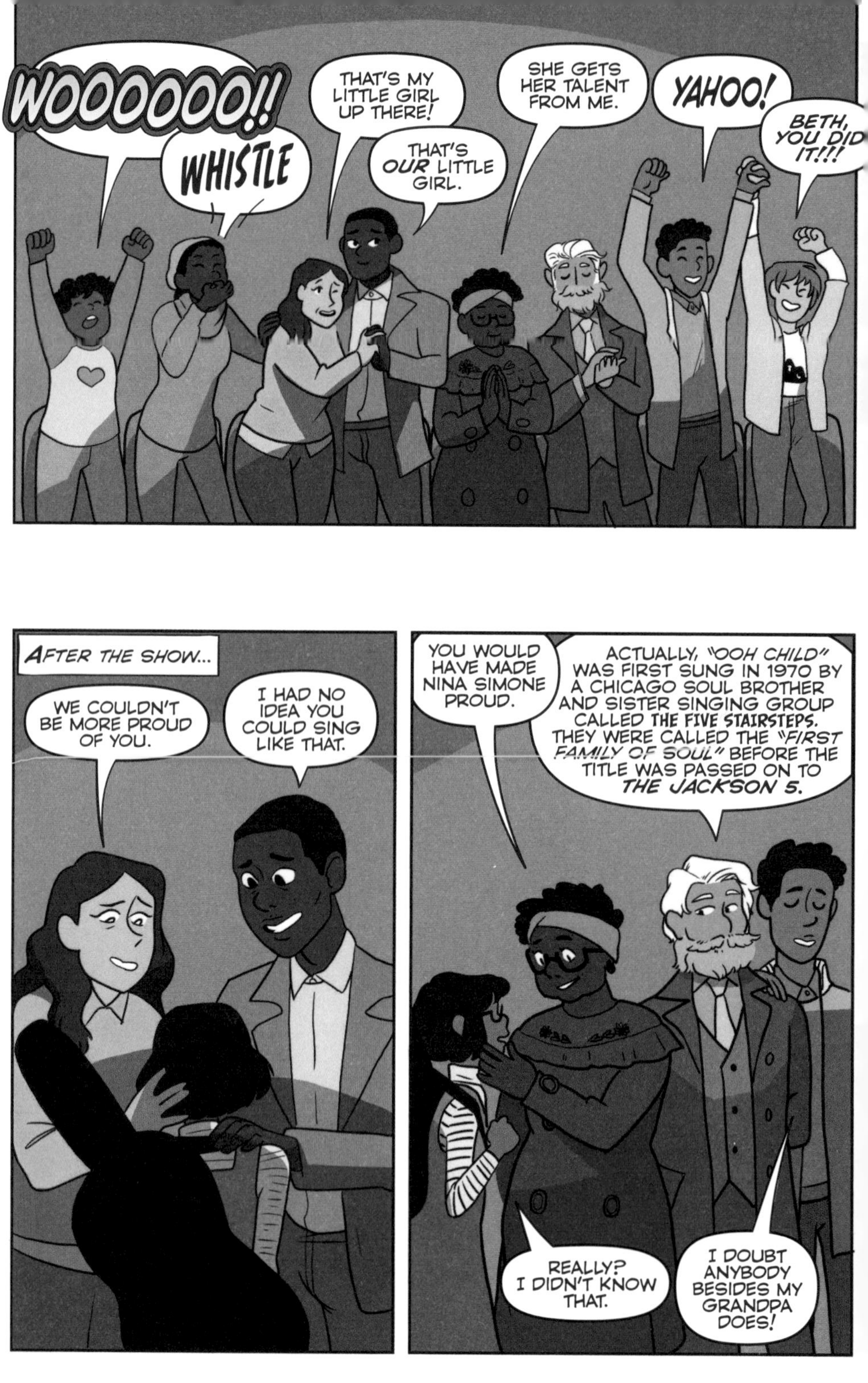
WOOOOOO!!
WHISTLE
THAT'S MY LITTLE GIRL UP THERE!
THAT'S OUR LITTLE GIRL.
SHE GETS HER TALENT FROM ME.
YAHOO!
BETH, YOU DID IT!!!
AFTER THE SHOW...
WE COULDN'T BE MORE PROUD OF YOU.
I HAD NO IDEA YOU COULD SING LIKE THAT.
YOU WOULD HAVE MADE NINA SIMONE PROUD.
ACTUALLY, "OOH CHILD" WAS FIRST SUNG IN 1970 BY A CHICAGO SOUL BROTHER AND SISTER SINGING GROUP CALLED THE FIVE STAIRSTEPS. THEY WERE CALLED THE "FIRST FAMILY OF SOUL" BEFORE THE TITLE WAS PASSED ON TO THE JACKSON 5.
REALLY? I DIDN'T KNOW THAT.
I DOUBT ANYBODY BESIDES MY GRANDPA DOES!

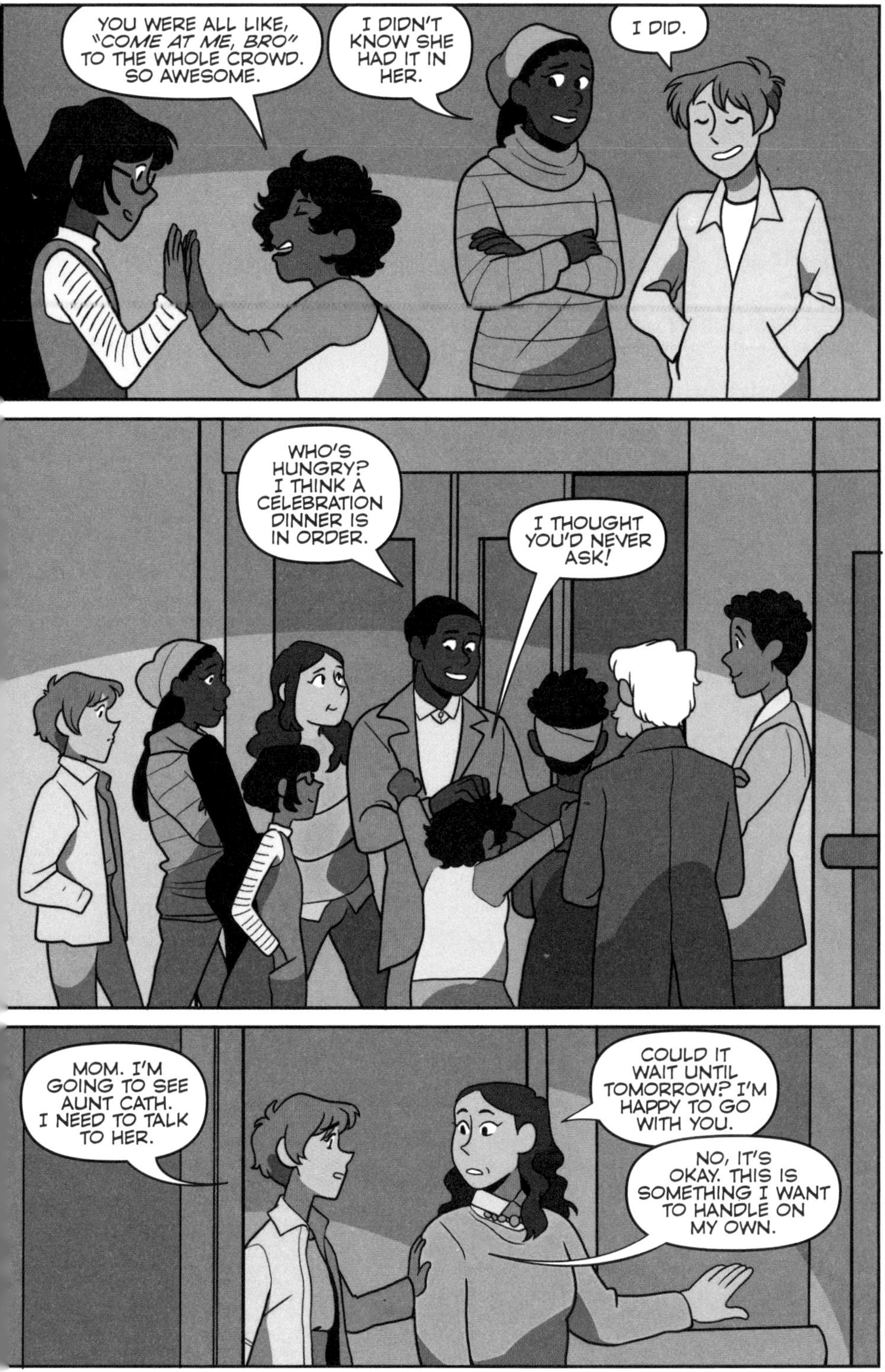
YOU WERE ALL LIKE, "*COME AT ME, BRO*" TO THE WHOLE CROWD. SO AWESOME.
I DIDN'T KNOW SHE HAD IT IN HER.
I DID.
WHO'S HUNGRY? I THINK A CELEBRATION DINNER IS IN ORDER.
I THOUGHT YOU'D NEVER ASK!
MOM. I'M GOING TO SEE AUNT CATH. I NEED TO TALK TO HER.
COULD IT WAIT UNTIL TOMORROW? I'M HAPPY TO GO WITH YOU.
NO, IT'S OKAY. THIS IS SOMETHING I WANT TO HANDLE ON MY OWN.

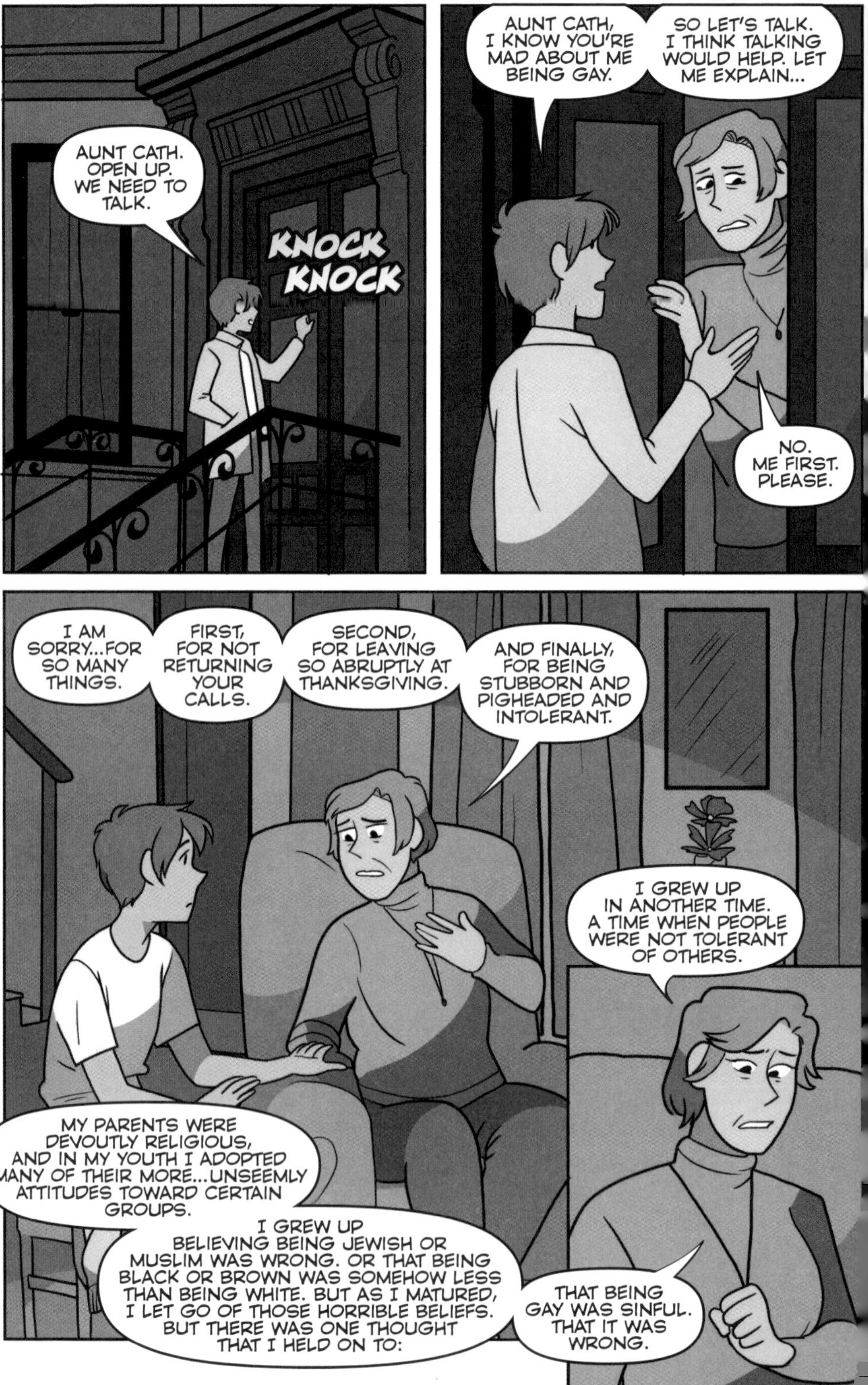
AUNT CATH. OPEN UP. WE NEED TO TALK.
KNOCK KNOCK
AUNT CATH, I KNOW YOU'RE MAD ABOUT ME BEING GAY.
SO LET'S TALK. I THINK TALKING WOULD HELP. LET ME EXPLAIN...
NO. ME FIRST. PLEASE.
I AM SORRY...FOR SO MANY THINGS.
FIRST, FOR NOT RETURNING YOUR CALLS.
SECOND, FOR LEAVING SO ABRUPTLY AT THANKSGIVING.
AND FINALLY, FOR BEING STUBBORN AND PIGHEADED AND INTOLERANT.
I GREW UP IN ANOTHER TIME. A TIME WHEN PEOPLE WERE NOT TOLERANT OF OTHERS.
MY PARENTS WERE DEVOUTLY RELIGIOUS, AND IN MY YOUTH I ADOPTED MANY OF THEIR MORE...UNSEEMLY ATTITUDES TOWARD CERTAIN GROUPS.
I GREW UP BELIEVING BEING JEWISH OR MUSLIM WAS WRONG. OR THAT BEING BLACK OR BROWN WAS SOMEHOW LESS THAN BEING WHITE. BUT AS I MATURED, I LET GO OF THOSE HORRIBLE BELIEFS. BUT THERE WAS ONE THOUGHT THAT I HELD ON TO:
THAT BEING GAY WAS SINFUL. THAT IT WAS WRONG.

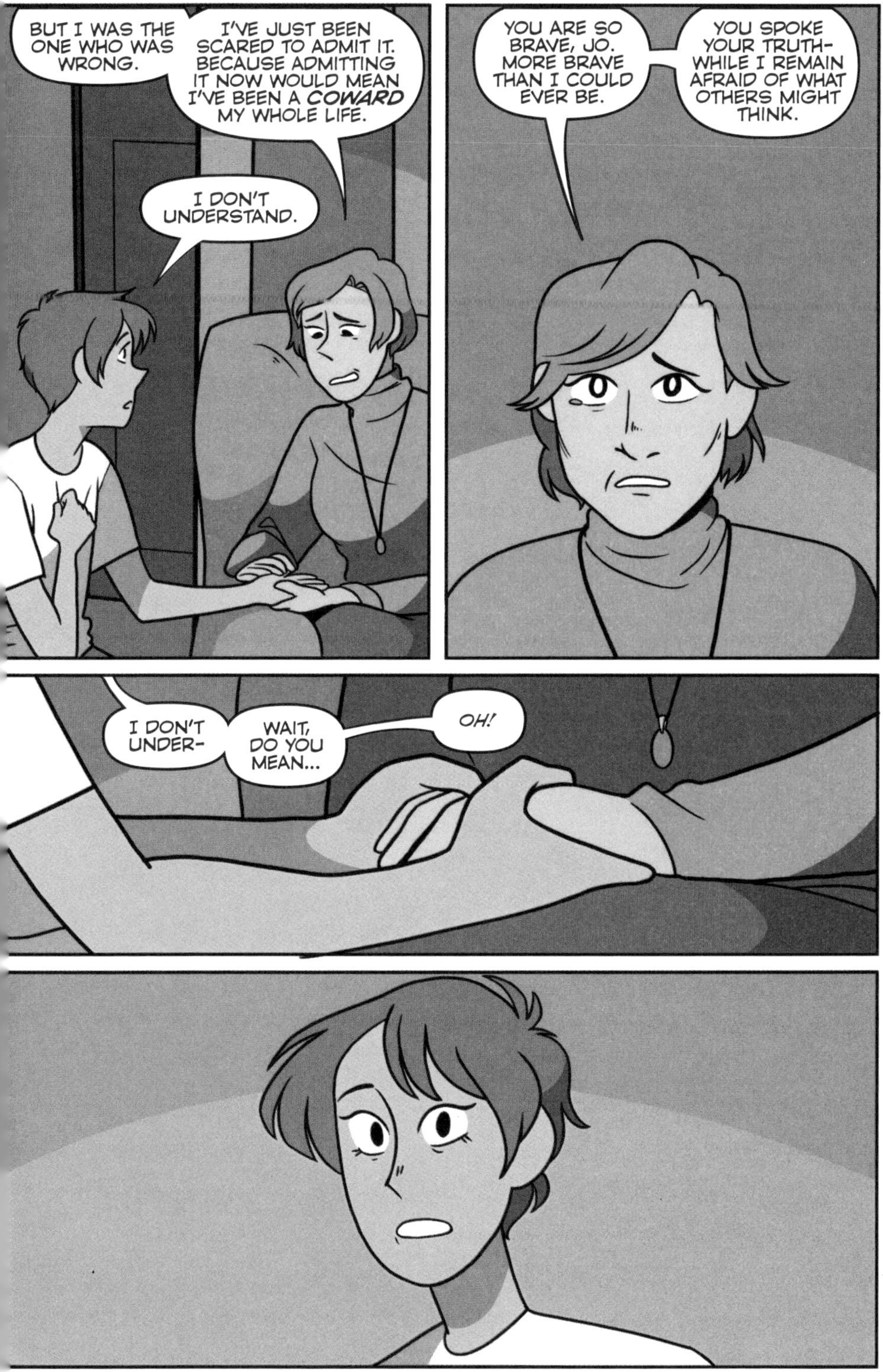
BUT I WAS THE ONE WHO WAS WRONG.
I'VE JUST BEEN SCARED TO ADMIT IT. BECAUSE ADMITTING IT NOW WOULD MEAN I'VE BEEN A *COWARD* MY WHOLE LIFE.
I DON'T UNDERSTAND.
YOU ARE SO BRAVE, JO. MORE BRAVE THAN I COULD EVER BE.
YOU SPOKE YOUR TRUTH- WHILE I REMAIN AFRAID OF WHAT OTHERS MIGHT THINK.
I DON'T UNDER-
WAIT, DO YOU MEAN...
OH!

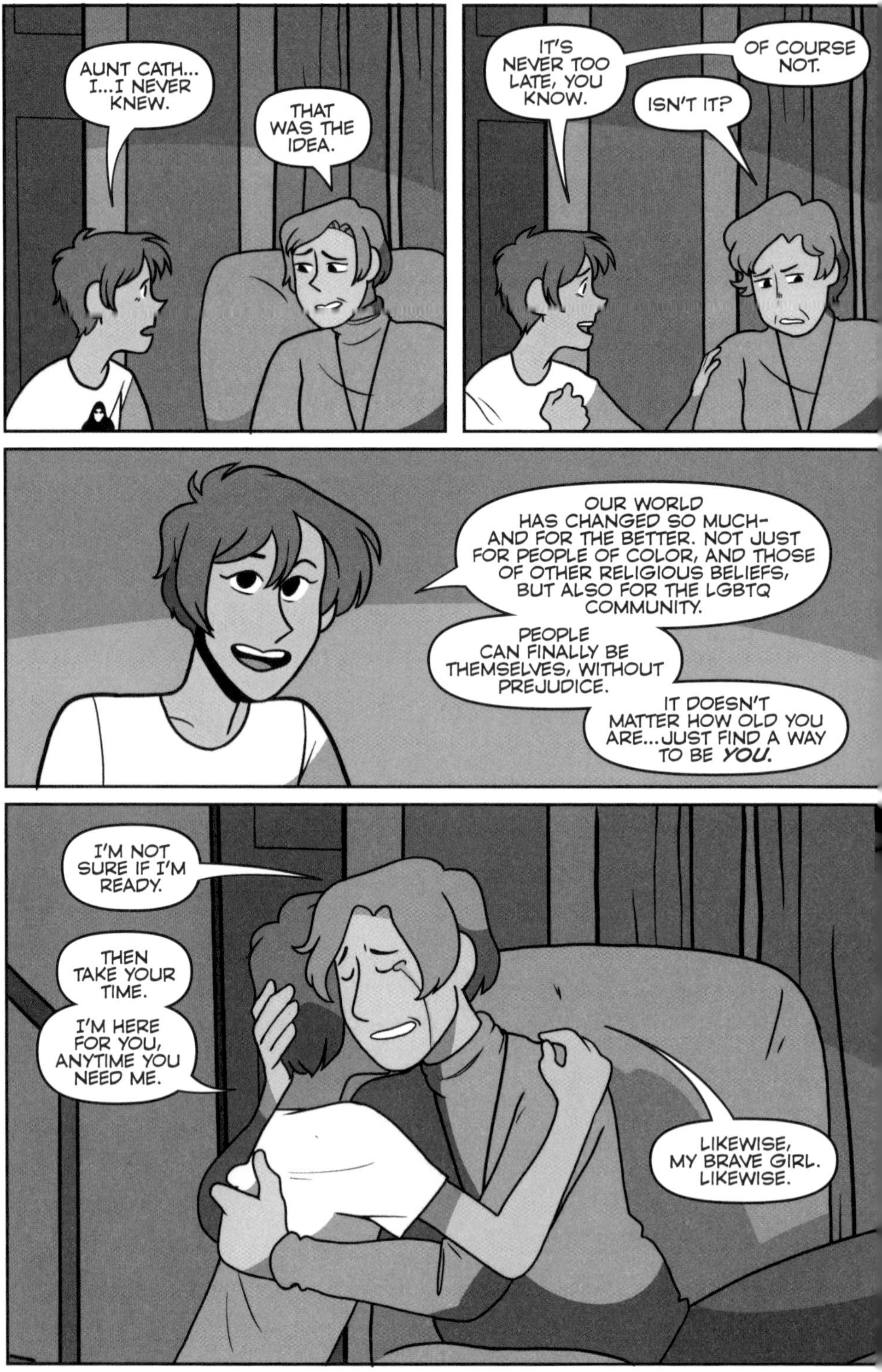
AUNT CATH... I...I NEVER KNEW.
THAT WAS THE IDEA.
IT'S NEVER TOO LATE, YOU KNOW.
ISN'T IT?
OF COURSE NOT.
OUR WORLD HAS CHANGED SO MUCH- AND FOR THE BETTER. NOT JUST FOR PEOPLE OF COLOR, AND THOSE OF OTHER RELIGIOUS BELIEFS, BUT ALSO FOR THE LGBTQ COMMUNITY.
PEOPLE CAN FINALLY BE THEMSELVES, WITHOUT PREJUDICE.
IT DOESN'T MATTER HOW OLD YOU ARE...JUST FIND A WAY TO BE *YOU*.
I'M NOT SURE IF I'M READY.
THEN TAKE YOUR TIME.
I'M HERE FOR YOU, ANYTIME YOU NEED ME.
LIKEWISE, MY BRAVE GIRL. LIKEWISE.

New Message

FROM: Madison March
TO: Alejandro Marquez, Laurie Marquez, Gammy Esther, Cathleen Burroughs, Mr. Bernstein, Kennedy Gardiner… (click to show more)
SENT: December 20

HAPPY HOLIDAYS FROM THE MARCH FAMILY TO YOURS!

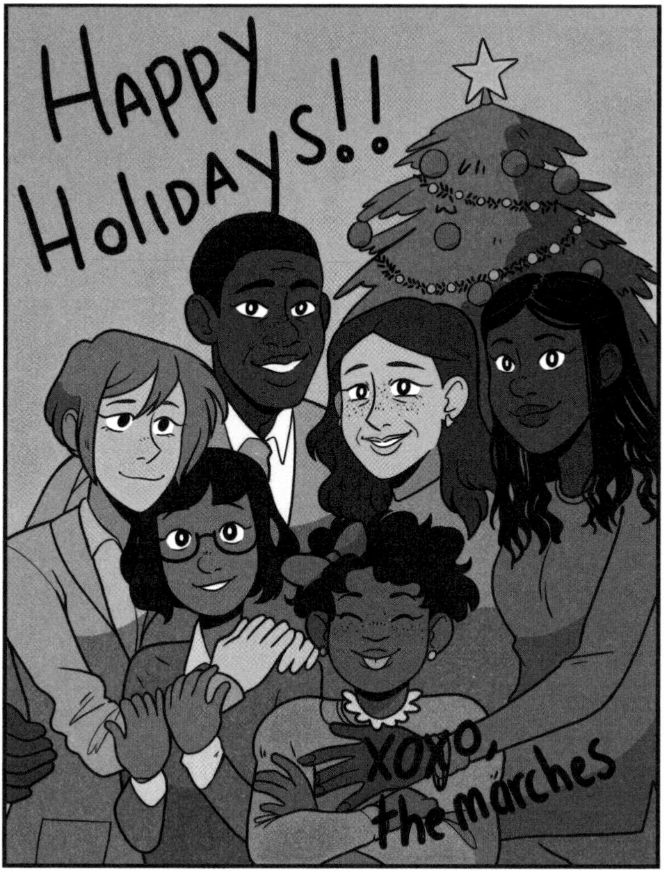

Happy Holidays!!
xoxo,
the marches

Send

CHAPTER 20

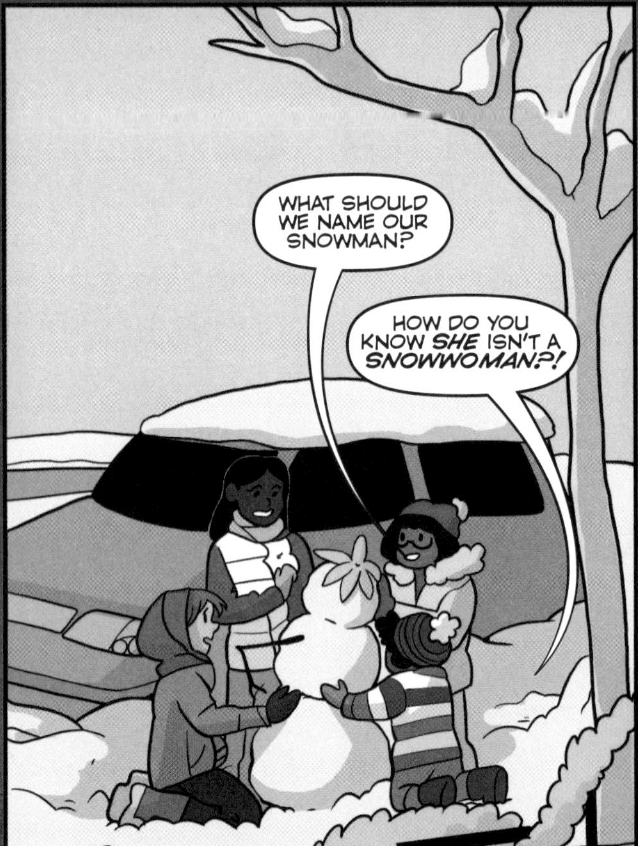
WHAT SHOULD WE NAME OUR SNOWMAN?
HOW DO YOU KNOW *SHE* ISN'T A *SNOWWOMAN?!*

March of the Marches...

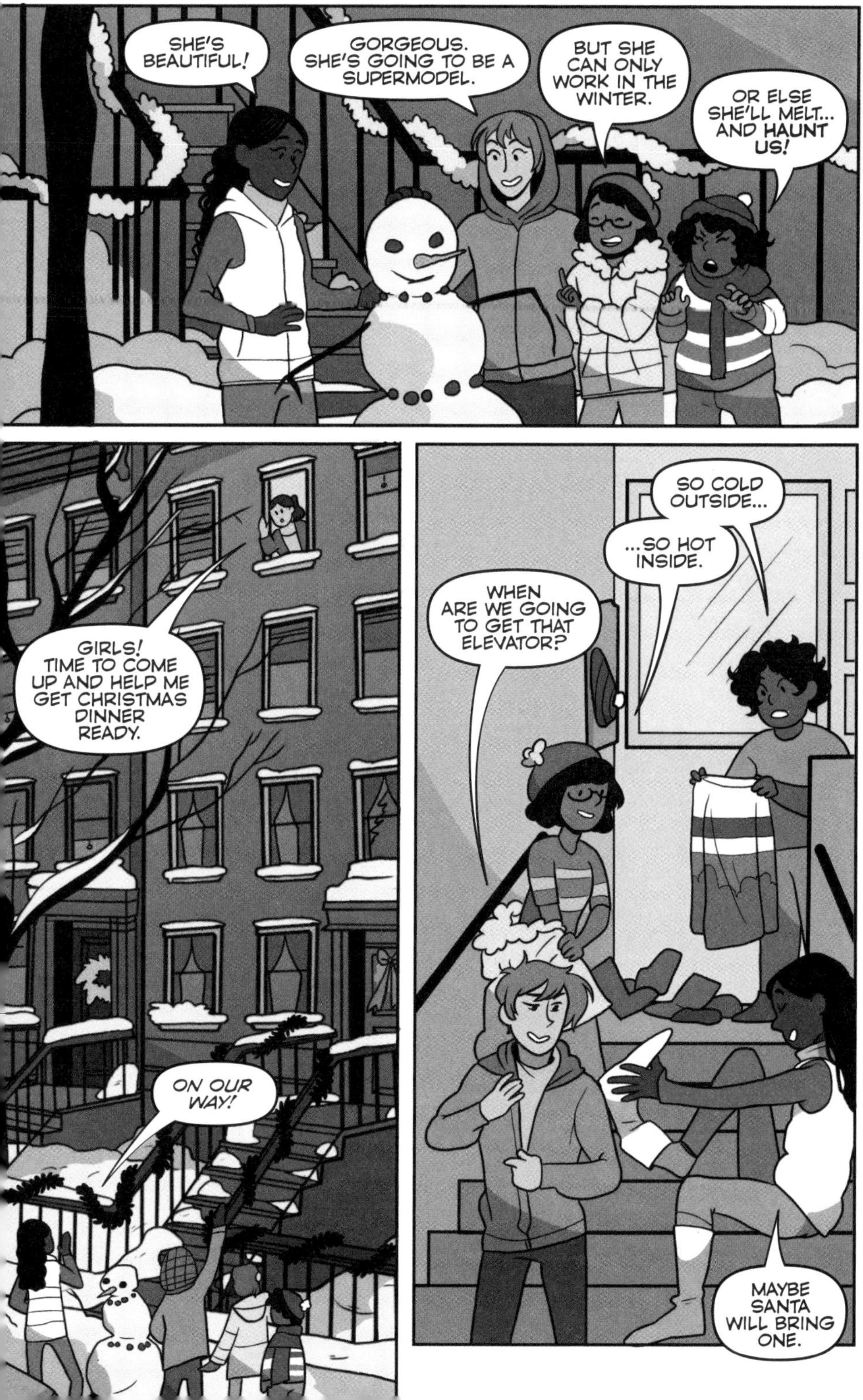
SHE'S BEAUTIFUL!
GORGEOUS. SHE'S GOING TO BE A SUPERMODEL.
BUT SHE CAN ONLY WORK IN THE WINTER.
OR ELSE SHE'LL MELT... AND HAUNT US!
GIRLS! TIME TO COME UP AND HELP ME GET CHRISTMAS DINNER READY.
ON OUR WAY!
WHEN ARE WE GOING TO GET THAT ELEVATOR?
SO COLD OUTSIDE...
...SO HOT INSIDE.
MAYBE SANTA WILL BRING ONE.

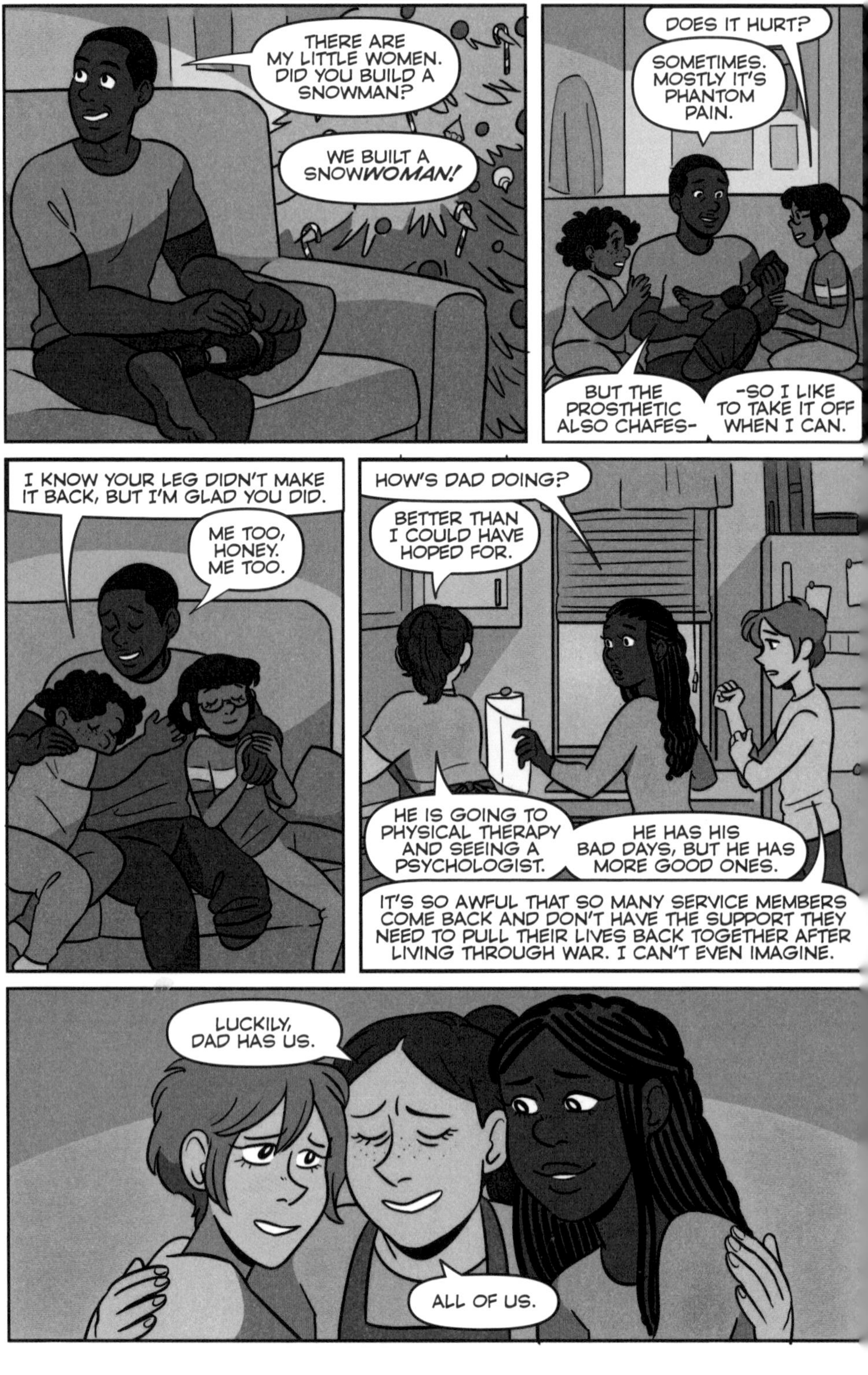
THERE ARE MY LITTLE WOMEN. DID YOU BUILD A SNOWMAN?
WE BUILT A SNOW*WOMAN!*
DOES IT HURT?
SOMETIMES. MOSTLY IT'S PHANTOM PAIN.
BUT THE PROSTHETIC ALSO CHAFES-
-SO I LIKE TO TAKE IT OFF WHEN I CAN.
I KNOW YOUR LEG DIDN'T MAKE IT BACK, BUT I'M GLAD YOU DID.
ME TOO, HONEY. ME TOO.
HOW'S DAD DOING?
BETTER THAN I COULD HAVE HOPED FOR.
HE IS GOING TO PHYSICAL THERAPY AND SEEING A PSYCHOLOGIST.
HE HAS HIS BAD DAYS, BUT HE HAS MORE GOOD ONES.
IT'S SO AWFUL THAT SO MANY SERVICE MEMBERS COME BACK AND DON'T HAVE THE SUPPORT THEY NEED TO PULL THEIR LIVES BACK TOGETHER AFTER LIVING THROUGH WAR. I CAN'T EVEN IMAGINE.
LUCKILY, DAD HAS US.
ALL OF US.

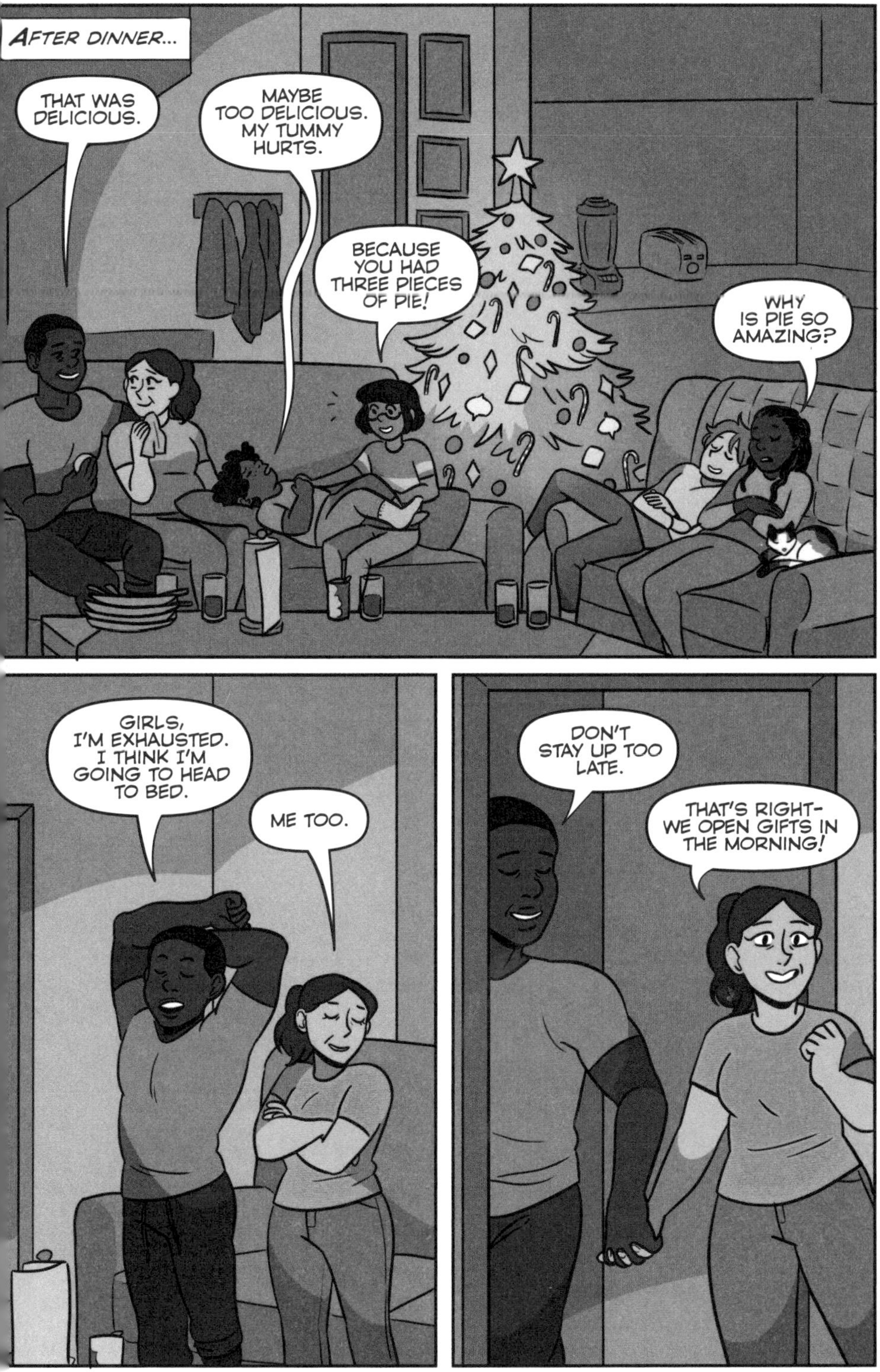
AFTER DINNER...
THAT WAS DELICIOUS.
MAYBE TOO DELICIOUS. MY TUMMY HURTS.
BECAUSE YOU HAD THREE PIECES OF PIE!
WHY IS PIE SO AMAZING?
GIRLS, I'M EXHAUSTED. I THINK I'M GOING TO HEAD TO BED.
ME TOO.
DON'T STAY UP TOO LATE.
THAT'S RIGHT- WE OPEN GIFTS IN THE MORNING!

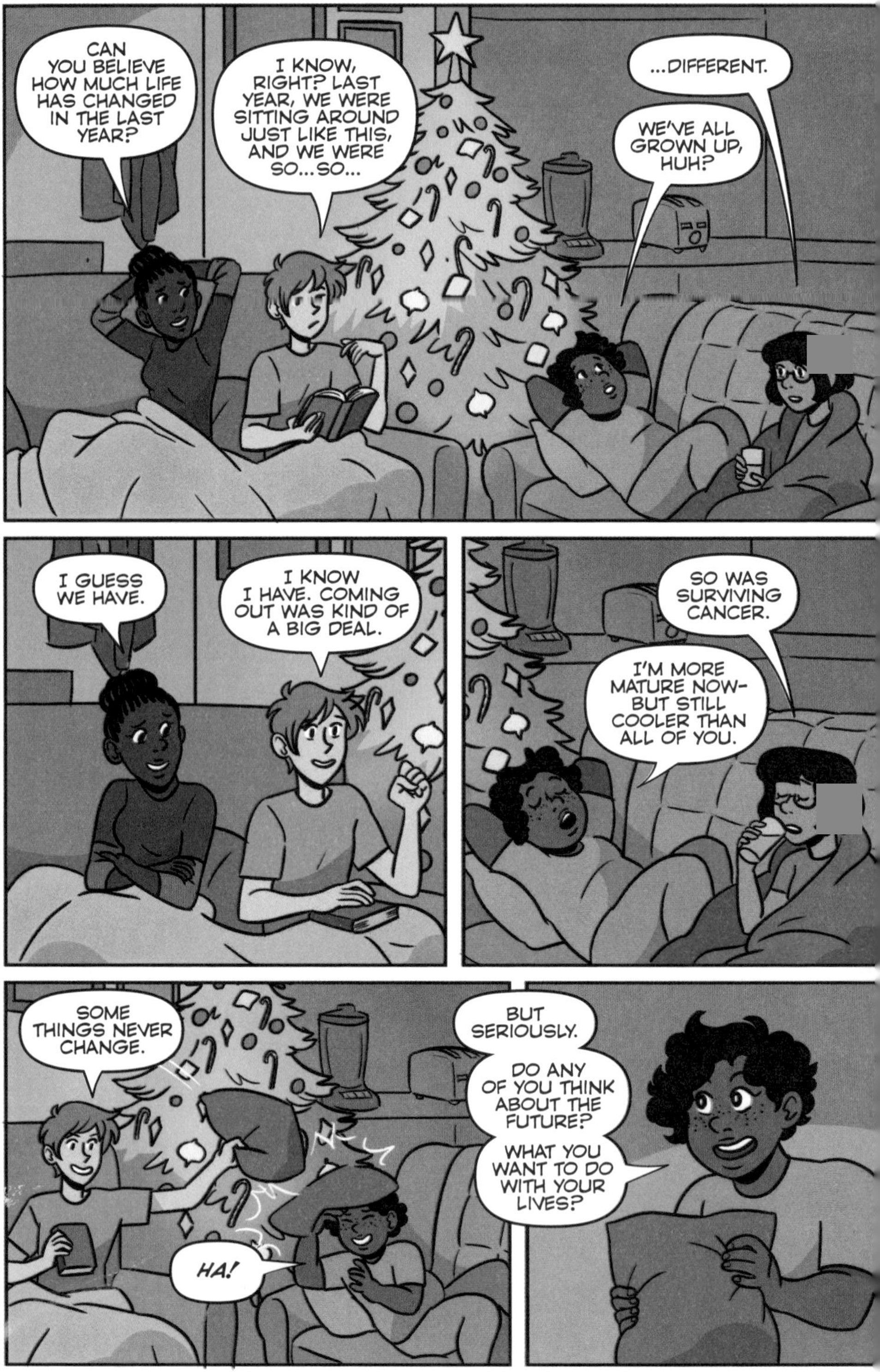
CAN YOU BELIEVE HOW MUCH LIFE HAS CHANGED IN THE LAST YEAR?
I KNOW, RIGHT? LAST YEAR, WE WERE SITTING AROUND JUST LIKE THIS, AND WE WERE SO…SO…
…DIFFERENT.
WE'VE ALL GROWN UP, HUH?
I GUESS WE HAVE.
I KNOW I HAVE. COMING OUT WAS KIND OF A BIG DEAL.
SO WAS SURVIVING CANCER.
I'M MORE MATURE NOW- BUT STILL COOLER THAN ALL OF YOU.
SOME THINGS NEVER CHANGE.
HA!
BUT SERIOUSLY.
DO ANY OF YOU THINK ABOUT THE FUTURE?
WHAT YOU WANT TO DO WITH YOUR LIVES?

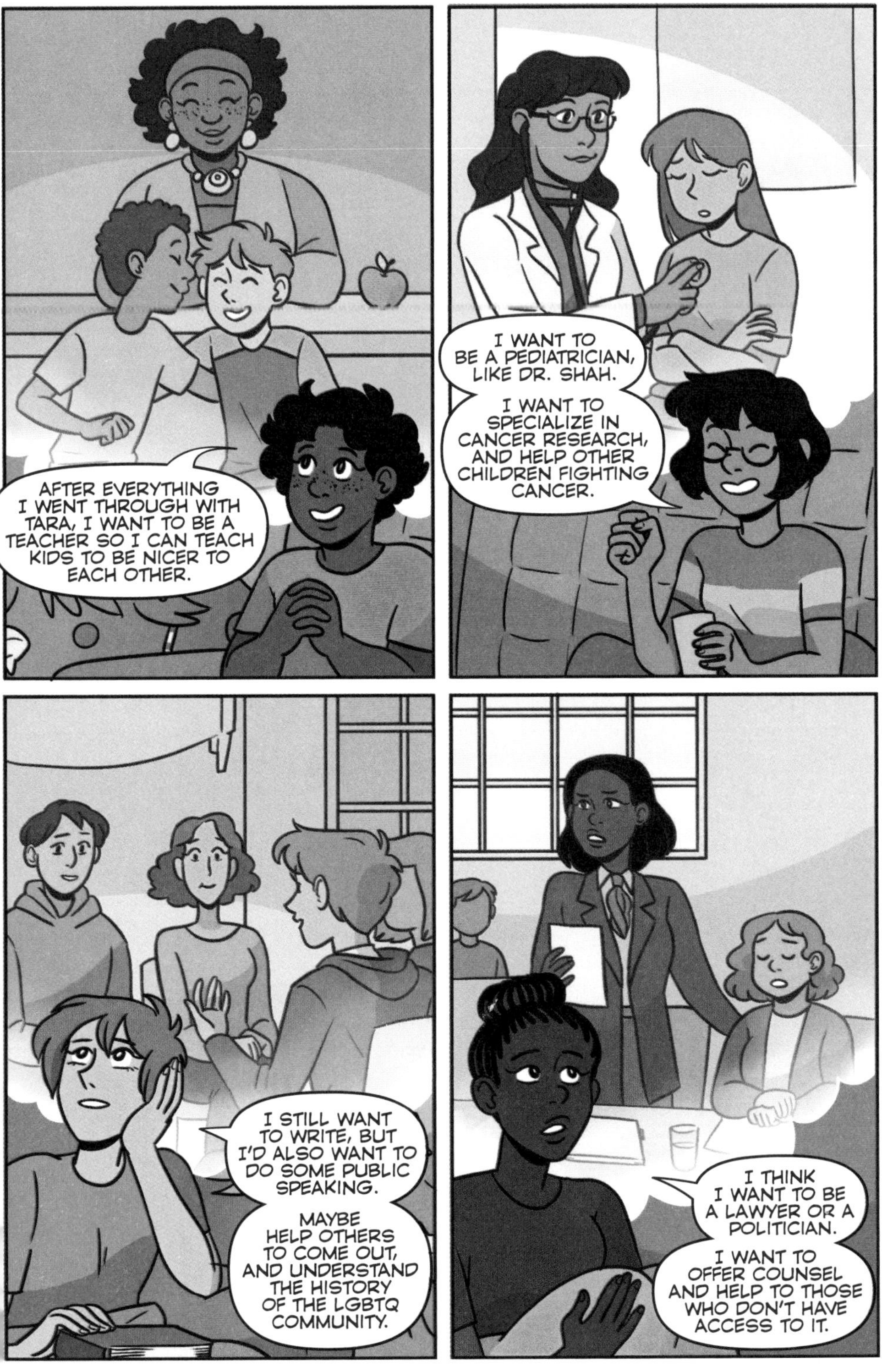
AFTER EVERYTHING I WENT THROUGH WITH TARA, I WANT TO BE A TEACHER SO I CAN TEACH KIDS TO BE NICER TO EACH OTHER.
I WANT TO BE A PEDIATRICIAN, LIKE DR. SHAH.
I WANT TO SPECIALIZE IN CANCER RESEARCH, AND HELP OTHER CHILDREN FIGHTING CANCER.
I STILL WANT TO WRITE, BUT I'D ALSO WANT TO DO SOME PUBLIC SPEAKING.
MAYBE HELP OTHERS TO COME OUT, AND UNDERSTAND THE HISTORY OF THE LGBTQ COMMUNITY.
I THINK I WANT TO BE A LAWYER OR A POLITICIAN.
I WANT TO OFFER COUNSEL AND HELP TO THOSE WHO DON'T HAVE ACCESS TO IT.

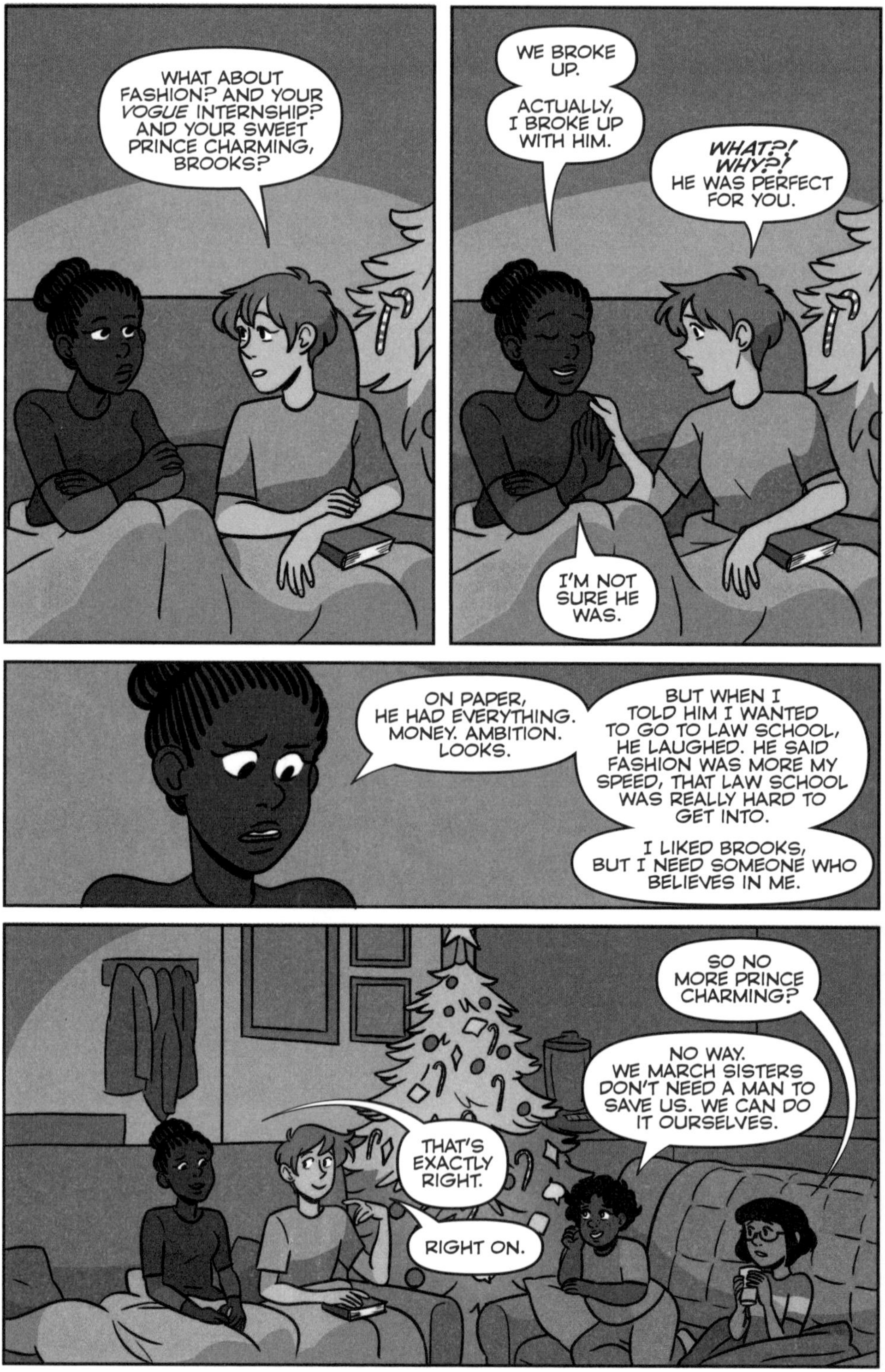
WHAT ABOUT FASHION? AND YOUR *VOGUE* INTERNSHIP? AND YOUR SWEET PRINCE CHARMING, BROOKS?
WE BROKE UP.
ACTUALLY, I BROKE UP WITH HIM.
WHAT?! WHY?! HE WAS PERFECT FOR YOU.
I'M NOT SURE HE WAS.
ON PAPER, HE HAD EVERYTHING. MONEY. AMBITION. LOOKS.
BUT WHEN I TOLD HIM I WANTED TO GO TO LAW SCHOOL, HE LAUGHED. HE SAID FASHION WAS MORE MY SPEED, THAT LAW SCHOOL WAS REALLY HARD TO GET INTO.
I LIKED BROOKS, BUT I NEED SOMEONE WHO BELIEVES IN ME.
SO NO MORE PRINCE CHARMING?
NO WAY. WE MARCH SISTERS DON'T NEED A MAN TO SAVE US. WE CAN DO IT OURSELVES.
THAT'S EXACTLY RIGHT.
RIGHT ON.

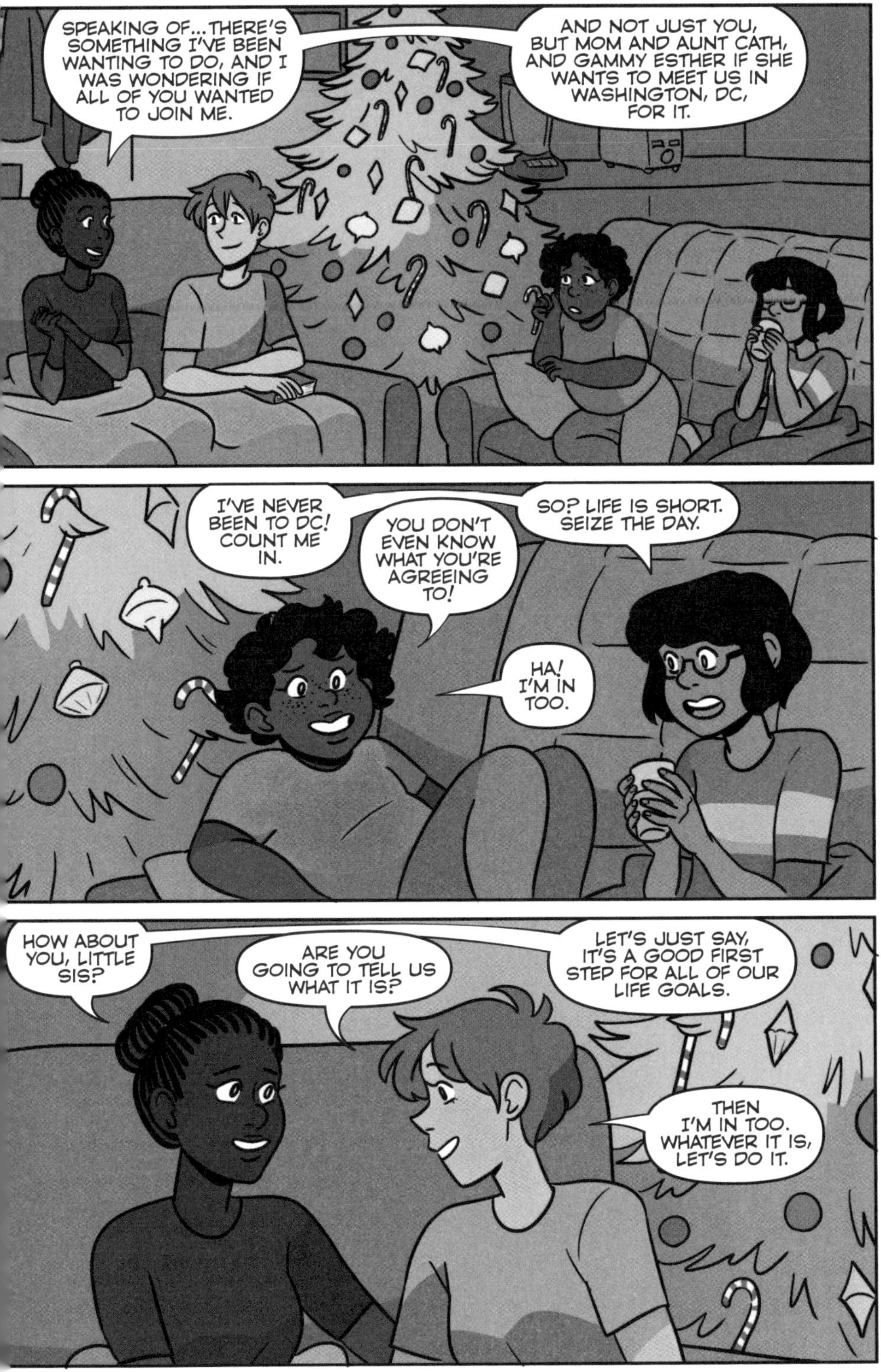
SPEAKING OF...THERE'S SOMETHING I'VE BEEN WANTING TO DO, AND I WAS WONDERING IF ALL OF YOU WANTED TO JOIN ME.
AND NOT JUST YOU, BUT MOM AND AUNT CATH, AND GAMMY ESTHER IF SHE WANTS TO MEET US IN WASHINGTON, DC, FOR IT.
I'VE NEVER BEEN TO DC! COUNT ME IN.
YOU DON'T EVEN KNOW WHAT YOU'RE AGREEING TO!
SO? LIFE IS SHORT. SEIZE THE DAY.
HA! I'M IN TOO.
HOW ABOUT YOU, LITTLE SIS?
ARE YOU GOING TO TELL US WHAT IT IS?
LET'S JUST SAY, IT'S A GOOD FIRST STEP FOR ALL OF OUR LIFE GOALS.
THEN I'M IN TOO. WHATEVER IT IS, LET'S DO IT.

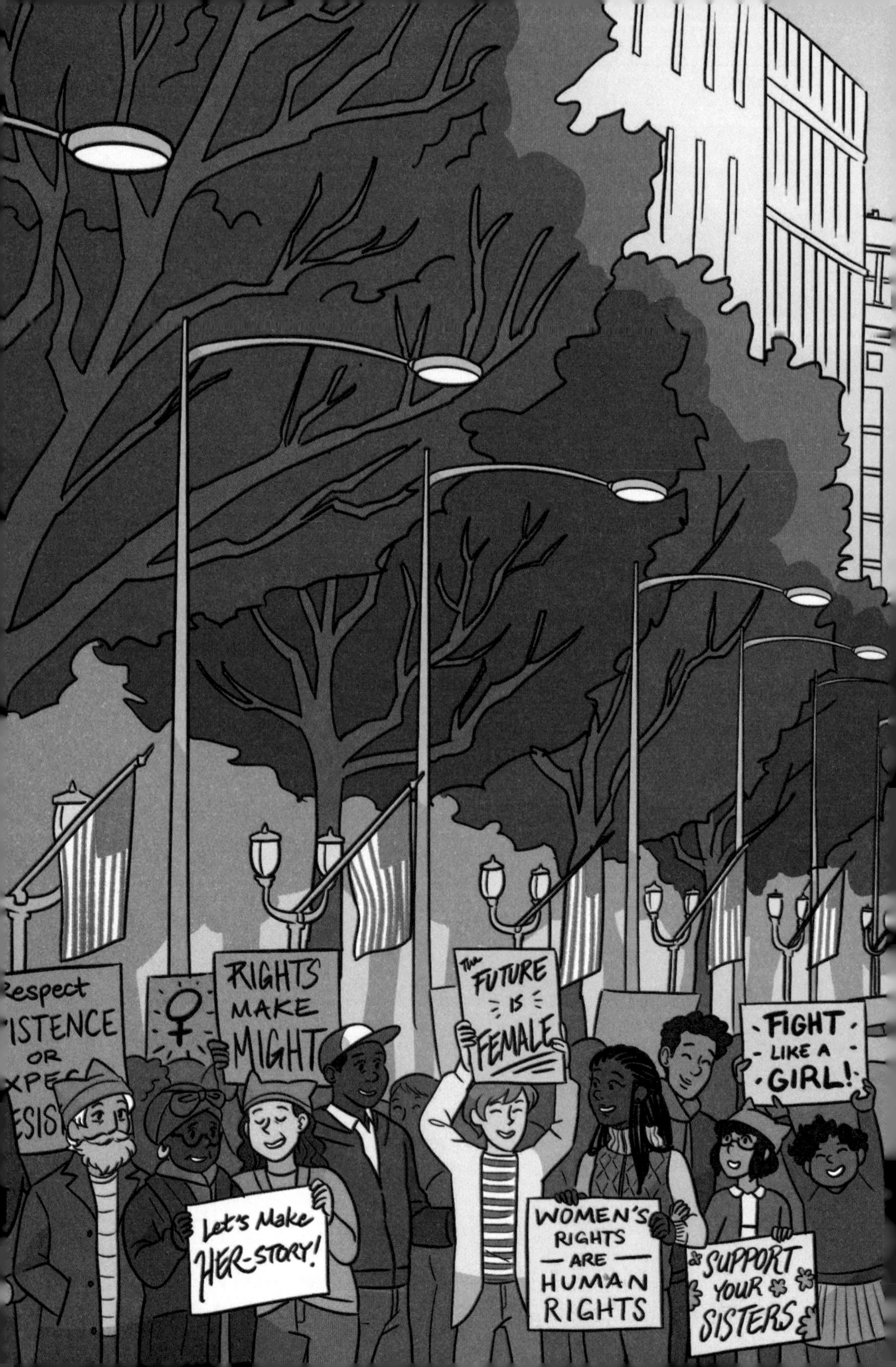
Respect
ISTENCE
OR
RIGHTS MAKE MIGHT
The FUTURE IS FEMALE
FIGHT LIKE A GIRL!
Let's Make HER-STORY!
WOMEN'S RIGHTS ARE HUMAN RIGHTS
SUPPORT YOUR SISTERS

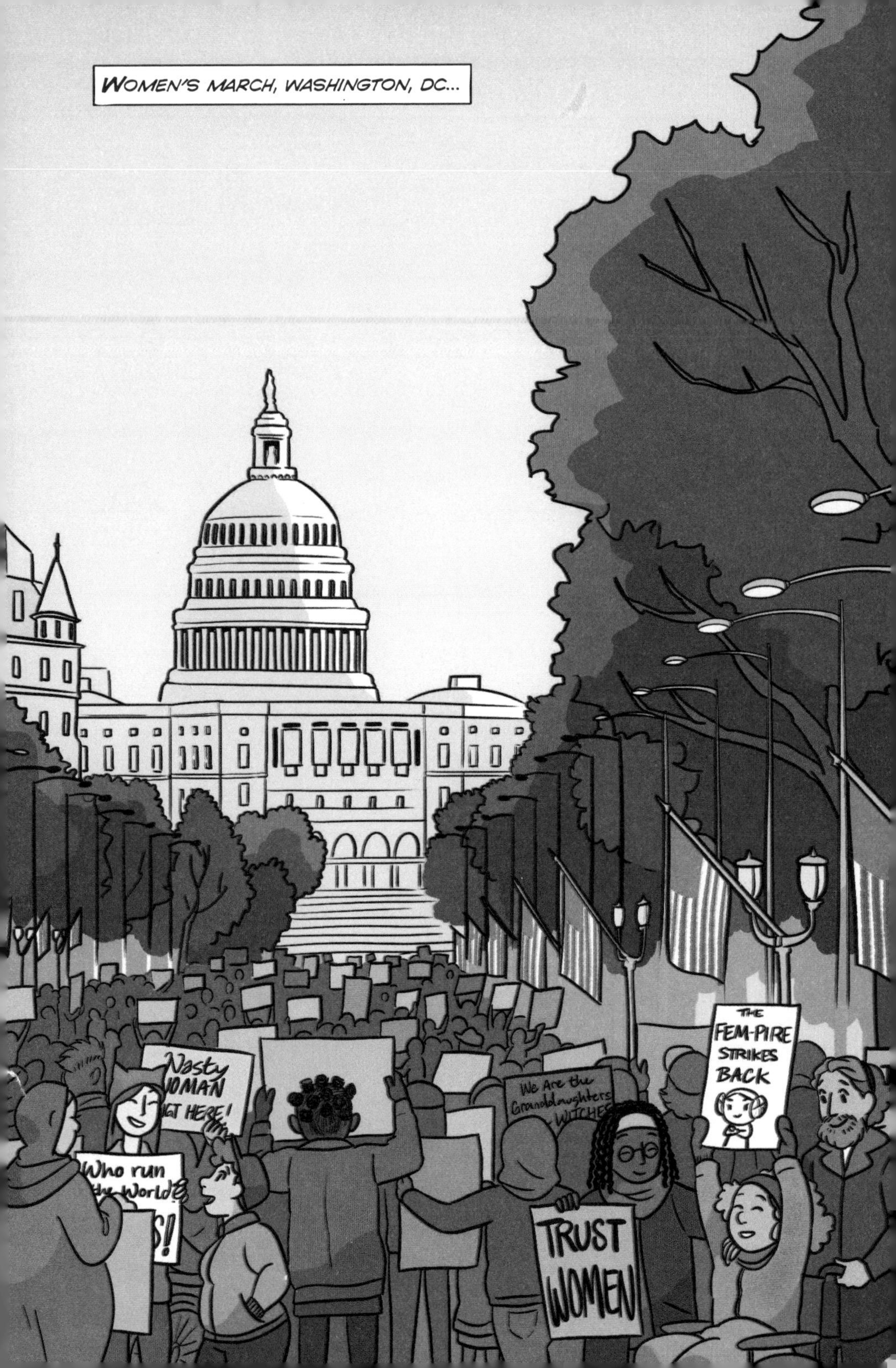
WOMEN'S MARCH, WASHINGTON, DC...
Nasty
WOMAN
HERE!
We Are the Granddaughters
WITCHES
Who run
World?
THE FEM-PIRE STRIKES BACK
TRUST WOMEN

January 21

Today I marched with my sisters, both figuratively and literally. And while the world isn't where it should be, it's on its way...

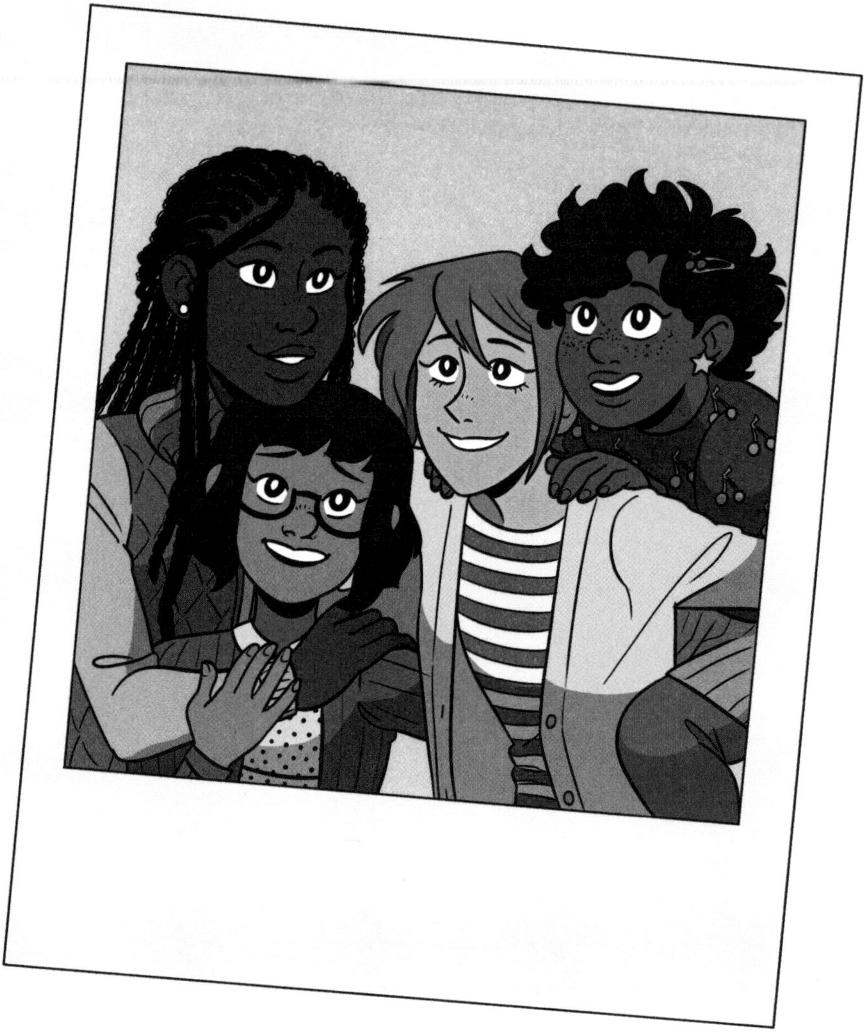

Louisa May Alcott

was born on November 29, 1832, in Pennsylvania. She was the second of four daughters of educator and social reformer Amos Bronson Alcott and social worker Abigail May Alcott. Despite a great deal of moving from place to place, Alcott received a formal education from her father. Her early instruction was rounded out with lessons from family friends, such as influential intellectuals Henry David Thoreau, Ralph Waldo Emerson, Theodore Parker, Margaret Fuller, and Nathaniel Hawthorne, who is best known for having written *The Scarlet Letter*.

Her family lived in poverty, which made it necessary for Alcott to work at an early age. She made money working as a seamstress, a governess, a domestic helper, a teacher, and, of course, a writer.

1847, the Alcott home became a safe house for the Underground Railroad, a network of secret routes used by enslaved African Americans to escape from the South to free states in the North during the early nineteenth century. This was not the only cause Alcott would take up in her lifetime. She also looked to empower women, who at the time had few rights and could not vote. Eventually, she became the first woman to register to vote in Concord, Massachusetts, in a school board election. It was a small step but an important one.

The 1850s were a difficult time for the Alcotts. In 1858, her younger sister passed away and her older sister married. Alcott's sisterhood—which had meant so much to her—felt as though it were breaking apart. With little money and no work, Louisa May found herself filled with despair. It was during this time she found a biography of Charlotte Bronte, discovering many parallels to her own life. Soon after, Alcott began writing for *The Atlantic Monthly*.

When the American Civil War began, Alcott served as a nurse until she became deathly ill when she contracted typhoid. Her letters home during this time would soon bring her critical recognition as a writer. But it was in 1868 that Louisa May Alcott finally found great success when her novel *Little Women* was published. *Little Women* was a semiautobiographical story of her own childhood growing up with her sisters. It is on that novel that our story is based.

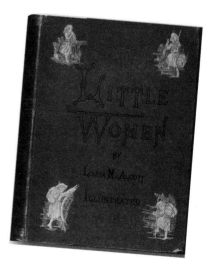

About the Creators

Rey Terciero, also known as Rex Ogle, has written and edited hundreds of books and comics for children and young adults. He is a queer writer who has always been drawn to strong female protagonists, including Elizabeth Bennet, Princess Leia, Jean Grey, and Hermione Granger. *Meg, Jo, Beth, and Amy* is his debut graphic novel.

Bre Indigo is a lover of astronomy, salmon sashimi, and open minds. She tells stories of gentle boys, tough girls, and those in between, with a focus on tolerance and the many faces of love. You can find her ongoing webcomic serie *Jamie* online at Tapas.

Gabrielle Rose Camacho is an aspiring artist and devoted cat lover. As this is her first big published project, she hopes to see more to come in paving the way for her career.

Johana Avalos Merino, better known as JAMpoots, is a Chicanx artist based in SoCal working on comics that deal with identity and the journey it takes to find one's self.

Joanne Kwan is a graphic artist and webcomic creator with a penchant for the odd and obscure. She has a passion and respect for history but is far from traditional and enjoys straying off the beaten path. All of her series can also be found online at Tapas.

Ryan "Toxin" Thompson is the creator of the fantasy webcomic series *Fauna Fairest* and *Drop Devil*. He has a profound love for all things colorful and a passion for exploring stories of growth and self-discovery. He tries to live a quiet life, far out of reach of the dangerous magical creatures he so often tells tales about.

A Larger World Studios is Dave Lanphear, Troy Peteri, and Joshua Cozine. They're letterjacks for comic book publishers all over the world. Join them online at Twitter and Instagram @A_Larger_World!